THE COMPANY OF STRANGERS

Lisbon 1944. In the torrid summer heat, as the streets of the capital seethe with spies and informers, the endgame of the Intelligence war is being silently fought. The Germans have rocket technology and atomic know-how. The Allies are determined that talk of the ultimate 'secret weapon' will not be realized.

Andrea Aspinall, mathematician and spy, enters this sophisticated world through a wealthy household in Estoril. Karl Voss, military attaché to the German Legation, has arrived embittered by his implication in the murder of a Reichsminister and traumatized by Stalingrad, on a mission to rescue Germany from annihilation.

In the lethal tranquillity of a corrupted paradise, Andrea and Voss meet and attempt to find love in a world where no one can be believed. After a night of terrible violence Andrea is left with a secret which provokes a lifelong addiction to the clandestine world, from the brutal Portuguese fascist régime to the paranoia of Cold War Germany. And there, in an ice-gripped East Berlin, as she discovers that the deepest secrets aren't held by governments but by those closest to you, she is forced to make the final and the hardest choice.

A consummate and passionate thriller, spanning Europe from the dark days of World War Two to the collapse of the Berlin Wall, by the Gold Dagger winning author of *A Small Death in Lisbon*.

THE COMPANY OF STRANGERS

Robert Wilson

HarperCollins*Publishers*

HarperCollins*Publishers*
77–85 Fulham Palace Road, London W6 8JB

The HarperCollins website address is
www.**fire**and**water**.com/crime

Published by HarperCollins*Publishers* 2001

1 3 5 7 9 8 6 4 2

A catalogue record for this book
is available from the British Library

ISBN 0 00 232669 8

Set in Janson Text
Typeset by Rowland Phototypesetting Ltd,
Bury St Edmunds, Suffolk

Printed and bound in Great Britain by
Clays Ltd, St Ives plc

*For Jane
and
in memory of my father
1922–1980*

ACKNOWLEDGEMENTS

I would like to thank Col. Peter Taylor (retd), Mrs Pam Taylor and Elwin Taylor for helping me with books, maps and information on Berlin in the 1960s and 1970s.

Ah, love, let us be true
To one another! For the world, which seems
To lie before us like a land of dreams,
So various, so beautiful, so new,
Hath really neither joy, nor love, nor light,
Nor certitude, nor peace, nor help for pain;
And we are here as on a darkling plain
Swept with confused alarms of struggle and flight,
Where ignorant armies clash by night.

Dover Beach by Matthew Arnold

Book One

Outlaws of the Mind

Chapter 1

30th October 1940, London. Night 54 of the Blitz.

She was running, running as she had done before in her dreams, except this wasn't a dream, even though with the flares dropping, as slowly as petals, and the yellow light, and the dark streets with the orange glow on the skyline it could easily be a dream, a horror dream.

She flinched at a tremendous explosion in a nearby street, staggered at the shudder in the ground, nearly ploughed into the paving stones face-first, legs kicking back wildly. She pushed up off a low wall at the front of a house and her feet were slapping against the pavement again. She ran faster as she saw the Auxiliary Fire Service outside the house. New hoses uncoiled from the engines and joined the spaghetti in the black glass street as they trained more water on the back of the house, which was no longer a house but half a house. The whole of one side blown away and the grand piano with two legs over the startling new precipice, its lid hanging open like a tongue lapping up the flames, which set off a terrible twanging as the fire plucked at the piano strings and snapped them, peeled them back.

She stood there with her hands over her ears to the unbearable sound of destruction. Her eyes and mouth were wide open as the back of the house collapsed into the neighbour's garden, leaving the kitchen in full view and oddly intact. A hissing noise of escaping gas from the ruptured mains suddenly thumped into flame and burst across the street, pushing the firemen back. There was a figure lying in the kitchen, not moving and with clothes alight.

She jumped up on to the low wall at the side of the house and screamed into the blistering heat of the burning house.

'Daddy! Daddy!'

A fireman grabbed her and hauled her roughly back, almost

threw her at a warden, who tried to hold her but she wrenched herself free just as the piano, the piano that she'd been playing to him only two hours before, fell from its precipice with a loud crack and a discord that reached into her chest and squeezed her lungs. Now she saw all the sheet music going up in flames and he was lying on the floor at the foot of the wall of fire, which the AFS where hosing down so that it hissed and sputtered, but didn't go out.

Another crack and this time the roof dropped, spitting whole window frames into the street like broken teeth, and crashed down on to the floor below, shedding great sledges of tiles which shattered on the pavement. There was a momentary pause, then the roof smashed through to the next floor and, like a giant candle snuff, suffocated the flaming music, crushed his supine body and dropped him amongst shafts of flaming timber into the bay window of the ground floor.

The warden lunged at her again, got a hold of her collar, and she wheeled round and bit his wrist so that he flinched back his hand. She's a wild one, this black-haired, gypsy-looking girl, thought the warden, but he had to get her away, poor thing, get her away from her daddy burning in the bay window in front of her. He went for her again, got her in a bear hug, her legs flailing, lashing out and then she went limp as a rag doll, bent in the middle over his arms.

A woman, white-faced, ran up to the warden and said that the girl was her daughter, which confused him because he'd seen the man who she'd been calling Daddy and the warden knew that the man's wife was dead in the kitchen.

'She's been calling for her daddy in the house there.'

'That's not her daddy,' said the woman. 'Her father's dead. That's her piano teacher.'

'What's she doing out here, anyway?' he asked, getting official. 'The All Clear hasn't sounded . . .'

The girl wrestled away from her mother and ran down the side of another house and into the garden, lit by the still falling flares. She ran across the yellow lawn and threw herself into the bushes growing against the back wall. Her mother followed. Bombs were still falling, the ack-ack was still pumping away on the Common, the searchlights swarming over the black velvet sky. Her mother was screaming at her, roaring over the noise, screeching with fright, savagely begging her to come out.

The girl sat with her hands over her ears, eyes closed. Only two hours before he'd held her hands, told her she was as nervous as a cat, stroked each of her fingers, squared her shoulders to that same piano and she'd played for him, played like a dream for him, so that he'd told her afterwards he'd closed his eyes and left London and the war and found a green meadow in the sunshine, somewhere where the trees were flashing with red and gold in the autumn wind.

The first wave of bombers moved off. The ack-ack fell silent. All that was left in the cold autumn air was the roar of the conflagration and the hiss of water on burning wood. She crawled out of the bushes. Her mother grabbed her by the shoulders, shook her backwards and forwards. The girl was calm, but her face was set, her teeth gritted and her eyes black and unseeing.

'You're a stupid girl, Andrea. A stupid, stupid girl,' said her mother.

The girl took in her mother's white raving face in the dark and yellow garden, her face hard and determined.

'I hate Germans,' she said. 'And I hate you.'

Her mother slapped her hard across the face.

Chapter 2

7th February 1942, Wolfsschanze, Hitler's East Front HQ, Rastenburg, East Prussia.

The aircraft, a Heinkel III bomber refitted for passenger use, began its descent over the vast blackness of the pine forests of East Prussia. The low moan of its two engines brought with it the bleakness of the vast, snow-covered Russian steppes, the emptiness of the gutted, burnt-out railway station at Dnepropetrovsk and the endlessness of the frozen Pripet marshes between Kiev and the start of Polish pine.

The plane landed and taxied in a miasma of snow thrashed up into the darkness by its propellers. A coated figure, huddled against the icy blast, slipped into this chill world from a neat hole which had opened up in the belly of the aircraft. A car from the Führer's personal pool waited just off the wing tip and the chauffeur, collar up to his hat, held the door open. Fifteen minutes later the guard at the gate of Restricted Area I admitted Albert Speer, architect, into the military compound of Hitler's Rastenburg headquarters for the first time. Speer went straight to the officers' canteen and ate a large meal with appropriate wolfishness, which would have reminded his fellow diners, if they'd had room for empathy, just how difficult it was to keep the latest far-flung corner of the Third Reich supplied.

Two captains, Karl Voss and Hans Weber, intelligence officers in their mid twenties attached to the Army Chief of Staff, General Zeitzler, had been standing outside stamping their feet and smoking cigarettes when Speer arrived.

'Who's that?' asked Voss.

'I knew you'd ask that.'

'You don't think that's a normal question when somebody you don't know walks past?'

6

'You forgot the word "important". When somebody important walks past.'

'Piss off, Weber.'

'I've seen you.'

'What?'

'Let's get back,' said Weber, chucking his cigarette.

'No, tell me.'

'Your problem, Voss . . . is that you're too intelligent. Heidelberg University and your fucking physics degree, you're . . .'

'Too intelligent to be an intelligence officer?'

'You're new, you don't understand yet – the thing about intelligence is that it doesn't do to be too inquisitive.'

'Where *does* this rubbish come from, Weber?' asked Voss, incredulous.

'I tell you one thing,' he said, 'I know what powerful people see when they look at you and me . . . and it's not two individuals with lives and families and all the rest.'

'What then?'

'They see opportunities,' he said, and barged Voss through the door.

They went back to work in the situation room, up the silent corridor towards Hitler's apartment where the Führer was still entertaining the Armaments Minister, Fritz Todt, whose arrival had terminated the situation meeting of that afternoon. As the young captains resumed their seats the two older men were still just about talking. Food had been served to them earlier by an orderly grown accustomed to glacial silences, split only by the odd cracking of a wooden chair.

Voss and Weber worked, or rather Voss did. Weber's head started toppling again almost as soon as they sat down in the airless room. Only the snap of his neck muscles jerked him awake and prevented him from flattening his face on the desk. Voss told him to go to bed. Weber's eyes ground in their sockets.

'Go on,' said Voss. 'This is nearly finished anyway.'

'Those,' said Weber, standing and pointing at four boxes of files, 'have to go out on the first flight in the morning . . . to Berlin.'

'You mean unless the Moscow flight is open by then.'

Weber grunted. 'You'll learn,' he said. 'Back to the monk's cell for me. It's going to be hard tomorrow. He's always bad after Todt's given his report.'

'Why's that?' asked Voss, still keen, still capable of doing an all-nighter for the East Front.

'The first place you lose a battle is up here,' said Weber, leaning over Voss and tapping his head, 'and Todt lost that one last June. He's a good man and he's a genius and that's a bad combination for this war. Good night.'

Voss knew Fritz Todt, as everyone knew him, as the inventor of the *autobahnen*, but he was much more than that now. Not only was he running all arms and munitions production for the Third Reich, but he and his Organization Todt were the builders of the West Wall and the U-boat pens that would protect Europe from invasion. He was also in charge of building and repairing all roads and railways in the Occupied Territories. Todt was the greatest construction engineer in German history and this was the greatest programme of all time.

Voss surveyed the situation map. The front line stretched from Lake Onega, 500 kilometres south-west of Archangel on the White Sea, through Leningrad, the Moscow suburbs and down to Taganrog on the Sea of Azov, off the Black Sea. From Arctic to Caucasus was under German control.

'And he thinks we're *losing* this war?' asked Voss out loud, shaking his head.

He worked for another hour or more and then went out for another cigarette and to wake himself up in the freezing air. On his way back he saw the good-looking man who'd arrived earlier, sitting on his own in the dining room and then, coming towards him outside the situation room, another figure, shuffling along with sagging shoulders as if they were under some penitential weight. The face was grey, soft and slack, falling away from its substructure. The eyes saw nothing beyond the immense calculation in his mind. Voss moved to avoid the man but at the last moment they seemed to veer into each other and their shoulders clashed. The man's face was reanimated in shock and Voss recognized him now.

'Forgive me, Herr Reichsminister.'

'No, no, my fault,' said Todt. 'I wasn't looking.'

'Thinking too hard, sir,' said Voss, dog-like.

Todt studied the slim, blond young man more carefully now.

'Working late, Captain?'

'Just finishing the orders, sir,' said Voss, nodding at the open door of the situation room.

Todt lingered on the threshold of the room, his eyes roved the map and the flags of the armies and their divisions.

'Nearly there, sir,' said Voss.

'Russia,' said Todt, his eye swivelling on to Voss, 'is a very large place.'

'Yes, sir,' said Voss, after a long pause in which nothing more was forthcoming.

'Maps of Russia should be room-sized,' said Todt. 'So that army generals have to *walk* to move their divisions, with the knowledge that each step they take is 500 kilometres of snow and ice, or rain and mud, and in the few months of the year when it's neither of those things they should know that the steppe is shimmering in silent, brutal, dust-choked heat.'

Voss shut up, mesmerized by the thunderous roll of the older man's voice. Todt backed out of the room. Voss wanted him to stay, to continue, but no questions came to mind other than the banal.

'Are you on the first flight out tomorrow, sir?'

'Yes, why?'

'To Berlin?'

'We'll stop in Berlin on the way to Munich.'

'These files need to go to Berlin.'

'In that case they'd better be on my plane before seven thirty. Talk to the flight captain. Good night, er . . . Captain . . .'

'Captain Voss, sir.'

'Have you seen Speer, Captain Voss? I was told he'd arrived.'

'There's someone in the dining room. He arrived earlier.'

Todt moved away, shuffling again down the corridor. Before he turned left to the dining room he turned on Voss.

'Don't imagine for one second, Captain, that the Russians are doing nothing about . . . about *your* situation in there,' he said, and disappeared.

No wonder the Führer was bad after Todt's visits.

Another half-hour passed and Voss went to fetch coffee from the dining room. Speer and Todt sat on either side of a single glass of

9

wine, which the older man sipped. The structural differences between the two men were marked. The one slumped with definite subsidence under the right foundation, the nineteenth century, Wilhelmine façade lined and cracked, the paint and masonry crumbling to scurf. The other cantilevered over at an impossible angle, his lines clean and defined, the modern Bauhaus front, dark, handsome, uncluttered and bright.

'Captain Voss,' said Todt, turning to him, 'did you speak to the flight captain yet?'

'No, sir.'

'When you do, tell him that Herr Speer will be joining me. He came in from Dnepropetrovsk tonight.'

Voss drank his coffee and on the way back to his work he had the strange and uncomfortable sense of silent machinery at work, out of his sight and beyond his knowledge. He turned into the situation room, just as SS Colonel Bruno Weiss came out of Hitler's apartment. Weiss was head of the SS company at Rastenburg in charge of Hitler's security and the only thing Voss knew about him was that he didn't like anybody except Hitler, and he had a particular dislike of intelligence officers.

'What are you doing, Captain?' he shouted down the corridor.

'Just finishing these orders, sir.'

Weiss bore down on him and inspected the situation room, the scar running from his left eye to below his cheekbone livid against his pale skin.

'What are these?'

'Army Chief of Staff files, sir, to go back to Berlin on the Reichsminister Todt's flight this morning. I'm about to inform the flight captain.'

Weiss nodded at the phone. Voss called the flight captain and booked Speer on to the plane as well. Weiss wrote things down in his notebook and went back to Hitler's apartment. Minutes later he was back.

'These files . . . when are they going?' he asked.

'They have to be at the airstrip by 07.30 hours this morning, sir.'

'Answer the question fully, Captain.'

'I will be taking them personally, leaving here at 07.15 hours, sir.'

'Good,' said Weiss. 'I have some security files to go back to the Reichsführer's office. They will be delivered here. I will inform the flight captain.'

Weiss left. An adjutant strode past. Minutes later he came back followed by Speer.

Voss, like Hitler (not an unconscious imitation), enjoyed working at night. He worked with the door open to hear the voices, see the men, to gain a sense of the magnetic flow – those drawn to and favoured by the Führer and those he rejected and disgraced. In the short time he'd been in Rastenburg, Voss had seen men striding down the centre of that corridor, medals, pips and epaulets flashing, to return fifteen minutes later hugging the wall, shunned even by the carpet strip in the middle. There were others, of course, who came back evangelized, something in their eyes higher than the stars, greater than love. These were the men who had 'gone', left the decrepit shell of their own bodies to walk an Elysium with other demigods, their ambitions fulfilled, their greatness confirmed.

Weber saw it differently, and said it with a cruder voice: 'These guys, they're all married with wives and families of lovely children and yet they go up there and take it up the arse every night. It's a disgrace.' Weber had accused Voss of it, too. Of sitting with his tongue out in the corridor, waiting for a tummy rub. It needled Voss only because it was true. In his first week, as Voss had laid maps down in a situation meeting while Zeitzler said his piece, the Führer had suddenly gripped Voss by the bicep and the touch had shot something fast and pure into his veins like morphine, strong, addictive but weakening, too.

The *Wolfsschanze* stilled into the early hours. Corridor traffic halted. Voss filed the orders and prepared the maps and positions for the morning conference, taking his time because he liked the feeling of working while the world was asleep. At 3.00 a.m. there was a flurry of activity from Hitler's apartment and moments later Speer appeared at the door looking like a matinée idol. He asked Voss if he wouldn't mind cancelling him from the Reichsminister's flight in the morning, he was too tired after his earlier flight and his meeting with the Führer. Voss assured him of his efficiency in the matter and Speer stepped into the room. He stood over the map and brushed a hand in a great swathe over Russia, Poland, Germany,

11

the Netherlands and France. He became conscious of Voss studying him and put his hand in his pocket. He nodded, said good night and reminded him to tell the flight captain. He didn't want to be disturbed in the morning.

Voss made the call and went to bed for three hours. He got up just before 7.00 a.m., called a car and he and the chauffeur loaded the box files, along with a black metal trunk which had appeared in the situation room addressed in white paint through a stencil to the SS Personalhauptamt, 98–9 Wilmersdorferstrasse, Berlin-Charlottenburg. They drove to the airstrip where, to their surprise, they found Todt's Heinkel charging down the runway. Voss could already feel the lash of Weiss's fury. He went to the flight captain who told him they were just testing the plane under orders from Hitler's adjutant. The plane circled twice and relanded. A sergeant with a manifest cleared the files on to the aircraft and they loaded them. Voss and the chauffeur drank a coffee in the canteen and ate bread and eggs. At 7.50 a.m. the Reichsminister's car pulled along-side and Fritz Todt boarded the Heinkel alone.

The plane immediately taxied to the end of the runway, paused, throttled up and set off down the snow-scabbed airstrip towards the black trees and low grey cloud of another grainy military morning. It should still have been dark at this hour but the Führer insisted on keeping Berlin time at his Rastenburg headquarters.

As he left the canteen Voss was arrested by the rare sight of SS Colonel Weiss outside the Restricted Area I compound. He was in the control tower, looking green through the glass, his thick arms folded across his chest, his pale face lit by some unseen light below him.

The continuous roar of the plane's engines changed tone and the wings tipped as it banked over the pine forest. This was unusual, too. The plane should have continued west, piercing the soft gut of the grey cloud to break through into the brilliant, uncomplicated sunshine above, instead of which it had rolled north and appeared to be coming back in to re-land.

The pilot straightened the wings of the plane and settled the aircraft into its descent. It was just reaching the beginning of the runway, no more than a hundred feet off the ground, when a spear of flame shot up from the fuselage behind the cockpit. Voss, already gaping, flinched as the roar of the explosion reached him. His driver ducked as the plane tilted and a wing clipped the ground, shearing away from the body of the plane, which thundered into the snow-covered ground and exploded with hideous violence, twice, a fraction of a second between each full fuel tank igniting.

Black smoke belched, funnelling out into the grey sky. Only the tailplane had survived the impact. Two fire engines stormed pointlessly out of their hangar, slewing on the icy ground. SS Colonel Weiss dropped his arms, jutted his chest, stretched his shoulders back and left the observation platform.

Voss grew into the iron-hard ground, his feet drawing up the numbing cold, transporting it through to the bones and organs of his body.

Chapter 3

Voss was driven back to Restricted Area I in silence, the dead hand of a full inquiry already on his shoulder. He pieced together the ugly fragments of information in his brain and felt his mind recoil in disgust. He began to see, for the first time, how a man could shoot himself. Until then it had been a mystery to him, on hearing of someone's suicide, how a man could bring himself to such a disastrous conclusion. He smoked hard until he was quite faint and prickling. He staggered up the path to the main building and realized on entering that the horrific news had preceded him by some minutes.

The dining room was full, but rather than being morbid with the news of the death of the most important and capable engineer in the German Reich, it was rife with the rumour of a successor. The monochrome mass of braid and band, oak leaf cluster and iron cross seethed like the bullring of the Bourse. Only one man was silent, head up, hair swept back, dark eyes shining under the thick straight eyebrows – Albert Speer. Voss blinked, sure as a camera shutter, and captured the image – a man on the brink of his destiny.

Voss took a coffee, fed himself into the knots of conversation and soon realized that anybody with anything to do with construction and transportation was in the room.

'Speer will take the Atlantic Wall, the U-boat pens and the Occupied West. It's already been talked about.'

'What about the Ukraine? The Ukraine is more important now.'

'You didn't forget that we declared war on the United States before Christmas.'

'No, I didn't, and nor did Todt.'

Silence. Heads swung to Speer's table. People were putting things to him and he was managing vague replies to their questions,

14

but he wasn't listening. He was coming to terms with a price. Appalled at the animal troughing around him, unwilling to accept anything that they attempted to confer on him, he was trying to justify to himself not only his presence there (for the first time and on such a tragic occasion), but something else whose nature he couldn't quite grasp. He seemed to be coping with a strong, unpleasant smell which had reached his nostrils only.

'He won't give it all to him . . . the Führer wouldn't do that. No experience.'

'He'll split Armaments and Munitions away from Construction.'

'You wait . . . the Reichsmarschall will be here any moment. Then we'll see . . .'

'Where is Goering?'

'At Romiten. Hunting.'

'That's only a hundred kilometres away . . . has anybody called him?'

'Goering will take Armaments and Munitions into his Commission for the Four Year Plan. He's in charge of the war economy. It fits.'

'The only thing that fits, if you ask me, is that one's face over there.'

'What's Speer *doing* here, anyway?'

'He was stuck in Dnepropetrovsk. He flew in with Captain Nein last night.'

'He *fetched* him?' asked a voice, aghast.

'No, no Captain Nein flew in there with SS General Sepp Dietrich and offered Speer a lift.'

'Did Speer and the general . . . talk?'

There was silence at that probability and Voss moved across to some air force officers who were picking over the details of the crash.

'He must have pulled the self-destruct handle.'

'Who? The pilot?'

'No, Todt . . . by accident.'

'Did it have a self-destruct mechanism on board?'

'No, it was a new plane. It hadn't been fitted.'

'What was he doing in a two-engined plane in the first place? The Führer has expressly forbidden . . .'

15

'That's what Todt was told yesterday. He was furious. The Führer waived it.'

'That's why they took the plane up for a practice spin.'

'And you're sure there was no self-destruct mechanism?'

'Positive.'

'There were three explosions ... that's what the flight sergeant said.'

'Three?'

'There must have been a self-destruct ...'

'There was none!'

Voss went to the decoding room to pick up any positional changes in the field. He took the decodes to the situation room. The corridor was silent. Hitler rarely moved before eleven o'clock, but on a day such as this? Surely. The apartment door stayed closed, the SS guards silent.

Weber was already working on supply positions in the Ukraine. He didn't look up. Voss leafed the decodes.

'SS Colonel Weiss was looking for you,' said Weber.

'Did he say what he wanted?' asked Voss, bowels loosening.

'Something about those boxes of files ...'

'Have you heard, Weber?'

'About the plane crash, you mean?'

'The Reichsminister Todt is dead.'

'Were those files on board?'

'Yes,' said Voss, stunned by Weber's insouciance.

'Shit. Zeitzler's going to be mad.'

'Weber,' said Voss, amazed, 'Todt is dead.'

'*Todt ist tot. Todt ist tot.* What can I say, other than it will brighten the Führer's day not to have that doom merchant on his shoulder.'

'For God's sake, Weber.'

'Look, Voss, Todt never agreed with the Russian campaign and when the Führer declared war on America, well ... poof!'

'Poof!?'

'Todt was a very cautious man, unlike our Führer who is ... what shall we say ... ?'

'Bold.'

'Yes, bold. That's a good, strong adjective. Let's leave it at that.'

'What are you saying, Weber?'

'Keep your head down and your ears out of that corridor. Do

your job, don't blabber, this is all that matters,' he said, and drew a circle around himself. 'You haven't been here long enough to know what these people are capable of.'

'They're already talking about Speer. Goering taking over ...'

'I don't want to know, Voss,' said Weber, closing his hands over his ears. 'And nor do you. You've got to start thinking about those files, how they got on that plane and why SS Colonel Weiss wants to talk to you, because if he wanted to talk to me after such a morning I'd have been in the toilet an hour ago. Start thinking about yourself, Voss, because here in Rastenburg you're the only one who will.'

The mention of the toilet sent Voss out of the room at a brisk pace. He sat in one of the stalls, face in hands, and passed a loose, hot motion which, rather than emptying him, left his guts writhing.

Colonel Weiss caught up with him while he washed his hands. They talked to each other via the mirror, Weiss's face disturbingly wrong in reflection.

'Those files ...' started Weiss.

'General Zeitzler's files, you mean?'

'Did you check them, Captain Voss ... before you took them into your care?'

'Took them into my care?' Voss asked himself, chest wall shuddering at the impact of this implication.

'Did you, Captain? Did you?' persisted Weiss.

'They weren't mine to check, and even if they were I wouldn't know why I would have to check a large amount of documentation irrelevant to me.'

'So who filled those boxes?'

'I didn't see them filled.'

'You *didn't*?' roared Weiss, throwing Voss into free-fall fear. 'You put boxes on to a Reichsminister's plane without ...'

'Maybe you should ask Captain Weber,' said Voss, desperate, lashing out at anything to save himself.

'Captain Weber,' said Weiss, writing him down in his book of the damned.

'I was doing him a favour putting the files on the plane in the first place, as I was for ...' He coughed at a garrotting look from Weiss and changed tack. 'Is this part of the official inquiry, sir?'

'This is the preliminary investigation prior to the official inquiry

17

which will be conducted by the air force, as it is technically an air force matter,' said Weiss, and then more threatening, 'but as you know, I'm in charge of all security matters in and around this compound . . . and I notice things, Captain Voss.'

Weiss had turned away from the mirror to look at him for real. Voss stepped back and his boot heel hit the wall but he managed to look Weiss straight in his terrible eye, hoping that his own stress, from the G-force steepness of the learning curve, was not distorting his face.

'I have a copy of the manifest,' said Weiss. 'Perhaps you should read it through now.'

Weiss handed him the paper. It started with a list of personnel on the flight. Speer's name had been added and then crossed out. Underneath was the cargo. Voss ran his eyes down the list, which was short and consisted of four boxes of files for the Army Chief of Staff, delivery Berlin, and several pieces of luggage going with Todt to Munich. There was no mention of a metal trunk for delivery to the SS Personalhauptamt in Berlin-Charlottenburg.

Voss had control of his panic now, the horizon firm in his head as he came up to the moment, or was it the line? Yes, it was something to be crossed, a line with no grey area, without no man's land, the moral line, which once stepped over joined him to Weiss's morality. He also knew that to mention the nonexistent trunk would be a life-changing decision, one that could change his life into death. It nearly amused him, that and the strange clarity of those turbulent thoughts.

'Now you understand,' said Weiss, 'why it's necessary for me to do a little probing on the question of these files.'

'Yes, sir,' said Voss. 'You're absolutely right, sir.'

'Good, we have an understanding then?'

'Yes, sir,' said Voss. 'One thing . . . wasn't there . . . ?'

Weiss stiffened in his boots, the scar dragging down his eye seemed to pulsate.

'. . . wasn't there a self-destruct mechanism on the plane?' finished Voss.

Weiss's good eye widened and he nodded, confirming that and their new understanding into him. He left the toilets. Voss reverted to the sink and splashed his hot face over and over with cold water, not able to clean exactly, but able to revise and rework, justify and accommodate the necessity for the snap decision he'd been forced to make. He dried his face and looked at himself in the mirror and had one of his odd perceptions, that we never know what we look like to others, we only know our reflection and that now he knew he would be different and it might be all right because perhaps he would just look like one of them.

He went outside for a smoke and to pace out his new understanding, as if he was wearing different boots. Senior officers came and went with only one topic of conversation on their hungry lips and two names, Speer and Todt. But by the end of that cigarette Voss had made his first intelligence discovery in the field, because the officers still came and went and they still had those two names on their lips but this time they were shaking their heads and the words 'self-destruct mechanism' and the 'incidence of failure' had threaded their way amongst the names.

It comes out of here and goes in there, thought Voss. The inestimable power of the spoken word. The power of misinformation in a thunderstruck community.

Voss went back to work. No Weber. He replotted the latest movements from the decodes. Weber returned, took a seat, braced himself against the desk. Voss kept his head down, looked at Weber through the bone of his cranium.

'At least I know you can listen now,' said Weber. 'You've passed the first Rastenburg test with an A and you don't have to worry about me and those files. I didn't fill them. I didn't seal them. I didn't even sign for them. Learn something from that, Voss. They're saying now that somebody must have accidentally pulled the self-destruct handle in the plane. We're all in the clear. Are you hearing me, Voss?'

'I'm hearing you.'

Voss did hear him, but only through the reel of film in his head which was full of the black metal trunk with its white stencilled address. His hands lifting the trunk and taking it into the plane where he jams it between the seats so it won't slide about – two of Zeitzler's boxes of files on top and two on the seats by the trunk. Todt comes on to the plane, preceded by his luggage, impatient to be away from the scene of his disastrous politicking and up into the light of the sunshine and the clear air where everything is comprehensible. He straps himself into his seat, not next to the pilot but in the fuselage where he might be able to do some work. The hold darkens as the door closes. The pilot taxis to the end of the runway. The plane steadies itself, the wings rock and stabilize. The propellers thrash the icy air. The pressure kicks in behind the old man's back and they surge down the runway flashing white, grey and black at the snow and ice patches on the strip. Then Todt sees the black trunk and some low animal instinct kicks in the paranoia and a terrible realization. He roars at the pilot to stop the plane but the pilot cannot stop. The velocity is already too great. He has to take off. The wheels defy gravity and Todt has a moment of weightlessness, a premonition of the lightness of being to follow. They bank in the steep curve, the trunk tight against the wall of the fuselage. Todt staring into the black Polish pine trees, or are they East Prussian pine trees now, Germanic Empire pine trees? Todt's weight has come back to him and he's in a panic now. He's seen the trunk before. He's seen it in his head and he knows what's in it. He knew what would be in it the night before and he woke up with the knowledge this morning and it was further confirmed by the flight captain who told him that Speer would not be on the plane. What was Speer *doing* here anyway? Todt and Speer. Two men who knew their destiny and had no hesitation in obeying. The plane's wings are still perpendicular to the ground. The black forest is still flashing past Todt's care-worn eyes. The wings flatten. They're going to make it after all. The pilot is hunched and roaring at the control tower. The altimeter winds its way down through three hundred to two hundred to one hundred and fifty and Todt is praying and the pilot is praying too, although he doesn't know why and that is how they enter the biggest noise, the whitest light. Two men praying. One who didn't like war enough and the other unlucky to be flying him.

And then silence. Not even the wind whistling through the shattered fuselage. Pure peace for the man who didn't like war enough.

'Everything all right in there, Voss?'

Voss looked up, dazed, Weber a blur in his eye.

'There was something else . . .'

'There was *nothing* else, Voss. Nothing that anybody wants to know. Nothing that I want to know. Those words stay in your head. In here we talk about military positions. All right?'

Voss went through the decodes. The black metal trunk slid into

20

a dark recess, the murky horror corner of his mind, and soon the white stencilled address was barely readable.

At 1.00 p.m. Hitler sent an adjutant to bring in his first caller of the day. The adjutant returned with Speer in his wake. Fifteen minutes later the Reichsmarschall Goering appeared in the corridor smiling and resplendent in light blue, his smooth jowls, shiny perhaps from the patina of last night's morphine sweat, juddered with each step. Half an hour later it was out. Speer had been appointed Todt's successor in *all* his capacities and the Reichsmarschall Goering's humour was reclassified as unstable.

Men from the Air Ministry sifted the wreckage for days and found nothing but seared metal and black dust. The black metal trunk with its white stencilling had ceased to exist. SS Colonel Weiss, under Hitler's instructions, conducted an internal investigation into the airport personnel and ground crew. Voss was required to supply his initials to the manifest alongside the four box files – posterity for his perjury.

The ice began to thaw, tanks whose tracks had been welded to the steppes broke free and the war rolled on, even without the greatest construction engineer in German history.

Chapter 4

18th November 1942, Wolfsschanze HQ, Rastenburg, East Prussia.

Voss wanted to remove his eyeballs and swill them in saline, see
the grit sink to the bottom. The bunker was silent with the Führer
away at the Berghof in Obersalzberg. Voss's work had been finished
hours ago but he remained at the situation table, chin resting on
his white, piled fists, staring into the map where a rough cratering
existed at a point on the Volga river. Stalingrad had been poked
and prodded, jabbed and reamed until it was a dirty, paper-flaked
hole. As Voss looked deeper into it he began to see the blackened,
snow-covered city, the cadaverous apartment buildings, the gnarled
and twisted beams of shelled factories, the poxed façades, the scree-
filled streets littered with stiffened, deep-frozen bodies and, alongside it, growing to midnight black in the white landscape and
becoming viscous with the cold, the Volga – the line of communication from the south to the north of Russia.

He was sitting in this position long after he could have gone to
bed, contemplating the grey front line that was now stretched to
the thinness of piano wire since the German Sixth Army had bal-
looned it over to Stalingrad, because of his brother. Julius Voss
was a major in the 113th Infantry Division of the Sixth Army. This
division was not one of those fighting like a pack of street dogs in
the ruins of Stalingrad but was dug into the snow somewhere on
the treeless steppe east of the point where the river Don had decided
to turn south to the Sea of Azov.

Julius Voss was his father's son. A brilliant sportsman, he'd collected a silver in the *epée* at the 1936 Berlin Olympics. He rode a
horse as if it was a part of him. On his first day's hunting at the
age of sixteen he'd tracked a deer for a whole day and shot it in
the eye from 300 metres. He was a perfect and outstanding army
officer, loved by his men and admired by his superiors. He was

intelligent and, despite his life of brilliance, there wasn't a shred of arrogance in the man. Karl thought about him a lot. He loved him. Julius had been his protector at school, sport not being one of Karl's strengths and, having too many brains for everybody's comfort, life could have been hell without a brother three years older and a golden boy, too. So Karl was taking his turn to watch over his brother.

The German position was not as strong as it might first appear. The Russians had trussed up ten divisions in and around the city in bloody and brutal street-to-street fighting since September and now, unless they could hammer home the death blow in the next month, it looked as if the rest of the German army would be condemned to spend another winter out in the open. More men would die and there would be little chance of the Sixth Army being reinforced until the spring. The situation was doomed to a four-month deep-frozen stalemate.

The door to the situation room crashed open, cannoned off the wall and slammed shut. It opened more slowly to reveal Weber standing in the frame.

'That's better,' he said, trying to put some lick on to his lips, clearly drunk, steaming drunk, his forehead shining, his eyes bright, his skin blubber. 'I knew I'd find you in here, boring the maps again.'

Weber swaggered into the room.

'You can't bore maps, Weber.'

'*You* can. Look at them, poor bastards. Insensate with tedium. You don't talk to them, Voss, that's your problem.'

'Piss off, Weber. You're ten schnapps down the hole and not fit to talk to.'

'And you? What are you doing? Is the brilliant, creative military mind of Captain Karl Voss going to solve the Stalingrad problem . . . tonight, or do we have to wait *another* twenty-four hours?'

'I was just thinking . . .'

'Don't tell me. Let me guess. You were just thinking about what the Reichsminister Fritz Todt said to you before his plane crash . . .'

'And why shouldn't I?'

'Because it's morbid in a man of your age. You should be thinking about . . . about women . . .' said Weber and, placing both hands on the table, he began some vigorous, graphic and improbable thrusting.

Voss looked away. Weber collapsed across the table. When Voss looked back, Weber's face was right there, giving him the wife's-eye view, head on the pillow, husband sweaty, lurid, tight, pink skin and wet-eyed.

'You shouldn't feel guilty just because Todt spoke to you,' said Weber, licking his lips again, eyes closed now as if imagining a kiss coming to him.

'That's not why I feel guilty. I feel . . .'

'Don't tell me, I don't want to know,' said Weber, sitting up and shunning him with a hand. 'Bore your maps, Voss. Go on. But I'll tell you this,' he came in close again, devil breath, 'Paulus will take Stalingrad before Christmas and we'll be in Persia by next spring, rolling in sherbet. The oil will be ours, *and* the grain. How long will Moscow last?'

'The Romanians on the River Don front have reported huge troop concentrations in their north-west sector,' said Voss, flat and heavy.

Weber sat up, dangled his legs and gave Voss the gab, gab, gab with his hand.

'The fucking Romanians,' he said. 'Goulash for brains.'

'That's the Hungarians.'

'What?'

'Who eat goulash.'

'What do Romanians eat?'

Voss shrugged.

'Problem,' said Weber. 'We don't know what the Romanian brain consists of, but if you ask me it's yoghurt . . . no . . . it's the whey from the top of the yoghurt.'

'You're boring me, Weber.'

'Let's have a drink.'

'You're stinking already.'

'Come on,' he said, grabbing Voss around the shoulders and barging him out of the door, their cheeks touching as they went through, horrid lovers.

Weber slashed the lights out. They put on their coats and went back to their quarters. Weber crashed about in his own room while Voss moved the chess game, which he was playing against his father by post, away from the bed. Weber appeared, triumphant, with schnapps. He crashed down on to the bed, hoicked a magazine out from under his buttocks.

'What's this?'

'*Die Naturwissenschafen.*'

'Fucking physics,' said Weber, hurling the magazine. 'You want to get into something . . .'

'. . . physical, yes, I know, Weber. Give me the schnapps, I need to be braindead to continue.'

Weber handed over the bottle, bolstered his wet head with Voss's pillow, whacking it into position with his stone cranium. Voss sipped the clear liquid which lit a trail down to his colon.

'What's physics going to do for me?' burped Weber.

'Win the war.'

'Go on.'

'Give us endless reusable energy.'

'And?'

'Explain life.'

'I don't want life explained, I just want to live it on my own terms.'

'Nobody gets to do that, Weber . . . not even the Führer.'

'Tell me how it's going to win us the war.'

'Perhaps you haven't heard talk of the atom bomb.'

'I heard Heisenberg nearly blew himself up with one in June.'

'So you've heard of Heisenberg.'

'Naturally,' said Weber, brushing imaginary lint from his fly. '*And* the chemist Otto Hahn. You think I don't stick my ear out in that corridor every now and again.'

'I won't bore you then.'

'So what's it all about? Atom bombs.'

'Forget it, Weber.'

'It goes in easier when I'm drunk.'

'All right. You take some fissionable material . . .'

'I'm lost.'

'Remember Goethe.'

'Goethe! Fuck. What did *he* say about "fissionable material"?'

'He said: "What is the path? There is no path. On into the unknown."'

'Gloomy bastard,' said Weber, snatching back the bottle. 'Start again.'

25

'There's a certain type of material, a very rare material, which when brought together in a critical mass – shut up and listen – could create as many as eighty generations of fission – shut up, Weber, just let me get it out – before the phenomenal heat would blow the mass apart. That means . . .'

'I'm glad you said that.'

'. . . that, if you can imagine this, one fission releases two hundred million electron bolts of energy and that would double eighty times before the chain reaction would stop. What do you think that would produce, Weber?'

'The biggest blast known to mankind. Is that what you're saying?'

'A whole city wiped out with one bomb.'

'You said this fissionable material's pretty rare.'

'It comes from uranium.'

'Aha!' said Weber, sitting up. 'Joachimstahl.'

'What about it?'

'Biggest uranium mine in Europe. And it's in Czechoslovakia . . . which is *ours*,' said Weber, cuddling the schnapps bottle.

'There's an even bigger one in the Belgian Congo.'

'Aha! Which is ours, too, because . . .'

'Yes, Weber, we know, but it's still a very complicated chemical process to get the fissionable material out of the uranium. The stuff they'd found was called U 235 but they could only get traces and it decayed almost instantly. Then somebody called Weizsäcker began to think about what happened to all the excess neutrons released by the fission of U 235, some would be captured by U 238, which would then become U 239, which would then decay into a new element which he called Ekarhenium.'

'Voss.'

'Yes?'

'You're boring the shit out of me. Drink some more of this and try saying it all backwards. It might, you know, make more sense.'

'I told you it was complicated,' said Voss. 'Anyway, they've found a way to make the "fissionable material" comparatively easily in an atomic pile, which uses graphite and some stuff called heavy water, which we used to be able to get from the Norsk Hydro plant in Norway – until the British sabotaged it.'

'I remember something about that,' said Weber. 'So the British know we're building this bomb.'

'They know we have the science – it's in all these magazines you're throwing around my room – but do we have the capability? It's a huge industrial undertaking, building an atomic pile is just the first step.'

'How much of this Ekarhe— shit do you need to make a bomb?'

'A kilo, maybe two.'

'That's not very much . . . to blow up an entire city.'

'Blow up isn't really the word, Weber,' said Voss. 'Vaporize is more like it.'

'Give me that schnapps.'

'It's going to take years to build this thing.'

'We'll be rolling in sherbet by then.'

Weber finished the bottle and went to bed. Voss stayed up and read his mother's part of the letter, which contained detailed descriptions of social occasions and was strangely comforting. His father, General Heinrich Voss, sitting out the war in enforced retirement, having made the mistake of voicing his opinions about the Commissar Order – where any Jews or partisans encountered in the Russian campaign were to be handed over to the SS for 'treatment' – would add an irascible note at the bottom and a chess move. This time his move was followed by the word 'check' and the line: 'You don't know it yet but I've got you on the run.' Voss shook his head. He didn't even have to think. He dragged the chair with the chessboard to him, made his father's move and then his own, which he scribbled on to a note and put in an envelope to post in the morning.

At 10.00 a.m. 19th November the first conference of the day got underway with a discussion over an enlarged map of Stalingrad and its immediate vicinity. No attempt had been made to alter the map to show the true state of the city. All it indicated was neatly packaged sectors, red for Russian, grey for German, like peacetime postal districts.

At 10.30 a.m. the teleprinters shunted into life and the phones started ringing. General Zeitzler was called from the room, to return minutes later with the announcement that a Russian offensive had started at 05.20 a.m. He showed how a Russian tank force had broken through the Romanian sectors and was now heading south-east towards the river Don, and that activity had broken out along the whole front to hold German forces in their positions. A panzer corps had been sent to engage the advancing Russians. Everything was in hand. Voss made the necessary alterations to the map. They went back to the Stalingrad situation leaving Zeitzler fingering the small flag of the panzer corps and rasping a hand over his sandpaper chin.

By lunchtime the next day news reached Rastenburg of a second large Russian offensive starting south of Stalingrad, with such huge numbers of tanks and infantry it was inconceivable that they'd had no intelligence.

The Stalingrad map was rolled and stacked.

It was clear that full encirclement of the Sixth Army was the Russian intention. Voss felt sick and empty as Zeitzler dragged him and his inexhaustible memory around wherever he went. Voss stood over Zeitzler's telephone conversations to the Führer, vomiting information which the Army Chief of Staff would use in a desperate bid to impress on Hitler the dire circumstances and the need to allow the Sixth Army to retreat. The Führer paced the great hall of the Berghof swearing at Slavs and hammering tables into submission.

Sunday, 22nd November was *Totensonntag*, the day of remembrance for the dead, and after a subdued service they heard that the two Russian forces were about to meet and that encirclement was a foregone conclusion. The Führer left the Berghof for Leipzig to fly on to Rastenburg.

As Voss began the monumental task of drafting orders for the phased withdrawal of the Sixth Army the Führer stopped his train en route to Leipzig and called Zeitzler expressly to forbid any retreat.

Zeitzler sent Voss back to his room and, to take his mind off the disaster, Voss pored over the chess game. In doing so he suddenly saw his error, or rather, he perceived his father's strength of position. He searched for the letter he'd scribbled days ago and found that one of the orderlies had posted it for him. He took out another sheet of paper and wrote one word on it. Resigned.

The Führer arrived in Rastenburg on 23rd November and after the initial shock of the Russian success nerves steadied. In the days

28

and weeks that followed the disaster, Voss witnessed the transformation of the Rastenburg HQ. It ceased to be a military installation and became instead the stuff of legend. Men would arrive, tear off their cloaks and capes and perform miracles in front of their glassy-eyed leader. Vast and powerfully armoured divisions, miraculously supplied, would appear and drive up from the south to relieve the stricken army. When, as in some bizarre game of three-card monte, this force failed to materialize, another maestro would whisk away a silken sheet and show fleets of aircraft supplying and resupplying until, brought back up to full strength, the Sixth Army would take Stalingrad, break the Russian encirclement and assume their position in Germanic legend. Everything became possible. Rastenburg became a circus where the greatest illusionists of the time came to perform.

At this stage, in the weeks leading up to Christmas, a sickness settled itself in Voss's gut. The news of men dying of starvation and cold, and the back to back shows from prestidigitators from all the forces, sealed off his stomach. His blue eyes sunk back into his head, his uniform hung off his ribs. He sipped water or schnapps and smoked upwards of fifty cigarettes a day.

In mid December an attempt was made to relieve the army from the south. The Russians stalled the attack and proceeded to smash the Italian army and decimate the air transport fleet. Still the Führer refused permission for the Sixth Army to retreat; his eyes seared the situation maps demanding deliverance.

Voss listened, first to the quality of the silence in the situation conferences, which were black, crushing and hideous, and then to the boot-licking apostles of the High Command who would pledge the impossible for one look of love from the Führer. He asked for a transfer to the front. Zeitzler refused him and, perhaps after seeing the bones appearing through the skin of Voss's face, went on Stalingrad rations himself. They became known as 'the cadavers'.

There had been no improvement in the German Sixth Army's position by the beginning of January 1943 and Voss, pale with his facial skin drawn tightly over his skull, found himself on his bed in his room smoking and sipping some of Weber's violent schnapps. He had two letters in front of him on the seat of a chair where he used to keep the chess games he played with his father. There'd been no chess since his resignation back in November. The two letters, both short, one from his father and the other from his brother, had presented him with a problem whose only solution involved calling on SS Colonel Bruno Weiss.

The *Kessel*, Stalingrad

1st January 1943

Dear Karl,

You know better than anyone our situation out here. I can only thank you for trying to send us the sausages and ham for Christmas but it was a lost cause. They probably never got off the airstrip. Real meat has not been seen for weeks. Krebs and Stahlschuss came up with some shreds of dried mule so that we managed to have some kind of celebration for the New Year. It wasn't as good as Christmas which, whatever happens to me now, will have been one of the greatest military experiences of my short career. It's difficult to believe in this unbearable environment that men can find (I've thought about this a long time to try to find the right word) such sweetness in themselves. They gave each other things which were their last and most important possessions and if they had nothing they made something from bits of metal or carved bone retrieved from the steppe. It was remarkable to find the human spirit so undaunted. Glaser has tried to have me taken to the hospital again (I'm yellow, and the legs are still badly swollen so that I can't move about) but I've refused. I never want to see that vision of hell again. I won't tell you. You must have heard by now.

I listen to the men and there's been a change in their mood now. Before the New Year they would say that the Führer will rescue them. Now, if they still think that, they don't say it. We are resigned to our fate and you might be surprised to hear that we are cheerful because, and I know this will sound absurd in the circumstances, we are free.

I think of you and am always your brother,

Julius

Karl read this letter over and over. His brother had never been one for the examination of the soul and his discovery of the nobility of man in these desperate circumstances was a revelation. Karl was sickened by the thought of playing on Weiss's side of the fence to get what he wanted.

Berlin

2nd January 1943

Dear Karl,
We have had another letter from Julius. His are not censored like some of the junior officers'. Your mother cannot read them even though he makes light of the terrible things around him. He seems so inured to the desperate circumstances that he doesn't see that what he considers normal is, to people in Berlin, unimaginable horror. I do not ask this of you lightly. I only ask this of you because I saw some of this pointlessness in the Great War. It goes against every military instinct I have but I would like you to do everything you can to get your brother out of that place. I know it is forbidden. I know it is impossible but I must ask this of you on behalf of your mother and for myself.

Your father

Voss lay back on the bed, his boots up on the metal bar at his feet, the two letters on his chest resting against his protruding ribs. He lit another cigarette from the one he'd been smoking. He knew that if anything happened to Julius it could potentially destroy his family. Since his father had been 'retired', he'd invested all his hopes and aspirations in his first-born son. He thought it possible that his father might be able to bear Julius's death in glorious victory but not, definitely not, in miserable defeat.

Voss swung his feet off the bed and slapped a sheet of paper on to the chair. He would have preferred to ask this favour of General Zeitzler but knew that he could not possibly grant him the request. SS Colonel Weiss was the only man with whom he had any leverage, if that was a word he could use when it came to the SS.

He began writing in his horrible, cramped scrawl, handwriting

31

that had developed because his brain always worked faster than his fingers. He balled his first attempt and tried again. He screwed that one up, too. He didn't know what he wanted for his brother. He wanted to save him, of course, but on what terms? Julius, his state of mind heightened to rare acuity, would not be easily duped.

Rastenburg

5th January 1943

Dear Julius,
The officer who will give you this letter will be able to get you out of your predicament, fly you out of the *Kessel* and eventually into hospital back in Berlin. You have a stark and terrible decision to make. If you stay, our mother and, you know this to be true, more especially our father will be heartbroken. You, his eldest son, have always been his lodestone, the one to whom he is naturally drawn, from whom he derives his energy and now, since his retirement, in who he has invested all his hope. He would be a broken man without you in his life.

If you leave, your men will not despise you but you will despise yourself. You will bear the guilt of the survivor, the guilt of the chosen one. This is possibly, and only you can answer this question, reparable damage. Whatever happens in our father's mind will not be.

I cannot believe I am having to deliver the burden of this choice to you in your desperate circumstances. In earlier attempts I tried to dress it up nicely, a temptation for Julius, but it refused to be pretty. It is an ugly choice. For my part, all I can say is that, whatever you decide, you are always my brother and I have never felt that there's any better man living.

Karl

Voss buttoned his tunic, put on his coat and went out under the icicle fringes of his hut into the frozen air. His boots rang on the hard, snow-packed ground. He entered Restricted Area I and went straight to the Security Command post from where he knew SS Colonel Weiss would be running his brutal régime. The other soldiers looked at him as he entered. Nobody came willingly into the Security Command post. Nobody ever wanted to talk to SS Colonel Weiss. He was shown straight in. Weiss sat behind his desk in a state of livid surprise, his white skin even whiter against the deep black of his uniform, his crimson stepped scar from his eye to cheek redder. Voss's nerve ricocheted around his stomach looking for a way out.

'What can I do for you, Captain Voss?'

'A personal matter, sir.'

'Personal?' Weiss asked himself; he didn't normally deal with the personal.

'I believe we reached a very special understanding between each other last February and that is why I have come to you with this personal matter.'

'Sit,' said Weiss, as if he was a dog. 'You look ill, Captain.'

'Lost my appetite, sir,' said Voss, lowering himself into a chair on shaky thighs. 'You know . . . the situation with the Sixth Army . . . is traumatic for everybody.'

'The Führer will resolve the problem. We will win the day, Captain. You will see,' said Weiss, giving him a wary look, already at work on the subtext of the words.

'My brother is in the *Kessel*, sir. He is extremely sick.'

'Haven't his men taken him to the hospital for treatment?'

'They have, but his condition did not respond to the treatment they have available in the field hospital there. He asked to be taken back to his division. I believe his condition is only treatable *outside* the *Kessel*.'

Weiss said nothing. The fingers he ran over his scarred cheek had well-cared for nails, glossy, packed with protein but tinged blue from underneath.

'Where are you quartered, Captain?' asked Weiss after a long pause.

It caught him off guard. He wasn't sure where he was quartered any more. Numbers tinkered in his brain.

'Area III, C4,' he said.

'Ah yes, you're next to Captain Weber,' said Weiss, so quickly that it was clear that his question hadn't been necessary.

33

The chair back cut into Voss's newly exposed ribs. You didn't build up any credit in Weiss's world, you always had to pay.

'Captain Weber is not a careful individual, is he, Captain Voss?'

'In what respect, sir?'

'Drunken, loose-tongued, curious.'

'Curious?'

'Inquisitive,' said Weiss. 'And I notice you don't disagree with my first two observations.'

'Forgive me for saying so, sir, but in my opinion Weber is the least inquisitive man I know, very concentrated on his task,' said Voss. 'And as for drinking . . . who doesn't?'

'Loose-tongued?' asked Weiss.

'Who's there to be loose-tongued with?'

'Have you been with Captain Weber on any of his trips to town?'

Voss blinked. He didn't know anything about Weber's trips to town.

Weiss played the edge of his desk one-handed, a tremolo finished with a rapped flourish.

'He has a very sensitive position right in the heart of the matter,' said Weiss. 'What do you two talk about when you're drinking together?'

Voss shouldn't have been shocked, but he was, at Weiss's apparent omniscience. A squirt of adrenalin slithered through his veins, panic tightened his neck glands.

'Nothing of importance.'

'Tell me.'

'He's asked me to explain things to him.'

'Like what? Chess?'

'He hates chess.'

'Then what?'

'Physics. He knew I went to Heidelberg before I was called up.'

'Physics?' repeated Weiss, eyes glazing.

Voss thought he sensed a nonchalance that made him think that this was perhaps dangerous ground, mine-sown.

'The evenings are long here in Rastenburg,' said Voss to cover himself. 'He teases me. He says I should be thinking of things more *physical*. You know, women.'

'Women,' said Weiss, laughing with so little mirth it became something else.

'He's more frustrated than he is inquisitive,' said Voss, aware that Weiss wasn't listening any more.

'So you would like to get your brother out of the *Kessel*,' said Weiss, opting for an alarming change of direction which left Voss thinking he'd said things he hadn't. 'Yes, in view of our earlier understanding I think that could be arranged. Do you have his details?'

Voss handed over his letter, wondering if the tiny morsel about Weber he'd offered was as good as a whole carcass to Weiss's paranoia.

'Rest assured,' said Weiss, 'we will get him out. I look forward to continuing our special understanding, Captain Voss.'

Voss heard nothing more from Weiss and he didn't put himself in the man's way. He wrote a note to his father saying that he'd put the process of getting Julius away from Stalingrad in motion, he was waiting for news and it might take a little time because of the shambolic state inside the *Kessel*. He avoided Weber and began to play against himself at chess without, curiously, ever being able to win.

A week later there was a conference in the situation room with all the senior officers in the *Wolfsschanze* present. It was a meeting that would change Karl Voss. A captain had flown in from the front and Voss had heard that he had been primed to deliver a speech on the real situation on the ground. Voss slipped into the meeting in time to hear the captain deliver his vision of horror. Lice-ridden men living off water and shreds of horse meat, others jaundiced with their limbs swollen to twice the size, hundreds of men a day dying of starvation in the brutal cold, the wounded at the airstrip left out in the open, their blood congealed to ice, the dead stacked on the impenetrable ground. The Führer took it, shoulders rounded, lids weighed down.

And then the moment.

The captain moved on to a complete rundown of the decimated fighting strength of every unit within the *Kessel* and without. Hitler nodded. Slowly he turned to the map and squeezed his chin. As the Führer's slightly shaking hand moved out from his side the captain faltered. Hitler stood a flag up which had fallen over and began to talk about an SS panzer division, which was three weeks

35

from the action. The captain's words still came out as he'd no doubt rehearsed again and again, but they had no meaning. It was as if all the conjunctions and prepositions had been stripped out, all the verbs had become their opposites, all nouns incomprehensible.

Silence, as the captain's boot squeak retreated. Hitler surveyed all his officers, his eyes beseeching, the terrible violence of red on the map below him flooding his face. Field Marshal Keitel, face trembling with emotion, stepped forward with a thunderous crack from his boot heel and roared over the deadly silence:

'*Mein Führer*, we will hold Stalingrad.'

At breakfast the next day Voss ate properly for the first time in weeks. Afterwards, as he headed to the situation room, he was called to the Security Command post. He sat down in Weiss's hard chair. Weiss leaned over and gave him an envelope. It contained his own letter to Julius unopened and with it a note.

The Kessel

12th January 1943

Dear Captain Voss,
An officer arrived today saying that he had come to pick up your brother. It is my sad duty to inform you that Major Julius Voss died on 10th January. We are his men and we would like you to know that he left this life with the same courage with which he endured it. His thoughts were never for himself but only ever for the men under his command . . .

Voss couldn't read on. He put the note and letter back in their envelope, saluted SS Colonel Weiss and went back to the main building where he found the toilets and emptied his first solid breakfast in weeks into the bowl.

The news that afternoon, of the final assault on the abandoned Sixth Army, reached Voss from a strange distance, like words penetrating a sick child's mind. Did it happen or not?

There was nothing to be done and he finished work early. The sense of doom in the situation room was unbearable. The generals crowded the maps as if coffin-side at a vigil. He went back to his quarters and knocked on Weber's door. A strange person answered it. Voss asked after Weber. The man didn't know him. He went to the next door, found another captain sitting on his bed smoking.

'Where's Weber?' he asked.

The captain turned his mouth down, shook his head.

'Security breach or something. He was taken away yesterday. I don't know, don't ask. Not in this . . . climate, anyway. If you know what I mean,' said the captain, and Voss didn't move, stared at him so that the man felt the need to say more. 'Something about . . . well, it's only rumour . . . don't hold with it myself. You wouldn't if you knew Weber.'

Voss still said nothing and the captain was sufficiently uncomfortable to get off his chair and come to the door.

'I know Weber,' said Voss, with the certainty of someone who was about to be proven wrong.

'They found him in bed with a butcher's delivery boy in town.'

Voss went to his room and wrote to his mother and father. It was a letter which left him exhausted, drained of everything so that his arms hung hopeless and unliftable at his sides. He went to bed early and slept, waking twice in the night to find tears on his face. In the morning he was woken up by an orderly and told to report to General Zeitzler's office.

Zeitzler sat him down and didn't stand behind his desk but leaned against the front of it. He looked avuncular, not his usual military self. He gave Voss permission to smoke.

'I have some bad news,' he said, his fingers pattering his thigh. 'Your father died last night . . .'

Voss fixed his eyes on Zeitzler's left epaulette. The only words to reach him were 'compassionate leave'. By lunchtime he found himself in the half-dead light, standing away from the edge of the dark pine trees alongside the railway track, a grey sack of clothes on one side and a small brown suitcase on the other. The Berlin train left at 1.00 p.m. and although he was heading into his mother's grief he could only feel that this was a new beginning and that greater possibilities existed away from this place, this hidden kingdom – the *Wolfsschanze*.

Chapter 5

17th January 1943, Voss family home, Berlin-Schlachtensee.

'No, no, they sent somebody to see us,' said Frau Voss. 'They sent Colonel Linge, you remember him, an old friend of your father's, retired, a good man, not too stiff like the rest of them, he has something, a sensitivity, he's not a man that assumes everybody's the same as himself, he can differentiate, a rare trait in military circles. Of course, as soon as your father saw him he knew what it was about. But you see . . .' She blinked but the tears fattened too quickly and rolled down her cheeks before she could get the clutched, lace-edged handkerchief to her face.

Karl Voss leaned over and took his mother's free hand, a hand that he remembered differently, not so bony, frail and blue-veined. How fast grief sucks out the marrow – some days off food, three nights without sleep, the mind spiralling its dark gyre, in and out, but always around and around the same terrible, hard point. It was a force more destructive than a ravaging illness where the body's instinct is to fight. Grief provides all the symptoms but no fight. There's nothing to fight for. It's already gone. Stripped of purpose the mind turns on the body and reduces it. He squeezed her hand, trying to inject some of his youth into her, his sense of a future.

'It was wrong,' she said, careful not to say 'he'. 'He shouldn't have placed so much hope in your letter. I didn't to start with, but he infected me with his . . . Having him around the house all the time, he worked on me until we became these two candles in the window, waiting.'

She blew her nose, took a deep, trembling breath.

'Still, Colonel Linge came. They went into his study. They talked for quite some time and then your father showed the colonel to the door. He came in here to see me and he was calm. He told me that Julius had died and all the wonderful things that Colonel

38

Linge had said about him. And then he went back to his study and locked himself in. I was worried but not so worried, although now I see what his calmness was. His mind was made up. After some hours sitting alone here I went to bed, knocking on his door on the way. He told me to go up, he'd join me, which he did, hours later, maybe two or three o'clock in the morning. He slept, or maybe he didn't, at least he lay on his side and didn't move. He was up before I was awake. In the kitchen he said he was going to see Dr Schulz. I spoke to Dr Schulz afterwards and he did go to see him. He asked him for something to keep him calm and Dr Schulz, he's very good, he gave him some herbal teas, took his blood pressure, which was high but to be expected. Dr Schulz even asked him, "You're not thinking of doing anything stupid, are you, General?" and your father replied "What? Me? No, no, why do you think I'm here?" and he left. He drove to the Havel, into Wannsee and out again, parked the car, walked along the waterfront and shot himself.'

No tears this time. She just sat back and breathed evenly, looking at nothing beyond the short horizon of her own thoughts which were: he didn't do it in his study, nor in the car, always a considerate man. He went out on the cold, hard ground and pointed the gun at the offending organ, his heart, not his head, and fired off two bullets into it. He froze out there. He was set solid by the time he was found, no walkers at this time of year, and short, bitter afternoons. She'd gone a little crazy that night he didn't come home. She woke up in the morning to find all the gardening tools laid out in the kitchen. What had she been thinking? She came to, her son's pulse thudding into her.

'On his desk are the letters he wrote,' she said. 'There's one there for you. Read it and we'll talk again. And put some coal on the fire. I know it's valuable but I'm just too cold today . . . you know how it gets into the marrow some days.'

Karl threw some pieces on the fire, put his hands in there for a second until the heat nipped them. He went to his father's study, his boots loud on the wooden floor of the corridor the way his father's were, so that Julius and he could hear them from the top of the house. Louder as he got heavier with the years.

He found the letter and sat in a leather armchair by the window, which still offered dim, late afternoon light.

Berlin-Schlachtensee

14th January 1943

Dear Karl,

This action I have taken is as a result of my unique perception
of a series of events in my life. It has nothing to do with
you. I know you did everything possible to get Julius out and
it was typical of him to make light of the seriousness of his
physical condition so that none of us could have known how
close to death he was. Your mother, too, is blameless in this.
She has given of her strength constantly and in the last two
years I have been an even more difficult man to live with than
I was before.

I have been overwhelmed by despair, not just because of
the sudden termination of my career, but also because of my
helplessness in the face of what I fear will be the direst
consequences for Germany as a result of our aggression and
the extent of our aggression over the past three years.

Don't misunderstand me. I, as you know, approved of
Hitler in those early years. He returned to the nation the belief
in ourselves which we had lost in that first terrible war. I
encouraged Julius into the Party as well as the army. I, like
everybody else, was inspired. But the Commissar Order, which
I vehemently opposed, was for a very important reason. Certain
things have happened and will continue to happen in Germany
and the rest of Europe while the National Socialists are in
power. You have heard of these things. They are truly terrible.
Too terrible, in so many ways, to believe. My stand against
the Commissar Order was an attempt to prevent the army
from acquiescing to these other, darker, politically motivated
and utterly dishonourable actions. I failed and paid the penalty,
a small one compared to the eternal damnation of the
German Army for conspiring in these appalling deeds. If we
lose this war, and it is possible, given the extent to which we
have stretched ourselves over so many fronts, that the defeat
of the Sixth Army at Stalingrad is the beginning, then our
army officers will face the same retribution as the brutes and
thugs in the SS. We have all been tarred by obeying the
Commissar Order.

This was the beginning of my despair and my removal from the battlefield compounded it in helplessness. When this abandonment of principle was combined with the leadership's utter failure to respond to the predicament of a far-flung army I realized that we were lost, that fundamental military logic no longer applied, that more than honour had been handed over with the acquiescence to the Commissar Order. Our generals have been emasculated, we will be run by the Corporal from now on. That this abysmal state of affairs should have resulted in the death of my first-born son was more than I could bear. I am no longer young. The future looks bleak amidst the wasteland of my shattered beliefs. Everything I stood for, believed in and cherished has fallen.

Two more things. At my funeral there will be a man called Major Manfred Giesler. He is an officer with the Abwehr. You will either talk to him if you believe in what I have said in the early part of this letter or you will not. That is your decision.

My body will be cremated and I would like you to scatter my ashes on a grave in the Wannsee church cemetery belonging to Rosemarie Hausser 1888–1905.

I wish you a happy and successful life and hope that you will once again be able to pursue your aptitude in physics in more peaceful times.

Your ever loving father

PS It is absolutely imperative that this letter be destroyed after you have read it. Failure to do so could result in danger for yourself, your mother and Major Giesler. If my predictions as to the course of this war prove to be correct you will see that letters containing such sentiments will carry heavy consequences.

Voss reread the letter and burnt it in the grate, watching the slow, greenish flames consume and blacken the paper. He sat by the window again in a state of shock at this, his first intimate sight of the workings of his father's mind. He gathered himself for a few moments; the conflicting emotions needed to be reined in before he went to speak to his mother. Anger and grief didn't seem to be able to sit in the same room for very long.

He went back to his mother who still sat in the same position, the light poorer but her scalp visible under her grey hair, which he'd never seen before.

'So,' she said before he had sat down, 'he told you about the girl.'

'He told me he wants his ashes cast on her grave.'

His mother nodded, and looked over her shoulder as if she'd heard something outside. The light caught her face, no sadness, only acceptance.

'She was somebody he knew, an army officer's daughter. He fell in love with her and she died. I think he knew her for all of one week.'

'One week?' said Voss. 'He told you this?'

'He told me about the girl, he was a totally honourable man, your father, incapable even of omission. His sister filled in the details.'

'But you're his wife and . . . I can't do this.'

'You can, Karl. You will. If it's his wish, it's mine too. Just think of it as your father being in love with the idea, or rather an ideal, that was not complicated or tarnished by the grind of everyday life. That is the purest form of love you can find. Perfection,' she said, shrugging. 'I can think of no better thing after what your father went through, than for him to rest with his ideal. To him it was a vision of peace that he failed to attain in life.'

The funeral took place three days later. There were few people, most of his father's friends were at one front or another. Frau Voss invited the few back to her house for some tea. Major Giesler was one who accepted. At the house Karl asked for a private word with him and they went into his father's study.

Voss began to tell him the contents of his father's letter. Giesler stopped him, went to the phone, followed the line to the wall and removed the pin from the socket. He sat back down in the leather chair by the window. Voss told him of his willingness to talk. Giesler said nothing. He had his hands clasped and was chewing on a knuckle, one of the few hairless regions of his body. He was very dark and his thick black eyebrows joined over his nose. He had a large, full-lipped, sensual mouth and his cheeks, razored that morning, already needed to be reshaved.

'I would understand,' said Voss, 'if you needed to make some inquiries about me before we talk.'

'We've already made our inquiries,' said Giesler.

Voss thought for a moment.

'In Rastenburg?'

'We know, for instance, how you felt about the . . . the death of the Reichsminister Todt,' said Giesler, 'and your . . . disappointment with the way in which good soldiers died needlessly at Stalingrad and, of course, you have an impeccable pedigree.'

Voss frowned, replayed some reels in his mind.

'Weber?'

Giesler opened his hands, reclasped them.

'Weber disappeared,' said Voss. 'What happened to him?'

'We didn't know he was a homosexual. There are some things that even the deepest of inquiries will not unearth.'

'But where is he?'

'He is in very serious trouble, which he brought on himself,' said Giesler. 'He behaved recklessly in a climate where scapegoats were eagerly sought.'

'He must have been under pressure . . .'

'Drinking is one thing.'

'How do you know I'm not homosexual?'

Giesler looked at him long and hard, that sensual mouth becoming unnerving.

'Weber,' he said after some time, as if perhaps that source hadn't been as reliable as he'd have liked.

'Well, he should know, although I'm not sure how. Women were not abundant in Rastenburg and those that were available . . .' he drifted off, disheartened by the turn the conversation had taken; this dip into the ignoble was not what he'd had in mind. This was supposed to be a courageous act and here they were parting the dirt.

Giesler had his answer. He didn't need to pursue this discussion further. He gave Voss an address of a villa in Gatow with a meeting time for the next day and stood. They shook hands and Giesler hung on, which at first Voss thought was another sexuality test but, no, it was a sincerity hold, a brotherhood clasp.

'Weber won't talk,' he said. 'It's possible he will survive, although he will never get back into Rastenburg. But it is something for you to think about before you come to Gatow tomorrow. It's not easy to be an enemy of the State – not, I hasten to add, an enemy of the nation, but *this* State. It is dangerous and lonely work. You will be lying to your colleagues every day for perhaps years. You will have no friends because friends are dangerous. Your work will require a mental fortitude, not intelligence necessarily, but strength and it is something you may feel you do not have. If you do not come to Gatow tomorrow nobody will think any the less of you. We will go our separate ways, praying for Germany.'

Voss slept badly that night in a torment over his part in Weber's arrest. At four in the morning, the death and debt hour, he found his mind crowded with thoughts of his father and mother, Julius and Weber, and it was then that he had a sudden perception of the power of words, of the business of communication. Once words are said nothing is the same. His father didn't have to tell his mother about Rosemarie Hausser, but he did. It must have established an unrecoverable distance, instilled a lifelong sense of disappointment in his mother with a short line, some words and a name. In his own crucial conversation with Weiss, which he had not been prepared for, he realized that it was not physics that had alerted him but the words 'physical' and 'women'. It had been a confirmation. It made him think that in talking to people you never know what they know, you never know what they think, and innocuous words can take on huge importance. He stopped writhing in his bed – he hadn't served up Weber, he'd just handed Weiss the spoons.

He went to Gatow the following afternoon, nervous as if it was a visit to the doctor, who might find a mild symptom the precursor of something deadly. He was met by a housekeeper who took him to a book-lined room at the back of the house. She gave him real coffee and a homemade biscuit. Giesler came in with a large man of military rectitude but who was dressed in a blue double-breasted suit. He was bald with a brown, clipped fringe of hair at the back and sides. He wore gold-rimmed spectacles. Voss was introduced but the man's name was never given.

They talked about his work at Heidelberg University and recent developments in physics. The man was knowledgeable, not expert, but he understood. The words 'fissionable material', 'critical mass',

44

'chain reaction' and 'atomic pile' were not mysterious concepts.

The conversation switched from physics to the Russians. Voss expressed his fear of them:

'They have no reason to be forgiving after what we have done to them. We have broken a pact, invaded their country, and brutalized the population. After the defeat we have suffered at Stalingrad it is possible that they will have the confidence to drive us back. If they succeed I believe they will not stop until they reach Berlin. They will punish us.'

'So you would see it as advantageous that we negotiate a separate peace with the Allies?'

'Imperative, unless we want to see Germany or a part of Germany in the Soviet Union. Perhaps we can even persuade the Allies that we are not the real enemy in this war and that . . .'

The man held up his hand.

'One step at a time,' said the man firmly. 'First we will work on your transfer away from Rastenburg. You will need some training, too. The Abwehr headquarters along with the Army High Command has moved south to Zossen and we now live for our sins in a concrete citadel out there called Maibach II. You will spend some months with us. The work you will be doing is very different – gathering information, running agents in the field – it's not the military intelligence that you know. After that we will send you to Paris and from there we will try to position you in Lisbon.'

'Lisbon?'

'It's the only place in Europe now where we can talk easily with the Allies.'

Voss lived with his mother while he completed his training in Zossen. She looked after him as if he was at school again and it was a comfort for both of them. It was a wrench when he was transferred to France in June.

He spent eight months in the Abwehr's French headquarters at 82 Avenue Foch in Paris and, furnished with his new perception of the power of words, saw the horrific consequences for others who hadn't yet come to the same understanding.

French and British men and women were arrested, sent to concentration camps, tortured and executed for what was, more than half the time, a totally imaginary situation. Both the Abwehr and the SD/Gestapo, who operated from next door, were playing what became known as radio games. Voss never worked out whether it was merely Allied stupidity or German infiltration into their intelligence operations at a very high level which enabled these deadly games to be played. Once an Allied radio operator was captured and his codename and signal extracted an Abwehr operator would continue broadcasting to London. Later when there were two security signals required, the Allies would reply simply reminding the operator that he'd forgotten his second signal but to continue. The baffled and angry radio operators soon supplied the second security signal to the Germans. Following these fictitious Abwehr broadcasts more agents and supplies would be flown into some misty French field and a reception from the Occupying force. These new agents' codenames were then used to build fictitious networks operated by the Abwehr and Gestapo, dispersing vast quantities of misinformation to the Allies. Meetings convened by operational Allied agents were frequently attended by Abwehr men using captured agents' codenames.

Occasionally Voss would stage arrests in the street to maintain verisimilitude.

Most intelligence activity was mirage and artifice. Very little was real. Intelligence, he discovered, was built on the foundations of the imagination and, in the case of the radio games, a blind belief in the veracity of technology. It was a terrifying concept, as terrifying as if the basic principles of physics or maths were completely wrong and whole academic disciplines had been built on falsehood and thus all discoveries were intrinsically wrong, all achievements bogus.

Voss also learned never to fall in love in this world. Lovers betrayed each other easily. Torture, the Gestapo's preferred method, was unnecessary. Just the insinuation of a lover's infidelity to a prisoner was as powerful as any of their appalling applications. The emotional betrayal played such devious and teasing tricks on the mind. Jealousy was inevitable in the loneliness of a cell. The darkness, with only the infected mind for company, created powerful images that at first disheartened and later so enraged and ravaged the prisoners that they would grasp at a new strength and in their vindictiveness bring down not just the lover, but all the connections as well.

This did not mean that Voss was celibate in his time in Paris – that was impossible and there was something to prove to Giesler too – but he kept his distance. A Frenchwoman called Françoise Larache taught him a different and darker lesson about love in the intelligence game.

They met when using the same bar. He would take a coffee in the mornings and find her watching him. He would stop off in the evening for a glass of something and she was often there at a table, smoking her strong cigarettes. They exchanged words and began to share a table, where he would watch her red lips connect with the thick tip of her cigarette, and her fingers pick off the flakes of tobacco from her pointed tongue. One night they went for a meal and back to his apartment where they made love. She was energetic and inventive, doing things on their first night which surprised him.

They became regulars of each other's company in bed, and as Françoise was quick to demand, out of bed as well. She pushed him to do things which were at first exciting and then became increasingly more reckless. She liked to make love on the balcony with people passing in the street below. She would lean back over the rail, her arms around his neck, and then suddenly let go so that he nearly lost her over the edge. They would have sex in doorways and on landings while people ate their dinner and table-talked. She would even cry out and the talk would stop inside. Voss would have to close his hand over her mouth. The greater the chance of being discovered, the more excited Françoise became.

Then one day in the autumn with the dried leaves rustling over the balcony, her mischievous eye, the one that glinted when she looked up at him from under her eyebrow, became darker, as if he was seeing deeper in and what was there was more sinister, taboo.

It started with a request that he spank her for being a naughty girl. Voss felt stupid with a grown woman over his knees and she had to encourage him to be serious and to be more severe. It didn't seem to be fun any more. He still lusted after her, but for Françoise the sex was being driven by something else. He became reluctant to play her games, she angry. They had furious arguments, monumental rows with flying objects, which would end in brutal lovemaking where each thrust into her seemed to be a payment back. He found himself reeling out of his apartment into the docility of occupied Paris, unable to believe what he'd participated in the night before, only knowing that it was powerful, intense and degrading.

Françoise's goading became worse. There was no fun now. She said terrible, unforgivable things and, although he could see what she was doing, he was a part of it too. There was no stepping back. She was forcing him to slap her, and not just a hysteria-breaking slap, a punishing slap. She wanted to be hit hard. She drove her face at him. The words came out slicing the air, lacerating, stabbing, each one honed to cut deep to the bone. They grappled and wrestled each other to the floor. She sunk her nails into his neck. He wrenched himself free and found his fist cocked back to his shoulder. He swayed, dizzy at what this had come to. Her face was suddenly soft, her eyes dreamy. This was what she wanted. He stood up, straightened his clothes. All lust gone. Her face hardened. He gave her his hand, she took it and he pulled her to her feet. She spat in his face. He pulled her to the door, grabbing her coat and handbag on the way, and threw her out of the apartment.

He made discreet inquiries. She was an informer, a collaborator. She delivered her countrymen, neatly trussed, to the Gestapo. The SD man Voss spoke to tapped the side of his head, shook it.

He saw her once more before he left Paris, walking in a snow-covered street on the arm of a huge, black-coated SS sergeant. Voss hid in a doorway as they went past. She was holding snow to the side of her face.

In mid January 1944 Voss was called to a meeting at the Hotel Lutecia. It was at night and the room in which the meeting was being held was dark. Only a small lamp lit one corner. The man he was meeting sat in front of the light, he had no face, only the silhouette of hair combed back, maybe grey or white. His voice was old. A voice that spoke as if under pressure, as if the chest was tight with phlegm.

'There are going to be some changes,' he said. 'It seems our friend Kaltenbrunner at the Reich's Main Security Office is going to get his way and bring the Abwehr under the direct control of the SD. God knows, they've been trying long enough. It is something we are going to have to live with. We want to be sure that you are in position with the right information for negotiation with the Allies before it happens. I understand you have been following the activities of a French communist intellectual, Olivier Mesnel, here in Paris.'

'We are in the process of disentangling his network. We haven't found out yet how his information is reaching Moscow or how his orders come in.'

'He has now applied for a visa to go to Spain.'

'He is ultimately heading for Lisbon,' said Voss. 'We were lucky enough to intercept the courier sent by the Portuguese communists asking him to go there.'

'Do you have any idea why he is required in Lisbon?'

'No, and I don't think Mesnel does either.'

'You will take this opportunity to follow him to Lisbon and to install yourself as the military attaché and security officer in the German Legation. When these changes come through, which could be next month, you will find yourself directly answerable to SS Colonel Reinhardt Wolters. He is not one of us, needless to say, but you must make him your friend. Sutherland and Rose are running the Lisbon station of the British Secret Intelligence Service, you will be talking to them directly, procedure is in the brief. There are some documents here which you should look at and memorize before you go and a letter which contains important information on microdot. You will use this information to open negotiations with the British. You must show them that we can be trusted, that our intentions are honourable and that the reverse is true of the Russians.'

'I'm not sure how the latter will be possible. I understand there is no Soviet legation in Lisbon.'

'That's true. Salazar won't allow them in. No atheists on Catholic Portuguese soil – which reminds me, we must make sure the Portuguese don't deny him a visa.'

The man seemed to laugh for no particular reason, or perhaps it was a wheeze that became a cough. He lit a cigarette.

'It is possible that Olivier Mesnel will lead you somewhere. He must be going to Lisbon for a purpose which I don't think, given his political beliefs, will be to take a ship to the United States.'

'At the Casablanca Conference it was decided that our surrender would have to be unconditional. We will have to offer something extraordinary for the British and the Americans to even consider breaking with the Russians.'

A long silence. Smoke rising from the chair drifted towards the lamp behind.

'Believe me, the Americans will be looking for any reason they can to cut themselves away from Stalin at the first opportunity, especially after the Russians have invaded Europe. At the Teheran Conference Stalin said that up to a hundred thousand German officers would have to be executed and he would need four million German *slaves* – that was his word – to rebuild Russia. This kind of talk is unacceptable to men of humanity such as Churchill and Roosevelt. If we can provide a catalyst . . .' he paused, struggled in his chair as if suddenly cramped, '. . . the Führer's death, I think, would be sufficient.'

Voss shivered even though it was warm in the room. The water he was easing himself into now felt deep and cold.

'Is that a planned action?'

'One of many,' said the man, as tired as if he'd planned them all.

Voss wanted to get away from contemplating the enormity of the statement.

'I've lost track of the development of our atomic programme. That could be important to the Allies. They've seen that we have the potential . . . can we put their minds at rest?'

'It's all in the documents.'

'How much time have we got?'

'We hope to make progress . . . like all things, in the spring, but by the end of the summer at the latest we must have results. The Russians have retaken Zhitomir and have crossed the Polish border – they're no more than a thousand kilometres from Berlin. We are being bombed to rubble by the Allies. The city is a ruin, the arms and munitions factories working at barely fifty per cent. The air force can't reach the new Russian arms factories on the other side of the Urals. The bear gets stronger and the eagle weaker and more short-sighted.'

There didn't seem to be any need of more questions after that and Voss was gestured towards the table where three fat files awaited him. He sat down and reached for the lamp. A hand landed on his shoulder and squeezed it in the same way that his father's used to – reassuring, giving strength.

'You are very important to us,' said the voice. 'You understand what is written in these files better than anybody, but we have

50

chosen you for other reasons too. I can only ask you, please, when you are in Lisbon, do not make the same mistake you made with Mademoiselle Larache. This is too important. This is about the survival of a nation.'

The hand released him. The man and his pressurized voice left the room. Voss worked until 6.00 a.m. going through the files on the atomic programme and the V1 and V2 rocket programmes.

On 20th January 1944 Olivier Mesnel was issued with an exit visa to travel to Spain. On the 22nd January Voss boarded the same night train as Mesnel, which left the Gare de Lyon heading south to Lyon and Perpignan, crossing the border at Port Bou and then on to Barcelona and Madrid. Mesnel rarely left his compartment. In Madrid the Frenchman stayed in a cheap pension for two nights and then took another train to Lisbon on the night of 25th January.

They arrived in Santa Apolónia station in Lisbon late the following afternoon. It was raining and Mesnel in his oversized coat and hat walked at funereal pace from the station to the massive square of the Terreiro do Paço, which Voss was surprised to see sandbagged and guarded in a neutral country. He followed the Frenchman through the Baixa and up the Avenida da Liberdade to the Praça Marquês de Pombal where Mesnel, dragging his feet, seemingly weak with hunger, entered a small *pensão* on the Rua Braancamp. Voss was relieved to take a taxi to the German Legation on the Rua do Pau de Bandeira in Lapa, a smart quarter on the outskirts of the city. SS Colonel Reinhardt Wolters had been expecting him two days earlier but welcomed him all the same.

On 13th February the Chief of the Abwehr, Admiral Canaris, was escorted out of the Maibach II complex by officers sent from the Reich's Main Security Office by Kaltenbrunner. He was taken to the house within the grounds where he packed and was then driven to his own home in Schlachtensee. On 18th February the Abwehr was dissolved and brought under Kaltenbrunner's direct control. The rain was clattering against the windows of the German Legation in Lapa when Wolters came into Voss's office to deliver the good news. As the SS man left the room, Voss was overwhelmed by a sense of loneliness, a man out on a limb at the westernmost tip of Europe with only the enemy to talk to.

Chapter 6

10th July 1944, Orlando Road, Clapham, London.

Andrea Aspinall collapsed on her bed in her room with the windows open, just back from another trip to the air-raid shelter – the doodle-bugs a menace, flying over at all times of day, not like the good old predictable nights of endless bombing raids in the Blitz. Some-times she toyed with the idea of not going to the shelter – listen for the low drone of the diesel-powered rocket, wait for its engine to cut out, take pot luck under its silent falling, test her boredom threshold.

She went to sit on the window ledge, her room at the top, old servants' quarters. She looked over the back garden through the lime trees to Macauley Road, four houses along, direct hit from a doodlebug, not much left, blackened beams, piled rubble but nobody home at the time. She caught sight of herself, only her head in the bottom corner of the mirror on the dressing table across the room. Long black hair, dark, nearly olive skin, twenty-year-old brown eyes wanting to be older.

She opened a packet of Woodbines, rested the filterless cigarette on her lower lip, let it stick. She struck a match on the outside wall, warm brick. Her hand came into the frame, she turned her face and accepted the light. She flicked her head back, unstuck the cigarette, let out a long stream of smoke and came back to herself in the mirror with her tongue on her top lip – being sophisticated. She shook her head at herself, looked out of the window – still a silly girl playing romantic games in the mirror. Not a spy.

She'd spent most of her life at the Sacred Heart Convent in Devizes where she'd been sent at seven years old when her great aunt had died and there'd been no one to look after her while her mother worked. That was why the piano teacher and his wife, who'd been bombed in their home during the Blitz, had been so important to her, they'd become family, looking after her through school holidays. The piano teacher was her father. She'd never known her own, the one who'd died of cholera before she was born.

They knew about discipline and religion at the Sacred Heart and not much else, but it hadn't prevented her from getting a place at St Anne's, Oxford to read maths. She'd done nearly two years of her degree when her tutor invited her to a party at St John's. At the party a large quantity of drink was served and consumed by dons, undergraduates and other people not directly associated with the university. These people floated around the room and occasionally moored themselves to some young person or other and engaged them in short intense conversations about politics and history. She went to more parties like this and met a man who took a particular interest in her, who was called simply – Rawlinson.

Rawlinson was very tall. He wore a three-piece suit, charcoal grey, a starched collar attached with studs to his shirt and a school tie which, if she'd known more, would have said Wellington and the military. He was in his fifties with all his hair, which was black on top, grey at the sides and combed through with tonic. He had only one leg and his prosthesis was stiff so that when he walked that leg swung in a semi-circle and he had to support himself with a duckhead-topped cane. She felt lucky because, while his conversation was the usual penetrative stuff, he participated with the charm of an uncle who shouldn't really take a fancy to his niece but couldn't help it.

'Tell me something,' he said. 'Mathematics. Has anybody ever asked you why mathematics? Interesting.'

Andrea, a little drunk, shrugged. Unprepared for the question, her brain ticked. She spoke with her mind elsewhere.

'You can get things to work out, I suppose,' she said, feeling instantly stupid, embarrassed.

'Not always, I shouldn't think,' said Rawlinson, surprising her, taking it seriously, taking her seriously even.

'No, not always, but when you do it's . . . well . . . there's a beauty to it, an inconceivable simplicity. As Godfrey Hardy said, "Beauty is the test. There's no place in this world for ugly mathematics."'

'Beauty?' said Rawlinson, baffled. 'Not something I remember from maths class. Fiendish is more the word. Show me beauty . . . beauty that I can understand.'

'The number six,' she said, 'has three divisors – one, two and three – which if added together come to . . . six. Isn't that perfect? And, seen in that same light, isn't Pythagoras's theorem beautiful too? So simple. The square of the hypotenuse is equal to the sum of the other two sides squared. True for all right-angled triangles ever created. What seems terribly complicated can be resolved into equations . . . formulae which go towards completing the . . . well, at least part of the puzzle.'

He tapped his cheek with a long finger.

'The puzzle?'

'How things work,' she said, hysteria mounting as the banality took root.

'And people,' he said; question or agreement, she wasn't sure.

'People?'

'How do *people* fit into the equation?'

'There are infinite possibilities in maths. Every number is a complex number. It can be real or imaginary, and real numbers can be rational or irrational. Rational like integers or fractions, irrational like algebra or transcendental numbers.'

'Transcendental?'

'Real, but non-algebraic.'

'I see.'

'Like π.'

'What are you saying, Miss Aspinall?'

'I'm talking to you in the simplest way possible, at the most basic end of mathematics, and already there are things you don't fully understand. It's a secret language. Only very few people know it and can speak it.'

'That still doesn't explain how people fit into your world.'

'I was just showing you that numbers can be complicated in the same way that people can be. And something else . . . I'm a person, too, with all the normal human needs. I don't always speak in algorithms.'

'Numbers are more stable than people, I'd have thought. More predictable.'

'I haven't come across an emotional number . . . yet,' she said, her hands feeling huge at her sides, flapping like albatross's wings, 'which is why, I suppose, it's possible to get things to work out . . . every so often.'

'Are solutions important to you?'

Andrea studied him for a moment, the question carrying interview weight. His eyes didn't flinch from hers. She lost the match.

'I do like to solve problems. That's the reward. But it's not always possible and working towards something can be just as satisfying,' she said, not believing it, but thinking it might please him.

After this string of parties her tutor sent her over to Oriel to talk to someone about 'matters pertaining to the war effort'. He sent her to a doctor who gave her a half-hour medical examination. She didn't hear anything for a week until she was called back to Oriel and found herself signing the Official Secrets Act, so, it seemed, that they could give her a course in typing and shorthand. She thought she was headed for a code-cracking centre, where she'd heard lots of other maths graduates had been sent, but they gave her some additional training instead. Dead-letter drops, invisible ink, using miniature cameras, following people, talking to people while pretending to be someone else to find out what they knew – role-playing, they called it. The minuscule arts of deception. They also taught her how to fire a gun, ride a motorbike and drive a car.

They sent her home at the beginning of July to wait for an assignment. A week later she was contacted by Rawlinson, who told her he was going to come to tea to meet her mother. It was important to establish normality at home, her mother had to be given something official about what her daughter would be doing but not, of course, the reality.

'Andrea!'

Her mother shouted up the stairs from the hall. She dabbed the coal of the cigarette out on the wall, put the butt back in the packet.

'Andrea!'

'Coming, Mother,' she said, ripping open the door.

She looked down the stairs to her mother's moon-white, but not so luminous, face at the curve of the bannisters.

'Mr Rawlinson's here,' she said in a stage whisper.

'I didn't hear him arrive.'

'Well, he's here,' she said. 'Shoes.'

She went barefoot back to the bedroom, put on her mother's

horrible shoes, laced them up. She sniffed the air, still smoky, still behaving like Mother's little girl. Definitely not a spy.

'She's very young, you know-. . .' She overheard her mother in the drawing room. 'I mean, she's nineteen, no twenty, but she doesn't act it. She went to a convent . . .'

'The Sacred Heart in Devizes,' said Rawlinson. 'Good school.'

'And out of London.'

'Away from the bombing.'

'It wasn't the bombing, Mr Rawlinson,' her mother said, without saying what it had been.

Andrea braced herself for the tedium of her mother behaving properly in front of strangers.

'Not the bombing . . . ?' said Rawlinson, feigning mild surprise.

'The influences,' said Mrs Aspinall.

Andrea rattled her heels on the tiles to announce herself, to stop her mother talking about 'goings on' in the air-raid shelters. She shook hands with Rawlinson.

Her mother's bra creaked as she poured the tea. What rigging for such a tight little ship, thought Andrea, feeling Rawlinson's bright, nearly saucy eyes on her neck, which heated up. Teacups rattled, raised and refitted on to saucers.

'You speak German,' he said to Andrea.

'*Frisch weht der Wind / Der heimat zu, / Mein Irisch kind / Wo weilest du?*' said Andrea.

'Don't show off, dear,' said her mother.

'And Portuguese,' said Andrea.

'She taught herself, you know,' said Audrey Aspinall, interrupting. 'Pass Mr Rawlinson some cake, dear.'

Andrea had been sitting on her hands and now found that the ribbing of her dress was printed on the back of them as she passed the cake. Why did her mother always do this to her?

'You have secretarial skills,' said Rawlinson, lifting the cake.

'She just did a course, didn't you, dear?'

Andrea didn't contribute. Her mother's porcelain face, still beautiful at thirty-eight years old but unyielding, turned hard on her. Andrea hadn't told her mother anything about what had gone on at Oxford other than what they'd told her to say.

'It's my job to find suitable staff for our embassies and high commissions. My department is very small and when we find someone with a foreign language we tend to snap them up. I have a position for your daughter, Mrs Aspinall . . . abroad.'

'I'd like to go abroad,' said Andrea.

'How would you know?' said her mother. 'That's the thing about young people today, Mr Rawlinson, they think they know every-thing without having done anything but, of course, they don't think. They don't think and they don't listen.'

'We're *relying* on youth in this war, Mrs Aspinall,' said Rawlin-son, 'because they don't know fear. Eighteen-year-olds can do a hundred bombing missions, get shot down, make their way through enemy territory and be up in the air again within a week. The reason they can do that is precisely that they don't think, you see. The *danger's* in the thinking.'

'I'm not sure about abroad . . .' said Mrs Aspinall.

'Why don't you come to my office tomorrow,' said Rawlinson to Andrea. 'We'll test your skills. Eleven o'clock suit you?'

'I don't know where you'd send her. Not south. She can't stand the heat.'

This was a lie, worse than a lie because the opposite was the case. Andrea, inside her dark skin, under her starling glossy hair, glared at her mother's translucency, at the blue blood inching its way under the alabaster skin. Mrs Aspinall had a Victorian's attitude to sun. It never touched her skin. In summer she wore marble, in winter the snow would pile on her head as on a statue's in the square.

'Lisbon, Mrs Aspinall, we have an opening in Lisbon which would suit your daughter's skills and intelligence.'

'Lisbon? But there must be something she can do in London.'

Rawlinson got to his feet, hauling his stiff leg up after him, shooting Andrea a conspiratorial look.

They followed him into the hall. Mrs Aspinall fitted him into his light coat, gave him his hat, smoothed the shoulders of his coat. Andrea blinked at that small, intimate action. It shocked her, confused her.

'You're going to be hot out there, Mr Rawlinson.'

'Thank you so much for tea, Mrs Aspinall,' he said, and tipped his hat before going down to the gate and out into the sun-baked street.

'Well, you won't want to go to Lisbon, will you?' said Mrs Aspinall, closing the door.

'Why not?'

'It's as good as Africa down there ... Arabs,' she added as an afterthought, making it exotic.

'I suppose it's because I speak Portuguese,' said Andrea. 'Why do you never let me say ...'

'Don't start on that. I'm not doing battle with you on that score,' she said, heading back into the living room.

'Why shouldn't I talk about my father?'

'He's dead, you never knew him,' she said, throwing her tea dregs into the pot plant, pouring herself another cup. 'I hardly did, either.'

'That's no reason.'

'It's just not done, Andrea. That's all.'

Something wriggled in Andrea's mind, something irrational like the first half of an equation, some algebra with too many unknowns. She was thinking about her mother smoothing Rawlinson's shoulders. Intimacy and what brought that intimacy. Rawlinson's leg. And why dead Portuguese fathers can't be mentioned.

Talking to her mother was just like algebra. Maths without the numbers. Words which meant something else. A question arrived in Andrea's head. One prompted by an image. It was a question which couldn't be asked. She could think it and if she looked at her mother and thought it, she'd shudder, which she did.

'I don't know how you can be cold in this heat.'

'Not cold, Mother. Just a thought.'

In the morning her mother produced one of her suits for Andrea to wear. A dark blue pencil skirt, short jacket, cream blouse, and a hat that perched rather than sat. Her nails were inspected and passed. After breakfast her mother told her to clean her teeth and left for work firing a volley of instructions up the stairs about what to do and, more important, what not to do.

Andrea took a bus to St James's Park and spent a few minutes on a bench before walking down Queen Anne's Gate to number 54 Broadway. She went to the second floor, her feet already hurting in the borrowed shoes, and the suit, built for her mother's slightly smaller frame, was pinching her under the armpits, which were damp in the heat. A woman told her to wait on a hard, leather-seated wooden chair. Sun streamed through the lazy dust motes.

She was shown into Rawlinson's office. He sat with his leg coming through the footwell to her side of his desk. Tea appeared and two biscuits. The secretary retired.

'Biscuit?' he asked.

She took the offered biscuit. The dry half detached itself from the sodden half.

'So,' said Rawlinson, pulling himself up straight in his chair, the air clear as after a storm. 'Nice to have you on board. There's just one question I have outstanding here. Your father.'

'My father?'

'You never include your father's details on any of your forms.'

'My mother says it's not relevant. He died before I was born. He had no influence and nor did his family. I . . .'

'How did he die?'

'They were in India. There was a cholera outbreak. He died, as did my mother's parents. She came back to England and lived with her aunt. I was born here at St George's.'

'In 1924,' he said. 'You see, I was interested in the Portuguese business. Why does Miss Aspinall speak Portuguese? And I found out that your father was Portuguese.'

'My grandparents were missionaries in the south of India. There were a lot of Portuguese down there from their colony, Goa. She met . . .'

'Your mother never took his name . . .' said Rawlinson, and steadied himself to pronounce Joaquim Reis Leitão.

'*Leitão* means "suckling pig",' she explained.

'Does it?' he said. 'I see why she never took his name. Not something you'd want to have to explain every day of the week . . . suckling pig.'

He sipped his tea. Andrea chased a piece of dry biscuit around her mouth.

'You've led a cloistered life,' said Rawlinson.

'That's what my mother says.'

'The Sacred Heart. Then Oxford. Very sheltered.'

'I spent time here during the Blitz as well,' said Andrea. 'That was a sheltered life, too.'

Rawlinson took some moments to find the joke and grunted, reluctant to be amused.

'So you'll be all right in Lisbon,' said Rawlinson, launching

59

himself out of the chair, cracking his leg a stunning blow on the desk.

'You'll be working as a secretary for a Shell Oil executive called Meredith Cardew,' said Rawlinson, speaking to the sky. 'Rather a fortuitous vacancy. Last girl married a local. The husband doesn't like her working. She's pregnant. There's been some accommodation arranged for you, which I will not attempt to explain but it is the crucial element of your assignment. How's your physics?'

'School Certificate standard.'

'That'll have to do. You'll be doing some translating work. German scientific journals into English for the Americans, so you'll have your work cut out, what with being Cardew's secretary and all. Sutherland and Rose are running the Lisbon station. They'll make contact with you via Cardew. A car will pick you up on Saturday morning and take you to RAF Northolt where you'll be given your documents for travelling to Lisbon. You'll be met at the airport by an agent called James – Jim – Wallis who works for an import/export company down at the docks. He will take you to Cardew's house in Carcavelos, just outside Lisbon. Everything you need to know at this stage is in a file which Miss Bridges will give you and which you will read here and remember.'

He turned his back to the sun. His face, backlit by the window, blackened. He held out his hand.

'Welcome to the Company,' he said.

'The Company?'

'What we call ourselves to each other.'

'Thank you, sir.'

'You'll do very well,' he said.

Miss Bridges sat her in a small room off her office with the file. It wasn't a long file. The changes that had been wrought in her life were small but significant. She would now be known as Anne Ashworth. Her parents lived on Clapham Northside. Her father, Graham Ashworth, was an accountant, and her mother, Margaret Ashworth, was a housewife. Their lives to date had nearly been too boring to read. She digested the material, closed the file and left.

She crossed St James's Park and The Mall and walked up St James's Street to Ryder Street where she knew her mother worked in a government office. She stood on the other side of

St James's to the entrance to Ryder Street and waited. At lunchtime the streets began to fill with people looking for something to eat. Men dived into pubs, women into teahouses. Her mother's white face appeared in the entrance to 7 Ryder Street and walked down to St James's. Andrea tracked her from across the street, into the park. Before the lake she took a right and chose a bench with a view of Duck Island and Horse Guards Road.

Rawlinson's distinctive gait was impossible to miss. He came from the other end of the park and joined her mother on the bench. They sat and looked at the ducks. Rawlinson's hand rested on the duckhead-topped cane. After some minutes he held her hand; Andrea saw the join just below the two slats of wood at the back of the bench. A roaming dog paused to sniff at their feet and moved on. Her mother turned to look at the side of Rawlinson's face and spoke something into his ear, only inches away. They stayed there for half an hour and then walked together, but unconnected, towards the bridge across the middle of the lake where they parted.

Andrea killed time in a reference library just off Leicester Square until the late afternoon. Rawlinson was punctual about leaving work. Andrea watched him swing his boom down towards Petty France and into St James's Park tube station. She followed him to a terraced house in Flood Street in Chelsea. A woman met him at the door, kissed him and took his hat. The door closed and through the lead-glass panes Andrea saw the coat coming off his back. The same coat that her mother had smoothed on to his shoulders the previous afternoon. Rawlinson's blurred outline appeared in the frame of the sitting-room window and collapsed out of sight into a chair. The woman arrived in the window, looked out through the net curtains directly into Andrea's stunned face and then up and down the street as if she was expecting someone.

Andrea walked back down to Sloane Square and caught a bus to Clapham Common, her feet in an uproar from the hard leather of her mother's shoes. She was furious at the years spent watching her mother laying the bricks to the austere edifice of her own hypocrisy. She limped home, dragged her tortured feet up the wooden stairs and collapsed face-down on the bed.

The next morning at breakfast her mother appeared in the doorway tightly bound in a burgundy silk dressing gown. Andrea felt her contemplating six or seven lines of attack before putting the kettle on – the English solution to personal confrontation.

'I got the job,' said Andrea.

'I know.'

'How?'

'Mr Rawlinson's secretary called me at the office,' she said, 'which was very considerate, I thought.'

Andrea searched her mother's back for clues. The scapulae shifted under the silk.

'Do you like Mr Rawlinson?' asked Andrea.

'He seems very pleasant.'

'Do you think you could like him . . . more?'

'*More*?' she said, rounding on her daughter. 'What do you mean by "more"?'

'You know,' she said, shrugging.

'Goodness me, I've only met him once. He's probably married.'

'That would be a shame, wouldn't it?' said Andrea. 'Anyway, I'll be out of here by the weekend.'

'What's that supposed to mean?'

'I'll clear my room out. You could take a lodger.'

'A *lodger*,' said Mrs Aspinall, aghast.

'Why not? They pay money. You could use a few pounds extra, couldn't you?'

Mrs Aspinall sat down opposite her daughter, who had a forearm either side of her plate, hands poised on the table top like spiders.

'What happened to you yesterday afternoon?'

'Nothing. After Rawlinson, I went to the library.'

'You're going away. You've got your whole life ahead of you. I'm staying here. I'll be on my own. Don't you think I'll be lonely? Have you thought about that?'

'That depends if you're alone.'

Her mother blinked. Andrea decided that the line was her parting shot. She looked back from the bottom of the stairs, her mother was still in the same position, the kettle whistling madly in her ear.

Andrea got straight down to packing her few clothes and books. Her mother thundered up the stairs. Half a minute of antagonistic silence opened up as she hovered outside the bedroom door. She moved off. Water ran in the bathroom.

Fifteen minutes later Mrs Aspinall came into Andrea's empty

62

room with only the case in the middle of the floor. All vestiges of her daughter already gone.

'You've packed,' she said. 'I thought you weren't leaving until Saturday.'

'I wanted to be organized.'

Her mother's face was indecipherable, too much going on at once for any emotion to make itself plain.

The complicated world of adults.

Chapter 7

Andrea landed in Lisbon at three in the afternoon, the adrenalin from her first flight still live in her veins. The heat slammed into her at the door of the aircraft along with the smell of hot metal, tar and vaporized aviation fuel. She took out the white-rimmed sunglasses her mother had given her to protect her eyes and took her first steps on foreign soil as Anne Ashworth.

The sun slapped down on the wide-open spaces of the airfield. The landscape beyond wavered in the rising heat. The trunks of palm trees snaked up to their frayed heads. The flat ground at their feet shone mirror bright. Nobody was moving out there, not even a bird, in the torrid afternoon.

The new airport, barely eighteen months old, had straight, hard, fascistic lines, its main building dominated by the control tower affright with antennae. Armed police moved around the halls inside looking at everyone, who in turn looked at no one, sank into themselves, tried to disappear. Andrea's dark face in the white sunglasses stood out and the customs officer selected her with two beckoning fingers and a cigarette trailing smoke.

He watched her with dark, long-lashed eyes as she opened her case, his lips invisible under a heavy moustache. Other passengers passed through with cursory glances over their luggage. The customs officer dismantled her packing, shook out her underwear, leafed through her books. He lit another cigarette, felt around the lining of the case, glancing up at her so that she stared off around the empty hall, bored. His eyes were rarely on the job but more frequently on her hips, or drilling into her bust. She twitched a nervous smile at him. His smile back showed black and brown rotten teeth, lichen-fringed. She flinched. His sad eyes hardened and he left the counter. She repacked the case.

The one man in the arrivals hall left no doubt as to his nationality. Blond hair combed back in straight rails, faint pencil moustache crayoned in, tweed jacket even in this heat, school tie. All that was missing was a lanyard with a pea whistle attached for bringing boys up short of the line.

'Wallis,' he said. 'Jim.'

'Ashworth,' she replied. 'Anne.'

'Good show,' he said, taking her case. 'You were a long time in there.'

'I was being shown some local colour.'

'I see,' he said, not sure what she meant, but still keen whatever. 'I'm running you out to Cardew's house in Carcavelos. They did tell you, didn't they?'

'You sound as if they might not have done.'

'Communication's abysmal in this outfit,' he said.

He threw her case into the boot of a black Citroën and got in behind the wheel. He offered her a cigarette.

'Três Vintes, they're called. Not bad. Not a patch on Woodies though.'

They lit up and Wallis drove at high speed straight into the heart of Lisbon, which at this hour and in the heat was silent. He hung an elbow out of the window, sneaked a look at her legs.

'First time abroad?' he asked.

She nodded.

'What do you think?'

'I thought it would be . . . older.'

'This is all the new building here. Salazar, he's the chap in charge, he made so much money out of us . . . and Jerry – you know, what with the wolfram, sardines and the like – he's building a new city, new motorways, a stadium, all this residential stuff – bairros, they call them here – all brand new. There's even talk of stringing a bridge across the Tagus. You'll see, though . . . when we get into the centre. You'll see.'

The Citroën's tyres squealed around a mule-drawn cart with eight people in it. The wooden wheels rattled over the cobbles. Dogs attached to the axle with string trotted in the shade, tongues lolling in the heat. The broad, dark faces of the women stared down without seeing.

'We'll take the scenic route,' said Wallis. 'The hills of Lisbon.'

Anne, as she now thought of herself permanently, leaned into him as they rounded the Praça de Saldanha, their faces suddenly close together, his with more than professional interest in them, giving her some girlish satisfaction. They shot down the hill into Estefânia, rounded the fountain and crossed high above another street on to Avenida Almirante Reis. Wallis built up speed down the long straight avenue. Overhead cables appeared, the tyres stuttered over the tramlines embedded in the cobbles. The ramparts of the Castelo São Jorge high above them were vague in the heat haze, the dark stone pines crowding a shoulder. They came into an area which looked as if it had suffered recent bomb damage and even the buildings still standing looked decrepit and crumbling, with grasses growing out of the walls and roofs, and the plaster façades scabbed and blistered.

'This is the Mouraria, which they're demolishing, cleaning the area up a bit. On the other side of the hill is the Alfama, best place to live in Lisbon when the Moors were here but they moved out in the Middle Ages. Scared of earthquakes. And, you know, that quarter was one of the few places that survived the big one in 1755. I tell you, it's like a *medina* in there, not too sanitary – and I should know, I was in Casablanca until last year.'

'What were you doing there?'

'Cooking things up in the kasbah.'

They came into a square whose centre was dominated by a massive wrought-iron covered market. Police, mounted and on foot, patrolled the area. The road was scattered with cobblestones torn up and thrown from the now pockmarked pavements. A *Manteigaria* on the corner had been half destroyed, no glass left in any of the doors and windows, and two women inside, sweeping up debris. The shop's awning was ripped but still showed the words *carnes fumadas*.

'Praça da Figueira. There was a riot here this morning. The *Manteigaria* was selling *chouriços* filled with sawdust. The rationing's bad enough without that, what with Salazar selling everything to Jerry. The locals got angry. The communists sent in a few *provocateurs*, the *Guarda* showed up on horseback. Heads got broken. There's two wars going on here in Lisbon. Us versus Jerry and the *Estado Novo* versus the Communists.'

'*Estado Novo?*'

'Salazar's New State. The régime. Not much different to the bastards *we're* fighting. Secret police – Gestapo trained – called the PVDE. The city's infested with *bufos* – informers. The prisons . . . well, you don't want to go to a Portuguese prison. They even used to have a concentration camp out on the Cape Verde Islands. Tarrefal. The *frigideira*, they called it . . . the frying pan. This is the Baixa, the business end of town. Completely rebuilt by the Marquês de Pombal after the earthquake. He was another hard man. The Portuguese seem to need them every few hundred years.'

'Need what?'

'Bastards.'

They rounded a square with a high column in the centre and went up a slip road off the corner. Wallis accelerated up the steep hill. A metal walkway crossed the street high above the buildings, connected to a lift.

'Elevador do Carmo, built by Raoul Mesnier. Gets you from the Baixa to the Chiado without breaking a sweat.'

They turned right, first gear up the hill. The difference of it all pouring into Anne. More policemen in khaki, guns in leather holsters. Peaked box caps. Shops with black glass and gold lettering. Jerónimo Martims' *Chá e café*. *Chocolates*. Broad pavements with black and white geometric patterns. Another turn. Another steep hill. Past a tram, groaning and screeching downhill. Dark impassive faces at the windows. Wallis pointed across her. The Baixa opened out below in squares of red-tiled roof. The castle still hazy, but now at the same level as them across the valley.

'Best view in Lisbon,' said Wallis. 'I'll show you the embassy then I'll take you out to the seaside.'

They drove around Largo do Rato and the Jardim da Estrela and turned left in front of a massive twin-towered, domed cathedral.

'Basílica da Estrela,' said Wallis. 'Built by Maria I at the end of the eighteenth century. She said she'd build a cathedral if she gave birth to a son, which she did. They started building it and the boy died two years before it was completed. Smallpox. Poor lad. But that's Lisbon for you.'

'That's Lisbon?'

'A sad place . . . suits those of melancholic disposition. Are you?'

'Melancholic? No. And you . . . Mr Wallis?'

'Jim. Call me Jim.'

'You don't seem to be that way inclined, Jim.'

'Me? No. No time for it. What's there to be sad about? It's only war. Let's go and see the enemy.'

He cut round the back of the basilica, up a short incline and then down into Lapa. They rolled quietly into a small square where a large mansion stood behind wrought-iron gates and high railings. A swastika flag hung from a flagpole above the door. Two limp phoenix palms stood in the garden. A flame of purple bougainvillea climbed above a window. The blue of the Tagus was visible over the rooftops. For once Wallis didn't say a word. The car dropped down a short hill, turned left and after a hundred yards Wallis nodded up the hill to where the Union Jack hung from a long pink building halfway up.

'We're practically neighbours,' he said. 'I won't drive you up there. There're always *bufos* hanging around outside looking for new faces, ready to report anything to the Germans.'

They went down the hill and came out at the Santos docks. Wallis turned right, heading west along the banks of the Tagus and out beyond the mouth of the estuary. The road hugged the coastline, the railway tracks alongside.

At Carcavelos, just by a large, brown, ancient fort they turned away from the sea and went through the centre of town and out the other side where they pulled up in front of a large, sombre house standing on its own behind a high wall. Two mature stone pines in the garden cast dark shadows over the windows. Wallis honked the horn and a gardener appeared from the shrubbery to open the gate.

'This is Cardew's house,' said Wallis, 'your boss at Shell, but your other bosses will see you first – Sutherland and Rose.'

Wallis lifted out her luggage, rang the door bell, got back in the car and reversed out. A maid came to the door, took her case inside and led her down the hall to a shuttered room where two men sat, one smoking a pipe, the other a cigarette. The maid closed the door. The two men stood. One tall and slim with brown hair swept back, introduced himself as Richard Rose. The other, shorter, with thick, black, undulating hair just said: 'Sutherland'. Both were in shirtsleeves, the room stuffy even with the french windows half-open on to the lawn.

Sutherland stared at Anne from under dark eyebrows. He had

blackberry smudges at the corners of his blue eyes. His skin was white and pasty. He pointed to a chair with the stem of his pipe.

'Wallis took his time,' he said.

'I think he gave me the introductory tour, sir.'

He worked on his pipe for a moment. His lips were oddly bluish, kissing off the pipe stem. He was a still man, no expression around his eyes or mouth and little movement in his body. A lizard, thought Anne.

'You're what they call *morena*,' said Rose. 'Dark. Dusky.'

'As opposed to *loira*,' she said. 'Blonde. Dizzy.'

Rose didn't like it, too cheeky on her first day perhaps. Sutherland smiled so fast and with such little breadth that all she saw was a brown column on the left side of his front teeth – discoloured from smoking.

'I didn't think your ability to speak Portuguese was part of your cover,' said Sutherland, his voice coming from somewhere down his throat, his lips parting to say the words but not moving.

'Sorry, sir.'

'This place . . . Lisbon,' he clarified, 'is . . . perhaps Wallis told you, a very dangerous city for the careless. You might think that the worst is over, now that we've landed in Normandy, but there are still some very critical situations, life and death situations, for men at sea and in the air. The idea of our intelligence operation here is to make those situations safer, not to exacerbate them with thoughtlessness.'

'Of course, sir,' said Anne, thinking – pompous.

'Information is at a premium. There's an active market on all sides. Nobody is innocent. Everyone is either buying or selling. From maids and waiters to ministers and businessmen. The overall climate is quieter. A lot of the refugees have been shipped out now, so the rumour circuit is tighter and there's less misinformation. We have won the economic war. Salazar no longer fears a Nazi invasion and he's closed the wolfram mines. We're doing our best to make sure that they don't get their hands on any other useful products. As a result we see things more clearly but, although there are fewer players on the pitch, and less complications, it has become a much more subtle affair because now, Miss Ashworth, we are in the endgame. Do you play chess?'

She nodded, mesmerized by the intensity of his passionless face, her own blood zipping around her body faster now that she was close to the current, the live wire. All her training seemed like so much theory. In less than an hour a new world had been peeled open – not just the place, Lisbon, but also an immediate sense of the power of the clandestine. The privilege of knowing things that nobody else knew. Smoke trailed from the pipe held just off Sutherland's face, curled through the sparse sunlight coming through the cracks of the shutters and disappeared up to the high ceiling.

'Part of your mission is a social one. There are no lines drawn here. Who is who? Who plays for whom? There are powerful people, rich people, people who've made a great deal of money out of this war, out of us and the Germans. We know who some of them are, but we want to know all of them. Your ability to speak Portuguese, or rather understand it, is important in this respect and, equally, that nobody should know of this facility. The same applies to your German. You will only use that in the office for translating these journals.'

'What specifically is it from these journals that the Americans are interested in?'

Sutherland beckoned Rose into the conversation, who gave a historical rundown of German nuclear capability from their first successful fission experiments back in 1938 through to Weizsäcker's discovery of Ekarhenium, the vital new element that could make the bomb. As Rose spoke, Sutherland watched the young woman. He didn't listen because he didn't understand any of it and he could see that she was struggling too.

'On 19th September 1939 Hitler made a speech in Danzig in which he threatened to employ a weapon against which there would be no defence,' said Rose. 'The Americans are convinced that he meant an atomic bomb.'

'You shouldn't worry about understanding any of this perfectly. There are probably only a handful of scientists in the world who do,' said Sutherland. 'The important thing is for you to understand the significance of this endgame that we're all involved in.'

'Why would the Germans tell you all this in a physics journal and published papers? Shouldn't this be top secret?'

Sutherland ignored the question.

'The fact is that the Allies have their own bomb programme. We have our own Ekarhenium, the 94th element, which for reasons of secrecy we refer to as "49".'

Brilliant, thought Anne, to switch the numbers round like that.

'In March 1941 Fritz Reiche, a German physicist on the run from the Nazis, passed through Lisbon on the way to the United States,' Rose continued. 'He was met by the Jewish Refugee Organization here and before they put him on a ship to New York we had a meeting in which he warned us that a bomb programme did exist in Germany. We now know that they're building an atomic pile for the creation of Ekarhenium somewhere in Berlin. We also know that Heisenberg went to see Niels Bohr, the Danish physicist, and that they had an argument about whether atomic warfare was the right way for physics to be going. A rift developed between the two men over the Germans' active bomb programme. Heisenberg also sketched out, in rough, the makings of an atomic pile. Since then Bohr has left Denmark and gone over to the Americans. You've been in London since June?'

'Yes, sir.'

'So you know about the doodlebugs ... the V1 rocket bombs?'

'Yes, sir.'

'We believe that these are the prototype rockets for launching an atomic bomb on London.'

It felt suddenly cold in the room despite the grinding heat outside. Anne rubbed her arms. Sutherland sucked on his pipe, which bubbled like a tubercular lung in the stem.

'Your day job in Cardew's office will be to microfilm the two German physics journals *Zeitschrift für Physik* and *Die Naturwissenschafen* and provide Sutherland and me with typed translations of any articles which pertain to atomic physics,' said Rose. 'More important than that is the accommodation we've managed to arrange for you in Estoril. Cardew has been working up a good social relationship with a fellow called Patrick Wilshere. He's a wealthy businessman in his mid fifties, with contacts and companies in the Portuguese colonies, mainly Angola. He is also Irish, a Catholic and not a lover of Great Britain. We have intelligence that he was selling wolfram, from his Portuguese wife's family's mining concessions in the north, exclusively to the Germans, as well as cork and olive oil from family estates in the Alentejo. He has offered Cardew a room in his considerable house for a lodger. He specified a female lodger.'

Sutherland looked to see the effect of this on his new agent. Her blood now felt as thin and cold as ether.

'What is expected of me?' she asked, clipping each word off.

'To listen.'

'You just said that he specified a female lodger.'

'He prefers female company,' said Rose, as if it was something he himself couldn't understand.

'What about his wife? Doesn't his wife live in the same house?'

'I understand that the relationship with his wife has . . . broken down somewhat.'

Anne began to breathe deep, slow breaths. Her thighs were sticking together under the cotton of her dress. Sweat seemed to be pricking out all over. Sutherland shifted in his chair. His first bodily movement.

'Cardew thinks she's suffered some kind of breakdown,' he said.

'You mean she's mad, too?' asked Anne, the scenario burgeoning in her mind.

'Not howling at the moon, exactly,' said Rose. 'More nerves, we think.'

'What's her name?' she asked.

'Mafalda. She's very well connected. Excellent family. Hugely wealthy. The spread they've got in Estoril . . . magnificent. Small palace. Own grounds. Marvellous,' said Sutherland, selling it hard.

'Do you mind if I smoke, sir?' she asked.

Sutherland broke out of his chair and offered her a cigarette from a silver box on the table. He lit it with a weighty Georgian silver lighter with a green baize bottom. Anne drew in heavily, saw Sutherland brightening in her vision.

'Tell me more about Wilshere,' she said, and as an afterthought, 'please, sir.'

'He's a drinking man. Likes to . . .'

'Does that mean he's a drunk?'

'He likes a drink,' said Rose. 'You do too, from the accounts of the Oxford do's. Quite a strong head on you, they said.'

'That's different from being a drunk.'

'Well, while we're about it, he's a gambler as well,' said Sutherland. 'The casino's practically at the bottom of their garden. Do you . . . ?'

'I've never had that sort of liquidity.'

'But you probably know something about probability, what with your maths . . .'

'It's not a particular interest of mine.'

'What is?' asked Rose.

'Numbers.'

'Ah, pure maths,' he said, as if he might know something. 'What drew you to that?'

'A sense of completeness,' she said, hoping that would do the trick.

'A sense or the illusion?' asked Rose.

'We might be talking about a lot of abstractions but what links them, the logic, is very real, very strict and irrefutable.'

'I'm a crossword man myself,' said Rose. 'I like to see into people's minds. How they work.'

Anne smoked some more.

'Crosswords have their own kind of completeness, too,' she said, 'if you're any good at them.'

Things were digging into her. Her bra felt tight. Her waistband knotty. She wasn't getting on with these two men and she didn't know how it had happened. Maybe that first exchange and the last one really had been too cheeky. Perhaps they'd seen one thing, imagined and extended their idea of her and she'd revealed something completely different. Was she this difficult?

'The thing about intelligence is that the picture is *always* incomplete. We deal in fragments. You, in the field, even more so. You might not always know what you're doing, you might not always appreciate the importance of what you hear. There are no solutions and, even if there were, you wouldn't have known the question in the first place. You listen and report,' said Sutherland.

'Something else for you to listen for in the Wilshere household, apart from people's names, has some relevance to the endgame we were talking about earlier,' said Rose. 'To make the doodlebugs, or any rocket for that matter, the Germans need precision tools. To make those tools requires precision cutting instruments. They need diamonds. Industrial diamonds. Those diamonds are finding their way in here on ships from Central Africa. We have tried searching those ships when they put in at our ports, like Freetown in Sierra Leone, but a handful of diamonds is not so easy to find on a 7,000-ton ship. We think, but we have no proof, that Wilshere is bringing in diamonds from Angola and getting them into the German Legation, where they are sent by diplomatic bag to Berlin. We don't know how he does it or how he gets paid for doing it. So anything you hear about diamonds and payment for them in the Wilshere household must be communicated, via Cardew, to us at once.'

'How do you want me to do that?'

'Wallis will look after that. You'll see him and arrange things with him.'

He glanced at his watch.

'Cardew had better take you up to the house now. It's getting late. I've told him to brief you on Wilshere and his wife, but I've also instructed him to exclude certain details which, for the safety of your cover, it would be better for you to find out yourself. I don't want you going in there knowing too much about the situation and not reacting correctly to ... developments. You're supposed to be a secretary. First time abroad and all that. I want you to be curious about everything and everybody.'

'That doesn't sound as if it's going to be too difficult, sir.'

Sutherland grimaced. The brown column of teeth appeared again and shut down just as fast. He went to the door and called for Cardew.

Chapter 8

Saturday, 15th July 1944, Estoril, near Lisbon.

Meredith Cardew drove Anne west past empty beaches. The sun was still high and the air crammed with heat, the sea in a flat calm, the Atlantic Ocean just licking at the sand. She didn't speak, still overwhelmed by that first meeting with Rose and Sutherland. Across the estuary Cardew pointed out the beaches of Caparica and further into the haze, discernible only as a smudge, the headland of Cabo Espichel. He was trying to loosen her up.

The saltine air that came through the windows brought back weekends by the sea before the war with her mother fully clothed and scarfed against the sun and wind, while her own young body went hazelnut brown in a day. It was easy to love this place, she thought, after London with its bombed-out, blackened houses, the drab grey streets piled with rubble. Here, by the sea, under the big sky, the palms and the bougainvillea flashing past, it should be easy to forget five years of destruction.

Cardew drove one-handed, clawing tobacco into his pipe with the other. He even managed to get the pipe going without sending them off down the rocks and into the sea. He was mid thirties, with thinning, reddish blond hair which had been razor cut up the back. He was tall, very long legs, and slim with a long nose and a facile smile working on the corners of his mouth. His baggy trousers flapped as his knees seemed to be conducting an unseen orchestra; the turn-ups were halfway up his shins, which were covered by thick beige socks. He wore heavy brogues on his feet.

What were the winter clothes like?

He smoked the pipe blowing stage kisses. His right arm had suffered a severe burn up to the elbow. The skin was shiny and patterned like sea fossils in rock.

'Boiling water,' he said, catching her looking, 'when I was a child.'

'Sorry,' she said, flustered at being caught out.

'Did Sutherland and Rose fill you in?'

'As much as they were prepared to. They said they'd purposely left some gaps.'

'Ye-e-e-s,' said Cardew, a frown of uncertainty rippling down his forehead. 'Did Rose say anything about Mafalda?'

'He said she was having a breakdown of some sort, not "howling at the moon", as he put it, just nerves.'

'I don't know what it is. Something to do with her husband perhaps, but it might just be a genetic thing. A bit of inbreeding back down the line. These big Portuguese families are known for it. Marrying each other's first cousins and the like and before you know it . . . I mean, look at the Portuguese royal family. A set of March hares if ever I saw one.'

'Isn't that all over now? The royal family?'

'Thirty-six years ago. Terrible business. The king and his son came up to Lisbon from the country, from Vila Viçosa in fact, not far from where Mafalda's family comes from, near the border. They arrived in Lisbon, trundling through the streets, both assassinated in their carriage. End of the monarchy. Well, it took a couple more years to fizzle out, but that was the effective end: 1908. Still, she might just be depressed or something. Whatever, she's not right, which is probably why Wilshere's looking for some company.'

'Female company, so I understand.'

Cardew shifted in his seat and looked as wary as a grouse on the Glorious Twelfth.

'Bit of a rum one, old Wilshere. He's broken the mould. Not your average chap.'

'Does he have children?'

'Only sons, who are away. No daughters. Probably why he wants female company. And here I am with four, for God's sake,' he said, a little gloomy. 'Sporting legacy gone . . . although the eldest one's school long-jump champion.'

'All is not lost, Mr Cardew.'

He brightened, bounced the end of his pipe by clenching his jaw.

'I think you'll like Wilshere,' said Cardew. 'And I know he'll like you. You've got that determined look about you. He likes girls with a bit of spunk. He didn't like Marjorie.'

76

'Marjorie?'

'My former secretary. The one who married a Portuguese and is now pregnant. The husband won't let her work, says she's got to lie down. Poor girl's got six months to go. Still, that's why you're here. Wilshere didn't take to her, anyway. She was a bit too English for his taste and he upset her. Yes, he can be a bit like that. If he takes to you, you're all right. If not he's . . . he's a difficult bugger.'

'He likes you.'

'Yes . . . in his way.'

'Aren't you a bit too English as well?'

'Sorry, old girl. I'm a Scot, both sides. Talk like a Sassenach but I'm a Scot through and through. Like Wilshere, in fact, he's Irish down to his heels but talks with a silver spoon in his mouth.'

'Or a hot potato . . . if he's Irish,' said Anne.

Cardew roared, not that he found it so funny. He was just the type who liked to laugh.

'What else is there to know about Patrick Wilshere?' she asked.

'He can be a charmer . . .'

'As well as a drinker and a gambler.'

'He rides, too. Do you ride?'

'No.'

'It's nice up there on the Serra de Sintra on horseback,' said Cardew. 'Sutherland told me you had a top-class brain. Maths. Languages. That sort of thing.'

'It didn't leave much time for anything else. I'm just not sporty, Mr Cardew. Sorry. I'm not much of a team person, I suppose. It's probably something to do with being an only child and . . .'

She pulled up short of saying 'and not having a father'. She had a father now, of course. Graham Ashworth. Accountant. She looked out of the window and ordered her mind. They passed large villas set in their own, almost tropical gardens.

'There're crowned heads of Europe sitting out the war in Estoril,' said Cardew. 'That's the kind of place it is.'

He turned off the main road at the Estoril railway station and drove into a square lined with hotels and cafés surrounding some gardens with palm trees and beds of roses, which gradually sloped up to a modern building at the top.

They passed the Hotel Palácio which Cardew told her was 'ours' and next door the Hotel Parque which was 'theirs'. They went round the back of the modern building at the top which proved to be the casino, and Cardew pointed out a narrow, overgrown passage and a gate in the hedgerow further up, which was the back way into the Wilsheres' garden. They climbed higher, right to the top of the hill, past gardens enclosed by privilege, hugging the towering phoenix palms and spiked fans of the Washingtonians, while the brash purple lights of bougainvillea tried to escape over the wall. Anne straightened her sunglasses on her nose, rested an elbow on the car window ledge, wished she had a cigarette going, which she thought would be the final detail of a leading actress's style, coming into her Riviera home.

'You didn't say whether you liked Wilshere,' said Anne, catching sight of herself in the wing mirror.

Cardew stared intently at the windscreen as if the entrails of squashed insects might lead him somewhere. They pulled up at an ornate gateway, walls curving up and scrolling against solid stone posts, each of which sported a giant carved pineapple on top. A tiled panel bore the words *Quinta da Águia* and the wrought-iron gates an elaborate *QA* design.

'Here's an insight into the man,' said Cardew. 'This place used to be called *Quinta do Cisne*, Swan House, if you like. He's renamed it Eagle House. His little joke, I think.'

'I don't get it.'

'He does business with the Americans *and* the Germans. Both countries use the eagle as their national symbol.'

'Maybe he's just being a gentleman.'

'How's that?'

'Making everybody feel comfortable . . . unless they're Marjorie,' she said.

The driveway was cobbled all the way up to the house, white with black geometric patterns, just as she'd seen on the Lisbon pavements. It was lined with pink oleanders, very mature, almost trees. They came out of the oleanders into a square in front of the house which had a fountain in the middle, water spouting from a dolphin's mouth. Lawn sloped away to distant hedges, a stepped, cobbled path ran down one side towards the bottom of the garden and the back gateway to possible financial ruin. The view reached to the hotels and palms of Estoril's main square, the railway station and the ocean beyond.

The house itself was vast and box-like, not an accumulation of extensions, not something organic that had grown with the owner's mind or fortune, but a house that had been planned, finished and never again added to. Its ugliness was disguised by the leafy frills of an ancient wisteria whose tributaries reached the eaves of the terracotta tiled roof. They walked to the pillared porch, Anne fretting about her case left in the car.

The door was opened by a grotesquely bent old man, his head at right angles to his body and turned sideways so that he could look Cardew in the eye. He wore a black tailed jacket and striped trousers. He was backed up by a small, wide woman also dressed in black with a white apron and cap. Cardew's Portuguese came out like an order for buttered scones but it was intelligible enough for the old man, who produced a length of cane from the back of his jacket and set off towards the car with the woman in tow. Another maid appeared, doing up her apron. She was even smaller than the first, with a face that had been pinched and drawn out to the length of a fox's. Tiny eyes, closed up by malnourishment in pregnancy, flickered in her head. There was an exchange and the maid set off across the black and white chequered floor of the dark hall which was surrounded by oak panelling, and stairs that joined a gallery above. A huge, tiered iron chandelier hung from the wooden roof.

On either side of the door through which the maid had disappeared were two glass cases full of brightly coloured, naïve clay figurines. Dark, uncleaned oil paintings in heavy gilt frames hung above them. In one, the stern face of a bearded ancestor appeared as if through battle smoke, the woman standing behind his chair was pale with dark rings around her eyes as if illness had been a way of life.

'Mafalda's parents,' said Cardew. 'The Conde and Condessa. Dead now. She inherited the lot.'

Behind them the old man and the maid staggered in with Anne's case suspended between them on the piece of cane. They started up the staircase and paused on the first landing. The old man held on to the shiny ball at the corner of the bannisters, panting. Anne felt the urge to get up there to help him and, sensing it, Cardew gripped her elbow. The other maid returned, taking tile-sized steps towards them, her foxy face nudging the air, suspicious, checking them for smells. Cardew steered Anne down the length of a wooden-floored corridor with a strip of carpet up the middle, tall mirrors on either side of mixed quality so that Anne appeared thin, chubby, wavy. A chandeliered dining room flashed past on the left. At the end of the corridor, just before the french windows out on to the back terrace, they turned right into a long, high room with six tall windows giving out on to the lawn. The shutters were open, the blue and gold designs on them faded from the fierce summer sun.

The quantity of furniture in the room gave the impression that there was a lot going on, that maps and compasses might have been helpful. This furniture was not in any way co-ordinated, colours clashed, brocade and velvet sat uncomfortably together, the muted carpets seemed embarrassed by the brashness and weight of it all. At the far end of the room was a carved marble fireplace which contained a frieze in bas-relief of an ancient people, Corinthians or Phoenicians, engaged in endless tussle with wild animals. Above the fireplace hung a painting, a hunting scene of wild and bloody savagery, with wild boar stuck and squealing and wounded dogs tossed in the air while mounted men with lances stared on.

Patrick Wilshere stood below this scene dressed in riding britches, boots and a loose, collarless white shirt undone at the neck. Cardew's description of him as 'rum' and 'not average' was typical understatement. Wilshere had stepped out of a novel from a different, more romantic age. His grey hair, swept back behind his ears, was long, long enough so that it rested on the first vertebrae of his back. He had a moustache whose waxed tips pointed upwards and his eyes were creased at the corners as if on permanent look-out for the source of all amusement. His hands had long elegant fingers and they cradled a cut-glass tumbler half-full of amber liquid. He nudged himself away from the fireplace where he'd been leaning.

'Meredith!' he called down the room, pleased to see him, hearty.

The maid stepped back and Anne followed Cardew through the watercourse between the furniture to the small backwater where Wilshere stood, still with the faint reek of horse about him.

'Sorry, haven't had time to change,' said Wilshere. 'Been out on the hills all day, just got back and needed a blast to put the wind back in my sails. You must be Anne. Pleased to meet you. Been travelling all day, I expect. Could do with freshening up. Get yourself out of that suit and into something more comfortable. Yes. MARIA! If you can't remember the maids' names just shout Maria and you'll get two or three.'

The maid came back and stood at the door.

'All tiny, these people,' said Wilshere, 'no bigger than fairies. Come from my wife's part of the country.'

He spoke in perfect Portuguese. The maid dipped and ducked in an attempted curtsy. Anne navigated the furniture to the door and followed the maid up the stairs and down a corridor to a room which would have been above the end of the living room. It was a corner room, with views of the sea and Estoril. There was a private bathroom which overlooked the terrace and, beyond some hedges, a grass tennis court, brown from the sun. The cast-iron bath had clawed feet holding on to small worlds. A shower rose the size of a frying pan stuck out from the wall. The maid left, closing the door. Anne waited for the footsteps to retreat, ran at the four-poster bed, flung herself at it wildly and writhed in luxury. She lay with her arms spread out, trying to encompass her new world.

She stripped, showered and changed into a pleated cotton skirt and a simple blouse which left her arms bare. She brushed out her hair, struck poses in the full-length mirror, pouting her mouth, flicking at her skirt, but still failed to match her surroundings.

She headed back down the corridor towards the stairs. A figure appeared at the far end of the gallery. A woman with a face whiter than her mother's and long grey hair down to the middle of her back. She wore a white nightdress. The woman faded into the darkness of a room, shut the door.

Mafalda the Mad, very Jane Eyre, she thought, and fled down the stairs.

Anne returned to the living room, which was empty. Wilshere was sitting on his own on the back terrace in front of a wrought-iron table with a cigarette box and the cut-glass tumbler, emptier. He had his boots up on an unoccupied chair opposite. She joined him.

'Ye-e-es,' he said, 'that's better.'

'What happened to Mr Cardew?'

'Sit down, sit down, won't you,' he said, pulling her down into a chair next to him, his palm rough on her bare arm. His green eyes stroked her all over and the hand held on to the soft part below her shoulder. His look was neither prurient nor penetrative, two other looks she'd had that day, but attentive, oddly intimate, as if they were old friends, or even stronger – lovers, maybe, who'd had a life together, parted and come back for another visit.

'Drink?'

How to play this? She'd been hoping to observe while Cardew talked but now she was in it. He likes a girl with spunk.

'Gin,' she said, 'and tonic.'

'Excellent,' he said, releasing her arm, calling a boy over, who Anne hadn't seen in the shade of the terrace.

Wilshere punched some words into him and drained his own glass which he handed over.

'Smoke?'

She took a cigarette which he lit for her. She blew the smoke out into the still, very hot evening. It smelled like burnt dung. The boy returned and laid out two tumblers and a small dish of black, shiny olives. They chinked glasses. The cold drink and the fizz of the tonic smacked into her system and she had to restrain herself from jutting her breasts.

'You'll probably want to go to the beach tomorrow,' said Wilshere, 'although I should warn you that our friendly dictator, Dr Salazar, does not agree with men and women disporting themselves semi-naked on the strand. There are police. An intimidating squad of fearless men whose job it is to maintain the moral rectitude of the country by sniffing out depravity at source. All those refugees, you see, brought their immoral ideas and fashions with them and the good Doctor's determined that it won't get out of hand. The three F's. Football, *Fado* and Fátima. The great man's solution to the evils of modern society.'

'*Fado?*'

'Singing. Very sad singing . . . wailing, in fact,' he said. 'Perhaps some of my Irishness has worn off in this sunshine. All that rain and terrible history, I should have a natural inclination for drink and melancholy thought, but I don't.'

'Drink?' asked Anne, archly, which earned a flash of white teeth.

'I've never felt the need to brood over things. They happen. They pass. I move on. Construct. I've never been one for sitting about, longing for previous states. States of what? Lost innocence? Simpler times? And I don't have much time for destiny or fate,

82

which is what *fado* means. People who believe in destiny are invariably justifying their own failure. Don't you think? Or am I a godless fellow?'

'I thought belief in fate was just a way of accepting life's inexplicability,' said Anne, 'and you still haven't told me how *fado* is supposed to stiffen moral fibre. How can fate or destiny be a social policy?'

Wilshere smiled. Cardew had been right about spunk.

'It's what they sing about in the *fado*. *Saudades* – which is longings. I've no time for it. You know where it comes from? This is a country with a magnificent past, a tremendously powerful empire with the world's wealth in their hands. Take the spice trade. The Portuguese controlled the trade that made food taste good . . . and then they lost it all and not only that . . . their capital was destroyed by a cataclysmic event.'

'The earthquake.'

'On All Souls' Day too,' he said. 'Most of the population were in church. Crushed by falling roofs. Then flood and fire. The perils of Egypt, minus the plague and locusts, were visited on them in a few hours. So that's where *fado* comes from. Dwelling in and on the past. There are other things too. Men putting out to sea in boats and not always coming back. The women left behind to fend for themselves and to sing them back into existence. Yes, it's a sad place, Lisbon, and *fado* provides the anthems. That's why I don't live there. Go there as little as possible. You have to have the right spirit for the city and it's not one that sits well with me. Pay no attention to *fado*. It's just Salazar's way of subduing the population. That and the miraculous sighting of the Virgin at Fátima . . . ye-e-e-s, Catholicism.'

'That must be hard work if they all died in church back in 1755.'

'Ah, well, you see, the good doctor's trained to be a priest, he's a monk *manqué* . . . he knows better than anybody how to control a population. You might have heard of the PVDE.'

'Not yet,' she lied.

'His secret police. His Inquisitors. They root out all non-believers, the heretics and the blasphemers, and break them on the wheel.'

She looked sceptical.

'I promise you, Anne, there's no difference except it's politics now and not religion.'

83

He beckoned the boy, who approached, whisky bottle in hand, and filled Wilshere's glass to within a quarter-inch of the brim. He took an olive, bit out the pit, and threw it unconsciously into the garden. He sucked the top off his drink, lit another cigarette and was surprised to find his old one still going in the ashtray. He crushed it out, flung a boot up on to the chair and missed. He looked at his watch as if someone had burnt his wrist.

'Better change for dinner. Didn't realize it was so late.'

Anne stood with him.

'No, no, you stay here,' he said, patting her arm. 'You'll do fine like that. Perfect. I still smell of horse.'

He did. And whisky. And something sour, which smelled the same as fear but wasn't.

'Will your wife be joining us?' Anne asked his retiring back.

'My *wife*?' he asked, turning on his boot heel, the whisky from his glass slopping on to his wrist.

'I thought I saw her . . .'

'What did you see?' he asked rapidly, drawing on his cigarette, which he then flicked away across the terrace.

'On the way down from my room. A woman in a nightdress . . . that was all. In the corridor upstairs.'

'What did Cardew say about my wife?' asked Wilshere, the savage edge to his voice even sharper.

'Only that he thought she was unwell, which was why I asked you . . .'

'Unwell?'

'. . . which was why I asked you whether she would be joining us for dinner, that's all,' finished Anne, holding her ground against Wilshere's sudden blast.

His top lip extended over the glass rim and sucked up an inch of whisky, the sweat from the alcohol in this heat standing out on his forehead in beads.

'Dinner's in fifteen minutes,' he said and turned through the french windows, clipping the door, which juddered in its frame.

Anne sat back down, a small tremble in the tip of her cigarette as she put it to her mouth. She sipped more gin, finished smoking and walked out on to the crepuscular lawn. Lights were on down in the town – rooms here and there in buildings, streets brought up in monochrome, the crowns of the gathered stone pines billowing like

84

thick black smoke, the railway station with people waiting, mesmer-ized by the track or staring off down the rails of past and future. Nor-mality, and next to this, the vast and threatening blackness of the unlit ocean.

Two squares of light came on in the house behind her. A figure came to one of the lit windows and looked down on her although, in the twilight, she wasn't sure if she was visible. She felt the drag, almost heard the sinister rattle of the pebbles as with the inevitability of tide she was being drawn into the complicated currents of other people's lives.

Chapter 9

Saturday, 15th July 1944, Wilshere's house, Estoril, near Lisbon.

The servant came out on to the lawn to get her, made her jump as she was lounging about in her own thoughts. She'd lost herself in the graininess where the town's light met the darkening air. She turned to the boy and found that the façade of the house was now lit by footlights as if it was a monument. It only came to her then. The freedom of artificial light. She hadn't thought about it looking down on the town. No blackout. This alarming country – free and yet forbidding.

She followed the boy. His thighs thumped out of the side of his trousers, massive as a weightlifter's. He walked her across the terrace, already cleared of her half-drunk gin and tonic, and on to the dining room halfway down the corridor. Three glass chandeliers hung over a table which had been shortened to fifteen feet for this, more intimate, occasion. Wilshere stood, almost at attention. He was dressed in a dinner jacket with a board-hard shirt front and black bow tie. He presented his wife, who was in a floor-length evening gown, breasts encased, waist pinched, skirts full of animal rustlings. Her hair was up and she wore a necklace of three large, set rubies. Her face still had the terrible pallor but it was not the alabaster whiteness of her mother's, more the ghastliness of unsuccessful junket.

Anne shook her hand which had been held out like a bishop's, waiting to be kissed. It was puffy, swollen by fluid retention, so that the knuckles were dimples. They sat. Anne, midway between their two ends, awkward in her informal dress. The light from the three chandeliers was surgically bright and harsh – operative.

A soup was served, greyish-green with a slice of sausage floating in the middle. White wine trickled into glasses. Mafalda refused the wine, placed her spoon in her soup and looked about. The wine

86

tasted of cold metal with a fizz like the end of a battery. The soup was replaced by a plate of three fish each, their eyes cataracted by frying. Anne's intestines screamed for a break to the shattering silence but Wilshere, unmoved, holding his knife like a scalpel, dismantled his fish expertly, while Anne reduced hers to a pile of bony hash. Mafalda's knife and fork tinkered around the sea bass and subsided. The fish were taken away. Large chunks of indeterminate meat flecked with red were served, clamshells rattled on the plates.

Anne, desperate to communicate, found her thoughts crashing about her head like a late-night drunk looking for food in a hotel kitchen. Mafalda corralled her meat on one side of her plate, the clams on the other, and laid down her irons. Red wine jugged into different glasses. It smelled of damp socks but tasted as complex as a kiss. Wilshere swilled it in his mouth, his lips pursed to a smooch beneath his joyous moustache.

'Your husband was telling me about *fado* this evening,' gasped Anne, having two goes at it, finding not just a frog in her throat but a whole fat toad.

'I can't think why,' said Mafalda. 'He doesn't know anything about it. Loathes it. Runs – no, sprints – to turn it off when it comes on the radio.'

Wilshere's jaws chewed over the meat in his mouth, interminable as cud.

'He was saying,' Anne pressed on, 'he was saying that they're songs about longing, about dwelling . . .'

Mafalda just rattled the cutlery on the side of her monogrammed plate and Anne shut up.

'I like that new girl. Amália,' said Wilshere. 'Amália Rodrigues. Yes, she's rather good.'

'Her voice?' asked Mafalda on the end of a coal-black look.

'I didn't know there was anything else to *fado*,' said Wilshere, 'or were you asking me whether I thought she had the spirit, the soul, the *alma* of *fado*?'

A twitch had started up around Mafalda's left eye. She stroked it down with her little finger. Anne looked from one end of the table to the other – the idiot spectator.

'Of course, she has marvellous . . .' said Wilshere, and his search for a word set the air quivering, '. . . marvellous deportment.'

87

'De*portment*?' scoffed Mafalda. 'He means . . .'

She reined herself in. Her small puffy fist banging the edge of the linen tablecloth a light thump.

'Perhaps I should have chosen something less contentious,' said Wilshere. 'We were merely conversing about our good friend the great Doctor and, of course, the three "F"'s came up. Perhaps we should have talked about history, but even that's a minefield. You'll be glad to know that I didn't make any mention of *O Encoberto*, the Hidden One, my dear.'

'The Hidden One?' asked Anne.

'Dom Sebastião,' said Wilshere. 'No, I didn't make any mention of him, my dear, I knew you'd rather tell Anne all about that yourself. My wife, you see, Anne, is a monarchist. A state that hasn't existed in this country for more than thirty years. She believes that the Hidden One, who was killed – ooooh, four hundred years ago, wasn't it? – on the battlefield of El Kebir in Morocco, will somehow return . . .'

Mafalda stood with some difficulty. Wilshere broke off. A servant was pulling back her chair and offering his shoulder for her to lean on.

'I'm not feeling so well,' she said. 'I'm afraid I will have to withdraw.'

She left the room without appearing to shift any of her weight on to the servant's shoulder, which she gripped in a fistful of material. She hadn't been that unsteady upstairs in her nightclothes. Mafalda gave Anne the shadow of a nod. The door closed with a brass click. Anne dropped back into the dent of her upholstered chair, traumatized. Her half-eaten meat was removed. Fruit salad appeared. Steps receded to the kitchen. They were left alone in the chandeliered glare, the red wine on a small silver tray in front of Wilshere.

'Words, words, words,' said Wilshere under his breath, 'it's only words.'

Earlier, out on the terrace Wilshere had been on his way up to drunkenness. The flash of anger at the mention of his wife had been a hiatus in the usual, uninterrupted progression. In the short fifteen minutes he'd taken to get changed he'd shot through drunkenness and regained sobriety, but with a difference. He was now capable of seamless transformations from belligerent to maudlin, from vindictive to self-pitying. Perhaps Cardew's estimation of the mental state of the occupants was the reverse. Mafalda was just unwell and the man drumming his stiff bib at the end of the table, contemplating the level of wine in his glass, was, if not mad, then close to it.

'Don't eat dessert myself,' he said. 'No sweet tooth.'

He chinked the edge of his plate with the spoon, drank the wine and poured the remains into his glass. The servants arrived with coffee. He told them to serve it out on the terrace. He finished the wine in a single draught as if compelled to drink it – condemned to death by poisoning.

On the terrace Wilshere forced a glass of port from another century on to Anne. This was no longer pleasurable drinking.

'Let's take a walk down to the casino,' said Wilshere after a prolonged silence in which his body became an impregnable fortification, behind which the man's mind had retreated to fight some internal battle. 'Run along and put your best party frock on.'

She put her only party frock on, one of her mother's from before the war. She looked down out of the bathroom window on to the terrace where Wilshere sat immobile. Refocusing on her own image in the glass she felt a crack of fear opening up. She remembered her training – the talk about mental stamina for the work – and breathed the panic back down.

She walked downstairs with her shoes in her hand, not wanting another confrontation with the spectral Mafalda. On the terrace she rejoined Wilshere, who was staring through the footlights into the wall of darkness. He jerked himself out of his chair, held her by the shoulders but not with the soft touch of her old piano teacher. His breath, an ammoniacal reek that could have blistered paintwork, made her blink. Sweat had appeared in the parted channel of his perky moustache. His mouth was no more than inches from her own. Everything in her body recoiled and a squeal moved up from her stomach. He let her go. Goose flesh flourished where his hands had been.

They walked through the curtain of light on to the lawn and round to the cobbled pathway that led down the garden. A half-moon lit the way. Not far from the bottom a path forked off to a summerhouse and a bower which had formed around some stone pillars providing a shelter of hanging fronds for a bench with a view out to the sea. It looked unused, as if the house's occupants had no need of such tranquillity but preferred the relentlessness of the dark halls and the corridors of their natural habitat.

They crossed the road under the dense darkness of the stone pines at the rear of the casino, a modern featureless building which knew that its attraction was not architectural. They joined the current of expensive-looking people going in – the rustle of taffeta, the sizzle of nylons and the crack of wads of freshly minted folding money.

Wilshere headed straight for the bar and ordered a whisky. Anne opted for a brandy and soda. As Wilshere lit her cigarette a meaty arm came around his shoulders. His slim body flinched.

'Wilshere!' said an expansive American voice, not looking at him but putting his head close as if about to touch cheeks. A hand stretched out towards Anne. 'Beecham Lazard.'

'The third,' said Wilshere, shrugging the American's arm off. 'This is Miss Anne Ashworth.'

Lazard was taller and wider than Wilshere. He was dressed in a dinner jacket too, but his was crammed full and bulging. He was younger than Wilshere by twenty years and had black hair with a precision-tooled side parting. His smile was faultless and his skin tone utterly consistent. There was something of waxwork perfection about him, both fascinating and repellent.

'We gotta talk,' said Lazard to the side of Wilshere's face.

Wilshere looked down his shirt front like a man on a high ledge.

'Anne is my new house guest,' he said. 'Flew in from London today. I was just showing her the wonderful place in which we live.'

'Sure thing,' said Lazard, releasing Anne's hand, which he'd been rubbing with a smoothing thumb. 'It's just about dates ... a few seconds, that's all.'

Wilshere, annoyed, excused himself and backed off to the entrance of the bar where they talked, jostled by others streaming past them. Anne fiddled with her cigarette and felt juvenile in her outfit. *Haute couture* Paris had shifted to Lisbon and the clothes on the people around her made her feel as if she was waiting for the jellies to come out at a tea party. She smoked as a diversionary tactic and cast about to compensate. Even that proved difficult. Her idle, confident gaze was easily met by others' with stronger, more demanding eyes. Her head snapped back to the mirrors and glassware of the bar, which reflected a multiplication of eyes, some drunk, some sad, some hungry, some hard – but all wanting.

'Americans,' said Wilshere, back at her side. 'No idea of the time or the place.'

He took her over to a table and introduced her to four women and two men. The foreign names rushed past like a hunt in full cry, all titles and ancestry, fanfare and heraldry. They spoke to Wilshere in French and ignored her. All they needed to know of Anne was apparent in her dress – some skivvy that Wilshere was tupping. He detached himself from their imploring jewelled and knotted fingers, and bowed.

'Has to be done, I'm afraid,' he said to Anne's cheek. 'Ignore the Romanians at your peril. Frightful gossips.'

They headed for the *caixa* where Wilshere wrote a cheque for some chips and they wheeled through the swing doors into the gaming room. He gave Anne an inch of his chips and went straight to the baccarat table, took a seat next to another slumped player and lapsed into dense concentration. Anne hung at his back, suspended in layers of smoke. Cards were drawn from the slab. The players turned up the corners. Sometimes they asked to stand, other times to draw and rarely they declared a natural. It was tedious unless you were one of the rivet-eyed players, who clenched the air in fists, hissing at their losses and uncurling, but only for a second, at their wins.

Wilshere's transformation was instant. All vestiges of amusement and ennui had left him. His interest now was only calculable in percentages, his intelligence reduced to a wavering telepathy with numbered suits. Anne diverted herself by computing the bank's advantage in the game and started to yawn. The gambling had sucked out the oxygen in the air. She wandered the room, keen to get away from the joyless backs of the baccarat players. No straying eyes connected with hers, money more compelling than lust in here. The room was quiet, but prickling with anticipation and torment. The yards of green baize and acres of carpet added stealth to wealth and hushed any sudden collapse of funds.

She was drawn to roulette. There was noise in roulette, especially when an American was playing, and the clicking of the ivory ball, playing its own *fado*, was almost a sweet distraction after the murderous cards. She joined the crowd, found herself embraced by it, welcomed, offered a cigarette, crushed and, in this familiar, slaughter-yard jostle, confirmed what she had known from the moment those swing doors had batted shut behind her. She was being watched.

It would have been easy enough to turn, to look over the heads bowed in supplication to the green baize god. It would have been easy to find the only other face in the room uncomplicated by numbers, unconcerned by the concentration of avidity. But she couldn't do it. The tension set in her neck, her head began to tremble. An arm snaked around her shoulder and dragged her into a damp shirt.

'Ladies for luck,' roared the American. 'Come on. Let's hear it for number twenty-eight.'

The American gripped her tighter. The croupier terminated the betting, span the wheel and set the ball in motion. Girls squealed. The ball began its chatter. Anne was clenched to the American's chest, harder. His smell as strong as roast meat. The ball played the flibbertigibbet – coy, tantalizing, coquettish – jumping in and out of bed, over the numbers' brass divides. Anne's head was almost on the man's chest now, such was his determination, and into the corner of her eye, back from the crowd, just inside the spread of light, came the strap of neck muscle, the prominent jawline, the hollow cheek of the one she knew was watching her.

He dipped his head. The cheekbones high against the blue eyes, the vulnerable mouth, the dented chin, the throat like a small fist framed by the straining neck. Seeing the eyes complicated matters. It was impossible to understand the motive, to accurately translate the look. Her throat closed up, heat prickled up her neck. She wrestled her eyes back down to the table but not to the squares and numbers, not to the black and red diamonds but to the soft, green felt that was easy on the mind. Her head clicked back up, jerked on a nervous string. Still there. His intent as close as thunder. A roar went up.

'*Vingt-huit*,' said the croupier.

The American's fist punched the underbelly of the smoke above, cigar in the corner of his mouth. Anne, released from his grip, fell forward and saw another girl on his other side still in the man's hug, tiny, thrush-sized with pointy breasts and a sharp beak. He kissed the little bird's head. The croupier raked in the dead chips, leaving the American's bet. He made his calculation and pushed a New York skyline back. Anne backed out of the crowd, sucked on her cigarette and headed for the baccarat tables. She had to concentrate on her walking, as if she had someone else's legs and feet, ones that might run off on their own.

Wilshere's back was still buttressed against the baccarat table, but now Beecham Lazard was sitting next to him. She held back from their orbit. The dealer had his back to the two men, preparing new slabs of cards. The American looked left and swept a stack of high-denomination chips across to Wilshere, whose shoulders widened for a moment and collapsed back.

Anne had to get out of the room, get away from the suffocating quiet of money, the fierce addiction of the gamblers, and away from those blue eyes. She headed for the padded swing doors. The way out of the asylum. She heard music from the Wonderbar and headed for it. She hid in the darkness, away from the lighted dance floor and smoked the cigarette down to her nails.

'Surprised to see you out on your own on your first night,' said a voice from below her.

The band's drummer enjoyed a roll and thrashed his cymbals. Jim Wallis was sitting at a table a few feet to her left, with a spare chair next to him. Across the dance floor, the face from the gaming room appeared at the edge of the light, swept round and fell back into the dark. She took Wallis's offer of a cigarette and drank some of his whisky and soda, which clawed at her throat. Blood smacked into her cheeks.

'I seem to be being followed already,' she said through the music.

'Not surprised,' said Wallis, almost miserable.

'I thought nobody was supposed to know who I am.'

'They want to, though,' he said and leaned into her with his lighter.

'I don't know what you mean.'

'You're beautiful,' he said, the flame wavering in her face. 'Simple as that.'

'Jim,' she said, warning him.

'You asked a question.'

'What are *you* doing here?'

'Waiting and watching,' he said. 'Do you want to dance . . . pass the time?'

'Aren't you with someone?'

'She likes roulette,' said Wallis, holding open his hands to reveal a man with shallow means.

He led Anne to the dance floor. The music started slow. They danced close but formally. She told him about the summerhouse and the covered bower which would make a good place for a dead-letter drop. She'd check it out the next day. The band leader announced a dance number and the couples multiplied on the floor.

She danced for half an hour and went into the powder room when the band took a break. By the time she arrived back at the bar, Wilshere stood on his own with his back to her, foot up on the brass rail, his elbow turned out so that she knew he was still drinking. She told him she wanted to get back to bed. He finished his drink with small ceremony and held out his arm, which she took and they went out into a night that was no cooler.

'These nights . . .' said Wilshere, panting, but without offering anything more, weary of them she could tell.

Wilshere's pace slowed as they reached the edge of the stone pines near the entrance to the garden. She thought at first that he couldn't face going back to the house, that smell on him again, which wasn't fear but like it. He disengaged his arm and put it around her shoulder. They moved on, she supporting him.

The moonlight coaxed the darkness of the garden to blue and Wilshere was staggering and snatching at the fat leaves of the hedge. He was sobbing from such a depth that it came out as a retch, as if he was trying to sick up this thing inside him, some horror tormenting his innards. He hugged her tighter to him. The sharp edges of the jacket stuffed with casino chips cut into her ribs. Anne's heels ripped over the uneven edges of the cobbled steps. They careened off the path and crashed through the hedge and landed, humped on top of each other, in the soft earth on the other side. Wilshere lay on his back. His face was slack, his breathing regular. She pushed away from his limp embrace and started at the sound of wildlife, large and loud, coming through the foliage. A white shirt front flitted, cuffs reached down to the comatose Wilshere.

'You're going to have to help me,' said the voice in quiet, accented English.

She helped Wilshere over the stranger's shoulder, chips cascading down his legs. He backed out of the hedge and set off at a steady lope up the lawn. The lights were off inside and outside the house. They went in through the french windows by the terrace.

'Where does he sleep?'

'I don't . . . I think . . . just put him in there,' she said.

The stranger sidestepped into the sitting room, threw Wilshere down on the first sofa and pulled off his shoes. Wilshere struggled with himself and fell silent. She went to the window and opened the shutter which the servants had closed against the morning sunshine. By the time she'd turned back the stranger had gone. Back at the window she saw him cross the moonlit lawn at a calm night-watchman's pace. He turned at the top of the path to look back, his face obscure. He trotted down the steps, his leather soles pattering the cobbles to silence.

Chapter 10

Sunday, 16th July 1944, Wilshere's house, Estoril, near Lisbon.

In the heat of the morning Anne lay in bed, a crack of light across the foot of the bed warming her ankles. The night's events crawled through her mind and she understood how quickly adults' lives could complicate themselves – a compression of thought and action in time, of too much happening in a confined space, of daily need and greed, triumph and disappointment – and how interminably slow a child's life was, how long the summers used to be with nothing in them. Her mind worked cyclically, coming round to fix on the same single image which had disturbed her even more than Wilshere's behaviour; the man's face, his look, intense and intent – inscrutable, too – threatening or benevolent?

She replayed the night to a final tableau in the casino. As she collected Wilshere from the bar Jim Wallis was sitting at his table with a girl. The girl was the song thrush from under the American roulette-player's arm. She was pretty, in the way of a porcelain doll, if a face that gave out so little could be attractive. It was a hard face that promised but never rewarded. Wallis's good nature might break itself against that face.

Her dress on the back of the chair was filthy. She recalled the catastrophe in the bushes. Wilshere fighting his way into unconsciousness, desperate to stop living with whatever he had in his mind. She threw on some clothes and ran downstairs barefoot. There was no Wilshere in the silent drawing room where dust motes rolled in the single shaft of light from the one half-opened shutter.

She ran out of the house, across the lawn, hot and rough underfoot, to the cobbled path and down to the bushes which she crashed through to find the soil raked over. The neat furrows twitched with ants. She felt around with her feet and fingers and found a casino chip of the highest denomination: five thousand escudos – fifty pounds. She crossed the path to the summerhouse and the pillared bower whose wooden crossbeams were overgrown with passionflower, its exotic purple and white tropical discs hanging above the stone seat. She placed the casino chip on the top of the left pillar to test her dead-letter drop.

The sun was already grilling her shoulders as she went back up to the house. She broke into a run across the lawn, thudded over the empty terrace and up to the french windows where Wilshere caught her by the arms so suddenly that her feet dangled for a moment. He brushed his thumbs over her hot shoulders, ran his fingers down her arms and off at her elbows so that she shivered.

'Mafalda doesn't like running in the house,' he said, as if this was a rule he'd just made up.

He was dressed as she'd first seen him, in riding gear, and if she expected to see a man dishevelled by his hangover, she was disappointed. He was fresh, perhaps in a way that had taken some work – washing, boiling, starching and ironing – but he was not the man who'd tried to throw himself into hibernation the night before.

'D'you fancy a ride?' he asked.

'You don't look as if you mean a donkey on the beach.'

'No-o-o.'

'Well, that's just about the upper limit of my riding experience.'

'I see,' he said, teasing his moustache up to points with his fingers. 'It's a start, I suppose. At least you've been aboard an animal before.'

'I don't have any clothes . . . or boots.'

'The maid's laid some things out for you on your bed. Try them on. They should fit.'

Back in her room the dirty evening dress had been removed and on the bed were britches, socks, a shirt, a jacket, and boots on the floor. Everything fitted, only the britches were a little short in the leg. She dressed, buttoning the shirt, looking out of the window, thinking that these were not Mafalda's clothes. They belonged to a young woman. Wilshere came striding back up the cobbled path, whacking his boot with his crop.

She turned, knowing she wasn't alone in the room. Mafalda stood in the doorway of the bathroom, hair down, wearing the nightdress again, her face shocked and taking in every inch of Anne as if she knew her and couldn't believe that she'd had the nerve to reappear in her house.

'I'm Anne, the English girl, Dona Mafalda,' she said. 'We met last night . . .'

The words didn't break the spell. Mafalda's head reared back, incredulous, and then she was away, the cotton nightdress wrapping itself around her thighs, her slippered feet striding the hem to full stretch. The floor in the corridor creaked as Mafalda disappeared in a sound of unfurling sailcloth. Anne pulled on the boots, a dark weight settled in her. If Sutherland thought that Cardew had successfully positioned her in this house without Wilshere's premeditation, he was wrong.

Wilshere was standing in the hall, nodding his approval as she came down the stairs and smoking.

'Perfect fit,' he said on the way to the car, a soft-top Bentley polished to new.

'Whose are they?

'A friend of Mafalda's,' he said.

'She seemed surprised to see me wearing them.'

'She saw you?'

'She was in my bathroom.'

'Mafalda?' he said, unconcerned. 'She's such a stickler for cleanliness. Always checking up on the maids. I tell you . . . you wouldn't want to be in service here.'

'She seemed to think I was someone else,' she said, pressing him.

'I can't think who that would be,' he said, smiling out of the corner of his face. 'You don't look like anybody else . . . that we know.'

They drove down to the seafront, turned right and along the new Marginal road to Cascais. Anne stared ahead, thinking of opening gambits to break through Wilshere's shiny, deflecting carapace. None came to her. They rounded the harbour, drove up past the block of the old fort and out to the west. The sea, with more swell in it than yesterday, pounded against the low cliffs and sent up towers of saltine spray through holes in the rock, which the light breeze carried across the road, prickling the skin.

'Boca do Inferno,' said Wilshere, almost to himself. 'Mouth of Hell. Don't see it like that myself, do you?'

98

'I only see hell how the nuns taught me to see hell.'

'Well, you're still young, Anne.'

'How do you see it?'

'Hell's a silent place, not . . .' he stopped, shifted again. 'I know it's Sunday but let's talk about something else, can we? Hell isn't my . . .'

He trailed off, put his foot down on the accelerator. The road broke through a clump of stone pines and continued along the coast to Guincho. The wind was stronger out here, blowing sand across the road, which corrugated to washboard, hammering at the suspension.

The hump of the Serra de Sintra appeared with the lighthouse at its point. The road climbed, twisted and turned back on itself – a grim chapel and fortification high above on a wind-blasted peak, naked of vegetation, looked out over the surf-fringed coast, now far below, tapering off into the Atlantic.

At the highest point the road turned north and into a thick bank of cloud. The vapour condensed on their faces and hair. The light sunk to an autumnal grey. Homesickness and gloom descended with it.

At the hamlet of Pé da Serra Wilshere turned right up a steep climb and on the first bend stopped outside some wooden gates flanked by two large terracotta urns. A servant opened the gates and they rolled into a cobbled yard in which vines had been trained to form a green canopy over a right-angled arcade. Piles of dung littered the stones and a Citroën was parked with its nose under one of the arches.

As the Bentley pulled up alongside, a man mounted on a black stallion came from behind the building. The horse stepped daintily around the piles of ordure, its hooves ringing on the damp satin cobbles. The rider, seeing Wilshere, turned his animal, the musculature in the horse's hindquarters straining to be out on the gallop. The horse snorted and tongued the bit. Wilshere shrugged into his jacket, introduced Anne to Major Luís da Cunha Almeida and tried to stroke the stallion's head, but the horse shook him off. The major was powerfully built, his shoulders as restless as the animal underneath him. His hands and wrists toiled with the reins while his thick knees and thighs gripped the horse's impatience. They exchanged a few words and the major turned his horse and trotted out of the yard.

The groom brought a large grey mare and a chestnut filly into the yard. Wilshere mounted the mare, took the reins of the filly and led it to some steps. The groom held the stirrup while Anne mounted. Wilshere arranged her reins for her, gave brief instructions, and they followed the major out on to the hills.

They walked the horses, climbing steadily through the pine on a sandy track through the forest. Wilshere retreated into himself, blended to the animal beneath him. Anne moved her body with the filly's strides, trying to think of a way into Wilshere, looking at the man in his silent place – his hell, he'd said. After three-quarters of an hour they arrived at a stone fountain and a low, miserable grey rock building, with a cross on the apex of its roof, which was submerged in the surrounding vegetation with the green streaks of damp clinging to its walls. Wilshere seemed surprised and annoyed to find himself at this spot.

'What is it?' asked Anne.

'Convento dos Capuchos,' said Wilshere, turning his horse. 'A monastery.'

'Shall we take a look?'

'No,' he said abruptly. 'I took the wrong road.'

'Why don't we take a look now that we're here?'

'I said no.'

Wilshere turned her horse and set her off back down the track. His own mare kept settling back on her hindquarters, raising her forelegs off the ground, apparently uncomfortable with the rider. They danced while Wilshere tried to wrestle her back down. Then he dug in his heels and let her have her head. They careered down the track, almost sideways, Wilshere bent over the horse's neck. They closed rapidly on the filly and, as they reached her, Wilshere leaned over and gave the animal a whack across the rump with his crop. Anne felt her horse start beneath her, tip back on its hind legs. Then the filly lunged forward, tearing the reins from her fingers and throwing Anne on to its neck so that the mane, coarse and bitter, was stuffed into her mouth.

The filly's fast hooves rattled over the dry stones and the hard-baked track ripped past underneath. Anne hung on to the mane with her cheek pressed to the smooth skin, felt the thick beam of muscle in the horse's neck, saw the animal's eye wild and white-edged with panic.

The track narrowed, the trees closed in. The filly's tongue was hanging out of its head as foam crept up her jaws. Branches snapped at their flanks, cracking against Anne's flattened back, whipping against the horse's chest, spurring it on. Adrenalin had burst into her system and yet she found herself detached – both on the horse and yet looking on, too.

They burst out of the trees and cloud into the brilliant sunshine, a rough brush underfoot. The wind crumpled in her ears. There was a clattering noise off to the right. A charging presence pursued by dust swirling in tight screws closed on her. The hot lathered flanks of the major's black stallion pulled alongside and a thick wrist gripped the strap of the bridle and the fractions crunched into each other to make slow seconds until they stopped altogether.

She pushed herself up straight against the major's arm, legs quivering.

'Where's Senhor Wilshere?' asked the major, in English.

'I don't know . . . I . . .' she ducked at the memory of him, crop raised, bearing down on her.

'Something frightened the horse?'

Anne, gulping at the air, working at the events in her brain, searched for any possible reason for Wilshere's bizarre action.

'Whose clothes are these?' she asked.

'I don't understand,' said the major, squinting at her.

'Mr Wilshere . . . did he come riding here with someone . . . before? Before me. Another woman?'

'You mean the American?'

'Yes, the American. What was her name?'

'Senhora Laverne,' he said. 'Senhora Judy Laverne.'

'What happened to her? What happened to Judy Laverne?'

'I don't know. I've been away some months. Perhaps she went back to America.'

'Without her clothes?'

'Her clothes?' he asked, confused.

'These clothes,' she said, slapping her thigh.

The major wiped sweat out of his eyebrow.

'How long have you known Senhor Wilshere?' he asked.

'I arrived in Portugal yesterday.'

'You didn't know him before?'

'Before what?'

'Before you arrived,' he said, solid, calm.

Anne filled her lungs with air, unbuttoned her jacket. The filly turned and put its head to the stallion's flank. High up on a ridge Wilshere appeared, white shirt against the blue sky, and waved at them. He worked the mare down through the brush and rocks and on to the path.

'I lost you,' said Wilshere, approaching them on the now subdued mare. As if that was all it had been.

'My horse bolted,' said Anne, not ready for confrontation, not in front of the major. 'The major rescued me.'

Consternation crossed Wilshere's face. It seemed so genuine that Anne almost accepted it, even though she'd seen he'd stripped off his jacket, which was strapped to the back of his saddle. Not the behaviour of an urgent man.

'Well, thank you, Major,' said Wilshere. 'You must be rattled, my dear. Perhaps we should head back.'

Anne eased the filly out from under the stallion's haunch. Wilshere gave the major a casual half-salute. They headed back down the path towards the dense cloud on the north side of the *serra*. The major stayed behind, motionless on his horse, solid as an equestrian statue in a city square.

They walked nose to tail back to the *quinta*, back into the gloom of the low cloud. Anne, mesmerized by the rhythm of the horses, replayed the incident; not Wilshere's madness, but the exhilaration of the adrenalin rush on the back of the runaway horse – fear had not been as frightening as she'd imagined. It seemed to tell her something about the faces in the gaming room of the casino, about the thrill and fear of gain and loss. Perhaps there was more thrill in losing – the morbid draw of possible catastrophe. She shuddered, which turned Wilshere in his saddle. She gave him a smile torn from a magazine.

They dismounted in the courtyard of the *quinta* and the groom led the horses away. Anne's buttocks and thighs felt like a cooling bronze's, the heat deep within, the surface set hard. The sweat in her hair was now cold, her muscles seizing as she followed Wilshere under the arches and into a rustic stone-flagged room with heavy wooden furniture, a dark family portrait and English hunting prints on the walls. Stags' horns pricked the palpable, mildewed air in the room. A macabre chandelier of antlers hung from the ceiling, unlit, over a refectory table set with plates of cheeses, *chouriços, presunto*, olives and bread. Wilshere poured himself a large tumbler of white wine from a clay jug and handed a clay goblet to Anne.

'Cheers,' he said. 'You'll need it after that.'

She was infuriated by his coolness and sank her wine. Questions backed up inside her. She wanted to find the join in his armour, prise it open, stick him with something sharp.

'Care for anything to eat?' he asked, diverting her, fluttering his hand over the food, not interested himself, gulping at the wine.

'Yes,' she said, 'I didn't eat breakfast.'

'Perhaps I shouldn't have dragged you out . . .'

'No, no, I was glad of it,' she said, facing off his mask of infallible politeness. 'I wanted to ask . . .'

'What?' he teased, an interruption to undermine her. 'What did you want to ask?'

'I wanted to ask about the major,' she said, not that interested in him, but he could be a lever, man against man. She took an olive from the table.

'What about him?'

'He seemed a very . . . ah . . . noble man,' she said, walking around to the opposite side of the table, grinding her teeth on the olive pit.

'Noble?' Wilshere asked himself. 'Noble. Yes, noble's . . . very apposite. He *is* a noble fellow.'

'Nobility sounds so old-fashioned these days,' said Anne, keeping her eye on Wilshere, who had come round to her side of the table.

'Something, perhaps, we associate with earlier conflicts,' he said.

'Except the major's not at war and yet he has . . .'

'Quite so, Anne, quite so. Perhaps because he was mounted on a horse, that made you think of nobility and other aspects of the chivalric code.'

'Other aspects?'

'Rescuing damsels in distress,' he said, blinking, almost batting his eyelids.

She peeled a length of skin off a slice of *chouriço*, Wilshere's presence close, unmistakably extortionate. He seemed like a small boy curious as to what would happen to a spider if he were to dismember it.

'I suppose if he'd had a red satin-lined cloak and a plumed tricorn hat . . .' she started, and Wilshere guffawed to the antler chandelier, reducing this little episode to some romantic nonsense. Anne gritted her teeth.

'Is that Mafalda's family up there?' she asked, pointing with her cup to the portrait of a group whose white faces stared out of the dark oil of the painting.

'Yes,' said Wilshere, without shifting his gaze from her. 'They used to come out here . . .'

'Hunting?'

'No, no, these trophies are from all over . . . Spain, France . . . I think there's even some Scottish ones up there . . . Yes, look, Glamis Castle. No. The family came out *here* to keep cool in the summer. Lisbon, you know, can get awfully torrid and the family seat is in the Alentejo, which is even more so.'

'And her family now?'

'Most of that lot are dead now. In fact her father died only last year. She took it very badly . . . been rather unwell as a result. Not good . . . as Cardew said . . .'

Anne paced the perimeter of the room. Below the antlers were photographs, hunting parties standing behind the day's slaughter, which in some cases was so considerable that the hunters were reduced to stick figures at the apex of thousands of rabbits, birds and some fewer deer and boar.

'Isn't that Mafalda,' asked Anne, surprised to see the woman young and smiling, gregarious amidst a group, 'with a gun?'

'Oh, yes,' said Wilshere, black against the grey light of the window, 'she's very handy with a twelve bore. Crack shot with a rifle too. I never saw it, mind, but her father told me she had quite an eye.'

'Mafalda,' said Anne, impressed.

She moved round to the portrait.

'Is she in this?'

'It's not that good, is it?' said Wilshere. 'She's third from the left, next to her brother.'

'And the brother?' asked Anne, face up to the two figures.

'Hunting accident . . . years ago, before I met Mafalda,' he said, almost confirming that he couldn't possibly have had anything to do with it. 'Tragic.'

'Mafalda must feel quite lonely now.'

Wilshere didn't answer.

Chapter 11

Sunday, 16th July 1944, Wilshere's house, Estoril, near Lisbon.

The heat steepened in the late afternoon, the Quinta da Águia slumped in silence. Anne's room on the west side of the house was hot, even with the shutters closed, and she couldn't sleep with the fan churning the stuffiness. She took her swimsuit, a robe and a towel and went down to the beach. Estoril was submerged in a haze, the sea blended into the sky.

There was no breeze in the gardens of the square. The palms hung their shredded heads in the heat. The cafés were empty. She crossed the road, the silver railway tracks, continued past the empty station and on to the beach. She woke up an attendant, who lay in the shade of one of the huts, gave him a coin and changed.

The beach looked empty at first, but as she walked down towards the sea a couple lying on the sand, arms linked, were given away by a dog digging at their feet. A woman in a white two-piece bathing costume stood up to reveal she'd been lying with someone in a dip in the sand. She wore white-framed sunglasses and was talking to a comatose man at her feet while smoking a cigarette in a short black holder. Anne sat on her towel twenty feet away from the woman, who whined loudly in an American accent.

'Hal,' she said.

'Yeah,' said Hal, drowsy, a straw hat over his eyes and a cigar burning out of the back of his hand which lay on his chest.

'I don't see why we have to be nice to Beecham Lazard.'

No answer. She toed him in the leg.

'Yeah, right. Beecham. Before you get going on Beecham, lemme ask you, what are we doin' here, Mary? What are we doin' in Lisbon?'

'Making money,' she said, bored to death.

105

'Right.'

'Except we ain't made none yet.'

'Right, too. Know why?'

''Cos you think Beecham Lazard's the key to success. Me . . . ?'

'Yeah, I know what you think . . . but he happens to be my only contact.'

She sat back on her heels and looked around. Anne studied the sand between her toes. Hal snored. Mary shook her head, stood and walked straight up to Anne.

'You speak English?'

'I *am* English.'

'Oh, great,' she said, and introduced herself as Mary Couples. 'I knew you had to be a foreigner . . . sitting on your own on the beach. Not a Portuguesey kinda thing to do.'

'No?'

'Not yet. The girls have shaken off their chaperones but they haven't quite got the idea of going some place on their own. You ever seen a Portuguese woman in a bar without a man?'

'I haven't . . .'

'Exactly,' she said, and removed the smoked cigarette from her holder.

Hal snorted, growled and continued snoring louder.

'That's my husband, Hal . . . over there . . . making all the noise,' she said, and looked at him, sadly, as if he was permanently crippled. 'He got stewed lunchtime. He got stewed last night in the casino. He was playing roulette. He won. He always gets stewed when he wins. He always gets stewed, period.'

'I was in the casino last night,' said Anne. 'I didn't see you.'

'I stay at home when he plays roulette.'

'Where's that?' Anne asked, being polite.

'A little place in Cascais. You?'

'I'm staying with the Wilsheres here in Estoril.'

'Oh yeah, nice place. Hal and I are going up there tonight for the cocktail party. You gonna be there?'

'I suppose so,' said Anne, digging a hole in the sand with her heel. 'Do you know many of the Americans round here? I heard you talking about Beecham Lazard.'

'Sure . . . he's not my favourite out of all of them . . .'

'Did you know a woman called Judy Laverne?'

106

'I heard about her. She was before my time. Hal and I have only been here a couple of months.'

'But you know what happened to her?'

There was a fraction of silence, a half-beat, before Mary replied.

'I think she was deported. Some confusion with her visa. She went to the PVDE, like you have to every three months, and they wouldn't renew it. She had three days to leave. I think that was it. Judy Laverne . . . ?' She repeated the name to herself, shook her head.

'You don't know why?'

'The PVDE don't have to give explanations. They're the secret police. They do what the hell they like and a lot of it's not nice. I mean, it's OK for foreigners, the worst that can happen is they deport you . . . no, that's not true, the worst that can happen is they stick you in jail and then deport you . . . but they don't *do* anything to you.'

'*Do* anything to you?'

'Torture is something they do to their own people,' she said, putting a new cigarette into the holder. 'Like Hal says, it's all palm trees and the casino on the surface and . . . You haven't been here very long, have you?'

'Didn't Judy Laverne work for somebody? Wasn't there anybody who could help her?'

Mary weighed that for a few moments.

'You mentioned Beecham Lazard,' she said.

'I was introduced to him last night . . . in the casino,' said Anne. 'She used to work for him?'

Mary turned down the corners of her heavily lipsticked mouth.

'If *he* couldn't keep her in the country, nobody could.'

'And what does Beecham Lazard do?'

'If you want to do business in this town – with anybody, with the government, with the Allies, with the Nazis, anybody – you gotta go through Beecham Lazard . . . that's what Hal says, anyway.'

'You don't like him . . . I heard you earlier.'

'Only because he likes to touch and I consider myself a bit of a museum piece these days . . . you can look and that's it,' she said, pushing the sunglasses up over her head and squeezing the bridge of her nose.

Mary Couples was no longer stunning. She *had* been, but the

107

green eyes under her dark hair didn't shine any more. They had the matt finish of someone who saw things a little more clearly. She was in her thirties and, although intact on the outside, the mind had been working from the inside and the first signs of that weariness, from the long years of holding things together, had crept into her face and started making a bed.

'So why couldn't Beecham Lazard help her?'

'What's your interest in Judy Laverne?' asked Mary, nailing Anne with a direct look.

'I found myself wearing her riding clothes this morning,' she said. 'I was with Patrick Wilshere out on the *serra*. I was just wondering why.'

'Welcome to Estoril,' said Mary, and the sunglasses dropped over her eyes.

'Does that mean Wilshere was having an affair with her?'

Mary nodded.

'And somebody arranged for her to be deported?'

'I don't know,' she said, irritated now. 'Ask Beecham Lazard. One of his pals is the Director of the PVDE, Captain Lourenço.'

'Are you saying that *he* got rid of her?'

Mary froze and then in a nervous reaction started checking herself for a lighter which was still lying next to Hal's heaving body.

'Gotta get a light,' she said, and staggered back to her husband, whose cigar was still trailing acrid smoke into the late afternoon.

A figure ran and plunged into the sea and set off in an explosive burst of crawl.

'The PVDE,' said Mary, handing her a cigarette, lighting it, 'is a state within a state. Nobody tells them what to do . . . Did you tell me your name?'

'No, I didn't. It's Anne. Anne Ashworth.'

'You working out here?'

'I work for Shell. I'm a secretary. My boss is a friend of Patrick Wilshere . . . which is why he offered me a room.'

'Who's your boss?'

'Cardew. Meredith Cardew,' said Anne, her insides congealing as Mary turned the talk around.

'Merry,' she said, 'that's what Hal calls him, which I suppose is fair. He's always smiling. Saying nothing, but smiling.'

'Yes, well, he's my boss.'

'You wouldn't have thought those two would have much in common,' said Mary. 'Merry and Pat. The oil executive and the ... maverick.'

'What's he being a maverick at?'

'That, Anne, is the nature of the maverick,' she said, drawing a large heart in the sand with her finger. 'Who knows?'

They smoked. Anne wanted to be out in the ocean, away from the American woman and her brass accent, away from the information exchange, away from what could be a knowledge debt.

'If I was you,' said Mary, scrubbing out the heart she'd drawn, 'I wouldn't get involved. Stick to the surface ... the palm trees and the casino. It's nicer that way.'

'Hey!' roared Hal, jerking awake, flinging the cigar off into the sand.

'Hal gets his fingers burned,' said Mary, to herself. 'Over here, Hal!'

Hal got to his feet, blew on his hand. Anne recognized him as the American who'd hugged her to his chest at the roulette table, the one with Wallis's songbird under his other arm. Mary introduced them. Hal acknowledged her, looked at his watch, told her they had to go. Anne watched them leave, knowing that Mary was filling Hal in on everything because Hal was looking back at her, either nervous, or as if he wished he'd done more than wave his burnt fingers at her.

Anne threw off her robe and walked down to the sea. She scanned the surface, which was empty. She tied her hair back, stuffed it into a cap. She waded in and threw herself on to the water and swam with quick strokes, hands knifing into the slow sea. She swam unconsciously, letting the complications slide off her body into her roiling wake, listening to the air and water ruckling in the hollows of her clavicles, feeling the brilliant coolness on her forehead. She hit a rhythm, her body rolled smooth as a sculling shell as she sucked in air from under her shoulder.

Her head came up just before impact. An intuitive radar. Bone hit bone. Her face slipped over his shoulder which caught her across the throat. Her arms flailed in a morass of sea and sunlight. She rolled off a man's hard shoulder, bubbles shooting out of her mouth. The light dimmed as she receded into the blue, his legs kicked in the frothing chaos above.

The peace was surprising, a slow noiseless calm, a place where panic couldn't reach. Even when her mother's face slipped through the gate of her memory, the burning house, and Rawlinson's leg, the nuns and $x = \frac{-b \pm \sqrt{(b^2 - 4ac)}}{2a}$ and the wheel turning and the ivory ball jumping, and Mary . . .

The hands in her armpits were an intrusion, the light coming down to meet her unwelcome, the air and water slashing into her lungs, brutal. She heaved and coughed out a ghastly hot acid liquor. She struggled and struggled as if it was all too new and real. She felt the lips on the back of her neck, heard quiet words against her skin, moving over her scalp. Her head rocked back and they were moving, the steady kick of his legs underneath her, his arm across her chest, the blue sky passing overhead and the notion of lying in a pram in the garden in Clapham.

He lifted her out of the water and lay her face-down on the sand. Sea water streamed out of her head in clear rivulets. She put a sand-coated hand to her head and pressed the fleshy protuberance on her temple. She puked without raising her head. The sand darkened into a continental archipelago.

Dead . . . and twice in one day, came the bizarre thought. Is this what happened when you left home? Was the world beyond parental guidance really this dangerous?

The man was talking to her distantly, the sound hollow, faint and echoing as if her head was under a bell jar. It was the same voice as last night. A face with prominent bones, bones so close to the surface they looked painful, the skin covering them too thin. Blue eyes. Blond hair. The cleft chin. An ambiguous face – strong and vulnerable, naïve and shrewd. There was a tightness round her throat again.

'Who are you?' she asked, scared now, eyes blinking, dropping from his neck to his small shrivelled nipples.

'Karl Voss.'

Chapter 12

Sunday, 16th July 1944, Estoril, near Lisbon.

She woke up lying on top of the bed, the counterpane rough against her cheek, a burning disc on her temple and her knees almost up to her chin. The window was open and the air was no longer thick with heat. Her back felt cool. The walls of the room were tinted to rose-water by the evening light. She rolled over to see a vast pink funnel of cloud taking up a segment of the light blue dome of the sky.

Her pillow was wet, an ear bunged with water and a low roar. She sat up, shook her head. Hot water trickled from her ear down her jaw. She stared between her splayed knees as snatches of dialogue emerged in the sloppy horizons of her mind.

'You're German, aren't you?' she'd asked, panting into the sand.

'Yes, I'm the military attaché at the German Legation in Lapa.'

Nobody's here for a holiday.

'Do I know you?'

'Not yet.'

'You're familiar.'

'I don't mean to be,' he said. 'I carried your friend up to the house last night.'

'Were you following me?'

'Your friend was drunk. I knew you were going to need some help.'

'I saw you before ... you were in the casino, watching the roulette.'

'No, not watching the roulette.'

The changing hut. Getting dressed in the hot wood smell, the sand rasping underfoot, the splintery planks furred at the edges. Him ... Karl, sitting on the platform outside in khaki trousers and a white open-necked shirt, plimsolls, no socks. Walking back with

111

him across the railway tracks and up through the gardens. No words. Nothing coming to her at all. His arm hanging next to hers, so close on a few occasions that the down on her forearm rose. At the garden gate behind the casino she could think of nothing else to do but hold out her hand.

'I didn't thank you.'

He shook his head, not necessary.

'And we had the whole Atlantic to swim in,' he said.

She walked back up the long steps to the house thinking 'not watching the roulette'.

She fell back on the bed, folded her hands over her stomach, the pink funnel in the sky reshaped itself into something like a Jewish candelabra. She thought about people not saying anything – the internal scream of silence inside Dona Mafalda, the black, empty lift-shaft behind Wilshere's impeccable manners and the complicated calm of Karl Voss.

Cars arrived outside the house, the drubbing of the tyres on cobbles as they rounded the fountain below. Doors slammed and opened the stopcock of gaiety. Hysterical, deadly vivacity sheared through the wistaria-clad walls below her window. The façade lights of the house came on, tearing the pink light out of the room and throwing yellow artificial bars and squares up on the ceiling.

Over the chair at the end of the bed was an evening gown, not her own, and a suspender belt and stockings. Without thinking, she stepped into the dress, leaving the more intimate wear. It was a modern cut of midnight-blue satin with a neckline that plunged. It matched a pair of satin evening slippers. A long, narrow box on the table with a faded gold name on the back contained a string of pearls. She put them on automatically. They were luminous against her skin, which had darkened in the couple of hours she'd spent in the sun. More cars arrived, more glass laughter shattered around the fountain.

'Henrique!' cried a girl.

'Françoise,' came the reply, '*la déesse de Lisbonne.*'

'*Dieter, wo ist meine Handtasche?*'

'*Ich weiss es nicht. Hast du im Wagen nachgeschaut?*'

And then an ironic voice over the top of the crowd.

'Oi! Myrtle! Weren't you who with me on the ships at Mylae!'

'Pipe down, Julian . . . you're drunk already.'

112

'Has that corpse you planted in your garden sprouted yet?'

'You're not even saying it right.'

'Bugger it.'

Anne's palms moistened as she looked down on the shining metal of the cars, the men in dark suits, the women in their jewels waiting for an arm. She brushed out her hair, pinned it up, smoothed her fingers over the collision point on her temple whose swelling had gone down. She applied lipstick, tried to look into herself beyond the black shining pupils. The dress made her feel confident, brought back that feeling of the actress in her as when she'd first arrived.

She walked down the corridor, but held back from the explosive laughter shooting up from the stairwell. Voices came from a room to her left whose door was ajar. The room was empty, not even a bed. The voices came from the fireplace. She counted off the rooms. She was above what must be Wilshere's study. She'd caught a glimpse of the book-lined walls, the desk and safe earlier in the day. She knelt by the mantelpiece, listened.

There were three men in the room below. Wilshere, Beecham Lazard and one other who spoke English with a heavy, guttural accent. Occasionally this voice and Wilshere's would lapse into German to clarify a point and Beecham's would cut in hard and fast: 'What was that? What did you say?'

It was clear, though, from what followed, that Lazard, far from being excluded from the conversation, was in fact joining with the German to apply pressure on Wilshere, who felt he had no need to step down from his position of strength.

'Say what you like,' said Wilshere, 'but I'm not going to release the goods until the Swiss have notified me that the funds have arrived.'

'Have we ever failed you, my friend?' said the German.

'No, but you know that's not the point.'

'Maybe you think that because of the Allied invasion of France we might be diverting funds away from this kind of activity.'

'That's your business. My business is to make sure that the goods are paid for. And as you know, they are not only my goods. I am representing a number of vendors . . . this is not a regular piece of business . . . not a parcel of this size and quality.'

'All I know is that there's a flight leaving for Dakar on Tuesday evening, which will connect perfectly with the Rio flight on

Wednesday morning,' said Lazard, 'and I want the stones on board.'

'Why so urgent?'

'We have a buyer lined up in New York.'

'And he's going to go away?'

'What's being sold might go to others.'

Silence for some time. Party murmurs. More cars arrived.

'The Russians?' asked Wilshere.

No response.

'When can the funds be in Zurich?'

'Friday.'

'Well, I can see that this is very different from the other business we've done,' said Wilshere. 'Is there anything you can give me that would help the people I'm representing to understand the unusual circumstances?'

'What do you mean?' asked the German brutally.

'Are you talking about a bonus?' Lazard nudged, the percentage man.

'Perhaps we could agree a bonus,' said the German, 'if we could see the goods.'

'Now it's my turn,' said Wilshere, gathering himself. 'Have I ever failed you?'

'Come on, Paddy,' said Lazard.

'Have I?' he asked. 'No. I haven't. I've followed your instructions to the letter. There's nothing under thirty carats in the parcel.'

'It's the value per carat that concerns us,' said the German. 'These are not the usual industrial quality. And whilst the last parcel we bought from the Congo was not entirely satisfactory, and we have confidence in your Angolan product, it does not mean that we're afraid to go back to Léopoldville.'

'But *my* goods are here . . . now,' said Wilshere. 'Ready to go to Dakar as soon as . . .'

'How much?' asked the German, the two words coming down with guillotine weight.

'What can you give me . . . in advance? To show your good intentions.'

'Escudos,' said Lazard.

'I don't want escudos, but . . . perhaps that commodity you use to buy your escudos?'

114

'Gold? That's all accounted for at the Bank of Portugal, it would be impossible . . .'

'Is it?' Wilshere cut in. 'I've heard there have been some interesting diversions since June the sixth.'

Silence. Brittle, frost hard, silence. Anne stared into the grate where a single dry fir cone lay on its side, its scales open, brown and black seeds showing. A floorboard creaked in the corridor. Her head turned slowly, her heart fighting between the two sacs of her lungs. A patch of nightdress flitted past the crack in the door.

She slipped out of her shoes, went to the door. Some strange wiring in her head reminded her of the luminous pearls against her skin and she covered them with her hand.

Mafalda stood on the threshold of Anne's room, looking back down towards the unlit stairwell. More neurotic night strolling?

'What are you talking about, Paddy?' asked Lazard, from down below.

Anne clenched her fists as Mafalda went into her room.

'A coincidence. The Allies invade Normandy. Salazar puts an embargo on wolfram exports.'

'Well, he's done that before.'

'But this time the embargo's effective. He's not worried about being invaded now. He's playing with the winners. My three mines up in the Beira have been closed down . . . officially. Boarded up. There's an Englishman roaming the countryside making sure of it. And yet . . . and yet . . .'

'Spit it out, Paddy.'

'The gold keeps coming in. Two consignments last month. If the price of tinned sardines had gone up that much, I think I would have heard about it and been in there.'

Silence again as the German digested Wilshere's perfect intelligence. Anne's neck shook with the tension. She padded down to her room, which was light and bursting with noise coming up through the open windows. Mafalda had the sheets peeled back. She was sniffing them like a dog over ground recently stained by a bitch.

Anne switched on the light. Mafalda stood between the bed and the window, blinking and bewildered. Anne stepped back in mock surprise.

'What are you *doing* here?' asked Mafalda.

115

'Isn't this my room?'

'Why have you come back?'

'Do you know who I am, Dona Mafalda?'

The older woman moved into the middle of the room, her breasts and the flesh of her thighs quivering against the cotton nightdress.

'If you young girls had any sense of honour, you'd know when to stay away.'

'My name is Anne Ashworth. I am English. I am *not* Judy Laverne.'

Mafalda winced at the name and her hands came up as if to cover her ears, except she'd already heard the offending name. She made for the door, brushed past Anne and fluttered down the corridor like a moth looking for another light source to baffle against.

Anne checked the corridors and went back to the empty room. Someone was resuming their seat in the room below. Wilshere and Lazard were alone.

'How did you know about those consignments going into the Banco de Oceano e Rocha?'

'Why? Didn't you?'

'Sure I did,' bluffed Lazard.

'Probably the same source then,' said Wilshere. 'The question is, do you know what the diamonds are going to buy in New York?'

'Dollars,' said Lazard, happy to oblige.

'And with the dollars . . . ?' said Wilshere.

'You're not feeling guilty are you, Paddy?'

'I know you like "Paddy", but I prefer "Patrick", is that all right, Beecham?'

'Sure, Patrick.'

'And what do I have to feel guilty about?' said Wilshere, to the sound of a striking match. 'I'm merely curious as to the raised tension, the established urgency to this particular deal. And, of course, the very specific requirements as to the quality of the goods, which are clearly designed to produce a market value of around one million dollars.'

'The answer is, I don't know,' said Lazard.

'*You* don't know?'

'That's what I said.'

'Then nobody knows,' said Wilshere, 'not even your old friends at American IG.'

'Maybe ... have you thought about *this*, Patrick? Maybe it's information we shouldn't know about.'

'The age of innocence, Beecham, is long gone.'

Anne went downstairs into the dark hall and along the unlit corridor to the back terrace where the cocktail party hummed in the yellow light coming up from the lawn. Cardew waved from some way off. She stepped into the crush of dinner-jacketed bodies, swiped a saucer of champagne from a passing tray and found her elbow cupped from the side. She turned into the white shirt and loose dark jacket of Hal Couples.

'You were talking to my wife on the beach,' he said, more friendly now.

'I've been even closer than that, Mr Couples.'

'Hal,' he said, mystified. 'Call me Hal.'

'Is your wife here?'

'She's in there somewhere,' he said, dismissing her, and produced a packet of Lucky Strike.

They smoked, sipped their drinks, sizing each other.

'You work for Shell. Mary told me.'

'That's right ... she didn't say what you did, apart from having to be nice to Beecham Lazard.'

'I work for a company called Ozalid. We sell machines that reproduce blueprints, you know, architectural drawings, that kinda thing. Lisbon's going through a construction boom so we figure we should be here selling our equipment ... a-a-a-nd waiting until they finish fighting in the rest of Europe and then moving in there ... making a lot of money on the way.'

'Interesting.'

'I'll be honest with you, Anne, and tell you ... it's not. But it *is* a living and when Ike gets to Berlin ... even more of a living. The state of that place ...' he said, shaking his head at the possibilities.

'You know I'm English?'

'You *are?*' he said, not that surprised but feeling he had to be.

'You know something about the English? We spent hundreds of years building our empire and in that time we made lots of money and yet – this is the strange thing – we're not allowed to talk about it. It's funny that ... We've been taught to think it's rude.'

'Hey, Anne, I'm sorry.'

'No need to apologize to me. It's just something I've noticed

about Americans. You talk about it, we don't. I think it's because
... well, my mother would call it showing off, drawing attention
to yourself, which is nearly a criminal offence in England.'

'It is?'

She remembered another rule from training – no irony with
Americans.

'It's the only reason we've kept the death sentence.'

'Tell your mother from me,' said Hal conspiratorially over his
glass, 'it's *all* about making money and if you don't talk about it
... you don't make it. I don't know how you limeys ever fall in
love.'

It made her wonder about her mother broaching the subject
with Rawlinson, helping him off with his wooden leg. Some things
just weren't meant to be thought about.

'I don't know,' she said, suddenly made lame by the idea.

'Stiff upper lip,' said Hal, showing her one.

'I don't think we like to look that stupid.'

Hal was looking at her differently now. She glanced around the
crowd and had a rush of freedom. Nobody knew her. She knew
nobody. She could be whoever she liked . . . as long as it was Anne
Ashworth.

'Do you play roulette?' asked Hal.

'We already did.'

'Did we?'

'Last night. I was on the other side from your *petite grive*.'

'My *petite* what?'

'Song thrush,' said Anne. 'And I wouldn't play roulette, Hal.
The odds are terrible.'

'Yeah, I guessed as much. You don't look the type.'

'You two finally met,' said Mary, coming between them.

'Yeah,' said Hal, dubious now, shifting on to his back foot to
see which way this would go.

'I was going to persuade Hal to give up roulette,' said Anne.
'Talk him through the odds.'

'I'd *love* you to do that.'

Beecham Lazard appeared at the french windows. Hal put his
arm around Mary and steered her away.

'Excuse us, Anne. Honey, there's Beecham, let's go talk to him,'
he said. 'See you later, Anne.'

118

'Bye, Hal.'

Mary rolled her eyes. They reached Lazard, who put his arm around Mary, buffed her shoulder. Anne finished her cigarette, socked back the tepid champagne, pleased with herself. A hand took the empty glass and replaced it with a full one.

'The bump's gone down,' said Karl Voss.

'I slept. I'm fine now,' she said, the social fluency she'd experienced with Hal freezing up inside her.

They stood shoulder to shoulder at the edge of the terrace looking at the party.

'I wanted to ask you something earlier, but I didn't want to appear . . . callous.'

'You mean, when in fact you *are* callous,' she said, the line coming out wrong – rude, not funny.

He laughed – both of them nervous.

'I mean it would have seemed . . . ah . . . scientific to have asked the question . . . or clinical.'

'Which was?'

'Whether while drowning you saw your life flash before you. It's what everybody says.'

'Does that mean old people take longer to drown?' she asked. 'All those reels to get through.'

'I hadn't thought of it like that.'

'I did see some things, but it's not what I would have called a whole life . . . more of a newsreel. Quite a dull one too. What would yours be like?'

'Well, not *Gone with the Wind*, if that's what you mean.'

'I haven't seen the film.'

'Lisbon is the only city in Europe where you can see it, maybe . . .' He stopped himself, remembered at the last minute where he was, who he was and who he was talking to. 'Maybe when life is less complicated . . .'

'Does life get any less complicated?'

'Possibly not,' he said, 'but there are good complications and bad ones.'

'We have a choice?'

'No, but to seize the good ones when they come along, that's the thing . . . like this afternoon.'

'That was an accident, wasn't it?' she said to the ground.

'Was it?' he asked, and turned to face the façade lights on the lawn.

Insects swirled high above their heads. The light took his face down to monochrome, white with black lines and grey cross-hatching. An artist's view. A geometrician's. She looked at him now, stared at him wide-eyed as a child, until she remembered in some ridiculous corner of her brain that it was rude to stare, and rude to point and rude to talk about money or food and rude to get down from the table without asking. The rules of rudeness. How could there be so many?

'What are you thinking?' he asked, turning his face to hers.

She reeled her mind in, ransacked it for some intelligent thought.

'About fate,' she lied, 'seeing as you brought it up.'

'I'm not sure there can be any fate in wartime,' he said. 'It's as if God's lost control of the game and the children have taken over . . . naughty children. Don't you think . . . ? We're in the hands of . . .'

'Ah, Voss, you haven't introduced me to your charming companion.'

The voice belonged to the German she'd heard in Wilshere's study, a voice as clipped as a shod hoof on cobbles. Voss held out his hand towards her, his brain frantically riffling the pages of memory. All blanks. He opened his other hand to the man next to him, who was tall, balding and held a pince-nez to his fattish face, which was broken up by a goatee beard, giving him the look of an academic, an art historian perhaps.

'General Reinhardt Wolters, may I present . . .' He turned back to her, his mind unjogged.

'Anne Ashworth,' she said. 'I'm staying here with the Wilsheres.'

'A beautiful house,' said Wolters, which it wasn't, 'a magnificent evening. Are you English, Miss Ashworth?'

'Yes, I am,' she said, bringing her defiance under control.

'Forgive me for asking. You sound it but don't look it.'

'I've been in the sun,' she said.

'I think you are new here . . . no? You must be quite surprised, coming from England into this . . .' He spread his hand out in front of him at nothing in particular.

'You mean the lights?'

'The lights,' he agreed, 'and the level of . . . fraternization with the enemy. We can all be friends in Lisbon.'

120

Wolters smiled with teeth gone yellow and a gap next to a canine. He was wrong. She didn't like being this close to the enemy, or at least this version of the enemy, but then Voss was the enemy, too.

'You're right, Mr Wolters, but it doesn't feel like war here,' she said. 'Perhaps if bombs were falling on us we'd feel differently about each other. As it is . . .'

She dipped her mouth to the champagne glass.

'Quite so, quite so,' said Wolters. 'Captain Voss, a word with you, please.'

Voss and the general nodded to her and they stepped off the terrace and walked beyond the façade lights into the matt black of the garden. She fingered the bump on her head thinking that this could be a hard school. She hadn't expected the lines to be so blurred. She hadn't expected someone like Karl Voss, military attaché to the German Legation, whom she knew even now she was looking for and waiting to come back.

'Some people are staying for dinner,' said Wilshere, touching her on the shoulder with two fingers. Always touching. 'You'll join us, won't you?'

He didn't wait for her reply because he was set upon by the pack of women Anne remembered collectively as the Romanians. She backed down the steps and retreated into the darkness. The party was already dispersing.

'*Je vous remercies infinement*' – she heard a woman's voice pitched hard against the soft night – '*mais on étés invités de diner par le roi d'Italie.*'

She turned her back, let her eyes grow used to the dark. There was no one on the lawn. She headed for the bushes, towards human noises which, as she neared them, made her veer suddenly away. Grunting, panting, the slap of skin. She stood in the lee of the bushes, confused. The noises stopped. Moments later Beecham Lazard appeared in a gap in the hedge, combing his hair back into its imperturbable shape, stretching his neck out of his collar. He loped back towards the house. A minute later, Mary Couples materialized in the same gap. She lifted the hem of her dress and brushed her knees. She threw her head back and shoved life into her hair.

Chapter 13

Sunday, 16th July 1944, Wilshere's house, Estoril, near Lisbon.

Anne hoped there would be someone English at dinner, Cardew and his wife perhaps, she'd seen him wave at the beginning of the party but only got to him at the end. She'd had time to pass on her dead-letter drop site and nothing more and they'd left for a dinner with a Spanish trade delegation. Now she looked down the table at two Portuguese couples, an Argentinian and a Spanish couple, Wolters from the German Legation, Beecham Lazard and, the only other single woman, an Italian contessa of some age and faded beauty.

Anne was seated between an Argentinian and Lazard on the window side. She was opposite a small Portuguese woman with hair curled tight to her head, who was wearing a dress made for someone more elegant. Wilshere sat at one end. His wife's chair was empty. Nobody asked after her.

A thick, smooth yellow soup was served from large silver tureens. Its only taste was faint and pewtery, perhaps from the ladle. Throughout this course Lazard kept his left leg pressed against her thigh while he spoke scrap-metal Portuguese to the woman on his right. She replied in perfect English, but Lazard's determination was unbreachable.

The fish course arrived, which was a tacit signal for all the men to start conversing with the woman on their other side. Lazard turned on Anne, looking her over like a complicated dessert, contemplating which bit to eat first.

'I met Hal and Mary Couples today,' she said, to divert him. 'Two of your fellow Americans.'

'Ah, yes, Hal,' he said, as if he were a distant relative, rather than the man whose wife he'd been tussling with in the bushes. 'I bet he talked to you about business. That's what Hal likes to do.'

'And roulette . . . and songbirds. A passion of his.'

'I wouldn't have believed it,' said Lazard. 'And what's your passion, Anne? I hope you're not going to say typing and shorthand.'

She opened up her fish, imitating Lazard, slitting it along the bone and levering the flesh away. She was glad of the distraction. What was her passion, now that she was Anne Ashworth? Not mathematics.

'Maybe I'm an old-fashioned good-time girl, but one who hasn't had a lot of practice. England hasn't been a good-time place these last few years.'

'Maybe I should take you out . . . show you the fleshpots of Lisbon.'

'Are there any?'

'Sure, we could have dinner in the Negresco, go to the Miami dancing bar, take a look in the Olimpia Club. They're all classy joints.'

He lifted away the bone and head of his fish, parted the white meat below.

'There was a riot yesterday in the middle of Lisbon just before my flight arrived. Somebody told me it was a food riot. Sawdust in the *chouriços*.'

'Communists,' said Lazard, as if they were a terminal disease. 'There's a lot of different worlds down there in the city, Anne, but roughly speaking they break down into two groups. The "haves" and the "have nots". You're a "have" and you'll have to get used to the "have nots" or stay out here in Estoril, where there's nothing but "haves".'

He put his knife and fork together over the skeleton of his fish and gulped down the remainder of his glass of white wine, which was instantly refilled. The plates were removed and, in the quiet while the meat course was served, the contessa made her first contribution of the evening, from one end of the table to the other.

'Now that Cherbourg has been lost, Herr Wolters, and the Allies are marching on Paris, what do you think your Herr Schickelgruber's going to do next?'

'Her again,' said Lazard, into his napkin.

Wolters took the insult face on, holding his glass by the stem and looking into the wine as if for some prescience. He pursed his goatee.

'The Führer, madam, is calm,' he said, batting back her rudeness, 'and as for marching on Paris, it may look a short distance on the map but be assured the Allies will meet with the fiercest resistance.'

'And the Russians?' she asked, without missing a beat.

Wolters gripped the edge of the table, shifted his buttocks on the brocade upholstery of his seat. All heads tuned in for some special intelligence. Only the clatter of the servants' spoons, dishing out the rice and vegetables, disturbed the quiet. Wolters looked as if he was tempted to turn the table up and over this venal bunch. He surveyed them in turn, apart from the English girl and the threadbare Milanese contessa, silently accusing them of getting fat from selling whatever they could lay their hands on to the Reich.

'It's true. The Russians have been enjoying some success,' he said, unruffled, measured, 'but don't believe for a moment that one hectare of Ger— . . . of French soil will be given up without the most bitter fighting the world has ever seen. There will be no surrender.'

His cold-blooded certainty shook nerves around the table, except for Wilshere's. He seemed amused at the fanaticism on display.

'You don't think they'll get rid of him . . .' started the contessa.

'*They?*' asked Wolters.

'Germans who would like there still to be a Germany after this business is all finished.'

'There will *always* be a Germany,' said Wolters, who'd never reached the cold, windy passage of this type of thinking.

'You still believe in miracles, I see.'

'We have ruled out nothing,' said Wolters who, suddenly aware that those words might appear ridiculous, added, 'Perhaps you are unaware of our unmanned rockets dropping on London.'

Eyes switched to Anne momentarily. They all knew by now she was English, from London.

'*This*,' he said, holding up a stiff finger, 'this is merely practice.'

The cutlery hovered over the china.

'We've been hearing about these miracle weapons from the German press for years,' said Lazard. 'Are they ready now?'

Wolters didn't reply but stabbed into his meat and ate wolfishly, as if the dish were Europe and he had plenty of appetite for it.

After dinner the women went into the sitting room to smoke cigarettes and drink coffee, the men filed into a room off the dining room where cigars and port had been laid on. Wolters joined shoulders with Wilshere as he rounded the dining table.

'Who was *she*?' he asked, loudly.

'La Contessa della Trecata,' said Wilshere, smiling.

'Is she a Jew?'

The Italian woman caught hold of Anne's arm as they walked down the corridor, her hand gripped and regripped the firm flesh.

'I am, of course,' she said, in her paper-thin voice.

'What?'

'Jewish. I insulted him too much . . . him and his Herr Schickel-gruber,' she said. 'But then . . . you're English, aren't you?'

'Yes, I'm staying here while I work in Lisbon.'

'What do you think of your Mr Moseley?'

'I think he is mistaken.'

'Yes,' she said, 'maybe I should learn something from you about choice of words. Mistaken. Needless to say, we are the only non-fascists here. The Argentines are *Peronistas*, the Spaniards are *Francophilos*, the Portuguese are *Salazaristocratos* and the German, well, you know what the German is.'

'And Mr Lazard?'

'*Capitalista*,' she said, dismissing him with a snort.

'And Mr Wilshere?'

'Unpredictable Irish blood. He is supposed to be neutral like Salazar, if you see what I mean. A man who admires one party whilst making money out of both. In Wilshere's case I think he *dislikes* one party while making money out of both.'

'So . . . not a fascist.'

The women sat around the empty fireplace, the two Portuguese fitting cigarettes into ostentatious holders. The contessa smoked hers straight, offering one to Anne. A maid poured the coffee.

'Has anyone seen Mafalda?' asked one of the Portuguese.

'I understand she's unwell,' said the contessa.

'For some time now,' said the Spaniard.

'We've been in the north,' said the other Portuguese. 'We're out of touch.'

'I've seen her,' said Anne.

'Well?'

'But I only arrived yesterday.'

'But you've seen her.'

'Yes.'

'Well, tell us.'

'It's just that . . .'

'We are all *friends* of Mafalda here,' said the Spaniard, which sounded threatening.

'Let the girl speak,' said the contessa.

'She seems to be confused,' Anne said, guarded.

'Confused. What's confused?'

'She seems to think I'm somebody else.'

'Mafalda? This is nonsense.'

'I told you,' said one Portuguese to the other in her own language. 'Didn't I tell you about the dress?'

'Whose dress is that?' asked the Argentine in English.

All eyes fell on Anne, except the contessa's – she stood at the fireplace smoking with her chin raised, the gossip well beneath her contempt.

'That's not your dress, is it?' asked the first Portuguese.

'If you let the girl draw breath, she'll tell you,' said the contessa.

'No, it is not my dress. Mine is being cleaned. This was left for me in my room while I was sleeping.'

'I knew it. It's come straight from that Parisienne's scissors in the Chiado. She's cut one for me.'

'Not the one you're wearing, I hope,' said the contessa.

'I think this dress and some riding clothes I wore this morning belonged to an American woman . . . and Dona Mafalda seems to thinks so, too. She has us confused.'

'Hoody Laberna,' said the Spaniard, throwing up her hands, triumphant.

The Argentinian's coffee cup flipped in its saucer.

'Hoody who?'

'Judy Laverne,' said Anne. 'I was told she was deported some months ago.'

'Who told you that?'

'Another American – Mary Couples.'

'What does *she* know?' said the Portuguese.

'The little *puta* wasn't even here,' confirmed the Spaniard, and her Argentinian friend laughed.

'Judy Laverne died in a car accident,' said the contessa, '*before* she was deported.'

'If you've been riding up on the *serra* you'll know the road,' said the Portuguese. 'She was on her way back to Cascais and she came off on that tight bend, just after the Azoia junction. There's a very steep drop. It was a terrible thing. The car exploded. She didn't stand a chance.'

'They say she'd been drinking,' said the other Portuguese.

'I don't know how they would know that,' said the contessa. 'The body was completely burnt.'

The string of pearls around Anne's throat felt suddenly tight. She pushed a finger up underneath them. How could Mary Couples not have heard about this?

'But why am I wearing Judy Laverne's clothes?' she asked.

'They were left, I suppose . . .' said the Portuguese. 'If you've come from England I imagine you don't have much of a wardrobe.'

Their eyes dropped away from her, swapped knowing looks amongst themselves. Anne felt hemmed in by the dress, these people and their society. The Argentinian with her hair scraped back so tight her eyebrows were up to her hairline. The Spaniard and her sexual suspicions, her tittering disdain for Mary Couples. The Portuguese and their gossip, sitting on their plump behinds, smoking out of their ridiculous holders. All of them desperate to show how much they knew about absolutely nothing. The contessa seemed to be the only decent person in the room.

'I hope none of you are suffering from the same confusion as Dona Mafalda,' said Anne. 'I might be wearing her clothes, but I'm *not* Judy Laverne.'

'Of course not, dear,' said the Portuguese, voice oozing. 'Whoever said you were?'

The condescension incensed her further and she knew she was going to overstep the mark.

'You all knew that Judy Laverne was Mr Wilshere's mistress and you've all made the assumption that because I've stepped into her shoes that *I'll* be his mistress too. Well, I'm not and I won't be, and never will.'

She should have stormed out then but two things stopped her. She knew how complicated it was to work around all the furniture in the room and . . . damn them. The contessa patted her on the arm. Anne wasn't sure whether it was reassurance or some friendly advice to leave it at that.

The air had stiffened up around the fireplace. Cigarettes and holders were stuck in the silence.

'Who do you think will get to Berlin first?' asked the contessa.

The question shot through the gathering and thudded into the wall like a flaming arrow. Everyone ignored it. The Argentinian and the Spaniard started talking about horse racing, the Portuguese went into an important name exchange. The house could have burnt down before they got round to responding.

Anne was left with the contessa. She asked her how she came to be in Portugal. The contessa told her she was on her own, living in a small *pensão* in Cascais. Her family had shipped her across to Spain in 1942 with the explanation that the war was getting closer. It was on the boat and the subsequent train journey to Madrid that she found out from other refugees why her family had done this. It was the first she'd heard of the Jews being rounded up all over Europe. There'd been no word from her family since.

'I think they have gone underground,' she said. 'They couldn't expect me to live like that at my age so they sent me away. In a few months this will be over and they will send for me. I am patient.'

As the contessa spoke her face roamed the objects in the room. The words came out detached from another mental process, which was working on her eyes and jaw. The words forced belief, while the subconscious battled against the unimaginable certainty that she was now alone. The clothes, the hairstyles, the painted lips, the eager teeth behind them, the soft fleshy tongues rooted in the hollow mouths, the incessant chatter in the room suddenly grated on Anne's ears like a steel butcher's saw ripping through bone.

A servant came to tell them the cars were ready. Anne supported the contessa to the door, put her into a car. As she was about to close the door, the contessa leaned forward, took her hand.

'Be careful with Senhor Wilshere,' she said, 'or Mafalda will have you deported, just like she did Judy Laverne.'

She let go of her hand. Anne closed the door. The car moved off after the others. The contessa's tired half-lit face didn't turn – the night, her friend, took her in for a few more hours until the start of another interminable, brilliant summer's day.

Anne left Wilshere saying goodbye to his guests and retreated to the back terrace, where she smoked in the uncomfortable light, all these lives suddenly pressing in on her own. The last car pulled away and the façade lights drowned in the darkness, dowsed to orange filaments that glowed like night insects. The smell of cigar smoke preceded a red coal crowded with ash. Wilshere sat down across the table from her, crossed his legs. Faint light from the house caught the rim of his glass as it went up to his lips.

'Another long day in paradise gone,' he said, the man stuffed full of its cloying sweetness.

She didn't respond, still thinking about the gross happenings of the day, trying to make them net, trying to see the profit, if there was any. Too much had happened. There was too much to be considered. That was the adult state. You might start swimming against the torrent of events and exchanges but then, after a while, you tired and let it all rush over you, until finally, like the contessa, it wore you away however hard the rock you were made of.

'Thinking anything interesting?' asked Wilshere.

'I was thinking,' she said, stopping her foot from nodding with the irritation building inside her, 'I was asking myself, why do you keep dressing me up as Judy Laverne?'

The words came out with their hard edges and she watched them in amazement as the points and corners of the toppling letters delivered their little blows to the dark face of the man opposite.

There was a long silence, filled only by the softest whistling of the crickets, in which Wilshere's presence intensified, his cigar glowing redder as he drew on the smoke.

'I miss her,' he said.

'What happened to her?' she asked, but not softly, still angry, and when he didn't immediately reply, she added: 'There seems to be some doubt. This afternoon I was told she was deported, this evening that she died in a car accident.'

'No doubt,' he said, something catching in his throat, the harsh smoke or the brute emotion. 'She died . . . in a car accident.'

Darkness and the descent of the night's cathedral cool brought the confessional to the table. A nightingale started up with hollow bars of song from the high vaulted trees and Wilshere's glass resettled on the table. The cigar seemed screwed into the night.

'We'd argued,' he said. 'We were up at the house in Pé da Serra. We'd been riding all afternoon and afterwards we started drinking. I was on the whisky, she, as always, drank brandy. The alcohol went to our heads and we started arguing . . . I can't remember

129

what it was about even. She'd driven up in her own car so, when she stormed out, she just drove off. I followed her. She was a good driver normally. I let her drive the Bentley whenever. But, you see, she was angry, angry *and* drunk. She drove too fast for the road. She went into a tight bend, couldn't hold it and the car shot over the edge. It's a terrible drop there, a terrible drop. Even if the petrol tank hadn't caught she'd have been . . .'

'When was this?'

'Some months ago. Early May,' he said, and the nightingale stopped. 'I fell for her, you see, fell all the way, Anne. Never happened to me before, and at my age, too.'

The way he said it, his reaching for the glass, made her think that perhaps the argument had been that Judy Laverne had not fallen in the same way or to the same extent as he.

'That argument . . .' she started, but Wilshere leapt to his feet, shook his head and arms, panic-struck, as if he'd felt himself slipping away somewhere to forget who and where he was. The cigar coal rolled to a corner of the terrace.

Wilshere turned his back on the lawn, let his head rock back to release himself from the thoughts he did not want. Anne was gripping her chair arms with her elbows and didn't see what Wilshere saw in the window above – Mafalda's white nightdress, her palms pressed against the glass.

Wilshere drew Anne up to her feet.

'I'm going to bed,' he said, and kissed her, the corner of his mouth connecting with hers so that her organs flinched.

Anne wasn't tired, too restless with aggregate knowledge. She took a couple of cigarettes from the box and some matches from a glass holder. She kicked her shoes off and walked across the lawn to the path and down to the summerhouse and the bower. She sat under the hanging fronds of the passionflower, pulled her heels up on to the edge of the seat and fitted a cigarette into her mouth, chin resting on her knees. She slashed a match across the stone seat and started in the flare of light. Sitting in the corner, ankles crossed, arms folded, was Karl Voss.

'You can frighten people like that, Mr Voss.'

'But not you.'

She lit the cigarette, shook the match dead, eased her back against the tiled panel behind.

'Is the military attaché from the German Legation watching this house?'

'Not particularly the house.'

'The people *in* the house, then?'

'Not all of them.'

A thin silver thread tugged her stomach tight.

'So what's going to happen this time?'

'I can't think what you mean.'

'You have a way of being on hand, Mr Voss.'

'On hand?'

'Around when you're needed, for carrying and life-saving, for instance.'

'I seem to have my uses,' he said. 'What for this time . . . who knows?'

He followed the tip of her cigarette. Her lips, nose and cheek glowed as she drew on it, burning that facial fragment on to his retina. He searched himself for words, like a man who's put a ticket in too safe a place.

'How well do you know Mr Wilshere?' she asked.

'Well enough.'

'Is that well enough to carry him home when he's drunk or well enough that you don't want to get to know him better?'

'I've done business with him. He seems honest. That's all I've needed to know about him so far.'

'Did you ever see him with his mistress . . . Judy Laverne?'

'A few times . . . they weren't hiding . . . at least not when they were in Lisbon. They used to go to nightspots and bars quite openly.'

'How did they look together?'

A long silence, long enough for Anne to finish the cigarette and crush it out on the underside of the stone seat.

'I didn't mean the question to be that hard,' she said.

'In love,' he said, 'that's how they looked.'

'But you had to think about it,' she said. 'Do you think it was two-way?'

'Yes, but what does anybody know from just looking?'

She liked that. It showed an understanding of unspoken languages.

'I've a cigarette, only one, if you want to share,' she offered.

He had his own in his pocket but he came and sat next to her. She found his hand with hers, put the cigarette into it. The match rasped and ignited between them. He held the back of her hand just as she had imagined somebody would. He drew a knee up and rested his cigarette hand on it.

'Why are you asking me these things about Wilshere?'

'I've been billeted with a man who dresses me up in his ex-lover's – no, his *late* lover's clothes. I don't know what that means except that it upsets his wife. He told me tonight that he missed her . . . the lover.'

'That could be true.'

'But you, as a man, you don't think that's strange?'

'He wishes that she wasn't dead. He's playing a trick on his mind.'

'Why should he do that?'

'There were things he left unsaid, maybe.'

'Or he feels guilty?'

'Probably.'

She slid the cigarette out of his hand, drew on it and eased it back between his fingers, feeling bolder with him now. Kissing by proxy.

'Did you hear about the accident?' she asked.

'Yes . . . I also heard that she was leaving.'

'Deported.'

'So they said.'

'You mean she might not have been? She might have *wanted* to leave.'

'I didn't know her,' he said, and shrugged. 'I couldn't say.'

They smoked again, fingers touching.

'Could you kill someone if they didn't love you?' she asked.

'That might depend on some things.'

'Like what?'

'How far I'd fallen. How jealous I was . . .'

'But you *could* kill . . . ?'

He didn't shoot the answer back. It took some ruminative smoking.

'I don't think so,' he replied. 'No.'

'That was the right answer, Mr Voss,' she said, and they both laughed.

He crushed the cigarette out with his foot. They sat in silence and when their heads turned to each other there was only inches between them. He kissed her. His lips changed physiognomies with a touch, fear and desire became indistinguishable. She had to wrench herself away, get to her feet.

'Tomorrow night,' he said to her back. 'I'll be here.'

She was already running.

She ran back up the path, sprinted to the back terrace and collapsed on the chair panting, acid in her lungs, her heart walloping in her throat. She slumped back, looked up at the stars, fought her heart back down behind her ribs, thinking stupid girl, that's all I am, a stupid little girl. The memory of the slash of her mother's white hand across her face in the garden in Clapham sat her up straight.

Fraternizing with the enemy, Wolters had called it. Fraternizing. Brothering. This was more than that. This was crazy and dangerous. She could feel herself coming off the silver tracks. She bent over, gripped her forehead with her fingertips. Why him? Why not Jim Wallis? Why not anybody else but him?

She picked up her shoes, exhausted now by her behaviour, no better than a heroine from a slushy romance. She went into the house, up the corridor into the hall, thinking how else do we learn about these things? Not from mothers. The clay figurines in their cabinet caught her eye, one in particular. She turned on the light, opened the glass doors. The figurine was one of several, not the same exactly, but developments on the theme. It was of a woman blindfolded. She turned it over, looking for some clue as to its meaning. On the bottom was the maker's name, nothing more. A blur closed in, a face sharpened as it appeared on the other side of the glass door. The skin on her scalp crawled and tightened.

Mafalda reached round the door and snatched the figurine from her hands.

'I just wanted to know what it meant,' said Anne.

'*Amor é cego*,' said Mafalda, replacing the figurine, closing the glass doors. 'Love is blind.'

Chapter 14

Meredith Cardew was writing in pencil on single sheets of paper directly on to his highly polished desktop. Anne was fascinated by the work, which seemed more like brush strokes, Chinese calligraphy, than handwriting. Nothing touched the page apart from the anchor point of his palm, protected by a handkerchief, and the lead of the pencil which he sharpened between bouts. His script was not legible even the right way up and looked Cyrillic or hieroglyphic rather than English. He only wrote on one side of the paper and only drew new sheets from a particular pad in the third drawer down on the right of his desk. Occasionally he lifted the sheet and brushed his handkerchief over the desk's polished surface. Was this eccentricity or security?

The debrief was long, more than three hours, because Cardew went over all the conversations at least twice and, in the case of the three-way discussion between Wilshere, Lazard and Wolters, five or six times. The word that seemed to bother him most was 'Russians' and he wanted to be certain that it was Wilshere who'd said it, that it had been interrogative and that there'd been no reply.

'Is that it, my dear?' asked Cardew, as his clock ticked round to midday and the heat outside finally caused him to remove his suit jacket.

'Isn't that enough, sir?' she asked, desperate not to fail at her first debrief.

'No, no, it's fine. It's very good. A very good weekend's work. You'll be coming into the office for a rest. No, excellent. I just wanted to be sure that we'd left nothing out.'

We? thought Anne and then the name Karl Voss, who'd been mentioned in passing on the beach and having a word with Wolters at the cocktail party but not, never, reappearing later that night down by the summerhouse. None of that exchange had found its way into the report.

'We've left nothing out, sir.'

'Well, now,' said Cardew, laying down his pencil, counting off the sheets and then clawing tobacco into his pipe, 'we might be about to see a very rare thing.'

Cardew swung round in his chair to face the window and its view of the heat cramming down on the red rooftops of Lisbon.

'We might be about to see Sutherland in a state of excitement,' he said.

The meeting was set for 4.00 p.m. in a safe house in Rua de Madres in the Madragoa district of Lisbon. Anne was to report to the PVDE in Rua António Maria Cardoso after lunch to confirm her residency and receive her work permit. From there she would go to Rua Garrett and buy cakes at the Jerónimo Martims cake shop and then walk to Rua de Madres where she would ring the bell to number 11 three times. To whoever came to the door she was to say:

'I've come to see Senhora Maria Santos Ribeira.'

If the housekeeper said that Senhora Ribeira was out, Anne was to reply with the line: '*Come what come may, / Time and the hour runs through the roughest day.*'

The housekeeper would then tell her she could come in and wait. Anne relished the absurdity.

Shortly after 4.00 p.m. *Macbeth* had been recited and Anne was sitting on a hard wooden chair in a shuttered room that was initially so dark Sutherland was not immediately apparent. He was sitting in a soft chair with wooden arms in a corner furthest from the window. Tea was laid out in front of him with an empty plate for the cakes. Behind him a crack had worked its way up the wall and finished in an estuary of lath at the ceiling. Sutherland volunteered to be mother, which she learned later from Wallis meant that he was pleased with her.

'Lemon?' he asked. 'Milk's a little complicated in this heat, although there might be some powder. Not the same, though, is it?'

'Lemon,' she said.

'No problems with lemons in this country,' he said, and sat back with his legs crossed, cup and saucer in hand, cake on the side. His first question was surprising but, she realized with more experience, typical.

'Wilshere . . . whacking your horse like that . . . what do you think that was all about?'

'Judy Laverne . . . I was wearing her riding clothes at the time.'

'According to Cardew's notes, or rather Rose's reading of Cardew's notes, because I still can't read a damned word of what that man writes, you didn't ask Wilshere what the hell he was up to, hitting your horse out of the blue, so to speak.'

'No, sir.'

'Any reason?'

'First of all I didn't want there to be any confrontation in front of the major and secondly, if he knew what he was doing . . .'

'You mean if he was conscious of what he was doing . . . ?'

'He would have apologized with an excuse, invented an accident.'

'Unless he *wanted* a reaction from you.'

'Of course, if he *wasn't* conscious then we are dealing with somebody who has a mental problem and he would have to be handled accordingly. I decided to bide my time . . . see what else happened.'

'You didn't think that perhaps he was testing your cover?'

The words cooled her innards, which with the heat stuffed into the room as thick as wadding, made her light-headed.

'I know this is a difficult situation, the sociability of the environment, but didn't you think of that?' he said, nibbling his cake.

'Yes, but I was thinking more about Judy Laverne . . . I'd been unsettled by Wilshere's wife's reaction to the riding clothes . . .'

'I think you should bring it up. Sooner rather than later,' said Sutherland. 'Make it plausible. You know . . . you didn't want to bring it up in front of Major Almeida, been thinking about it a couple of days . . . that sort of thing. Give him chance to apologize and make his excuses.'

'And if he doesn't?'

'You mean if it *was* an unconscious act? Well, then it would appear that whatever happened between Wilshere and Judy Laverne has made him a somewhat unpredictable entity.'

'And who was this Judy Laverne, sir?'

'Ah, yes,' he said. 'A mess. A terrible mess. I don't know whether we'll ever get the full story on her. She used to be a secretary at American IG.'

'What's American IG?'

'The American sister company of IG Farben, the German chemical conglomerate,' said Sutherland. 'And, as *you* know from what you overheard in Wilshere's study, Lazard had been an executive with American IG too. As far as I can make out, Judy Laverne had lost her job with them back in America and Lazard invited her over here to work for him.'

'So, she wasn't working for the Americans.'

'In intelligence? The Office of Strategic Studies, you mean? Another one of their brilliant euphemisms, I must say. No, no, I don't think she was, although there seems to be some confusion here. It seems that they were trying to get her to do some work for them but she was very loyal to Lazard, and enjoying herself with Wilshere, so didn't want any part of it. We don't know what they were after from Lazard, still don't. Totally obsessive about secrecy, these Yanks – and this even after D-day, which, Christ Almighty, must . . .' Sutherland reined himself in, pinched the bridge of his nose, screwed the tiredness up in his fist and threw it on the floor.

'Do we know that she died in a car accident?' asked Anne. 'There was some confusion about deportation.'

'Her visa renewal had been turned down by the PVDE, *that* was true. She had three days to leave, true as well. And she did meet her death in a car that came off the road around the Azoia junction . . .'

'You don't know why she was being deported?'

'No, nor did the Americans. In retrospect we thought they might have arranged it, pulled her out when she wouldn't play ball, but they deny it. They say it was as much a surprise for them as it was for Judy Laverne.'

'The Italian contessa said that Mafalda arranged for her deportation.'

'You can take that with a pinch of salt,' he said. 'Beecham Lazard is very close to the PVDE director, Captain Lourenço. He'd have found out.'

'Do you think Lazard suspected that she was being approached by the OSS?'

'Possibly.'

'Do you think his suspicion might have been stronger than that?'

'If he thought she was *working* for the OSS I don't think he'd have just arranged for her deportation.'

'You mean he'd have killed her?' asked Anne. 'Well, she did die.'

'In a car accident.'

'You're satisfied with that?'

'The PVDE came down on it hard and fast, wrapped it up in a matter of hours – don't like a song and dance over foreigners' deaths. They sent a full report to the American consulate. The Americans accepted it, or at least they didn't react. More tea?'

She drank the first cup down. He poured more. The air became breathable again.

'So, you don't think my position is vulnerable.'

'As long as you maintain your cover, no,' said Sutherland. 'We didn't exactly position you, remember. We took advantage of an opportunity given to Cardew by Wilshere as a result of their relationship. The background to it is strong. Cardew's secretary getting pregnant, wanting to leave . . . all that. But *you* tell me . . . what's your worst fear?'

'That Judy Laverne *was* working for the OSS, her cover was blown and Wilshere or Lazard killed her.'

'Do you think Wilshere could have killed her?' he asked, suddenly following the crack in the wall up to the lath estuary. 'You say he loved her. Our reports of them being seen together in Lisbon indicate the same.'

What does anybody know from just looking, she thought. Voss's words, which she'd so admired, suddenly began to create doubts in her own mind about his interest in her.

'How would you feel,' she said, 'if you found that the woman you loved was a spy, was spying on you? You'd start thinking that her love was part of the cover, wouldn't you? And that would make you very angry, I'd have thought . . . that your trust had been so completely abused.'

'*If* she was an agent, which she wasn't.'

'You asked me for my worst fear.'

'And I say it has no basis in fact and that even if it did I doubt Wilshere could have killed her . . . Lazard, on the other hand . . .'

'*That* makes me feel safe.'

Sutherland writhed in his seat, exasperated by what he saw as nothing but an irrelevance to the real intelligence operation.

'You have to stop thinking about Judy Laverne,' he said. 'She has nothing to do with your assignment.'

'But she could have a bearing, surely,' she insisted.

'We've examined the possibility of Wilshere positioning you so that he can control the flow of information or disinformation going out. We have decided that it was a game he didn't need to play, so why, when there is so much at stake, play it?'

'He's a gambler. Cardew said.'

'Yes,' said Sutherland, taking out the chip which had found its way back to him from the dead-letter drop. 'What is this?'

'One of the many chips that Lazard swept over to Wilshere in the casino.'

'But, you see, to me this is not a man who is gambling. This is a man who sat at a baccarat table and took a pay-off. He is someone who is playing certainties.'

Anne blushed at her own stupidity. She was losing this. Her mind was not concentrated on the information at hand. She'd been distracted by what she thought Sutherland would probably have called emotional nonsense. And not just Judy Laverne's.

'One other question . . . the man who helped you up to the house with Wilshere?' asked Sutherland. 'You didn't say . . .'

'He didn't make himself known.'

'But clearly someone who was following you.'

'It wasn't Jim Wallis.'

'Yes, well, I'd asked him to keep an eye on you but not to get too close. If he humped Wilshere up to the house that is what I would call . . .'

'Then we have a mystery man.'

'They're all mystery men,' said Sutherland.

'Except for Beecham Lazard.'

'Yes, he seems quite straightforwardly venal . . . although I was surprised by this business with Mary Couples.'

'Perhaps the Couples are more desperate than we think.'

'Well, now, here's something interesting. You say he worked for Ozalid?'

'That's what he told me.'

'We were talking about American IG earlier,' said Sutherland. 'Among the companies they own are General Aniline & Film, Agfa,

Ansco and . . . Ozalid. GAF supplied khaki and dyes for military uniforms, which gave their salesmen access to every military installation in the United States. All military training films were developed in Agfa/Ansco labs. All blueprints of military installations were made by Ozalid.'

'And all that information found its way back to Berlin?'

'It was a phenomenal breach of security, but it all changed in 1942 after Pearl Harbor,' said Sutherland. 'They had a spring clean . . . as they say.'

'And one of the people swept out was Beecham Lazard?'

'Which was why he came here . . . but as a free agent. He doesn't work exclusively for the Germans, but he has those high-level contacts, he's trusted by them . . .'

'And by the Americans.'

'It seems so,' said Sutherland.

'So, given that they worked for connected companies, it's possible that Hal Couples and Beecham Lazard already knew each other?'

'We're not sure.'

'Do you know when Couples started working for Ozalid?'

'We've asked for more information from the Americans. It takes time.'

'What would Hal Couples have for sale that could possibly be of interest to the Germans on a continent thousands of miles away?'

'Quite. The dogs are on their doorstep, why should they want to know the state of the kennels?' said Sutherland, sucking on his empty pipe, desperate for a smoke. 'Now look, let's not jump to conclusions about Couples. The Americans will come back in their own time. From our side we'll be watching all the Lisbon/Dakar flights. Your next task is to get into Wilshere's study and find any information you can about the provenance of these diamonds, where they're being held, how this business is going to work . . . anything. If Wilshere *is* holding these diamonds you work out a system with Wallis to let him know if and when the gems leave the house.

'Now, personalities . . . Wolters you know about. I think he revealed himself sufficiently at the dinner. To give you an idea, he took up this post at the beginning of the year as an SS Colonel. When the head of the Abwehr, Admiral Canaris, was removed from office he was promoted. He is now an SS General. He is effectively running the German Legation. Who else? The Contessa della Trecata. I notice you gave her a very sympathetic review. Do not talk to her. She is dangerous for the very reason that she elicits sympathy. The others, well . . . you know, I think.'

'You haven't mentioned Karl Voss.'

'The military attaché is an Abwehr man. He reports directly to Wolters,' said Sutherland, stopping in the middle of the room, on the brink of offering additional material but deciding against it.

'Major Almeida?'

'Portuguese Army officer. Don't know which side his bread is buttered, so steer clear,' he said. 'That's it, isn't it?'

If there were other things, Anne couldn't think of them. What she thought, at first, was the stress coming from Sutherland seemed to have pushed everything else out of the room. It was only later, as she made her way down to the station, that she realized it could have been something else – ambition. This could be Sutherland's big moment of the war.

Karl Voss was happy, although he didn't quite know it yet. He was at that stage of happiness where his behaviour could still be classified as normal – no unconscious outbursts of laughter, no running skips in the street, no profligacy to beggars – but a change had taken place. His insides were weightless, his step was light on the uneven cobbles, he hopped off pavements, trotted over tramlines, made way for struggling ladies, even in the dire heat he couldn't put a foot wrong. He looked up and out too. He noticed things in an unintelligent way for the first time in years. Façades of buildings, panels of tiles, shop fronts, railings, dogs flaked out in the square, a girl hanging out washing from a high window, dust on the leaves of the trees, and the blue sky, even the blue sky beyond the skeletal arches of the Igreja do Carmo, destroyed in the earthquake and left as a monument to Lisbon's dead. He was at that stage of happiness where he no longer looked down or inwards. He wasn't thinking about his situation any more.

He broke into a run as he saw people coming across the metal walkway. The *elevador* had just arrived. He made it to the lift, which descended to the Baixa. He took the steps down to the Rua do Ouro two at a time and headed towards the river at a fast walk. He crossed the road to the building of the Banco de Oceano e Rocha which at this time of the day was closed. He looked up and down the street for the car he'd arranged to meet him outside the bank. He didn't mind the five-minute wait, which was unusual for him. The car arrived, he rang the bell to the offices on the first floor. Fifteen minutes later he was sitting in the back of the car with a small but heavy case beside him.

Chapter 15

Anne sat in a railway carriage opposite a Portuguese couple in their sixties with a dog at their feet, which had legs too short for its body and bulging eyes. The man had a goitre the size of a cantaloupe hanging from his neck. The woman was so small her feet didn't touch the floor and her left leg was swollen to twice its normal size. Anne didn't want to look at them but each time she turned away from the view out to sea, of a three-funnelled ship pumping black smudges into the bleached sky, their eyes were on her, even the dog's. It was only on the third occasion, as she let her gaze drop from thyroid to dog, that she noticed the couple's hands were clasped between them, resting on the seat.

She leaned her forehead against the window. The silver train curved out in front, reflecting the ocean in its glass panels. A sand-bank surfaced outside the Tagus estuary, the surf peeling back from its brown hump. She had an irrational desire to be out there, alone, simple, offshore from the complexities of the city. She glanced back over her seat. Jim Wallis had his head down in the *Diário de Notícias*. He looked up but not at her. They'd spoken earlier about the diamonds – how she would signal if the gems left the house. She turned back to the sea. Her mind circled back to the same spot – Karl Voss, Abwehr.

She would have to stop this . . . this what? What was it she had to stop with Karl Voss? A kiss. Was that anything? She told herself not to think. The Rawlinson gambit – the *danger*'s in the thinking. Just finish it. Simplify the equation. Reduce the variables.

Forget Judy Laverne. Let her into the bracket and she was the quickest route to a blown cover.

Sutherland wanting her to break into Wilshere's study. Was that

143

the right thing to do? Was that an unnecessary risk? Surely the Americans were right, Lazard was the man to watch. He was the go-between.

She was leaning forward, her eyes were unconsciously drilling into the soft neck of the woman in front of her. She eased back. The train braked with a screech of metal as they came into Paço de Arcos station. The old couple got up and left the carriage, the woman on the man's arm, the dog shuffling behind.

The image of Karl Voss returned, stronger now.

They hadn't said anything to each other. They'd smoked a cigarette. Touched lips. Nothing had happened but everything had changed. They didn't know each other and would never know anything of each other, except what was allowed to be known, and none of that was true. But then how much do we want to know about each other? Everything? Everything except that which sustains our interest – the mystery. To know that is to kill it.

Her thoughts multiplied. Squared. Cubed. Ramified to the nth.

She walked up through the square in Estoril. The heat was still terrible but a dying heat now, one that was slumped against the buildings, sagging in the stillness of the palm trees. She felt drowsy, needed to lie down after a long day, after long hours spent running around in her head.

The path up to the house seemed longer. She stumbled across the lawn and went into the house through the french windows at the back. There were voices in the drawing room. She put her head in. The Contessa della Trecata and Mafalda stopped talking. Sutherland hadn't mentioned Mafalda, probably written her off as a sad case. The contessa patted the sofa.

'Come and tell us about the real world,' she said.

Mafalda, in a blue tea gown, was wearing the plaster cast of her own face – white, still and void.

'The real world of dictation and typing has not been very interesting today.'

She tried to excuse herself but the contessa insisted. She sat on the sofa.

'Don't they let you out?'

'I went to the PVDE for my papers, that was all.'

'But lunch, you have to have lunch.'

'Mr Cardew is very demanding.'

'I'm surprised a young girl like you should want to come to a backwater like Lisbon . . . to be a secretary.'

'I tried to join the WRENS. They wouldn't have me. Medical. Lungs.'

'You seem to be running around here all right,' said Mafalda, as if this was the kind of cat-house behaviour she'd had to get used to.

'In London I can hardly get to the end of the street without . . .'

'Those peasoupers,' said the contessa. 'Shocking.'

'My mother thought it was the bombing.'

'Yes, well that would fit, wouldn't it?' said Mafalda, as if it was meant to but didn't, not in her mind. 'Nerves can do strange things.'

'What does your father have to say on the matter?'

From nowhere came the image of her mother sitting on her like a bully girl at school.

'My father? I don't have . . .' She checked herself, the image of her real mother had crowded out her surrogate parents. 'I don't have the faintest idea. He doesn't have an opinion.'

'Most odd,' said Mafalda. 'My father was always inquiring after our health. Probably should have been a doctor.'

'I never knew my father,' said the contessa.

'You've never mentioned him,' confirmed Mafalda.

'He was overseeing the loading of one of his ships in Genoa. A piece of cargo swept him overboard. He drowned before they got to him. My mother never recovered from it. It made her a very bitter, difficult woman. Nothing ever came up to standard in her view. She survived to a great age on the strength of it.'

'My mother's a very difficult woman too,' said Anne, the words out before her teeth could clamp down on them.

'Well, I'm sure there was some sadness in her life which has made her like that.'

'Does your mother do anything with herself?' asked Mafalda.

She lost it. The thread was just plucked out of her hand. She couldn't think what her mother did. Even her name had gone. Ashworth, yes, but her first name.

'She does what everybody's doing these days,' she said slowly, waiting for the jog which never came. 'She works for the government.'

That wasn't it. It would have to do. She would have to relearn that. Why couldn't she think of her name? It was like forgetting the most famous person in the world at the moment. Retrain the mind. *Gone with the Wind*, lead actress ... Clark Gable was the lead man and the lead actress was ... Scarlett O'Hara ... come on, think.

'Are you all right, dear?' said the contessa. 'This heat today has been ...'

'I'm sorry, did you ask something? It *has* been a long day. I should really ...'

Why has this happened? This has never happened before. Your role is Miss Ashworth. You play the part. The lines are ...

But reality had crept back in. All she saw was the audience. There were no lines. In her head there was only panic.

'Mafalda just asked about your father, that was all. Is he in the fighting?'

'No,' she said, trying to swallow but not being able to, her mind even forgetting the motor reflexes.

'No?' asked the contessa, both women riveted to Anne's crisis.

'No,' she reiterated, tears coming now, tears of frustration. She couldn't think of his name either, nor his profession. The only name that arrived in her head was Joaquim Reis Leitão. 'He's dead.'

'Not in the bombing?' said Mafalda, appalled.

'You're upset,' said the contessa, 'perhaps you should lie down.'

'No, not in the bombing,' said Anne, buying herself seconds, waiting, hoping for the part to come back to her. She looked down at Mafalda's feet, exactly where the prompter would have been in the theatre.

All I need is a name and it will all fit again.

'So what happened, dear girl?' asked the contessa, insistent, interested.

A car pulled up outside, the radiator grille visible at the corner of the window. Mafalda announced her husband's return.

'This heat,' said Anne, getting to her feet. 'Will you excuse me.'

She staggered from the room, set off down the corridor at a half run, a whining in her ears, a whining buzz like a reel paying out line to a sounding fish. She ran past Wilshere coming through the front door, swung up the stairs, felt his eyes rippling on her through the mahogany bannisters. She got to the bedroom door, shut it behind her. Sick. Had she thrown it away? She collapsed on the

146

bed. The breathing came back. The swallowing, too. How had she become this fragile? She took stock, an egg count. Cracks only. No omelette. She drank some warm water from the jug at her bedside.

The simplest cover story known to man . . . but who knows it? She undressed, ran a thumb down her wet spine, held her dress up to the window. A dark patch ran down the centre of the back. Nobody knows. She stood under the tepid shower, soaped herself, rinsed off the sweat. Nobody knows. She towelled herself dry, lay naked on the bed with just the towel over her. The PVDE knows. She wrote it on their form. Graham Ashworth. Accountant. But not deceased. It had all come back. Finally. The simplest cover story ever.

Another car arrived. She levered herself off the bed, wrapped herself in the towel, went to the window. Just who she didn't want to see. Karl Voss got out of the driver's seat, went round to the passenger side and pulled out a briefcase which hung heavily on his arm. Her stomach tightened. The silver thread tugged again. He stopped in front of the door. Anne pressed her eye to the glass to see him at that acute angle to the house. He ran a hand over his bony features, preparing a new face.

She dressed and went down the corridor to the empty bedroom over the study. Voss's voice came up the stairwell. She sat at the fireplace. Small talk, the clink of bottles on glass, the gush of soda. She imagined his lips on the thin rim of the crystal.

'Another brutally hot day in Lisbon?' said Wilshere.

'There's more to come . . . so they say.'

'When it's like this I think of Ireland and the soft rain falling endlessly.'

'And when you're in Ireland . . . ?'

'Exactly, Herr Voss. It's only variety we're after.'

'I never think of Berlin,' he said.

'There's a different rain falling over there.'

'My mother's moved out to relatives in Dresden. She was in Schlachtensee. All the bombers flew over her on their way to Neukölln and . . . perhaps you don't know this, but air bombing is a very inaccurate science. She had three land in the garden. Unexploded, fortunately.'

'I didn't know that about air bombing.'

147

'But if you bomb enough . . .' Voss trailed off. 'Tell me some-thing, Mr Wilshere. What do you think of the idea of a single bomb that could completely annihilate a whole city? People, build-ings, trees, parks, monuments . . . all life and the product of life?'

Silence. The wood ticked. A huff of breeze shambled through the exhausted trees outside. A cigarette was offered and accepted. Chairs creaked.

'I wouldn't think it possible,' said Wilshere.

'Wouldn't you?' asked Voss. 'But if you look at history it's the only logical conclusion. In the last century we were standing in formation, blasting each other with inaccurate muskets. By the beginning of this century we were cutting each other down with very precise machine-gun fire and shelling each other from miles away. Twenty years later we have thousand bomber raids, tanks crash through countries bringing them to heel in a matter of weeks, unmanned rockets fall on cities hundreds of miles away. It stands to reason, given man's creativity for destruction, that someone will invent the ultimately destructive device. Believe me, it's going to happen. My only question is . . . what does it mean?'

'Perhaps it will mean the end of war.'

'A good thing then?'

'Yes . . . in the long run.'

'A good observation, Mr Wilshere. It's the short run that's the problem, isn't it? In the short run there would have to be a demon-stration of the power of the device and, of course, a demonstration of the ruthlessness to use it, too. So it's possible that before the end of this war, depending on which side has the device, Berlin, Moscow or London could cease to exist.'

'That's a terrible thought,' said Wilshere, without conveying it.

'But the only logical one. I'm predicting that this war generation will invent what H. G. Wells said they would invent at the end of the last century.'

'I've never read H. G. Wells.'

'He called them atomic bombs.'

'You've taken an interest in this.'

'I studied physics at Heidelberg University before the war. I keep up with the journals.'

It was difficult to judge the silence that followed, whether awk-ward or ruminative. Voss broke it.

'Still, this is nothing to worry us here in Lisbon, where the sun shines whether we like it or not. I have brought your gold. It has been weighed at the bank as you will see from their receipt, but if you wish to verify that . . .'

'That won't be necessary,' said Wilshere, moving across the room. 'I'll want you to count these to confirm that you've received one hundred and sixty-eight stones.'

'We've arranged for the quality to be checked tomorrow morning.'

'I'm sure there won't be any problem but I'll be here all day tomorrow if there is.'

The trickling of metal slipping against metal as Wilshere dialled in the combination to his safe. Silence while Voss counted the diamonds and Wilshere paced the room. A signature was applied to paper. The door opened. Voices entered the hall. Anne went back to her room and hung her wet towel out of the window. Her sign to Wallis.

Voss drove back to Lisbon, followed by Wallis. He went straight to Lapa and the German Legation where he presented Wolters with the receipt and the stones, watched him count them out and put them in the safe.

Voss walked back in the darkening evening to his one-roomed apartment overlooking the Estrela Gardens and basilica. He showered and lay on his bed smoking and sinking into a drowsy sensuality. He wanted to bring her here, not that it was Lisbon's best apartment, but it was a place to be alone, away from the eyes, a place where the moment wouldn't have to be snatched. There would be time for . . . there would be time and intimacy. He ran his hand up his stomach and chest, drew on the thick white end of the cigarette, felt the blood rush, the prickle and the brain smoothing out into the warm evening.

'I am not alone,' he said, out loud, conscious of being absurdly dramatic – the melodrama of the Berlin cabaret singer to a bored audience.

He laughed at his insanity and ramped his head up on his elbow. With no warning the faces of his father and brother came to him. His eyes filled, blurring the room, and the long hot day drew to a close.

Chapter 16

Monday, 17th July 1944, Estrela, Lisbon.

At 9.30 p.m. Voss got up, dressed, picked up a newspaper, drank a coffee at the corner café and went to his customary bench in the Estrela Gardens. He sat with the newspaper on his lap. People walked under the trees. There was a sense of relief after the brutal heat of the day. Most of the women were well dressed – in expensive silks if they could afford it or high-quality cottons if they couldn't. The men, if they were Portuguese, wore dark suits and hats. If they were foreigners, the richer ones were dressed in linen, the poorer in material too thick for the weather. Money had filtered through Lisbon.

Voss blinked, saw the scene through a different lens, saw the other people in the gardens. These were not men and women enjoying an evening stroll. These were the sweat of the city. They oozed out of the dark, polluted buildings, seeped out of the cheap *pensões*, which stank of the drains, leaked out of the stuffy attics in rinsed underwear dried crisp in the sun. They were looking for the odd escudo to weigh down the damp pockets creeping up their thighs. They were the watchers, the listeners, the whisperers, the fabricators, the rumourmongers – the liars, the cheats, the conmen and the crows.

One of this number sat on Voss's bench. He was small, emaciated, unshaven and toothless with black eyebrows that sprouted an inch from his head. Voss tapped the bench with his newspaper and some of the man's sour smell wafted towards him. His name was Rui.

'Your Frenchman hasn't been out of his room for three days,' said Rui.

'Is he dead?' asked Voss.

'No, no, I mean he's only been out for coffee.'

'And he drank that on his own?'

'Yes. He bought some bread and tinned sardines too,' added Rui.

'Did he speak to anyone?'

'He's scared, this one. I haven't seen anyone so scared. He'd turn on his own shadow and kick at it in the street.'

You would too, thought Voss. Olivier Mesnel had come from Paris where he had only one enemy, to Lisbon where he has two, the Germans and the PVDE. Who'd be a French communist here?

'Has he made any more trips to the outskirts of town?'

'Those trips to Monsanto, they seem to drain him too much. This is a man who has few reserves left . . . not for what he's doing.'

'Tell me when he does something. You know the form,' said Voss, getting up and leaving the newspaper, which Rui started flicking though to find the twenty-escudo note slipped between the sports pages.

Voss left the gardens at the exit closest to the basilica and headed for the Bairro Alto down the Calçada da Estrela, looking behind him for a taxi but also checking that there was no *bufos* on him. A cab pulled up and he let it take him to the Largo do Chiado. He thought about Mesnel. He worried about him. Always the same worries. Why would the Russians choose such a man for intelligence work? The hopeless loner, the seedy neurotic, the unwashed loser, the . . . the liver fluke, the mattress flea.

Voss left the cab and walked at pace up through the grid of the battered cobbled streets of the Bairro Alto to a *tasca* where they where grilling horse mackerel outside. He took a seat in the darkest corner with views out of two doors. He ordered the mackerel and a small jug of white wine. He ate with no enthusiasm and washed it back with the wine, fast so that he couldn't taste its sharpness. Nobody showed at the two doors. He ordered a *bagaço*. He wanted that ferocity of the pure, colourless alcohol in is throat. He smoked. The cigarette stuck to the sweat between his fingers.

Anne tried the study door. It was unlocked and empty. She moved on to the sitting room. Dark. On the back terrace Wilshere sat alone at the small table smoking and drinking undiluted whisky from a tumbler. She sat. He didn't seem to notice her but kept up his silent vigil on the empty lawn, while moving the heavy, dark furniture of his doubts and concerns around in his head.

She was trying to work out how she was going to fit Sutherland's orders into her strange relationship with Wilshere. She had no ease with the man. Whatever charm Cardew said he possessed must be reserved for men. With her he was either disconcertingly intimate or unfathomably distant. Either stroking her, kissing the corner of her mouth or thrashing the hide off her horse. The man's wealth had insulated him from ordinary mortals, it was always a job to think how to tease his brain towards interest.

'Dinner ready?' he asked, exhausted by the notion.

'I don't know, I've been upstairs.'

'Drink?'

'I'm all right, thank you.'

'Smoke?'

He lit her cigarette, tossed his own and lit another.

'I will have that drink, after all,' she decided.

'João?' called Wilshere, to no response. 'I thought it was awfully quiet. You know, I don't know whether we're going to get any dinner tonight.'

He fixed Anne a brandy and soda from the tray.

'I'm not hungry,' she said.

'They *should* give us something. Mafalda confuses them sometimes, I think.'

'When we were riding yesterday,' said Anne, deciding on a frontal assault, 'why did you hit my horse?'

'Hit your horse?' he said, sitting slowly.

'You remember my horse bolted?'

'Yes,' he said, but careful now, uncertain of other things, 'she did bolt.'

'It was because you hit her with your crop as you rode past.'

'I did,' he said, a statement, but on the edge of a question.

'Why was that? I didn't want to bring it up in front of the major. I was thinking that it might have had something to do with this girl Judy Laverne. I've been worrying about it.'

'Worrying?'

'Yes,' she said, realizing now that she'd drawn a blank.

His eyes turned furtive in his head. It scared her. Sutherland had been wrong. This had not been the right thing to do.

'I thought it was . . . I thought it was maybe my mare that had spooked the filly, coming up on you so fast like that.'

She had the image of him clear in her head – half standing out of the saddle, crop arm raised, intent on damage.

'Perhaps that was it,' she said, grasping at anything conciliatory. 'Was Judy Laverne a good horsewoman?'

'No,' he said, close to vehement now, 'she was a *brilliant* horse-woman. Fearless, too.'

He socked back the whisky, drew savagely on the cigarette and bit his thumbnail, staring through her, wild for a moment.

'I think I'll go and see what's happened to dinner,' he said.

The lawn darkened another degree. She gulped her brandy. Her confidence in Sutherland had evaporated. Whatever this was, her presence here, it was *all* to do with Judy Laverne.

Voss left a few coins on the table, the meal costing so little it was difficult to imagine the lives of those providing it. He walked back down to the statue of Luís de Camões, did a circuit under the trees of the people sitting on the stone seats who were not interested in him. He headed down the Rua do Alecrim to the railway station at Cais do Sodré and bought a ticket to Estoril. He sat in one of the middle carriages of the almost empty train. Just before the train was due to pull out he left the carriage and walked back up the platform. There was nobody following him. The guard blew his whistle. He stepped into the first carriage of the moving train.

In Estoril he walked up through the gardens to the Hotel Parque. He watched the cars and people from under the palm trees, waited until the pavements were clear and crossed the road. He walked towards the casino and, in a single movement, opened a car door and swung in behind the wheel. He started the car, drove behind the casino and down the other side of the square. He headed west, through Cascais and out to Guincho, where the long stretches of straight road showed him that he was not being followed.

The road climbed up the Serra de Sintra past Malveira, past the bend in the road where the American woman had come off, past the Azoia junction, through Pé da Serra, down to Colares and then back up the north side of the *serra*, past a dark village, some unlit *quintas*. After some kilometres he pulled off the road and parked the car deep in some trees. He crossed the road, went through an iron gate and down a cobbled track into the gardens of Monserrate.

Twenty yards down the track he was joined by a man behind and a man in front, who shone a torch in his face.

'Good evening, sir,' said an English voice. *'What is the worst of woes that wait on age?'*

The man with the torch spurted laughter, while the one at Voss's rear whispered softly in his ear.

'What stamps the wrinkle deeper on the brow?'

Voss sighed but remembered his lines:

'To view each loved one blotted from life's page,
And be alone on earth, as I am now.'

'It's not as bad as all that, sir. We're all friends here, as you know.'

The English and their sense of humour, thought Voss. This was Richard Rose's work, the writer. He had the whole of the Lisbon station spouting the classics.

'Learn while you work,' he'd said. 'It's our way of handling the serious business.'

The three men walked down to the unlit building in the centre of the gardens. The first time Rose had met Voss here he'd told him that the gardens had originally been landscaped by an eighteenth-century English aesthete called William Beckford, who'd had to leave England in a hurry or face the noose.

'What had he done?' Voss had asked, innocent.

'Buggered little boys, Voss,' said Rose, eyes shining and alive to the possibilities. 'The love that dare not speak its name.'

He'd confirmed it in German too, just to make sure Voss understood, to see how straight the tracks were that Voss was running on.

They arrived at the strange palace built in the middle of the last century by another English eccentric. The lead escort pointed with his torch down the Moorish colonnade to some open glass doors at the far end. Voss was relieved to see Sutherland there with Rose, the two men sitting on wooden chairs in the deserted room with the light from a hurricane lamp shuddering up the walls.

'Ah!' said Rose, standing up to greet Voss, *'the wandering outlaw of his own dark mind.'*

'I'm not sure I understand you very well,' said Voss, blank, unamused by Rose.

154

'It's nothing, Voss, old chap, nothing,' said Rose. 'Just a line from the poem that provides your codename . . . *Childe Harold*. Did you know that was written just down the road in Sintra?'

Voss didn't respond. They sat, lit cigarettes. Sutherland sucked on his empty pipe. Rose removed three small metal goblets from a leather holder and half-filled them from a hip flask.

'We've never thanked you properly for the information on the rockets,' said Sutherland, raising his cup to Voss, striking the note he wanted for this meeting, steering away from Rose's more reckless style.

'Didn't stop them falling, of course,' said Rose, arm over the back of his chair, 'but cheers, anyway.'

'At least you were prepared,' said Voss. 'And you tested the craters?'

'We tested the craters.'

'And I assume you found that what I said was true.'

'No evidence of radiation,' said Sutherland. 'Conventional explosives. But it doesn't mean we're no longer concerned.'

'We're of the opinion that they were test flights,' said Rose.

'Given the seriousness of the situation in Italy, France and the East, do you think the Führer is of the temperament to spend his time in testing?' said Voss.

'The flight path of the rockets?' asked Rose. 'Yes, we do . . . until such time as Heisenberg has developed the atomic pile to create the Ekarhenium, as you call it.'

'We've been through this before. Heisenberg and Hahn have been explicit. There is no atomic bomb programme.'

'Heisenberg wasn't explicit to Niels Bohr, and Niels Bohr is with the Americans now and he, along with others, has convinced them that Germany's made serious advances, you're damned close.'

Voss closed his eyes which were sore in his head. Some smoking ensued.

'We know you didn't bring us all the way out here just to talk us through that one again, Voss,' said Sutherland. 'You're never going to convince us . . . and even if you did, we wouldn't be able to convince the Americans, what with all the evidence they've been accumulating.'

'There's probably only twenty scientists in the world who know what any of this is about,' said Rose. 'Even you with your years of physics at Heidelberg University wouldn't understand what it entails. You might have grasped some theory but don't tell us that you, here in Lisbon, could have the first idea of the practicalities. This is innovative science. Brilliant men see things differently. Short cuts can be made. Heisenberg and Hahn are two such men. It would take a lot more than your word to send us back to London telling our people not to worry.'

'I have something else for you,' said Voss, sick of this endless battering and getting nowhere – intelligence services the world over only believe what they want to believe, or what their leadership wants them to believe.

Sutherland leaned forward to hide his excitement. Rose cupped his knee in the stirrup of his hands, tilted his head.

'We have completed some negotiations and are now in possession of a number of diamonds, which are not of industrial quality. They have a value in excess of one million dollars. These diamonds, which I have just delivered to the German Legation in Lapa, will be handed over to Beecham Lazard, who will be travelling tomorrow via Dakar and Rio to New York. I understand he will be acquiring something with the proceeds of the diamond sales which could advance or lead to the acquisition of a secret weapon programme for Germany. I don't know what exactly he is buying or from whom, or even whether it is in New York.'

'You said "secret weapon" – how do you know that much?'

'I am reporting to you what has been heard in Germany, that there is talk of a secret weapon in Berlin and this has now reached the Führer. The best confirmation of this that I can offer is that, at the moment, we have insufficient funds in Switzerland to buy the diamonds outright and to make up the shortfall we had to take a loan of some gold from the Banco de Oceano e Rocha. That gold would not have been released without the highest authority from Berlin. I would suggest that it is worth following Lazard to New York.'

'We'll tail him from Lisbon.'

'I wouldn't put anybody on the flight,' said Voss. 'He's a very cautious man. Even our own agents won't make contact until he arrives in Rio.'

'We'll check him on and check him off,' said Sutherland. 'Can I have a word, Richard?'

156

The two Englishmen went out on to the colonnade and as they went down some steps and on to a steep lawn out of sight Voss heard their opening exchange:

'You can't put this to him now,' said Sutherland.

'On the contrary,' said Rose, 'I think the timing is perfect.'

Voss pressed the sweat out of his eyebrows with the edge of his thumb. Five minutes and the two men were back. Sutherland was, as usual, grave and Rose's reliable levity was turned off. They'd gone out English and come back very serious men. Voss felt something turning in his bowels.

'We're going to make a communication with Wolters through our usual channels,' said Sutherland.

'Your usual channels?' asked Voss. 'I'm not sure what that means.'

'We have a way of letting Wolters know about intelligence we want him to hear.'

'Real intelligence?'

'Yes, the real thing.'

'You mean threats?'

'Sometimes.'

'And you're going to tell me first . . . to see how I react?'

'Not exactly,' said Rose. 'We know how you'll react. It's just that we think the information you've given us makes you a member of our club.'

'I don't like clubs,' said Voss, suddenly revealing things about himself. 'I'm not a member of any.'

'It's also important that you know that this message to Wolters has nothing to do with the intelligence you've just given us.'

'The communiqué that will be given to Wolters tomorrow will be as follows,' said Sutherland, his voice so low that the other two had to lean in to him: 'If we do not have an unconditional surrender from Germany by the 15th August, by the end of that month an atomic device will be dropped on the city of Dresden.'

Voss lost the ability to swallow. It was as if what his mind was refusing to accept was also being rejected by his body. The sweat, which had gathered in his hair and eyebrows from the hot night and the heat of the hurricane lamp, now broke and flowed over the taut skin of his drawn features, so that he had to wipe his cheeks as if he was crying. He thought of his mother.

'Are there any other circumstances, apart from unconditional surrender, in which this could be prevented from happening?'

The two men opposite him thought about the meaning of unconditional surrender.

'Well, I suppose . . . Hitler's death might do it . . . as long as Himmler didn't take over, or anyone like him,' said Rose.

'If we got cast-iron proof that there was no atomic bomb programme, or we had the exact location of any laboratories and the crucial scientists involved in the programme – Heisenberg, Hahn, Weizsäcker – so that they can be destroyed . . . then possibly the action could be . . .' said Sutherland.

'It would save a great number of lives,' said Rose.

'But not many of them in Dresden,' said Voss.

The two Englishmen stood. Voss felt broken in the middle, his legs not operational. As they left, Rose, not a normally demonstrative man, patted him on the back. Voss sat alone for a quarter of an hour until his motor responses normalized. He picked up the hurricane lamp, went out of the room and handed it to the remaining agent, who stood at the edge of shadow under the Moorish arches of the colonnade.

'A beautiful evening, sir,' said the agent, dowsing the lamp.

Voss's legs didn't work the pedals very well on the way back. He scared himself taking hairpin bends with one foot flooring the clutch and the other still on the accelerator. The tyres had squealed, the engine howled, and the steering wheel slithered through his wet hands. He found himself thinking of Judy Laverne coming off the same road and wondered whether this was what had happened. Something terrible had been said to her, some terrible revelation and she'd given up, thrown herself away, exhausted by man's capacity for inflicting horror.

He took a walk on the beach at Guincho for twenty minutes to stop his legs shaking, to see if the Atlantic rollers could thump out the dark empty space in his chest and guts. But all he'd felt was the ground trembling beneath him and its reverberation through the cast of his body. He'd thought about something Rose had quoted to him in a previous meeting. Something about hollow men. He couldn't remember it precisely, but Rose's first words, as they'd met that evening, came back to him. *The wandering outlaw of his own dark mind*. Yes, that was what he'd become. Alone out here, between the earth and the sea. Nobody. He was nobody any more. Modelled. Fabricated. Moulded. Cast. And with no way back to the old Karl Voss. The one that . . . the one that used to what? Believe in things? Admire people? The Führer? Pah! He was lost. That Rose. He says these words and then: 'Nothing, Voss, old chap, nothing.' It *is* nothing. He's right. Karl Voss is nothing but a hunted man. Hunted by himself.

He'd been drawn back to the car, winched to it. He sat behind the wheel, held his head out of the window, rested his chin on the ledge and smoked, staring at the ground. He drifted deeper into his dark mind, retreated until, panic-struck by his wanderings over that empty landscape, he started the car and headed back to Estoril.

Voss parked up somewhere between the Hotel Parque and the casino. Smoking was all that was holding him together. He lit one cigarette from another. He strode up towards the casino. He wasn't thinking any more. He was doing. He was desperate. He walked past Jim Wallis in his car without noticing. He went straight into Wilshere's garden without checking his rear. Wallis had to run to catch up with him and even then he only just saw Voss's back disappearing into the bower next to the summerhouse. Wallis slowed, eased back into the hedge, waited.

Chapter 17

Tuesday, 18th July 1944, Wilshere's house, Estoril, near Lisbon.

It was 2.00 a.m. Anne lay on the bed, pinned to it, absorbed by the ceiling, waiting for time to shift. She wasn't thinking about what she had to do – search the study. She was floating in and out of fantasy and reality, between Judy Laverne and Wilshere, Karl Voss and herself.

Wilshere said he missed Judy Laverne, said he'd fallen. They appeared to be in love according to Voss and others. Now Wilshere was using her to remind himself of Judy Laverne. To torment his wife? To torment himself? He *had* struck the filly. He'd been angry, deranged by the vision of her. He'd wanted to drive her away, to banish her from his thoughts.

Did Karl Voss know what she was? Was he on an operation or did he, in the heart of the paranoid city, see this as one of hers? Would it ever be possible to know what was real? She decided that she wouldn't see him again or rather that she wasn't going to put herself in that position. There would be no visit to the bottom of the garden tonight. There was too much that was unknowable. The equation would never simplify. The variables would mount. The additional logic would defeat itself. She didn't have the tools to prove any part of the solution. In the end the silver thread would stop tugging.

It was time to go to work. She walked the dark corridor, her shoulder brushing the wall. She waited at the gallery above the hall. The wood in the house groaned after a day spent straining against the heat. Moonlight lay in a blue rhombus across the chequered tiles. She went down the stairs, stepped around the moonlight, past the cases of Mafalda's silent figurines. *Amor é cego.* She walked the length of the house and unlocked the french windows to the back terrace in case she had to get back in that way after escaping out of the window. She went back to the study, let herself in, closed the door behind her.

She crossed the room, opened the window behind the desk and moved a plant on the window sill three inches to the right. She lifted her nightdress and took a torch from the waistband of her knickers. She sat in Wilshere's chair and surveyed the night-lit room.

The books in neat, leather-bound collections filled the walls. Two paintings on either side of the door, one of men in Arab dress on camels in a desert scene, the other of a fishing boat dragged up on a mist-filled beach. Ireland, perhaps. One corner was African, with three masks mounted on the wall, the one at the apex maybe three-foot long with inch slits for eyes and mouth, the mask never more than six inches across through its entire length. Hair, a kind of rough hemp, sprouted from the top. The mouth even appeared to have teeth.

She listened again to the settling house and painted the desktop with her torch beam. A blotter, two old newspapers, a pen and ink tray, tidy. She opened the central drawer. One block of clean paper and beside it a single sheet with a four-line stanza accompanied by jottings in the margins, the odd word crossed out and the replacement word connected by a line. The stanza seemed to read:

> Crow black in the middle night
> Around the marchers come for another fight.
> No boots, but claws scratching through the dust,
> No armour, but shells blistered with rust.

That was how it stood at the moment, but it looked as if there were more drafts to be done and even then it would find its way to the bin. The wastepaper basket was empty. She drummed her chin with her fingers and shuddered. If that was what Wilshere had teeming through his mind of a night – ghostly, dark, restless, seething with ugly energy – maybe he *was* going mad. She had a memory flash, a story of her mother's when she'd visited a cave in India – alone but with the sense of not being alone. Above her, covering every inch of the roof of the cave, were hanging, sleeping bats. The sight of the dormant army, their jostling folded wings, had turned

161

her mother and sent her out in a crouched sprint into the sunlight. Was that the inside of Wilshere's cranium?

She opened all the desk drawers; some were empty, most of little interest. The bottom one was locked. She shifted books in the bookcase, she lifted pictures, she checked the fireplace. To the left of the fireplace in the darkest corner of the room was the cabinet where Wilshere kept his safe with a combination dial lock. She went back to the desk. She listened. Hands moist now. First nerves creeping in. House noises growing into something else in her mind. Footsteps on a stair. Stop breathing. Sweat under her breasts. She stood up. Remembered her training: never leave a warm chair. She opened all the drawers again, checked the roofs and sides. Central drawer, at the back, stuck with something resinous, a key.

It opened the bottom drawer; inside was a single thick book bound in very soft untooled leather, its plain unlined pages covered in the same handwriting as the stanza of poetry. There were dates. A diary, which at a quick glance she could tell was personal. Day after day with no mention of business. Started 1st January 1944. The initial entries were rarely more than a couple of lines long – observations such as: '*4th January. A rare frost. The lawn quite white. The low sun turns it back to green in a matter of moments. Not what you'd call an Irish frost. It would be quite something to have real foot-stamping weather for once.*' '*23rd January. Heavy storm out at sea. Drove out to Cabo da Roca, walked the coast to Praia Adraga. The rain driven off the ocean, lacerating. Waves clawed at the rocks and shot up the cliff faces. Rollers on the beach like I've never seen. Thunderous. Had to run to stay out of their clutches.*'

A man overwhelmed by tedium or positively reflective? Hard to tell. The first entry of more than a few lines came on 3rd February and coincided with Beecham Lazard introducing his new assistant, Judy Laverne. '*I've never seen such a mouth. So wide and what lips! The bottom one so plump I just wanted to put my finger to it, feel its soft cushion. And bright red lipstick which rings all her cigarette stubs, which I've kept.*' Infatuated from the first moment. Karl Voss shuttled through her brain.

She skimmed the pages. They ride almost every day, in invigorating rain, in sunshine that was never so brilliant, under magnificent turbulent skies. There's no such thing as bad weather now. They sleep together in the house at Pé da Serra. Wilshere has fallen. He can't keep the pen off the page. Her blue-black hair, her marble breasts, her hard, ¬ink, shilling-sized nipples, her jet strip, not triangle, of pubic hair. It was embarrassing, it was touching, it was so private it made the sweat trickle down Anne's ribs. Until the end of April.

'*25th April. Lazard has lost his head. He spends too much time in Lisbon. He's reading bizarre things into normal everyday life. That's what happens if you spend too much time in that city – everybody watching each other – anyone's bound to look odd eventually. Why shouldn't Judy meet another American? She's American. She wants to talk to her own people. So what if they go for a walk through the Igreja do Carmo. It's something to do. Were they holding hands? No. I don't see what he's getting at . . .*'

The tirade continued to the bottom of the page, by which time Lazard's words had wormed their way into his mind and laid their eggs. The parasites proliferated. Doubt scuttled from page to page, a black spider against the white paper, desperate for the dark safety of the book's spine. The lyricism vanished. Wilshere's open, flowing italics tightened, his hand cramped on the page. Lazard reported another meeting in *A Brasileira* café with a different American. He has them followed to the Pensão Londres where they stayed for an hour. Jealousy took root, spreading, ravaging like couch grass. Wilshere was in a torment. Lazard haunted the pages, as reliable as any Iago. Then in early May Judy Laverne announced that the PVDE had refused to extend her visa. She was going to have to leave. Wilshere was sick. He wrote things. Terrible things. Things that should never have been written down, in language that shouldn't be known, couldn't be known by anybody outside hell. The page was spattered with ink dried to a coppery blood, the paper had been torn up by the blade of the dry, frustrated nib. Anne turned the pages, the empty pages, pages that could have been full and ripe, to the end of the book where, on the inside of the back cover, were six sets of numbers and letters – R12, R6, L4, R8, L13, R1.

This time the creak of the wooden stair was followed by the slap of a leather slipper on the tiled floor of the hall. Anne wiped the diary clean with her sleeve, replaced it in the drawer, shut it, turned the key. Light from the corridor appeared in a line at the foot of the door. She found the resin in the central drawer, restuck the key, straightened the chair, stepped on to the sill and out of the window, pulled the plant across, shut the window. The door opened. The light came on in the study. She crouched, her back was as cold as cod, her nightdress soaked through. Wilshere drew up his chair, sat down. She ran across the lawn and down the path to the summerhouse.

In the study, Wilshere leaned back in his chair rubbing his fingers. He sniffed the air. Wisteria. He stood and pushed the unfastened window open, rubbed his fingers again. He looked below the window ledge and then up at his shadow reaching out across the empty lawn.

Anne slowed at the bottom of the path. Her heart rattled against her ribs. Her throat was tight, constricted, as if the neckline of the nightdress was strangling her. She pulled up the hem and wiped her face, pushed the torch into her knickers. She looked back up the path, shook herself out and went into the bower. Voss lay on his back on the stone seat, asleep. She started to turn. He sat up, ran his hand down his face.

'I'd given up on you,' he said.

Her breasts were still heaving under the cotton.

'I didn't think you were going to come,' said Voss, pinching the sleep out of his eyes.

'I didn't intend to,' she said, moving into the darkest corner behind him.

He swivelled on the seat.

'You didn't *intend* to,' he repeated.

'No.'

'You're scared,' he said. 'I can see.'

'And why shouldn't I be?' she said, the blade of her mother's voice in her own.

'Of me?'

'We're enemies, aren't we?'

'Out there,' he said, and his hand caught the edge of the moonlight.

'There's more of out there than there is in here.'

'True . . . but what's in here is ours.'

'Is it?' she asked. 'Do you think that? How am I to know that?'

'Because we're talking like this.'

'We can talk, but I still don't know if you're . . . honourable.'

'Which is why you didn't intend to come,' he said. 'So why did you?'

'I ran out of cigarettes.'

He laughed. Her organs went back to their places. Spies in love. Bloody hopeless. Would they ever tell each other anything? He offered a cigarette.

'You're probably a spy, Mr Military Attaché,' she said, taking one. 'I work for Shell, the oil company. A sensitive economic commodity.'

'Everybody's a spy,' said Voss, searching himself for a lighter.

'In Lisbon, maybe.'

'Anywhere,' he said, lighting their cigarettes. 'We all have our secrets.'

'Spies have even more.'

'It's just their job and they're dull secrets.'

'You seem to know.'

'It's wartime and I work in the German Legation; there are secrets all over.'

'Which is the problem. Where does the job end?'

'So you think, for instance, that attraction is easy to act,' he said. 'Love, too?'

She sucked on the cigarette, her cheeks sinking in sharply, drawing in the smoke to disguise the race around her heart, the fast blood standing the hairs up on her arms, itching around her teeth.

'It depends,' she said, flicking her ash, dizzy now from the nicotine rush.

'I'm listening,' he said.

'It depends, say, if the object of your affection is predisposed to that kind of attention.'

'That sounds like experience.'

'Not personal.'

'How did you find out?'

'I read it in a book.'

'Is that the sum total of your experience?'

'There's nothing wrong with learning from people who write books.'

'My mother told me that in affairs of the heart no rules apply.

165

No one's love is the same as anybody else's. Comparisons don't work. Even love between two people can't be relied on to stay the same,' said Voss.

'Your *mother* told you that?'

'I was *her* child. My elder brother was my father's.'

'Do you know what she meant?'

'Probably that loving my father was hard work. She did it, but he never made it easy for her,' said Voss.

Silence, Anne waiting for him to continue, praying for him to continue. Voss, staring into the ground, prepared himself to tell it for the first time.

'In the beginning,' he said, as if this was now legend, 'my father was an exciting man, an army officer, my mother . . . a beautiful . . . well, girl, I suppose. She was sixteen and she thought she'd found true romantic love until one day he told her that there'd been someone else. A girl he'd loved, who'd died. Those few words wrung out all the romance from their so-called "true love". But what was she to do? Suddenly not love him when she knew she did? They married the next year in 1910. Four years later he went to war and for four years she hardly saw him. He had some leave . . . enough to create my brother and then me but when he did come back home in 1918, on the losing side, he was a different man. Damaged. He wasn't exciting any more. My mother said he was like a house with the windows bricked in. So she had to find a different way of loving him, and she made it work for twenty-odd years . . . until the next war.

'My father was a principled man – one of those generals who spoke out against some of the orders given to the army before the Russian campaign – it cost him his job. They retired him, sent him home. Now he was a man who was not only no longer exciting, but bitter, too. Then my brother was killed at Stalingrad and that was the end for my father. He shot himself, because as far as he was concerned he'd lost everything. He didn't say it, but my mother was not enough. That was how I found out. In a letter he asked me to spread his ashes over the first woman's grave and my mother, who *still* loved him, made sure that I did it.'

Silence while Voss turned that over, reploughed it into his mind.

'That, I think, is what she meant,' he said. 'Are you still scared of me?'

'Not of you.'

'By me?'

'No.'

'Someone's scared you.'

'Patrick Wilshere.'

'Why?'

'I read his diary tonight,' she said, drawn in by the intimacy.

'Like I said, we're all spies.'

'I find his behaviour . . . threatening. I wanted to know what he was thinking.'

'And now?'

'More so. It wasn't a relaxing read.'

'What did the diary say?'

'That he was madly in love with Judy Laverne until Lazard told him he'd seen her in Lisbon with other men. He became insanely jealous and, although it wasn't actually in the diary, there were things written that would suggest that he would have happily seen her dead.'

'I don't see what bearing this has on you.'

'I don't know what I'm doing here. I don't know why he has invited me into his house but I'm certain that it wasn't to give a secretary somewhere to sleep.'

'Tell me.'

She told him about the riding incident on the *serra* and the subsequent conversation with Wilshere. He lit two more cigarettes from the coal of his own, handed her one.

'And when you confronted him he did not appear to have been aware of his actions,' Voss repeated. 'So now you think that Wilshere is deranged, has drawn another woman into his orbit to punish her for the crimes, real or imagined, committed by the first. No, I don't think so.'

That annoyed her. Dismissing the silly girl.

'What does the omniscient Military Attaché think, then?'

'Sorry,' he said, 'I wasn't being patronizing. I don't disbelieve you. I just think there is more to it. Wilshere is a complicated individual. He wouldn't position you simply to satisfy his need for vengeance, although sexual jealousy is a very potent force. No. He has seen an opportunity in having you there. By confronting him with the riding incident you have revealed a weakness to him. He can no longer rely on himself. He is . . . leaking. It *could* make him more dangerous.'

'And everything had been going so well,' said Anne.

'It's strange that the English don't have a word for *sang froid*, and yet the French, who rarely exhibit it, do.'

'If you take things too seriously it could feed your inclination to give up.'

'We Germans take everything seriously.'

'But unfortunately it doesn't seem to work with you.'

Voss's laugh was barely a grunt. He hadn't expected to find anything funny after what he'd been told.

They sat in the accumulative silence of a moment when life goes one way or the other. Two people who knew that words would not continue the thing. A move was needed, possibly two. Then the words could restart but in a different light, in a light that others wouldn't be able to see and would shake their heads at, mystified.

He threw his cigarette on the floor, hers went after it, the coals smouldered on the black floor, smoke strayed into the moonlight. Their lips searched the dark. Touched. It was not a tender moment. There was too much desperation. And just as she'd thought she would let him have her there, on the stone seat, at the edge of moonlight, she remembered the torch in her knickers and other small details fell in afterwards so that she knew there would have to be another time and place.

He told her to come to his apartment after work the following afternoon. He would leave the downstairs door open for her. She stroked the bones in his face with her hands, like a blind person wanting to remember.

She went back up to the house, adrenalin slick in her system. Her feet found the steps of the back terrace, her nose the smell of cigar smoke. She stepped into a sudden funnel of torchlight.

'What are you doing?' asked Wilshere, voice liquid, floating between inquiry and menace.

'It was too hot to sleep. I've been walking in the garden,' she said. 'And you?'

His slippers clapped his heels as the beam of light compressed between them. She put a hand up to shield her face.

'I wasn't tired,' he said. 'I was lying in bed thinking too much.'

168

He snapped off the torch, slipped it into his pocket, tossed his cigar.

'You look cold now,' he said.

'No,' she replied, her skin tight as blubber, 'not cold.'

He held her arms and kissed her. Tobacco bitter. Whisky sour.

'Forgive me,' he said in a voice that wasn't asking. 'You were irresistible.'

She unwelded her feet from the stone floor.

'I'll lead the way,' he said almost gaily, and set off torch in hand through the french windows, the beam swaggering from wall to wall. She followed him up the protesting stairs, revulsion seething in her chest.

As she entered her room, Wilshere blew her a kiss.

On the other side of the gallery, Mafalda's door shut.

Voss arrived back in Lisbon close to 4.00 a.m. He was beyond tiredness. He parked outside his apartment and checked his dead-letter drop in the gardens. Although he checked it regularly this particular one was used infrequently and he was surprised to find something in it. A coded message asking him to go, whatever the time, to an address in Madragoa which belonged to a colonel of the Free Poles. He walked down the Calçada da Estrela and turned right into the narrow streets of Madragoa.

He found Rua Garcia da Horta and went into the building, which was always open, and up the narrow stairs to the first floor. He knocked on the door twice, then three times, then twice again. The door opened a crack and then all the way. He went into the dark apartment, following the colonel, who didn't speak but pointed to the open windows where he spent most of the night trying to get cool. Still not used to the heat after a lifetime in Warsaw.

Even without being able to see the man in the room clearly, he knew that sitting in a chair to the side of the window was the same man he'd spoken to in the Hotel Lutecia in Paris at the end of January.

'Drink?' he asked, holding up a bottle.

'What is it?' asked Voss.

'I don't know what the colonel called it,' he said, 'but it's rough.'

He poured him a measure into a wine glass.

'How is it going with the British?' he asked.

169

'Very badly,' said Voss. 'They don't believe a word I say except, of course, after it has happened. Then they thank me and tell me how much they have suffered and follow that up with threats.'

'Threats?'

'They're threatening to drop an atomic device on Dresden in mid August unless they get an unconditional German surrender.'

'Doesn't that sound like bluff?'

'They're very nervous about our nonexistent bomb programme. The Americans even more so.'

'What more do they want?'

'Nothing much,' said Voss, scathing. 'The deaths of all our major scientists – Heisenberg, Hahn, Weizsäcker, the lot. The location of all our research laboratories so that they can be bombed to rubble, and the death of the Führer, as long as he's not replaced by another National Socialist leader.'

Silence while the man turned his head and lit a cigarette.

'You have been alone a long time, I know. It has been very hard. The British are making what they see as necessarily cruel demands. But they are the only ones we can rely on. We have to tell them everything we can in the hope that they will relent,' he said. 'You will tell them about the V2 rockets. You can tell them they can bomb the laboratories in Berlin-Dahlem to dust if that will make them feel better. And you may tell them that the Führer will be assassinated around midday Berlin time in his bunker in the *Wolfsschanze* on 20th July.'

Voss was stunned. The alcohol trembled in his glass. He drank it automatically. The man continued in his quiet voice.

'Your job, once you've received the signal that Operation Valkyrie has started, will be to take control of the German Legation here in Lisbon. It may require strong methods. If SS General Wolters does not obey your orders you will shoot him without hesitation. Do you have a gun?'

'Only one from the legation which I have to sign in and out.'

'The colonel will provide you with a firearm.'

'Is this certain?'

'We have been close several times but have been frustrated at the last moment by changes in schedule. This time the Führer is fixed at the *Wolfsschanze* and *we* are going to *him*. This is the most certain we have ever been, which is why you are being informed

170

and can pass it on to the British. I hope this means you won't be alone for much longer,' he said. 'One last thing before you go. Olivier Mesnel?'

'Olivier Mesnel, as far as I am informed, does nothing except have occasional, unspeakable assignations with gypsy boys in the caves on the outskirts of the city.'

'The colonel has found that he's making contact with a communist courier who visits him in the Pensão Silva on Rua Braancamp. The colonel believes that whatever Mesnel is giving him will find its way back to the Russians.'

'I don't know what he *can* be giving him. He never goes out.'

'Then perhaps he's receiving instructions. The point is that whatever he's involved in could help us with the British. If we can show that the Russians are not to be trusted it will help our cause.'

Chapter 18

The man in the dark suit sat with his hands clasped and jammed between his knees. He was tense and the natural hunch his occupation had given him gave the impression that he was about to sustain a series of blows across the shoulders. His hat sat on the table in front of him. A black homburg. The drag of the heavy bags under his eyes made his long face longer, his sadness sadder.

'Couldn't you find anyone else?' asked Voss, looking at him through the glass panel of the door. 'In all those jewellery stores off the Rossio? There must have been someone local, surely.'

Hein, one of Voss's subordinates, didn't say anything but let his hand do the talking. They were too gabby down there.

'Where did you find him?'

'The Jewish Refugee Commission.'

'Did he volunteer?'

'Kempf said he'd find out about his family for him.'

'And did he?'

Hein gave Voss a diagonal look and shrugged.

'Well, he won't talk, that's for sure,' said Voss. 'Where's he from?'

'Antwerp. Worked a lot with Belgian Congo product.'

'Keep Wolters away from him.'

'That's probably your job, isn't it, sir?'

'What's his name?'

'Hirschfeld ... er ... Samuel Hirschfeld,' said Hein, morose now.

Voss went in, shook hands with the man and told him to set up his equipment. The man, wordless, opened a wooden case and lifted out his scales, weights, tweezers, eyeglass and a square of worn dark velvet.

172

Voss knocked on Wolters' door, waited the customary beat, announced the diamond assessor.

'Bring him in, Voss, bring him in.'

'I've just told him to set up in the other room.'

'Each stone individually weighed and valued.'

'Yes, sir.'

'And someone in the room with him at all times.'

'Yes, sir.'

Wolters lobbed him the bag as if it was nothing more than a sack of marbles. Voss went back to the Belgian, who declined his offer of a cigarette and went to work.

Jim Wallis had filed his report at 8.00 a.m. and gone home to bed. Sutherland read it shortly afterwards and smoked a whole pipe bowl thinking about it. At 9.30 a.m. Cardew sent a coded message to the embassy and an hour later Sutherland and Rose were in a safe house just off the Largo do Rato with Anne sitting, knees pressed together, handbag on top, just like the virgin Sutherland had imagined her to be.

She took them through last night's business. Sutherland whistled through the now empty pipe, annoying her. He checked the numbers she gave him from Wilshere's diary. They talked about the safe, its make, whether there was a key as well as a combination. He told her Cardew would arrange for her instruction on how to open the safe. Anne continued the story, same as she had for Cardew. How Wilshere had surprised her in the study, how she had left via the window, how she wandered the garden and the final incident on the back terrace. Sutherland nodded her through it.

'Your report is incomplete,' said Sutherland.

'I don't think so, sir.'

'Perhaps you've forgotten something.'

'No, I'm sure I haven't.'

She was sweating in the close, curtained room. The light from the single overhead bulb was jaundiced after the fierce brightness of the street. Nausea turned in her stomach.

Sutherland bared his teeth where they were gnawing into his pipe stem.

'Your angel,' Rose prompted.

She blinked. Jim Wallis. She *had* forgotten about Jim Wallis, who they'd sent to keep an eye on her. Free-fall sweat.

The mournful notes of a knife-grinder's flute sounded in the street below.

'From the beginning,' said Sutherland, drilling her.

She told him about Karl Voss. The casino. The man who carried Wilshere back to the house. The beach. The cocktail party. The first and accidental meeting and the second, observed by Wallis, the unintentional one.

'You may recall that I told you that Voss was with the Abwehr,' said Sutherland.

'Yes, sir.'

'Have you spoken to him about any of our business?'

'No, sir, I haven't. He thinks I'm a secretary at Shell.'

'Karl Voss is an experienced officer,' said Sutherland. 'He's been with military intelligence in Zeitzler's team in Rastenburg. He's worked at the Zossen headquarters in Berlin, Avenue Foch in Paris and now here in Lisbon. Do you for one moment think he doesn't know how to play the . . . toy with the romantic illusions of a young woman?'

'All I can tell you, sir, is that I haven't told –'

'Have you . . .' Rose interrupted bluntly. 'Have you had a *physical* relationship with Voss?'

'No, sir.'

'That's something,' said Rose. 'He's a charismatic man, Voss. Very successful with the ladies. You wouldn't have been the first and you most definitely wouldn't have been the last.'

Rose's toxic words entered her intravenously. They went straight through her heart and into her head where the virus multiplied into a fever. Anger came first, a torrential rage, followed by cold, hard jealousy. They ran a circuit in her head, chasing, chasing but never catching up with the words, which remained intact, clear, defined as in the first moment that they were spoken.

'Can I make a suggestion?' said Sutherland, not looking for an affirmative. 'That you leave Captain Voss to his womanizing and concentrate on your job.'

Her handbag hung from her grip like a bad puppy as she went over to Sutherland, put him in her shadow.

'I did not have sex with him,' she said firmly. 'I have not spoken to him about our business.'

'If you had, my dear, you'd be on the first plane back to London,' he said, those blackberry smudges under his eyes swollen with insomnia. 'Dismissed.'

By the time the Contessa della Trecata arrived at the German Legation at 11.00 a.m. the shade temperature was in the low nineties and the British agents were settled into their routine, watching from apartments at the side and rear. Sutherland had put additional men in cars in the backstreets, while their paid *ardinas* – the newspaper boys – walked the hot *calçada* barefoot, ready to flag them and set Operation Dragnet in motion.

The contessa, wearing a petrol-blue silk dress cut to the mid calf of her still excellent but unsteady legs, climbed the few steps into the legation, eyed the swastika flag hanging dead over the doorway and fluttered her fan under her chin. She was taken upstairs to a gilded chair outside Wolters' office where she sat, fanning herself, in the still corridor. Voss watched her through the door from behind the hunched diamond assessor.

She was called into Wolters' office. They didn't shake hands. No contact was an understood part of their arrangement. Wolters puffed his cigar heavily as if fumigating his office.

'I know you see it as part of your cover, but could you be a little . . . a lot less rude when we're in company?' said Wolters.

'I'm sorry to have overplayed my part.'

'I can only think you used to be on the stage.'

The contessa accepted this small humiliation.

'What do you have for me?' asked Wolters.

The contessa set off in French, their common language, and the usual, baroque elaborations began to scroll the thick air of the room. Wolters slumped in his seat, fitted his cigar into the side of his mouth, between the gap in his teeth. He was used to the contessa's embellishments, the magnificent constructions of stylish detail which were the accompaniment to the tiny morsels of intelligence she brought. For him it was like tugging aside four hundred petticoats until ah! – yes, the ankle. But not today. He banged the edge of the table, which sent the contessa's fan off under her chin.

'Tell me,' he ordered.

175

'The British girl staying at the Wilsheres' house is a spy.'

'Evidence?'

'Dona Mafalda's seen her wandering the house at all hours and she's lied on her residency form to the PVDE about her father. To them she has said that he is an accountant and alive, to me that he is dead.'

'Is that all?'

The contessa wanted to round it out, give it body and depth, to disguise what in fact she was doing. She attempted to fill the silence. Wolters snapped her shut. He stood to drive her out. Her head ducked and trembled as she became the cringing bitch.

'My family,' she asked, 'have they been found yet?'

Wolters dropped his eyes to her. What was it to be today? Hope or no hope? He felt good.

'They've been found,' he said. 'We'll be moving them shortly. They were in Poland.'

'In Poland?'

'I am busy,' he said, and pointed to the door.

Voss glanced up from the diamond assessor as the contessa left. Samuel Hirschfeld signed a receipt for the small sum he'd been paid for the work.

'I'll go now,' said Hirschfeld, wiping the palms of his hands on his knees.

'Pack your things but wait for one moment.'

Hirschfeld tried to sit back in his seat but couldn't, his acid stomach churned around his ancient ulcers and tipped him forward. Voss took the diamonds and Hirschfeld's calculations across to Wolters, who was standing at his window looking down on the nonchalant but significant activity in the Rua do Sacramento à Lapa.

'Isn't this unusual?' asked Wolters, taking the paper from Voss, pointing to the street. 'I mean they watch us, we watch them, but this . . . this is excessive.'

'They're on to something, sir.'

'Or somebody's told them something,' said Wolters, no vaudeville menace but quiet, with weight.

'What did the contessa have to say?' asked Voss. 'She was quick today.'

176

'Yes,' said Wolters, 'I kept her on the leash this time.'

Voss frowned behind Wolters' shoulder.

'It was the usual thing,' said Wolters. 'Telling me things I already know. A baroque recital for a crumb of the obvious. Ach! These revolting people. They lick the hand that beats as eagerly as the one that feeds.'

He shook his hand as if saliva still clung to it.

Voss preferred Wolters in this mood. The man who knew, the man who was in total command of the multiplicity of strands that only his iron fist could hold.

'Today's treat?' said Wolters, over his shoulder. 'Today's smear of caviar on toast?'

'Yes?' said Voss, letting Wolters dangle it in front of him.

'The English girl in Wilshere's house is a spy. Really? Does that Milanese strumpet think we are fools?'

'Clearly,' said Voss, his head crammed full.

'And now this –' said Wolters, nodding at the street, shaking with false mirth. 'Ants.'

He turned his back to the window, a silhouette against the brightness of the day. He threw himself into his chair, stamped his foot.

'We will crush them.'

'The parcel came out at close to one million one hundred thousand dollars,' said Voss.

'That should do it, don't you think?'

'As I'm sure you're aware, you and I haven't discussed anything beyond Lazard flying with these stones to Rio and on to New York, sir,' said Voss. 'Should I know what will happen there?'

'I don't want Lazard to be bothered by any of your people in Dakar,' snapped Wolters. 'Don't have him tailed, he's nervous enough as it is. Doesn't know who's who any more. Let him get to Rio in peace and we'll pick him up there and make sure he gets to New York.'

'And the return journey?'

'That depends on the success of the negotiations.'

'Very good, sir,' said Voss, getting to his feet, hoping to lure Wolters out by his own reticence.

Wolters was disappointed with Voss's deference. He burned with the brilliance of his plan. He wanted Voss to try harder, to work on him, to tease more out of him.

'I understand the need for secrecy, sir,' said Voss, making for the door. 'I can only offer my help.'

'Of course, Voss,' said Wolters. 'Thank you. Yes. This . . . *this* will be the single most important intelligence event of the war and you will have been a part of it. *Heil Hitler.*'

Voss matched Wolters' salute and left with some of what he'd wanted, which was confirmation of his assumption of the day before, that the diamonds were involved in the purchase of the Führer's 'secret weapon'.

Kempf handed Voss the extracts from their dead-letter boxes. Voss read them through. Kempf stood at ease, hands behind back, eyes forward as if on parade.

'What's going on, sir?'

'What do you mean, Kempf?'

'It's like Piccadilly Circus out there, sir. They'll be driving on the left-hand side of the road by the end of the day.'

'I don't doubt it.'

'Beg your pardon, sir?'

'We're getting a little more attention than usual.'

'It's "Ring a ring of roses" out there, sir.'

'What was that, Kempf?'

'It's an English nursery game, sir.'

'You're very knowledgeable, Kempf.'

'Had an English girlfriend before the war, sir. She was the nanny from across the road. They were the only games she knew, apart from . . . but we won't go into that, sir.'

Kempf drifted into a momentary blissful state. Voss smiled.

'I can't tell you anything, Kempf. I'm in the dark myself.'

'The Jew's still waiting, sir. The stone man.'

'Damn,' said Voss. 'I forgot about him. Hein said you made him a promise.'

'You know how it is, sir,' said Kempf. 'I'll move him along then, shall I?'

'I'll go, Kempf. I'll go.'

Hirschfeld was a little wild in the eye by this stage. Voss released him. His little feet clattered down the stairs and didn't stop running until they were beyond the gates in Rua do Pau de Bandeira.

Voss sat in Hirschfeld's vacated warm, damp chair, tapped his lips with a finger. One of the dead-letter drops had revealed that Olivier Mesnel had made a move and not to the caves of Monsanto to perform any of his ghastly acts. He'd gone to an address in Rua da Arrábida off the Largo do Rato.

Voss left the legation. Kempf had been right, the *ardinas* were as good as selling *The Times*. He bought a *Diário de Notícias* and headed downhill, down the cobbled, stepped streets and into the Rua das Janelas Verdes. He turned into the dark, stone steps of the Pensão Rocha and climbed slowly up to the courtyard writing down the address and pushing it inside the newspaper with a twenty-escudo note. He took a seat at a table. The clientele, exclusively men, eyed him over and around their own newspapers, not all of them today's. The waiter, a boy, stood next to him, barefoot, trousers tied up with string.

'Bring me Paco,' said Voss.

The boy walked through the tables, watched by the printed pages of the newspapers. He went into the *pensão* and did not return. Paco appeared some minutes later, a short, dark Spaniard from Galicia, with no forehead between hair and eyebrows and sunken cheeks that had known hunger from birth. He sat at Voss's table, cheap suit, shirt buttoned to the throat, no tie and the faint smell of urine.

'Are you sick?' asked Voss.

'I'm all right.'

'Looking for work?'

He shrugged, looked away, desperate for work.

'I bought you this newspaper. There's an address. I want to know how it's used. Don't take any friends.'

Paco closed his eyes once. One of the newspapers behind him folded, upped and left.

'Any new faces?' asked Voss.

'Not here.'

'In Lisbon?'

'There's been talk of an English girl.'

'Anything?'

'She's a secretary for Shell,' he said, eyes dead, heading towards sleep. 'Lives in a big house in Estoril.'

'Is that it?' asked Voss, putting two packets of cigarettes on the newspaper.

'She's working,' he said, economic.

'How do you know?'

'I've been watching Wallis,' he said, shifting a shoulder. 'I think he's looking after her.'

'Be quick,' said Voss, and got out of there.

Back at the legation there were four cars in the short driveway between the gate and the steps up to the building. Voss went upstairs and stood in one of the front windows overlooking the intersection of Rua do Pau de Bandeira and Rua do Sacramento à Lapa. It was lunchtime and from underneath him people began to pour out of the legation building, an unusual number at once. Some got into the cars, others headed for the gates, which were now fully open. The cars all left in different directions. The streets were suddenly crowded, the *ardinas* flagging left and right in the confusion. In moments there was a traffic jam and people streamed off the pavements in between the cars. Men who had been walking like extras in a movie were now in a farce, looking up and down the four possible exits in complete indecision. Voss walked through the empty building and down the stairs. Wolters met him on the way up, grinning.

'We finally gave them something to do,' he said.

Beecham Lazard leaned against the ship's rail of the small trans-Tagus ferry. There were four cars on board and over seventy passengers. He'd seen his man come on at the ferry terminal at Cais do Sodré and had worked around him from several angles to make sure he was clean. The ferry was crossing to Cacilhas and everyone was on deck to catch the cooler air on the water. The ferry made slow going through the crowded river of cargo boats and liners waiting to dock and the low, muscular tug boats looking for work. Black smoke from a ship's funnel joined the haze on the river, scarfing the high sun. The colonnade of the huge square of the Praça do Comércio behind them was soon vague behind a humid gauze.

Lazard completed another circuit of the ferry and walked into a gap on the ship's rail next to his contact man, who'd been one of the crowd coming out of the legation for lunch. They knew each other by sight. They switched identical briefcases and parted,

Lazard now with the diamonds. Fifteen minutes later Lazard stepped off the ferry and walked to the Cacilhas bus terminal, where he took a ride along the south bank of the Tagus to the village of Caparica and then down to the ferry station at Porto Brandão. He waited there for half an hour until the ferry arrived and took him back across the river to Belém and the old 1940 Expo site. He checked his back walking around the docks, and crossed the railway tracks through the Belém train station. He took a short walk up to a house on the Rua Embaixador.

He'd rented a small apartment on the first floor. He took off his dark grey suit and put on a light blue one. He took a white hat with a dark band out of the wardrobe and laid it on the bed. He closed the other suit and briefcase into the now empty wardrobe. He checked the empty street, picked up the telephone and dialled a Lisbon number. He spoke to a man with a Brazilian accent.

'Did you pick up my laundry?' asked Lazard.

'Yes,' he said, words from a wooden actor, 'and it had all been ironed.'

Lazard hung up, annoyed, and checked his watch. He was running early. Hours to go before check-in. He took off his jacket, moved the hat to one side and lay down. Important thoughts hung in his brain like large harbour fish. His mind drifted through them until he came across something that would help pass the time. Mary Couples kneeling at the foot of the hedge with her dress bunched up around her waist, her underwear stretched between her thighs, the dark crease through her white bottom, the tan lines from her bathing costume, his thumbs hooked around the two straps of her suspender belt, her shoulders lunging forward with each of his thrusts.

Why had she done it? He was quite used to having the lewd suggestions he made to her pearl-studded lobes turned down. Why had she acquiesced suddenly and degraded herself in such a fashion? He was sure she didn't even like him.

From there it was a short hop to the thought that Mary didn't like Hal much, either, and probably not herself too. These thoughts excited him. Could she be pushed further? He entertained himself by making unacceptable proposals to Mary Couples. His hand stroked the seam of his fly as his mind dropped further into his cold, dark world.

At 4.30 p.m. he swung his legs off the bed, straightened his trousers, put on his jacket, the white hat and a pair of sunglasses. He picked up a suitcase and briefcase in matching caramel leather, both monogrammed BL in dark red lettering. He walked down to the taxi rank and asked to be taken to the airport where he checked in his suitcase. He sipped coffee in the lounge and picked out the British and German agents loitering in and around the airport building.

At 5.45 p.m. he went to the toilets, urinated, washed his hands until the room was empty and took the cubicle closest to the wall in which there was yesterday's sports newspaper *A Bola* on the cistern. He locked the door, removed his hat and sunglasses and passed them under the cubicle wall with his briefcase. He removed his suit and red tie and the brown English brogues which followed the hat which was still sitting on the floor. His eyes widened. He checked the newspaper. It was the right one. He had a sudden hysterical vision of a stranger staring at a hat, briefcase and a bundle of clothes, puzzled and then affronted, followed by an interview with the GNR in his stockinged feet.

A dark suit appeared under the cubicle wall. A black hat, a dark blue tie, a pair of black Oxfords, no briefcase. Lazard dressed, left the toilets and walked directly out of the building to the taxi rank and took a cab into the centre of town and a train from Cais do Sodré to Belém.

At 6.20 p.m. a man in a light blue suit, white hat and sunglasses, carrying a caramel briefcase with BL in red on the side, boarded the evening flight to Dakar. As the plane took off the exhausted agents from both sides made their reports.

Sutherland, still shaking at the morning's catastrophe, slumped in his chair, beckoning tobacco into his pipe. Rose let himself into the office, leaned over the desk.

'We seem to have clawed something back from that fiasco outside the legation this morning.'

'Lazard's on the plane?'

'Let's hope Voss's intelligence is correct and he has the diamonds with him.'

'Voss has asked for another meeting.'

'Already?' asked Sutherland.

'He's rated it even higher priority than last night.'

Voss, having made his dead-letter drop to the British on the way back from the legation, sat in the Estrela Gardens waiting for Paco. He tapped his knee with yet another newspaper, thinking this business was an editor's dream. When this war was over there'd be a circulation drop of a thousand because one thing nobody ever did was *read* the newspapers, which were heavily censored. There was also the question of the Portuguese journalistic style, which was not dissimilar to Wolters' description of the contessa's intelligence reports, except there were the four hundred petticoats and then, damn, no ankle.

Paco dropped on to the bench. He smelt worse, as if he was sweating some disease out of his system – something bad like yellow fever or plague. In fact, Paco had a black rim to his lips on the inside of his mouth, reminding Voss of yellow fever's common name – black vomit.

'Are you sure you're not sick?' asked Voss.

'No sicker than I was at lunchtime.'

'You said you were all right then.'

'I'd been lying down,' he said, resting his knees on his elbows, hunched forward as if constipated.

'So what's the matter?'

'I don't know. I'm always sick. So was my mother and she lived to be ninety-four.'

'Go and see a doctor.'

'Doctors. Doctors . . . they just say: "Paco, with you the good Lord should have started again." Then they charge some money. I don't go to doctors.'

'What about the address?'

'It's a communist safe house.'

'How do you know?'

'They're not careful. The PVDE will find that place in no time.'

'Give it a few days, Paco.'

'*I* won't tell them. Those Reds,' he said, shaking his head, 'they'll advertise it in their magazine, *Avante*, on the property rentals page.'

Paco's face strained into the closest expression he could get to a laugh but only managed to look as if he was passing a belligerent stool.

Voss walked up to his apartment with the uneasy feeling that he could catch something from Paco. That Paco could be the death of him.

Chapter 19

Tuesday, 18th July 1944, Voss's apartment, Estrela, Lisbon.

Voss was sitting on the back of his sofa, looking out of the dormer window of his top-floor apartment over the Estrela Gardens and the square in front of the basilica. Anne had already come out of the gardens and he'd recognized Wallis leaning against the railings, reading the predictable newspaper. He was interested to see how she would deal with Wallis, who glanced up as she crossed the square and entered the basilica. Wallis took up a position in the shade by the entrance, lit a cigarette, rested a foot behind him against the wall. Pigeons took off from one of the basilica's towers, performed a circuit, relanded. A nun mounted the steps, brushing past Wallis. Two boys with shaved heads, filthy shirts and bare feet sprinted out of the gardens pursued by a policeman with his truncheon out. His cap came off, bounced off his back. Voss put his hand into the cold, wet towel sling he had hanging from the bolt of the window, testing the cool of the wine bottle. He smoked, flicked ash down the tiles in front of the window.

'How much time do you spend looking out of that window waiting for your girlfriends?'

He twisted and fell back awkwardly on to the sofa. She was sitting in a wooden armchair with her feet out of her shoes. Her face was set hard, not lovely, not how he remembered it in the kind flicker of a match flame. He smiled. This is what he liked about her – always challenging. He started forward but came up against some unseen field which repelled him, pushed him back on to the sofa.

'Where do I fit in?' she asked. 'Which shift?'

He smoked hard, thinking, glancing up at her.

'You can throw one of those across,' she said.

He got up again.

'Throw it.'

He threw the packet, which she caught one-handed. She picked up a book of matches from the table, read the cover. She lit her cigarette.

'The Negresco,' she said. 'You know, Beecham Lazard offered to take me there one night. He said it was *the* place to be seen in Lisbon for elegant couples ... people like, for instance, Judy Laverne and Patrick Wilshere, I should think. Is that where you take yours?'

'My what?'

'Of course, *I* don't even get to see the inside of the Negresco,' she said. 'I get a glass of lukewarm white wine, and then what? I suppose it's bed.'

She glanced at the bed visible through the door to the bedroom, a single, ascetic, hard-looking anchorite's cot, rather than a Lothario's empire bed, decked in shot silk and notched with conquests. She dragged on the cigarette.

'Is this an English thing?' he asked. 'One of those humorous things that we Germans don't understand.'

Her glare was fierce, oxyacetylene harsh. Voss didn't take his eyes off her in case she threw something. He crushed out his cigarette in the ashtray on the table between them. Drew back, slow movements as if with a wild animal. He wasn't sure how to proceed now, like a comedian who's tipped his audience over into tragedy and can't get them back. Her eyes shifted to the bedroom again and then around the living room, taking in the shelf with three books and a family photograph, two landscapes on the wall, the bottle of wine in the towel, the carpets beaten and clean, the dark red sofa with two dents, neat.

'I don't like to be one of a crowd,' she said.

He nodded, taking it in, not understanding. He checked the room, as she had, to see if there were answers amongst his few possessions.

'Are you an honourable man, Mr Voss?'

'I've never been to the Negresco, if that helps.'

She flung the book of matches at him. They fluttered and landed in no man's land.

'I know,' he said, 'but I've never been there. They were given to me.'

186

'Who by?'

'Er, Kempf, I think.'

'*Mein Kempf*, no doubt,' she said.

He studied her, the small, silly, throwaway pun taking its time to work through the confusion of the initial minutes. He blurted a laugh, then a wheezing chuckle, followed by an open-mouthed belly roar and finally silent hysteria, which was fuelled by Anne's maintenance of the steel line of her unsmiling lips. She held it for a minute until Voss's madness filled the room and the thought occurred to her that this was a man who must be kept very short of decent jokes, which set her off. 'I bought some wine,' he said, wiping tears out of the corner of his eyes with the knuckle of his thumb.

'And glasses?'

He left the room, came back with two tumblers. She watched his movements, his face. Boyish. Eager to please. Tenderness, which had been tied up outside the door, managed to creep in and settle under the table.

'I'm thinking,' he said, 'that somebody has told you something about me.'

'That you're a womanizer.'

'Funny,' he said, 'I don't know anybody in Shell. Oh, except Cardew, I know Cardew to say hello to . . . but not to exchange my private life with him . . . and he's married, he wouldn't go to the Negresco, couldn't possibly have seen me even if I had been there.'

They drank the first glass of wine quickly and Voss repoured, Anne with her eyes on him, not letting him go for a second – Sutherland's words gone now, her day on the rack forgotten.

'So you *are*,' she said.

'A womanizer? To be honest, Anne . . . and honourable with you . . . there's been the opportunity here in Lisbon, but not the inclination. I work and I sleep. There's little time in between. Whoever told you . . .'

'They had their reasons,' she said.

'They?' he said. 'A collective attack. It seems one can make enemies in Lisbon without even trying.'

'*He* was being protective.'

'You know what I'd like?' said Voss, looking at the door. 'That in here it's just us.'

There was a pause while all the unwanted guests got out. Anne walked over to where he was sitting on the sofa on trembling legs. She threw her cigarette out of the window and put a hand through his hair while she drained the glass of wine. She kissed him and he groaned as if something had snapped inside him. He pulled her on to the sofa, her neck rested on the back, her hair spread out all over. They kissed madly, knowing that the kissing wasn't going to be enough. Her tumbler rolled across the floor.

Voss pulled away, rested his neck on the back of the sofa, held her hand. Her eyes drifted around the room taking in the softening light, the warm air. She knew that everything was going to happen here, that her whole life was going to take place in this room. He kissed her knuckles, turned to her, spanned her slim waist with his hand, moved it up her ribcage, felt her shivering underneath. She rolled towards him, held his face, searched the fragile contours. He ran a hand down her spine so that she pushed her hips to him. She pulled at the knot of his tie, inexpert, reduced it to a hard nut. He pulled the tie off over his head, tossed it away and found the hem of her dress, the warm, smooth skin of her leg. He watched as she undid his shirt buttons, better with those. She tugged the shirt out of his trousers, pushed her hands up his body. He bent down, kissed her knee, her thigh, each touch of his lips welding him to her. She undid the buttons of her dress so that it fell open. He kissed her stomach, her breasts still encased in their bra. She peeled his shirt back off his shoulders, down his arms, cuffing his hands behind him. He wrestled with himself, like a madman in a straitjacket. She shrugged off her dress, unhooked her bra. He hopped about, tearing off his shoes and socks, threw his trousers, showering money, keys and coins. He pulled her away from the dress which was left open on the sofa, ravaged.

He walked her to the bedroom, took off his shorts and sat on the narrow bed. He kissed her stomach, drew her knickers down her long legs. Their bodies tensed as they touched in full-length nakedness. He kissed her all over, each individual rib, the tiny, hard, brown nipples, while her hands found every bone and muscle in his back.

They looked into each other's faces as he eased into her, the pain twitching around her eyes. She loved his bony hardness, the trace of hair that joined his nipples, the ridges of his stomach straining under the thin, stretched layer of skin. She looked down his body to the dark join and wanted all of him. She brought her knees up and dug her heels into the dents in the sides of his buttocks, spurring him on.

She woke up with her lips on his skin, her head on his chest rising and falling. Beyond the cliff of his ribs, down the flat landscape of his stomach, his penis slept. She reached for it, examined it, played with it, almost politely, until it enlarged and she became more strenuous. Her tongue flickered over the salty skin on his ribs. The tendons in his feet surfaced as his toes curled away from the end of the bed. His thighs twitched, his stomach quivered. She turned to his creased face, his closed eyes, his open mouth straining against the sweet agony so that she had to kiss him, lightly on the lip, while in her hand he leapt.

He rolled and looked through the bedroom door. She was kneeling on the sofa, naked, her elbows up on the window ledge, her face to the evening light, birds sweeping across the square of sky in the frame. His eyes traced the cello of her body. He went to her. She glanced at him over her shoulder and then back to the sky. He put his hands on either side of her elbows on the window ledge, kissed her back, each individual vertebra from bottom to neck, until she trembled. She reached behind, pulled him in to her, rested her chin on her arms, felt her nipples harden against the cracked paint of the window ledge. His hands held her at the cello's waist, the hardness of his thighs feathering against the back of her legs, and the bells started up for evening Mass. He took it as some sort of signal and began in earnest. She braced herself against the window, threw her head back laughing at the profanity of it, the bells so loud they could both shout at the reddening sky and not be heard.

Naked, they sat at either end of the sofa, her knees between his, a single glass of wine on top and a shared cigarette, no light in the room. He'd asked about her family and she was talking about her mother, her real mother, and Rawlinson – but not by name – with his wooden leg. How her mother had got her the job because she didn't want her daughter to hear her with her peg-leg *beau*, helping him off with it at night, leaning it up against the wall and finding

189

her waxing and polishing it in the mornings for him before he went to work. Voss was laughing, shaking his head at the irreverence, never heard a woman speak like this before. He asked about the father, who was dead, nothing more, but she wouldn't look at him.

'I want to get dressed and go for a walk,' she said, 'with you. Like lovers would . . . afterwards.'

'It's not safe here,' he said. 'The city's different. Everybody's watching . . . As you said, oil is sensitive.'

'Oil,' she repeated, eyes wandering.

'It's all right to meet at a cocktail party, Anne, but . . .'

'I want you to call me Andrea,' she said.

'Andrea?'

'Not a question . . . a name.'

Voss stood up and looked out of the window, surveyed the square and what he could see of the gardens. He knelt back down, said the words into her mouth.

'I was interested to see how you'd lose him . . . Wallis.'

'You knew it . . .' she said, their eyes locked.

'I saw you go into the basilica.'

'There's always more than one way out of a church,' she said. 'How long have you known?'

'The contessa gave a report to Wolters,' he said, sad at how work had come back into the room like an engine starting up, ruining silence. 'And others have noticed you.'

'I didn't last very long.'

'Everybody knows everybody in Lisbon by now,' he said, and then as an afterthought, striding ahead: 'All we have to do is hang on, survive, until the end.'

He wiped the thoughts of Beecham Lazard on a plane to Dakar, of another plane that could fly over Dresden just as the leaves were turning red and gold.

'It's already dark,' she said. 'We'll walk. I'll hold on to your arm. I want to show you something.'

'We can't leave together,' he said and gave her directions to a small church in the Bairro Alto.

Olivier Mesnel had spent the afternoon and evening stretched out on the floor. His room was like a furnace, his mattress thin and stuffed with something horrible like half-ground bonemeal, so it was always more comfortable lying on the floor on the strip of frayed carpet. His mind wouldn't leave him alone, wouldn't stop questioning him like some ghastly inquisitor off in the dark. Why had the Russians chosen him for this? How could they possibly think he was capable of such an act?

His stomach was shot, completely burnt away, a rag of threadbare tripe. He would never be the same, digestion was something that had happened to him as distant as learning biology at school. He couldn't remember his last solid motion, he would check the bowl to make sure he hadn't given birth to his innards. He was carcass. Carcass with a mind that scribbled inside, like the mosquitoes at night close to his ear.

He stood on his thin, shaking legs in the ludicrous sleeves of his pants, his buckled chest panting in a dishcloth vest. He stepped into his trousers whose waistband still had residual damp from the morning walk to Rua da Arrábida. Traffic gushed on the Rua Braancamp. He pulled on a shirt and jacket, a dark tie. He dabbed the sweat out of his moustache. He sat on the edge of the torture bed, his pelvis painful to his fleshless buttocks. The revolver which he'd taken delivery of that morning from the local communists lay under the pillow. He slid it out and reminded himself of its workings, checked the chambers, four bullets only. Enough.

'Russians,' he said to himself, a snippet from the tape of his thoughts. 'Why have the Russians chosen *me* to be an assassin? I'm an intellectual. I study literature. And now I fire bullets into people.'

At 9.30 p.m. he found himself sweat-slicked on the edge of the city so unable to control his fear and apprehension that he'd taken to walking backwards for several paces at a time until the inevitable had happened and now one side of him was covered in street dust, his left arm dead below the elbow and an imprint of the revolver on his flank.

Rui and his partner were following Voss's orders and shadowing him from behind and in front, used to the man's problems after all these months. They were bored. They knew, as always, where he was heading. It was a hot night and they didn't want to be out in it, especially not following the Frenchman. When they arrived at the Monsanto hills they let Mesnel get ahead so that he could perform his usual disgusting business with the gypsy boys in the caves. They lay down in the burnt, dry grass and talked about cigarettes which neither of them had.

Mesnel waited for his two shadows as he had done on a number of occasions before when he'd come to these meetings. He satisfied himself that they weren't following, turned away from the caves and began the brutal ascent to the Alto da Serafina and the view-point high above the western end of Lisbon. He sat exhausted on a rock and stared open-mouthed at the aura over the city, its dark-crowded edges pricked with light, a view of a different galaxy. Sweat dripped off his chin. He wanted away from this. He wanted Paris. A Paris that would be free in months, maybe weeks. He would have survived the occupation but . . . the Russians had asked him to do this thing. For the Party.

'You can't see the mulberry trees this time of night,' said the American voice behind him, soft, a presence that had been there all the time watching him.

'The worm turns it to silk,' said Mesnel, to identify himself.

'You alone?'

'You know I'm alone. My apostles are down there, as usual, lying in the grass talking about football. Benfica. Sporting.'

The American moved around him, stepped on to his rock and then in front of him, his face not visible.

'So what did you get for me?'

Mesnel sighed. A hot breeze blew from the city bringing stink and pollution.

'You did see your guys?' asked the voice. 'I told you this was the last chance.'

'As you know it's not so easy without a Russian mission in Lisbon.'

'We been through that a few times already.'

'But I did see them, yes.'

'So what did they offer for the opportunity not just to become an atomic power but to prevent the Germans from becoming one, too?'

'They didn't,' said Mesnel, shifting his position, his hand easing over towards the hardness on his left hipbone.

'They didn't?' said the American. 'Do they understand what we've been talking about? That this is a unique opportunity to get on even terms with the United States in the production of an atomic bomb. Did they really understand that? I know you're a university man, but did you tell them right?'

'I told them correctly . . . as you told me. They understand,' said Mesnel, 'but they're not interested.'

'How long have we been talking, Monsieur O?'

'Some months.'

'Some months? It's been nearly five months. And it's after five months that they decide they're not interested?'

'Monsieur, you can't just pick up the phone in Paris and call Moscow. We haven't even been able to call London for four years. Imagine what it's like. It all goes by courier . . .'

'You're boring me.'

Mesnel moved his hand again.

'And don't move.'

'I only want to wipe my face. It's a hot night, monsieur.'

The American, who'd had his hand in his pocket, released the safety catch on his revolver, took it out of his pocket and rested it on Mesnel's forehead.

'What is this?' said Mesnel, bowels liquefying as his own hand closed over the butt sticking out of his waistband. He heard the hammer click back.

'It's a Smith & Wesson revolver, Monsieur O.'

'I'm only the messenger,' said Mesnel.

'Are you?' said the American. 'I don't know who you are any more, but you're not the guy who's brought me a Russian offer which I've been waiting for very patiently for five months.'

'They've seen your sample drawings of the structure of the pile, just as you gave them to me. They had better intelligence themselves from inside the American project. That is all. There is nothing to be gained from shooting me . . .'

'They have better?'

'That's what they said. They have their own people in America.'

The revolver slipped on Mesnel's greasy forehead. He fell to one side. The American fired, grazing Mesnel's head. Mesnel tore out his own revolver but the American was on him. The revolver back in his face, on his eye, jammed into the socket with anger.

'Just the messenger, Monsieur O?'

'Not now, monsieur, please,' said Mesnel, close to tears. 'It's nearly the end of all this. Paris will be liberated in weeks. Please, monsieur, it's nearly all over.'

'I know,' said the American, nearly kind. 'It's just policy.'

A second shot and the whining finally stopped in Mesnel's head.

Rui and Luís had heard the first shot, it brought them to their feet.

'What was that?' asked Rui.

'Don't be an idiot, *homem*.'

'What do you think?'

The second shot.

'I think that the boys in the caves don't have guns.'

They ran down the hill, split up and walked back into the safety of the well-lighted city.

Voss was waiting for her in the shadows of the church in Largo de Jesus. They came together as if they'd been a week apart. She as excited as a child, wrapped her arms around his neck, crushed the tendons. He held her, nearly paternal. She kissed him, moulded herself to him.

'Now can we walk,' she said.

They went behind the church, through the back alleys, across the Rua do Século and into the narrow streets of the Bairro Alto. Relief had come for the people of the Bairro with the cool of the night. Their windows and shutters were open and there was the smell of fried onions and garlic, the grilling of fish. Families murmured on the other side of lace curtains and the tentative plucking of the strings of a Portuguese mandolin joined the rattling of feet on the cobbles.

A woman's voice started up, sang a single tremulous phrase and stopped, as did the people in the street. Women appeared in doorways, dark women, dark as dates, feet bare under their colossal skirts hiding ranks of children. The lovers leaned back against a flaking wall to listen. Another phrase, a wail to silence, the words not discernible, comprehensible only as a terrible sense of loss or the pity of it. The voice rose again. They listened, despite having found what this voice had lost. All love born with an innate understanding of its fragility.

They pushed through the streets, always walking across the steep slope, until they broke out into the Rua São Pedro de Alcântara.

194

They walked up the hill following the silver threads of the tramlines until they reached the boarding stage of the funicular. They crossed the road and drifted under the dark trees and along the railings of a small park as the lighted carriage of the funicular began its groaning descent.

They were alone. The lights of Lisbon were spread out before them across the Baixa below and up to the medina of the Alfama and the Castelo de São Jorge. She leaned against the railings, dragged him to her by the lapels, wanted to squeeze him into her.

'Is this completely normal?' she asked.

'I don't know,' he said. 'I've only been in love once.'

'Who with?' she asked, those few words opening up an abyss.

'You,' he said, 'crazy.'

She laughed, relief flooding the momentary chasm, and realized the absurd frailty of any commitment. It all hung by threads and words could sabre through them.

They talked, lover's talk. Talk unbearable to the ears of normal mortals with jobs and attic rooms and small coins for the rest of the week. Talk that married people might hear in small snatches in cafés and bars and shake their heads. Talk that might make a wife look at a husband and try to remember if he'd ever said things like that. Talk that was so interesting that Anne forgot there was a world with cigarettes until Karl produced a crumpled packet and they held on to the bars of the railings and smoked.

The Baixa below them began to fill with mist drifting up from the river. Buildings blurred, their lights diffused. The castle glowed in grainy luminescence. Anne leaned back into him, fists clamped to the railings below his.

Karl looked at his watch.

They walked back through the Bairro, the streets and doorways still full of people, Voss nervous now, looking for faces he knew, who knew him. They split up and took different routes back to the Estrela Gardens. Voss ran back up to his apartment and found the gun given to him by the colonel from the Free Poles. He wanted it with him now at all times. He wasn't just protecting himself any more. He put the gun in its cloth back in the tool box in the boot. He picked her up from a dark street by the gardens and took her back to Estoril, the glare of the headlights butting against the sea mist that hung just off the coast. The air cool on that side. He dropped her in a street away from the casino, crushed a kiss on to her lips and took his usual long roundabout route to the gardens of Monserrate.

Chapter 20

There'd been a bad scene in the kitchen at Hal and Mary Couples' small house in Cascais in the late morning. The heat had just worked its way under the roof and there seemed to be nowhere in the house where the distance between them could be described as comfortable. So they stood on either side of the kitchen table, holding on to the chair backs, shouting at each other over a pair of soiled and crumpled knickers.

'Maybe you should ask yourself,' screamed Mary, 'maybe you should ask yourself what you're doing going through my dirty laundry.'

'But I'm not,' said Hal, 'because that was not the crime.'

'Crime? Since when has it been a crime? Maybe that says more about you, Hal Couples, than it does about me.'

'I'm just asking you, who you did it with and why. You tell me and it's finished. We'll work it out and move on from there.'

She leaned over the chair back, heavy breasts. His eyes flickered from her face to her cleavage and back up.

'Beecham Lazard,' she said, a whisper over the crumple of white cotton on the table.

His face twitched on one side as if she'd slapped it.

'You *slept* with Beecham Lazard?' he said, the words coming out piecemeal from his perplexed mind.

'Not *slept* exactly,' she said, straightening up.

'When?' he asked, sharp as a hatchet.

'At the cocktail party.'

'You went upstairs at Wilshere's cocktail party?'

'Not upstairs. We found someplace in the garden.'

Hal squeezed his eyes shut with his fingers and thumb, gripped the flesh over the bridge of his nose.

197

'I don't get it,' he said to himself. 'I thought you hated Beecham Lazard.'

Mary was unnerved. She'd expected, wanted, a different reaction, more explosive, more physical. If there'd been a crime, there should be punishment. But not this, not reason, because there was no reason, not one that had surfaced in her mind.

'We've been living a long time like this,' she said.

Hal's guts went cold. He reached for the half-smoked cigar in the ashtray, plugged in its chewed end, relit it.

'There's been some pressure,' he said, to get some thinking time, to keep at bay what was coming out in the room.

'The man and wife bit,' she said, and pushed her arms together so her cleavage swelled, 'you know . . . but not.'

Hal puffed hard. What is this? He stared at the underwear, blinked at it. She's cracking up. For Christ's sake, push back the stuffing, doll, we've only got twenty-four more hours of this to go.

'Maybe you should go and pick up the mail,' he said.

She nodded, backed away from the table, turned into the hall. She checked herself in the mirror, applied lipstick. She left the house. He watched her hips walk down the street. He picked up the underwear, went back to the bathroom and laid it on the lid of the laundry basket where he'd found it. Women don't leave their underwear lying around like that, he thought, and tipped the lid over.

Hal Couples – Harald Koppels – had been an Ozalid salesman in Los Angeles for twelve years when the FBI came to him one night in early 1942 and gave him two options: jail on a spying charge or work for the government. He was divorced and living alone and he could see that this could be the undramatic end to what had been a short life. He took their offer, turned Ozalid inside out for them and GAF and Agfa, too. Handed them all the names of anybody of whom he had the slightest suspicion of spying. He did his bit, but they kept that hook stuck in his gullet and wouldn't let him off. One last job, they said. You're going to Lisbon to look up an old friend. This is your new wife, her name's Mary, she's going to keep an eye on you. What they didn't say was: Don't go to bed with Mary, it makes her nuts. He went to bed with her, but it wasn't what he wanted, so he slept in the spare room and took his fun where he could find it. Mary started to go nuts.

*   *   *

198

Now it was night and they were sitting in the living room, Mary with her feet up on the sofa, reading a fashion magazine, fanning herself with the pages. She hadn't eaten all day, had a stomach full of olive sticks and could have used the dry martinis to go with them. She wanted to talk to him but he'd been in professional mode all afternoon, preparing his product, the strips of microfilm with the plans, the dots with the building specs. He fed film into the seams of the buff envelope, attached microdots to the documents to go inside. She clapped her heel with her shoe, the foot nodding in the corner of his eye, the beat in his ear. He didn't look up.

'Oh, Hal,' she said, back in her wifey voice, 'I can't wait 'til we get back.'

He nodded. She flicked the pages, sighed.

'I'll meet him on my own if you want,' he said, a vague hope.

'It's not what he's expecting,' she said, her voice grating, as if this was a trip to a difficult in-law.

Maybe he should let her have the drink. That might help. He went into the kitchen, fixed two Tom Collins with lots of ice. They drank, but it didn't smooth him out. He finished the work.

'You ready?' he asked.

'As I'll ever be, Hal.'

He put a dark jacket on over his dark shirt, ran a comb through his hair.

'You look nice, Hal.'

He fixed her with a look. She unpinned it, went over to him and brushed off his shoulders, straightened his lapels, made the hair on the back of his neck stand up.

'It was only sex, Hal,' she said from behind him. 'Nothing important.'

'Yeah, but it wasn't part of the brief,' he said. 'We don't know what it means when we get up there. How it's going to affect the deal we're doing with him.'

'It won't mean anything, Hal,' she said. 'Now that I know.'

There it was again.

'Mary,' he said, 'I'm not sure who you are any more – what you want.'

'I'm your wife, Hal,' she said, and that worried him. 'All I want is a little kiss and let's get going.'

He went to kiss her forehead but she tilted her head back and fastened her lips on to his, they were wet and cool from the ice, they were sucking, penetrating and their teeth clashed. It was like eating a mollusc on the half-shell.

She brushed past him into the hall. He followed her dark blouse, black skirt, stockings and soft leather pumps. They got into the car and started driving out of Cascais, heading west on the Guincho road. He checked the rear view and her all the way.

He'd tried to make the OSS pull her out, but she was their agent. He'd insisted that her behaviour could threaten the assignment, but of course, when she was with them, she was always fine. 'It's too important for personal considerations,' they'd said. Now look. The woman's mind unravelling like bad knitting.

'We'll be all right,' she said, 'you'll see. After this we'll get back together and it'll just be you and me.'

She rested a hand on his thigh, kneaded the muscle, and Hal's sole inspiration for getting through the night was a decision to just go along with it.

'Florida,' he said.

'The Keys,' she said. 'You ever been to the Keys?'

'Fishing,' he said, and her hand moved higher and the little finger strayed over his fly.

He removed her hand from his crotch, kissed the back of it, held it on his knee and rubbed it with his thumb.

'They run rum up from Cuba,' she said. 'We could do that.'

'I thought you were talking about a holiday.'

'I was . . . but maybe we could live there, you know . . . the two of us on an island.'

He'd have been pushed to spend ten minutes with her in New York City, let alone a lifetime on a Florida Key. She slipped down the leather seat of the car, rested her neck on the back and let her head loll, wanting him to look. Her skirt had ridden up her thighs to the stocking tops. She stretched her legs out and drew her heels back up but this time with her knees open.

'We'll get tight on our rum,' she said. 'Drink all the profit.'

She laughed and took his hand off the steering wheel and put it on the inside of her thigh, part on the stocking top, part on the

200

hot skin. He swallowed. Christ, this is what happens when you go with it.

'We'll do it on the beach in the open air and it won't matter, not like it does here, with all the bathing suit police.'

She drew the hand up to the apex. He yanked it away as if he'd touched red-hot iron.

'Jesus Christ, Mary, where's your goddamn underwear?'

'You know I don't like blasphemy, Hal.'

'Where is it, for God . . . where is it?'

'I don't have any clean.'

'You can't . . .'

'Nobody's going to know.'

He rubbed the side of his little finger which had come into contact with her damp sex. It itched. The car climbed up through the pine trees of the *serra*.

'This is business, Mary,' he said. 'This is the work, now.'

Her face hardened. She sat up, pushed the skirt back down. The one eye Hal could see had a nasty determination to it. They turned away from Malveira and headed towards Azoia.

'Did I ever tell you about Judy Laverne?' asked Mary.

'No,' he said flatly. He didn't want to hear about her from Mary. He'd liked Judy Laverne. She was one of the few people in American IG who'd been spotless, but it hadn't mattered, she was linked to Lazard, the OSS made sure she was fired.

'That's where she came off the road,' said Mary, as they rounded the bend.

Hal changed gear, turned hard right up a dirt track, doubling back on himself. Mary looked down on the old crash site. Hal slowed and dowsed the lights.

'There were no skid marks in the road,' she said. 'The guys from the OSS said that if the car had been moving at speed the impact point would have been much further down the hill.'

'What are you saying, Mary?'

'I'm saying her car was rolled off.'

Hal was driving with his face up close to the windscreen, the darkness impenetrable amongst the pine trees. They crawled along the ridge.

'By who?' he asked.

'Who do you think?'

'Maybe she wasn't moving that fast.'

'Anyway, it's kinda sad, don't you think?'

'What?'

'That she wasn't even working for us. She'd turned us down and they didn't have anything on her, not like they had with you.'

'So why did they roll her off, Mary?'

'It's a mystery, Hal,' she said. 'A sad mystery. She was crazy about Wilshere. Crazy about him.'

Hal stuck his head out of the open window to see if the visibility was any better and because he didn't want to hear Mary any more, not when she was talking about people being crazy about each other.

They connected with another track, turned right and began a slow descent into the back end of the village of Malveira. The first building they came to was a partially built villa which overlooked the rest of the village on the main road below. The house had a roof and walls but the windows were boarded up, the land around full of builder's detritus, not much evidence of recent work.

They took hurricane lamps from the boot and a flashlight. Mary walked on ahead with the envelope containing all the microfilmed plans. Hal pocketed a small revolver which he'd hidden earlier in the tool box and followed her. They let themselves in with a key, which Hal knew where to find. They lit the lamps, put them on a table made of a board supported by bricks. Hal sat on a column of stacked bricks. Mary paced the room. There was some threat in the way she moved, the careful placement of each foot. He tried to think of some small talk to smooth her out but none came to mind in the heat and smell of cement. At 11.30 p.m. a car pulled up outside. Mary went to one of the boarded-up windows, peered through the crack.

'It's Lazard,' she said.

Mary was applying lipstick, using a hand mirror with the torch balanced in a niche in the wall. Hal and Lazard made the usual identifying exchanges and Hal opened the door.

'Hi, Beech,' said Mary.

'Hal . . . Mary,' said Lazard, shaking hands, except Mary kissed him on the cheek, too. He was sweating and she wiped her lips afterwards.

'Hot night,' said Hal.

'I thought it'd be cooler up here.'

They stood around for a moment, uncertain as to how this business should be conducted.

'I don't have much time,' said Lazard, knowing the flight was due to land in Dakar in an hour.

'Give him the envelope, Hal.'

Hal wanted to hit her, keep her mouth shut. Lazard noted the palpable friction, handed over the diamonds.

'I'm just going to have to check these over quickly,' said Hal.

'Sure,' said Lazard, calmer by the second.

'This your place, Beech?' asked Mary.

Lazard nodded.

'Whyn't you show me around while *Hal* does his work,' she said, and wiggled the flashlight, whose beam happened to be on Lazard's thigh. Hal wouldn't have minded breaking her teeth. Lazard shrugged. Hal went to the table, laid a piece of velvet on the board and poured the diamonds on to it. Mary took Lazard by the arm and went off into the house. Hal watched them leave, the torch beam bouncing around the walls, their voices echoing in the distant rooms. He went to work. Minutes passed.

'We're just going upstairs, Hal,' Mary called, sing-song, from deep in the house.

Back to the stones, Hal counting them, making the basic visual tests as he'd been taught, just to make sure he wasn't getting glass. A noise stopped him. A noise over the loud whistling of the cicadas in the hot, still night. Was that grunting? He didn't believe it. He stood up. Mary's voice, loud and clear. Oh! Yes!

She thinks she's goading me . . . Jesus.

He sat down, shaking his head. Only minutes and it'll all be over. Mary's voice cut through, almost a shriek this time, overplaying the pleasure. She never liked it that much. Hal knew.

Silence. A tense, rock-hard silence. Then a crash, bodies upsetting something, falling into or over . . . He took the gun out of his pocket, moved through the ground-floor rooms to the bottom of the stairs. Not a sound inside the walls . . . only mosquitoes or tinnitus.

Hal walked sideways up the stairs, back to the wall, no bannister on the open side. On to the landing, cracks of light around the

203

boarded window on the far wall. The moon up high now outside. Light came from a doorless room, low light, floor height. He stepped into it. The flashlight lay on the wooden boards. He put the gun into the room first. Against the wall, to the right, Mary lay on her front, the wooden board of a workman's table underneath her, the bricks toppled. She had a length of hemp rope wrapped around her neck so tight that her eyes were halfway out of her head. Her skirt was up over her buttocks, black suspenders, disappearing tracks. A black smear from the crack of her bottom that ran down the back of her thigh to her stockings. Blood.

Hal swallowed hard against the gristle of his Adam's apple, acid rising from his stomach. Nobody had mentioned this kind of thing in any of the briefings. The muzzle of Lazard's revolver screwed itself into his neck.

'Oh, Christ,' said Hal, the horizontals going in his mind.

'Kneel down, just there, behind her,' said Lazard. 'I'll take the gun as you go down.'

Hal's legs shook so much he dropped to the floor as if he'd been rabbit-punched. Lazard slipped the gun out of his wet grip and took hold of Hal's jacket collar to keep him steady.

'Now crawl over to her feet.'

The sweat ran off Hal, sweat and tears because he knew this was it. He'd survived, made it through to the last minute and instead of the new beginning, it was the end of everything. Wasted years. Holy Christ. His head was shaking from side to side as he inched towards Mary's fallen heels.

'Drop your pants.'

He undid his trousers.

'And your undershorts.'

He pushed them down and saw, now, what Lazard had done, what he'd done as he held her by the reins of his garrotte. He wanted to vomit.

Lazard put the gun to Hal's temple, pulled the trigger, the noise thunderous and ringing in the room. He let Hal fall forward. He came to rest with his face in the middle of her back, his groin on her buttocks.

Lazard put the gun into Hal's slack hand and took the front-door key from the dead man's pocket.

Downstairs he poured the diamonds back into the bag, cleared the velvet and Hal's eyeglass. He knocked one of the boards out of a downstairs window, locked the house up, got into his car and drove up into the pine forest of the *serra*.

Chapter 21

Tuesday, 18th July 1944, Monserrate Gardens, Serra de Sintra.

Just before midnight Sutherland, Rose and Voss were in the Moorish pavilion sitting on their usual chairs, smoking, apart from Sutherland, and drinking from Rose's steel tumblers.

'Two nights in a row,' said Rose. 'I hope it's worth it. It's no small operation to secure this place.'

Rose always had his difficulties.

Voss was preparing his words, small words which could accumulate to mean a future for Germany and an end to destruction or the bleak possibility of life under the Russian knout.

'Did you make your communiqué to Wolters?' asked Voss.

'You haven't spoken to him?' asked Sutherland.

'Not since that fiasco outside the German Legation this morning, no.'

'Yes,' said Rose, 'what was that all about?'

'Incompetence on a large scale,' said Voss, 'rather than the usual small-scale idiocies, which are an everyday occurrence in the intelligence world. I assumed you thought my services dispensable. What do you think Wolters made of it? He actually said to me that somebody must have told them something.'

Rose and Sutherland stared at the chequered floor. Voss remembered postal games with his father. Chess. Strong central pawn.

'You said last night that there were two possibilities for Germany to achieve a conditional surrender.'

'Did we?' asked Rose. 'I thought we said that we wouldn't drop an atomic device on Dresden if you would give us the means to destroy your bomb programme or you disposed of your leadership. That's not an offer of conditional surrender.'

'Does that mean,' said Voss, getting to his feet, 'that even if we fulfil those conditions you will not open negotiations?'

Silence, as they watched him move towards the door. There was the smell of sea and pine in the room, clean, as if it might have been possible for things to work out after all.

'It would strengthen your position.'

'That doesn't sound like a "yes".'

'But it's not a "no" either, Voss.'

'I have information about a secret weapons programme. I have the locations of our research laboratories. I have very important intelligence about the German leadership. However, before I give you any of this I must have some assurances. Assurances which, after months of us talking and me giving the highest quality information, have still not been given.'

'We're not just British any more, Voss,' said Sutherland. 'We're Allies.'

'I know, but what do I have to show after months of giving you intelligence? No assurances, only an appalling threat.'

'You told us about the V1 rockets,' said Rose. 'You were right. They came. They fell.'

'With conventional explosives. I told you that, too.'

'One of your . . . compatriots told us, months ago now, that Hitler would be assassinated,' said Rose.

'Still nothing,' said Sutherland.

'We told you about the U-boats,' said Voss. 'We pushed your false intelligence about the June landings in the Pas de Calais to the German leadership. Every day I receive reams of intelligence from your man sitting in his attic room in Lisbon, concocting his stories about British defences and aerodromes and God knows what rubbish, and I pass it on, as if it's the genuine article, not a word out of place . . .'

'Yes, yes, and yes,' said Sutherland, 'but, of that, what has been persuasive enough for us to break agreements with our Allies?'

'Let's be *more* specific,' said Rose. 'With an ally who has so far sacrificed millions of his countrymen to repel an invading army, which in turn has given *us* the opportunity to take the advantage on the western front. If we turn on the Russians now I doubt there'll be peace in Europe for a hundred years.'

'You'll see what'll happen,' said Voss. 'You'll end up with your

207

friends, the Bolsheviks, on your doorstep and you know how it is with them, with Stalin. You can't talk to the man. He'll give you nothing except the cold wind from the steppes.'

'He hasn't failed us yet,' said Rose. 'It would be impossible for us to . . .'

'Tell us, Voss,' said Sutherland, scything through the world politics on which none of them would have the remotest effect. 'By telling us, you at least give yourself a chance.'

Voss had retaken his seat and found that he was now crouched over his knees as if racked by some terrible colic. He sat up and back, drew on his cigarette, drank his drink. That other world came to him, that distant planet less than fifty kilometres away where there had been certainties – a trembling ribcage in his hands and, beyond the bars, the railings, some kind of hope, the faintest possibility.

'You all right, Voss, old man?' asked Rose.

Voss stood up again, another attempt to get away from this, to leave this dried husk, this slough of skin, the knotted nerves and stupid bones underneath.

'Drop of whisky, perhaps, would that help?' said Rose, leaning over with the flask, chugging the spirit in so that it splashed cold on Voss's hand. Voss licked it, found the taste of her in the web between thumb and forefinger and gnawed at it.

'You still there, old man?'

'I look forward,' said Voss, thinking she would be proud of him, 'to seeing you kiss Stalin on his red, moustachioed lips.'

'Now look here, Voss,' said Rose, and Voss did, daring him, thinking where's your sense of humour now, Richard *verdammt* Rose?

Sutherland held up his hand between the two men.

'We are Lisbon station, Voss. That is who and all we are. We communicate everything back to London. We are not able to make political decisions or offers. We can only do what we are told. London is very appreciative of your intelligence . . .'

'We are helping you win the war,' said Voss. 'A war that is nearly over, that will see Europe change, that could see – if you persist with your romantic attachment to the East – half of it sheafed under the scythe and beaten with the hammer. Is that what you want?'

'Very poetic,' said Rose, deadpan.

208

'It's not our decision,' said Sutherland. 'We put your case, believe me. We put your case very strongly.'

'And my reward?' asked Voss, holding out his hands. 'An atomic device will be dropped on Dresden. I thank you for it.'

'Long night ahead of us, you know, Voss,' said Rose, walking behind Sutherland to the fireplace.

'What we *can* do,' said Sutherland, 'is look after *you*.'

'Look after *me*?'

'Here in Lisbon,' said Rose. 'You know how it is when you start losing a war. Start spit-roasting the traitors.'

'For God's sake, Richard,' said Sutherland.

Rose crossed his legs at the ankle, made a suave Noël Coward gesture with his cigarette hand. 'It's true, isn't it?'

'You could be comfortable in Lisbon,' said Sutherland.

'As long as you like your women *morena*,' said Rose, staring into him.

Their argument twitched in Voss's mind. They know something. Wallis must have seen something. But when?

'Do you think my personal safety has been an issue in any of this?' asked Voss. 'Do you think I play this game to save my own skin?'

Sutherland felt instantly shabby, disgusted. Rose, not so.

'It's an option,' said Rose, light as duck down.

These men are no better than SS Colonel Weiss at Rastenburg, thought Voss. Not only is there never any credit with them, but they're paid . . . they're paid not so much to open the chink into the light, but more to find the slimy crevice into the sweaty cavern of men's shameful needs.

'What he means,' said Sutherland, nauseated by Rose himself, 'is that we will make sure you don't go down. If they're closing in on you and we hear about it, we'll get you out.'

'But that is not why I am here. I thought you understood that,' said Voss, directly to Sutherland. 'I'm here . . . I'm here . . .'

'Yes?' said Rose.

Why was he here? What was his motive? He'd never examined it to be put into words. He'd only assumed it. His country? No, that wasn't right. That wasn't precise.

'Why *are* you here?' pressed Rose, taking delight in Voss's discomfiture.

'I'm here because of my father,' said Voss, and nearly wept at the thought of it. 'I'm here because of my brother.'

Sutherland looked mortified. Rose had hoped for something more kitsch – I'm here to save my country from the Russian bear – that would have satisfied. That could have been punctured.

Voss resumed his seat, looked around the room, felt the quality of their silence. Rose? Damn him. Sutherland. He'd tell Sutherland.

'A new type of rocket will be launched at the end of next month,' said Voss, speaking before he was even aware of it himself. 'It's long range and, unlike the V1, which I understand has been named the doodlebug, it is totally silent. It also weighs fourteen tons.'

'Fourteen tons!' said Sutherland.

'Now come on, Voss,' said Rose. 'What's going to be the payload on something like that? Don't tell us . . .'

'I *am* telling you, if you're prepared to listen. It is these rockets that Hitler is calling his miracle weapons, *but*,' he said, raising a finger, 'they will still be carrying conventional explosives.'

'Where are the rockets?' asked Sutherland, cutting Rose dead.

'Underground. They're in the Harz mountains, not far from Buchenwald. They'll be nearly impossible to destroy from the air.'

'I can't believe . . .' started Rose.

'You'll *have* to believe me.'

'So what is Wolters buying from Lazard?' asked Rose. 'Don't tell us Lazard's coming back with a million dollars' worth of TNT.'

'Lazard is out of our hands now. You'll only find that out when you pick him up in New York. I doubt, if he has any sense, that he'll be wandering about with a case of atomic material.'

'It's an interesting coincidence, though,' said Rose. 'The new, bigger rocket and Lazard's trip.'

'That's why you have to be careful . . . not to lose Lazard,' said Voss. 'Either way you might like to bomb the research laboratories in Berlin-Dahlem. It will give you small satisfaction. I've told you again and again, and you must know from your own research, that the industrial activity to produce the substance of an atomic bomb would be enormous. Unmissable. Germany has neither the money nor the material.'

'But you have Hahn and Heisenberg.'

'They are scientists, not wizards. They are just like Dornberger and von Braun.'

'The rocket men?'

'The difference with Dornberger and von Braun, though, is that *they* have the necessary materials to build rockets. The other two men only have a small half-working cyclotron, a little heavy water left from Rjukan. Even their precious uranium will be thrown at the enemy now that the wolfram supply has been closed off.'

Sutherland checked his watch.

'You said something about the leadership.'

'What time is it?' asked Voss.

'Past midnight.'

'Tomorrow on 20th July some time before midday, Hitler will be assassinated by a bomb planted in the situation room at his headquarters in Rastenburg,' said Voss, calmer about it now, but still expecting to make a big impression.

'How many times did we hear that from Otto John in March?' jeered Rose.

'But not from me . . . now,' said Voss. 'The assassination will launch Operation Valkyrie. I will arrest or shoot SS General Wolters and any other SS men in the legation. At that point, gentlemen, I hope and presume we will be able to start our proper negotiations.'

'And if the assassination attempt fails?' asked Sutherland.

There was a knock on the glass of the door. One of the agents under the colonnade asked permission to interrupt. Rose went outside, talked to the man behind the closed door.

'To answer your question,' said Voss. 'Few of us, if any, will survive but it will be a deliv—'

Rose wrenched the door open, slammed it shut behind him. The glass rattled in the frame.

'Lazard wasn't on the plane when it landed in Dakar,' he said.

Chapter 22

Anne walked the warm, quiet streets until she came out into the casino square. She skirted the parking area, keeping to the deeper shadow beneath the dark spread of the trees. She was looking for Jim Wallis but he wasn't there, not sitting in any of the cars. She went into Wilshere's garden, through the gate. Waited. Still no Wallis. She knew she should go back up to the house and get some sleep before working on the safe in the early hours of the morning but she didn't want to see Wilshere. She went down to a café in the square, straightened herself out in the ladies room and looked for Wallis, expecting to see him in the bar looking after her again. She found an empty table, ordered a brandy and soda. Still no Wallis, but people. She needed to be amongst people. She stayed there until the waiters started turning up the chairs. She walked back up to the house and sat in the darkness of the bower until 1.00 a.m.

She took the shoes off her aching feet and went back up to the house whose windows were dark. She thought about the safe, wondered if she should just go straight in now and open it, but exhaustion hit her as she tripped across the lawn and she stood for a moment rolling her head on her shoulders, thinking of Voss and the room over the Estrela Gardens. Her eyes were half-closed ready for sleep when she went up on to the back terrace, nudged into a piece of the garden furniture which jabbed her thigh.

'Ah,' said Wilshere, as if he'd been waiting all evening, relief in his voice. 'Been working late?'

She was irritated to find him there, sitting at one end of a bench with bottle and glass in front of him, two packets of cigarettes piled on the table.

'I went out with someone from work.'

'Where did you go?'

'The Negresco,' she said. 'I'm tired.'

'Shell must be paying well these days,' he said, and patted the bench beside him. 'Have a seat.'

'I've had a long day.'

'Drink?' he asked.

'I just want to go to bed.'

'Just a quick one. Keep an old man company on a long, hot night.'

She dropped her shoes, sat on automatic, yawning.

'Nothing complicated, if you don't mind,' he said. 'Have to get it myself. Servants really are off tonight.'

'All of them?'

'Like to be alone sometimes,' he said. 'You don't know what a strain it is to be with people all the time. Never have the place to yourself. Never . . . private. So . . . every so often . . . we pack them off. They've all got families around here. Bit of peace and quiet. Remind myself how to make a sandwich.'

He made her a brandy and soda, which she didn't really want. He lit cigarettes, sat on the bench with his arm along the back.

'They say the weather's going to break,' he said.

'There was a fog in Lisbon.'

'Yes, that's supposed to mean something but I can't remember what.'

His finger came to rest on her shoulder. She glanced at it, set her jaw. She shifted her shoulder while crossing her legs and looked him in the eye, so that he'd know that these invasions were not allowed any more. It signalled something to him. He held her look, returning her cold, hard stare with a slack, expressionless face. The sexual confidence she had to stare him down vanished, and was replaced by undiluted panic. It wasn't her life she was afraid of losing so much as everything that had just started. To be nothing now, to cease to exist after the beginning of something new would be terrible. She turned away from him.

'Why am I here?' she asked, taking a large slug of the brandy, needing a bottle to see this one out. 'Why did you invite me to come and stay at your house?'

'To spy on me,' he said, quite calm.

Her breathing shallowed, the blood drained out of her lips, how cold they went. She put the cigarette to them knowing from her short study of the history of spying that nobody says something like that without having drastic intentions.

'Spy?' she said, a lame effort at denial.

'Cardew's an amateur. Most of the rest of them think they're not. Rose, Sutherland, all the people they've sent to my door. Do you think I could have supplied Germany with diamonds through-out the war without knowing who's who in the SIS and all their stupid tricks? Amateurs, the lot of them. The local drama group could do better.'

It was so still, not even the smoke moved off. Her brain crashed through the possibilities. All she'd heard in this house had been gifted to her. Parcelled. Not one piece of unconsidered information. Lazard. The diamonds. New York. If that was so, there were no variables left. She worked out the equation. Lazard – American IG – Ozalid. Lazard had known Hal Couples before. Hal Couples, still working for Ozalid, had picked something up and was now selling it for the diamonds supplied by Wilshere.

'Hal Couples,' she said.

'Bravo,' he said and clapped, a slow sardonic clap. All he could manage for the local drama group.

'What does he have that's worth that sort of money?'

'Nuclear know-how,' he said. 'The core to the atomic apple. Don't ask me the ins and outs.'

'You'd let Lazard sell that to the Germans?'

'You're too involved with your own game to see what's happen-ing on the other pitch.'

'What other pitch?'

'Anything the Germans do to bring closer a united Ireland is fine by me,' said Wilshere. 'They can reduce London to ashes and we'll run the dogs out of the north.'

She needed to talk. That would extend things. She had to unbal-ance Wilshere but even then, no Wallis, no back-up.

And why me? That was another thought that was not helping her.

Wilshere moved down the bench, put his arm all the way around her, his warm dry palm cupped her shoulder – no sex, avuncular now. The only idea that came up in her head and wouldn't go away was Judy Laverne, Wilshere's weakness.

214

Why not play out her theory? What had been her greatest fear had probably been Wilshere's too. Keep twisting the blade stuck in his ribs, see what happens when steel grates against bone.

'There was somebody, wasn't there, who got through?' she said.

'None of them . . . they were all hopeless.'

'You're forgetting Judy Laverne. She was a professional. When did you find out about her?' she said, and Wilshere's arm flinched.

'Find out what?' he asked.

'That Lazard wasn't quite telling you the truth.'

'Lazard?' he said, more intrigued.

'He tried to persuade you that she was seeing other men, didn't he?' she said, dredging up the diary. 'He must have known she was a spy, though. Why do you think he'd do a thing like that? Or maybe you know already.'

She could almost hear him blinking. He gripped her arm hard, squeezed the flesh.

'You wouldn't have thought that someone like Beecham Lazard would bother with Shakespeare.'

'Shakespeare?' he said, confused.

'*Othello*,' she said. 'He doesn't seem the cultured type, does he? I think it must have just been an innate understanding of the . . . of the manipulative power of jealousy. I suppose if he'd done it the other way round – told you that she was a spy first – he wouldn't have had the same measure of control over you, would he? And that's what Lazard's after in all his dealings, isn't it? Control. Whose idea was it to get me to come and stay, yours or his?'

'I know what you're doing,' he said.

'*You* are hurting my arm,' she said, feeling stronger now.

He stopped squeezing, stroked instead.

'What's going to happen to you has already been planned,' he said, 'but keep talking, you're amusing me.'

'But you don't answer, do you?' she said. 'I don't think you're being fair.'

She reached for her drink. He grabbed at her arm, then let her pick up the glass, put it down for her. They smoked.

'I was relieved at first,' said Wilshere.

'That she was a spy?'

'It explained everything,' he said, and Wilshere's confirmation spooled out the ramifications.

'Except one thing, surely.'

'Ye-e-es,' he said, and never had the affirmative been so despairing.

'How did it come out . . . that she was working?'

'Beecham caught her. She got careless one day, disturbed things on his desk, which made him watchful. So eventually he left the office and came back suddenly to find her . . . *in flagrante.*'

'What was she looking for?'

'The diamond trail. There're two ways to stop rockets falling on London. One is to bomb the launch sites, except that bombing isn't accurate and rebuilding the damage is comparatively easy. The other way is to stop the rockets being built in the first place. Cut off the diamond supply, no more precision tools . . . end of rocket programme.'

'How did the Americans know that Lazard was the broker between you and the Germans?'

He seemed on the brink of an automatic answer but then stopped to think. Maybe it wasn't so obvious.

'They knew about him from when he was an executive at American IG.'

'I mean specifically diamonds?'

'I suppose it must have just . . . They knew he was handling a lot of business for the Germans . . . so they put her in there.'

'But who told you she was after the diamond trail?'

'Lazard, of course.'

'But how did she get to you? I'm sure Lazard doesn't leave notes around his office saying four hundred carats of diamonds from Wilshere received 20th May 1944, does he?'

'I think . . . I think what it was . . . it was that she saw Lazard and I together in the casino.'

'One of your little transactions with the high-denomination chips?'

'Yes.'

'And the only way she could think of getting close to you was to fall in love with you?'

Wilshere's cigarette travelled to his lips on trembling fingers. He drank heavily from his glass, topped it up again from the bottle.

'Lazard caught her, as I said. She talked her way out of it brilliantly. She was so ... charming ... so vivacious. It was impossible not to believe every word she said. Lazard accepted her cover story and that night came to see me. He said...' Wilshere swallowed hard, 'he said she had to be ... what were his words? Neutralized, that was it ... she had to be neutralized before she could be pulled out. I was vehemently against it. I didn't ... I couldn't believe it ... And, I mean, why kill her? What did she really know, after all? Let her go, I said. But Lazard said that it wasn't the way things worked, that he had to know what she knew, and what the Americans knew about his operation, so that he could protect his business. I still couldn't accept it. He said: "You'll see, Paddy, she'll be here tomorrow telling you she's got to go ... mother's dying or something, and that'll be it. We'll be exposed." What else did he say? Yes ... that was it: "I know you're sweet on her, Paddy," he said, "but she's a spy. Whatever there is between you and her isn't real, not from her side anyway. We're going to have to cut her out." My God, as if she were a cancer or something.

'I saw her that night. We met in the casino. We danced, played cards, some roulette, had a few drinks. I walked her home. We made love in her single bed and, you know, she wasn't just calm ... she was serene. She was serene and appeared deeply happy. Lazard was wrong, I thought. He just had to be wrong.'

Wilshere hugged Anne to his chest. Smoked the cigarette down to his fingers, which were steadier now that the story was coming out. He lit another and drank more. Anne was silent, her desperate thoughts being interfered with now by Karl Voss and whether that was 'real' and how do you know what's true about anybody anyway? Karl Voss hadn't known about his father's first love. Throwing his ashes on a stranger's grave. And, unbidden, like a piece of dream from the night before that suddenly becomes clear, the image of Mafalda appeared, taking the clay figurine out of her hands, the blindfolded woman – *Amor é cego*. Love is blind.

'The next day Lazard called to say that Judy's visa had not been renewed by the PVDE. She had two or three days to leave. We both called Captain Lourenço but he claimed it was out of his hands. There was nothing he could do. Lazard went to see him, offered money ... nothing. We knew then it was political. Lazard offered Lourenço money just to tell him why she wasn't getting a visa. He said one word – *Americanos*. It was as Lazard had said ...

they were pulling her out. Later Lazard found out there was a petrol contract attached to the deal. I was sick. I did actually vomit. Lazard said we had to act. He told me to get her to drive up in her own car to Pé da Serra . . . that it would be our last day's riding out on the *serra* or something like that. He met us there.'

Wilshere stopped for a moment, his eyes fixed on something so far away that it had to be in the middle of his mind. His grip tightened again on Anne's shoulder. Anne needed the support. Terrible things were happening to her. There was no part of her body that wasn't reacting to the appalling realization of what had happened, that only she, at this moment, understood. Her flesh stood away from her, the body's covering repelled by the calculations of the mind. Air was hard to come by, or she couldn't get the necessary oxygen from it. Wilshere ploughed on, unmoved.

'I spoke to Judy first. She denied everything. She was very convincing, but as soon as I started the questions I saw the fear in her. And she did everything she could, everything. She told me how much she loved me, how I should come with her to America, how different it would be over there, away from the war. And . . . and . . . I didn't believe a word of it. Her fear in that first instant. It was something terrible. I'd reached the pinnacle, the zenith of . . . total love and in that moment it was all dust.

'Lazard took over. He took her off to the stables. He said I shouldn't go. I didn't go. I couldn't watch that. He had to find out what he had to. He tied her up, beat her. I didn't . . .'

He shook his head, denying it all. The part that hadn't happened. Anne was shaking, her heart pattered fast and tight, fingers on a hard drum skin. Wilshere consoled her, rubbing her arm, feeling the goose flesh.

'Lazard put her in the car. She was barely conscious. He forced brandy down her. He drove her to the Azoia junction. I followed in Lazard's car. Lazard pushed me to help him drag her across into the driving seat. I couldn't bring myself to touch her. He sent me back to the car to get the jerry can he had in the boot. He told me cars don't burst into flames on their own. He poured the petrol in all over her. She was slumped over the wheel, the back of her dress all torn and bloody. The petrol fumes brought her round and she flung herself back and it splashed over her face and hair. She started coughing and spluttering and I didn't hear it at first. But even then

218

she was saying . . . she was saying: "But I love you, Patrick. I love you."'

His voice cracked, and he coughed against the emotion in his chest.

'We pushed the car to the edge. Lazard gave me the matches. He was holding the steering wheel. I lit the match and as the wheels went over I tossed it in. I tell you – it went up like a bomb.

'We drove back to Pé da Serra. I got drunk. I got so drunk I woke up in the stables, lying on the cobbled floor in the morning fog and I didn't know who or where I was.'

Anne started to struggle but Wilshere crushed her to him so that she thought her chest wall would collapse under the pressure. She went limp. Fell across him. He kissed her temple, stroked her hair. She sobbed into his shirt.

'Why are you crying?' he asked.

She couldn't speak. She held on to him and wept. He cradled her, strangely . . . paternally.

'Lazard will be here soon,' he said.

Anne sat up, still choking. She drank the brandy down in two gulps, wiped her face with the back of her hands.

'Don't run away,' said Wilshere, who got up and brought the brandy bottle over.

He poured her a large measure.

'No soda,' she said, and lit one of his cigarettes.

Wilshere put the bottle on the table, breathed in the still night with a sense of relief, as if he'd come to terms with something. The brandy glass rattled against her teeth. He took it from her. She brought her heels up on to the edge of the bench and hugged her knees.

'I'm going to tell you something now,' said Anne. 'I'm going to tell you something you won't believe.'

'Then why tell it?'

'Because it's the truth and it's something you should know, even though you might find it hard . . . you might find it unbearable.'

'Believe me, Anne, when I tell you that I can bear anything now. Anything. Nothing is unbearable to me.'

'But not this,' she said. 'Not this.'

'Tell me.'

'The report I made to Sutherland on Monday afternoon about

my first weekend in your house . . . the first part of it . . . was all about Judy Laverne. You know why. You knew what you were doing. I was very worried about the significance of your actions. I thought I was vulnerable. Sutherland, to try and calm me down, told me what he knew about Judy Laverne. He said that she used to work for American IG where Lazard was an executive until after Pearl Harbour. The OSS decided that the company represented a security risk because of its German connections and had to be cleared of all spies and vetted. Judy Laverne subsequently lost her job, probably because of her link with Lazard, who'd been asked to leave on suspicion of dealing for the Germans. When Lazard heard, he invited her over to Portugal to work for him.'

She stopped. Wilshere had drawn up a chair and was sitting opposite her, staring into her as if she was a prophet and every word counted towards his salvation.

'Go on,' he said, desperate to hear more about Laverne. 'Go on.'

'She arrived in Lisbon, started working for Lazard, and the OSS made an approach. They asked her if she would pass on information about Lazard's business dealings. She refused point-blank. She was totally loyal to Lazard, who'd helped her out with a new job. The OSS didn't have anything on her. They left her alone. I asked Sutherland about her deportation order. He said the Americans categorically denied that they had anything to do with it. The first time I met the contessa, you remember I helped her to the car, and as I closed the door for her she said: "Be careful with Senhor Wilshere or Mafalda will have you deported, just like she did Judy Laverne."'

Wilshere's chair shot back away from him. He stood holding on to his head. Anne was not sure whether he was trying to stop hearing what she was saying or whether he was trying to wrench out what he'd just heard. The lines of his face deepened in his agony, as if he'd felt that first tightening in his chest, a prelude to what could only possibly mean death.

'How conclusive was Lazard's proof to you that she was a spy?' asked Anne. 'From what you've told me, you accepted *his* word on everything. But did he actually *show* you anything and did she ever, even in her direst moment, even as Lazard beat her in the stables, even as she went over the edge soaked in petrol, did she ever admit anything that would lead you to believe that she was a spy?'

Wilshere was staring at her through the bars of his fingers, a man caged by his own torment.

'Did he?'

If he did, Wilshere couldn't think of it, didn't have to think of it. He knew.

'You said that it was her fear when you finally questioned her that made you believe in what Lazard had told you, that changed your love to dust. Wouldn't *you* be scared if your lover suddenly made these accusations, wouldn't *you* find that the most terrifying experience, that the man you love more than yourself is questioning your trust? It would be like a dagger in my breast,' she said, 'it would be like seeing the life flowing out of a mortal wound.'

'Shut up!' he said, almost a hiss from behind his hands.

'*Amor é cego,*' she whispered. 'Lazard at least knew that.'

Wilshere didn't seem to know where to put himself, like a man with barbed wire insides, every inch of life was a writhing torment. He dropped to his knees, crawled to the table as if he was remembering the benefits of prayer from a religion he'd dropped decades before. His face came out from behind his hands. He looked like one of Dante's heroes.

'But why?' he said. 'Why?'

Anne barely had to think. Her day on the rack after she'd been told of Voss's womanizing came back to her. The moment that he'd said he'd only been in love once. There was only one answer.

'Because Lazard was in love with her himself.'

No other words could have had that effect. They were so evidently true that they had a calming influence on Wilshere. He stood up, dusted his trousers down, drank a finger of scotch and looked at her, looked through her.

'I don't have any proof of that, Mr Wilshere,' she said, feeling stupid using his name formally like that when they'd just been so close, closer even than lovers could ever hope to get. 'How could I?'

'Of course not,' he said. 'I see that. Nobody could have known that . . . except me.'

'Did Judy Laverne say something?'

He smoothed his moustache with thumb and forefinger, madly, obsessively until all amusement from those turned-up points had been ironed out of it. Throughout this exercise he nodded, as if he had a tic in his mind. Then his face relaxed, his head turned away from her and a smile wandered across his lips.

Beecham Lazard walked up the steps on to the terrace. He was carrying a briefcase and a jacket. He was sweating, but the machine-tooled parting was still in place.

'You look hot, Beecham,' said Wilshere. 'I'm afraid we don't have any ice out here. Can I get you a drink?'

'You know what I'd really like, Paddy,' he said, without bothering to correct himself, using the name Wilshere didn't like. 'I'd really like a bourbon. But I guess that's out of the question, so I'll take a scotch and . . . be generous, Paddy, we're celebrating. I got the plans.'

Lazard waved an envelope as Wilshere handed him the drink. They all stood. The men touched glasses, ignored Anne.

'Let's go to the study,' said Wilshere. 'We'll finish the business there. You'll have to come too, my dear. Can't have you slipping away.'

They carried their glasses up the corridor, filed into the study, Anne in the middle, Lazard prodding her in the back with his finger so that she turned on him.

'You're not my problem,' he said quietly, just between the two of them.

'Problem?'

'I was never wild about the idea of using you,' he said, 'although . . . you're prettier than Voss.'

'Voss?'

Lazard and Anne sat in chairs in front of the desk. Wilshere leaned against it, stared intently at Lazard, who'd put the briefcase on the floor, settled with his jacket and the envelope across his lap, and was sipping scotch unaware of Wilshere's attention. A floorboard creaked above their heads without concerning either man.

'I figured we didn't need two lines of communication to the boys at Lisbon station,' Lazard said to Anne. 'Voss was enough, but Paddy wanted you, didn't you, Paddy?'

'Voss is with the Abwehr,' said Anne.

222

'Don't tell me you didn't know he was a double?' said Lazard, laughing. 'That's how the limeys operate, isn't it, Paddy? Nobody knows what anybody else is doing. It makes life easier for people like us.'

'Why did you need me as well?' Anne asked Wilshere.

'Because,' said Lazard, leaning over the arm of his chair, 'he was very disappointed by somebody else and he thought the Allies should be made to pay for that.'

'I was having a very interesting conversation with Anne, here, before you arrived, Beecham.'

'Oh yeah, what was that about?' he asked, uninterested.

'Well, naturally she was concerned about her future so she was doing a lot of thinking and talking in the hope that she would be able to persuade me that it wasn't going to be necessary for her to be . . . what's that word you use again, Beecham? It always escapes me.'

'Neutralized.'

'Yes, neutralized. Nobody likes to be neutralized. Made neutral. Neutered. I suppose all those words come from the same . . . Latin *ne . . . uter* . . . not either.'

'I don't know what you're getting at, Paddy.'

Nor did Anne.

'We got to talking about somebody else, whom we'd had to neutralize . . . because she'd proved herself untrustworthy,' said Wilshere. 'My disappointment, you call her.'

'You know, time is not on our side, Paddy.'

'Anne told me it wasn't the Americans who arranged for Judy's visa not to be renewed. It was Mafalda. And you know, come to think of it, she'd be one of the few people with influence who could . . . yes, family's very important here, Beecham. Your name gets you a long way, even with people like Captain Lourenço – *especially* with people like Lourenço . . .'

'I really have to move now, Paddy.'

'You've got nothing to say to that . . . Beech?'

'Look, I just came by to tell you we're celebrating . . .'

'Is that the only reason you came by . . . Beech?' asked Wilshere. 'It's something I've been thinking about. Why does Beecham Lazard have to come and see me tonight, his last night in Portugal? Is it to celebrate and say goodbye? Just that?'

223

'Apart from a few little things we gotta tie up, yeah, I think that's it.'

'Are you sure it's not because you had to take one last look at your masterpiece?'

Wilshere was being very strange. Lazard saw it, too.

'I don't collect art,' said Lazard.

'*I* am your masterpiece,' said Wilshere, and Anne's skin came alive – the scalp clung to her head, the hair straining against it.

Lazard's face went dead, only his eyes darted around the room, from Anne, to Wilshere, to the safe. His waxy cheeks twitched out a laugh.

'I asked Anne this question,' said Wilshere " 'What sort of a man would tell another that his lover was seeing other men, then tell him that she was spying on him, and when her visa is not renewed tell him that it was her spymasters pulling her and then not just make him complicit in the murder of his lover but actually get him to light the match, to burn her alive? What sort of a man would do that? *Why* would he do that?" And you know what she said?'

'Paddy, you just *told* me this girl has been trying to get herself off the hook . . .'

'Listen to this line, Beecham, the words . . . are you ready? She said: "Because he was in love with her himself." How does that sound to you?'

Wilshere was standing over him now, tall, wild, as if he'd been out riding on a blasted heath all night.

'Are you OK, Paddy?'

'No, I'm not,' he said, dropping his hands on to the arms of the chair, pushing his face up close to Lazard's. 'You know what Judy Laverne said to me after the third or fourth time we made love? No, you don't, because she would never have said it to you, she could never have been that blunt. She said: "Beecham's got a crush on me . . . he's kind of in love with me, but . . ."'

Wilshere coughed, wretched, gasped. Lazard's arm had shot out and buried itself in Wilshere's crotch – in it was the Smith & Wesson revolver. Wilshere staggered back, thumped against the desk, dropped to his knees holding on to himself.

'Want to be neutered, Paddy?' said Lazard. ' "Not either"? Is that what you want?'

Lazard locked the door, put the key in his pocket. Wilshere was doubled up. Lazard kicked him hard in the leg and toppled him over.

'Get over to that safe, Paddy,' said Lazard, and kicked him again. 'Go on, Paddy.'

He laid into him with his feet, both feet, and then he trampled on him, jamming his heels down into the inert body, strutting and jabbing as if he was a ram asserting his mating rights. Anne rushed at Lazard. He grabbed hold of her front – dress, bra and breast – flung her across the room.

He hauled Wilshere across to the safe.

'Open it, Paddy. Open the safe.'

'She said . . . she said . . .' Wilshere struggled to get the breath to talk, 'she said, "I like Beecham, I like him a lot. He's been very good to me, but physically . . ." Are you listening to this? "But physically . . . he disgusts me." Did you get that, Beecham? "He disgusts me."'

Lazard raised the revolver.

'You hit or shoot me and you'll never get this safe open,' said Wilshere.

Lazard strode across the room, sheafed Anne's hair, wrapped it around his fist and dragged her to the safe.

'Was that what you couldn't bear, Beech? That there she was with me, a man more than twice her age, and it wasn't you and it would never be you.'

Lazard tore a bottle of brandy out of the cabinet above the safe and poured it over Anne's head.

'Do you want to see this again, Paddy? Do you? Do you want to watch another one of your beauties burn?'

He took a Zippo lighter out of his pocket, flicked it open and swiped it across his leg. The flame came up a lazy yellow.

'That's enough, Beecham, I'm opening the safe. Put out the light,' roared Wilshere. 'I said, put out the light!'

Lazard waved the flame, the brandy was vaporizing quickly in the heat. Anne was paralysed, the smell strong as ammonia in her nostrils. He clicked the Zippo shut, threw Anne down, across the floor in front of him. Wilshere pulled himself up to the safe, entered the combination into the dial. Lazard brushed the muzzle of the revolver up and down Anne's leg, pushing the hem of the dress up further each time.

'Look at this, Paddy,' said Lazard.

Wilshere opened the safe, tugging on the heavy door. He reached in and closed his hand around the revolver he kept in there, thumbed back the hammer. There were no further questions he had for Lazard. He turned. Lazard looked up from Anne's exposed leg. The bullet, which should have gone through his head, tore Lazard's throat out. He fell back, dropping his gun, applying both hands to the massive black haemorrhage where his Adam's apple used to be. A gargling, coughing noise broke from Lazard's body as his hands panicked around his throat, trying to stem the gouts of blood.

'Get the door key,' said Wilshere, grim as winter.

Anne crawled over to Lazard, searched his pockets, the body now in some terrible state of spasm as life clung on, or struggled away.

'Open the door,' said Wilshere. 'We're going to finish this all now.'

He grabbed Anne's wrist and dragged her past the figurines, *amor é cego*, across the hall and up the wooden stairs, the panelled wall, Anne hardly able to keep her feet, until he suddenly stopped.

Mafalda stood at the top of the stairs in her nightdress. She had a leather cartridge belt slung over her shoulder and a twelve-bore shotgun in her hands. After the shot and what she'd heard coming up through the fireplace, she'd known who was going to be next. Anne took one look at her and decided that nothing was up for discussion. She twisted her wrist out of Wilshere's grip, hurled herself over the bannister into the hall, as Mafalda pulled both triggers. Wilshere took the double quantities of shot in the chest. It ripped him open, tore everything out. Everything that had ever troubled him.

Mafalda didn't pause. She broke the gun, the spent cartridges popped out. She reloaded, turned her shoulder and put both barrels into the ceiling. The massive wrought-iron chandelier, fixed to the ceiling by a metal plate, parted from the splintered wood. A quarter of a ton of chandelier headed for the floor. Anne scrabbled across the chequered squares. The chandelier crashed into the tiled floor, sending out shrapnel of black and white chippings. Mafalda reloaded, walked down the stairs, calm, professional, work to be done. Anne hobbled down the corridor to the french windows, which she now saw were shut. Had Lazard locked them? The seconds it would take to try might be vital. Mafalda skirted the fallen chandelier, saw Anne sidestep into the drawing room, slowed down, checked her weapon, triggered the triggers, proceeded.

Chapter 23

Wednesday, 19th July 1944, Monserrate Gardens, Serra de Sintra, near Lisbon.

Voss sat alone in the dark palace. Rose and Sutherland had run for their cars and headed back into Lisbon. The agent from the colonnade came in, lowered the flame on the lamp and picked it up. He waited while Voss applied his fingertips to his temples, trying to force in the energy to think.

After a minute of the agent swinging the lamp and watching the effect on their shadows, Voss stood. The agent led him up through the trees to his car. Voss stared at the steering wheel, the agent looked in on him.

'You have to put the key in the ignition, and turn it, sir,' said the agent. 'That way the motor starts. Good night, sir.'

Voss pulled out and drove back to Sintra, past the palace of Seteais, blue and silent in the moonlight. He took the high road above Sintra town and drove through the unlit village of São Pedro heading south to Estoril. Check Wilshere first, he thought, there was a chance that Lazard would go there if they were in this together, and check Anne, too. Then go back to Lisbon.

In the open country between the *serra* and the coast he pulled off the road under some pines trees. Another thought: whatever Lazard was doing had been a carefully planned operation; Voss would represent a threat to that plan. He went to the boot and lifted out the tool box. From the cloth bag he removed the Walther PPK, well-oiled and loaded. He checked it, laid it on the passenger seat and drove into Estoril from the north, heading down to the sea and the casino square.

He walked up the garden, the night air full of barking dogs that had been set off by Wilshere's shot. He heard Mafalda put both barrels into Wilshere. He was running by the time the next two barrels were emptied into the ceiling. He hit the lawn at a sprint and slowed, checking the windows of the house. Light in the study only, then light in the drawing room and Mafalda holding the twelve bore with the cartridge belt still over her shoulder, sweeping the room like a hunter in a copse.

He ducked, ran across the lawn and hit the wall close to the last window. Mafalda had got up on a coffee table and was looking amongst the furniture.

'Judy,' she said in a little voice, coaxing a kitten. 'Judy.'

Now he could see Anne hiding behind the sofa at the far end of the room, crouched with a dark stain around the neck and shoulders of her dress. He ran to the back terrace, eased open the doors of the french windows and stood in the doorway of the sitting room. Mafalda had her back to him. He raised the Walther PPK.

'Put the gun down, Dona Mafalda.'

Mafalda turned slowly, the twelve bore at her hip.

'Put it down, slowly,' said Voss, checking her face.

He stepped behind the corridor wall as the shot crashed through the open doorway and ravaged the plaster beyond. Voss stepped back into the frame as a large vase hurled from the far end of the room shattered on the edge of the table on which Mafalda was standing. She lost her balance, fell, the gun slipped off her hip, the stock thudded into the floor. The blast ripped into her nightdress, rolled her off the table – a crack as she hit the floor. Voss was on her in a second, pulled open the shredded nightdress, her left breast gone, the blood – thick, arterial, important – flooded into her ragged lungs, drained out.

Anne crashed across the room. Voss tucked his gun into his waistband. Outside, the ringing bell of a police car started up in the distance. Anne, oddly calm, seeing everything slowly now, walked quickly back into the study. She opened Lazard's briefcase, slapped the envelope on top of the velvet bag of high-quality gems, scraped the contents of the safe into it, which included a few white paper sachets of other diamonds and some documents, shut the briefcase and left the safe open with the gold bars still in it. Headlights flashed through the front door into the hall. She and Voss ran out on to the back terrace and on through the hedge to the perimeter wall at the back of the property. Over the wall they walked briskly downhill and back towards the casino, which they avoided because

229

a crowd had gathered outside. The town dogs were still barking and howling into the night.

They drove down the Marginal without exchanging a word. Voss hung on to the wheel as if it was a cliff face, Anne pulled her heels up on to the seat, jammed herself into a corner and hugged her knees, shaking. Lisbon was fogbound and strangely cool. They went to Estrela, parked and walked up to the apartment. He ran a bath, lit cigarettes, poured out some harsh *bagaço* he kept in the kitchen. He took her into the bathroom, stripped off her dress and put it in the basin to soak. He bathed her as he would a child and towelled her dry. He put her into bed, where she cried for an hour; the images of the burning woman, the innocent burning woman with love and petrol in her throat in the furnace car, refused to go out. He washed her dress, hung it up by the window. He stripped, got into bed behind her, pulled her back to his chest. They stared into the dark corner of the room. She told him everything that had happened.

Dawn came early with a faint mist by the window and woke them up out of short, deep sleep and back into hard fact. Her forehead was pressed against his back, her arm over his chest. His hand was resting on her hip. She knew he was awake, could hear his brain ticking.

'Lazard and Wilshere knew you were a double,' she said, the words reverberating up his spine. 'Lazard told me last night. Does that mean Wolters knows?'

He didn't reply but brushed his thumb over her hip bone, back and forward. He was staring at the briefcase under the table. He imagined Colonel Claus Schenk von Stauffenberg going into the *Wolfsschanze* situation room (or would it be in the new bunker, whose five-metre thick walls he'd never seen), positioning his briefcase, being called out to the telephone, the explosion and then the end of all this and a return to real life – which, of course, would not be possible, to go back, to return. There was only one direction in this life and that was relentlessly forward, away from old states of comparative innocence and on to new states, the images collecting in the brain to be shown in one horrific flash should you be unfortunate enough to drown.

'Did you hear me?' she asked. 'You can't go back.'

'Back?' he asked, momentarily confused.

'To the legation,' she said. 'They know you're a double.'

'I have no choice,' he said. 'I have to go back.'

'If you come with me now to the embassy . . .'

'I can't. I have my duty.'

'What duty?'

'With any luck, tomorrow will be the beginning of the end and I have to be there for it. I have my part to play.'

'Take the case,' she said. 'It's got everything in it . . . the diamonds . . . the envelope with the plans, everything you need to survive.'

'I can't take the case. I can't do that. If Wolters gets those plans, everything I've worked for will have been for nothing.'

'Then take the case and leave me the envelope. At least you'll salvage the diamonds.'

'If I take the case I place myself at the scene. They will know I was at the house. There are three dead bodies there including Lazard, who was supposedly brokering a deal for us. It will be difficult.'

'You invent something. If you go back empty-handed I don't know how you'll be able to survive. You'll have nothing to bargain with. Nothing that proves you're not a double.'

'It won't make any difference. My only chance to hold Wolters off, if he knows I'm a double, would be if I gave the briefcase to him complete and saved his intelligence coup from disaster. I won't do that.'

He got up, made coffee which they drank without sugar because he hadn't picked up his ration. They shared a dry biscuit. It felt like the spare meal of a condemned man who no longer had an appetite for life. Voss looked at his watch and then out of the window.

'The sun will burn this off in no time.'

'When do I see you?' she said, suddenly made desperate by his insouciance.

'That will be difficult. You're going to be in trouble, too. There'll be a lot of explaining. I'll be here in the evenings, if you can come . . . come, but not tomorrow. I will be here at five thirty on Friday. If something happens . . . if I'm not here . . . call this number and ask for Le Père Goriot. He'll tell you.'

He gave her a number and the lines of code. She didn't want to hear them. They made her feel dark, cavernous. He gave her keys to his apartment. They kissed, a brushing of the lips, and he handed her the briefcase. He followed her out of the room, watched her go down the stairs, looking up at him as she went, until her face disappeared in the dark well.

He went to the window and waited for her. She walked up the short hill behind the basilica and at the top she turned and waved, one straight arm salute, which he returned.

She went straight to work and a one-hour debrief with Cardew, who pushed her to tell him everything not just about the débâcle in the Wilsheres' house but about Voss as well. Once Wallis had lost her, Rose and Sutherland had been on to him, and now he wanted to give them as full a picture as possible about her movements. He was annoyed.

At 9.30 a.m. she was sitting in the room of the safe house in Rua de Madres in Madragoa. Rose and Sutherland were there and two Americans, OSS men from the American consulate.

The men took up their positions around the room, Sutherland and Rose in the chairs, the Americans standing by the walls. No explanation was given for the Americans' presence.

They asked for her story, the same story she'd given Cardew, from the moment she left the Shell building the previous afternoon. It meant she had to start where she didn't want to – with Karl Voss. Sutherland was still annoyed after receiving Cardew's report. Rose was prurient. The Americans were baffled.

'How long were you with him?' asked Sutherland.

'Five hours or so.'

'Where?'

'Part of the time in his apartment but we went for a walk in the Bairro Alto, too. Then he drove me back to Estoril.'

'How long were you in the apartment?'

'Two to three hours.'

Silence while the Americans' boredom settled. This was not why they were here.

'Did you have . . . relations?' asked Rose.

'Yes, sir,' she said, bold now, and one of the Americans raised

232

his eyebrows, smirked, straightened his tie. 'We *are* lovers, sir,' she added.

'Was that all it was?' asked Sutherland.

'What else could it have been, sir?' asked Anne.

They moved on to Estoril. They went through what had happened in Wilshere's house four or five times until the Americans were satisfied and got to their feet.

'Do you mind?' asked one of them to no one in particular.

He opened the briefcase, removed the envelope, looked it over and tapped it on his fingernail.

'Pity,' he said, and the two Americans left the room.

Rose took the empty chair, played a quick piece up and down the arms, not chopsticks, more Mozart. It annoyed Sutherland.

'Pity?' asked Anne.

'The OSS were running an operation without telling us,' said Sutherland, more drained than ever before. 'When I heard Lazard wasn't on the Dakar flight I contacted them. By then they had permission to talk to us about Hal and Mary Couples. They asked what you were doing and I told them that you were an observer. Their only comment was that you should "maintain that status".'

'And what were the Couples doing?' she asked.

'Hal Couples worked for Ozalid. He was spying on military installations while selling them Ozalid machines. The OSS turned him and he cleaned out the American IG stable for them. This was his last job. They put one of their agents with him and sent him to Lisbon with a set of plans. I think I told you that Bohr was being debriefed by the Americans about the German atomic programme. He had with him a sketch that Heisenberg had given him the year before. He thought it was an atomic bomb. The American scientists saw something different – not a bomb but an atomic pile ... something that could make fissionable material for use in a bomb in quantity.'

'Wilshere called it the core to the atomic apple.'

'Artistic mind, that Wilshere,' said Rose.

'The Americans have been worried by the quality of the physics coming out of Germany in the last five years. After debriefing Bohr they were concerned about Heisenberg's loyalties. Was it to physics or the Führer? They decided that, although he might not be a fanatical Nazi, he was sufficiently drawn to the excitement of progress that he might be developing a bomb. With the German rocket capability this became a somewhat worrying prospect.'

'So if the Couples were working for the OSS, what did they have for sale?'

'Some cleverly constructed plans that would have built a very dangerous atomic pile. The intelligence the Americans would get back after the documents were received would have given them a clear indication of how close the Germans were to including unconventional explosives in their rockets.'

'You mean Karl Voss could have taken the case, he could have given General Wolters the envelope, that was what the Americans wanted, that would have been the perfect solution?'

Sutherland and Rose said nothing. Anne's eyes filled with tears which rolled down her face, bit into the corners of her mouth and dripped off her jaw on to her still damp dress, silent as soft rain off the eaves.

Voss had been right. By the time he arrived at the legation the sun had burnt off the mist and the temperature was already in the high twenties centigrade. He called Dakar airport and asked them for a report on the Rio flight. It still hadn't taken off. He went straight in to see Wolters with this diversionary piece of information and was astonished to find him cheerful and expansive.

'So maybe it will be a little cooler today, Voss,' he said.

'I don't know about that, sir,' he said. 'Just to let you know, sir, the Dakar/Rio flight still hasn't taken off.'

'Thank you, Voss, I had that checked. I hope that wasn't a report you received.'

'No, sir, I cleared all our men away from the airport.'

'Keep it that way.'

Voss was dismissed. He went to his office light on his feet again, threw himself into his chair. Happy.

'You in love, sir?' asked Kempf.

Voss whipped round, hadn't seen him there in the corner of the room, leaning up against the window.

'Just had a good night's sleep, that's all, Kempf. First cool night in weeks. You?'

'What, sir? Sleeping well?'

'Or in love?'

'Not that sort of love, sir. Not the sort that makes you happy.'

'What sort, Kempf?'

'The sort that makes the first piss of the morning absolute agony, sir. Think I've got myself a dose.'

'Take the morning off, Kempf.'

'Thank you, sir.'

Voss lit a cigarette, stretched his feet out and saw the cello of Anne's body at the window and the thick black sash of her hair over one shoulder. The phone rang. He listened, hung up and left the legation, buying his usual newspaper as he went.

He walked down to the Pensão Rocha with nothing on his mind apart from the blue Tagus in front of him and ships easing past, visible though the gaps in the buildings heading for the Atlantic.

He took his usual table in the courtyard, laid the newspaper in front of him, saw a small item at the foot of the front page. The PVDE announced that a communist cell had been captured in a safe house in Rua da Arrábida. The same place where Mesnel had been visiting and he'd sent Paco to check. Paco, thought Voss. You have to be careful of Paco. He has only one loyalty – money. A few minutes later Rui lowered himself into the chair opposite.

'Your Frenchman was shot last night. Dead,' said Rui.

'Tell me.'

'We followed him to the caves, as usual. He went off to do his business and we left him to it, except we heard a shot, two shots. We went back up there this morning. Somebody found the body around six o'clock. The PVDE were up there because he was a foreigner, so I didn't get too close. He'd been shot in the head at the viewpoint of the Alto da Serafina.'

'That's it?'

'I heard he was found with a gun on him,' he said, 'and some PVDE men were talking about a triple killing up in a big house in Estoril. Two foreigners and a Portuguese woman from a big family.'

Voss drummed the tabletop, gave Rui a cigarette which he pocketed without thinking.

'Do we do anything?' asked Rui.

'You wait,' said Voss, and left the newspaper on the table.

The PVDE had been hard at it since they arrived at Quinta da Águia at close to 2.15 a.m. They were working conscientiously to

235

hide the fact that they had been unimpressively late on the scene. The first phone call about gunshot noise from the Wilsheres' house had come in around 1.50 a.m. and had been discounted as carpet beating. By 2.00 a.m., however, there'd been another four calls, each reporting the same thing, gunshots – one quite loud, followed by two very loud and then two not so loud – and so it was that two PVDE men and two GNR men reluctantly got into a car and drove up to the Quinta da Águia with the bell on, just so that everyone in the neighbourhood would be woken up and they could feel important.

At 6.00 a.m., because of the names of the dead found in the house, Captain Lourenço was informed and once he took a personal interest in the investigation the servants were rounded up and later in the morning a search began for the Englishwoman, whose address on her visa application was given as Quinta da Águia. They were waiting for her at the Shell building when she came back from Rua de Madres. They put her into a car and drove her to the PVDE headquarters on Rua António Maria Cardoso where there was intense activity as the reports of three other murders were being filed.

Sutherland and Rose had gone through Anne's story and come up against a serious difficulty – the hours spent in the café after Voss had dropped her placed her in Estoril. They had hoped to be able to hide her at the Cardews' house – dinner and then too tired to go home, stayed the night. The time at the café made this impossible. They toyed with the idea of the truth, omitting her presence at the Wilsheres' house but confirming that she spent the night with Voss – but it would compromise Voss. They'd hammered away at the problem until Anne put the idea of Wallis.

Jim Wallis was found. He'd spent the night alone. A story was plugged into him – that Anne had dined with the Cardews, been dropped at the *quinta*, gone to the café, waited and waited for him, left, met him outside and gone back to his apartment in Lisbon. There were some shaky elements, not least of which was that Anne had never been to Wallis's apartment and Wallis had a landlady. Anne was instructed to play her interrogation coy and reticent until the murders were disclosed and then, well, natural instincts would prevail. As she walked to the Shell building she elaborated the germ of the lie until it was an infection of perfect reality in her mind.

She was desperate for it to work, her fear being that they would keep her locked up without charge for as long as they wanted to.

The PVDE worked on her throughout the morning as more and more information came in. The Frenchman, Mesnel, whose revolver had not been fired, had been shot twice, grazed once and mortally wounded the second time. The bullet in Mesnel's body matched that of the Smith & Wesson lying near Lazard's body, with his fingerprints on it, in the Wilsheres' house. The sides and underside of Lazard's car, found outside the casino, were covered in cement powder and sand, and the tyre tracks matched those left at the site of the half-built villa belonging to Lazard where the bodies of the Couples had been discovered. The PVDE inspector was not convinced, by the way the bodies lay, that Hal Couples had done this unspeakable thing to his wife, strangled her and then shot himself in the head. As a scenario he didn't believe it, and he said as much in his initial report to Lourenço, who had the benefit of an autopsy on Lazard which revealed blood on his penis and undershorts.

By the end of the morning Lourenço saw it like this: Lazard had shot Mesnel in Monsanto, driven to Malveira, raped and strangled Mary Couples, shot Hal Couples with the man's own gun. He had then driven to Estoril where there had been a disagreement, resulting in Wilshere shooting him with a gun probably kept in the safe. Wilshere had then been shot by Mafalda on the stairs and Mafalda had apparently shot herself by accident in the sitting room. There were some questions. Why did Mafalda put both barrels into the ceiling? Had she first attempted to kill her husband by dropping the chandelier on him? It seemed unlikely. Why was there the stink of brandy in the study, an empty bottle, a stain on the floor, but no stains on any of the bodies? Why, if the motive was robbery, was the safe open with four bars of gold in it? It wasn't long before Lourenço was convinced that there was somebody missing from the scene.

None of this information filtered down to Anne, who was in Room 3 with a single interrogator who asked a lot of questions and took copious notes. She told him how she had dined with the Cardews (tomato soup, mutton stew and cheese), gone to a café for a drink and then gone back to the Wilsheres' where she'd overslept in the morning, taken the train to Lisbon and walked to work, arriving late. He drew the story out of her again, chipping away at her for more detail and getting it, masses of it. What she wore in bed, her dreams, whether she heard anything in the night (no), breakfast with Mr Wilshere (Dona Mafalda rarely attends), the walk to the station, the beauty of the morning sunshine coming through the mist, the cool after the terrible days of swelter. It was only after she was asked for a third rendering that Anne began to appear concerned.

The PVDE man gathered the copious notes and left the room. She was there on her own for an hour (early lunch for the interrogators) and she developed some worry, which was not hard to do.

At 12.15 two men came in and it was immediately different. They had strong alcohol and coffee on their breath and the words that came out on the back of it were ugly – liar, thief, murderer. She asked for a cigarette. They hit the table with their fists. They stood on either side of her, each with one hand on the back of her chair and the other on the table in front. They hemmed her in, breathed on her and told her what had happened at the Quinta da Águia the night before. She winced, shrank, paled and looked down into her hands, her shoulders shaking, her back shuddering under the implacable eyes of the two PVDE men.

They gave her a cigarette, pulled their chairs around to the side of the table and smoked with her. One gave her his handkerchief and it was to him that she revealed her affair with Jim Wallis. Two *agentes* were dispatched. They picked up Wallis within the hour. During that hour Lourenço received a report in which he was informed that officially Lazard had left the country from Lisbon airport on a flight to Dakar the previous afternoon. This complicating development had the effect of clarifying everything to the PVDE chief, who treated this detail as confirmation that only foreign intelligence services could possibly have made such a fantastic mess.

Voss returned to the legation and put a call in to his contact at the PVDE who told him the names of the three murdered people in the Quinta da Águia. He went straight across to Wolters' office and asked to see him urgently. They sat in the darkened office, shutters closed to the high sun, only cracks of intense light around the edges.

238

'I've had some disturbing news which I don't fully understand,' said Voss. 'One of the agents I've been using to follow the French communist Olivier Mesnel reported to me that he was shot last night. The agent went up to Monsanto in the morning to where the body was found and overheard two PVDE men discussing a triple murder in a big house in Estoril. I've just contacted the PVDE who've confirmed the names of the three dead as follows: Mr Patrick Wilshere, Senhora Mafalda de Carmo Wilshere and Mr Beecham Lazard.'

Wolters' face was perfectly still, the only movement in the room was the cigar smoke trailing from his fingers. The phone rang, more urgent than usual to Voss's mind, and he sat back to admire Wolters' collapsing world.

The call was from Captain Lourenço demanding to see a representative from the German Legation in his office in Rua António Maria Cardoso. This was how Voss came to be sitting at the hottest point of the day staring at the PVDE chief's back as he stood looking out of the unshuttered window in the vague direction of the São Carlos theatre. Voss was still thinking about Wolters, convinced that the general was as stunned by Lazard's murder here, in Portugal, as he was himself.

'It's been very hot these past few days,' said Lourenço. 'I've been glad my office faces east . . . not that it makes that much difference. In Lisbon, you see, it's the humidity that throttles.'

'You should get out of the city more, sir,' said Voss.

'I would. I'd love to . . . if people would give me the time.'

'Surely . . .'

'People like yourself, Senhor Voss.'

'Me, Captain?'

'What's going on, Senhor Voss?'

'You've confused me now, sir.'

'I don't think so, Senhor Voss. You don't strike me as a man who confuses easily,' said Lourenço. 'I'm looking at six murders, five of them foreigners. I'm quite certain that that is a record for one night in Lisbon and it is one record I am not proud of holding.'

'Were any of them German?' asked Voss. 'Is that why . . . ?'

'No, none of them were German. That is why you're here,' said Lourenço. 'I find it interesting that the military attaché has been sent, don't you?'

239

'I was sent because I was on hand,' said Voss, wondering how long his dumb show could continue.

'This *is* an intelligence matter, Senhor Voss,' he said, settling behind his desk, smoothing his moustache with his fingertips. 'So, please, let's not walk around each other for an hour.'

'We are as shocked by last night's . . .'

'Yes, yes . . . please, Senhor Voss, the point.'

'We were expecting some goods from Senhor Lazard, that is true,' said Voss. 'But we were expecting him to leave the country in order to procure them. In fact, we *know* he left the country and we were very surprised to find him still here and even more –'

'What were the goods?'

'Well, I say "goods" . . . what I mean is that he left with diamonds in order to buy dollars. We have a hard currency problem in Europe.'

'So he should have had some diamonds on him?'

'I don't know about on him, but they should have been in his possession, unless they were being carried by the man who boarded the Dakar flight impersonating Mr Lazard.'

'Don't try to confuse the issue, Senhor Voss. It's very clear in my mind. All I want to know is why Lazard should shoot a Frenchman in Monsanto, drive to the Serra de Sintra to rape and strangle Senhora Couples, shoot Senhor Couples and then go on to Estoril where I am sure he was about to shoot Senhor Wilshere.'

'I'd like to propose the theory that Senhor Lazard was operating in his own interests,' said Voss. 'Have the Allies been forthcoming about Senhor and Senhora Couples?'

Lourenço's dark eyes didn't leave Voss's face as they lit up with his first idea of the afternoon.

'Ah, yes, now I see . . . is it possible he was using your diamonds to buy something from Senhor and Senhora Couples? Then, having got what he wanted, he killed them. The only problem is that Senhor Couples, according to the American consulate, is a salesman for a company which makes printing machines for use in the construction industry . . . she was his wife. There's been gossip that she was having an affair with Senhor Lazard, which I find hard to believe. What was the value of the diamonds?'

'Why?'

'I would like to know, Senhor Voss.'

240

'I meant why do you find it hard to believe that Senhor Lazard would be having an affair with Senhora Couples?'

'The details of her death were not pleasant . . . You will have noticed that I used the word rape . . . that was . . . I was being . . . ach! . . . the man was an animal,' said Lourenço, throwing his hand away. 'And who is this Frenchman? That's another thing.'

Voss dipped his head, sorry that he was unable to enlighten.

'Have you spoken to the English girl who was staying at the house, she must . . . ?' said Voss.

'She knows nothing. She wasn't there,' he said. 'She said she was there. She said she had breakfast with Wilshere in the morning and went to work, but the reality . . . I don't know . . . foreigners.'

'Foreigners?'

'She was off with her English boyfriend somewhere in Lisbon . . . These women . . . she only arrived here on Saturday. I should have been born . . .'

Lourenço trailed off. Voss survived the jolt, which had started out as fear, turned into a wild, irrational jealousy and finished as happiness. He lost Lourenço's words as he stared across the street at the sun blinding the windows of the building opposite.

Wolters listened to Voss's report of the interview with Lourenço in hard silence, his eyes blinking once a minute as if that was part of the process of taking in the disaster. A million dollars lost, the most valuable supplier of industrial diamonds dead, the plans, which would have taken them a step nearer to a secret weapon, well, where were they? Did they ever exist?

'What do we know about this?' asked Wolters, the process of shifting blame already starting in his head.

'What we know is useless to us,' said Voss, relishing this moment, wanting to be able to share it with someone – this was what happened when the SS took over Abwehr intelligence operations.

'But we do know something?' he asked, clutching.

'We know that someone calling himself Beecham Lazard boarded the Lisbon/Dakar flight. According to Immigration in Dakar he arrived safely but nobody of that name was on the Dakar/Rio flight which has now taken off . . .'

'Yes, yes . . . I know these things.'

Voss studied him, looking for confirmation of his theory, but

Wolters was expressionless. There was nothing in his face to show whether he knew what Lazard had been doing, whether this had been part of the game – a bluff to the SIS and the OSS to focus their attention outside Portugal. Whatever. It had gone wrong.

'*I* will write the report of this matter,' said Wolters. '*I* will send the report personally to Berlin. Is that understood?'

Voss waited until evening to see whether a report came out of Wolters' office. Only Wolters himself came out and that was to leave the legation for a cocktail party at the Hotel Aviz and then dinner at the Negresco afterwards.

Voss left the building at 7.00 p.m. and went back to his apartment where he knelt at the window smoking, drinking his preferred rubbing alcohol and watching the square, waiting, waiting for tomorrow to finally arrive.

Because he never took cabs it had been a long walk for Paco to the small park above the Santa Clara market in the Alfama district. He had been told that the information he was going to be given would certainly be worth the very long walk from Lapa across the city. He sat under the trees with a view over the church of Santa Engrácia, wondering whether this was a dangerous place to be. Behind him, watching him, was someone else who was also reflecting on the same building, which was still incomplete after 262 years' work. Paco sat back and tried to enjoy the warm night air of the empty park and watched the lights of small craft inching their way across the Tagus which was as big as a small sea at this point.

The voice that came to Paco from behind him was not Portuguese. He had heard this kind of voice before. It was a voice incapable of relaxing. It was an English voice and only capable of speaking barely comprehensible Portuguese. The park was so dark that even when he turned round he couldn't see who was speaking. He didn't like this voice. Paco didn't *like* anybody. But he especially didn't like this voice because it belonged to someone who wouldn't make themselves known, the type who would always be on the edge of light, just in the shadows.

'Ah yes, Paco. Beautiful up here, isn't it? Especially at night. Very quiet. Hardly aware of the city.'

Paco didn't reply. These were just some of the things that Englishmen said.

'I have something for you, Paco. A piece of information. Something that you could use at the right moment. I can't tell you when that moment will be. It might be tomorrow or the next day. You will listen and watch as you always do and you will decide the correct moment for you to go with this piece of information to the man who will pay you well.'

'Who is the man who will pay me well?'

'This isn't anything that should go to the PVDE.'

'*They* do not pay me well.'

'Then that is good,' said the English voice. 'The man who will pay you well is SS General Reinhardt Wolters of the German Legation.'

'He will never see me. Why should such a man want to see Paco Gomez?'

'There is no doubt that he will want to see you with this piece of information.'

'Tell me.'

'You will tell him that last night you saw his military attaché, Captain Karl Voss . . . you do know who I mean, don't you, Paco?'

'Certainly.'

'You will tell him you saw Captain Karl Voss with the English girl . . .'

'The English girl who works for Shell, who lives in the house of Senhor Wilshere?'

'Yes, that girl. You will tell him that you saw them walking together in the Bairro Alto last night,' said the English voice, 'and that they are lovers. That is all.'

Chapter 24

Thursday, 20th July 1944, PVDE Headquarters, Rua António Maria Cardoso, Lisbon.

Anne was released in the morning at 9.00 a.m. She was met by Cardew who took her straight off to his home in Carcavelos, where she showered and changed into some clothes borrowed from his wife. Anne insisted on going into work. She needed to be occupied, she said. She didn't say that she needed to be in Lisbon with a chance of seeing Voss.

They drove back into Lisbon. She typed for the rest of the morning and then began translating articles on physics from the *Naturwissenschafen* journal. She looked at the clock constantly, so frequently that the hands stopped moving.

Voss sat in his office looking at the clock giving Berlin time which, because of the Führer's insistence that all parts of the Third Reich should operate on German time, meant that he was also looking at Rastenburg time, *Wolfsschanze* time. It was midday and in a matter of minutes Colonel Claus Schenk von Stauffenberg would be positioning his briefcase, maybe he had already positioned his briefcase and was waiting to be called to the telephone, praying to be called to the telephone in the *Wolfsschanze* signals room. Voss tried the bottom drawer of his desk, which was locked. It contained the Walther PPK given to him by the Free Poles colonel which he'd brought into the building that morning and was going to be used to take control of the German Legation.

'You all right, sir?' asked Kempf.

'Yes, yes, just stretching my back, Kempf,' said Voss. 'You better?'

'Not better exactly, sir.'

'You should stick to English nannies, Kempf.'

'Thank you for the advice, sir. I'll try to remember that the next time I'm drunk, down at the Santos docks surrounded by sailors,' said Kempf. 'I'll put out the call for an English nanny . . .'

'Point taken, Kempf.'

'If you're trying to get into that drawer, sir, I'd . . .'

'No, no, Kempf. Just stretching.'

'I was going to say, a good kick will sort it out. I know that desk.'

'No, no, no, Kempf. It's just a way of bracing myself, that's all. Let's go through the mail. You have brought the mail with you?'

Kempf stalled.

'Go and get the mail, Kempf.'

Voss sat back, his whole body in a lather.

Paco lay on his bed curled in a tight ball, with his kneecaps pressed into his eye sockets, tears leaking out at the excruciating pain in his stomach. After the Englishman had given him his intelligence gift he had also pushed a hundred-escudo note into his pocket and with this Paco had gone back through the Alfama district where he'd stopped and eaten his first meal of the day. He had been stupid to choose the pork. Pork in this heat . . . and you never knew how long they'd kept it there, rotting in their kitchens, these filthy people. As soon as he'd tasted that sharpness he should have stopped. It was the sharpness of vinegar which they used to disguise the age of the meat. He'd spent the whole night crouched over the stinking toilet, vomiting between his knees, while his innards streamed out of his backside. When he was empty, when he was no more than a dry, flattened bladder, he'd crawled to his room and dry-retched until dawn, while a fever wrung out the little moisture left in him, so that the yellowing bedsheets were soaked through. The boy had come and made him drink water and the wire spring of his abdomen had contracted, doubled him over so that his vertebrae stuck out of his back under his paper-thin skin. Only at midday did his stomach release him, let him stretch out and fall into a prickly sleep, from which he would jolt awake at the strange and ghastly images that surfaced in his mind.

At lunchtime Anne went to the Estrela Gardens, sat on a bench and watched people, checking if she was being followed. She went into the basilica and out again and up the wooden stairs to Voss's apartment. She let herself in, he wasn't there. She wandered about the rooms, tested the sofa, sat on his bed and looked at his family photograph, the three men in it. The father and Julius looked alike, broad, strong men with dark hair and eyebrows, handsome, sporty. They were in uniform. Voss was wearing a suit and a student scarf. He had the same fair looks as his mother and, it seemed to her, the same light-coloured eyes and vulnerable bone structure. She held the image of the mother up to her eye to see if any of that sadness she must have felt, that disappointment at not being the love of her husband's life, was evident. It wasn't, she looked happy.

She put the photograph down on the bed, went to the dresser, rummaged amongst his clothes in the drawers and found a small package of letters tied with ribbon. She read the letters, the need for a sense of his presence was too strong for her to consider privacy. The letters were in date order and most of them consisted of a few lines from his father finishing with a chess move. She flipped through them in a state of vague contentment until she reached Julius's letter, dated New Year's Day 1943. She found herself crying, half blind with tears, not seeing the deserving end of an invading army but the unfolding of a family tragedy – a father's desperation, a brother presenting Julius with his terrible choice and then the final letter from the unknown lieutenant. She retied the ribbon, tucked the letters back in the drawer and took some of his hairs out of his brush and comb. She went to the bathroom even hungrier for him now and fingered his shaving gear, thumbed the badger brush, sniffed the razor to see if there was something of him on it. Nothing. She had to go, yet she wanted to leave something of herself for him but nothing legible, or personal so that it could be traced back to her. She went to the dresser, plucked a hair from her own head and wove it amongst the bristles and hairs in the brush.

Voss watched the Berlin clock move around to 5.00 p.m. The hour at which it would be certain that Stauffenberg would be back in Berlin after the three-hour flight from Rastenburg. Still nothing. Voss forced himself to stay still, sitting at his desk he went through papers again and again, reading nothing, taking in nothing, being nothing.

Wolters had kept his secretary working late and now she was leaving the building, her heels clopping on the tiled hall, skipping down the stone steps to the driveway and into the hot evening of the city. Voss sat back in his chair, elbow up on the arm, thumb supporting his chin, forefinger sweeping over his lips back and forth, eyes blinking once a minute in the thickening silence. Wolters stirred out of his office. Voss tracked the creaking leather of the man's shoes until they reached his door. The handle turned.

'Ah, Voss,' said Wolters, 'working late?'

'Thinking late, sir.'

'Would you care to join me for a drink? I've just taken delivery of some rather fine cognac.'

Voss followed him back to his office where Wolters laid out the glasses and poured the brandy.

'What were you thinking about, Voss?'

Lines sprinted through Voss's mind, none of them usable. Wolters' lips hovered over the rim of his glass, waiting. Alternatives did not immediately present themselves to Voss. His head was too full of what should be happening now in Berlin.

'It was nothing important,' he said.

'Tell me.'

'I was wondering why Mesnel was armed. Had I been running him, I would not have used him for assassination work. That was all.'

Wolters' face darkened. He stuck two fingers into his collar, pulled at it to let some of the blood drain into his body. Voss raised his glass. They drank. The alcohol smoothed Wolters out. He lit a cigar.

'I have been thinking about something, too,' said Wolters. 'I have spoken to Captain Lourenço myself now. It seems that he is under the impression that there were two people who left Quinta da Águia alive on that Tuesday night.'

'Why two people?'

'The situation in the drawing room where they found the body of Dona Mafalda.'

'What was that?'

'A vase had been thrown the length of the room. The vase was one of a pair that belonged on the mantelpiece.'

'Yes.'

'And there was evidence of shot having peppered the wall of the corridor beyond the living-room door,' said Wolters. 'Captain Lourenço thinks that Dona Mafalda was shooting at someone in the doorway and that another person, at the far end of the room, either wanted to distract her or hit her with the vase. The vase smashed, startling Dona Mafalda, who lost her footing and accidentally shot herself as she fell. Captain Lourenço doesn't think that the person who was shot at in the doorway could be the same as the one who threw the vase from the other end of the room, which is why he now thinks that there are two people unaccounted for. I have been thinking, Captain Voss . . .'

'Yes, sir.'

'I have been thinking that I would very much like to talk to those two people and that what they took from the Quinta da Águia that night could be very interesting to us.'

'Yes, sir.'

'I want you to use your considerable intelligence resources to find those two people.'

The phone rang, jolting the two men in the smoke-layered stillness. Wolters picked up the phone and Voss heard the urgent voice of the switchboard operator, a corporal in the telegraph room. Von Ribbentrop, the Reichsminister for Foreign Affairs, was on the line. Wolters checked his watch, just after 8.00 p.m. He asked Voss to leave the office for a moment, take his glass. Voss paced the corridor for some minutes and then collapsed behind his desk, suddenly exhausted, nerves shot, knowing that von Ribbentrop calling Lisbon at this hour was not a good sign. He gulped the brandy, which slipped down like burning silk. He lit a cigarette, watched his trembling fingers until they stilled, then sat back and smoked. Did they delay again? But von Ribbentrop calling on the evening of such a day. They must have failed. The gun. He must get the gun out of the building. If a gun is found in his desk he will be finished. Now they will be looking at everyone, especially the ex-Abwehr men.

Wolters left his office, his shoes smacked down the corridor in triumphant strides. He flung open the door. Voss found himself looking up, hunched over his cigarette like a prisoner in his cell.

'A attempt was made on the Führer's life this afternoon,' Wolters announced, excitedly. 'A bomb was placed in the situation room in the *Wolfsschanze*. It exploded right underneath the Führer's feet but ... it must be a sign, it must be some sort of a turning point ... he has only been lightly wounded. An incredible thing. The Reichsminister said that, had they been in the new bunker, nobody would have survived ... as it was, they were in Reichsminister Speer's blockhouse, the bomb blew out the sides, releasing the blast, eleven people were injured, four of them seriously. Reichsminister von Ribbentrop is uncertain but he thinks that Colonel Brandt and General Schmundt have not survived their injuries. The Führer has a slight concussion, burst eardrums, damage to his elbow and splinters from the table have been blown into his legs, but he has assured everyone that he will be back at work tomorrow. The coup has been defeated. The terrorists are being rounded up in Berlin as we speak. It is a great day for the Führer, a great day for the Third Reich, a terrible day for our enemies and a great day for us, Captain Voss. *Heil Hitler.*'

Wolters clicked his heels and shot his arm out. Voss stood and responded in kind. They went back to Wolters' study, replenished their glasses and toasted the survival of the right, the victory of justice, the defeat of terrorism, death to the conspirators and many more until the bottle was finished and Voss reeled out of the office drunk, desperate and clammy with fear. He went sweating back to his desk, removed the gun from its drawer and jammed it down his trousers where it stuck into his groin, but he was numb to pain. He picked up his briefcase, crammed his head into his hat and left the building in the tunnel of his own mind. His eyes, pricked by the heat, were glassy as an old man's and as he walked from Lapa to Estrela he stumbled over the *calçada* of the pavements and cobbled streets, his cheeks wet with tears – drained from rejoicing with Wolters, released from the tension of the past weeks and bleak with his vision of the future.

At the top of the Rua de São Domingos à Lapa he looked back down the hill at the limp Union Jack outside the British Embassy. A tram rumbled past, people stared out at him, looking without seeing, two boys hanging off the back yelled, seemed to be beckoning him. Anne's words spoken into his back that morning came to him and he took two steps down the hill, saw himself knocking on the British Embassy door, his welcome into the sanctuary and then a terrible settling. The emptiness of defeat, the end of his cause while others, unbent by setbacks, endangered by his resignation, continued their struggle, his struggle.

He crossed the street, turned right down Rua de Buenos Aires, which was hot and stinking with the remains of a dead dog in the gutter. He dithered over the carcass, the bared teeth in the snout fierce in death, the intestines strewn and flattened across the road. He bared his own teeth at the thought of Wolters swaggering away from his costly intelligence fiasco into a new age of anti-conspiracy zeal, a place where his kind could shine, deflecting all critical scrutiny. Voss walked on at pace towards the back of the basilica, the brandy, hot and acidic, rising in his gullet.

Anne lay in bed in Cardew's house listening to the excited whispered chatter of his daughters next door. Her empty stomach had been unable to accept any dinner, she'd redesigned the landscape of her plate consuming nothing, as Dona Mafalda used to do. The ghastly images marched across her unclosed eyes of the innocent Judy Laverne, tearing down into the ravine in a cage of flame, Wilshere's clawed fingers trying to prohibit entry of the worst possible truth into his mind, Lazard trampling the tortured Wilshere, Lazard's torn throat after the ear-splitting blast from the gun from the safe, Wilshere's ruptured chest as he fell back down the stairs and Mafalda's missing left breast, the dark hole filled with black, central blood, the pallor of her life-drained face, the uncoloured lips. War in the living room. No different to the bombs that had fallen into her piano teacher's house on the corner of Lydon Road in that other life that she'd lived, except this had been so personal.

She could feel her mind restructuring. These were sights, sounds, smells and emotions which could not be accommodated in the soft, pliable naïveté of her life of just last week. They'd been gulped, forced, packed in, rammed down her gullet, so that she thought she could never be hungry again, so that her mind would never lack for this terrible nourishment which trembled her fingers, shuddered her insides, crawled over her skin to the top point of her scalp. She knew then, lying under the open window in the vague, indirect moonlight, how much Voss mattered. He was the only one who knew. He was the only one who could comprehend. He would be her salvation, the one who could order this fresh chaos and make it sad, documentary reading.

She was living for 5.30 p.m. Friday 21st July 1944. As long as there was this one last time everything else would work out. It would be like the clue, the code, the recipe for an equation which would give her the unknown value of x.

Her thoughts sped like silver fish out of the light into the darkness of sleep and she dreamt for the first time the dream which would be hers for years. She was running through the streets of an unknown city – buildings, monuments that were all foreign to her. It was hot. She was dressed in a slip but there was snow on the ground and her breath was visible. She was heading for somewhere where she knew she would find him and she found the door in an unlit alley. There was yellow light coming from the door, painting the cobbles gold. She ran up the wooden stairs and she found she knew the stairs and that her heart and mind were full of hope, that she knew she was going to see him, that he would be waiting for her in the room at the top, their room. She was running faster and faster up the stairs, more landings . . . more landings than she could remember, so many landings and new flights that she began to worry that this wasn't the stair, the right house, the correct street, the real city. But then the door appeared, the right door, behind which she would find him, and she hung exhausted on to the handle, preparing herself for the sight of his face, the bones pushing up under his skin in the way that made his face unique, and she threw open the door, and there was nothing, there was no floor, there was no room, there was only a hot, dry wind over the frozen city and she was falling into the dark.

She woke in a flash of light on a black horizon. Dawn had settled into the room, comfortable as a pet. Her scalp was drenched in sweat, her heart thumping between the walls of her chest like a hard ball thrashed by a madman. Was this it? Was this the mind's new régime?

She got dressed like an old person, consciously putting each foot through the leg hole of her knickers, drawing them up to her waist. She harnessed herself in her bra. Her dress hung off her differently. The hairbrush bit into her scalp as it had never done. The mirror showed her someone who was so nearly her that she had to lean forward to see what was missing from her face. It was all there, all in the right order, no anagram but a nuance. That was something unbearable to a mathematician, because a nuance meant that

251

something was just slightly wrong, the logic had foundered and thrown up, not an error, but just the *nuance* of one, something that was deep in the logic, perhaps a small line somewhere in a mass of equations, something that would be immensely difficult to find and root out, something that might mean you'd have to start all over again ... from scratch. But there was no starting again for her. This was it for the rest of time. A change that would have to be accepted, housed, hidden from view. And for no reason at all her mother came to mind.

She had breakfast. She let coffee trickle down her throat, no solids. Family conversation careered around the table, vectors that never reached her. Cardew drove her to work beside a sea so blue it made her ache.

Dawn came up in Sutherland's office gradually painting him into a corner of his room in the embassy where he'd sat all night after hearing news of the failed assassination attempt, smoking bowl after bowl of tobacco in his pipe. The empty pouch now lay on the floor along with loose strands of shag and dead matches from the overflowing ashtray on the arm of the chair. He'd been thinking about everything, everything that had ever happened to him, including the one thought that he'd never allowed, from the moment he'd received the letter back in 1940 telling him that she'd died in an air raid. How had he dealt with that? Everyone had someone who'd died in an air raid, he was no different. And now here he was, exhausted, completely shattered, the tiredness so profound that it had gone through all his organs and leaked into his bones, sucking on the marrow.

The responsibilities which Richard Rose wore like a summer suit hung off Sutherland's shoulders like a yoke of full pails. The losses from various operations stacked up in his mind, like coffins in a carpenter's yard. This time, though, he would not make the same mistake. He would pull Karl Voss, codename Childe Harold. He would get him out. The man had been right about everything and now, with the failure of the assassination attempt and what Anne had told them, he was in terrible danger, his identity as the military attaché in the German Legation held in place by paper walls. As soon as Rose came in he would announce the operation. Voss would be on his way to London and taking a debrief by evening.

Rose announced himself with a roll of knuckles on the door at 9.00 a.m. He walked in to what he thought was an empty room, not seeing Sutherland still in his chair behind the door.

'We're pulling Voss out today, Richard,' said Sutherland.

'Good morning, old boy,' said Rose, spinning on his heel. 'Just came to talk to you about these decodes.'

'After the failed coup he's sitting in a house of cards ... one breath from the wrong direction and the whole lot'll come down around him.'

'To be frank, I'm surprised he's not here. He must have heard hours before we did ... should have come knocking straight away, if he could.'

Sutherland was unbalanced. For some reason he'd expected resistance from Rose. Rose always hated losing sources. The battles they'd had.

'Checked his whereabouts, old man?' asked Rose.

'Not yet.'

'Well, if he's gone to work that should give us some idea of how he feels about the situation himself.'

'We pull him, Richard. I won't tolerate ...'

'Of course we do, but we can't drive up Rua do Pau de Bandeira calling for him to come out, can we, old chap?'

Old boy, old man, old chap ... just call me Sutherland, he thought, raising himself out of his chair, his arm curiously tingling, his left foot dead.

'Are you all right? Look damned pale to me.'

'Been up all night,' he said, trying to shake life back into his foot.

'Steady on.'

Sutherland was suddenly seeing the world at floor height, a landscape of carpet and furniture legs, with an atmosphere of dust motes and broken sunlight. He didn't understand it and he couldn't articulate his inability to comprehend. His mind ticked like a gramophone needle stuck in a groove.

At 10.00 a.m. the ambassador assembled everyone in the German Legation and gave the same announcement that Wolters had made to Voss the night before. The opening of the speech that followed was about betrayal, treason and terrorism. Wolters, the

253

disciplinarian at the headmaster's side, surveyed the room with the eyes of a bird of prey, so that everyone glued their looks to the picture of the Führer above the dignitaries' heads. The ambassador finally asked them to rejoice in the tragedy averted and led them into an exultant *Heil Hitler!* which rattled the windows. They went back to their offices like chastened schoolchildren after assembly. The world was no different as they streamed back to their desks, only now there was an undertow which was black and uncertain. An undertow that would be random in its search for a scapegoat.

Voss sat at his desk in the legation, sweat at the back of his knees trickling down his calf muscles to his sock tops. He had woken at 5.00 a.m. on the sofa with his tie still up to his neck. He'd clawed it down to his chest, popped the stud at his throat, gulped in air that was at its coolest now but only for an hour. He'd stripped, gone to the bed and found the photograph face-up on the pillow. He put it on the shelf, laid down and found the faintest smell of her on his pillow, sunk his face into it and then looked up through the bars of the bedhead at the plaster beyond and those words came to him again:

'Lazard and Wilshere knew you were a double. Lazard told me last night. Does that mean Wolters knows?'

He'd showered, shaved and walked naked to the chest of drawers to find the top one open a crack and his brush in a different position. He turned it over and saw the single long black thread of hair, doubled back four times through his own.

Now he was giving Hein and Kempf a solid good morning. Cheerful. All black thoughts banished to the black metal trunk with the white stencilling at the back of his mind. Now he thought of fields of buttercup. Shadows of clouds blown across the face of the sun moving over the flowers at summer's speed. He briefed Kempf and Hein about the two people who were presumed by Lourenço to have been in the Quinta da Águia but were still unaccounted for. He sent them out to put the word on the streets and told them that all reports must come to him first and none of them must be written. This would be a verbal operation. Kempf and Hein looked at each other. There was no such thing.

'These are direct orders from SS General Wolters,' said Voss.

'Nothing written?'

'That's what he said. He will make the written report to Berlin when the matter has been resolved.'

Kempf and Hein left the legation and drifted into the cafés and dark bars, where the occupants took their time to develop after the fierce light of the street and who, on hearing the word from the legation's men, downed their tumblers of wine and waded out into the crushing heat.

Voss stayed in his office, smoked and took some small comfort from moving his thumb up and down, nose to hairline. It had to be that only Lazard and Wilshere had known that he was a double. That Wolters' knowledge stopped at Anne as the informer positioned by Wilshere to send the British chasing after the wrong Beecham Lazard. How else could he be surviving this débâcle? Nobody knew that he'd been in the house. Lourenço had bought Anne's story. He was surviving. The next hours were critical, but what would come back from the street? Had anyone seen him and Anne walking in the Bairro Alto? The cigarette trembled in his mouth. He drew too hard and burnt his lips.

That morning, when the sweat of the city oozed out of their attics, their threadbare *pensões*, their stuffy rooms and dark bars they found the streets zipping with the new blood of fresh news. They sucked it in, this strange tribe, like cannibals who have to eat it to make something their own. They regurgitated it into the mouths of others, with new morsels added from their own inventive minds. The rumours grew and then multiplied when an ambulance reversed into the gateway of the British Embassy, stayed for five minutes and sped out, bell ringing, heading for the Hospital São José. The city ran a fever until lunchtime when those who'd made their small piece piled their olive pits, ate their fish and chewed their bread.

Except Paco.

Paco woke up at three in the afternoon, still dry-retching. He told the boy to bring him a jug of lemon water with salt dissolved into it. He drank it, forcing it down his throat, crying at its sourness. It revived him instantly. He went downstairs on shaky legs and sat, like a patient, under a shade in the sunlit courtyard. He found a half-smoked cigarette in his pocket which, when the boy bought him a herbal tea, he lit for him. He spoke to the boy, and because

255

he was the only one who ever spoke to the boy with consideration, the boy told him things, told him everything that had happened whilst he'd been sick. Paco sat back and knew that his time had come, knew that this was the moment the Englishman had spoken about. Now it was only a question of timing and money.

The tea made him sweat and he thought he should go back upstairs and lie down, but then a Portuguese lowered himself on to the wooden chair opposite.

'I didn't see you this morning,' said Rui.

'I was sick.'

'You missed it all.'

'I don't think so.'

'You could have made your piece.'

'There's time.'

'So you do know something,' said Rui. 'I knew if there was anybody who would know something it would be Paco.'

'What do I know?' asked Paco.

The Portuguese sat back from the table to size up the state of Paco's mind, see if there was anything written on his face. He offered Paco a cigarette, a generosity which in Paco's experience was unusual.

'You heard about the murders?' asked the Portuguese.

'I heard there were six deaths. I don't know how many of them were murders.'

'Three people died in Estoril.'

'In the Quinta da Águia . . . where they had the robbery.'

'The husband killed the American. The wife killed the husband. But who killed the wife?'

'I thought it was an accident,' said Paco.

'Nearly.'

'Who got the loot?'

'Exactly.'

'Haven't they asked the English girl who was staying at the house?'

'She wasn't there . . . off fucking her boyfriend . . . that Englishman you see down at the docks . . . what's his name?'

'Wallis,' said Paco, screwing his fist on to his chin so that, for the first time, Rui knew with certainty that Paco held cards.

'There's money in this, Paco.'

256

'From whom, and how much?'

'The Germans, and that depends.'

'Not the PVDE.'

'No.'

'Is it interesting for them to know that the *inglesa* is lying?' asked Paco, and Rui went very still. 'That her lover is *not* Jim Wallis?'

'I don't know.'

'What do they want to know?'

'The identities of two people who left the Quinta da Águia on the night of the killings.'

'I can tell them something from which they will be able to draw their own conclusions.'

'How much?'

'But I will only talk to General Reinhardt Wolters . . . nobody else.'

'How much?'

'Fifty thousand escudos.'

'You're crazy.'

Paco closed his eyes, dismissing the notion. Rui nodded in sudden comprehension.

'You think it's all over?' he asked. 'Time to get out?'

'For me,' said Paco. 'You belong here.'

'Buy yourself some land, is that what you're thinking?'

Paco shrugged. Exactly that. Back to Galicia. No more selling water in the Alfama as he'd done in the years before the war. His own piece.

The Portuguese told him not to move and ran down the steps and back up Rua das Janelas Verdes, leaping up the *calçada* steps towards the British Embassy and swinging left to the German Legation, arriving at the gate with his lungs in rags. He babbled to the gate man and the very correct woman in reception. He dripped on the floor by her desk as he watched the muscles stand out in the backs of her bare legs as she climbed the stairs. She was back in seconds and didn't bother coming all the way down but beckoned him to follow her. He held his hat over his groin as he told Wolters the news, saw his eyebrows rise when he said the *inglesa* was lying, heard the explosion as he gave the price.

'Fifty thousand to know why the Englishwoman was lying,' roared Wolters. 'How much are you taking?'

257

'Nothing. I swear to you. Nothing.'
'Bring him.'

Voss had felt something different. There was something distinctive about urgency in forty degrees Centigrade. He opened his door a crack, saw the receptionist scuttle out of Wolters' office and down the stairs. She came back up with Rui dripping with sweat. He waited. Rui came back out, rattled down the stairs. Voss crossed to the window, watched him swing on the gate post and sprint down Rua do Pau de Bandeira. As far as Voss knew, this was a man who never ran. He put an eye to the crack of the door. Wolters crossed the corridor to the safe room, returned with blocks of escudo notes. Expenses.

Voss went back to the window and smoked hard, so hard that the nicotine closed the walls in around him. He waited for a lifetime, which in normal currency was only twenty minutes. The Portuguese came back down Rua Pau da Bandeira, trying to make Paco walk faster, but Paco, as Voss knew, had only one pace.

As they came up the stairs, Voss leaned against the door jamb, half in the corridor. Rui knocked on Wolters' door, holding Paco by the arm. Very valuable merchandise. Paco glanced over his shoulder at Voss and in one shameful lowering of his eyelids communicated everything Voss needed to know.

Voss didn't go back into his office. He walked straight down the stairs and out into the barbaric heat, forcing his legs down the driveway in casual strides. He slipped out of the gates with a nod to the gateman and as his foot hit the cobbles of the street he heard the first shout. There was no need to look back. He leaned into the thick air and ran.

He sprinted down Rua do Sacramento à Lapa; the sun at his back needled straight through his jacket and shirt. Sweat popped fatly in his hair. He heard the boots on the cobbles behind him, put his head down, lifted his knees and stamped his feet harder into the pavement. A tram thudded across the entrance to the street, heading downhill towards the British Embassy. He hit the corner fast, coming out into the street and swinging wide and right in behind the tram. He ran between the silver rails, gaining on the tram as its brakes bit and the wheels screeched. The Union Jack appeared blue/red/white high in the corner of his eye. Then he saw the group who'd come out of the legation and run the other way, down Rua Pau da Bandeira, up Rua do Prior and were aiming to cut him off at the embassy gates, which they could because no gateman alive would understand such urgency in this heat. He closed on the tram, where two barefoot boys were hanging off the back, looking at the foreigner in amazement. Voss lashed out at the rail, once, twice, caught it. His feet flailed wildly until they found the ledge. He pressed his streaming face to the glass, a woman inside stepped back, nudged her companion, who turned and looked affronted. Voss worked his way round to the blind side of the tram and it wasn't until it slowed into the left-hand bend that he heard the group behind him roaring at the other pursuers to change direction. The tram picked up speed downhill. One of the runners fell over himself and brought down others in his wake, a few continued down the hill but quickly gave up.

Cardew told Anne he'd bring the car around to the front of the Shell office building. He was looking after her, she knew it, keeping her close. The news of Sutherland's collapse had shaken them both, but the feeling of Rose's new hands on the helm had been immediate. She was on the leash now, not exactly mistrusted but a variable that Rose did not like having in his calculations. She went into the ladies powder room and left, via the back of the building, and headed straight for Estrela and the basilica. She let herself into Voss's apartment, saw the photograph back on its shelf, inspected the brush to find her strand of hair missing. She sat on the back of the sofa, drew her dress up to her thighs to keep cool and smoked out of the window while looking down into the square between the gardens and the church. It was a few minutes past five o'clock.

The tram came to a halt on Calçada Ribeiro Santos just on the other side of Avenida 24 Julho from Santos station and Voss leapt off and on to the pavement. The liners and cargo ships in the docks beyond seemed, at first, an interesting place to lose himself, stow away even, but the risk of being picked up by the port police and taken to the PVDE was too high. He preferred the idea of getting into the maze of streets around the Alfama and disappearing until nightfall, when he could make contact with Sutherland.

The tram seemed to be stationary for a long time and Voss

looked around for cabs, which were rare now in this part of Lisbon with the fuel shortages. His shirt had become a second sodden skin under his suit. He emptied the jacket pockets into his trousers, keeping his eye on the road back up to Lapa from where he was expecting his pursuers. He tried to remember if there'd been any legation cars around. There'd been none in the driveway. At that moment the tram slowly pulled away again just as he heard the sound of a set of tyres squealing and thudding over hot cobbles. Voss hopped on to the ledge at the rear doorway of the tram, pressed himself against the folding door. A black legation Citröen, two chevrons on its grille, the windscreen crowded with faces, drove down Calçada Ribeiro Santos with two wheels up on the pavement.

The tram was painfully slow as it moved away from Santos, as if the electricity in the overhead cables was suddenly draining away into the Tagus. The legation Citroën overtook, with two men leaning out of the windows, straining to see into the tram. Voss crouched. The tram's speed increased suddenly as it moved out of Madragoa into the Bairro Alto. If he could stay with this tram until Cais do Sodré he knew he could get a cab from there into the old medina of the Alfama district and they'd never find him in there, with all the alleys and staircases, the *tascas* and shops, the crowds and chaos of the early evening.

The Citroën pulled up and parked across the tramlines in the Rua da Boa Vista – the bonnet was up but nobody was looking in the engine. A man stood forward from the car with his hand up to stop the tram. Voss worked his way around to the back and came off at a run and kept his momentum up some *calçada* steps. He saw Kempf's big fist reach out, the finger pointing, and heard the crack of leather soles on cobbles as three men gave chase. He wasn't worried about Kempf – heavy, and his system riddled with pox, he wasn't going to last in this terrain and heat – but the young men behind him were fit and fired up with Wolters' zeal. Voss cut through a small *largo*, sprinted up *travessas*, and got into his stride down the Rua do Poço dos Negros. The tram he wanted was just ahead of him, one that would take him through the Baixa and up into the Alfama. He felt oddly unpursued. There was no sound of running behind him. He glanced back at an empty street and he suddenly thought that he was going to get there, that he'd lost them. He tore off his jacket and hurled it into an open doorway and ran, taking big strides, feeling strong, feeling elated. He put his head back and stared up at the light sky above the canyon of the narrow street and his running thoughts suddenly met stationary ones. His knees juddered as he came to a halt. He looked at his watch. It was 5.15 p.m. He'd stopped between the silver threads of the tram tracks. He looked back down the empty street, dropped his hands to his knees, hung his head and knew that he was lost.

Anne would be in his apartment.

They would go to his apartment. They would find her and they wouldn't just kill her.

He stopped a cab going in the opposite direction and directed the driver to the rear of the Estrela Gardens. He sat in the back, a stripe of sun across his thighs, and felt himself suddenly on the other side of the impossible knot. He rolled up his shirtsleeves as the cab pulled in by the roundabout at the bottom of Avenida Álvares Cabral. He paid the driver and went into the gardens, heading for the basilica. He walked, a brisk walk through still, hot, empty gardens – the shade, the sun, the black, the white. He felt a strange exhilaration and in other times he would have stopped to examine it in his head, but this time he knew. He was happy. My God, he was happy. And he remembered Julius writing from the *Kessel* at Stalingrad and knew now what he'd meant. He was free.

He stepped out of the gardens, through the iron railings and looked up and she was there at the window, waiting for him just as he'd expected. At that instant he knew that out there in the blinding sunlight of the square, in the whirling hub of the paranoid city, he was not alone and that nothing else mattered.

She saw him as soon as he stepped out of the gardens and threw her cigarette down the slope of the tiled roof. She leaned out of the window, kneeling on the back of the sofa. She was going to wave at him, but now she saw he was in shirtsleeves and that he'd raised his arms above his head, a strange thing to do. They came at him, running across the square and from left and right. A car appeared from nowhere. He was making no attempt to run. He stood like a sporting hero, expecting adulation from the crowd. He let one arm fall by his side, leaving the right arm raised in a salute. He swiped the air above him and with that gesture said it all – goodbye and get out.

The car pulled up in front of him. They scrummed him in. Anne ran for the apartment door, heard boots thundering up the wooden stairs. She turned back to the dresser and grabbed the package of letters and the Voss family photograph. She climbed out on to the roof, up and over the dormer window and lay there under the brutal sun while they crashed about in the room beneath her, chiselling and hacking at the air with their German voices.

Above her the sky was rediscovering itself in an aching blue after the slow bleaching of the long afternoon. A flight of pigeons took off from the bell towers of the basilica, the first of the evening strollers arrived in the fading gardens and a knife-grinder played on his sad pipes in the street below.

Chapter 25

This is not a diary. I am not allowed to write a diary. I think it must be rule number one of spycraft. I know that if I'm to survive this, with my mind intact and my nerves not so close to the surface that I bristle like a cat at the slightest movement, I must find a way of getting, if not all, then at least a part of it out of me. A release of pressure ... is that what I mean? At the moment it is like a tumour which, because it is of the body, even if it is cell structure gone mad, it is treasured and nurtured by my biology. I can't do anything about it. More blood supply attaches to it. It grows bigger, sucking from all corners like some beastly embryo. I've tried to contain it. I've tried to cordon it off. I've tried to shut it away in an attic room like a crazed aunt. But I can't get the lid down, it broke through the ropes, it's rampaging around the house breaking everything it can lay its hands on.

I've tried to breathe it out of me, speak it out of me, even vomit it out of me, anything to stop what it's doing, which is taking me over. I lie on my back at night, the package of his letters and the Voss family photograph on my chest with only the grainy ceiling in my vision. I breathe very shallowly. The breath coming out in an ooze like bad air from a swamp and through this ooze I say the words, the words that are a part of it. 'Are you alive or dead?' I couldn't keep this up for long because it didn't seem to be a question any more about KV's continuing existence. I began to take it personally. There ... I've smiled, nearly laughed reading that back. This could be working, except that even now I can see what I'm doing. I'm describing it and what it does to me but I'm not writing what it is.

What has happened to me? Nothing. I have sustained no physical injury apart from a bump on the head. I have only seen and felt things. This is how my brain works. Rationally. Logically. I am only two weeks older than when I left London. I am still the same height and weight. There is only one physical difference. I am no longer a virgin. But what was that? A hymen. An unseen membrane. There was hardly any pain, perhaps a little blood – I didn't inspect the sheets. No, what I've come to realize is that the difference between now and then is that rather than living in a state of expectation, I am living in hope. Why am I hoping? Why am I desperately hoping?

All that time ago, in that different age, that first night in the casino, Voss was just a presence, nothing more. When he carried Wilshere up to the house he was just a body, mechanically useful. We didn't meet until we clashed in the sea and we hardly spoke afterwards. How is it that in nearly drowning me he came to take responsibility for my life? I saw him again at the party. What did we talk about then? Nothing much. Fate ... that was it, what else would we have talked about? What did he say? 'It's as if God's lost control of the game and the children have taken over ... naughty children.' He said something else but down at the bottom of the garden, something about Wilshere and Judy. 'What does anybody know from just looking?' A spy's words, or maybe not. He said something else along those lines too. 'Everybody's a spy ... we all have our secrets.' His parents and theirs. Mine. What do I know about mine? We are formed by our secrets. They enter us like bullets. No, that's not it. Like diseases. Bullets are a sweet release if they kill you, crippling if they don't. Disease is more like it. One moment you are healthy, the next you are ill. You have caught something. Secrets are an emotional disease. You cope with it or you don't. Stubbornness helps. My mother is a stubborn woman. Am I? What is my disease?

The next time we met was in his flat. I was so angry. I've never known anger like that. Hot rage. With my mother I'm like ice. A sentence from Rose and I was mad. A few lines from KV and I wasn't. Tender and making love and then the walk. The walk. I'm crying now. Why am I crying about the walk? Yes, it was on the walk that he said, 'I've only been in love once.' I died at that moment, until he said, 'With you, crazy.' When the world dropped away from me then, I saw how anything could happen. How Lazard could have infected Wilshere's mind. How he would believe Lazard over the veracity of his own heart. I know because I'd been falling into the ravine until he said those words: 'You . . . crazy.' How could that be? *Amor é cego*. Mad Mafalda's blindfolded doll.

The last time. Not the very last time. The last time to touch. After the horror. He took charge of me again. He bathed me, towelled me dry, put me to bed as if I was a child. That's what a lover is. Everything. Father, brother, friend, lover. Then lying there with the importance of it all in the briefcase, in the room. That first time he'd said something about 'when we're in here I want it to be just us', and it was, but only that once. The other times we always had our terrible guests.

He made the decision, the important, noble decision, the only one a man like that could make. Wolters will not get his hands on those plans. And for what? All for nothing. Some trick by the Americans. Is that my disease? That he put himself in terrible danger for somebody else's idiotic game, which probably wouldn't have worked anyway. He would have been a hero to both sides if he hadn't been so damned noble. No. That's not it. That's just the world's disease. What's mine? What am I going to have to grow around?

The last time, only to see, not to touch. The irony is in the brevity of the moment. Voss's economy has produced the heaviest burden of all. That fearless walk from out of the dark gardens into the fierce heat and sunlight, his hands up, telling me he was caught. The salute, like my own when I left him that morning with the briefcase in my hand. Love and admiration in one. And the warning. Swiping the air as they came for him. Get out. I was the only one who would have understood him. Get out, Andrea.

I know things now that I didn't know then. Rose and Sutherland were having their first planning meeting about how to get Voss out of Lisbon when Sutherland collapsed. Rose has told me that the PVDE were looking for two people whom they believed had left the Quinta da Águia alive that night. Wallis told me that one of the *bufos* from the Pensão Rocha had seen Voss and I together in the Bairro Alto. The *bufo*, a Galician, had been seen going into the German Legation on that last afternoon. Voss had got out of the legation. He was on the run but he'd come back. It was thought that he'd left something in his flat, something vital to the Allied

265

cause. That could have been the only reason why he would do such a foolish thing as to go back. Nobody knew. But I knew.

This is my disease. But can I write it? I wish it were as impersonal as an equation, all algebra meaning something else. My disease is that I made him go for a walk in the Bairro Alto and we were seen. My disease is that he came back to get me out of his flat. To save me . . . again. My disease is that I have almost nothing of him and yet he has left me with everything.

This is my hope. This is my desperate hope. Not a cure. The cure is to have him back. This is a remission. How many times have I counted the days? How many times have I gone back to 30th June and counted. I was due the day before yesterday and I'm never late.

Chapter 26

30th July 1944, Cardew's House, Carcavelos, near Lisbon.

Anne burnt the crumpled pages in the grate, including the blank
pages underneath, all the way down to the first undented sheet.
She lit a cigarette with the same match and drew on it, knowing
that these would be her friends for life. The writing of her disease,
her assessment of it, her diagnosis of it was consumed in a green
flame until only the blackened negative remained, the copper of
the ink still legible. She beat it with her shoe until it had all broken
up and showered in flakes and specks on to the swept stone below
the grate.

There had been only fractions of seconds when her thoughts
had not been full of Voss. Even the lighting of a cigarette brought
thoughts of his unwavering hand in the darkness of the garden.
Nothing else came to her. Numbers didn't matter any more. Her
work was automatic. Every thought, however disconnected, found
its way back to Voss or a reference to him.

Now there was a difference. The written confession had brought
about some containment. Her mind no longer galloped away from
her, which it had done when she'd heard that Voss had been
smuggled out of Portugal and back to Germany for interrogation.
During those days she'd found herself amongst terrible imaginings
of dark, sobbing cells punctuated by bright, searing light and questions, endless questions. Questions to which there were no answers,
and questions to which all possible answers would be inadequate.
She'd been told about torture, and the detail, which had been at a
manageable distance in a rainy springtime lecture theatre in Oxford,
could now make her writhe in the morning sunshine.

She crushed out the cigarette and for the first time in a week
lay down on her bed and slept six straight hours, no dreams. She
woke up without the normal electrical jolt as her mind hit the

thousand-volt reality. She was on top of the bed. The room warm and glowing pink from the setting sun. Her body felt languorous, as if she'd been walking all day. An exquisite lassitude seeped through her muscles. She stretched to full length like a cat with all day on its mind and had a memory flash so vivid she rolled over to check that the room was empty.

She was six years old, her mother was sitting by her on the bed, cigarettes and cocktails mingled with her perfume, which was different for parties – spiky, exotic. She had her hand on Anne's shoulder, who had been sleeping. The material of her dress wasn't making the usual quiet rustlings but was racked with creaks and convulsive friction. Anne had seen through the slits of her eyes that her mother was crying and not quiet tears. She had been too sleepy, too overwhelmed by the weight of slumber to even put a finger to her mother's knee. In the morning her mother had returned to her usual cool strictness and Anne had forgotten the moment.

A thought unravelled itself. Rawlinson and his missing leg. An odd notion about the integrity of integers, the missing fraction ruining the completeness. What about the invisible missing fraction or the unseen additional one? The structure altered, the equation would never work out. Mad thoughts manipulating maths to emotions, and yet there was such a thing as a nuance.

The Cardew children were already in bed. Anne went down for dinner which was eaten late in high summer and, this evening, out in the garden under the liquid yellow light from Cardew's hurricane lamps. There was a crowd. A chair was pulled out for her and, when the face of the man who had helped her re-entered the light, she saw that it was Major Luís da Cunha Almeida, the man who'd stopped her horse from bolting.

They ate cheese, *presunto* and olives with fresh bread. Cardew poured wine brought by the major from his family estate in the Alentejo. Mrs Cardew served the fresh seafood while the servants went to the village bread oven to collect the lamb, which the cook believed tasted better having been slow-roasted since the middle of the afternoon.

They all ate the lamb, even the servants in the dimly lit kitchen. The potatoes, which were glued to the bottom and sides of the clay roasting tray, were sticky with meat juice and pungent from the garlic and rosemary. The meal returned Anne to her tribe like a rider, horseless on the open plain, who'd made it back to civilization.

At the end of the evening the major asked her if she would like to go out for a drive with him one evening the following week. She didn't say no. He settled on Wednesday.

As she went up to bed, Cardew intercepted her at the bottom of the stairs. He patted her shoulder, gripped it.

'Glad to see you've pulled through, Anne,' he said. 'Terrible shock, I imagine . . . but good show.'

In bed she thought that this was what it was like to be English. This is how we handle things. We're natural spies. We never wear anything on the outside. Napoleon was wrong, we were not *une nation de boutiquiers* but a nation of secretkeepers. We all know you can't say a word with a stiff upper lip.

Richard Rose agreed to see her on Monday afternoon. A positive psychological report must have made its way to him because until now he'd refused to see her. They'd said he was busy, but Wallis had told her that, unlike Sutherland, Rose preferred to keep his distance. He wasn't going to risk discomfort in front of an emotional woman. Rose into women didn't go. They were indivisible.

It was the last day of July and there'd been no relenting of the heat. Rose sat behind Sutherland's desk in the room shuttered against the sun which hammered that side of the embassy building in the afternoons. She sat in the hot gloom, an indistinct, ignorable figure, while Rose read through papers, signed them off. He rubbed his bare elbows as if they were sore from desk work. He muttered excuses. She didn't respond. She knew she wasn't a welcome presence. Sutherland's secretary had been replaced by someone called Douggie who didn't look up when he was spoken to but pointed with his pen. Rose spoke while stacking his papers.

'How d'you fancy staying with Cardew?'

'As his secretary?'

'Thinks a lot of you, he does,' said Rose. 'You'd still be doing the translation work, of course. Very important work, that.'

'I thought that was just my cover.'

'It was, yes. But you can't work as an agent any more, can you? Not here in Lisbon. And given the flap on at the moment we're going to have a job to replace you immediately. London don't want

269

to move you yet. Cautious buggers. They'll have a file on you by now . . . in Berlin.'

That word 'Berlin' shot past her like a bird in the room.

'If you think that's the best use of my abilities . . .'

'We do,' he said, too quickly, '. . . for the moment.'

'You know that I do want to continue with the Company, sir.'

'Of course.'

'If my involvement in the last operation is going to have any bearing on my future . . .'

'Your *involvement*?' he said, pinching his lips, looking her in the eye for the first time.

'That my actions resulted in the loss of a valuable double agent.'

'You shouldn't blame yourself for that, you know,' he said, his face bearing an approximation of pity. 'You were inexperienced. Voss . . . yes . . . he should have known better. A terrible risk he took. Madness, really, for such an old hand.'

'Has there been any news?' she asked, matter of fact, wringing the pathos out of her voice.

'What do you know?'

'Only that he was taken back to Germany.'

'There were two others on the same plane. Men who'd been kidnapped off the streets of Lisbon just like Voss. One of them, Count von Treuberg, has since been released. He told us that Voss had been packed in a trunk for the flight. They were all taken from Tempelhof to the Gestapo HQ in Prinz Albrechtstrasse in the back of a van. Von Treuberg spoke to Voss, who was not in good shape. He saw him once more on the day he was released.'

Rose fell silent. Anne stared into the floor. Her head weighed heavily on the cords of muscle in her neck.

'Voss had undergone three days of intensive interrogation. Von Treuberg was shocked.'

Anne's insides froze and her breathing shallowed.

'Are you sure you want to hear this?'

'I want to know *everything*,' she said with vehemence.

Rose fetched a thick file from the grey metal cabinets that now lined the room.

'The operation you were involved in with Voss took place at a very sensitive moment for the Third Reich.'

'The coup attempt, you mean?'

'SS General Wolters was running an intelligence operation which he hoped was going to be one of the great successes of the war. It's in the nature of the losing team to believe that they can suddenly turn things around with a miracle. His operation was a disaster. He's lost a lot of money and one of the main pipelines for diamonds to the Reich. Voss is his scapegoat. Taken by itself, the botched operation might earn Voss a reprimand and a nasty transfer, but in the light of the 20th July assassination attempt it becomes more serious, which is better for Wolters. Wolters will want to implicate him in the coup attempt, which, at this distance, you might think is improbable except that *we* know that Voss knew what was going to happen. He gave us notice, so it was clear he was involved. Given that he's an old Abwehr man, the only one left out here, we're of the opinion that his part was to take control of the legation in Lisbon. If that is the case and there's a single strand of evidence pointing to that sort of level of involvement . . .'

Rose let his sentence drift, lit himself a cigarette.

'Then what, sir?'

He opened the file, picked the pages apart with his nail and turned them as if they were ancient scriptures.

'The investigation of senior Wehrmacht officers is being carried out by the head of the Reich Main Security Office, SS General Ernst Kaltenbrunner. He's a lawyer, which you might think is a good sign until you've seen a photograph of him. Sinister-looking brute. Total fanatic . . . intensely loyal. He will . . . he hasn't shirked his duties. Thousands of people have been rounded up. Men, women, children . . . anybody with a family connection or otherwise to any of the known conspirators has been brought in for questioning. All other suspects are being interrogated by an SS Colonel Bruno Weiss. He used to be head of security at the *Wolfsschanze*, Hitler's Rastenburg HQ in East Prussia. If he were younger he could be taken for Kaltenbrunner's son. I don't know where they breed them.

'I have no doubt that these men will find something amongst the thousands of depositions because it is in the nature of ordinary people to write things down when they shouldn't, say things that should never be said and babble uncontrollably when they're scared. Voss's chances are not good. If he is charged he will appear in the so-called People's Court presided over by the most disgraceful judge ever to find his way into the law, Roland Freisler, where, if the evidence is even vaguely positive, he will be sentenced to be executed, and if it's not, he will certainly end up in a concentration camp where he's very unlikely to survive.'

Rose flicked through the file. Anne sat rigid in the chair.

'Apart from what we've heard from von Treuberg there is no other news,' said Rose, more concerned with his file. 'If I were you, Miss Ashworth, I'd forget about him. Live your life. It's the nature of war.'

Anne stood on shaking legs, on knees that unless she locked them straight would buckle. She turned to the door.

'You'll continue with Cardew, then?' he said to the back of her head.

'Yes, sir,' she replied, and staggered out of the room into the corridor.

Anne worked with an intensity that unnerved Cardew. She rarely looked up and took no more than a quarter of an hour for lunch. On Wednesday evening she went out with Major Luís Almeida. They drove to Cascais and ate a fish meal. She didn't recall what fish. She remembered the way the major didn't take his eyes off her throughout the meal and even when he was driving, so that she had to brace herself occasionally to get him to look ahead. She knew then that she would be all right because she didn't want to die. She feared death, which she hadn't a week ago. She began to orbit nearer to the outer edges of normality as each day passed and another onion skin of insulation wrapped itself around her disease, her growth, which had been rendered benign now by the absence of any trace of menstrual blood.

The major, on holiday for the whole of August, intensified his campaign and took her out nearly every night. She never turned him down. She only refused to ride horses. His presence was a comfort, his attention close to avuncular. Their talk was formal, inquisitive without being intimate. She preferred that. She could retreat into herself while she was with him and he wouldn't pressure her. She knew that she was changing and that it was for her own protection. It was making her different and she couldn't help that difference materializing into distance. She would find herself in a crowd at a lunch, never aloof but always alone. Society took her in and she let herself become a part of its edifice, not as a brick in its wall but more of a gargoyle spouting out of a corner.

On a mid August Saturday night Anne sat with the major outside a café in the main square in Estoril. He'd tried to persuade her into the casino but she wasn't ready for that yet, if ever. It was eleven o'clock and still hot. She had no appetite for food or drink. She proposed a walk along the front, away from the holiday bustle, the family scenes, the fractious palm trees. The major was glad to stretch his legs.

They walked the promenade above the beach. There was a little light from a crescent moon, no wind and the air was soft. Waves came in as phosphorescent ripples, collapsing on to the beach and running up to merge into the sand. She took his arm. Her heels made the only sound above the muted ocean.

She stopped to breathe it in and the major put his arm around her and she realized that he'd misinterpreted her motives. It wasn't as if she hadn't expected it. It was just that she'd never managed to think any further than it happening. She turned to him and put her hands up on his chest to keep him at bay but he wasn't tentative like Voss. He crushed her to him and kissed her on the mouth for the first time, long and hard, so that she was struggling for breath and completely unmoved.

His staidness vanished. His manner, which was normally governed by a stronger gravitational pull than that on most humans, giving him his granite-like dependability and solidity, broke its moorings and he became all ardour and expression. She was stunned by the transformation. He held her face in his hands and told her over and over how much he loved her, so that the words lost their meaning and she didn't listen to them, but began to think whether this was perhaps a Portuguese trait – to be hermetically sealed receptacles for mad passion.

He was breathing the words into her mouth, as if trying to make her say them back to him, and she was remembering his profound enjoyment of food, how eating one meal would remind him of the wonder of another. Wine to him was like a favourite piece of music. He drank it with his eyes closed, let it flow through him as if it was Grand Premier Cru Mozart. The flowers he bought for her he seemed to enjoy more himself – plucking a bloom, he wouldn't just sniff it, he would inhale it. It struck her that he was a sensualist and she'd hardly been aware of it because he had no talent for conversation but only physical pleasure.

He snapped her back into reality. He was holding her by the shoulders and willing her to respond, his forearms trembling as if he was restraining himself from crushing her. He was demanding that she marry him, but she couldn't find any words to begin to explain the complexity of her situation.

'Will you? Will you?' he asked, again and again, his English heavily accented so that each demand came from deeper and deeper down his throat like a man drowning in a well.

'You're hurting me, Luís,' she said.

He let her go, running his hands down her arms, hanging his head, suddenly ashamed.

'It's not so easy,' she said.

'It *is* easy,' he replied. 'It is *very* easy. You only have to say one word. Yes. That's it. It is the easiest "yes" you will ever say.'

'There are complications.'

'Then I am happy.'

'How can you be happy?'

'Complications are surmountable. I will talk to anybody. I will talk to the British Ambassador. I will talk to the Chairman of Shell. I will talk to your parents. I will . . .'

'My mother. I only have a mother.'

'I will talk to your mother.'

'Stop, Luís. You must stop and let me think for a moment.'

'I will only let you think if it is to overcome these complications, if it is to see that complications . . .' he said, running out of words for a second until he announced, 'Complications mean nothing to me. There is no complication that I cannot . . . that I cannot . . . *Raios*! . . . what is the word?'

'I don't know what you want to say . . . overleap?'

'Overleap!' he roared in agreement. 'No, no, not overleap. Overleap means that it is still there . . . behind you maybe, but still there. Vanquish. There is no complication that I cannot vanquish.'

She laughed at a vision of Luís with sword and shield flashing in the sun, blinding the complications.

'I can't answer you,' she said.

'I am *still* happy.'

'You can't still be happy, Luís. I haven't said anything.'

'I am happy,' he repeated, and he knew why, but he didn't want to say that it was because she hadn't given him the alternative, perhaps even easier, reply.

She crawled into bed at two in the morning. Luís wouldn't let her go home. His earlier boldness had given him new fuel to burn and he couldn't stop. He took her into Lisbon and they danced at the Dancing Bar Cristal. Luís had never been so animated and she realized that he could only speak when he was doing something else. As soon as they went back to the table for a rest he would fall back into silent contemplation of unknown complications until he could bear it no longer and he'd drag her back on to the floor. There he talked as if he knew something she didn't. His family, their estate outside Estremoz in the rural Alentejo, 150 miles east of Lisbon, his work, the barracks he was posted to, which luckily was in Estremoz, and all was related to how their life would be together, how she would fit into his world.

Anne slept and dreamt her dream and woke in a panic with the certainty that she would not be able to survive this pace. Like a fallen rider with a foot still trapped in the stirrup, dragged along at the whim of the horse, she needed a release, she needed control, but she could not bring her intelligence to bear down on the complications. The different strands knotted too quickly.

She asked herself a question. Why shouldn't she marry Luís? She didn't love him was not an answer, it was the reason she wanted to be with him. That she was still in love with Voss did not make any sense. Richard Rose had been brutal in his prognosis. The whole point of her involvement with Luís was to survive her guilt. That she was carrying Voss's embryo was the impediment, which, as soon as the thought occurred, was dispatched. It scared her, not in shivers of panic, they were surface qualms. This was core fear, a deep moral fear. Only religion did this to you, she thought. All that stuff the nuns had crammed into her head about guilt and evil, it shook her up, disorientated her. She paced the room to confirm the ground under her feet, to calm herself, to tether herself to what she now understood, which was that she *had* to marry Luís *because* she was carrying Voss's child.

She sat on the bed inspecting her hands. She had been young. She had been green and whippy, but now she could feel the brittleness of age creeping in and the breakability that came with it. Alone on her single bed, in the high August heat, with the cells multiplying inside her, she shivered in the cold shadows of society, the Church, her mother. She made her decision and even while making it the Catholic inside her knew that there would be some cost, some bloody awful price to pay later on. She would marry Luís da Cunha Almeida and her secret would sit with her other one, they would be joined like Siamese twins, individual but dependent on each other.

The morning light had a new clarity. The thick heat of the last few days and nights had been cut by a fresh, saltine zest from the Atlantic. The sun still shone in a clear sky but bodies felt less like carcasses. The Serra de Sintra was no longer vague in the haze and the palm trees applauded in the square. Out from under the close doom of night, Anne saw things differently. There was hope of a solution. She would talk to Dorothy Cardew. The women, between them, would get things out on the table where they could be examined.

The maid took the Cardew girls to the beach mid-morning and Anne found Dorothy on her own, sitting with her sewing box in the living room. She was working on a sampler, tackling the 'e' of 'Home'. Meredith was outside reading in the garden, his pipe signalling his enjoyment. Anne moved around the room, circling before landing, waiting for a way in. The needlepoint was badly at odds with what she had trampling through her mind. Dorothy Cardew eyed her, made mistakes in the sampler, gave up on it.

'Luís has asked me to marry him,' said Anne, which knocked Dorothy back into the cushions.

Anne registered the total relief in Dorothy's face. Good news after all.

'That's marvellous,' she said. 'Wonderful news . . . such a good man, Luís.'

And that was the end of it. This was not a day for trouble. The clear air, the breeze in the pines, the birds talking up the day so that anything other than good news would seem ill-mannered.

'Yes,' said Anne, the word dropping out of her like a drunk from a bar.

'You must let me tell Meredith.'

The scene developed, transformed from the one Anne had inside her head. Dorothy skipped to the french windows and called for her husband, hopping up on to one leg as she did so.

'Good news, darling,' she called.

Meredith slammed his book shut and scrambled like a fighter pilot. He joined his wife at the french windows, breathless, eager.

'Luís has asked Anne to marry him.'

A flicker of disappointment. Hitler hadn't surrendered after all.

'Congratulations!' he roared. 'Terrific chap, Luís.'

'Yes,' said Anne, another brawler ejected into the street.

A quizzical look from Cardew. Had he seen something? Had he sensed something other than spoken words in the room?

'Have you said anything to anyone?'

'Not yet.'

'Best talk to Richard first . . . could be complicated.'

'Yes.'

'Marvellous news, though . . . couldn't hope for a better chap than Luís. Terrific horseman, too,' he finished, as if that could be an enormous help in a marriage.

Anne's smile creaked into position. This was the future – words taken from her and put into a common language, the language of the receiver, never her own. It pricked her eyeballs because that was one of Voss's talents – an understanding of many languages but more especially the silent ones.

The following Tuesday Anne sat in the Estrela Gardens watching children, waiting for time to pass before heading into Lapa for her meeting with Rose. The children ran over the thousand changing shapes on the ground as the breeze rippled the sunlight through the trees. The pace was slowing at last. The relentlessness was still there but that breathless speed had gone. Now there was the sense of large forces manoeuvring, something perhaps to do with what was happening in Europe as the Russian, American and British armies bore down on the rubble of the Reich.

She walked to the gates opposite the basilica and looked up to the room where she'd been waiting only a few weeks ago. A maid was cleaning the window, a disembodied hand appeared and flicked a cigarette out. At her feet the silver tramlines embedded in the cobbles headed off down the hill of the Calçada da Estrela towards São Bento and the Bairro Alto where they would cross and connect with other rails but would never deviate from their dedicated path. What on one night had seemed like an exquisite thread tugging her to a hopeful future, now appeared as a terrible certainty from which the only way out was derailment and disaster.

She sat in front of Richard Rose again, who was not ignoring her but, because it was after lunch, was lounging back in his chair with a cigarette in his hand and either smoke in his eye or contempt tempered only by shrewdness.

'Cardew told me your news,' he said.

My news, thought Anne, dissociated from it already, a messenger for someone else.

Rose waved his match at her, tossed it into the ashtray. It enraged her, God knows why.

'When we trained you as an . . .'

'With all due respect, sir, you did not train me as a translator. I arrived with that ability on board.'

'When we trained you as an *agent* and the subsequent assessment of your training arrived here in Lisbon, I . . . *we* didn't perceive you as an emotional character. Everything pointed towards you being logical, rational, even clinical. That was why we liked you.'

'*Liked* me?'

'On paper you were perfect for the assignment,' he said, sitting back, flourishing his cigarette, stabbing the smoking end in her direction, goading her. 'You were female, very intelligent, excellent at role-play, of . . . beguiling looks, but also determined, clear-headed, detached . . . in short, perfect for the work.'

Silence while Rose inspected his cigarette box, seeing if that had been enough to elicit more reaction.

'You arrived,' he continued, 'and we were immediately impressed by the way you entered into your role. Good information. Strong social involvement. Excellent handling of some difficult personalities. Everything going swimmingly until . . .'

Rose blew out smoke in an exasperated jet.

'Even logical, rational, clinical people can fall in love,' said Anne.

'*Twice?*' asked Rose.

The cold, cutting edge of the word sliced into her. Its unjustness pushed her on to the defensive.

'It was you who told me to forget about Voss,' she said, 'that there was no hope for him.'

'I did, but . . .' he said, and let that hang with the smoke, accusatory, before dismissing it with a flick of his fingers. 'So, now you'd like to marry Major Luís da Cunha Almeida?'

'He has asked me. I want to know if it's possible,' said Anne. 'I don't intend to allow it to affect my work . . . the work which you indicated that I would be doing in the . . . until further notice.'

'There is the small question of identity,' said Rose. 'If you want to get married I don't see why you shouldn't, it's just that you will have to marry under your cover name and you won't be able to have any member of your family present. As far as the Portuguese are concerned you are Anne Ashworth and will have to remain so.'

'My name changes anyway.'

'Quite.'

'You should know that I broke my cover story.'

'How?'

'I was emotionally . . .'

'Just tell me how.'

'I told Dona Mafalda and the contessa that my father was dead.'

'I doubt that will be a problem. If it is we'll say that you were emotionally distraught, that your father died very recently in an air raid and you've been unable to accept it. On application forms you always put him down as alive but he is in fact dead. We'll arrange a death certificate. Finish.'

And that was the end of the matter. The end of Andrea Aspinall too. She stood and shook hands, headed for the door.

'We've had news of Voss, by the way. Not good,' he said to the back of her head. 'Our sources tell us that he was shot at dawn in Plötzensee prison last Friday with seven others.'

She slipped through the door without looking back. The corridor rocked like a ship's in a heavy sea. She concentrated on each stair going down to the street, nothing automatic, nothing certain. She breathed in the clear air, hoping it would somehow dislodge the obstruction in her chest, this fishbone, this piece of shrapnel, this sharp chunk of crystalline ice. She screwed up her face, doubled over and ran up the hill towards Estrela. It felt like a heart attack and, when she reached the gardens, she found that she could think of nothing else but crossing the road to the basilica and hiding herself in the darkest corner.

Inside, she crossed herself and collapsed on to her knees, face in the crook of her elbow and the word 'never' repeating itself in her mind. She was never going to see Voss again, never going to be herself again, never going to be the same again. The pain loosened itself from the wall of her chest and moved up to her throat. She started crying, but not crying as she'd ever cried before, not bawling like a child, because this pain was pain that could not be articulated. It had no human sound. Her mouth was wide open, her eyes were creased shut. She wanted her agony to find some superhuman screech so that she could get it out of herself but there was nothing, it wasn't on her scale. Scalding tears coursed down her cheeks, acid streaks to the corner of her mouth. Snot and saliva poured out of her, hung in quivering skeins from her mouth and chin. She seemed to be crying for everything, not just herself but Karl Voss, her dead father, her distant mother, Patrick Wilshere, Judy Laverne, Dona Mafalda. She didn't think she would be able to recover from such crying, until a nun put a hand on her shoulder and that jerked her upright. She wasn't ready for nuns, nor the dark sweat box of the confessional.

'Não falo Português,' she said, smearing her face around with a ball of sodden handkerchief. She crashed through the pew into the aisle and ran for the door. Out in the sun, the breeze was still blowing. It went clean through her louvred ribs.

Book Two
The Secret Ministry of Frost

Chapter 27

16th August 1968, Luís and Anne Almeida's rented house in Estoril, near Lisbon.

The night before her flight to London Anne had another running dream. Almost every night since coming back from the vicious fighting in the Mozambique war she'd had running dreams. Sometimes she would be running in daylight, but most of the time it was twilight. This time it was dark and enclosed. She was running down a tunnel, a rough tunnel like an old mine. She had a torch in her hand which was picking up the black shiny walls and the uneven floor, showing the imprint of some old tracks, narrow gauge. She was running away from something and she would occasionally look over her shoulder to see only the blackness she'd left behind her. But there was also the sense of running towards something. She didn't know what it was and she could see nothing beyond the hole of light made by her torch.

She ran desperately. Her heart pounded and her lungs felt pierced. The torchlight began to waver. The beam flickered and yellowed. She shook the torch but it dimmed further and she found herself looking into the fading filament of the bulb, her breath suddenly visible as if it was cold. Finally it was totally black. No source of ambient light presented itself. Fear crawled up her throat and she tried to scream but nothing would come. She came awake with Luís holding her in his arms and she was crying as she hadn't cried in over twenty years.

'It's all right, it's only a dream,' he said, the obvious surprisingly comforting. 'She'll be all right. You'll be all right. We'll all be all right.'

She nodded into his chest, unable to speak, knowing it was more than that but going along with him. It had been a turning point. That subterranean river, which snatched people's lives and drove them harder and faster over the quick rocks, through the boiling water, down the chutes and cataracts, had just grabbed her again. The strong current was wrenching her away from her quiet past, slow at the moment, but the pace was gathering beneath her.

She didn't go back to sleep but lay on her side looking at her husband's broad back, blocking the sound of his violent snoring with thoughts that hadn't occurred to her in more than two decades. The news of her mother's illness had saved them from a formal separation after she'd refused to accompany him to yet another African war but, having arrived at the brink, she now found herself picking over her life, re-examining it in the new light of an uncertain future. One which was sending her back to London and her husband and son, colonel and lieutenant, fighting together in the same regiment in another independence war in Guiné in West Africa.

That other new beginning, twenty-four years ago, came back to her like biography, an objective fascination with another person's more interestingly led life but, somehow, subjectively dull. She saw herself on her wedding day on a belting hot morning in Estremoz. How she was able to appear happy because she was glad that Luís had been so desperate to marry her, he'd rushed her into the ceremony giving her no time to think of the complications she was carrying inside her down that aisle. It had also meant that when her baby arrived three weeks late there was no suspicious discrepancy in the dates between her wedding night and the birth of *their* son on the 6th May 1945.

That had been unforgivable. She still felt the pang of guilt as fresh as on the day she'd announced her pregnancy to Luís. The happiness he radiated, the tenderness with which he held her, cut through to her terrible twin secrets, jabbed them awake so that as Luís's joy grew sweeter, hers could only sour. It was then that she understood the true nature of the spy. The work she'd been doing for Rose and Sutherland hadn't been anything like spying. What she'd done to Luís was spying. Watching him believe in her, admire her, love her, while she silently betrayed him every moment of every day. It was why, she supposed, the punishment meted out to spies throughout the ages had always been cruel and swift.

So much had happened after they were married that she couldn't understand when looking back on it, especially that first year, why it all seemed so flat. All the decisions she'd made – those lonely nights spent in the confines of her mind – had determined the following decades and yet they came back to her with such rational clarity, devoid of excitement, mere measures for the continuation of her existence.

The long weekend of the wedding had seen the beginning of a seismic shift in her view of the world. Snapshots entered her head of Luís's family, the Almeidas, and how they ran their estate in the depths of the rural Alentejo on principles she'd come across when studying the Middle Ages under the nuns. On the morning after the wedding, driving around the estate in a small cart with Luís, they'd come across workers of all ages, even small children, clothed from head to foot against the dry, unbearable heat, reaping corn by hand. She saw them again later sitting under a cork oak, eating the meagre rations provided by the estate and wincing with disgust at the barely edible food. She recognized some of the men who'd been brought in to sing at the wedding feast – slow, beautiful, melancholy songs, which had all the Almeidas, even the men, in tears.

She'd taken Luís to task about the treatment of these people and he hadn't answered her. It had always been like this. She was about to importune Luís's sister, hoping for a more sympathetic response, until the sister, showing her around the kitchens, described, almost with glee, how they pickled the olives with swathes of broom to make them more bitter so the farmworkers wouldn't eat too many. As she'd travelled back to work in Lisbon on the train, an action regarded as treachery by the Almeidas, who thought she should remain with her new family, she found ideas forming in her head, new ideas about a fairer way of life. Ideas which would mean that she wouldn't have to think too much about herself.

She rolled on to her back, turned away from Luís and his animal gruntings. She'd been lying in this same bed twenty-four years earlier with the baby growing inside her as rapidly as her guilt with all its Catholic foundations and she'd known then that there would have to be some payment for what she was doing. A heavy sum would be extracted and she'd hoped then, as she did now, that her unpredictable God would see fit to confine His punishment to her alone.

Her eyelids became impossibly heavy, even against her horror of re-entering the dark tunnels of her dreams, and she slept until Luís, at his morning toilet, woke her.

If her mother hadn't been seriously ill she would have given up at the airport and gone to Guiné with them. She made a fool of herself outside the departures lounge. Luís had to prise her arms from around Julião. She wept in the toilet until her flight was called. As she flew she didn't eat but drank gin and tonics and sat at the back, smoking on her own. She couldn't seem to propel her thoughts forward. Like last night all they wanted to do was drift back listlessly over the past. This time it was her son, Julião, who occupied the foreground of her mind. How she'd failed him and he in turn had failed her.

She'd learned something about genetics on the day he was born. Looking into his face, screwed up against the harsh hospital light, she knew instantly that this child's personality was neither hers nor Karl Voss's and she hadn't been so astonished when Luís, the proud father, had picked him up and said:

'He's me, isn't he?'

In that moment the Voss family photograph came into her mind – the father and his eldest son, Julius, who'd died at Stalingrad – and she knew that this was who Luís was holding.

'I think we should call him Julião,' she said, and Luís had been jubilant that she'd chosen his grandfather's name.

It had been so poignant when they left the hospital two days later on VE day. They drove down the hill from the Hospital São José into the Restauradores to find it full of people waving Union Jacks and Stars and Stripes and jabbing the air with victorious fingers and V-shaped placards. She noticed blank flags being waved, too, and asked Luís what they meant.

'Ach!' he said in disgust, pulling away from the crowd. 'They're the communists. The hammer and sickle is banned by the Estado Novo so they wave these rags . . . I see that and I'm sick, I'm . . .'

He hadn't been able to continue and she couldn't understand his vehemence. So they'd left it, the thin end of the wedge already jammed in between them.

The first black day had come twenty months later when, after trying every siesta and every night to conceive another baby and after three consultations with different gynaecologists, Luís went to see a doctor, a private one, not an army doctor, not for this. He took Julião with him for comfort and, she suspected, to show he'd already struck once.

He returned home, stunned and morose. The doctor had told him something he hadn't been prepared to believe and, on taking the first blast of Luís's outrage, let him look down the microscope himself. The doctor had said it could easily happen. A man, especially one in an active profession and a horseman, could go sterile.

Luís sat outside on the verandah in the January cold, staring at the slow, grey heave of the Atlantic. He was immovable and inconsolable. Anne, looking at the back of his bowed head, knew now that she'd never be able to tell him. After some hours she tried to coax him back in but he wouldn't respond. He even lashed her hand away from his shoulder. She sent Julião out to bring him round. He eventually picked the boy up, sat him on his knee, held him tight and when the two came back in an hour later she knew that something had been resolved. He formally apologized to Anne and looked down on his son's head in such a way that she knew, and it was almost with relief, that Julião would be the focus of Luís's life.

As the plane began its slow descent the adrenalin trickle started. They touched down at Heathrow just after midday. The taxi drove into London past office blocks, endless rows of houses, through traffic, and she knew she was in a foreign country. It was not her own. This was a country which had moved, was moving. She realized how stultifying Salazar's Estado Novo had become. In the first glimpses of London on a summer's afternoon driving through Earl's Court, seeing men with long hair, wearing red flared velvet trousers and vests, vests like the peasants wore except in bright colours and bleached with circles, she realized what Portugal was missing. This lot wouldn't have lasted ten minutes on the streets before being picked up by the PIDE.

The cab driver charged her two weeks' housekeeping to take her to her mother's house on Orlando Road in Clapham.

'It's on the meter, love. I doesn't make it up,' he said.

She paid and waited for him to go, prepared herself. The last time she'd seen her mother was Easter 1947, Luís had been on exercise and she'd flown back to London for a week. It had not gone well. London felt like a beaten city – grey, still rubble-strewn and ration-carded and peopled by dark-clothed shadows. Her mother had shown little interest in Julião and had made no alterations to her social or work arrangements, so that Anne had found herself alone with her son in the Clapham house for most of the week. She'd returned to Lisbon furious and since then she and her mother had phoned rarely, written letters which were strictly informative and exchanged presents neither of them wanted at Christmas and birthdays.

The only change in the street was a new block of flats where her piano teacher's house had been bombed out on the corner of Lydon Road. She walked up the path to her mother's house behind the privet hedge and had a momentary panic at the sight of the red-stained glass panels in the front door. She rang the door bell. Feet clattered down the stairs. A priest opened the door, saw the shock in her face.

'No, no,' he said, 'nothing to worry about. I was just dropping by. You must be the daughter. Audrey said you were arriving today. From Lisbon. Yes. Nice bit of weather we're having here so ... yes ... well, come in, come on in.'

He took her case. They stood in the hall, inched around each other for a moment. Familiar furniture appeared over the priest's shoulder like better company at a cocktail party.

'She's having a good day today,' he said, trying to recapture her attention.

'She still hasn't told me what's wrong with her,' said Anne. 'I tried to ask her last night on the telephone but she's being evasive.'

'Good days and bad days,' said the priest, who although bald, looked as if he was her age.

'Do *you* know, Father?'

'It would be better coming from her, I think.'

'She said it was serious.'

'It is and she knows it. She even knows how long ...'

'How *long*?' she said, shaken by it, not prepared for that level of finality. 'You mean ... ?'

'Yes. She's always playing it down, just says it's serious, but she knows it's only a matter of weeks. Weeks rather than months ... so the doctors are saying.'

'Shouldn't she be ... in hospital?'

'Refuses to stay. Won't have it. Can't stand the smell of the food. Said she'd rather be on her own at home . . . with you.'

'With me,' she said, out loud but to herself. 'Forgive me, Father, but you seem very cheerful, given . . .'

'Yes, well, I always am around Audrey. Most extraordinary woman, your mother.'

'I have to admit that I am quite surprised to see you here. I mean, she was never . . .'

'Oh yes, I know. Somewhat lapsed.'

'I mean, she's always been religious and quite strictly Catholic . . . that's how she brought me up. But as for . . . going to church, priests, confessions, Holy Communion, all that . . . no, Father . . . ? You didn't say . . .'

'Father Harpur. That's Harpur with a "u",' he said. 'Look, I'd best get going. I've put the tonic in the fridge.'

'Tonic?'

'She likes a gin and tonic at about six.'

'Is she in her room?' she asked, suddenly desperate for him to stay, help her through this . . . any awkwardness.

'No, no . . . she's out in the garden sunning herself.'

'In the *garden*?' she said, looking up the stairs.

'She just asked me to put something in your room . . . that's why I came from upstairs.'

'No, of course, but you said she was out in the garden in the sun.'

'Yes.'

'Have you heard my mother's confession?' she asked.

'Yes, I have,' he said, startled by the change of tack.

'Did she tell you when she last went to confession?'

'Thirty-seven years ago. It *did* take several days.'

'Well, that was probably the last time she sat out in the garden, too.'

'No, that would have been when she was in India.'

'Yes, I suppose it was.'

'You must go to her,' he said. 'I must get back to the church.'

They shook hands and he slipped out the door, black and silent as a cat burglar, a soul saver. She took her bags up to her room, which had been painted and new curtains hung. There were flowers on the dressing table. All her old books were on their shelves, even her battered, balding teddy lay on her bed like a valued but stinking hound. The smell of cigarette smoke drifted up from the garden and she saw herself twenty-four years younger sitting in front of the mirror, pretending to light a cigarette from a suitor's hand. She ducked to see herself in the glass, to inspect twenty-four years' worth of damage, but there was little on the surface. She could still grow her hair long if she wanted to and it was still thick and black with only the odd white strand, which she plucked out. Her forehead was smooth, although there was a little creasing around the eyes, but the skin of her face rested on the bones, there was no sag in her cheeks. Well preserved, they called it. Pickled. Pickled in her own genetic recipe.

On the lower floor she pushed open her mother's bedroom door. There was the strong scent of lilies masking another odour – not death, but the decay of live flesh. She shied away from it, went down to the hall, clicked across the black and white tiles to the kitchen and out into the garden. Her mother sat in the sun under a broad-brimmed straw hat with a tail of red ribbon. She had her neck back, her face up to the sun and the high trees which, in full leaf, screened the back of the houses behind. Smoke from a cigarette rippled out of her dangling hand. A tray sat on a stool and an empty chair next to it.

'Hello, Mother,' she said, nothing more momentous coming to mind.

Her mother's eyes sprang open in shock – shock and, she saw, joy.

'Andrea,' she said, as if she was crying the name out of a dream.

She kissed her mother. There was a moment's awkwardness as she crossed over to kiss the other cheek.

'Oh yes, of course, both cheeks in Portugal.'

Bony fingers fumbled across Anne's shoulders, thumbed her clavicle, seemed to be searching for something.

'Sit, sit, have some tea. It's a bit stewed but have some all the same. Did Father Harpur leave you a scone? He's a bugger for those scones.'

Her mother was thin. Her body had lost its compactness, the sturdiness. If there was any creaking now it wasn't from the bra or corsetry clasped to her but from old bones unoiled in their joints. She was wearing a flowery tea gown, and a loose light coat, cream and sky blue. Her pale face when kissed had lost its cool firmness. Now it was slack and soft, warm from the sun. Her features were still fine but faded and she'd lost that severity that had been so tiresome. For someone who was dying she looked good, or perhaps it was just what she was emanating.

'You met Father Harpur.'

'He let me in. I was surprised, I must say.'

'Really?'

'But he was very cheerful.'

'Yes, we do get on, James and I. We have such a giggle.'

'Giggle' wriggled like a worm in her mouth. Anne shifted in her seat.

'He told me he was your confessor.'

'He is, yes. And no, that wasn't much of a laugh, I have to say. He's a poet too, did he tell you?'

'We only met on the doorstep.'

'A good poet, as well. He wrote a very fine poem about his father. The death of his father.'

'I didn't think you liked poetry.'

'I didn't. I don't. I mean, I don't like that self-important stuff. People wandering lonely as clouds . . . you know. It's not me.'

There was a long pause while a wind worked its way through the trees and Anne had the feeling that she was being prepared for something. Softened up.

'Poetry's different these days,' said her mother. 'Like music, clothes, the sexual revolution. Everything's changing. You probably saw it on the way back from the airport. We even won the World Cup . . . was it last year, or the year before . . . anyway that was novel. How are Luís and Julião?'

Silence, while her mother smoked the cigarette to the end, her eyes closed, eyeballs fluttering against the thin lids.

'Tell me about Luís and my grandson,' she insisted gently.

'Luís and I had a bad falling out.'

'What about?'

'About the wars in Africa,' she said, immediately steeling up, not wanting to, but that was what politics did to her.

'Well, at least it wasn't about boiling his egg too hard.'

'He knows that these wars are not . . . if there is such a thing . . . good wars. They're not just.'

291

'He's an army officer, they're not normally given the choice, are they?'

'He should have kept Julião out of them, though . . . and now they're both in Guiné, or at least they will be in a few days' time.'

'It's what men do if they join the army. Combat is what they think they've always wanted from that life, until they get into it and come face to face with the horror.'

'Luís has even seen the horror. That first time back in '61 when we went to Angola . . . terrible . . . the things he told me he'd seen up in the north. But he's been hardened . . . inured to it. God knows, he might have even perpetrated some of the appalling atrocities they reported in Mozambique. No, there's no doubt that Luís knows. He knows absolutely what it's like. But the fact is, *he's* a full colonel, it's Julião who'll be in the front line. Julião's going to be the one who's leading the patrols out into the bush. The guerrillas . . . sorry, I have to stop, I don't really want to . . . I just can't think about it.'

Her mother reached out her hand and Anne thought she wanted more tea at first but found it clawing a way up her leg towards her own. She gave it over and her mother stroked it with a papery palm.

'There's nothing to be done. You'll just have to wait it out.'

'Anyway, that's why we had the falling out. I was supposed to go with them and I refused. Your call saved us from a formal separation.'

Some drops fell on the back of her hand and she thought it was raining and looked up to find the trees blurred as tears leaked down her cheeks. She was crying without knowing it, without understanding why. The start of some difficult unbuckling.

The sun dropped behind the trees. They went inside. Anne rattled ice cubes into glasses, poured the gin and tonics, sliced the lemon, thinking about the new openness of this undiscovered person she'd known all her life, working out the best way in.

'You mustn't spend any of your own money while you're here,' said her mother, shouting from the living room. 'I know what life's like in Portugal and I have plenty. It's all going to be yours in a few weeks so you might as well use it now.'

'Father Harpur said it'd be better if *you* told me what was wrong with you,' said Anne, handing over the G&T, blurting it out, unable to keep up the light pretence.

Her mother took the drink, shrugged as if it was nothing much.

'Well, it started as a stomach ache, one that went on all the time, no respite. Nothing would cure it – camomile tea, milk of magnesia – nothing would even ease it. I went to the doctor. They prodded and probed, said there was nothing to worry about. Ulcer, perhaps. The pain got worse and the men in white coats got their machines out and had a look inside. There was nothing wrong with the stomach but there was a large growth in the womb,' she said, and sipped her drink, frowned.

Anne's own insides quivered at the news, at the thought of something terrible and life-threatening growing inside of her.

'Could I have a tad more gin in mine?' asked her mother. 'They always want to tell you how big it is – the tumour, I mean – as if it's going to be something that you're proud of, like those gardeners at country shows with spuds the size of their grandmother and tomatoes like boxers' faces. I've also noticed that the smaller tumours are always fruit. It's about the size of an orange, they say. I assume it's to give you the impression that it can be easily picked. Once it's bigger than a grapefruit they give up and thereafter it's bladders. They told me mine was the size of a rugby ball, which is a game I've never even followed.'

They roared at that, the glib release, the gin slipping into their veins.

'They took it out. I told them to send the damn thing to Twickenham. These chaps, though, they didn't laugh. Deadly serious. Said they'd taken everything out, kit bag, tubes, the lot – but they didn't think it had been enough. I told them I wasn't sure I had anything else to hand over and they said it was too late anyway. The secondaries were already established. A black day that was. Mind you, I never thought I was going to go on and on, not with the Aspinall track record. Death,' she said finally, 'it runs in the family.'

Anne cooked a piece of lamb, slow-cooked it with garlic and potatoes in white wine.

'I'm dying in here,' her mother shouted, still in the living room.

'I'm dying for another drink and from the wonderful smell of your cooking.'

'It's the way the Portuguese cook lamb,' said Anne, appearing at the door.

'Marvellous. We'll have some wine too, and none of that Hirondelle rubbish I give to Father Harpur. No. In the cellar there's a 1948 Chateau Battailley Grand Cru Classé which I think will suit the occasion of my daughter's return.'

'I didn't know you were interested in wine.'

'I'm not. Not enough to go out buying that sort of stuff. It's all Rawly's. You remember old peg-leg Rawlinson. He left it to me in his will.'

'You were still seeing him?'

'Good Lord, no.'

'But you were, weren't you? Back in '44.'

'Is something burning?'

'Nothing's burning, Mother,' said Anne. 'That was why I was packed off to Lisbon, wasn't it? You and Rawlinson.'

'I'm sure there's something . . .'

'There's no point in denying it, Mother, I saw the two of you in St James's Park after my interview with Rawlinson.'

'Did you now?' she said. 'I knew *something* had happened that day.'

'I followed you from your office in Charity House in Ryder Street.'

'Yes, well, I was working for Section V in those days. That's where Section V was. Rawlinson was in recruitment. I recruited you . . .'

'You *recruited* me?' said Anne.

'Yes, I recruited you, with Rawly's help, and made sure you didn't get sent anywhere dangerous. Thought you'd be safe in Lisbon.'

'Was that all?'

'Yes,' she said, going a little sheepish.

'But you wanted me out of the way as well, didn't you?'

'It wasn't the sort of thing a young girl should know about her mother,' she said, writhing in her chair. 'It was embarrassing.'

'But not now.'

'God, no. Nothing embarrasses me now. Not even dying embarrasses me.'

*   *   *

294

They sat down to eat. Her mother drank the wine and ate tiny scraps of the food. She apologized for not having an appetite. After dinner her mother was sleepy and Anne took her up to bed, helped her get undressed. She saw that frail white body, the small breasts gone to flaps of skin, her belly still swathed in bandages.

'We'll have to change the dressing tomorrow,' she said. 'If you don't mind.'

'I don't mind,' Anne said, pulling the nightie down over her mother's head.

Her mother washed, cleaned her teeth, got into bed and asked for a goodnight kiss. Anne felt a pang at the roles reversed. Her mother's eyes fluttered against sleep and the alcohol.

'I'm sorry I was such a useless mother,' she said, the words slurred and gargling in her throat.

Anne went to the door, turned out the light and found herself thinking about what she'd started on the plane – of her own inadequacy, how she'd loved Julião but always kept him at a distance.

'I'll explain everything,' her mother said, into the dark. 'I'll explain everything tomorrow.'

Chapter 28

Anne sat on her window ledge in the dark, the soft breeze blew through the cotton of her nightdress, rustled the trees at the bottom of the garden, drowned out the slow thunder of the city. A half-moon lit the lawn blue and there was the occasional faint few bars of music coming from a record player a few houses down. If she could have disembodied the sharp chunk of anxiety over Julião's safety she could have called herself happy. She was home and, after all the bitterness between her and Luís, now found herself near someone who had suddenly become reliable and all because of words, a few hours of words. A few hours to break the deadlock of forty-four years. Her mother not the person she'd ever known, behaving as if nothing was any different, as if she'd always been like this. Had the prospect of death done that? Given her a sense of freedom, of nothing to lose. She shivered. Old Rawly had been the tip of the iceberg, something that had broken the surface at the time. There was more. 'I'll explain everything.' That was the problem with becoming a different person, or returning to the original, everybody around you is changed as well. A little sickness crept into her stomach, a flutter in the gut. The nausea of truth taking off.

She was trying not to remember things but it was impossible, under these circumstances, not to look back. She tried to concentrate on the easy details – how she'd carried on working even after the war to the disgust of the Almeidas, Cardew leaving Shell at the end of '45 to go back to a different career in London and how that prompted her to start studying for her seventh-year exams to get a place to read maths at Lisbon University, none of her own qualifications being acceptable. But cutting into these bland facts were the other sharp, undeniable truths. Luís had drawn Julião to him,

296

made him *his* son, not hers, and she hadn't resisted it and, at the time, she couldn't think why.

She'd busied herself with her maths and political observations. The harsh treatment meted out to the *ganhões*, the day labourers, employed at subsistence wages by the Almeidas' foremen was little different from what the city workers suffered in the factories and on construction sites. Under Salazar's fascist régime the conditions were terrible and any treacherous talk of union representation was rooted out by the *bufos* and the troublemakers handed over to the renamed, but equally brutal, PIDE. Her perception of these injustices hardened her and not just to the perpetrators. Luís became less of a husband, a more distant figure because he was away a lot, but also she thought of him as the father of her child – a job description whose irony never failed to make her uncomfortable.

She veered away from the start of that kind of thinking, lit a cigarette and paced the room, saw her first day at the university back in the autumn of 1950. The meeting with her tutor and mentor, João Ribeiro, a stick man built from pipe cleaners, a deathly pale individual who ate nothing, drank endless coffee in the form of small strong *bicas* and smoked packets and packets of Três Vintes. He was in constant pain from his teeth, of which only two were a yellowish white, the rest being brown, black or not there. From their first meeting, since he'd interviewed her for the place, he'd known that he had a brilliant student in front of him and they became close. When, a few months later, looking out of his window, they saw the arrest of several students and a professor by the PIDE, they exchanged a look and then risked some views on the matter. He felt safe because she was a foreigner but he was taking a risk, especially knowing that her husband was an army officer. After that groundbreaking moment their tutorials became maths and political symposiums and after some weeks João Ribeiro received permission to introduce her to some officials of the Portuguese Communist Party.

They were interested in her curriculum vitae although the written version didn't include her war service, but because there'd been Portuguese communist collaboration with the British Secret Intelligence Services at that time, they were aware of her role and were interested in her training. The communists had been decimated by a series of successful PIDE infiltrations and the subsequent arrests had included one of the main resistance leaders, Alvaro Cunhal. They wanted to make use of her SIS training to implement some safety measures within the cadres.

It became routine that after their tutorials João Ribeiro and Anne would throw themselves into Party work. She introduced a protection system whereby cell members would never know the identity of their controller, and all new members were given passwords, which were regularly changed. With João Ribeiro she developed new encryption codes for documents which, even when the PIDE raided a safe house in April 1951, proved to be uncrackable as there were no further arrests. Over the spring she introduced the whole idea of cover and initiated training programmes in role-play.

After the arrest of Alvaro Cunhal, the central committee had begun to suspect that they had a highly placed traitor in their ranks. Anne and João Ribeiro concocted a series of dummy operations in which each member of the central committee's discretion was tested with specific pieces of information leaked to them. Manuel Domingues, one of the most senior party members, failed the test. If Anne still thought she was engaged in intellectual games it changed that night. Domingues was interrogated and revealed to be a government spy and provocateur. *A Voz*, the Salazarist newspaper, reported the discovery of the body the next day, 4th May 1951, in the Belas pine forest north of Lisbon. He'd been shot, or rather executed, as she'd forced herself to accept.

In 1953 they launched the rural Communist Party newspaper, *O Camponês*, whose avowed aim was so close to Anne's heart – to campaign for a daily minimum wage of fifty escudos. The workers won their demands after a series of punishing strikes and brutal pitched battles between peasants and police, but not before a young and pregnant woman from Beja, Catarina Eufémia, was shot by a GNR lieutenant to become a martyr and symbol of the brutality of the régime. Her image emblazoned the front of *O Camponês* countrywide.

Anne stopped in her tracks across the room and looked up out of herself and realized that steely obsessiveness had returned. In falling back on those memories, she'd forgotten or rather been able to put aside, the moments of . . . what had she called it? Domestic pain. That made it sound like knife cuts and toe stubs, which is

298

possibly what it had been, but they added up, maybe that was it, they added up.

In the morning her mother didn't tell her anything. She was sick and in pain. Anne changed the dressing on the livid, black-stitched scar across her mother's stomach. Her mother took pills and drifted, floated on a cloud of morphine through the slow, hot day. The next day was the same. Anne called the doctor. He inspected the wound, looked into the old woman's dull eyes, tried and failed to get any sense out of her. He left saying she'd have to go into hospital if she didn't come round. It must have penetrated her mother's unconscious state because it rallied some of her old stubbornness. She didn't take morphine the next day and slept through the morning.

The brilliant sunshine of the first days had been taken over by a growing oppression. The clear heat had become thunderous and the pressure leaned against the windows. Her mother ate a little lunch and read the newspaper. Anne took tea with her in the bedroom, sat facing the window with her feet up on the ledge. Her mother was sweating and held a damp flannel in her hand.

'It used to get like this in India before the monsoons came. The later the rains, the worse the heat. Everybody else went up to the north. Houseboats in Kashmir . . . that sort of thing. We . . . the missionaries, stayed. Terrible heat,' she finished savagely.

'It was the same in Angola.'

'What places for women like us to have been. They died in the streets in Bombay . . . just dropped to the floor like old carpets.'

'The smell,' said Anne.

'I don't think I could have lived with all that endless decay.'

'How do you mean?'

'If I'd stayed in India.'

'Would you have done?'

'No,' she said, after some time, 'no, I wouldn't . . . I couldn't have stayed.'

'Why not?' asked Anne, pushing now, sensing that they were coming to the nub of it.

Her mother stared at the lump of her feet at the end of the bed.

'You'd better bring me that box from the dressing table,' she said.

It was a reddish box and on the lid were carved two stylized figures, a man and a woman. Indian. Her mother opened it and tipped the contents of her jewellery on to the bedcover.

'This is beautiful,' she said and pushed her thumbs into the corners of the box below the hinges. The bottom of the box dropped like a jaw and two pieces of paper fell on to the sheet. 'You see, on the lid are the lovers and underneath are their secrets.'

The light outside had turned yellow. The sunlight strained against some dark centre like an old bruise. It screwed the pressure down in the room and the perspiration came up on their skins.

'You'd better sit down,' said her mother, and reached for her spectacles, which she held in front of her eyes without unfolding.

'Is this going to be a shock?' Anne asked.

'Yes, it will be. I'm going to show you who your father was.'

'You told me you didn't have any photographs of him.'

'I lied,' she said, and handed over one of the pieces of paper from the box.

On the back was written *Joaquim Reis Leitão 1923*. She turned it over. There was a photograph of a man in a light suit.

'Is there something wrong with this photograph?' asked Anne. 'Or the light? Perhaps it's just old.'

'No, that's what he looked like.'

'But . . . he seems to be very dark-skinned.'

'That's right. He's Indian.'

'You said he was Portuguese.'

'He was . . . partly. His father was a member of the Portuguese garrison, his mother was a Goan. Joaquim was a Catholic and a Portuguese national. His mother,' she said, and shook her head, 'his mother was stunning. You take after her, thank heaven. The father . . . well, he was a good man, so I understand, but beautiful? . . . Perhaps the Portuguese are different on their own turf.'

'My father was an *Indian*.'

'Half Indian.'

Anne took the photograph to the window but the light was so bad she knelt by the bedside lamp trying to discern the features.

'You look like the mother . . . lighter-skinned but . . .'

Anne squeezed the picture as if it was flesh and she was trying to extract something, not a splinter, but a tincture of life.

'So why couldn't you stay? Was it the cholera?'

300

'This was before the cholera.'

'What was before the cholera?'

Her mother dabbed her face and neck with the flannel.

'It's going to break soon,' she said. 'The weather.'

'They did all die in the cholera outbreak, didn't they?'

'Both my parents died in the cholera outbreak but that wasn't until 1924. This was in 1923.'

'When you got married? I was born in 1924 so . . .'

'We were never married. It didn't happen like that.'

The thunder rumbled way off in Tooting or Balham. The room was lit only by the bedside lamp which suddenly flickered and went off. The two women sat still in the ghastly light of the approaching storm.

'Was this your confession?'

'Yes. Father Harpur showed me his poem about his father afterwards. It was a great help for me. For the first time I managed to make sense of things . . . understand my stupid self.

'I fell in love with Joaquim. Madly in love. I was completely crazy for him. I was seventeen. I didn't know anything. I'd had this strict Catholic upbringing. The convent and then the mission. I knew nothing about boys . . . men. Joaquim was being trained by the Portuguese in medicine. My father got on well with the Portuguese. All Catholics together, I suppose. The Portuguese used to send the mission medicine and staff. One day they sent Joaquim. I was working as a nurse in the hospital at the time so I met him on his first day and everything I'd ever been taught, all my religious education, all my fear . . . it all went out of the window when I saw Joaquim.

'It was physical. He was the most beautiful human I'd ever seen. Dark brown eyes with great long lashes and skin like sanded wood. I just wanted to touch him and feel the texture of him on the palm of my hand. He had beautiful hands, too. Hands that you could watch doing anything and they'd lull you. I'm banging on, I know, but it was an incredible thing for me at the time. To have this feeling inside of me of, of . . . I never know how to say this because it was too many things at once – certainty, beauty, joy. You know what Father Harpur said? "Like faith, you mean?" And that would have been it . . . if sex was allowed to come into faith.'

'Sex,' said Anne, the word falling out of her mouth, prickly, like a horse chestnut, which grew to the size of a sea mine in the room.

'Yes. Sex,' said her mother bluntly. 'And before marriage, too. You'd have thought they'd only just invented that, the way they go on about it these days. Joaquim and I couldn't keep our hands off each other. We had the opportunity in the mission hospital at night. We even had a bed. We were young and reckless. I tried to keep count of the days . . . tried to be careful, but we were both incapable. I got pregnant.'

The thunder rolled nearer. The sound of the wooden tumbrel on a cobbled street was south of the Common now, the smell of rain already coming in through the windows. The pressure cracking. The electricity in the air fizzing.

'That was a terrible day. Joaquim was away, back in Goa. I'd been praying to come on. My father couldn't believe my sudden devotion. And one day it hit me. Two weeks after I should have had my period it came to me that this was it and I panicked. I lay in bed at night, my brain in a flat spin, trying to imagine myself standing in front of my father . . . you didn't know my father. It was inconceivable to have to tell him that I was pregnant and, not only that, I was pregnant by an Indian. I mean, they liked Joaquim very much. They loved the Indians but . . . mixed marriages. No. The Portuguese were different in that respect, they've always mixed with the locals in their colonies, but the British . . . a white British Catholic girl and a Goan. It wasn't possible. It was against the laws of nature. No different to homosexuality in those days. So, I panicked. I made up a story. I invented this very detailed account of how I'd been raped and become pregnant.'

'By whom?'

'A man. A fabricated man. One who didn't exist. It was easy to act it out. I mean, I was so damned upset anyway . . . almost mad at what I was having to go through.'

'And Joaquim?'

'He still wasn't there. The Portuguese had sent another medical student for a couple of weeks. I was on my own. I was in a desperate state and I knew something had to be done. So I told my father I'd been raped, broke down and wept in front of him, fell at his feet. Literally, I was a heap on the floor. I cried until I retched. My father called the police. The local police was headed by a fellow called Longmartin. He was one of those fearsome, muscular types,

302

quite small, wire-brush moustache and with a neck in a permanent state of rage. He came round and took my statement, the statement of my completely flawless story. He also spoke to my father. I don't know what was discussed. I think perhaps they were asking my father whether he wanted it kept quiet in the district that his daughter had been raped. How open the investigation should be. I don't know. What I did know was that once those words of mine were uttered, they changed everything. I don't know where I got this from, my own mind, Father Harpur, a book . . . I don't know. The fact is that something started with a lie can only beget other lies, like a bad bloodline it will continue through to its terrible end.'

The wind thrashed through the trees, rattled the sash windows in their frames.

'What did Joaquim say when you told him?'

'There was nothing to be said. It was a *fait accompli*. He was racked with guilt that he'd brought this upon me . . . as if in some way I'd been unwilling in the whole affair. I've never seen anyone in such a torment of anguish. He was appalled that I'd had to take this stigma upon myself. The stigma of a defiled woman. He felt totally responsible. He wanted to go to my father. He wanted to take the blame.'

'Oh, my God . . . and did he?'

'You haven't heard the half of it yet.'

The first drops of rain hit the window. The smell of it on the hot tarmac filled the air. Thunder cracked overhead and lightning blitzed through the room. The net curtains billowed in the bay window and the roof took the full force of the colossal downpour.

'The way it happened,' her mother said, raising her voice over the roar of the rain, 'was that the police caught somebody. Yes, there's a crash course in colonial justice in this, too. They came to the house, Longmartin and two of his constables. They wanted me to identify someone. This was ten days after my supposed attack. I had myself under control by then, but when my father came to my room and told me I had to go with Longmartin, I went straight back into the terror. Of course my father said he'd go with me but Longmartin was a clever little bastard, that's why he'd brought the two constables along with him. There was no room in the car. He wanted me on my own. I rode in the back with him and he told me what was going to happen. There would be a line-up of six

303

men, all Indians. They would be standing under the light behind some mosquito netting and I would be in the dark, so I'd be able to see them but they couldn't see me. I nodded through all this and then Longmartin started to say something else. He went from being the straightforward, almost brutally frank, police officer to somebody altogether quieter, more threatening, hopping backwards and forwards over the line of implication.

'He said that he was glad that they'd been able to clear this matter up. They were just beginning to have second thoughts about what had happened because they hadn't had the first glimmer of a clue. None of their informers had come back with anything except some rubbish about a Goan student at the mission. All the locals hate Goans, he said, because they're Catholics. Little hints but with an accumulative weight. By the time we reached the police station I was convinced he knew my game, so when he whispered in my ear as I went in front of the line up: "Third from the end." I didn't hesitate. I walked the line and went straight back to the third man from the end, whom I'd never seen before in my life, and pointed him out.

'Longmartin was very pleased. He took me straight home and handed me back to my father and said: "Very brave girl, your daughter, Mr Aspinall. Very courageous. Looked him in the eye and pointed him out. Very plucky, I must say." I hung by his side, a broken, spineless creature, while he snapped me up into pieces with his savage little ironies. I even thought I heard derision in his voice. I went to bed and, when I wasn't lying on my back staring sleepless into the mosquito net seeing that man's face behind it, I was writhing about as if ... as I had been before they took this damned tumour out.'

'So Joaquim wasn't involved in the end.'

'Things were already going wrong in India. I know it was another quarter of a century before the handover but colonial rule was already in trouble even then. It had only been four years since that terrible business in Amritsar when General Dyer machine-gunned all those unarmed demonstrators. There was unrest everywhere. The man I'd pointed out was a leader of one of the local Hindu resistance militias. Longmartin had wanted him for years. When the Indians heard the charge against their man, they rioted and marched on the mission, but Longmartin was well prepared. The troops stepped in and broke it all up.

'Joaquim couldn't stand it. Everything had gone to dust. Our physical desire for each other had vanished. We could hardly bear to be in the same room as each other because we were so tormented by the developments. He saw it all as his fault. He was six years older than me and should have known better etcetera, etcetera. Now a man was going to hang in all probability because of him. He was outraged at the injustice. He said it would never have happened in Goa. He demanded to know my lie . . . how I'd said the rape had occurred. And he was fierce about it, Andrea, totally frightening. I told him everything and he handed himself in to Longmartin, admitted to raping the English girl, gave him my story verbatim.'

'And Longmartin accepted it?'

'I imagine Longmartin was furious. It was probably the one thing he hadn't anticipated. If you're ignoble yourself you can't foresee another's nobility. I know he would have resisted it strongly. I don't know what Joaquim said to persuade him but I think he must have scared him, given him a few ideas about how bad the rioting could get if the Hindus had categoric proof of their man's innocence. The end of it was that the Hindu leader was released and Joaquim was . . . Joaquim . . .'

Her mother was suddenly struggling against the unseen torment. She lay back, head thrown against the bedstead, her mouth wide, black and gaping, her shoulders convulsing with each chest-wrenching hack. She collapsed to her side. Anne sat next to her, put a hand to her shoulder, remembered that night when she was a child, her mother after the party sobbing to herself. Gradually the bird-like body underneath her calmed, the eyes opened and stared blankly into the room.

'Joaquim died in police custody,' she said. 'The official line was that he "committed suicide", hanged himself from the bars of his cell. Another version was that Longmartin was punishing him for ruining his little plan and he overdid it. As far as everybody was concerned, not just my parents and the people at the mission, but the whole town, Hindus and Muslims alike, justice had been done. Ten days later I was put on a ship to England. It was my peculiar fate that I, as the instigator of the whole rotten business, was to survive all of them. Thousands died in the cholera outbreak the following year including my parents, the Hindu resistance leader

305

and Longmartin. As a nurse in the hospital my chances would not have been good. As it was I became a living monument to my own moral cowardice. And Joaquim, the most honourable of men, died ... reviled by everyone ... even his father wouldn't collect the body and he was buried in an untouchables' grave on the outskirts of town.'

The rain moved off. The air blown into the room was cool and clear and brought with it the freshness of wet earth and mown grass. Her mother strained to sit up. Anne propped her up on the pillows. In her hand was the other piece of paper from the box.

'So that was my tale full of sound and fury. Shakespeare was right. It all comes to nought in the end. The slate is constantly wiped clean,' she said, and handed Anne a letter. 'This was the first, last and only letter he wrote to me ... from jail. One of the Hindu leader's men brought it to me. Read it. Read it out loud for me.'

Dear Audrey,
I feel clean for the first time in many days. My body is filthy, they don't let me wash, but inside I am scrubbed clean, the walls newly whitewashed and the sun bright against them so that I can hardly bear to look. I am happy in the same way that I was happy when I was a small boy.

You must believe me when I tell you that what I did was for the best. What would have become of our love with that man's death between us? Better that we should hold it as something that was good and true although not to be. I know in these short lines that I might not be able to persuade you that none of what has happened is your fault. I am suffering the consequences of my own mistakes. You must sail away from here into the rest of your life with a clear mind and the knowledge that you have been my only true love.

Joaquim

'It's not an excuse,' her mother said, 'but an explanation.'

Chapter 29

Autumn 1968, Orlando Road, Clapham, London.

The days shortened inch by inch towards the end of summer. The number of 'bad days' increased. If Audrey got out of bed it was only for a few hours in the afternoon. They spoke in the lucid moments before the pain took hold and the morphine smothered it.

Anne made a study in the room next to her mother's, put a desk in front of the window with one of her many photographs of Julião at one corner and read Number Theory books during the day and Jane Austen at night. When she wasn't reading she was thinking and smoking and watching the way the smoke was drawn up though the lampshade and into the dark.

One afternoon there were kids playing in the street, all gathered around one boy who was explaining the rules, and she saw herself years earlier looking out on to the lawn in Estoril at Julião and his friends. He'd only been eight years old and yet all the boys looked up to him, faces rapt with admiration, and she could only think of Julius and his last letter from the *Kessel* at Stalingrad. His men. It had started an ache in her chest. It was during the time they were launching *O Camponês* and she realized then that Julião was a passion she could have allowed herself, a cleaner, warmer passion than the politics she'd chosen, except it was a passion she didn't feel she deserved and it was one she feared, too. She could never rid herself of that sense of a payment due. She photographed Julião all the time, despite some dim memory telling her that primitive people thought that it was a theft of the soul. To her it had been a constant confirmation of his existence but now, fingering the frame on the corner of her desk, she wondered if it was her way of loving him at a distance.

* * *

307

She didn't sleep much in this period. Her mother would call out at all times of night and Anne would sit with her until she drifted off again. They covered old ground, her mother added detail to incomplete pictures.

The great aunt who, on Audrey's parents' death, had inherited and lived in the Clapham house with her niece and the illegitimate child, had died and left it all to Audrey when Anne was barely seven years old. Audrey had been working in Whitehall as a secretary for five years. The job had been arranged for her by her aunt and when she died it meant there was no one to look after the child, which was why Anne was sent to the nuns early.

'It was your Great Aunt, my Aunt G, G for Gladys, who started this régime of discipline. She was strict with both of us and I just carried it on. It wasn't me at all but it was a useful persona to hide behind.'

'What were you hiding from?'

'Your curiosity,' she said. 'My own guilt. I was quite different at work. I think I was seen as a bit of a good-time girl, always on for a drink, always ready for a party. I learned how to laugh. A loud laugh is very useful in England.'

'You must have had . . . offers.'

'Of course, but I didn't want anybody getting too close. Rawlinson was perfect. I have to say, there was something about his missing leg that attracted me. I couldn't fathom it at the time, especially as the only man I'd ever known had been physically perfect. It occurred to me only the other day that this was what I thought I deserved. I didn't want the full commitment so I didn't go after the whole man. I certainly wasn't his only girlfriend, either.'

'I followed him to Flood Street.'

'That was his wife. They didn't do much together. She never knew about the wine even. Terrible . . . the secrets, aren't they? We were bloody masters, Rawly and I. It's funny how they know, isn't it?'

'Who?'

'The Company. Once the war got going I was transferred into the Ministry of Economic Warfare. I was good with numbers . . . only numbers, mind, not *your* hieroglyphics. Secretaries in those days did most of the work and it was all top-secret stuff. They liked me. And when they moved Section V up from St Albans to Ryder

Street they sent me over there to keep an eye on the money.'

'What was Section V?'

'Counter Intelligence. And you know who was running it? Kim Philby. Yes, Philby was there from the beginning. I couldn't believe it when he fled to Moscow. 1963. It was a cold day. January some time.'

'You were talking about how they know.'

'Yes. How they know the ones who can keep a secret.'

'And?'

'They find the ones who've already got a secret to keep. I'd be useless now. Thrown it all away. Tell anybody anything, me. They'd call me Blabbermouth Aspinall and give me my cards.'

'And you were still working for the Company after you retired?'

'Oh yes, still in banking. You'll see them all at the funeral . . . except him.'

'You liked Philby?'

'Everybody did. Great charmer.'

Audrey suddenly directed her to the chest of drawers, left-hand side, under the bras and knickers, to a small leather box. Inside was a medal on a length of ribbon.

'That's my gong,' said Audrey. 'My OBE.'

'Why didn't you tell me?'

'My great triumph!' she said, punching the air weakly. 'Not much of one after forty years' service.'

'I'd liked to have known.'

'Now, yes. Now that we're talking,' she said. 'You know, it wasn't just because of Rawly that I sent you away. I *did* want you to be safe but . . . I wanted you out of my sight, too. You were a constant reminder of my weakness, my cowardice. You remember I couldn't stand the heat either. It brought back India. Terrible headaches.'

That night Anne sat even longer at her desk, the Jane Austen open but unread in front of her, just her own still reflection in the dark glass of the window pane and the trail of smoke rippling from the ashtray. After the afternoon's revelations she was thinking of her own secret life, which had continued after she graduated from Lisbon University with an offer from João Ribeiro to do a postgrad thesis on the new hot topic – Game Theory.

309

She'd snatched at the chance. Julião, under Luís's constant supervision, was becoming more embroiled in his young male world and drifting further from her already weakening orbit. Two years later she was stunned and a little sickened when he announced that he'd joined the boy's brigade, Mocidade, without asking her. To Anne, Mocidade was no better than the *Hitler Jugend* and it was only João Ribeiro who was able to mollify her, by saying it was a completely natural thing for a boy to want to do, to go off walking and camping in the hills with his friends.

It was then that the secret work had become even more important to her. She knew it was irrational but she saw Julião's actions as defiance, even, God help us, betrayal. The boy spent all his time with Luís, he was a brilliant sportsman and horseman, he was good at maths but not brilliant and he had a complete blindspot for physics. All that, and his pride in the Mocidade uniform, made her think that her son was all Almeida, that there wasn't a drop of Voss left in him.

It had come to her one day, as she was taking the train into Lisbon and looking at the faces in the carriage, that it was her secret life that made her different. She knew it brought her excitement but it was at that moment that she began to think it was bringing meaning, too. She lived for her document encryption sessions with João Ribeiro, the long meandering walks to the safe houses and secret printing presses of *O Camponês* and *Avante*, the role-playing sessions, the whole mechanics of the clandestine struggle.

For her husband she felt occasional affection, for her son – unconditional, if distant, love, for her mathematics – an objective, intellectual interest, and for her secret work – a deep need, an addiction stronger than the cigarettes she smoked end to end with João Ribeiro and the caffeine in the coffee they drank. It was what defined her.

She even recalled lying in bed one night next to Luís's snoring and feeling suddenly sufficient, enclosed, whole. She was thinking that guilt was being assuaged. Her secret work for social justice was an endless 'Hail Mary', penance for her self-confessed sins. It was part of the process of purification. And just as she arrived at this point she'd shaken the nonsense out of her head. She was a communist, an atheist – it had been muddled thinking.

She replenished her glass of brandy, found another packet of

310

cigarettes and couldn't help immersing herself in the real glory years. In 1959 João Ribeiro and Anne planned what became, a year later, the brilliant and successful escape of their leader Alvaro Cunhal from the Peniche prison in the north of Portugal. They followed this with an even more outrageous scheme which would bring the attention of the world to the suffering of the Portuguese people. In January 1961 a group of Portuguese communists hijacked the cruise liner *Santa Maria* in the Caribbean. She referred to those two operations as the glory years but, looking back on it, they'd been short-lived. That was the high point of João Ribeiro's fame within the PCP. It was downhill after that. Members of the central committee became uncomfortable with his success and, when there followed a number of inexplicable arrests of communist cadres, suspicion seemed to fall automatically on João Ribeiro and his foreign assistant. João was sidelined into dull Party work but heard there was a plot to have Anne deported. He split away from her, told her to stay at home and destroy anything that could compromise her with PIDE.

Anne spent a month pacing the drawing room of the house in Estoril, smoking severely, waiting for the knock. Luís was away on exercise almost constantly. The knock never came. Her exit from the resistance stage arrived when Angola blew up in February 1961 and Luís and his regiment were sent out to quell the rebellion. Six months later, when the initial crisis was over and the fighting contained in the north of the country, she'd arrived by boat in Luanda with a sixteen-year-old Julião.

She sat back from the desk, turning the tumbler of brandy in her hands. She'd expected more from her memories. She'd expected some kind of emotional intensity to come with them but, as when she'd woken up from the nightmare back in Lisbon, it had come back to her as newsreel. She looked in on her mother who was fast asleep, the air rushing into her gaping mouth, and realized that she'd been more replenished in a matter of weeks than she had been by two decades of living.

Before the end of August the weather changed. A chill wind blew in from the north-east and summer was over. Audrey remained in bed all day, sailing on morphine. She muttered to herself, babbled lines of poetry while kids screamed outside and a football boomed against a car. A man, cross, roared at them and after a pause a small voice piped up:

'Can we have our ball back?'

'No, you bloody can't.'

Anne sat with her mother, holding her hand most of the day, squeezing it like a pulse, mulling over those endless days spent on the verandah in Angola while Luís fought the rebels and Julião played war in the garden. How it had all been leading to what she saw at the time as Julião's next betrayal, which was his dramatic announcement in 1963 on his eighteenth birthday that he'd been accepted by the Military Academy for Officer's Training. Why did she still think of it as betrayal? As if she'd spent years developing his political consciousness. A crack opened up in her mind and she'd just got her eye to it, her eye to a small chink of truth, when her mother suddenly said:

'You never told me about Karl Voss.'

It jolted her, whipped her head round to her mother, whose eyes were closed, her breath baffling and ricocheting in her throat.

'Mother?' she asked, but there was no reply.

Now there was regret at a chance missed. Her mother, working in Section V, must have seen the progress reports, must have read about her indiscretion with their double agent, the military attaché of the German Legation. In all their time together Anne hadn't spoken about Karl Voss and she'd had no intention of doing so. This was her mother's time, her mother's confessional. Earlier Audrey had urged her to go to Father Harpur several times. Anne even liked Father Harpur but she wasn't going to see him because she knew what he'd ask of her. He would compel her to tell Luís and Julião the truth and, whilst she could live with Luís's contempt, she would not be able to bear Julião's disdain. Now she thought that she should have told her mother, that it wouldn't have mattered. She wouldn't have made any demands. She would have listened and taken the secret to the grave with her.

She wrote a letter to a friend of João Ribeiro's, a mathematics professor at Cambridge called Louis Greig. His name and address had been given to her on her last afternoon in Lisbon while she'd put into action a half-measure, as she'd called it. She'd given João Ribeiro a wooden box from Angola containing the Voss family photograph and letters for safekeeping. She didn't want Luís to come across them if it ever came to him clearing her out of his life.

Louis Greig replied to her letter by return, urging her to visit. She responded, telling him about her mother but also jotting down some of her recent ideas and asking if there were any course possibilities, not in her doctoral thesis subject, Game Theory, which was a dead duck by now, but more in the line of pure maths. He wrote back saying that João Ribeiro had made contact and that there were definite possibilities for someone of her calibre. It was then that she began to see her half-measure as a full one and asked herself if she was ever going back to Portugal.

When she'd gone back to Lisbon in the past, from the various African wars, she'd gone back as the same person to find everything changed. Arriving back from Angola in 1964 she'd found the whole resistance movement stalled. Alvaro Cunhal had gone to the Soviet Union. João Ribeiro had spent two years in prison, his wife had died, he'd lost his job at the university and was now living in a single room in the Bairro Alto on very little money. The PCP had shunned him and he'd told her it was all over.

As it happened, she hadn't had much time to take it all in because the Mozambique rebellion started and Luís, with all his experience, was immediately posted to Lourenço Marques. It was in that tactically more brutal war that she and Luís began to fall apart. The Mozambique commander introduced techniques used by the British in Malaya and the Americans in Vietnam, giving the locals a stark choice – co-operate or face unrelenting suffering and death. News of the atrocities reached Anne in the army compound. She had pointless, violent rows with Luís. She threw things at him. She taunted him about the justice of the colonial wars, whether wars designed to maintain Salazar as an emperor were fit wars for his son. Luís spent more time in the mess. Anne drank cheap brandy and fulminated on the verandah.

She remembered the rage of that time as she sat with her first gin and tonic of the evening, with Louis Greig's reply on the desk in front of her, and knew she wasn't going back to that. She'd made the break. She'd had all that time to change, sitting on verandahs in Africa, but it had taken these few weeks with her mother, in the middle of a city striding into the future, to shrug off half a lifetime's inertia.

*   *   *

313

On 30th August she sat with her mother for the last time. Father Harpur had given her the Last Rites. She hadn't spoken a coherent word for twenty-four hours and it was clear the end was coming. At 2.00 a.m. Anne couldn't stay awake any longer. She stood to leave. Her mother's hand tightened and her eyes sprang open.

'They will come for you,' she said. 'But you must not go with them.'

Her eyes shut. Anne checked her pulse, shuddering at the ideas behind her mother's lurid visions. She was still there, breathing shallowly. Anne went to bed and overslept until midday. She woke up groggy, with her face crushed and creased. Her mother's room seemed more silent than usual and she knew there was nobody living beyond her door.

Her mother lay on her back, eyes closed, one arm out on the bedclothes. The slightly decaying lilies brought by Father Harpur from his church could not mask the odour of life's fluids curdling. Her face was quite cold. Anne looked at the body with a total absence of grief and realized the body meant nothing to her, that this was something that could be put in the ground.

She called the doctor and Father Harpur. She made herself coffee and smoked a cigarette in the kitchen. The doctor came and pronounced her dead and wrote out the death certificate. Father Harpur called a funeral director and stayed until tea, when the men came and removed the body. He left saying he would give a Mass for her mother the following morning. She went up to her mother's room after they'd gone. The bed was made. Audrey's slippers, swollen by the shape of her feet, lay beside the bed and it was that which reminded Anne of her loss.

The funeral was held on a cold, wind-whipped day. She'd followed her mother's instructions that a large party was to be held afterwards. The house was stocked with sherry, gin and whisky and she'd made a hundred sandwiches by dawn. She was still stunned by the extent of her mother's legacy, which included the Clapham house and a little over fifty thousand pounds in cash and investments. The solicitor said she never touched any of the capital left by her aunt. He also gave her a key to a safe-deposit box, number 718, held at the Arab Bank on the Edgware Road.

In the church she sat alone in her pew. Father Harpur gave a moving sermon about service to God, one's country and oneself. Afterwards, as the congregation converged on the grave site, Anne felt that unmistakable tug of the silver thread. As the men and women and a few older children moved through the old stones towards the dark oblong hole, she suddenly felt part of the race. This is what we humans do. We live and we die. The living salute the dead, however small the life, because we have all trodden the same hard track and know its difficulties. We will all go this way, into the ground or the air, president or pauper, and we will have all succeeded in one thing.

As they lowered the coffin it began to rain, as if on cue. Umbrellas exploded overhead, droplets formed on the varnished wood. Father Harpur said the blessing. Anne threw the first handful of soil and remembered something, but incorrectly, 'In your end was my beginning.'

Back at the house she began to see faces, rather than heavy coats and hats. They introduced themselves: Peggy White – assistant in Banking. Dennis Broadbent – Archives. Maude West – Library. Occasionally people just gave a name and she knew not to pursue it further. All the time one man kept finding his way into the corner of her eye. A fat, balding man. Someone waiting for his moment. Anne went into the kitchen for more sandwiches. He followed her, stood in the doorway, brushing the strands of hair across his bald pate with his hand.

'You don't know me, do you?'

'Should I?

'You should . . . we were lovers once. Don't you remember? We spent a night together in Lisbon,' he said, smiling.

'I would have remembered that.'

'We did,' he said, '. . . on paper.'

'Jim Wallis,' she said.

They kissed on both cheeks.

'Fat and bald,' he said. 'I didn't age well. You look just the same.'

'Give or take a crow's foot.'

'You married,' he said, 'just after they moved me out.'

'Yes. Are you . . . yet?'

'I'm on my second now. Spent too much time in Berlin to keep my first. But I'm in London these days. Any children?'

'A boy. Julião.'

'Is he here?'

'No. He's a soldier . . . in Africa.'

'Ah yes, with his father.'

'You knew that much.'

'I was always interested, Anne,' he said. 'And not just on paper.'

'But now you're married . . . again.'

'Yes, two children from the last marriage. One of each.'

'And you knew my mother.'

'We all knew Audrey. Very important to be on the right side of Audrey, you know, when you're putting through your expenses and that. Bit of a stickler, she was. Never let it interfere, though. After the grilling there was always a drink down the pub. Yes, we were regulars at The French in Soho, she and I. Very sad. Going to miss her. We'll all miss her. Especially Dickie.'

'Dickie?'

'Surprised he didn't come back for a snort. Dickie Rose.'

'You mean Richard Rose?'

'*Lui-même*. You remember, took over from Sutherland when he blew up that time in Lisbon in '44. Dickie's heading for the high table now. Had a bit of a clearout after Kim left us in '63. Bad year that, with Profumo and all. Given him a clear street though. It'll be *Sir* Dickie before long and we'll all have to bow and scrape.'

'Richard Rose was a friend of my mother's?' she said, incredulous.

'Oh yes, Audrey had a knack of picking out the high-flyers. Big fan of Kim's, too. Bloody mortified when he pushed off. We all were. Smoke?'

He offered a B&H, lit it with a petrol lighter. They smoked and Wallis helped himself to three sandwiches stacked on top of each other.

'Shouldn't really,' he said. 'Bread's the killer for me. Got any plans, Anne, or is it Andrea?'

'It's still Anne.'

'Back to *Lisboa?*'

'No, I don't think so.'

'I see.'

'I did my bit in Angola and Mozambique. I'm not doing it in Guiné with both of them fighting.'

'Quite understand. Don't know what they're doing there in the first place. Mad war. Bad war. Can't afford it. Can't win it. Best chuck it all in, you ask me. I mean, what's it all worth? Peanuts. Peanuts and cocoa ... some door mats. Can't go throwing your money after that sort of thing. Pull out, Doc, that's what I say, pull out. The darkies'll be at each other's throats in minutes. Look at Biafra.'

'I thought I'd try and do some research at Cambridge.'

'Still doing your sums?'

'I've graduated in long division now, Jim.'

'Well *done*. Isn't it all about Game Theory these days? Strategy. How to keep the Russian balls in a vice. That sort of thing.'

'You should be a lecturer, Jim. Bring strategic thinking down to earth.'

'Tried it. Got pelted by the students at the LSE. Called me a fascist. They had a sit-in before my next lecture and that was it. Bloody long-haired ... they got somebody to come in and talk to them about disarmament instead. Don't know how the bloody layabouts learn anything.'

'You're sounding like a boiled colonel from Bagshot.'

He wheezed a laugh through his cigarette smoke.

'We're a dying breed,' he said, 'but we're needed. Have you seen a picture of Brezhnev? D'you think he's going to listen to someone wearing an Afghan, smoking pot and burning joss sticks? Actually I preferred Khrushchev. He said things, you know, blinked occasionally.'

'You only liked Khrushchev,' said a voice from the corridor, 'because you've got the same Philistine taste in art.'

'Ah, Dickie. Wondered where you'd got to. Just said to Anne here, unusual of you not to come back for a stiffener.'

Richard Rose had his greyish hair combed back with tonic. His eyes were still bright and his full lips twitched as if there was the prospect of a kiss. They shook hands. He brushed imaginary lint of his dark blue suit.

'What was it Khrushchev said about modern art, Jim, that you so wholeheartedly agreed with?'

'The lashings of a donkey's tail,' said Jim, in cod Yorkshire.

'Pure peasant. Potato farmer, no, shire horse. That was Mr K.'

'Drink, Mr Rose?' asked Anne, keen to get away from him.

'I'll fetch,' said Wallis. 'What'll it be?'

'Pinkers, I think, if you've got it.'

'The angostura's out there,' she said, annoyed with Wallis.

'My condolences, Anne,' said Rose, smoothly. 'Very fine woman, your mother. Tremendous. When she retired she left an unfillable gap.'

'I don't think she ever thought her services were that indispensable.'

'Perhaps not, but she gave style to her work, that's what's irreplaceable. Conscientious, severe even, but a great sport, too, terrific fun.'

They ran through the same question and answer exchange as she had with Wallis. That Rose was still unmarried was all the information he parted with.

'Who did you say you were talking to at Cambridge?' asked Rose.

'I didn't, but his name is Louis Greig.'

'What's his game?'

'I'm not sure any more. It used to be Game Theory back in the fifties and early sixties but I think he's moved over . . .'

'Ah yes, come to think of it his name has appeared here and there. Strategist. Think-tank bod.'

'Probably.'

'He was at RAND over in California for a while in the fifties,' said Rose, confirming it to himself. 'Research and Development, know what I mean?'

'That must have been after he finished his doctoral thesis at Princeton.'

'He's not a Yank, is he?'

'Eton and Cambridge.'

'Mmm,' said Rose, running aground on Anne's frosty shores.

Wallis turned up with the pink gin.

'To Lisbon station,' said Wallis, raising his glass.

'The good old days,' said Rose. 'My . . . we were all innocent then.'

'Here's another from the 1944 team,' said Wallis. 'This really is Lisbon station now.'

A man's hand thrust a pipe between the two men's shoulders and struggled through the gap between. He kissed her on both

318

cheeks before she had time to take him in. He held her shoulders at arm's length and looked her up and down like an uncle.

'I'm so sorry,' said Meredith Cardew, 'so terribly sorry, Anne. Shock for us all, wasn't it, Dickie, when she called us back in July. Brave woman. My God, I don't think I could have taken it as well as she did.'

He released her but kept an arm around her shoulder as if she were his protégée.

'Quite a little reunion,' said Rose. 'We're only missing Sutherland.'

'Poor chap,' said Cardew.

'Pinkers, Merry?' asked Wallis.

'I should say.'

'How's Dorothy?' Anne asked Cardew.

They were all gone by two in the afternoon. Wallis was the last to leave. He was supporting Peggy White, assistant Banking, who'd neglected the sandwiches and was paying heavily for the seven pink gins on an empty stomach. Anne cleaned up the house and sat at the kitchen table thinking about Wallis and Rose, how the two men, in their own way, had looked her over, sized her up for something. Rose couldn't be thinking of a job, not given their mutual dislike, but that was how it had felt. Wallis? Maybe Wallis was just looking for an affair. Bored with wife number two already. It seemed that family life was going to the dogs in England. No more sweating in the dark about getting pregnant. You just took the Pill and did what the hell you liked. Salazar would die rather than allow the Pill, Franco too. Her thoughts rushed down that trail until she arrived at her own family, split up, thousands of miles apart, the men fighting, and she found herself crying, alone in her big house, her mother's clothes already gone to the Oxfam shop, the worms already nosing against the smooth varnish of the coffin.

319

Chapter 30

7th September 1968, England.

Anne took the train up to Cambridge. She bought a newspaper at the station and for once reading the *Guardian* made her happy. On the first page of the foreign news section was an article about Dr Salazar, who'd been rushed to the Cruz Vermelha Hospital in Lisbon after suffering a collapse. A doctor announced later that an intercranial subdural haematoma had been found, and she smiled at how typically Portuguese that was, they could never have just said a blood clot on the brain. The article finished with a statement from a consultant brain surgeon who said that the Head of State would have to undergo an operation to remove the clot.

The sun broke through the clouds and streamed into the railway carriage. Anne lit a celebratory cigarette and mentally toasted the end of the fascist régime and its colonial wars in Africa.

Louis Greig had rooms in Trinity College overlooking the quad. He smoked cigars, a Swiss brand called Villiger. Anne smelt them from the bottom of the stairs and imagined a place in a state of controlled chaos, full of papers and books filed only in the occupant's mind. His rooms, though, were unexpectedly tidy. There was no loose paper. A section of the bookshelves was stacked with ring-bound notebooks, several hundred of them, and they were filed in bunches tied with different-coloured ribbons. Greig had not succumbed to the usual sartorial eccentricities of the maths don, such as socks and sandals with shiny grey trousers that ended above the ankle, a tweed jacket with elbow patches and a tie featuring a real bacon and egg motif. He was bald, but his remaining hair was cut close to his head, which was big and square. His body was solid, strong and fatless. From the way his shoulders and chest were packed into his suit jacket he appeared to be a regular at some sort of heavy physical exercise.

He was lounging back in his chair with a pair of black brogues up on the corner of the desk when she came in. By the time she'd closed the door, he'd leapt to his feet, skirted the desk and was behind her, a dark presence. She held out a hand. His felt hard and calloused like a farmer's. He kissed her knuckle. She smelt a faint cologne mingled with the cigar tobacco. He didn't let go of the hand but led her round and lowered her into a leather sofa. He sat opposite her on the front lip of an armchair. Close up she put him somewhere in his early fifties, but well taken care of.

'João Ribeiro did say you were exceptional, although he omitted to say in his letter that it was in a most evident way, too.'

'There were things he didn't tell me about you as well,' she said, batting his flattery off into the room. 'How you met, for instance.'

'Oh, João came here for a symposium on primes, I think. Then I went to Lisbon before I headed off to Princeton and gave a short series of lectures on Diophantine Equations.'

His eyes didn't leave her face. His hands, clasped together, fingers steepled, pointed at her. His head was sunk into his muscled shoulders and he'd dug his heels into the base of the armchair as if he was about to launch himself, dive into her. A metallic excitement uncoiled high in her stomach. She hadn't felt such brazen interest for more than twenty years. She had difficulty trapping questions long enough in her mind to ask them.

'Somebody I met the other day thought you'd been at RAND,' she said.

'I was. Two years. Bit of a hothouse that, all those brains steaming away under one roof . . . not totally dissimilar to working at Bletchley Park with Alan Turing during the war. That delayed my doctoral thesis, which was why I ended up in Princeton in the mid fifties. Then RAND . . . Santa Monica, you know, there's only two types of weather on the West Coast. Sun and fog. I missed my seasons. Nothing like an iron-hard frost and weak sunshine behind bare trees.'

'I missed the leafy summers and the smell of mown grass.'

'Who was it, who said I'd been at RAND?'

'Someone at my mother's funeral, I don't remember who.'

'I'm sorry. João didn't mention that.'

'I haven't told him yet.'

'He's been having a miserable time of it, João. Reading between the lines of his letter.'

'Maybe things will get better now. Did you read the news today?'

'About Salazar, yes. They say he won't be able to work again.'

'That might be good news for me, too,' she said, and sensed her reluctance, registered that first twitch of guilt.

'Oh you mean your husband and son fighting out in Guiné, yes, João said that you only *might* come . . . but here you are, so . . .'

They talked maths for what seemed like a short time because they got lost in the exchange. Greig was aggressive, starting most of his counter arguments with the words: 'That's trivial,' but Anne was an elusive opponent who, as soon as he'd nailed her down, tantalized him with another alluring possibility. By the end they'd hammered out a brief for a research paper. Greig said he would make inquiries about a place for her at one of the women's colleges.

She caught the train back to London and sat in a full carriage of American tourists who'd clearly journeyed down from Scotland and had thought that plaid made great jackets. Black Watch, yes, maybe, but Macleod? She couldn't believe them and suddenly felt like a staring hick. She went out into the corridor to smoke a cigarette and let her mind get crowded out by Louis Greig's physical presence, their intellectual connection and the smell of his cigars still on her coat. She put her face out of the window, her back to the wind so that her long black hair rushed past her face, blinkering her vision. The silver rails streamed out of the back of the train to Cambridge and she felt that tug again. She turned her face into the wind, the full blast of it too much to bear so that tears started in her eyes. Her hair flew behind in a thick lash and she was laughing at her life picking up speed, at the idea of events rushing towards her. Things, finally, happening.

The next day it rained and she sat in the dungeon dark of the Clapham house waiting for the telephone to ring, which it didn't. In the evening the rain stopped and sodden sunshine lapped into the room. She walked to her mother's grave and found that two expensive wreaths had been laid amongst the other bouquets – no names on them, only that of the florist's in Pimlico. She wandered amongst the other stones, her heels sticking in the turf, and took tea in a coffee house in Clapham Old Town. She ate cake and

322

thought she might have imagined the attraction between them, overdecorated it in her mind. He was probably married. The lack of a wedding band meant little in England. She turned her own ring which wouldn't slip over her knuckle any more. Why would he be interested in her when there were all these sexually revolutionized twenty-two-year-olds on campus? She walked back home, skidding on the mash of autumn leaves and soggy litter.

The telephone was ringing as she opened the door and the five short steps to it made her breathless. Greig told her that he'd had the go-ahead from the head of the maths department, that he'd arranged a postgrad place at Girton, that application forms were being sent and accommodation was being looked into. He'd expect her to be up by the beginning of October.

She drank gin and tonic that night before supper and enjoyed one of Rawly's Pomerols with a pair of lamb chops. She went to bed drunk and woke up repentant.

London, still swinging in the sixties, rejuvenated her – the wild fashions, the incredible variety of music after Portugal's monotony, the sheer amount of stuff to buy. She bought winter clothes, went to Biba, wore jeans for the first time, smoked Gitanes, wondered why her mother had an entire collection of Herb Albert and his Tijuana Brass and ate her first hamburger at a place called a Wimpy Bar. It tasted like hell in a cotton wool bun. She did some practical things too, like getting the estate agents in to rent out the house on short company lets.

The application forms for the university arrived on the same day as a letter from João Ribeiro. The letter had been opened and read by the censors in Portugal, the tip of the flap stuck back down with glue. It was written in one of their codes and she had to dig out a copy of Fernando Pessoa's collected poems from the reference library to translate it.

Dear Anne,
You will have heard our good news by now but you will also,
no doubt, have seen from the state of this envelope that,
whilst the leader of the Estado Novo languishes brainless in
hospital, his security measures are still firmly in place. We hoped
for much but there has been no change. The government is
now in the hands of Marcelo Caetano, who is more

approachable than our old friend but, in getting the top job, will now find how much he owes to his pals in big business, the Church and the military. Nothing, I fear, will change. In fact, his first speech was directed at the ultra-right in which he said that the Portuguese, who have grown accustomed to being ruled by a genius, must now adapt to the government of common men. He's a donkey to Salazar's stallion and all we will get from him is a sterile old mule. I hope I am wrong. I hope the colonial wars end tomorrow and that the Portuguese can take their place among the civilized people of Europe.

I have lost three more teeth to the man in the street with the pliers. He told me that he is also a cobbler and I have given him my shoes to repair. He is taking care of me from head to foot.

I think of you and wish you all success.

João Ribeiro.

She smelt the letter, hoping to find some whiff of the sea, grilled horse mackerel or a freshly poured *bica* – smiling at herself as she fell for the Portuguese *saudades*, the longings – but all she caught was João's melancholy – despair tempered by humanity – which had penetrated the paper from the sweat of his hand.

Her pen hovered over the application forms, still undecided about one thing, still confused by the implications of João's letter. The telephone rang. She answered it in the chill hall and missed the man's name but heard that he was from the Portuguese consulate and would like to come and see her. She asked him what it was about but he declined to tell her. Only in person, Senhora Almeida. She agreed and hung up, only realizing then that he hadn't had to ask for her address.

He was there in less than an hour introducing himself from in front of his sticking-out ears as Senhor Martims. He was no more than five foot high and wore a black belted raincoat like a schoolboy's. They sat over coffee. He stroked his moustache downwards over his top lip obsessively, as if this was part of diplomacy, that he should never be seen speaking. They settled and his features became still and grave so that Anne immediately felt panic-struck

324

and wanted to run from the room. He removed a letter from his pocket and held it on his knees which were pressed together. Anne saw her own name in Luís's handwriting. Senhor Martims looked down, gathered himself. His English came out quickly and barely made it through the gap between his teeth.

'It is my sad duty to have to inform you, Senhora Anne Almeida, that your son Captain Julião Almeida was killed in action four days ago in Guiné.'

There was a long silence. Senhor Martims' words did not penetrate her through the normal channels. She didn't hear them. They were hard words which hit Anne in the face, like torn-up cobblestones in a riot. They bruised their way in. They were not comprehensible as language. She understood them only as pain. Senhor Martims couldn't bear this silence in which he could only imagine the destructive power of his fast factual words. He started again and added more.

'Your son was leading a patrol in the forest and they were ambushed by guerrillas.'

Senhor Martims repeated it for her and she nodded at the words which headed off at different angles into the room.

'The guerrillas ambushed the patrol and your son, who was leading, was shot in the neck and chest. The fighting continued for an hour and his men were unable to come to his aid. By the time they had fought the guerrillas away your son had died from loss of blood. I am truly very sorry, Senhora Almeida.'

There was colour in these words, not just black and white information, and sound, too. They flung images into her head. The green forest, hooting and screeching. The first dull shots – cracks of poisonous sound. The red of blood on his neck and chest, darkening the green of his uniform. Julião lying in the long grass, the bullets zipping above him and the sky beyond the dark canopy, white, bleached to a harsh, glaring white, but growing dimmer as his life leaked into the pulsating ground, the heart beating under Africa.

'I am very sorry,' Senhor Martims was saying again, almost chanting. 'I have no way of softening this blow. This is the very worst thing to happen to a mother. I . . . I . . .'

Anne thought she should be crying, that she should be wailing her heart out, but these words had taken her to a much darker place. Crying was too small for this. You cried when you hit your finger with a hammer, not when the abyss has opened up inside you. She dug her elbows into her ribs to hold herself in. More words were coming her way from the small man but she was stopping herself from being split in two. The concentration for this was so hard and pure that the new battery of words came to her incomplete.

'. . . he felt responsible . . . fellow officers . . . nothing stupid . . . service revolver which I'm afraid he turned on himself . . . depressed . . . very proud . . . this terrible tragedy . . . two outstanding servants of their country. He left this letter addressed to you, Senhora Almeida.'

She didn't take the letter. She couldn't move her arms from her sides. Senhor Martims, at a loss, placed the letter on the arm of the chair.

'Do you have family here?' he asked, looking into her eyes as if she was shut in a box and he was peering through a slit.

'My mother died at the end of August,' she said. 'I have no family here.'

'You have no family?' said Senhor Martims, aghast. 'No friends?'

'Maybe . . , in Lisbon . . . still.'

'Friends of your mother?' he asked. 'You shouldn't be alone after such news.'

The only name that came to her was Jim Wallis and she said it. Senhor Martims found the number and spoke to Wallis in a murmur. Senhor Martims stayed with her, pacing the room, looking at the unopened letter on the arm of the chair, waiting for Wallis to arrive.

In her head she saw herself with her face out of the train window. These were the events that were rushing towards her, but blinded by the wind, they were just a blur, a sense of impending incident. Looking back she'd seen the silver rails but only through the incoherence of her own streaming hair. Now she was seeing a pattern, a terrible tragic pattern – her mother's story, her father's death, Julius Voss perishing at Stalingrad, his father's suicide, Karl's capture and execution, their son's death, the suicide of the surrogate father. 'Lies beget lies,' her mother had said, you have to tell another to keep the first one going. But tragedy is the same. It follows bloodlines. The one thing she'd never expected to be was tragic –

some jittery middle-aged woman, living alone in a large cold house, never going out because she could anticipate the next lightning strike. And here she was, a tragic figure. Pitied by Senhor Martims because she was a mother who'd lost everything and had no family. It made her angry and she tore open Luís's letter to see what he had to say for himself.

Dear Anne,
It is late and I've been drinking. The drink is not doing what it is supposed to do. I'm sweating and words, which were never my strength, float past me, but the pain, which should be dull by now, is still there, diamond hard, piercing, not one edge of it blunted.

The night and the noise of the insects are crowding me. My friends, fellow officers, have gone to bed. They see that I have taken it well. But I have not.

You and I left each other on bad terms because you thought that these wars were wrong. I saw it before – that first time in Angola – and I see it clearly now, but it is too late and I have lost everything – my son, and because you can never forgive me, you as well. The two of you were all that mattered to me and without you the future has no value.

I was never a man to do this sort of thing. I always savoured life. Perhaps if I wait I could persuade myself out of it and live the unendurable existence. But now, with the heat pressing against the walls, the vagueness of the world beyond the mosquito netting, the great distance between us and the colossal absence – I have no strength for it, no courage. Forgive me this, if not the other.

Your husband. Luís

She folded the letter up in its envelope and stuffed it down the side of the chair. Senhor Martims had stopped pacing and was now thinking about the English as a race. The words pity and admiration came to him. Why can't they explode? Why can't they squeeze out a tear? If she'd been Portuguese she'd have ... she'd have fainted or fallen to her knees, wailing, but this ... this bottled silence, this strapped-down stoicism. How do they do it? *Sang froid*, that was it, cold blood. The English were emotional reptiles. And as soon as he'd thought it he felt guilty. This was not the time for such thoughts. This woman ... the suffering ... it was unimaginable. Her mother as well.

But Senhor Martims was wrong. He didn't know it, but he was walking at the foot of a volcano. Plates had moved inside Anne, chasms had opened up and this boiling rage of molten rock was seething to the surface. Her hands, which were clasping her knees, trembled against her body's geology.

'Thank you, Senhor Martims, for coming to see me,' she said, her voice quaking. 'Thank you for your sympathy. I'll be all right now. You can go back to the consulate.'

'No, no, I insist on staying until Mr Wallis arrives.'

'I would like some moments to myself beforehand, that's all. If you would be so kind as to ...'

She engineered him out of the door. He went to his car and waited. Anne didn't go back into the sitting room but found the darkness of the dining room a comfort. She fell towards the table, retching with something too big to vomit out and barked her shins on a chair. The sharp physical pain was blinding and she stumbled over the chair, crashing with it to the floor. She lashed out at it with savage kicks, ripped the heel off her shoe.

'You fucking ... you fucking ... you little fucker,' she spat from between gritted teeth and, amazed at finding the available vocabulary, hauled herself to her feet.

She grabbed the back of the chair and dashed it against the wall. The back and rear legs split away from the seat and she brought this down with all her strength on another chair and broke off the two legs. She smashed the back into the wall and saw it splinter into matchwood. She took the front legs and seat and reduced that, too. She stood back, panting. The china quivered in the dresser. She threw open the doors, took out a plate and hurled it against the wall, another plate and another, the destructive satisfaction of it thrilling up her ribs. She swung each one harder and, as she got tired, she dredged up a screech of agony to launch the next plate with increasing venom. Just as her arm began to hang limp from her shoulder and her chest felt too full of organs, jostling for room, she found herself engulfed by a damp raincoat and Wallis whispering into her ear. More incomprehensible words.

She was taken up to a bedroom, her mother's room, and put into bed. A doctor was called, who came and sedated her. He left valium for later. She lay like a figurine in a cotton wool-filled box. The outside did not penetrate and inside was curiously muted, no thought or feeling could reach its pin-sharp conclusion.

She floated for what seemed like days and came into daylight with a strange woman in the room. She had to claw her way back into reality, a physical effort. The woman explained herself. Jim Wallis's wife. Anne tried to edge back towards what had happened but found herself removed from it. There was a padded bulwark between this new point and her past. She knew what had happened, the steel-fastened lock of muscles around her shoulder reminded her of that. She even saw the drift of shattered china up the wall but she could not recapture any of the intensity of the moment. She felt curiously bereft. The thought of her dead son and husband elicited sadness, which produced bleak, but quiet, weeping but there was no madness. She missed that madness. It had been right for the moment. Now she felt split, completely disconnected, not just from the incident but from the whole of her old life. The memories of it were as intact as they had been in the weeks while her mother lay dying, only now it wasn't even biography but more like history. It frightened her, this change of perception, until she realized that it was a modus vivendi, a truce after a mortifying exchange of artillery.

Wallis came by in the evening to relieve his wife. They talked on the landing outside the room. The day's report. Calm. Wallis sat on the bed, took Anne's hand. The front door slammed below.

'I'm back,' she said.

'It looks like it.'

'How long have I been . . . out?'

'Three days. Doctor's orders. He thought it best, in view of your mother as well.'

'Am I still on drugs?'

'Less than before, which is why you're back with us but probably a little fuzzy.'

'Yes, a little . . . fuzzy.'

She dressed as if she was watching herself do it and they ate something downstairs, the cutlery loud on the plates. Her surroundings, although sharp and recognizable, appeared unusual, as if oddly lit. Wallis asked her what she was going to do with herself, but carefully as if she might be considering . . . what did they call it? Something stupid. The strangest thing was that the thought hadn't occurred to her – to kill herself. She assumed that she'd instinctively locked on to that stubbornness that her mother had possessed as well.

'I don't know,' she said. 'My life seemed to picking up some kind of momentum before this, I should try and recapture that, I suppose.'

'I could get you a job if you want.'

'Who with?'

'The Company, of course,' he said. 'They still haven't filled Audrey's position to Dickie's satisfaction. Every time someone new starts in the job Dickie just shakes his head and says, "Irreplaceable", and that's it.'

'Thanks, but Richard Rose and I, you know . . . I think I'm going to do this research project at Cambridge.'

'Any time you need help, Anne, we're here.'

Then something did come back to her and in focus. The reason why she'd hesitated to fill in her university application forms.

'There is something you could do for me now,' she said. 'You could get me my name back, my identity. I wouldn't mind being Andrea Aspinall again.'

Chapter 31

1968–70, Cambridge and London.

Her last act as Anne Ashworth was to go to Lisbon for the burial of Julião and Luís. Because of the African heat the bodies had already been cremated in Guiné but there was to be a Mass in the Basílica da Estrela and a burial service at the family mausoleum in Estremoz.

Anne stayed in the York House in Rua das Janelas Verdes in Lapa. The evening before the funeral she walked the familiar streets past the British Embassy on Rua de São Domingos, turned right into Rua de Buenos Aires, left into Rua dos Navegantes and down the railed slope of Rua de João de Deus. She hadn't been back in this neighbourhood for twenty-four years and, when she first saw the swaying jacarandas below the white dome of the basilica, she'd expected the memories to rush at her like excited children, but they held back, sidled off.

She stood in front of the old apartment building, its façade still the same with the green and blue tiles, black diamonds, the plaque, commemorating the death of the poet João de Deus, was still above the door.

She joined the Almeida family group on the steps in front of the basilica and, even though they'd never liked her, the foreigner, they took her in, accepted her in their mutual grief. They walked into the basilica together, Anne on Luís's mother's arm, and it confirmed to her what she knew about the Portuguese – they understood tragedy, it was their territory and they were united with anybody who was in it with them. They sat all night through the vigil – keeping watch over the urns.

Mass was held in the morning. Few people other than family came. The friends of Luís and Julião were all in Africa, fighting the wars. The Almeidas took the urns to Estremoz where they were

331

laid in the family mausoleum, alongside other coffins, bunked on top of each other like soldiers in the barracks. The wrought-iron door was closed on the dead and their photographs placed in frames on the outside: Luís, as he'd always been in front of the camera, solemn, almost as if he was attending his own funeral, and Julião, still ready for life, his smile unbroken.

She stayed a night with the Almeidas and headed back to Lisbon on the train the next day. In the evening she went to see João Ribeiro, the last loose end to be tied before she flew out the next morning. João was living in a different room, but still in the heart of the Bairro Alto. He greeted her, kissing her hard on both cheeks and holding her tight to his thin body. She pulled away and he was weeping, pushing his handkerchief up under his specs until he realized it was easier to take them off.

'So, this is what has happened to me. This is what you do to an old man. How can you leave for such a short time and still make me so happy to see you? And sad. I am sorry for all your losses. More than anyone should have to bear in a lifetime, let alone a month. Life can be a brutal beast at times, Anne.'

'You should know, João,' she said, looking around the spartan room, his worn circumstances.

'This . . .' he said, sweeping his arm around, 'this is nothing to what you have had to endure.'

'You lost your wife, your job, the work that you loved.'

'My wife was always sick. It was a blessed release for her. The university? Under this régime it can't teach anybody anything. How can you learn with the newspapers printing their daily lies. And my work? I *have* work. This room is better than the last one, isn't it?'

'What work?'

'I teach arithmetic to children and their mothers how to read and write. I am a true communist, a better one now that I live among the people. They feed me, clothe me, look after me. But you . . . you must tell me what you are going to do after these terrible events.'

'There's only one thing I can do,' she said. 'I seem to have reached some sort of finality and yet I'm still here. I have to continue. I have to start again.'

She told him about Louis Greig and the research project and

they talked mathematics until a woman brought a tray of plates and grilled sardines and they sat down to dinner.

'It's not a bad life for an old man,' said João. 'My meals cooked, my washing done, my room cleaned and *fado* in the evenings. Perhaps this is how we should all live. I find it harmonious.'

The woman came back, cleared the table and left coffee and brandy.

'They know you are important to me,' said João, 'so they're making a fuss. They wanted to cook you something special but I told them sardines was what you liked, that you were one of us . . . as indeed is Louis Greig, for all his wealth.'

'One of us?'

'A mathematician and a communist.'

'I'm surprised. He told me he worked at RAND after Princeton.'

'But *after* McCarthy's witch hunts and anyway he's always been . . . safe.'

'His wealth, you mean.'

'His father owns a few thousand hectares of Scotland and is a Conservative MP, who I think was even in the shadow cabinet for a while. Louis went to Eton and never bothered with politics as an undergraduate. He kept himself clean and his eye on the larger game.'

'What about those lectures he gave here?' she asked. 'You, João Ribeiro, renowned communist, Head of Maths, must have invited him?'

'Me? No. That was the beauty of it. Dr Salazar invited him. Louis's father had business interests in Porto. Wine, I think. Connections were made, the invitation given. Louis was delighted. It looked like cast iron on his CV.'

'And you and he talked.'

'I was looking after him.'

'So he knew about you?'

'At his level the Communist Party is global.'

In the morning she sat outside Café Suiça in the Rossio square, taking a coffee and a last *pastel de nata* for what she thought would be a long time. Beggars nagged at her table – a man with no hands and his pocket held open with a stick, a woman with one side of her face burned, barefoot kids swatted away by waiters. She paid for her coffee and went to a street of jewellers nearby and had her wedding band sawn off. The jeweller weighed it for her and paid her cash. She went back to the Rossio, distributed the money around the beggars, got into a taxi and left with a flight of pigeons for the airport.

The plane taxied to the end of the runway. As the engines built up power she waited for her favourite moment except that, as they were throttling up, she felt a rising surge of panic instead. She was terrified by the juddering of the plane's structure as it hurtled down the runway, had to close her eyes and fight the panic back down her throat as the wheels left the ground. The sense of nothing under her feet had never occurred to her before but now, as the plane powered into a steep climb, she felt powerless, rigid with fear at the approaching moment, when God might give up the pretence, let them drop from the sky and she would die in the company of strangers, unknown and unloved. They levelled out. A stewardess walked the aisle. The No Smoking light went out and Anne fought her way into her bag for her stalwart supporters.

Back in London Wallis came round for a drink on his own. He had a passport in the name of Andrea Aspinall, a national insurance number, everything she would need. They talked about Lisbon. He looked at the red dent left on her finger by the missing wedding band. Andrea steered the conversation round to his wife.

'She's a good girl,' he said. 'We get on, you know. She's self-sufficient, too. Doesn't need me around all the time. Don't have to worry about her at parties.'

'Is that important?'

'Don't like them clingy, Anne. Sorry, Andrea. Bit of space, if you know what I mean.'

'To play the field?'

'Well, yes, I suppose that's what I mean. Not that I have much luck these days.'

'Did you ever have any luck with that French songbird in Lisbon?'

'Everybody had luck with her except me,' he said, and rubbed his money fingers. 'Nothing's changed.'

'Maybe you wear your heart on your sleeve, Jim.'

334

'You think that's it?'

'We all want a bit of mystery, don't you think? You should be good at it. You *are* a spy, for God's sake.'

'Never much good at that malarkey, Andrea. Admin, that's me now. I was always talking too much. Not like you. Very spare with words, you are.'

'I wasn't then.'

'And now?'

'Had a bit of my stuffing knocked out, that's all.'

'Sorry. I didn't mean to be glib,' he said. 'It's a pity you're off to Cambridge.'

'You don't need me to give you mystery lessons.'

'No, no. Thought you'd come and work for us. Get you a job at the drop of a hat, you know that.'

'Even with Richard Rose in charge?'

'Dickie's not operating at a departmental level any more. He's practically government. Way back from the front line, he is.'

'Why's he going on about my mother's irreplaceability then?'

'Old school . . . they went back to the forties. He still took her out to tea once a week even after she retired.'

'Tea?'

'Their euphemism for a four-hour session in The Wheatsheaf. Christ, Audrey could put it away. Never saw her even stagger. Bloody marvellous sight. It was Dickie's way of keeping his finger in the pie. Audrey . . . Auders, as he called her. Follow Auders, he used to say. She knew everything. You always do if you're running the money.'

'I'm going to Cambridge, Jim.'

'Yes, yes, of course you are. All I'm saying is that if it doesn't work out . . . I'm, we're, the Company is here.'

Wallis tried to kiss her on the mouth as he left – five double G&Ts inside him and one down his shirt – she turned her face the fraction necessary so that he wouldn't feel bad. He stumbled down the path. She closed the door and watched him through one of the unstained diamonds of glass. He got into his car, started the motor and looked through the windscreen straight at her before pulling away. She didn't understand that look. It wasn't disappointment, vague humiliation or even anger. It was the look of a man who was working

335

on something and it was a long way from the bluff bonhomie that he churned out in her company.

She rented the house out to an American couple for a year. She went up to Cambridge on the train to find herself suppressing that same surge of panic she'd had on the plane coming back from Lisbon. Louis Greig had arranged a flat for her on the first floor of a semi-detached house in a leafy street not far from the station. She started work straight away but couldn't seem to remember the old social skills to make friends in her department. She became afraid of dead time. The English autumn was dark and squally. The rain scratched at her windows and she kept her head down because, if she stopped to look at her reflection in the glass, she might see dread in the empty room behind her.

Greig was away in Washington for the first two weeks which meant she had two Sundays when, in the early evening, *Songs of Praise* would come up from the television below her and Julião would appear in her head, lodge himself in her chest and she would pace the room until the pain went back into its crack, like a snake into a wall. At seven o'clock the pubs opened and she was always there with a half of lager, orbiting some sporty crowd of raucous and ebullient undergrads.

Greig came back in mid October and Andrea presented her first paper to him which he crushed as mercilessly as one of his cigar butts. He sent her out into the rain feeling empty, useless. She went back to her flat and lay on the bed, wondering whether her middle-aged brain was too hardened into its old patterns to be able to think originally any more. Greig came by in the late evening, hung his mac and umbrella behind the door and apologized for his brutality. Relief spread through her. He brought wine, something good from the Trinity cellars and a triangle of brie stolen from high table. She asked about Washington. He grumbled about the Yanks, how spoilt they were over there. He asked about Lisbon. Apologized for not inquiring earlier, he'd just had an ugly meeting with the dean about budgets. They talked about the Portuguese, the Almeidas, João Ribeiro.

'He's teaching arithmetic,' said Greig, amazed. 'The man could knock off Diophantine Equations before breakfast. What's he playing at?'

'Being a true communist, he says.'

'But he doesn't have to teach long division to street kids, for Christ's sake.'

'He's satisfying local demand. They don't need Diophantine Equations to sell their fish door to door.'

Greig's eyebrows seemed to float from his head with boredom. 'Isn't Salazar dead yet?' he asked.

'No, but still *hors de combat.*'

'That man's driving his country back to the Middle Ages,' he said. 'A thousand miles from his hospital bed there've been students rioting in the streets of Paris. The whole of European youth is on the move. We're in the middle of a cultural revolution while the Iberian Peninsula is in the hands of Edwardian stiffs, throwing money away on empire and grinding their people down into some pre-industrial slavery. They'll never recover. Sorry, Anne, I'm ranting . . . nothing like a good rail against our old fascist friends.'

'It's Andrea now . . . I wrote to you.'

'Yes, yes, of course it is. What's all that about?'

'I was a field agent for the Secret Intelligence Services in Lisbon during the war.'

'My God.'

'For some complicated reasons and a smattering of political embarrassment I had to get married under my cover name, which I was stuck with for twenty-four years until last month. Now I'm starting again. A clean slate for Andrea Aspinall.'

She was surprised to find Greig impressed. Bletchley Park hadn't perhaps had the kudos of action in the field. Cracking Enigma didn't have the dashing image. The keenness she'd seen in their first interview returned to his eyes, nailing her to the bed she was sitting on, did something strange to the muscles in her thighs.

'You're lucky we don't bother too much with proof of qualifications.'

'You're lucky I'm here at all,' she said, playing to him now, hands reaching shakily for some self-confidence. 'They wanted me for a job.'

'They?'

'The Company, as we call ourselves. The SIS. My mother worked for them, too. All her work cronies turned up at her funeral.

Some of them I knew from the forties in Lisbon. They were looking for staff.'

Greig leaned back in his chair. Andrea stretched herself out on the bed, propped her head up with a hand, sucked on her cigarette and tried to remember whether this was how seduction worked . . . if she ever knew.

'You're a dark horse,' he said.

'I'm dark,' she said, flatly.

He laughed, uneasily, suddenly finding blood converging on parts of his body – neck, groin – finding swallowing and crossing his legs suddenly a problem.

Her mother had been wrong. Sex *had* been revolutionized over the last twenty years or maybe Rawly had been much more of an interesting partner than Luís. After their first kiss she'd reached to stub out her cigarette and Greig had told her to carry on smoking. He put his hands up her skirt and she felt his hands shake as he found her suspenders and the bare skin above her stocking tops. He stripped down her knickers, roughly. He knelt before her, bent his head down between her thighs, cupped her buttocks with his rough hands and drew her to him.

He made love to her expertly. He was unembarrassed at making his demands and, continuing the tutor/pupil relationship, taught her things about men, like a tennis coach demonstrating grip. He asked her not to close her eyes in mock ecstasy but to keep them open, looking at him at all times, especially when she was kneeling in front of him. She ricocheted between embarrassment, lust and disgust. She was doing things within a matter of hours that Luís had probably never heard of and the discovery of this deep carnality in herself was disturbing, but oddly gratifying, too.

She fell asleep in the early morning and woke up alone, the morning so dark that she thought it was dawn when in fact it was close to eleven o'clock. She fingered her lips, which were sensitive, bruised. Her legs were as stiff as if she'd been out riding. In her gut she was both desolate and rampant. In her head she was ashamed and excited.

She had a bath and found herself rooting around for her best lingerie. She made herself up as she'd never done to go to the maths department and dressed in her new autumn clothes. He

338

wasn't in the department. Her postgrad colleagues stared at her from beneath their crackling nylon shirts, their drip-dry, ever-creased Crimplene trousers. She moved on to Trinity and bumped into him coming out of the porter's lodge. He had his face turned back and he was holding his hand out.

'Come *on*, Martha,' he said. 'For heaven's sake.'

A woman, dazzlingly kempt, with styled blonde and lustrous hair, and a floor-length brown coat with a French silk scarf around her neck, took Greig's hand. Andrea stepped back, preparing to run. Greig turned, saw her.

'Anne,' he said.

'Andrea,' she replied.

'You're so awful with names,' said Martha, whose American accent grabbed the adjective and made of it innards on a butcher's floor.

Greig introduced his wife, asked Andrea to drop by his rooms at tea time. He pressed the automatic release on his umbrella, which burst open like a giant bat, and they headed out into the rain.

It had happened as quick as murder and the change was no less devastating. Andrea watched his broad back heading into town, Martha's narrow shoulders leaning into him. Desolation, bleak as the rain-slivered wind off the Fens, sliced into her.

She went home and thumped into the bed in her damp coat. The earlier emptiness had now been replaced by a full roll of barbed wire jealousy. Why anybody thought it was green, she couldn't fathom. Jealousy was a multi-edged blade and whichever way it turned it cut you.

By tea time she was exhausted and the walk back to Trinity in the rain was the trudge of a soldier making his way back to the front but, and she couldn't fail to notice this, she was going back. It was that inevitable. Choice was not in it.

Greig took the coat from her antagonistic shoulders, hung it up and showed her the leather sofa.

'I could see you were surprised by Martha,' he said softly. 'I thought João would have told you that much, but then it's not a natural way for his mind to think. Must have been a terrible shock. I'm sorry.'

She had nothing to say. All the savagely planned words suddenly seemed amateur, naïve.

'I hope you don't think that last night meant nothing,' he said. 'It wasn't just a one-off.'

Hope surged to absurd heights. What was she? Twenty again? Not one inch of emotional progress since girlhood.

'You're a beautiful woman. Extraordinarily gifted. Mysterious . . .'

'And your *wife*?' she asked, the word hacking through the air, serrated edge.

'Yes,' he said, simply – no excuses, no apologies, no denials.

She had questions stacked up inside her like punch cards for a computer programme but they were all binary banal and some of them, if asked, might have answers she didn't want to hear. What am I to you? A comfortable lay. A convenient screw. A charitable poke. That last one hurt because she knew how needy she was.

Greig sat next to her on the sofa, took her hand as if she was a patient. Where *did* he get those rough hands from? Nobody got hands like that from chalking equations on a board. His words leaked into her head like myrrh – exotic, nearly meaningless, except her insides quivered at them.

'The first time I met you I knew you were going to be important to me. I didn't intend to stay last night with you, but I just thought we'd suddenly connected and I couldn't resist that connection. The chance of knowing you, of getting closer to you. The way you smoked that cigarette, stretched across the bed . . . I was yours.'

As he spoke his hand came to rest on her knee. She knew, she saw what he was doing and did nothing about it, because she wanted this to happen. The coarse skin of his hand snagged on the nylon stocking as he pushed it up between her legs, over the stocking top, the soft skin on the inside of her thigh, until he brushed a hard finger over the outline of her sex beneath her best silk. The carnal jolt rushed up her spine, but something older, atavistic, recoiled. She stood and lashed her hand across his face. The slap fizzed on her palm. His face reddened. She slammed the door as she left.

Hours later she was back looking for him in the quad. No lights on in his room. She found his address from the porter's lodge and stood outside his house on the other side of the street, still wearing the same clothes, her make-up repaired. At 11.30 p.m. a light came on upstairs and Martha appeared in a bay window to close the curtains. Another light came on in the hall. The front door opened and Louis came out with a short-haired dachshund on a lead. She crossed the street, came at him between two parked cars and startled him as surely as if she'd had a knife.

'I'm sorry,' she said, partly for startling him, partly for the slap.

'I probably deserved it,' he replied, and continued on his way.

'You were taking advantage of me,' she said, catching up with him.

'I was,' he said. 'I admit it, but I couldn't help it.'

The dog trotted between them, doggedly disinterested in human drama.

'Do you have any idea what this is like for me?' she asked. 'I've been married for twenty-four years. You're only the second man I've known.'

The lie so smooth she even believed it herself. It stopped him in his tracks. The dog continued, yanked the lead tight, walked back huffily, looked at their feet.

'How am I supposed to know these things?' he asked. 'You don't tell me anything about yourself. And from my side, well, I sensed something. I was attracted to you. I did what any man would do. I went for you. It has nothing to do with my past, my marriage, your past or your previous marriage. It was just the moment.'

'And this afternoon?'

'I couldn't help myself. I find you irresistibly sexy.'

'Your wife,' she said, the word cutting her at the back of the throat, 'she looks . . . she seems very . . .'

'If I want strength, pragmatism, and efficiency, she's my girl. You have to understand, Andrea, Martha runs our lives, hers and mine, as a controlled experiment. My career, my work – what's that geared to? To achieving pinnacles of logic, zeniths of rationale. That's a mathematician's lot. Somewhere along the road I need passion, mystery, humour, for God's sake.'

They carried on walking. The dog leading, jaunty now that they were on the move again. They came on to an open expanse, a football pitch, and he let the dog off the lead.

'I thought you were walking into this with your eyes open,' he said.

'I was, but not with full information.'

The wind buffeted them. His mac flapped open. Her hair

341

streaked across her mouth and nose as if she were under the veil. He peeled her hair back, pushed his hand round the back of her neck and pulled her to his face. They kissed as they had done the night before. She pushed her hand into his jacket and up his shirted back. The dog reappeared, circled, snorted and tore off again.

The ground rules laid out, they started their affair. In that first term, the longest they ever spent together was after Sunday dinner when Martha, who was bored by the Senior Common Room, had an early night and Louis, instead of passing round the port, cycled to Andrea's flat and stayed there until 2.00 a.m. He also had a brass bed in his rooms in Trinity and they would occasionally take a tutorial in there. On spring afternoons they would go to his allotment, he was a gardener (those rough hands were from digging and planting), and she would read her paper to him while he worked and afterwards they'd lie down on the rough wooden floor of the shed amongst the forks and spades. Some evenings, if she became desperate, she would wait for him to walk the dog and join him on black, blustery nights. The dog would run off and they'd manage as best they could on a park bench, Louis looking around wildly as car headlights skirted the common.

The next term, when it was too cold to sustain anything in the frost-hardened air, they would slip into the back of his car, which he took to parking down the street from his house. They would trap the dog lead in the door and she'd end up with her face pressed against the quarterlight of a window, her breath fogging the glass, the dog outside looking up at her, questioning.

She couldn't believe what was happening, what she was doing. He would ask her to do things. Things like role-playing, which at first thought seemed absurd and, in practice, faintly disgusting but then she found herself doing them and as she did them more they would become less repellent, until they didn't seem revolting but were stimulating and then almost normal.

When he left her, as he did all summer to go to the States to idle on the beach with Martha and her family in Cape Cod, she stayed in Cambridge, researching to forget him. She lay awake at night, at first trying to work out what it was all about without ever be able to define her nebulous need for him and then realizing that she knew all along. With her mother, son and husband gone she felt unmoored, empty. Louis, her mentor and teacher, tethered her, filled her up. But the realization made no difference to her state and she saw that although this was what she expected of Louis, it never quite happened and yet it could . . . it could.

She had thought, at first, that Martha was the only barrier to her future happiness until it had occurred to her that Martha's presence was a part of the intensity. She and Louis were both hooked on the subterfuge – the secret meetings, the late-night assignations, the sense of the forbidden.

Memories of another age, another secret love leaked into her head to confuse the present.

During the next academic year Louis sensed a change in her, a change he did not like. She appeared confident. Louis responded by becoming slapdash about his other liaisons. Andrea would arrive just as another girl left, reapplying her lipstick. She found an earring in his room, a tiny pair of knickers, a used condom. Andrea never mentioned any of these finds. He had already become hostile and she didn't want to antagonize him further. That next summer he left for Cape Cod without saying goodbye.

She became prone to spontaneous bursts of crying which stopped as abruptly as they started. When the library shut for that summer she couldn't bear to go off on her own for a lonely holiday near families and lovers. Even when Jim Wallis invited her down to his cottage in the south of France, she couldn't face being with him and his not-so-new wife.

She stayed in Cambridge and counted the days to the beginning of term like a child with an advent calendar. As her loneliness crowded around her in her first-floor flat and the usual haunts of the undergrads fell silent, she sought out other pubs with life and noise, pubs whose regulars were labourers and builders, people who actually ordered pickled eggs from the jars behind the bar and ate them. She woke up in the mornings feeling as if she'd drunk everything including the wringings from the beer mats. She shuddered and squeezed the pillow to her face in a pathetic attempt to block out the creature she'd become.

Louis turned up late, three weeks into term. She was happy even when he trashed her summer's work, even when she could smell another woman on him.

343

As the Christmas break of 1970 approached she didn't know what to do with herself. She saw no way out. She was disgusted by her own weakness – announcing to herself every morning that this was the last time, that she was going to abandon the project, go back to London. Then she would methodically get dressed in her best clothes and go and visit the man who had made her into this.

Waking at four in the morning she would force herself to think of the good things from her life. She couldn't touch on Julião because her failure there was still too painful, but she went back to those last days with her mother and found things to sustain her. Her father's nobility. Her mother's honesty. Her own feelings of love for the woman she'd despised so much. She replayed conversations, thought about Rawly and his wine. His wife. And Audrey telling her that she only deserved the three-quarters man that Rawly was. Had the same happened to her? Was Louis all that she deserved, all that she wanted?

At the end of November she went to his rooms in Trinity, as usual, like the programmed toy she'd become. He barked at her from the door to go straight to the bedroom. He'd begun to enjoy command. She'd just undressed with Louis standing in the doorway, when they both heard Martha's voice at the bottom of the stairs. Martha never came to his rooms. It was an unspoken agreement. He shut Andrea in the bedroom. Martha came into his rooms without knocking. Her New England voice cracked like a whip. They were continuing a row they'd had the night before about going to New England for Christmas, rather than up to Louis's father in Scotland. Andrea, paralysed, sat naked on the bed and stared at the door. She thought she was praying for it not to open, but realized that this was just some superficial horror of social embarrassment, that in fact she *wanted* Martha to open the door. It would do something. It would move her situation one way or another.

Martha was breaking Louis down, dismantling him so effectively that Andrea thought that it wasn't a row about holidays at all. What was Martha doing here? Martha answered the question as if she'd heard it.

Martha opened the door.

She didn't open it gently. She was making a point. She flung it open. It swung round, smacked against the wall and slammed back

344

shut in a fraction of a second – shutter speed. The image from both sides indelibly printed. Andrea naked on the bed. Martha transfixed.

The door was not reopened. It didn't have to be.

The silence was as crystalline as frost.

This time it wasn't Martha's voice that cracked like a whip. The slap must have stilled the quad. A door slammed. Louis burst into the room, tore off his trousers, wrestled her back on to the bed and pinning her wrists lunged into her and rammed her with directed, shuddering vehemence. It didn't take long and he collapsed on top of her. She shifted under his weight. He released her wrists, rolled off her and sat with his head in his hands for minutes.

'Fuck,' he said, after some time.

Andrea sat on the other side of the bed, back to him.

'I've always wondered how you and Martha stayed together,' she said, as if this might be some consolation.

'Because her father's a senator,' he said.

'Was that all?'

She rolled up a stocking and pulled it on, another.

'There's somebody I've been wanting you to meet for some time,' he said.

His words nauseated her. It was as if he'd been preparing her, bringing her to the right psychological pitch for some bad news. He went to the sink, washed himself, towelled between his legs. He pulled on his undershorts, trousers, flipped the braces over his shoulders, looking at her all the time, contemplating the new situation.

She reached for a cigarette and some tissues, wiped herself between her legs, lit the cigarette. She dressed without washing. She needed to soak for a week to get rid of this sordidness.

He made tea in his study. They sat at his desk. He stirred his tea a long time for a man who didn't take sugar.

'Who do you want me to meet?' she asked.

'Someone in London.'

'In London,' she said on automatic, now that the situation was changing she didn't want it to.

'We can't continue here.'

'You mean *I* can't.'

He went back to stirring his tea.

'This is an opportunity, a unique opportunity.'

'For you to get rid of me,' she said. 'I know bad news, Louis. I don't need it sweetened.'

'This is a job,' he said. 'And I know you'll be good at it.'

Chapter 32

1970, London.

They went to London on separate trains. Andrea had a nasty British Rail breakfast, cardboard toast and grey coffee. She smoked instead and wanted it to be pink gin time. Louis still hadn't told her who she was going to meet and he was no clearer on his cryptic remarks about the unique opportunity. This was what they had become. Not telling. Not talking. Circlers of each other. Unequal lovers. Bad maths. Mere satisfiers of each other's strange psychosexual needs.

Louis's intensity emanated from one source – his cock. What he admired in her was not what stirred him. He never talked about her beauty, her brain, her mystery as he had done before in those days which a madman might have called their courting. He was driven by the sex, but she had no idea what the connection was in Louis's head that was running his desire. As for herself, she didn't want to think about herself – a pair of scaley claws scratching about in the dust.

The train came into King's Cross Station. As it shunted to a halt and she reached for her bag she nearly grasped something about Louis, a nuance which wouldn't come back to her, but which had something to do with control.

She went to the RAC club in Pall Mall as instructed and asked for Louis Greig. The man at the desk gave her an envelope which contained a very long list of instructions. Go to Waterloo, take a train to Clapham Junction, then a bus to Streatham, another train to Tulse Hill, a bus back to Brixton and on and on. She set off on the interminable journey, annoyed with Louis for not telling her so that she could have worn flatter heels. She thought about the instructions as she made her way to Waterloo and found herself

347

instinctively checking her tail. The instructions had the quality of spycraft about them. And on the bus from Tulse Hill to Brixton the man sitting next to her leaned over and said:

'Ours is the next stop.'

They got off on the Norwood Road and went into Brockwell Park. Her new companion took her to the bowling green in the middle, nodded her towards the clubhouse and disappeared. She was unaccountably excited as she tried the loose Bakelite handle of the clubhouse door. The interior was unlit and dark on what was now an overcast late November afternoon. In the weak light by the window, Louis sat with his back to the wall next to a thickset man in a dark, heavy overcoat and a grey-brimmed hat with a black band. She trod the wooden boards to where the men were sitting. The smell of creosote filled her nostrils. They were talking in low voices and she realized they weren't speaking English. They were talking in a language which she thought she should understand, it had the same sounds as Portuguese.

Louis and the man stood up and the light caught their faces. Andrea realized that this man must be a Russian. He took off his hat. His hair had the quality of wire wool.

'This is Alexei Gromov,' said Louis. 'He'll tell you where to go afterwards.'

He shook hands with the Russian and left, his retreating feet sounding like those of the first lord vacating the stage for the tragedians' big scene. Her heart was pounding in her chest, her system so shot through with adrenalin that breathing became a concentrated act and sweat formed on odd patches of her body.

Gromov's face had the stillness of someone accustomed to very cold weather, as if evolution had made the nerves retreat from the surface, to make life more bearable. His eyes seemed deep set in his head, not wary, but viewing with the advantage of cover. He showed her to a chair which he positioned so that her face was in the weak daylight and his head was backlit.

'We've been following your career with interest,' he said slowly in English.

'I'm not sure I've ever had one.'

'Politics is a belief. You might not practise it all the time, but it's always there.'

'You mean we communists never suffer from disillusionment?'

'Only if you've decided against the human race. Communism is of the people, for the people, by the people,' he said, opening his hands in front of him.

'And the state?'

'The state is merely structure,' he said, boxing his hands this time.

'Can't you be disillusioned by mere structure and still be for the people?'

Gromov found himself down an alleyway he didn't want to be in. He wasn't an ideologue, he'd never been strong on dialectic, and anyway it wasn't the purpose of the meeting. Greig had warned him of her cleverness, but seemed to have made a massive assumption about her commitment.

'We had heard that you were very committed to the cause,' he said.

'That depends on who you've been talking to.'

'One of our guests in the Soviet Union. A Portuguese guest.'

'I'm not sure that I know any.'

'Comrade Alvaro Cunhal.'

'I don't believe we ever met.'

'You planned his escape. A very bold and daring strategy.'

'I planned it, yes, but not alone,' she said, and for some reason it triggered off an old strain of anger. 'Do you know who planned that with me?'

'I think it was João Ribeiro, wasn't it?'

'Do you know what happened to him?'

Gromov shifted in his seat, the ride still uncomfortable, silently cursing Greig, who'd said she was psychologically prepared for the work.

'He left the party, didn't he?'

'They kicked him out, Mr Gromov. After nearly forty years of active, anti-fascist resistance, after some of the best operations ever planned against the *Estado Novo*, they kicked him out. Why *was* that?'

'The report said there'd been a security breach.'

'No. It was structure, Mr Gromov. Structure kicked him out.'

'I don't follow.'

'The central committee thought he was getting too big for his boots. They thought he was threatening their positions in the party.

So they planted their innuendo and rumour and João Ribeiro, one of the best, most loyal servants to the cause was removed from his office in the party. He ended up in prison and lost his job, Mr Gromov.'

'I'm not sure I understand.'

'Ask the central committee of the Portuguese Communist Party of 1961–2.'

'I can see you're angry.'

'He's a good and trusted friend. The PCP treated him badly.'

'I promise you a full investigation,' said Gromov, having no intention.

'Now tell me what you want,' she said, surprised at herself, angry and forceful now that she was out of Louis's orbit.

Gromov's hands were fists turned in on his knees. He'd lost the initiative in this meeting and he badly needed to get it back if this woman was to do what he wanted.

'We are entering a critical phase in our relationship with the West,' he said.

'And with the East, now that China's got the H-bomb.'

'It's not relevant to our relationship with the West.'

'Except that you're surrounded and you've made the West nervous after the Prague Spring.'

Maybe he should have asked Louis to stay and bring this wretched woman under control. She was impossible.

'In order for us to proceed into the next phase, the negotiating phase, we need to ensure that we have the very best quality information.'

'You want me to spy for you,' she said. 'You want me to give up my life, my research, my . . .'

'Love affair?' he asked. 'No, not necessarily. You'd only be in London.'

Love affair. That unbalanced her. How much detail had Louis given him? Those words. Love and Affair. They didn't really describe what was going on between Louis and her. But he'd said love affair and that meant that Louis must have said the same. She found herself suddenly on the downward spiral, clutching at the ludicrous to find hope.

'We want you to go and work for the British Secret Intelligence Service,' said Gromov, leaning in on her, seeing he'd hit home with something, but not sure what. 'If you are still sympathetic – no, I mean if you still believe in what *we* are trying to achieve, then we would like you to contact your old friend, Jim Wallis.'

'Jim's in Administration.'

'That is very good,' said Mr Gromov thickly, as if advertising cakes.

'Does that mean your aim is for specific or general intelligence?'

'You unnerved me earlier, Miss Aspinall.'

'I apologize if I was over-aggressive.'

'I thought you might have suffered an ideological shift,' said Gromov, thinking that's better, this is the tone.

'My argument was with the central committee of the PCP of 1961–2.'

'Some people when they come into some money, property . . . experience a change of view,' said Gromov, turning the knife now that it was in, punishing a little. 'From being in the street they are suddenly up high, looking down.'

'I've spent more than half my life in Portugal and its colonies under the dictatorship of Dr Salazar. You should have no fear of the bourgeoisie claiming me.'

'Yes. It is good, perhaps, that you have seen things from a different perspective.'

'I'm surprised Louis didn't put your mind at rest. If you didn't know already, he would have told you that I've lost a son and a husband to a fascist, capitalist, imperialist and authoritarian state.'

'It is refreshing to find someone both intellectually and emotionally motivated. I am sorry I doubted you. I don't know how I could have done, given your pedigree.'

The significance of that final word did not penetrate at first. She found herself thinking what exactly her pedigree was and got sidetracked by her earlier statement about Portuguese imperialism and the colonies. Gromov watched her mind at work from behind his glacial façade.

'Do you mind if I smoke?' she asked.

'Not at all.'

She scratched through the contents of her handbag, rooting around in her mind at the same time. She found a cigarette. Gromov provided the light. The word came back again with its full force – pedigree.

'Are you saying, Mr Gromov, that my mother used to work for you?'

'Yes, I am,' he said. 'She was an excellent servant of our cause. Her position within the Company's administration was vital.'

'I'm not sure . . . I'm not sure that . . .'

'She was never very clear to us about her motivation. You understand that some people who work for us are anxious to establish their reasons. It assuages their feelings of guilt. Your mother was not one of these. She was never a clandestine member of the Communist Party, for instance, like you were.'

'How was she recruited?'

'Kim Philby recruited her during the war.'

'Did he shed any light on her motivation?'

'Only that it was for very deep emotional reasons, which she was not prepared to divulge,' said Gromov. 'This is our preferred motivation. Those who do it just for the money . . . well . . . they are already demonstrating an untrustworthy capitalist tendency. We remunerated your mother for the considerable risks she undertook but she told me once that luxury made her feel very uncomfortable.'

'Was it you who laid those wreaths on her grave?'

'Yes. One was from me, the other from Comrade Kosygin. It was a small way of honouring her service.'

'She worked in banking.'

'A very interesting position.'

'I'm sure they've found someone satisfactory by now. It's been four years since she retired.'

'Just approach Jim Wallis . . . remind him.'

'You said there was something specific.'

'I don't think I answered that question,' said Gromov, on a roll now. 'But there is, yes. Something that your mother had been working on before she retired. As you know, the shared culture and language of the two Germanys makes our job of planting agents very easy and they are extremely difficult to uncover unless they are betrayed. We are in the process of entering into discussions with the West and, specifically, with the West German Chancellor, Willi Brandt. We have some very well-placed sources who are gathering excellent material to aid us with our negotiations. We have lost some of those agents, not important ones at the moment,

352

but we don't want to lose any more. We are also losing the odd high-level defector to the West which is causing us a lot of ... embarrassment. The problem is that since Philby left the Company our knowledge at an operational level has been very poor.'

'But not nonexistent. You do have people?'

'Your mother was one. Her retirement was a great blow. In spycraft, as in business, money is everything. It pays for things. You follow the money trail and you find out who it is paying.'

'That sounds simple.'

'Except that your mother traced every penny and concluded that the traitor on our side was either not receiving funds or receiving funds from a different source within the British Intelligence Service. We have since discovered that there is no separate source of funding for overseas operations.'

'So, you have a traitor who is not motivated by money.'

'It's even rarer than that, Miss Aspinall,' he said, which irrationally annoyed her for the second time. 'We have a traitor who is operating without expenses. Not many of our officers, KGB or Stasi, are prepared to fund treacherous operations out of their own pockets. These officers are privileged, but they are paid in Ostmarks and roubles, which don't go very far over the Wall.'

'So he gets his money from somewhere.'

'Possibly *she*. We are not even that far down the road.'

'By the sound of it you think whoever it is, is in Berlin.'

'Yes.'

'And you've looked at all your agents with access to West Berlin, checked their backgrounds and nothing's come up?'

'It's a long process.'

'But you've been doing it.'

Gromov shifted a foot, his first noticeable movement.

'It's in progress.'

'But easier and quicker through me?'

'You will be rewarded.'

'My reward will be to see João Ribeiro restored to his position on the central committee ... if he wants it.'

'It will be done,' said Gromov.

'The other thing is, Mr Gromov, that this will be the only operation I will perform on your behalf. I have ideological faith but I do not have the same quarrel with my country that my mother

353

did. I also suspect that this is the end of my research project at Cambridge. I imagine that I will have to tell Jim Wallis that it didn't work out. It will be a burned bridge. I'll need work. Admin within the Company may not be such a bad job, but I don't want to be a permanent *spy* there.'

Gromov nodded. He would work on her. She would come round to him in the end.

'The only clue we have on the identity of the traitor was something your mother overheard back in '66 from Jim Wallis. It was a codename she'd never heard of before and she could find no existing financial record for it. The name was: Snow Leopard.'

'Well, they're rare, aren't they, Mr Gromov?'

'Very rarely seen indeed,' he replied. 'I come from Krasnogorsk in Siberia, not far from the Mongolian border. At that point the Sayan mountains form the frontier, which is the natural habitat of the snow leopard. My father took me hunting when I was sixteen and while Wall Street was having its magnificent crash I shot the one and only snow leopard I have ever seen. My wife wears it today as a jacket when we go to the ballet.'

Andrea sat on a bench, high up in Brockwell Park, overlooking the Dulwich Road. The wind had got up and one side of her face was frozen, the eye tearful and her nose red. She hoped this discomfort would prompt some reasoned thought as to why she had just committed herself to spying for the Soviet Union. She had given Gromov good reasons. She wanted João Ribeiro to be rehabilitated. She had hinted that she was motivated in part by the death of her son and husband. Gromov had thrown up the pedigree business. It would appear that this was her family tradition. He'd also brought Louis Greig into the game. Her lover. Had she been considering that? Was it important not to disappoint Louis? His standing with Gromov would be enhanced. Would hers with Louis? Was that what she wanted? Were any of these the real reasons?

Then it struck her. The thought that had nearly penetrated at the end of the train journey. Control. Everyone, in this business and out, was looking for control. Louis had taken her as his lover because the secret of it gave him control over Martha. Andrea went along with it, with his demands, because she wanted to control Louis. As Louis sensed his control over Andrea waning, he drove her back into a vulnerable state. She allowed it, she wanted it, because she perversely interpreted this as regaining control over Louis by giving him what he wanted. She wanted to go back into the Company because, the spy's fantasy, it would give her ultimate control. Perhaps that was it after all.

This had become her nature. Gromov had talked about pedigree, and he was right. She was her mother's daughter. Her mother's revenge for Longmartin's injustice had been twenty-five years of treachery against her country. She wondered if she'd confessed that to Father Harpur.

Unable to stand the cold any longer she left the park. Gromov had told her that she was to meet Louis Greig at Durrant's Hotel in George Street in the West End which, it occurred to her, was not far from the Edgware Road. She checked her handbag to make sure she was still carrying the key to safe-deposit box 718 at the Arab Bank. She took a bus to Clapham Common and the tube into the West End. She came up into Oxford Street from the Marble Arch tube station and walked up the Edgware Road, wondering what instinct in her had prevented her from looking in the box before now.

Within half an hour she was sitting alone in a cubicle with the oblong stainless steel box, hands sweating, unaccountably nervous. Inside the box were sheafs of ten-pound notes. She didn't have to count them because there was a note in her mother's hand showing a total of £30,500.

Outside in the autumn wind she hailed a cab and, leaning against the passenger door, thought for a few moments and made her decision. She asked the driver to take her to King's Cross Station. She took the afternoon train back to Cambridge and spent the evening packing her things. She went to the pub, ordered a double gin and tonic and called Jim Wallis.

Chapter 33

15th January 1971, East Berlin.

The Snow Leopard stood three feet back from his living-room window and looked down from his fourth-floor apartment on to the empty packed snow and ice between the five concrete blocks which constituted his part of the not-so-new development on the Karl Marx Allee. He was smoking a Marlboro cigarette in a cupped hand and watching, and waiting, and thinking that life had become all about numbers – three feet, four floors, five blocks, all surrounded by nothingness, white, white zero snow. No cars. No people. No movement.

The two apartment blocks immediately opposite were completely unlit, not a square of light to be seen, not even the hint of someone stretching in a half-dark room, preparing for another all-night surveillance of nobody. The sky above was a muffled grey. The noise level was close to what city people knew as silence. The Snow Leopard's wife snored quietly in the bedroom, her door open, always open. He cocked his head as one of his two daughters squeaked in her sleep, but then his face went back to the window, his hand back up to his mouth, and there was the unmistakable taste of export America.

He went into the kitchen, dowsed the butt and threw it in the bin. He shrugged into his heaviest coat. It was minus twelve degrees outside, with more Russian snow due during the day. He put his hand to the radiator. Still working – glad they weren't on the tenth floor where the heating probably wasn't and State plumbers as rare as Omaha steak around here. He reviewed the situation one last time. Quiet. Two a.m. His time of night. His type of weather. He crammed a brimmed hat on to his head, picked up his uniform, which was protected by brown paper, and left the apartment, taking the stairs down to the garage.

He put his uniform in the boot and got into his black Citroën. He drove slowly over the ice-packed roads until he reached the cleared Karl Marx Allee, which had been the Stalin Allee, until Uncle Joe had been Khrushchevified, and then Brezhneved. He turned left, heading into the centre of town and the Wall. There was no traffic but he checked the rear view constantly. No tail. At Alexanderplatz he turned left on to Grunerstrasse, crossed the River Spree and parked up in Reinhold-Huhnstrasse. He took a brisk walk into an unmarked building, flicked a pass at two guards, who nodded without looking, and dropped down two flights of stairs into the basement. He went through a series of swept and swabbed tunnels until he reached a a door which he unlocked. This door, which he relocked, gave on to a small hallway and in four short steps he was walking southwards down Friedrichstrasse on the West side of the Wall.

He walked quickly and crossed the street at the Kochstrasse U-bahn. A hundred metres later he paid ten Deutschmarks to a swarthy, moustachioed man in a glass cubicle under a neon sign which read Frau Schenk Sex Kino. He entered through a large heavy leather flap and stood at the back, unable to see and unable to work out what was happening on the dark screen. Only the soundtrack told him that several people were approaching ultimate satisfaction with customary and prolonged ecstasy while the camera locked itself unerringly on their biological detail. Porn, he thought, the desecration of sex.

He reached the side wall of the cinema and walked slowly down to the front and another door, which let him into a passage lit by a single red bulb. A ginger-haired man, the same width as the passage, stood at the far end with his hands in front of his groin. Close to, the Snow Leopard could see that the man had the eyelashes of a pig. He handed over another ten marks and opened his coat. The man patted him down, squeezed his pockets.

'Number three is free,' he said.

The Snow Leopard went into number three cubicle and closed the door. There was a binful of used tissues and some wishful graffiti on the walls. Beyond the tinted glass panel there was a girl kneeling on the floor with her face turned sideways, cheek to the ground, eyes closed, tongue roving her lips and her behind as high up in the air as it would go. She was fingering herself. He turned his back on the

357

scene, checked his watch and tapped on the plywood wall. No answer. He tapped out his code again and this time received the correct reply. He took a roll of paper, a coded message, from the cuff of his coat and pushed it halfway through a hole drilled in the wall. It was removed from the other side. He waited. Nothing came back. A few minutes later the next-door cubicle was vacated.

He waited more minutes, his back to the glass panel, until there was a polite knock on the door. They always knocked, just in case. He followed another man down a passage, which curved to the right past other cubicles. The man opened a door to the left and waved the Snow Leopard through. The lighting returned to neon normal in this part of the building.

'Second on the left,' said the man, to the back of his head.

He went into the office. A man with a substantial belly stood up on the other side of a desk. They shook hands and the man offered coffee, which he accepted. The Snow Leopard laid a small white sachet on the sports page, which the man had been reading. The man set the coffee down, picked up the sachet, closed his newspaper and laid out a piece of dark blue velvet. He emptied the sachet on to it. He inspected the diamonds visually first, divided them up and then weighed them on a set of scales he had on top of the safe in the corner of the room.

'Three hundred thousand,' he said.

'Dollars?' asked the Snow Leopard, and the man laughed.

'Are you OK for cigarettes, Kurt?' he said, showing how seriously he took the attempt at negotiation.

'I've got plenty.'

'Did you bring any of those Cuban cigars with you this time?'

'What are we celebrating?'

'Nothing, Kurt, nothing.'

'That's why I didn't bring any.'

'Next time.'

'Only if it's dollars, not Deutschmarks.'

'You're getting to be a capitalist.'

'Who? Me?'

The man laughed again, asked him to turn his back. The Snow Leopard sipped his good, strong, real coffee down to the grounds and turned to find six blocks of money on the desk. He put them into the lining of his coat.

'Which way out?' he said. 'I don't want to go back through there like I did the last time.'

'Left, right, keep going until you get to a door and that'll put you into the Kochstrasse U-bahn.'

'Why couldn't I come in that way?'

'That way we don't get the twenty Deutschmarks entrance fee from you.'

'Capitalists,' said the Snow Leopard, shaking his head.

The man boomed another laugh.

The Snow Leopard got back into his Citroën on the East side of the Wall. He headed north through the old Jewish quarter of Prenzlauer Berg on the Schönhauser Allee. He took a right after the Jewish cemetery and, as the street narrowed, went up on to the pavement and parked under the arch of the *ersterhof* of a huge and decrepit *Mietskasern* in Wörtherstrasse. He waited with the engine running and then rolled into the first courtyard of the old nine-teenth-century rental barracks, the terrible fortress-like forerunners to the kind of place he was now living in himself. He parked up and crossed the courtyard to the *hinterhof*, the back building, which never saw any sunlight. It was silent. The place was deserted, the living spaces totally uninhabitable, the damp, at this time of year, frozen on the walls. Chunks of plaster and concrete lay scattered across the stairs and landings. He knocked on the metal door of an apartment on the third floor. Feet approached from the other side. He took a full-face ski hat out of his pocket and pulled it over his head.

'*Meine Ruh' ist hin*,' said a voice.

'*Mein Herz ist schwer*,' he replied.

The door opened. He stepped into the heat.

'Do we have to have such depressing lines from Goethe?'

'I'll be changing to Brecht next week.'

'Another cheerful soul.'

'What can I do for you, Herr Kappa?'

The Snow Leopard took off his coat, laid it on the chair and removed an American passport in the name of Colonel Peter Taylor from the lining. Amongst its pages was a loose passport-size photograph.

'You know the deal. Take the old one off, put the new one on.'

The man, late thirties with bland, unnoticeable, dark features opened the passport, leafed through it with the familiarity of a border guard, which was what he had been fifteen years before. The nine years he'd spent in prison as a member of a five-man ring who'd been caught smuggling people to the West had not dulled his attention to detail, but rather sharpened it to a professional level.

'This is genuine,' said the man, looking up out of the corner of his head.

'It is.'

'I'll need forty-eight hours.'

'I want an entry stamp, too. I'll give you the date later.'

'Five hundred . . .'

'Same as the last time then.'

'Five hundred down and five hundred when I finish.'

'Since when did your rates double?'

'Like I told you, Herr Kappa, passports are the window into people's lives. I looked into this one and it seemed . . . cluttered to me.'

'Cluttered or sparse, it shouldn't affect your work.'

'That's the deal, Herr Kappa.'

The Snow Leopard took his uniform out of the boot and changed in the car. He went back to the Schönhauser Allee and headed north under the pillars of the S-bahn. He kept going and passed under the Pankow S-bahn, where he turned right and, as he pushed on, began to come out of the urban sprawl through Buchholz. Just before Schönerlinde he had to show his papers at a police post and was saluted and allowed through without even a glance into the back seat. He drove through the small village and headed north again through Schönwalde and into the pine forest beyond. A fine snow began to fall just as he turned off the road to Wandlitz and by the time he reached the guardhouse to the Wandlitz Forest Settlement, the idyllic lakeside village reserved for the ruling élite, he was swearing out loud. The snow was going to slow everything down.

The guard cracked his heels together and saluted.

'To see General Stiller,' said the Snow Leopard.

'Herr Major,' said the guard, and raised the barrier.

He drove through the settlement to the corner reserved for the Ministry of State Security, the Stasi, and parked up outside the villa belonging to General Lothar Stiller. The wind was blowing hard, buffeting against the buildings, needling the fine crystals of snow into the still sensitive side of his face. He'd think afterwards whether he'd heard anything, or if it had just been the thump of the wind on the edge of the villa.

He did hear something as he walked up the path to the front door, the snow swirling, feinting left and right, on the steps up to the porch. It was the door knocking against the latch. He pushed it open with a thick gloved finger and stepped into the dark carpeted hall.

Light came from a crack under a door to the left. It opened on to the remains of a party – three shot glasses for schnapps and vodka and larger glasses laced with the scum of beer foam. There was nobody in the room, but a tie lay on the back of one of the chairs. He skirted the furniture and headed for the general's bedroom.

He didn't see him at first. There was only a bedside lamp on and a bad sulphurous smell in the room. He turned on the main light. General Stiller was naked and kneeling in the corner of the room, hunched over an armchair on the back of which his light blue uniform was neatly laid out. There was a large, dark red stain over the pocket of the jacket which was working its way up to the medal ribbons on the chest. The white shirt next to it was flecked with blood. The bad smell was from the streak of diarrhoea down the general's hamstrings and spattered over his calves.

The Snow Leopard held a hand over his mouth and inspected the body. Stiller had been shot at point-blank range in the back of the neck. He knelt by his side. The exit wound was huge, an appalling mash of skin and bone and an ugly black hole where the nose should have been. The eyes seemed to be staring agog, as if amazed at seeing what had been a good-looking face sprayed over the back of the chair.

The Snow Leopard reached under the chair and came up with a ball of lacy underwear. He stood and took in the room. Four strides and he was in the bathroom. He pulled back the plastic curtain to the bath. She was lying face-down, peroxide blonde hair, black at the roots and now horribly reddened. She wore a black suspender belt and black stockings.

Back in the bedroom he flung back the covers. Something heavy hit the floor. The gun. A Walther PPK, no suppressor. He held it in his gloved hand, went back to the living room, opened the door opposite the curtained window of the front room. The girl's clothes were on the back of the chair. The bed had seen some action, all the covers hung off the end like a thick tongue and there was a large stain on the bottom sheet. He checked the rest of the house. Empty. The back door was open. The wind had eased up and the snow was now falling thickly. No tracks.

He picked up the phone and thought for a full minute of his options. He had to be careful. They always said that the phones in the Wandlitz Forest Settlement weren't tapped but anybody would be mad to believe that, given the ubiquity of the Stasi, and he should know.

Half of the money he had on him was due to a Russian, the KGB General Oleg Yakubovsky, and he would really have liked to call him and ask his opinion at this moment but that risked pointing a finger. There was no possibility of just driving away as he was logged in at the guardhouse. He knew he only had one option but it was worth fidgeting around his head just in case he miraculously came up with an alternative. But there was none. It had to be General Johannes Rieff, Head of Special Investigations.

Rieff's voice was thick with sleep.

'Who is it?' he asked.

'Major Kurt Schneider.'

'Do I know you?'

'From the Arbeitsgruppe Ausländer.'

'What time is it?'

'Five thirty, sir.'

'I'm not used to being disturbed for another two hours.'

'There's been an incident at the Wandlitz Forest Settlement. General Stiller has been shot and there's a dead girl in the bath who . . . is not his wife.'

'Frau Stiller hasn't been a girl for a long time, Herr Major.'

'The girl has been shot too . . . in the back of the neck.'

'What are *you* doing there?'

'I came to see General Stiller.'

'Yes, and that's quite normal at five in the morning, is it?'

'We frequently meet before office hours to discuss internal business.'

'I see,' he said, as if that was one of the world's most unlikely events. 'I'll be with you in an hour. Stay there, Major. Do not touch anything.'

Schneider put the phone down, sniffed the gun in his other hand. It smelled of oil, as if it had not been fired. He checked the magazine. Full. He tossed the gun back on to the bedclothes.

He inspected the ashtray in the middle of the table in the living room. Three cigar butts, one badly chewed, six cigarettes, three with brown filter, three with white, all six with lipstick, different colours. Two women. Three men. The women not drinking. He went to the kitchen. Two champagne saucers by the sink, both with lipstick, an empty plate with the faint smell of fish. One bottle of Veuve Clicquot in the bin. The girls came out for a talk, see how they were going to play it.

He opened the fridge. Three tins of Beluga caviar, Russian. Two bottles of Veuve Clicquot and one of Krug. One bottle of lemon vodka encrusted with ice in the freezer.

He went back into the spare bedroom where he found the girl's clothes, his brain just beginning to motor now. He swept a hand under the bed, lifted the covers. The handbag. He emptied it on to the stained bottom sheet. One passport. Russian, in the name of Olga Shumilov, her blonde hair perfect in the photo. He put everything back, threw the bag under the covers, suddenly remembered the original business and all the money in his coat.

He took the blocks of money out of the lining, stuffed them in the pockets and went to the car. He fitted the three packets under the front passenger seat and went back up the snow-covered path. Heavy flakes landed on his shoulders, he felt their delicate touch on his forehead.

He found a clean ashtray in the kitchen, began some serious smoking and light-headed thinking. The money, minus his twenty thousand Deutschmark tip and sixty thousand for Russian expenses, was to be split evenly between Stiller and Yakubovsky, who was waiting for him in the KGB compound in Karlshorst. The way the scam worked, as far as he'd been able to discover, was that Yakubovsky procured the diamonds, which arrived by diplomatic bag from Moscow. Stiller had set up a number of buyers, including whoever was the owner of the Frau Schenk Sex Kino chain. Not Frau Schenk, was all he knew. Schneider himself was just one of the sad old leg men who worked as an aide to Stiller and his Stasi friends, and who were occasionally on the end of a hard-currency bonus.

He was trying to work out why he thought this was a KGB job, even though the Russians had the tendency to shoot the other way round, through the face taking away the back of the head. He also couldn't quite square the girl being there. It was an inside job, of that he was sure, and *deep* inside, because admission to the Wandlitz Forest Settlement was very selective. Only the East German leader, Secretary General Walter Ulbricht, and his central committee members, plus top armed forces men and high-ups in the Stasi, or MfS as they saw themselves.

Stiller was not short of friends or enemies. There would be little sobbing over his grave. Certainly the handkerchief of the chief of the MfS, General Mielke, would not find its way up to his eyes at the funeral. General Mielke only tolerated Stiller because of the man's special relationship with Ulbricht, and his status as Ulbricht's head of personal security. Mielke and Stiller had the same interests, venality and power, which were competitive rather than complementary. Even so, it was unlikely that Mielke would take him out of the game, and certainly not so ostentatiously, unless . . . back to the Russians. Perhaps the Russians had styled the execution and left one of their operatives as a decoy. This was pure paranoid thinking, of the type that could only possibly raise its head in East Berlin and it didn't come close to answering the fundamental question, which was: What had Stiller done wrong? He really had to speak to Yakubovsky about this, and preferably this morning.

Schneider's mind spiralled in and out from the incident without getting any closer to its meaning. All he knew, as a pair of headlights swept the front of the house, was that a death of this magnitude was going to see large forces manoeuvring for position and creating massive problems for him.

He let Rieff into the dark hall. The general, a heavy, dark man of about the same height as Schneider, stamped the snow off his boots. It was already ankle-deep out there. Rieff stared at the sole-patterned clods of snow on the mat and stripped off his brown gloves and peaked cap, preparing himself. He brought a strong smell of hair tonic with him.

'Do I know you, Major?' he asked, jutting his jaw, crushing his greying eyebrows together.

'I think you would have remembered,' said Schneider, clicking the hall light on.

'Ah, yes, your face,' he said, peering or wincing at him. 'How did that happen?'

'Laboratory accident, sir . . . in Tomsk.'

'I remember you now. Somebody told me about your face. Sorry . . . but you're not the only Schneider. Where's General Stiller?'

Schneider led the way, stepped back at the door. Rieff swore at the stink, slapped his thigh with his gloves.

'The girl?'

'Bathroom on your right, sir.'

'Probably shot her first,' he said, his voice echoing from the tiled room.

'General Stiller's gun is on the floor over there, sir. It hasn't been fired.'

'I thought I told you not to touch anything.'

'I came across it before I called you, sir.'

Rieff came back into the living room.

'Who's the girl?'

Schneider faltered.

'Don't treat me like an idiot, Major. I didn't really expect you to stand about with your thumb up your arse until I arrived.'

'Olga Shumilov.'

'Good,' said Rieff, slapping his hand with his gloves. 'And what were you and General Stiller up to?'

'I beg your pardon, sir?'

'Simple question. What were you up to? And don't give me any shit about work. The general's work habits were minimal.'

'That's all I can do, sir. That's all we discussed. They were minimal because he was an excellent delegator, sir.'

'Goodness me, Major,' said Rieff, sarcastically. 'Well, I'll let you think about that one and you can answer it in your own time.'

'I don't have to think about it, sir.'

'What would I find if I searched your car, Major?'

'A spare tyre and a jack, sir.'

'And this villa? What would we find in here? A piece of rolled-up Russian art? An icon? A nice little triptych? A handful of diamonds?'

Schneider was grateful for his burnt face, the mask of impenetrable plasticated skin which had no expression or feeling, other than it itched when he sweated. He kept his hands jammed in his pockets.

'Perhaps General Rieff has privileged knowledge about General Stiller's affairs . . .'

'I have *extensive* knowledge about his *privileged* affairs, Major,' said Rieff. 'What was in the fridge?'

'Material suitable for the refreshment and entertainment of Russian officers, sir.'

'Material?' snorted Rieff. 'He taught you well, Major.'

'He's my senior officer, sir. I'm stunned to see him in this state.'

'*I'm* surprised there weren't *two* girls in the bath . . . and a boy in the bed.'

This was true. There'd been some scenes. Schneider had heard and kept himself away from them.

'I hope I did the right thing in calling you, sir. It had occurred to me that this was sufficiently serious for General Mielke to be contacted.'

'I'm taking care of this, Major,' said Rieff severely. 'Where are you going now? I'll want to talk to you.'

'Back to the office, sir. I might be lucky to get there in time in this weather.'

'You don't fool me, Major,' said Rieff brutally. 'I've seen men who've met flame-throwers.'

Schneider, unsettled by the observation, didn't bother trying to correct him. He gave his salute and left.

His Citroën crawled through the heavy snow, back through the dark villages buried in silence. Snow-piled cars with two black fans scraped from their windscreens crumpled towards him, a swirl of moths in their headlights. He couldn't see out of the back window. Inside he felt muffled, suffocated. He opened the window a crack and breathed in icy air. This was a disaster, a complicated disaster. Rieff was going to brick his balls. Clack! He was no longer protected by the thick, rusting hulk of Stiller's corruption and that was the end of finance for his extra-curricular activities. A thousand marks for the American colonel's passport, that left nineteen thousand marks and then what? Unless. He could give Yakubovsky his half and keep Stiller's. Tempting, but insanely dangerous. His face didn't need the addition of a black, torn hole like Stiller's. He resealed the window, lit a capitalist cigarette.

The thump of the windscreen wipers lulled him. The warm, smoke-filled cocoon of the car was a comfort. He came into the centre of town. The snow-filled vacant lots, the crumbling buildings re-mortared white, the shells of deserted houses with their steps and window ledges stacked thick with pristine snow, all looked nearly presentable. How democratic snow was. Even the Wall, that raised scar across the face of the city, could look friendly in the snow. Icing on the cake. The death strip tucked up under a blanket. The watchtowers Christmassy.

He slewed the car into the Karl Marx Allee and joined the serious morning traffic of farting lines of two-stroke Trabants and Wartburgs, their black exhausts blasting and splattering the snow, already sludging up to pavement level. He eased through Fried-richshain into Lichtenberg and took a left before the Magdelen-strasse U-bahn into Ruschestrasse. He took one of the privileged parking spots outside the massive grey block of the Ministerium für Staatssicherheit. The only sign that this was the Stasi HQ was the number of Volkspolizei outside and the aerials and masts on the roof. The building itself was called the Oscar Ziethon Krankenhaus Polyklinik, which Schneider thought made it the largest mental institution in the world. Thirty-eight buildings, three thousand offices and more than thirty thousand people working in them. It was a town in a single block, a monument to paranoia.

He went through the steel doors, flashing salutes left and right, and went straight up to his office. He stripped off his coat and gloves, refused his secretary's grey coffee and called Yakubovsky on the internal phone. They agreed to meet on the HVA floor, the Hauptverwaltung Aufklärung, Main Administration Reconnais-sance or Foreign Espionage and Counter-espionage Service.

Yakubovsky's eyebrows came before him. Schneider wondered why a man prepared to shave his face clean every morning couldn't see the necessity of hacking back the brambles of his eyebrows. They saw each other and the Russian nodded and turned his grey back, which was wide enough to be tarmacked rather than clothed. Yakubovsky puffed on a thick white cigarette, from which he was constantly spitting flakes of black shag from his tongue. They began a slow walk. Yakubovsky's fat, slack as a brown bear's, shuddered under his uniform. Schneider delivered his news. Yakubovsky smoked, spat, turned his mouth down.

'The money?' he asked.

'It's in the car.'

'All of it?'

Tempted again, but no.

'Yes, sir.'

'Come to Karlshorst, five o'clock.'

'General Rieff is in charge of the investigation.'

'Don't worry about Rieff.'

Yakubovsky sped away suddenly, leaving Schneider jostled in the corridor.

At 4.15 p.m. it was dark. The snow had stopped. Schneider cleared his car windows front and back. He drove home first to see if Rieff was having him tailed. He parked up and stripped his DM19,500 from one of the packages. He drove a slow circuit of the blocks of flats before coming back on to the Karl Marx Allee and heading east down the Frankfurter Allee. He turned right into Friedrichsfelde, past the white expanse of the Tierpark, under the S-bahn bridge and then left into Köpenicker Allee. The KGB headquarters was in the old St Antonius Hospital building on Neuwiederstrasse. His ID card was taken into the guardhouse. A call was made.

He parked where he was told, pulled the packets of money out from under the seat. An orderly came out to meet him and took him up to the third floor, through an office he knew already and into a living room beyond, which he didn't. Yakubovsky sat upright in a straight-backed leather chair, next to a fire burning in the grate. He was smoking the last inch or so of a cigar. Schneider thought about the ashtray in Stiller's villa. It made him nervous but he told himself that anybody could smoke cigars.

The orderly appeared, carrying a tray on which there was a steel bucket of ice with a bottle of vodka stuck in it. Alongside was a plate of pickled herring and black bread, two shot glasses and a fresh pack of cigarettes with Cyrillic script over them. The orderly backed out, as if Yakubovsky was a man to keep an eye on.

The Russian crushed out his cigar. The end was soggy and

368

chewed up. Schneider twitched under his coat. He handed over the packets of money.

'Don't let me keep you from your guests,' said Schneider. 'I've already taken my twenty thousand marks. There's two hundred and eighty thousand left.'

'You're my guest,' he said. 'And you'd better take some more. There's not going to be anything for some time.'

He fished out a sheaf of notes from the lucky dip, which Schneider slipped into his pocket. Thick. Fifty thousand marks at least.

'Take off your coat. We need vodka.'

They tossed off three shots quickly, the vodka freezing cold, viscous and lemony. Schneider tried to loosen his neck off, his shirt collar chafing his scarred flesh. Yakubovsky threw pickled herring down his throat as if he was a performing elephant seal.

'Stiller is dead,' he said, which was no progress at all, but baldly stated the facts and filled the muffled silence in the room. The fire cracked off a spark up the chimney. More vodka. The good side of Schneider's face felt smacked. Black bread revolved in Yakubovsky's mouth like tights in a washing machine.

'Do you know who did it, sir?' asked Schneider, his voice sounding like someone else's in the room. 'And what was the Shumilov girl doing there? She was one of your agents, wasn't she?'

Yakubovsky tore open the pack of cigarettes like a savage and got one going.

'This is a delicate situation,' he said. 'A *political* situation.'

'Forgive me for being forward, sir, but you were there last night, weren't you?' said Schneider, the vodka steaming him open. 'Who else was there? That should throw . . .'

'I can understand your nervousness, Major. You probably feel exposed . . . out in the open,' said Yakubovsky from under his dark and threatening eyebrows. 'I *was* there, with General Mielke, if that satisfies your curiosity. We left at midnight. Stiller was shot about five hours later.'

'And the girls?'

'The girls arrived as we were leaving. They came with Horst Jäger.'

'The Olympic javelin thrower? What the hell was he doing there?'

'I understand he has quite a javelin in his trousers,' said Yakubovsky, eyebrows off the leash. 'And he doesn't mind throwing it about . . . or who's watching.'

'So who was the other girl?'

'Not one of ours, a girlfriend of Jäger's.'

'So when did Jäger and his girlfriend leave?'

'Four o'clock, according to the guardhouse.'

'Why was Olga Shumilov killed?'

'Because she happened to be there, I suspect.'

'And why *was* she there?'

'Probably to make sure that Stiller didn't go home,' said Yakubovsky. 'And under the circumstances, Major, I don't think you need to know the answers to any more of your questions. I've already told you that this is a *political*, not an intelligence, matter and that should indicate that any greater knowledge could bring its own pressures. Have some herring.'

They drank some more, finished the food. The Russian signalled the end of the evening by holding up Schneider's coat for him to get into. As he shrugged it up on to his shoulders Yakubovsky spoke quietly into his ear.

'We won't be seeing each other again on the same footing as before, you understand. Should anything happen to you, I will not be able to help. It would be inadvisable to use my name.'

The half-bottle of vodka prevented Schneider's fear from reaching the ends of his nerves which meant that the hair on the back of his neck stayed smooth as a seal's.

'Can I ask how strong General Rieff is in this matter, sir?'

'He is very well positioned. Look at his career before he became Head of Special Investigations.'

'And is he well-intentioned towards either of us?'

'No, Herr Major, he is not,' said Yakubovsky. 'He is of the ascetic school. A hair-shirt man.'

Outside an icy wind had got up and in the short walk to the car it effectively flayed his coat off him. He sat at the steering wheel, tearful, panting with the alcohol in his system. He stuck gloved thumbs into his eyes to stem the tears and force some concentration into his brain.

Yakubovsky was telling him that this was a KGB job and that the hidden agenda was political and, hard as it was to believe, bigger

370

than himself. A Moscow directive, but aimed at what? And leaving Rieff so powerful.

Nothing came to him.

He started the car, drove back to the main gate and out on to Neuwiederstrasse. The sloppy suspension and his drunkenness threw him about the cockpit as if he was on a rollicking fair ride. He stopped on Köpenickerstrasse, pulled into the kerb near one of the still visible storm drains. He was gritting his teeth and hammering the steering wheel with rage and frustration. He took out the wad of Deutschmarks, felt their newness, sniffed their ink. New money. Real money. But too much of it if you were in the unexpected position he'd just found himself. He added his own tip to the bundle of notes, opened the door and threw the lot down the storm drain. Now he would even have a problem getting that passport back.

He drove home, parked up in the garage underneath the apartment block. He locked the car door, staggered to the stairs and walked into the sudden flare from a pair of headlights. Two men approached from the darkness behind, their shoes gritty against the cement.

'Major Kurt Schneider?'

'Yes,' he said, licking his lips.

'We'd like you to come with us for a . . . little word.'

Chapter 34

December 1970 to January 1971, London.

Andrea sat at her desk, the same desk that her mother had occupied for more than twenty years doing the same job. The work was not difficult and it meant that she met everybody who was doing any kind of operational work, and they all talked to her because they wanted to keep her sweet and lenient over their expenses sheets.

Andrea had had to endure a long interview with Dickie Rose, as he was now known, and a shy man called Roger Speke, who would only ask her questions through Dickie Rose and never directly. She had found out nothing about either of them, neither their work, nor their job titles. Meredith Cardew had seen her, too, but that was more of a chat about old times – Lisbon, sardines on the beach, and whether the restaurant Tavares was still running. It was only as she was leaving that she happened to mention how surprised she was to find him in the Company.

'Yes, well, got a taste for it during the war,' he said. 'Bored at Shell, so when I came over on a trip I arranged an interview. Stupid move, really. I'd have been much better off in the oil world but, you see, that was the other thing. Dorothy was fed up with the travelling, wanted to come back to the UK.'

'To London?'

'Good God, no, we bought a house in Gloucestershire. Happy as Larry out there. The girls have left the nest now, of course. All married. So now it's just grandchildren and the dogs.'

'And you've got the Company.'

'Heading for retirement now. Best days behind me. Berlin in the fifties, that was the time. We must have a drink, Anne . . . catch up on old times. Come over to the flat one of these cold evenings, keep an old man company.'

'I'm Andrea now, Meredith.'

'Of course. Sorry. Yes. And sorry about Luís and Julião. Jim told me the awful news. Terrible shock.'

The way he said it, as if it had happened last month and just as she was leaving, took her back a quarter of a century to the house in Carcavelos. Another terrible shock, as he put it. It set something off in her chest, a bird batting against her rib wall trying to get out.

She started in the early December. Wallis took her on a tour of the building. He reintroduced all the people who'd been at the funeral party. Peggy White, who'd assisted her mother in Banking. John Travis in Documentation. Maude West in the Library and Dennis Broadbent in Archives, who was the only one with anything to explain to her.

'I've got you down here as a Grade 5 Blue and Yellow. Grade 5 is medium security, Blue is for banking and Yellow is for Foreign, which means you're restricted to looking in files in that range and anything with a security rating of 5 and under. We all start on 5.'

'What's the highest?'

'Grade 10 Red. You can look at anything with that, including the Hot Room, but there aren't many Grade 10 Reds. Five in the whole building in fact and one of them is "C".'

'The Hot Room?'

He pointed to a door which had a card punch and a number pad by the jamb.

'All Top Secret and Operational.'

'What are the other colours I'm not allowed to look at?'

'Green is for Home/MI5, boring as hell. White is for Personnel, which you'll be cleared for in a few weeks' time.'

'Pink? Is there any Pink?'

'Yes, there is as a matter of fact.'

'What's Pink?'

'Sex.'

'Is that kept in the Hot Room too?'

'Under lock and key.'

'Who's got the key.'

'Roger Speke.'

'It's always the quiet ones, Mr Broadbent.'

'Just like your mother,' said Broadbent, laughing. 'Uncanny.'

*　　*　　*

Peggy White took her through the Banking procedures, sipping her way through glasses of water, as her small lips pursed themselves over International Money Transfers, Expense Sheets, Contingency Funds, Emergency Funds, Quarterly Finance Presentations, Cash Flow, Budgeting and all the other bean counting jargon.

'It's been pretty quiet recently. The last big flap was '68, after the Prague Spring. Agents flying this way and that. The money going all over. Your mother was retired by then. Yes, the Prague Spring did for her replacement. Terrible hash she made of it. Anyway, we really thought that was going to be it, you know. The Reds were going to pull back the Iron Curtain, charge through, and keep going until they hit Holyhead. Still, it's all died down now. I do love it when the days hurtle by like that. To be honest, they're dragging at the mo'. But . . . with the Russkies, anything can happen.'

Andrea settled into the work and made friends with everybody, especially Broadbent. He would leave her alone in Archives so that she could wander the files which she hadn't been cleared for and she could also watch who had access to the Hot Room. Only Rose, Speke and Wallis ever used it. Broadbent revealed that there was a card with magnetic tape and a set of four numbers was issued every week by Roger Speke.

By mid December she'd been through most of the main body of the archives and found nothing of any interest and no reference to the Snow Leopard anywhere. Ten days before Christmas the Americans finally moved out of her house in Clapham and Andrea left Wallis's attic room and set up at home. She met Gromov again at the bowling green in Brockwell Park. He told her what she already knew, that she was going to have to gain access to the Hot Room and look at the operational files to find any reference to the Snow Leopard. If she could get him a card he would arrange for a duplicate to be made overnight. Once she had that, all she had to do was get the weekly number code. Easy. Easy for Gromov in his big coat with his chilled face sucking his one capitalist weakness, sherbet lemons.

She went back to watching the Hot Room users and where they kept their cards. Wallis and Rose were less frequent users than Speke and they kept their cards in their wallets. Speke, who went twice a morning, kept his in the breast pocket of his jacket. She watched Speke for a week and noticed that he only did Hot Room work in the mornings. Grade 10 Red files were not allowed to be removed from the Hot Room. The men worked in there and could only take notes. No photocopying.

She noticed that Speke was a very correct man, fastidious in his manners and dress, the sort who always had a comment about the single vent versus the double vent, and he never worked with his jacket on. He would wear it between rooms but would always remove it before sitting down. He wore a cardigan underneath the jacket and the jacket was always hung on a hanger on the back of his door. The only problem was that she never had access to Speke. He didn't speak to her, or anyone for that matter, apart from the other section heads. He left at five thirty every afternoon and never stopped for a drink. She wasn't surprised that he hadn't been at the funeral – not her mother's type.

She was getting desperate and thinking about how she was going to find out who the fifth card holder was when an expense sheet appeared on her desk with a request for more funds. She checked back in her files and found that the agent, codenamed Cleopatra, should still have had £4,500. Cleopatra's base was given as Tel Aviv. The Middle East was Speke's section.

She waited until two minutes before lunch and knocked on Speke's door. He was standing by the window, looking out on to Trafalgar Square, hands in pockets, stretching the cardigan out in front of him. He was startled to see her and made for his desk as if he had a gun in it. Andrea was sweating under her woollen suit, her blouse sticking to the small of her back. She handed him the expense sheet and talked him through it. He scratched the end of his nose and blinked behind his bifocals. He reached for his phone. She told him she'd be back in the morning. He stood as she backed away. He headed for the window again. Andrea opened the door. Speke stooped to fuss over a plant on the mantelpiece. She put two fingers in the breast pocket and lifted the card, closed the door.

Back at her desk, Peggy White asked her if there was anything wrong.

'Institutional central heating, Mrs White. I can't take it.'

'Your mother was just the same,' she said.

Andrea went out for lunch and queued for a passport photo in Charing Cross station. A man stood behind her. She went into the booth and slipped Speke's card behind the sample photos board. She stood and waited for her photos to be developed. The man behind her came out after his session but didn't wait. Her photos came out. A few minutes later the man's came out black.

The following morning there were two cards in the letter box at home, original and copy. She got to work early, in case Speke went straight to the Hot Room. He arrived. She gave him a few minutes and went to see him. He still had his jacket on. She blinked the intensity out of her eyes, slowed herself down. He was at his window again, looking out on the brittle, frosty morning. Speke, poor, portly Speke, who liked ten minutes to recover from his tube journey in the morning, stiffened.

'I'll come back,' she said.

'No, no, no, what is it?'

'Cleopatra's expense sheet.'

'We must change that codename, you know.'

'I agree. It's absurd to think such mundane things of Cleopatra.'

'Quite. One day we'll find at the bottom: one asp – £3 9s 6d,' he said, and laughed at his own joke. Poor Speke, he'll never be able to go decimal.

'Let's hope not, Mr Speke,' she said. 'Shall I take your jacket?'

'Oh . . . thaggadee,' he said, five options colliding in his brain.

She lifted the jacket off his shoulders, replaced the card, hung it up.

'You're right,' he said, 'Cleopatra should not be requesting more funds. I shall send him a message forthwith. What do you think it should say . . . Miss Aspinall?'

'I wish you all joy of the worm?' said Andrea, knowing that Speke would appreciate Shakespeare.

Speke's laugh came out higher pitched than a hyena's in the bush at night.

'That might be a little too sinister,' he said, 'but excellent nonetheless. Put the wind up in Tel Aviv. Nothing wrong with that.'

Andrea came away exhausted. These things seemed so easy in films but they tore her nerves to shreds, like stealing sixpences from her mother's purse, except it was ten years in Holloway for this kind of domestic pilfering. And she still had to get the weekly access code. And she still had to get into the Hot Room with enough time to achieve something. She knew what she was up against in there. Hundreds of files, and that was just the Berlin/Soviet section.

Cardew asked her over for drinks and supper in his flat, a one-bedroomed affair in a mansion block in Queen's Square, Blooms-bury. They drank gin and tonics while Cardew made a Bolognese sauce in his galley kitchen, *Don Giovanni* on the record player.

'Spag Bol's my staple,' he said, looking a bit sad from behind, grey trousers hanging off his backside. 'I think I'm going to try something else but I always gravitate towards the minced meat and the tins of tomatoes. Pathetic, really. We ate so well in Lisbon.'

'I miss the fish,' she said. 'I even miss the salt cod and I never thought I was going to miss that.'

'Fish only comes in a finger these days,' he said. 'You know, I liked the salt cod with the cured ham on top. Ever try that? One of our girls came from up north and that was how they did it up there.'

'Doesn't Dorothy ever come down and cook you something up . . . or go to the theatre?'

'Dorothy wouldn't be seen dead in London. Hates the damned place. Filthy dirty. Full of Flash Harrys. I'm all right, Jack, and eff you, is how she sees it. Pity, really. Lonely old life I lead down here. G&T, Spag Bol and opera in the evening.'

They ate the pasta and salad, started on the second bottle of red. Cardew's conversation drifted towards work.

'Yes, the fifties were terrific once we got rid of bugger boys Burgess and Maclean. Thought we were right on top of the game, only to find it was a complete bloody farce, with George Blake spoon-feeding the KGB the whole Berlin works and Kim in London doing the dirty here. Made fools of us all. Khrushchev said to Kennedy once that we should give each other a list of all our spies and we'd probably find they read the same. Too bloody right. Another drop, dear?'

He refilled the glasses. Sweat glistened on his top lip. He was on his way.

'It's much more secure now,' said Andrea. 'They seem to have cut admin away from operations. We're all boxed off. Nobody knows what anybody else is doing.'

'As if that was the bloody problem. They've got completely the wrong end of the stick, as per u. Nothing was leaking out of admin. It was ops, that was the holey bucket. Now we sit trussed and blindfolded in our offices, not daring to do a damned thing. And they put us all through the wringer back in the sixties, I can tell you. I held on to my Grade 10 Red status . . . a lot of the others didn't. Plenty of early retirements, one or two arrests. Gutted the Company. Barely ticking over now.'

'I don't see much of you in Archives,' she said. 'Flashing your Grade 10 Red status.'

'Not the way I do things, Andrea. Not my style. Never been a bookworm. Not like Speke. He loves those files. That's his nest. He's the one who devised the system. Gave us all our little bloody cards. Comes round every Monday morning and tells us the weekly code numbers. I can never remember the damn things. Once he told us the numbers and forgot to reprogramme the lock, decided there'd been a security breach and they set the dogs on us again. Yes, he was a bit sheepish after that, old Speke. Bloody right, too.'

They finished the wine. Cardew put on the *Magic Flute*, poured himself a whisky and a brandy for Andrea. He stood in front of the gas fire and conducted an imaginary orchestra. The whisky bottle found its way to the rim of his glass once every half an hour and after the third he hunched himself over and made a ghastly face and said:

'The Bells, The Bells,' as he poured himself another, trying to divert attention from the fact that he was hitting it hard. It was Teacher's, too.

Andrea sipped through her brandy and said she had to leave. At the door Cardew held her coat to his chest in a neck lock, very drunk now, eyes fluttering.

'Don't suppose you'd care to make an old man happy?' he asked, and before she could disappoint him, 'no, no, no, bloody ridiculous thing to say. Four sheets to the . . . no, ten sheets to the wind. Don't know what I'm saying. Take no notice. Always thought a lot of you, Anne. Yes . . . liked you very much. Very, very much. Very . . .'

'Can I have my coat please, Meredith?'

'Sorry, sorry, sorry. Course you can. Strangling the poor fellow.'

He helped her into it and at the door planted a ludicrously chaste but very wet kiss on her cheek.

'Wonderful,' he said, and fell back against the wall.

The next Monday morning, the second week in January, she was in Cardew's office when Speke came to give the numbers. She witnessed the absurd sight of a grown man whispering in another's ear behind a cupped hand. As soon as Speke left the room Cardew wrote down the numbers on a pad.

'Don't know why I bother,' he said. 'But you know the one time I did need to go to the Hot Room and I went to ask Speke to repeat the week's numbers, the bugger wouldn't tell me. Worse than school here, Andrea. If anywhere could be worse than Charterhouse.'

As she stood at the end of the meeting she read the numbers off upside down. She had one week's access. Now she had to get past Broadbent.

Broadbent worked from nine to five thirty with an hour off for lunch. Usually he cleared the archive room and locked up while he went for his sandwich and pint in the Coach and Horses in Soho. Andrea persuaded him to let her stay. He could lock her in there while he went out.

'Just for a few days while I get on top of this,' she said. 'It's getting all the background that's so important, Mr B. Peggy White can only tell me so much.'

'I'm surprised Mrs White can tell you anything,' said Broadbent, swigging his hand. 'That's not water she's knocking back, you know.'

He locked her in the archive room. She sat reading her files for five minutes and went to the Hot Room. She slipped in the card, punched in the numbers and the lock clicked back. She took off her shoes and put them on the table. She'd been washing herself in non-perfumed soap since this campaign began and she hadn't washed her hair over the weekend to make sure she was odourless. She went straight to the Berlin/Soviet section and went through all the active personnel files, each one fronted with the agent's codename. There was no Snow Leopard, but there was a file headed Cleopatra, which she opened only because of the business with Speke and the curiosity of finding a Middle East agent in the Berlin section.

According to the file Cleopatra was not working out of Tel Aviv but was in the Political Section of the Secret Intelligence Service in Berlin recruiting KGB officers for intelligence purposes. She memorized the recruited names, all Russian except one German. The back of the file opened in a gatefold and showed the monies paid to the men and the totals. None of the amounts were insignificant. She looked at the dates. She went back to the front of the file. Cleopatra had been installed on 1st August 1970. She replaced the file, looked around the room, found the London section. There was no admin section and all files were headed with codenames. There was a click, the same click as when she'd opened the Hot Room door herself, but not from her end of the room. The noise went through her like a slaughterer's bolt.

She snatched her shoes from the table. The noise had come from beyond the stacks to the right. Another click as the door shut. Footsteps on the lino floor. She moved alongside one of the Dexian stacks with their woodchip shelves. Speke walked down the aisle on the far side, a cardboard folder under his arm. There was another door. It should have been obvious. How were the section heads expected to access files after hours? She backed behind the stack, viewed him from between the files, looked at her watch. She had twenty minutes before Broadbent was due back. The sweat seemed to pounce out of her.

Speke threw his folder down and went to a caged section beyond the Soviet/Berlin area. He took out a bunch of keys connected to his trousers by a chain and unlocked a padlock at the front, opened the barred doors. He let his fingers play along the shelves and pulled out a file. He went back to the table in the middle and put it down. He removed his jacket, hung it on the back of the door, sat down and opened the file. He went through the papers until he got to a buff envelope, put his hand in and drew out a set of colour photographs. A small groan emanated from deep in his throat and he looked around suddenly and directly at her so that everything in her retreated to her spinal column. Speke laid the photographs on the table and leaned forward over them. In the foreground was a naked woman on all fours with a man in front and a man behind. Broadbent hadn't been joking. This was Speke's personal erotica section. The needle of the second hand on the wall clock behind Speke flickered as it devoured each chunk of time. Speke sat back and then jolted forward as he picked up some other unseen detail.

By five to two Andrea's physiognomy had changed. The desire to scream that had been confined to her throat had now spread over her entire body. She couldn't swallow, she couldn't blink, her brain had seized, its cogs crunched together like a traumatized gearbox. The second hand flickered two hundred and thirty more times until she was sinking her teeth into pure air.

Speke suddenly looked at his watch, started, packed up the photographs, slung the file back together and threw it into the caged section. He relocked it and headed for his door so quickly that Andrea barely had time to shift around the end of the stack.

She heard the lock go, the door shut. She counted to fifteen, forced the seconds out of her. Then slammed her card into the door and tapped out the numbers. No click. The lock didn't shoot back. She tapped the numbers again. Nothing. She knew the numbers were right. She never made a mistake with numbers and not with this number. This number was a famous number. This number was 1729. No mathematician could forget that number. It was the smallest number expressible as the sum of two cubes in two different ways. Her brain was crashing down a cresta run of pure panic, white, white, white.

She took two deep breaths. Slowed everything down. Tried the numbers backwards, thinking Holloway, Holloway. The lock clicked back. Broadbent's keys were rattling in the outer door. She sprinted to the desk, threw her shoes down and hit her chair so hard with her behind that she had to save herself from crashing to the floor.

'Still here, then?' said Broadbent.

She rattled a pencil between her teeth. Started as she noticed him.

'What?'

'Still here?'

'To be honest with you, Mr B., I wasn't.'

'Oh, really?'

'I went to Lisbon for lunch. Grilled lobster and white wine on the terrace.'

'All right for some,' he said, monotonous, morose.

Her stomach disentangled itself from her heart and lungs and headed south.

She met Gromov at night in a safe house just off Lordship Lane in Peckham or East Dulwich. A balding, grey-haired man let her into the semi-detached house halfway down Pellatt Road, behind a hedged front garden of various gnomes at work. She followed his large rubber-soled slippers into the living room where Gromov was sitting by a tiled fireplace, with a clock on the mantelpiece and a figurine of a woman in a bonnet with a trug of flowers. The Russian looked awkward with his still, grey face next to a print of two sweet little girls entitled 'Nature'.

'I don't think I've ever been to this part of London before,' she said. 'Brockwell Park, now Lordship Lane. I thought it was all supposed to happen on Hampstead Heath.'

'Not at this time of year, and in the summer it's full of civil servants with their boys in the bushes.'

'I had no idea.'

'Some of them are our boys,' he said, and didn't laugh.

'You're everywhere, Mr Gromov.'

'Nearly.'

She told him that there was no record of the Snow Leopard in the active personnel files and Gromov nodded as if this was common knowledge. She said she hadn't had time to look through the operations files because of Speke and she made it clear that she wasn't going to try again, given the dangers.

Gromov blinked, accepted it, not upset at all. His reconciled silence needled her. She told him about the Cleopatra file and got his attention. He was pleased to see that she was operating off brief. She told him of the oddity of the file, Cardew's insights into the Company, the atmosphere of distrust, the rift between ops and admin. She gave him details of what was in the file. Gromov still did not register surprise.

'There were six names on the list,' she said.

'Six?' he said. 'Are you sure there were six?'

'I was a postgrad mathematician until six weeks ago, Mr Gromov. I can count.'

'Give me the names.'

'Andrei Yuriev, Ivan Korenevskaya, Oleg Yakubovsky, Alexei

Volkova, Anatoly Osmolovsky and one German, Lothar Stiller.'

'This will have to be checked,' he said brutally.

'Checked?'

'You have done very well.'

'How do you *check* this, Mr Gromov?'

'I send somebody else in ... somebody with Grade 10 Red status.'

Hard silence from Andrea.

'You have proved yourself,' said Gromov. 'That was what was important about this exercise.'

She was furious.

'Do nothing until you hear from me again,' he said and went to his coat.

He handed her an envelope.

'What's this?'

'Five hundred pounds.'

'I don't want your money.'

'Your mother wasn't so proud,' he said, and she remembered safe-deposit box number 718 sliding back into its wall.

At the weekend Louis Greig appeared outside the house. He rang on the door bell and she didn't answer it. He stayed there, pacing up and down the pavement outside, checking the front-room window and peering through the stained-glass panels of the front door. He went away and came back after lunch and she knew she was going to have to see him or be besieged in her own home.

She wanted to confine him to the doorstep but he stepped straight past her into the hall. He looked hunted. His customary neatness had gone. His hair stood up so that he appeared frayed. His eyes were dark with sleeplessness.

'I've been trying to find you,' he said.

'I was staying with a friend until ...'

'Yes, the Americans, your tenants, told me.'

'I've only just moved back in,' she said, keeping it banal.

'Martha and I were in the States.'

'So you went in the end.'

'She went and I followed on later,' he said. 'I was going crazy in Cambridge.'

There was a very long silence in which the stink of his desperation

383

became unbearable. She couldn't think of anything to alleviate it.

'I'm sorry,' he said, his lips thinning to white lines as he pressed them together, trying to keep the extent of his wretchedness to himself. It made her feel cruel. 'I just . . . I can't . . . I'm completely desperate, Andrea.'

'There's nowhere for this to go, Louis. It's finished.'

'Couldn't we . . . ?'

'What?'

'Talk?'

'We have. You're forgiven. Now go.'

'It's just that I can't . . . I have to be with you. I can't stop thinking about you.'

'How do you think about me, Louis?' she asked, turning vicious. 'On the park bench, in the back seat of the car, on your brass bed . . . in the potting shed?'

He grew more agitated.

'Martha's left me,' he said. 'We . . . we could be together . . . properly.'

'No.'

He brushed back his flyaway hair, again and again, touched his anxious face.

'Couldn't we . . . ?'

'No.'

He closed his eyes, bringing himself to the marks. The real reason he was here.

'Just one more time,' he said. 'Please, Andrea. Just one last time.'

She was revolted by him and opened the door.

'Just touch me how you used to touch me,' he said. 'Don't you remember . . . out on the common . . . the way you, the way I taught you to.'

'Get out, Louis.'

He swallowed.

'Just one touch and I'll go.'

She got behind him and shoved him out. There was surprisingly little resistance. He'd gone kittenish. She slammed the door on him. He put his face up to the glass panels.

'Don't you remember how it was, Andrea? Don't you remember?'

*   *   *

384

At work on Monday morning the atmosphere had changed. There was palpable tension like she'd only ever felt at school when something had gone drastically wrong. Peggy White was already halfway down her first glass of watery gin and it wasn't even five past nine.

'They want to see you,' she said.

'They?'

'All the section heads. They're in Speke's office.'

Andrea was panting. Her heart beat in tight spurts and tapped like a knuckle against a high rib. She'd left the card with Gromov. She'd been careful all the way. It had taken her for ever to get to Pellatt Road making sure she wasn't tailed. She covered her nose and mouth with her praying hands, closed her eyes, said a few words to a God she'd forgotten and knocked on Speke's door. Cardew opened it. Speke was at his window in his cardigan. Wallis leaned against a wall in the corner. She was asked to take a seat in a chair in the middle of the room. Speke moved back to his desk. Cardew loomed to her left.

'This is intimidating,' she said. 'I hope I haven't been too hard on your agents' expenses.'

'It's not meant to be,' said Speke. 'It's just serious, that's all.'

'I haven't even been here long enough to make a quarterly statement,' she said. 'I don't see how I . . .'

'This is something different, Andrea,' said Wallis, sitting on the bars of the radiator in front of the window.

Her fingernails were blue with cold.

'Wallis has been running a double agent in East Berlin for the last six years,' said Speke. 'None of us here knows anything about him, no name, nothing. All we know from the quality of his intelligence is that he has contacts in both the KGB and the Stasi. Apart from his intelligence, which has always been perfect, he has facilitated a number of defections. He has managed to retain complete anonymity by being self-financed and not demanding any payment. We have no idea how he finances himself but he has always been able to meet the not inconsiderable expenses that his work demands. However . . . now there is a problem.'

'Well, there's plenty of money in both Emergency and Contingency,' she said.

'Thank you,' said Speke.

'This isn't a banking matter,' said Wallis.

'The agent was in the process of arranging a defection of a man whose specialized knowledge would give us a more complete understanding of ICBM deployment in the Soviet Union. Now a number of things have happened which have made the agent's life awkward. We need to give him temporary support until he can get this defector out. After that he can disappear back into his cover and rebuild his system.'

'Support? What sort of . . . ?'

'Operational support.'

She looked at the faces of the men around her. They looked back.

'I'm admin,' she said, quoting Jim Wallis back to them.

'At the moment,' said Speke.

'I was trained as an agent back in 1944. My active service was less than one week and, as Jim knows, that wasn't entirely successful.'

'But it wasn't your fault, Andrea,' said Wallis. 'The whole operation was a cock-up from the start.'

'But surely you can find someone with a bit more experience than me. I mean, Cold War espionage is . . .'

'Not so different,' said Cardew, 'the Americans still don't tell us what they're doing and the West German BND have their own agenda. A week's training in Lisbon back in 1944 will stand you in very good stead.'

'The point is,' said Wallis, 'our man doesn't want anybody with experience. He doesn't want anyone with a track record in post-war espionage. He wants someone, as he puts it, with a clean bill of health.'

'Then there must be someone in training. I mean, it's ridiculous to send a bean counter on operations.'

The men looked at each other as if this might well be the case.

'It's the fact that you've just started here from a ready-made background that's decided us,' said Cardew. 'There's nobody in training at the moment who we could get into East Germany as easily as you.'

'East Germany?'

'You have a very particular background,' said Speke. 'We've spoken to the head of the maths department in Cambridge and it seems that there would be some point in you paying a visit to a Professor Günther Spiegel, who is a senior lecturer at Humboldt

University in East Berlin. An invitation is in the process of being arranged for you.'

'In the process sounds as if . . .'

'There's a certain amount of urgency,' said Speke.

'It sounds as if you're not giving me any choice in the matter.'

'You *could* refuse,' said Speke.

'And we would lose a very valuable defector,' said Wallis. 'And possibly an agent, too.'

Silence while they let the weight of that press on her conscience.

'This Gunther Spiegel,' she said, after a lengthy pause, 'is he one of us?'

The men leaned back, the pressure subsided.

'No, no, he's a maths professor. He's your ticket in and out, that's all.'

'And what am I expected to do?'

'Do as you're asked. Think on your feet,' said Speke.

'Who is the defector and am I supposed to be involved in helping with that?'

'You will be told who the defector is in due course, and yes, you will be expected to assist.'

'And who do I do this for?'

'Contact will be made.'

'How will I know the contact?'

Speke nodded at Cardew and the two men left the room. Wallis tore a piece of paper off a pad and put it on his knee.

'He will ask you this question,' he said, writing.

He handed her the paper. It said: 'Where do the three white leopards sit?'

'And what would be your reply?'

She wrote: 'Under the juniper tree,' and handed it back.

'I knew we could rely on you,' he said, and lit the paper, threw it in the metal bin.

'Does he have a codename?'

Wallis leaned over, put his lips to her ear and whispered:

'The Snow Leopard.'

Chapter 35

15th January 1971, *East Berlin.*

The first hint that the Snow Leopard had that this might not be a civilized little chat was when one of the men asked for his car keys. Schneider was put in the back of their car with the other man and they drove in convoy out of the estate and on to the Karl Marx Allee. The second hint came when they didn't go to the Stasi HQ but headed north of Lichtenberg, to the Hohenschönhausen Interrogation Centre where the meat wagons used to arrive bringing food for the massive Nazi kitchens during the war but now emptied out live, suspicious flesh for questioning in the dark cellars known as the U-boat.

His name was logged at the front desk and the contents of his pockets and wrist watch were put into a buff envelope, which one of the men took, along with Schneider's coat, to a room down the corridor. There they asked him to strip down to his underpants and take off his shoes. The clothes and shoes were added to the coat and taken away. The remaining man told him to put his hands up the wall and spread his legs. A man in a white coat appeared and searched him thoroughly – hair, ears, armpits, genitals and the final indignity of the greased, gloved finger in the rectum. He was taken back out into the corridor and downstairs to the cellars. Behind a soundproofed door he entered a sodium-lit cavern of freezing cold and hellish noise. Loudspeakers relayed endless torture sessions of men screaming and screaming, until it seemed impossible that their larynxes could take any more. They put him in a cell with no furniture whose concrete floor was scattered with shards of ice. They locked the door and left him in total darkness. A few minutes later a light of surgical brightness came on and after half an hour he did what he'd heard other inmates of the Hohenschönhausen used to do. He knelt on the floor, made fists

388

of his hands in front of him and rested his head on top of them. He disappeared into his thoughts. He was well aware of Stasi methods. They were not beaters and bludgeoners. They played the long game, the slow, psychologically destructive game. After a while he moved beyond these thoughts into a region where nothing happened, where the physical being was suspended, senseless, like a bat in daytime.

He heard the key in the door and stood to attention, face screwed up in agony under the light. They took him back up to the room where he'd been searched. He asked for a cigarette. They ignored him, sat him on a chair and left him with the door open. He waited for the psychological point to be made and after a few minutes his wife and two daughters filed past in the corridor.

'Kurt?' said his wife, confused.

'*Vatti*,' said the girls.

They were moved on. He was taken back down to the cell with the knowledge that his wife and daughters were being questioned and the apartment searched. Still calm. They knew nothing and he'd always made sure there was nothing in the apartment. No spy paraphernalia, no illegal currency, no documents. Thank God he'd dropped off the American passport on the way up to Wandlitz.

It was probably past midnight when they came for him again. They took him into an interrogation room. Two chairs, no table, a panel of mirrored glass on one wall and maybe an audience beyond. They stood him in the middle of the room and started the questions, endless questions, repeated endlessly, which, whatever tangent they appeared to come in on, always ended up probing the same nexus. His relationship with Stiller, Stiller's activities in West Berlin, Stiller's interest in the Arbeitsgruppe Ausländer.

It was a softening up process and Schneider allowed himself to be softened. He let his head loll and jerk up as if out of sleep. He paid out confusing lines, let them pick up on them and truss him up with them later. He constantly asked for things – cigarettes, coffee, water, the toilet. They circled him, drove the questions into him from all angles, worked his brain over like a piece of dough. His knees buckled after six hours standing and they forced him to stand in 'the statue' – leaning against the wall, arms outstretched, weight supported by the fingertips. The pain was quite quickly excruciating. Answering the questions became almost impossible, just barely audible words between grunts of agony.

After three hours alternating between standing to attention and 'the statue' he didn't have to pretend so hard. One of the interrogators disappeared for some minutes and then brought back his shirt and trousers. They told him to dress and then marched him down corridors and up stairs until they reached an unmarked door, which they shouldered through. He was left in an office with a desk and two chairs. He sat in one of the chairs and instantly fell asleep.

He came to with his face being lightly batted by a pair of thick brown gloves. He focused on General Rieff, sitting on the edge of the desk, performing this task of light dusting.

'There's some coffee for you on the side, Major,' he said.

Rieff was going to have to do a lot better than this to break him down.

The general threw him a packet of Marlboros and held out a light.

'There's a bread roll there, too, some butter, cheese.'

'You're killing me with kindness, General. What do I have to do?'

'If you want to, you could start by telling me why you killed General Stiller and Olga Shumilov.'

Schneider sat back, crossed his legs, drew on his cigarette.

'Even you know that's not true, General Rieff.'

'Do I? We've had an autopsy done. You might care to read the report. Time of death should interest you.'

Schneider took the paper, ran his eyes down it.

'Between five and six in the morning,' he said. 'That's very convenient.'

Schneider helped himself to coffee, broke the roll, buttered it, added a slice of cheese. He chewed his way through it, taking his time, showing that Rieff's scare tactics weren't working.

'Where's the gun, General Rieff? There's no gun.'

'On the contrary, we've found General Stiller's Walther PPK on the floor with two bullets missing from the magazine. You might like to read the ballistics report.'

'It might make predictable reading.'

'The good thing about a life sentence in a labour camp, Major,

390

is that it's never as long as the original life would have been. Yours would probably be all over in a matter of fifteen years.'

'Rather than breaking down the bag man, General Rieff, I should have thought your time would be better spent pursuing General Stiller's real murderers. You must know by now who was in that villa . . .'

'Don't be ridiculous, Major,' roared Rieff. 'If you're going to persist with that kind of attitude I'll send you back downstairs, and for a little more than ten hours this time. A week should see you right. You'll have a brain like calf's-foot jelly by the end of that.'

Schneider drank the coffee down, cleared his mouth of bread and cheese, poured himself another. He picked up his still smoking cigarette and returned to his seat.

'I can't think what there is for me to tell you that you don't know already. I imagine you were on the receiving end of some of General Stiller's generosity, yourself. You know that he was operating beyond the limits of a general's pay. You know that he was venal and depraved. I can supply the unsavoury detail, some of it titillating in its salaciousness, but I'm not sure how that will . advance your cause.'

This seemed to strike Rieff as true, because he suddenly had the look of the bull surveying the shattered china shop, wondering what he was doing with all this porcelain crunching underfoot.

'What were you doing for General Stiller in West Berlin?'

'I was running errands for him,' said Schneider. 'That's what I was, General Rieff, and you know it, an errand boy. I'm not proud of it but I was given no choice in the matter.'

'What were these errands?'

'From the questions you asked me in the villa you know this already. Diamonds. Art. Icons. Selling them to the West.'

'So who was running the Russian end of this operation?'

'That I can't tell you.'

'You don't know?'

'If I did, General Rieff, and you acted on it, how long do you think I would last?'

'Was it General Yakubovsky?'

'I can't answer that,' said Schneider. 'But that should be enough for you, shouldn't it?'

Rieff nodded, walked once around the table.

'Did you ever make contact with foreign agents?'

'I work for the Arbeitsgruppe Ausländer. It's my job to deal with foreigners, following them, checking their contacts . . .'

'I mean, on behalf of General Stiller.'

'This was only ever about hard currency, General Rieff,' said Schneider. 'It was never treachery.'

'Ninety per cent of spies betray their countries for money.'

'I'm sure it's not as simple as that,' said Schneider.

'Have you ever heard of a foreign agent codenamed Cleopatra?'

'No. Which agency is she with?'

'The British Secret Intelligence Service.'

'In West Berlin?'

'Yes.'

'How is she relevant?' asked Schneider.

Rieff didn't answer. He walked around his desk and slumped in his chair, thinking. Here was a man caged by his own paranoia, determined to know everything about everybody, and when he didn't know something it ate into him. He didn't know who Cleopatra was, or how she was relevant.

'You think that Stiller was contacting an agent called Cleopatra and selling intelligence to the West?' asked Schneider.

'Yes, I do, and I think you were making that contact. You were his creature, Major Schneider.'

'I have never contacted any agency on his behalf. I did what I was told to do – picking up for him. And *you* know that once you've been asked to do something like that you can refuse, but your future will look bleak. I did what Stiller asked and if I hadn't I wouldn't be here, but there would be someone else in my place, you can be sure of that.'

'Until I've cleared up this business you're not going to do anything for anybody,' said Rieff.

'I'd like to remind you, General, that I *did* call you when I found Stiller's body and you should know from the guardhouse that I did that within ten minutes of arriving at the Wandlitz Forest Settlement. The incident was also sufficiently serious for General Mielke to be informed, but I left that for you to do.'

Schneider thought it a point worth reiterating.

'That's why I'm going to release you, Major. I'm not going to let you travel to the West any more and I'm keeping your car for the moment, but you're free to go.'

'Free? You think I can do my job properly under these circumstances? If you're going to send me out under twenty-four-hour surveillance I might as well stay in here.'

'If that's what you want . . . I'll get the guards to take you back down,' said Rieff. 'If not, the rest of your clothes are behind you.'

No, he didn't want to go back downstairs. Fresh air. *Berliner Luft.* That was what he needed. He dressed in his unstitched clothes, the shoes parted from their uppers, his coat with the lining stuffed in the pocket, the buff envelope in the other. He stood in the middle of the room, putting his watch back on, thinking up a negotiating stance.

'A car will take you back to your apartment,' said Rieff.

'If I can get you information on Cleopatra, will you give me freedom of movement?' asked Schneider. 'I can find out. I have the contacts who can find out, but I'm not going to compromise my network doing it.'

'I won't let you out of East Berlin, if that's what you're after.'

'I just don't want people on my back.'

'I'll give you forty-eight hours without surveillance, then you report back to me.'

The car dropped him off outside his apartment block. It was six in the evening. He flapped up to his apartment in his ruined shoes, found his keys in the bottom of the buff envelope. His wife was sitting with the girls, playing cards in the living room. He kicked off his shoes, took the rush of his two daughters into his arms, clasped the tiny ribcages under their woollen cardigans, kissed the tight smooth cheeks of the ones who loved his own ruined face without question. He put them down. Elena, his Russian wife, sent them to their room. They sat at the table with coffee and brandy and smoked at each other, while he talked her through the surface of his problem with Rieff. He asked her if they'd been treated badly and they hadn't, just made to wait around before being taken back to the apartment. He asked if the apartment had been searched. She handed him a Polaroid of one section of the living room. Polaroids which would enable them to put the apartment back as they'd found it.

'They must have dropped this,' she said.

'I suppose they could have wrecked the place if they'd wanted to.'

Elena, who seemed to have some natural understanding of these kind of events, went into the kitchen and made supper. She was always calm, not through any innate serenity, but more out of an acceptance of the workings of the State. Schneider, cleaned up and dressed, sat at his desk and wrote out a coded note. They ate supper as a family and the girls went to bed. At 10.00 p.m. he went out. Elena didn't ask for any explanations. She never asked him questions. She was watching women's volleyball on the television.

Schneider walked up to the Karl Marx Allee, past the Sportshalle where the volleyball his wife was watching was being played. He went into the Strausberger Platz U-bahn station and back out again. He turned right down Lichtenberger Strasse heading for the Volkspark Friedrichshain. Rieff had been as good as his word. He was clean. He hovered in Leninplatz around the new statue of the great man, taking a last look around him to be sure. The nineteen metre statue, backed by red granite blocks, looked ahead, smiling benevolently on the grim city. He cut across the square into the dark, snow-covered park, made his dead-letter drop and walked back home.

Elena was already asleep. She slept with the bedroom door open, even now, in case the girls needed her. He watched her calm face as she slept, a woman at peace, an unquestioning person. He wondered if there was a part of herself that he didn't know about, that she was living her life for, because he only ever saw her engaged if she was with him or the children. She could watch television until the screen went blank. It didn't matter what. Secretary General Ulbricht boring a trade delegation, the four-man bobsleigh team, Brezhnev overseeing the weaponry of the Soviet Union in Red Square, skilaufen. She was never bored, but also never took any greater interest than what appeared on the screen. She didn't read newspapers or books. She used television to fill in time between engaging with those that mattered to her.

Schneider cared for her. He'd tried to push himself beyond just caring but it required taking her with him, and she was an unwilling traveller. In fact, she didn't like physical travel either. She'd hated leaving Moscow to come to this halved, tormented city. She was envious of his trips back there, even if they were for shudderingly dull conferences and hair-raising debriefs with KGB seniors. He brought back caviar, which he thought she might consider killing for, yes, that was a passion – fish eggs, roe. He should have taken some from Stiller's fridge but that would have given Rieff another stick to beat him with. He suddenly felt exhausted, almost too tired to undress. He wanted to just lie down, scratch a cover over himself, some leaves perhaps, hibernate, dissolve for a season and wake up in spring.

It was late. Schneider's body craved more sleep. The covers weighed a hundred kilos. Leaving the warm sheets was like struggling out of the arms of a woman, but not Elena. She wasn't the type. She was already up, giving the girls their breakfast. They never made love in the mornings. He couldn't bear her looking over his shoulder to make sure the girls weren't at the door. She couldn't bear . . . all that mess, as she put it.

In his office twenty-four hours of paper had built up on his desk. Twenty-four hours of endless reports on what this foreigner had drunk in which bar, who that diplomat had lunched with at what restaurant, what that businessman had said to which girl and what they had done together . . . sometimes with photographs. Nothing surprised him, except that any work was done by these people at all. They were either drinking, eating or fucking. He leafed through, reading the summaries only, his eyelids heavy. At 11.00 a.m. he was summoned to a meeting in the HVA Dept XX, which handled dissidents and was overseen by the KGB General Yakubovsky. He put a call through to the general, hoping for a corridor chat, but he wasn't in.

The meeting was opposite a colonel, who informed him that another deal had been concluded. The sale of two East German politicals had been agreed and there was to be a handover on the Gleinicke Bridge on Sunday at midnight. Schneider would be the driver. This surprised him. It meant that his under-investigation status was not yet common knowledge. Rieff had put him back into the sea.

After work he passed by the Volkspark Friedrichshain and picked up from his dead-letter drop. The note was short. A British intelligence agent posing as a British Steel delegate, codenamed Rudolph, would meet him in the usual place, a deserted *Mietskasern* in Knaacke-strasse in the Prenzlauer Berg district at 10.00 p.m.

Schneider performed his family duties and went out into the cold night to catch a bus to the Alexanderplatz and then a U-bahn to Dimitroffstrasse. From there it was a short walk to the *Mietska-sern*. He passed under the arches and crossed the courtyards of the massive boarded-up complex and went up the staircase of the *Dreiterhof* to the fourth floor. He went to a room above the arch and waited. He was half an hour early. He was always early.

He took the full-face ski hat out of his pocket and fitted it on to his head. He didn't pull it down because the wool itched against his scarred flesh. Twenty-five minutes of refrigerated silence passed and he saw the British SIS agent arrive. He rolled down the ski mask. The footsteps came up to the top floor and approached. He stopped them with his introduction and received the right password back. He clicked on a torch for the SIS man, who had always been annoyed by his codename and especially at this time of year. They went to a table, stood over it and Schneider produced cigarettes which they lit up. Rudolph looked very young for this kind of business, not even thirty. He had the feeling of an undergraduate about him – dissolute, uncaring, loose – a very bad combination for a spy, thought Schneider.

'What's the problem?' asked Rudolph, staring fixedly at the ski mask.

'Apart from the ones outlined in my note, you mean?'

'You asked about Cleopatra. How's that relevant?'

'That's what I want to know,' said Schneider. 'I've got somebody standing on my neck. I said I'd find out about Cleopatra for him.'

'What's the background?'

'My funding comes from extra-curricular work I do for General Stiller . . .'

'Ulbricht's head of personal security . . . the one who got shot yesterday with a girl.'

'Olga Shumilov . . . KGB. I didn't know what to make of it. Still don't. I had to call General Rieff.'

'Who's he?'

'Well, the last time I bumped into him was years ago and he was running the HVA Dept X, which is Disinformation and Active

Measures. I don't know where he went from there,' said Schneider, 'but now he's operating under the umbrella of the Ninth Main Directorate, which is the Stasi's investigative arm.'

'That sounds a very Kafkaesque department.'

'General Rieff is putting me through the wringer. So far only my fingers have gone through. A little bit of pain to see if there is anything more to come out. I don't want him to feed me all the way through . . .'

Rudolph sniggered.

'Sorry . . .' he said. 'Just an image . . . that's all.'

'You should try it. A quick twelve hours in the U-boat in Hohenschönhausen would further your education.'

'Carry on . . . sorry.'

'He mentioned Cleopatra, asked me who she was. In return for staying off my back, I said I'd get him some information.'

'Well, now . . . Cleopatra,' said Rudolph, preparing himself, 'you might find this surreal.'

'It's all surreal,' said Schneider.

'This, even more so. Cleopatra is an American idea. She recruits senior KGB officers. She pays them for intelligence. That intelligence is then circulated around the SIS, CIA and the BND. Between the British, American and German intelligence agencies we try and work out from the disinformation the KGB seniors supply and the real information we're getting from our reliable agents . . . a picture.'

'My God.'

'It's what it's come to. Nobody knows what's real any more, so we examine and qualify untruth to get closer to the truth.'

'I don't know whether I can get Rieff to believe that. He's old school, you know.'

'They're all old school on this side of the curtain. That's why everything stays the same. You've got flat-earthers in charge.'

'Thanks for that, Rudolph,' said Schneider. 'What did Stiller have to do with Cleopatra?'

'His name was put forward for recruitment by General Yakubovsky. Stiller was the only German on the list.'

'And the only one to get shot,' said Schneider, and they lapsed into silence.

'Do you want London's theory?' asked Rudolph.

'Might as well, seeing as we're here.'

'Yakubovsky wanted to get rid of Stiller.'

'Doesn't make sense. Yakubovsky's making money out of Stiller's contacts in the West.'

'What if he's been told by Moscow that Stiller's got to go? All his commercial concerns go out the window. Oleg's job is on the line.'

'Why would Moscow want to get rid of Stiller?'

'You said he was Secretary General Walter Ulbricht's personal security man.'

'*You* said that.'

'Wouldn't that suggest they're trying to weaken Ulbricht?' he said. 'They take Stiller out of the game. He's corrupt and deserves to go. If Ulbricht cries foul, Moscow shows him he was on the take, not just for money but intelligence as well. Ulbricht has to swallow his bitter little pill.'

'What's wrong with Ulbricht?'

'Brezhnev thinks he's too full of himself. So full that he thinks he doesn't have to pay attention to Moscow any more. He's getting to be a loose cannon ... and then there's all that stuff with Willi Brandt.'

'What stuff?'

'Ulbricht hates him. You remember Erfurt, March last year. Willi got a big reception. Crowds cheering him outside his hotel window. Biggest crowds ever in East Germany for a pol. And if you don't know Ulbricht, we do. A CIA man said to me the other day: "That guy Walt's got a personality cult following ... of one."'

'We all want to be loved ... even communists.'

'Well, it's made Ulbricht a difficult customer to handle. Brezhnev doesn't want the West riled up, what with the Chinese and their H-bomb in the east. And if he wants to keep the whole communist edifice in place he has to make it look as if he's moving, when in fact he's still on the same old treadmill. Hence détente. Given Ulbricht's antipathy to Brandt, Moscow doesn't think his contribution to any negotiations is going to be positive. *Ergo* they want to give Walter his cards and find someone who will toe the line and be less of a maverick.'

'That makes sense, Rudolph,' said Schneider, surprised that the boy had it in him.

'Well, there's as much truth potential in it as anything else, I suppose.'

'Another thing . . .' said Schneider. 'The money. I need money.'

'Don't we all,' said Rudolph, still dazzled by the brilliance of his analysis.

'To get Varlamov out, Rudolph.'

'Oh, yes, sorry, I'd forgotten about him.'

'I'll need help too. The kind of help that's not going to compromise me.'

'OK. First of all, the money. London have assured me that they're going to deliver your money with a one hundred per cent guarantee of anonymity. They also said you can spill it about Cleopatra. She's a closed operation. I think that should keep you snug with General Rieff, by the sound of it.'

'Or it might just increase his already very suspicious mind,' said Schneider. 'He accused me of being a double today.'

'The way the money is going to come to you, I have been assured, will make you cast iron with Rieff, with Mielke, with Yakubovsky, and with Lord Leonid Brezhnev himself, too.'

Chapter 36

16th January 1971, safe house, Pellatt Road, London.

Gromov sat in the armchair in the front room of the safe house in Pellatt Road. He'd slipped his shoes off and was warming his toes on the tiled hearth. Andrea sat opposite, not wanting to smell whatever vapour was coming off Gromov's feet. She had just reported the conversation with the section heads and Gromov was digesting it, along with two biscuits which had showered crumbs down his front. She lit a cigarette and tossed the match into the fire over Gromov's wriggling toes.

'A very interesting development, don't you think?' said Gromov, flat as beer from the drip tray.

'It seems to be progress.'

'Is this a money-related problem that the Snow Leopard has?'

'Wallis said, "It's not a banking matter."'

'Not a banking matter, yes. So what is his problem?'

'Something to do with the defector?'

'The defector. An expert in ICBM deployment in the Soviet Union,' said Gromov. 'There is a Russian physicist due at Humboldt University to give two lectures, attend a dinner, receive a prize, and spend the night before returning to Moscow. His name is Grigory Varlamov.'

'Is he a known defection risk?'

'If he was we wouldn't be sending him to Humboldt University,' said Gromov. 'When do you leave for Berlin?'

'Tomorrow morning.'

'Varlamov arrives the following day ... in the afternoon and stays for twenty-four hours,' he said, and then, thinking out loud: 'If Varlamov's satisfactory defection is the goal of the SIS's operation then what could be giving the Snow Leopard his problem? If it's not money, it must be that his situation has changed and, for whatever reason, he's finding it difficult to manoeuvre.'

Gromov came up with a crumpled white paper bag of the sort given in sweet shops. He offered it to Andrea and she turned her head. He fished out a miniature rugby ball of yellow sherbet lemon and threw it in his mouth. He rattled the sweet around on his teeth.

'You gave me Cleopatra's list,' he said. 'There was a name on it that shouldn't have been there. When I sent that list back to Moscow I was told that General Lothar Stiller who was Secretary General Walter Ulbricht's personal security chief did not have permission to enter that operation.'

'Was?'

'Stiller couldn't come up with any explanation that could save him,' said Gromov, and Andrea whitened. 'No, no, no . . . nothing to do with your intelligence. I've since learned that he was already under a death sentence. It was the KGB who put his name forward to Cleopatra. His appearance on the list in London was just some paperwork to legitimize his termination.'

'To whom?'

'The East Germans, of course. If we show them categoric proof that their man is a traitor – on file as a traitor in London – there can be no argument.'

'Why did Moscow want to get rid of Stiller?'

'He was a disgrace to communism and because of his corruption or his generosity, whichever way you choose to look at it, he had a comprehensive and far-reaching power base within the Stasi. And that is all I'm prepared to say at the moment. There's a political angle to this development that cannot be discussed. My point is that the Snow Leopard's problems started after Stiller's death.'

'So now you are investigating Stiller's contacts?'

'I said they were comprehensive and far-reaching. We have begun an investigative process but there are hundreds of people involved and given that Varlamov will be arriving in East Berlin within the next thirty-six hours, and presenting the SIS with twenty-four hours to get him out, we have very little time. Breaking men down *takes* time. Your action will be faster, more direct.'

'Do you really expect me to believe that?' said Rieff.

'I told my contact you wouldn't,' said Schneider, who'd just finished telling Rieff the bare bones of Operation Cleopatra, no theory, no mention of Stiller, just that the Americans had set it up to buy Soviet intelligence with the certain knowledge that they were receiving KGB disinformation from which the Allied Intelligence services hoped to be able to draw conclusions as to the real picture.

'It's absurd.'

'It's the point at which we have arrived in the . . . er . . . *impasse*,' said Schneider, which seemed to strike home with Rieff, because he gave a little jump in his seat.

'You know, it would be typical of the KGB,' he said.

'What?' asked Schneider, dismally stirring the rough Cuban sugar into his weak black coffee.

'That the KGB should mount an operation without telling us *and* without showing us any of their results.'

'What's there to show?' asked Schneider. 'That we've reduced the enemy to such absurdities? I suppose it might improve morale.'

'You think morale is low?'

'I mean give an extra fillip to our already high morale.'

'You don't fool me with that plastic face of yours, Schneider. The result of your so-called laboratory accident,' he said scornfully.

Schneider didn't like this about Rieff. The way the man hugged you to him, conspiratorially, and then thumped you in the gut just as you thought you were friends. He said nothing.

'In your work for the AGA you meet a lot of foreigners,' said Rieff. 'You must have quite an extensive network on both sides of the Wall.'

'I've been working at it for seven years.'

'In those seven years have you ever come across an agent code-named the Snow Leopard?'

'No, I haven't. Why do you ask?'

'Because I want to find him.'

'What's his game?'

'He's a double, who's successfully blown several of our under-covers in the West as well as having arranged at least three high-profile defections.'

'Has he been operating long?'

'In the region of six or seven years.'

'I'll put the name around my network, see if I come up with anything.'

'I doubt anyone will.'

'Why not? It's very difficult to operate completely anonymously. You shouldn't be so pessimistic, General.'

'I only doubt it, Major, because I think *you* are the Snow Leopard.'

Andrea took an Interflug flight into the Schönefeld Airport in East Germany. The East Germans had only been prepared to accept her as a visiting mathematician to Humboldt University if she came as a guest of the DDR, although it didn't mean they paid for her flight or hotel, which were expenses she would have to cover in hard currency.

She went through a lengthy document check, during which her two letters of invitation, one from the chancellor of the university and the other from the head of the maths department, Günther Spiegel, were verified by telephone. Her luggage was dismantled and left for her to put back together again, but there was no personal search. She made a currency declaration and bought the standard twenty-five Ostmarks from the State bank. A driver sent by the university was waiting for her, with her name misspelt on a card. He took her straight into the centre of town, into the flattest city she'd ever been in, and dropped her at the Hotel Neuwa on Invalidenstrasse. He didn't speak a word, not of his own volition and not to answer any of her questions.

She ate lunch on her own in the hotel. A terrible piece of gristly pork with a mush of red cabbage and waterlogged potatoes. The driver returned and took her in his usual surly silence to the university. He led her up the stairs to the first floor, pointed to a door and left. A woman answered her knock and, in asking her to come in, offered her the first words of welcome since she'd been in the country. She had an initial meeting with Günther Spiegel, who at the end of it asked her to attend one of his lectures later in the afternoon with a group of his postgrad students.

She found her own way to the student canteen, where she sat alone with a cheap coffee, but even nastier than on British Rail. People looked at her but nobody dared to approach. After her lecture with Spiegel he invited her back to his apartment for dinner.

'I would have asked you earlier,' he said, 'but it had to be cleared first.'

Back in the hotel she found that her room had been searched, her clothes unpacked and repacked with near precision. She ran water into the bath, stripped naked and peeled off a dressing from the small of her back and unpinned a sanitary towel from the gusset of her knickers. She opened them and removed twenty thousand Deutschmarks in soft used notes which she wrapped in tissue.

The bath water was lukewarm and brown, and whatever was suspended in it making it brown clung to the soap, producing a frothy scum on top of the water like effluent. She dressed, putting the money in the small of her back just below the elastic of the waistband, always in the bathroom. She lay on the bed and read a book, turning the pages without taking in a word. Reception called at 7.30 p.m. to tell her the driver was waiting for her downstairs. He took her on a short drive to a modern development called Ernst-Thälmann Park.

Günther Spiegel's apartment was on the eighth floor of a high-rise block overlooking the statue of Ernst Thälmann himself, all thirteen metres of black Ukrainian marble. Spiegel stood with her at the window, shaking his head, drinking wine as they looked out over the flat expanse of the city, still covered with a crust of ice-hardened snow.

'We moved here from a beautiful nineteenth-century tenement in Belforterstrasse because the old place was falling to pieces, the plumbing didn't work and the electrics were life-threatening, all of which the State refused to repair. They insisted we move here. It was brand new. And now it's as bad as the hundred-year-old places. You have been fortunate to find the lift working, although the eight-floor climb means that for the first hour you are warm when the central heating breaks down and, of course, State plumbers hibernate in winter . . . it's well known.'

The meal was marginally better than the one in the hotel and both Herr and Frau Spiegel apologized separately for the poor quality of the meat.

'The State moved into pig production in a big way recently,' said Spiegel, 'so now we get no vegetables and all our terrible meat is sold to the West for pet food.'

'Your poor dogs,' said Frau Spiegel.

After the meal Spiegel beckoned her into the bathroom and

asked her if she had any spare hard currency. He must have done this before, and with visitors more important than she, because he showed no signs of embarrassment or humiliation.

He told her they would have to find a taxi near the S-bahn station because the usual driver was off for the night. They went down together and found one cruising the estate. Spiegel spoke to the driver while Andrea got into the back.

The cab driver didn't go back the way she had come, but headed off down Greifswalderstrasse and kept going until a park appeared on the left.

'Volkspark Friedrichshain,' he said.

They headed along the south side of the park and passed a statue.

'Statue of Lenin,' said the driver, in bad English. 'New. Nikolai Tomski.'

'I'd prefer to go straight back to my hotel,' she said.

'No problem.'

He turned back into the centre and headed into the Prenzlauer Berg district.

'Volksbühne . . . theatre,' he said, their eyes meeting in the rear-view mirror.

'Hotel Neuwa, Invalidenstrasse,' she replied. 'Please.'

'Patien',' he said.

At the Senefelderplatz U-bahn he bore right up Kollwitzstrasse, past the Jewish cemetery and right on to Belforterstrasse, where Spiegel had said he used to live. The driver turned left again, checking his mirrors all the time.

'Water tower,' he said. 'Nazis use to murder people in cellar.'

Andrea didn't say anything this time.

'Good. You relax now,' said the driver.

He crossed the Kollwitzplatz, keeping on the Knaackestrasse, and swung hard left into a *Mietskasern*, driving swiftly under the entrance arch, through a courtyard and another arch, until he parked up in the total darkness of the second courtyard. He opened her door, took her by the arm and led her to the staircase.

'Top floor. Right side,' he said. 'Hand on the wall. Very dark. I wait for you.'

She shivered, not cold, involuntary, as if fingertips had brushed her ribs.

* * *

405

The Snow Leopard saw the car arrive and put on the ski hat. He had arranged two piles of cement blocks on either side of the table as stools to sit on. He had a torch in his pocket. He heard the uncertain steps coming closer, feet searching across each landing to the next flight. He yawned until tears came into his eyes. He was surprised to find so much adrenalin in his system. He pulled the mask down over his face.

The feet reached the top floor and moved down the corridor. He turned on the torch, pointed it at her feet, stroked the stockinged ankles with the light. She stopped, he asked her where the three white leopards sit and she replied. He led the feet into the room and laid the torch on the table. The fog from their breath met at the edge of the low light. He took out a packet of Marlboros and a lighter. She slid one out. He lit her face with the yellow oily flame from his petrol lighter. His hand shook. She steadied it. He lit his own cigarette and there followed a long silence of the sort that rarely happens at the beginning of a meeting.

'They said you would wear a mask,' she said, to break the deadlock.

'Do you mind if I look at your face? Shine the torch in your face?' he asked.

'If that would help . . . we'll have to know each other properly eventually . . . I expect.'

He shone the torch at her from several angles. She looked straight ahead without closing or screwing up her eyes. The defined circle of light in his hand trembled.

'Do you mind if I turn it off for a moment?' he asked. 'I need to hear your voice without distraction.'

'That's fine.'

He turned off the torch. They sat in darkness, only the two coals of their cigarettes provided any light. His heart was like thunder, no distinct beats, just a tremendous roll of noise in his chest.

'Do you know me?' he asked.

'How could I?' she said. 'I don't know what you look like.'

'What does anyone know from just looking?'

Silence.

'You're the expert,' she said. 'You're the spy.'

'Everybody's a spy,' he said. 'We all have our secrets.'

'But . . . but you're the professional.'

'Unpaid. Remember. That's why you're here.'

'Ah, yes, the business,' she said, relieved. 'I have your money. Twenty thousand Deutschmarks.'

'You'd know me by my voice now, wouldn't you?' he asked. 'You listen carefully.'

'I don't know how you've arrived at that conclusion.'

'They say a child will always recognize its mother's voice.'

'But I'm not your child,' she said, something shaking inside her or rather outside, as if there was an earth tremor, something completely strange. 'Can we have the light on now, please?'

'Would the same apply to a lover?' he asked, ignoring her. 'Between lovers?'

'It's not the same, is it? It's not a blood tie.'

'Have you ever been in love?'

'I haven't risked coming here to discuss that with a total stranger.'

'Of course. Not to talk about those kind of secrets . . . but other ones . . . duller ones.'

Silence again.

He pulled off his mask, flattened it on the table.

'Would *you* answer the same question from someone you didn't know?' she asked.

'I might.'

'Have you ever been in love?'

'Only once.'

'Who with?' she asked, her heart undecided about its next beat.

'You . . . crazy.'

She coughed against the sudden knot in her throat. Her cigarette wavered in the dark.

'Now do you know me?' he asked.

No answer.

'Do you?'

'Yes,' she said, and after another long silence, 'I'm not sure I know myself.'

'We've changed . . .' he said, almost blasé, distant, 'that's normal. Isn't that completely normal? I'm not as I used to be either.'

He recognized his own coldness and reached over, found her hand.

'Let me see your face,' she said.

'I've only half a face you'll remember.'

'Just show me.'

'The good news or bad news?'

'Where I come from, we always ask for the bad news first.'

He turned his head to the right, switched on the torch and held it at table height so that he looked ghostly, ghastly, horrific.

'That's the worst news,' he said.

He turned his head to show the other profile, and there was Karl Voss, almost as she'd first known him. She put her fingertips to his face, touched the bones which were still prominent, still vulnerable under the tight skin.

'That's the slightly better news,' he said. 'A Russian flame-thrower grilled the other side.'

'They told me you'd been shot in the Plötzensee Prison.'

'A lot of us were,' he said. 'I was in a line up but they were firing blanks that day. Scaring us to death.'

'Rose said you were involved in the July Plot.'

'I was. I was their man in Lisbon.'

'How did you survive that?'

'I happened to be interrogated by a man called SS Colonel Bruno Weiss who, although he was a very nasty piece of work – I think they hanged him in '46 – was someone I knew from my days in the *Wolfsschanze*. I had a particular connection with him there.'

He stopped, because she was looking at him, transfixed, tears rolling silently down her face.

'It *is* me,' he said. 'I *am* here.'

'Can *you* believe it?'

'No. I'm trying not to think about it.'

'I'd forgotten you.'

'Had you? That wouldn't surprise me. I imagine you were told something, a few lines, I don't know, maybe only several words. Voss has been shot. They were wrong, that's all.'

'This is what Rose told me, he said: "We've had news of Voss, by the way. Not good. Our sources tell us that he was shot at dawn in Plötzensee Prison last Friday with seven others." That's what he said. Those were his words.'

'I never liked Rose but he did happen to tell you the truth. Perfect intelligence. It was a Friday. Yes. And there were eight of us. We were shot too . . . but only shot at.'

'That lie has . . .'

'It wasn't a lie . . . only an untruth. I doubt he knew and if he did, he probably thought it would make life easier for you. You were young. You could recover.'

'No,' she said, quickly. 'It made it hard, incredibly hard. If I'd known you were somewhere, even if I couldn't see you, there would still be possibilities. That word "never" would not have got stuck in my vocabulary.'

'You're angry.'

'Because I thought this could never happen, I've never considered it. If I had, anger is not what I would have expected. I'd have thought that we'd flood back into each other's arms, like they do in films, but it's twenty-seven years, isn't it, Karl? It's the nature of frost that after time it becomes permafrost. It doesn't thaw out in ten minutes, and definitely not in this climate.'

'It *is* cold,' he said. 'And you're right. I never had to live with the loss. That would have been hard.'

Silence again.

'It's warmer when it snows,' he said, and she knew he was thinking.

'Then let's talk,' she said. 'Tell me about that particular connection to Bruno Weiss.'

Silence while he finished the cigarette, rubbed his thighs up and down, went back to that black trunk with the white stencilled address in the furthest recess of his memory.

'I planted a bomb for him, which killed a great man,' he said. 'Fritz Todt. A *great* man and *I* killed him. I didn't know that I was killing him, but I did and afterwards I entered the world of SS Colonel Bruno Weiss and, what's more, I accepted it. I didn't just keep my mouth shut. I went a step further and planted a lie for him. He sort of returned the favour some time later by trying to help me get Julius out of the *Kessel* at Stalingrad but . . . it was too late.'

'But he got you off the hook after the July Plot.'

'Off the hook, yes,' he said, thinking about the irony of that. 'He chose to believe me, that was all. There were others, who I knew were innocent, whom he chose not to believe and he tortured them and executed them. But me . . . he didn't exactly let me go. I ended up reduced to the ranks on the East Front. But even there, you know, this appalling luck pursued me and within a few months the shortage of officers was such that I was back in a captain's uniform. Some of my men said I was "blessed", as if that could possibly be the right word for being allowed to continue in that hell.'

'That depends on what you believe.'

'Yes,' he said, almost aggressive. 'What do I believe in?'

'Perhaps, like me, you'd begun to think there's nothing beyond the door into the dark.'

'That's true. I certainly didn't want to see behind that door. Not then. I can't think why. There was every reason. Being embraced by the dark should have been a relief.'

'And the Russian flame-thrower?'

'I'd like to tell you that was purification by fire, but I think it was just simple luck again. We were retreating, every day we were retreating in front of that Russian onslaught. We were on the outskirts of Berlin. I was pushing a car out of a mudhole so that my men could get a piece of artillery through and, as I grunted against the back window, I came face to face with General Weidling, who was an old friend of my father's. He recognized me but couldn't place me. We had one of those absurd chats, where a world war seems to stop for a few minutes, and he tried to think where he'd seen me before but I'd already changed my name by then. It had been easy enough in the confusion, amongst all that death and destruction, to pick up some ID tags. My men knew my history, they even came to me with Captain Kurt Schneider's documents one day, found them on a body in a shell crater. They knew it would be hard for me if later the Russians traced me back to the Abwehr. Military intelligence. Spying. It never looks good. So I told Weidling I was Kurt Schneider but, as with Bruno Weiss, Weidling and I had made some strange connection and he asked me how well I knew Berlin. I'd lived there all my life before going to Heidelberg so I knew it very well. He ordered me to take him to the Führer's bunker, which I did, and when I got him back in one piece he made me a member of his staff. My men couldn't believe it.

'It helped being on Weidling's staff but I wasn't out of the war. Occasionally the fighting caught up with our constantly mobile HQ – it was all street to street, house to house with the Russians.

410

Terrible fighting. Terrible loss of life. And one day some of the original Kurt Schneider's luck caught up with me and I got my leg stuck under some rubble after a tank blasted a hole in a house wall. A Russian cleaned out the room with a flame-thrower. I was left for dead and picked up only after the fighting had more or less stopped.

'When the Russians found out I'd been on Weidling's staff I was given some medical treatment and eventually flown to Moscow on a planeload of loot. They did some rough repair work on my face and I was taken to a prison camp north of the city called Krasnogorsk 24/III. Weidling was being interrogated in Moscow and one day the NKVD came to see me when they heard that I'd been in the Führer's bunker with him near the end. I told them everything I'd seen, which wasn't much, waiting at the bottom of the stairs while Weidling delivered the latest atrocious news . . . but I embellished. Then I mentioned I'd studied physics at Heidelberg University and I slipped in Otto Hahn's name, and that was it – anything to get out of that camp.

'They interviewed me, sent me to some technical centre in Moscow and then out to Tomsk, where I was a lab assistant in a research laboratory for twelve years, until 1960. I married and, maybe because of my father-in-law's contacts, I was offered a place at the M-P school, which was the Soviet Intelligence Academy in Moscow. I leapt at it, because they said it would get me back to Germany. They gave me a Berlin posting in '64, so here I am – Major Kurt Schneider, Ministry for State Security, Arbeitsgruppe Ausländer – I monitor foreign visitors to East Berlin. *Wilkommen nach Ost Berlin.*'

'You're married.'

'With two daughters. And you?'

'I was married. I got married straight after I was told that you'd been shot. I had to. I thought I had to at the time.'

'Yes, of course. Any children?'

She stared into the table. The wood was stained with rings from mugs and glasses, creating a series of Venn diagrams. Connections. Overlaps. Differences. She opened her bag and took out a photograph of Julião. She slid it across the rough surface. He tilted it towards himself. Frowned.

'My God,' he said.

'I called him Julião.'

'But that's extraordinary,' he said, flicking the corner of the photograph, until finally he took the torch to it and inspected the face minutely.

She fought it back down several times – the instinct to lie, to dissemble, still strong, even in front of the one person who she could and should tell.

'The Portuguese and their *fado*,' she said. 'Do you remember that?'

'We heard some that night we went walking in the Bairro Alto.'

'It seems we're destined to live our lives in minutes and hours, instead of years and decades. My life's been two weeks long, where everything that has happened to me is as a result of that short fortnight and its endless repercussions.'

He flicked the torch up at her, to see if her face said more than her words.

'Why do you think he looks like Julius?' she said.

He stood up, paced the room, snatched at the cigarettes and lit two up, gave one to her in passing.

'I can't think,' he said. 'I can't think. Don't talk. I can't hear. I can't speak.'

Her hands trembled the cigarette to her lips. Her lips trembled the cigarette back into her fingers. She laid it on the edge of the table, interrupted his pacing, grabbed the lapels of his coat.

'Where is he?' he asked. 'Just tell me where he is, so that I can imagine him there.'

She was suddenly aware of how cold it was in the room. Standing close to, they were immersed in each other's breath. The air was freezing in her mouth and nostrils, chill in her lungs, ice around her temples.

'He's dead, Karl. He was shot and killed out on patrol in Guiné in Africa in 1968. He was a soldier . . . like Julius.'

For a moment he looked as if he'd breathed in pure frost, it stiffened him, froze his guts and weighed him down. He slumped on to the cement blocks, his head hanging from his shoulders, as if suddenly broken. He took her limp hand and put it to his good cheek, shook his head against it, not so cold now.

'No wonder you don't know yourself,' he said.

'And you?'

'Living my son's life in fifteen seconds . . . it's not the same. Losing a child after a lifetime, that's an unbearable thing.'

'Like your parents did,' she said, automatically because she'd thought that years ago, too.

'Yes,' he said, and stared into the concrete floor.

His head came up slowly. His eyes fixed on a thick crack in the plaster of the wall. He followed it up to the ceiling, where it parted into two thinner cracks, which eventually merged into nothingness.

'Tell me,' she said.

'I'm thinking.'

'You haven't stopped thinking since you shone that torch in my face.'

'Now I'm thinking what I was trying not to think earlier.'

'And failed.'

'Yes, I failed . . . I've been wondering why Jim Wallis would send *you* to contact me.'

'Did Jim recruit you?' she asked, a feint, a diversion.

'*I* recruited *him*,' said Schneider. 'He came over to East Berlin on a trade delegation, soon after I got here. He was fat and bald, but I could still see that schoolboy's face of his staring out. He was travelling under some name or other, but I knew it was him. I had him picked up, grilled him, had him with his claws stuck in the ceiling. Then I personally drove him back to the delegation and told him who I was. I proved it to him as well . . . using your names. Anne Ashworth, Andrea Aspinall. I'd already decided that the only way I could make myself feel better about what I'd become – this Stasi officer who spies on foreigners – was to work against the system from the inside, use my position to get defectors out and point the finger at East German undercovers in the West. I said I'd work for him on condition that he was the only person to know about me and that there would never be any link between me and British Intelligence. Complete anonymity. No money to be allocated to me so that I could never be traced. But he's clever, Jim, because he remembered that there *was* a link. The original link. You.

'And our arrangement was all working perfectly . . . until I came under investigation after the KGB shot General Stiller, which I can only think was a political assassination with top-level authority from Moscow, because since then I've been under some very heavy

413

internal pressure. I needed help, Russian help but, as you can imagine, my KGB friends deserted me so . . . Jim comes up with a plan to give me support without compromising my conditions of service. Or to use the words of the contact agent, in a way that would leave me "cast iron with Lord Leonid Brezhnev". And what does Jim do? He sends *you* to contact me. Which means . . .' he said, looking not at her but into her, organ-deep.

'What?' she said, shuddering under that look.

'You're working for them, aren't you? The Russians. And Jim knows it, too. You're a double,' he said. 'It's clever, isn't it? And very sick, too. This *is* a cold war, they're right on that. The level of absurdity is such that nothing can be believed, or is believed any more, except the old reliables. Wallis would never let me fall through the net because I am one of the few agents he's got on this side of the Wall who delivers consistently good intelligence. He will do anything to protect me. He will use my only love, because he knows that she is the one person in this world who would never give me up.'

Silence.

'Or is he wrong?' he asked, raising a corner of his forehead where there should have been an eyebrow. 'Did they scrub your brain, Andrea?'

'He's right,' she said quietly.

'My luck holds,' he said. 'But yours doesn't.'

'Why not?'

'Jim's decided to sacrifice *you* for me.'

'How?'

'You've been sent by the Russians to find me. The Snow Leopard. And now?' he asked. 'Now you're *not* going to find the Snow Leopard because you won't give me up to the Russians. So, as a double agent, what the hell are you going to do?'

'I'll say I never saw you.'

'They won't believe you. What have you been doing this last hour? They'll check with the hotel. Everybody's watching everybody else. This is wartime Lisbon cubed.'

'I didn't see your face.'

'But what can you say you were actually doing for an hour?'

'We were planning the Varlamov defection together.'

'And that's it? You never see me again? The Russians won't

accept that. There will have to be another meeting and they'll want to know about it. If you don't find the Snow Leopard . . . you might not be going back to London.'

'Do your thinking, Karl.'

'That's all I can do.'

'I'll do anything, you know that.'

'Anything?

'Except give you up.'

'Maybe you won't have to give up *the* Snow Leopard, just *a* Snow Leopard,' he said, and then to himself, 'Whatever . . . Jim's going to have to do without Varlamov.'

Chapter 37

17th January 1971, East Berlin.

She lay on the bed, not sleeping, always uncomfortable, always some part of her uncovered and cold because the cover was too small and she got cramped with her knees up to her chest. She writhed and rucked up the bottom sheet, which was too short as well. What's the matter with this country, that they torture their guests with linen?

They had kissed, and she still felt the halfness of that kiss on her lips. The one half as she remembered it, the other smooth and hard like a beak, but not of a bird, more like a squid. Strange that it hadn't repelled her when the idea of it was so unpleasant. His new imprint.

He'd asked her why she was working for the Russians and the lies queued up with amazing alacrity, ready to file out: In Portugal I grew to hate fascism. I became a communist out of resistance to fascism. I loathed the authoritarian imperialism of the *Estado Novo*. I lost a son and a husband in the maintenance of empire. It was all very impressive, but she used none of it. It was all unacceptable, more than a disgrace, to attempt to speak those words to his lashless, browless eye. Even the loyalty to João Ribeiro, which she'd used to beat Gromov, looked tarnished in the glow of that torch between their half-dark faces, their visible breath joining in the cold air. She'd started on that new line of thinking, her need for control, everyone's need for control, but even without being able to see him clearly, she knew he wasn't having any of it.

'When I was in Lisbon, Richard Rose was always throwing lines of literature at me,' he said. 'He gave me a line once from a poet, who he told me afterwards was called Coleridge. I'd never heard of him. The line was "the secret ministry of frost". How silently and stealthily frost transforms the world. We don't know it's hap-

416

pening until we wake up on a white, still morning with everything frozen in its moment. Perhaps this was supposed to be a vision of beauty, I don't know. But one morning, before I'd made contact with Jim, when I was sitting in a car, out on surveillance, I saw the secret ministry of frost. It had been raining and then the temperature started to drop. It happened in front of me, no secrecy. The water hardened on the windows around me into clear slivers of ice at first, and then, as it grew colder, they crystallized, blurred and whitened until I couldn't see out and nobody could see in. And it hit me, threw me into a blind panic, that this was what had become of me. I had disappeared under the secret ministry of frost, I was impenetrable, I was blank ... except that it wasn't frost. It was hate. I hated myself, what I'd become.'

She lay now, cold in her bed, thinking about her mother, because it was easier to think about her than to get personal. She remembered her mother's remoteness, her white moon face, peering up the stairwell out of the dark hall, that hardness of her cheek, the coldness of her hands, the unreachable mother trapped behind her frosted windows. She'd come to see her hate of Longmartin clear enough, but had she ever taken it that one step further, as Voss had done? Father Harpur might know. She might have confessed to him that she was betraying her country and found salvation that way.

Andrea propped her head up, lit a cigarette, placed an ashtray on her chest. She already felt different, still too trussed up by fear, perhaps, to see it clearly but she was beginning to understand the simple beauty of the 'whitewashed walls' in her father's last letter to her mother. The cleanliness. She'd been lucky, or was it a different destiny for her, to find the one person to whom she could possibly admit her appalling weakness? In the drear light behind the curtain she saw how she'd been formed by that weakness. How she'd used her strengths to hide it. How that weakness had become her secret. That was an equation. Secrets equal weaknesses. She sucked on the cigarette and savoured the irony that it was her secrets, those weaknesses, that had made her unknowable. They gave her mystery and they made her attractive, too. Some men, like Louis Greig, knew it and used it to satisfy their own depraved needs. The others were hopelessly misinformed.

There was a knock on the door. She stubbed out the cigarette.

Another knock, more urgent. He'd told her the Russians would come for her and that it would be in the night. She opened the door. A man stepped past her, another stayed in the corridor. The man stood at the window, told her he'd come to take her to General Yakubovsky and that she should get dressed.

The Snow Leopard had watched her leave. She hadn't let him keep the photograph, more cautious this time around, and right, too. He kept his eye to the crack in the boarded window and counted her steps across the courtyard to where the taxi driver was waiting. That kiss. He touched the ruined half of his mouth. Had that kiss disgusted her? Something shuddered in his torso, a wrack of old pain. Seeing her, opening that black trunk, bringing back all those dark memories. His mother's death, perhaps, in the firestorm of Dresden. Was that it? He braced himself against the window, eye still to the crack, as the taxi pulled out of the *Mietskasern*. Another shudder. Pain streaked across his chest. He coughed as if he was hiding and was desperate not to be heard. He dropped to his knees and sobbed into the back of his gloves, over the years of not knowing, over the years that he would never know, and that possibly he might never have known. Julius, his father and mother all staring into the camera, behind his son's unbreakable smile.

He pulled himself together. He collected up the cigarette stubs, stamped the ash into oblivion. He took a different route out of the *Mietskasern* and crossed Wörtherstrasse into another. He went to the *hinterhof* and up to the third floor, trying to remember his Brecht, pulling the mask over his face and knocking on the door.

'*Und der Haifisch, der hat Zähne,*' said the voice.

'*Und die trägt er im Gesicht,*' he replied.

This time the man offered him a drink, which meant that this was not going to be a smooth operation. *Molle mit korn.* Beer with schnapps. Not the time of day for it, but it seemed right. They knocked back the schnapps and sipped the beer.

'Is it ready?' asked the Snow Leopard.

'Except for the entry date.'

'I don't need an entry date any more.'

'It's not going to make it any cheaper, Herr Kappa.'

'It should.'

'I know who this is,' said the man. 'I've been reading the newspapers.'

'I'm amazed someone like you bothers with those rags.'

'He's Grigory Varlamov. The physicist. He's going to give a couple of lectures. They're going to present him with a medal at some dinner and then what? Hup, hup over the Wall. You've got to be crazy, Herr Kappa.'

'I'm not asking you to go with him. Just to do your job.'

'This is very, very cluttered, Herr Kappa.'

'Did I ask you to sign your work? Nobody's going to look at this and come knocking.'

'If you take Varlamov over the Wall the heat's going to come down hard on all of us. Nobody will move a muscle for months.'

'Just tell me.'

'I'm doing myself out of a job.'

'You're nearly there.'

'I've got people I have to run. People who've collected their wolf's ticket years ago . . . they rely on me.'

'Keep going.'

'Five thousand.'

'And finally we have it. The price of freedom.'

'Five thousand.'

'I heard you the first time,' he said, steeling up. 'Let's see the work.'

The man left the room and returned to find the Snow Leopard counting out the money. The man was relieved.

'It's the best bit of work I've done for a long time,' he said.

Schneider looked at the passport, held it up to the light, sipped his beer, suddenly weighed down by sadness. He put the beer down, handed over the money, slipped the passport into his pocket.

'Who've you spoken to about this?' he asked.

'I never speak to anyone.'

'You'd better count that money.'

The man thumbed through the notes. Schneider hit him hard in the throat. The man went down and Schneider knelt on his chest and jammed his gloved fingers into the man's windpipe and held him, looking up at the door so that he didn't have to see the man's face. The fist in the throat had taken everything out of the man. He died with barely a struggle. Schneider picked up the money, cleaned out his two glasses and stood over the body. He was angry at what the man had forced him into but he felt ruthless, too. He wasn't going to leave a man like that out there, with Andrea taking her risks.

'Stupid,' he said, and left.

Andrea sat in the back of the car, the two men in front speaking in Russian, animated, talking about football, she gathered from the head movements. She smoked her duty-free cigarettes and thought about his body. The body she had just held, had put her hands into his coat and grasped, was thin and hard as a rail. She knew from looking at his throat, the veins standing out of his neck, that he had not put on any weight and when she put her hands on him he seemed even thinner than she remembered. His big bones protruded, large hard knuckles around his shoulders, elbows, wrists. He'd told her that his two years in Krasnogorsk on bread and vegetable soup, with the odd piece of fish, had left him like this. He couldn't flesh out however much he ate. It was as if there was something else inside him eating the food, a worm, or something bigger, a snake. Thin or not, she still wanted him. She still had the taste of his salt in her mouth, even after all these years.

The car turned off the main street and into another. A white expanse, which disappeared into greyer lines to black, flashed past in frames. The word 'gulag' formed in her brain, stuck in her throat, which was not a good sign.

She'd asked him about his wife. Elena. A Russian. He'd said he'd married her out of loneliness. He didn't know her, but he thought that was because there was little to know. His girls. He loved his girls. His wife made him feel lonely still, but his girls filled him up.

This was how they'd been together a quarter of a century on. A generation between meetings, and yet no time at all.

They pulled up at the barrier to the St Antonius Hospital, the car's exhaust crowding the foot of the guardhouse. Minutes later they were stomping up stairs and down corridors, through an office, into a living room where General Oleg Yakubovsky, the fat man with the eyebrows Schneider had told her about, was standing in front of the fire, warming his buttocks. She introduced herself. He offered coffee, or something stronger. She took both. He seemed pleased.

'You have made contact with the Snow Leopard,' said Yakubovsky. 'We watched you get into the taxi in Ernst Thälmann Park but decided to let you have your first meeting alone.'

'I'm not sure where we went. The driver took me on a tour. A park, a statue of Lenin.'

He asked her to describe where they'd met and what the Snow Leopard looked like.

'I didn't see his face because he was wearing a ski mask. He was taller than me by some inches. He wore gloves and a grey coat. He was broad, thickset but not fat. The only skin I saw was at his neck between the mask and the collar of his shirt. There was some dark hair and his skin colour was dark, too. The shape of his head was wide, square. It looked like a heavy head.'

'What did you discuss?'

'I gave him twenty thousand marks and an American passport in the name of Colonel Peter Taylor. He spent some time inspecting the passport, but he never removed his gloves.'

'What colour were the gloves?'

'Brown.'

'What does he intend to use this passport for?'

'To get Grigory Varlamov into the West.'

Yakubovsky didn't react.

'You were with him a long time,' he said.

'I wouldn't know.'

'Your taxi didn't come back to the hotel for over an hour.'

'I was building his trust. He was very nervous. I told him about myself. I wanted him to talk about himself, but he was cautious. I told him I was attending lectures at Humboldt University where Varlamov is due to perform. I wanted him to make use of me, but he was a very difficult man, General. He said he needed twenty-four hours to change the passport photo and then he would need to get the passport to Varlamov. I offered again and this time he accepted. We've agreed to meet again and finalize how I should approach Varlamov.'

Yakubovsky wrote out two numbers on a card, which she should ring when the Snow Leopard made contact again. He told her she would be followed from now on and she protested, saying that it was too dangerous, that she didn't want to lose him when they were so close. Yakubovsky agreed, reluctantly. She finished her brandy. He held her coat.

421

'The Snow Leopard also said that this would be his last job for some time. That his position was changing in line with some unspecified political shift here in the DDR. He said he would be going back into cover.'

Yakubovsky walked her to the door.

'This place where we met,' she said. 'It was massive. Hundreds and hundreds of rooms, on four floors, building after building.'

'Yes. The *Mietskasernen* were built as accommodation for working men and their families in the time of Frederick the Great. They're no better than slums.'

'If the Snow Leopard had any chance to run I doubt you'd find him in that place, even with a whole battalion of men. There must be lots of ways in and out. There's probably access to the sewers. It's his place of choice.'

'What is your point?'

'Mr Gromov, back in London, told me that the only Snow Leopard he ever saw was back in 1929 in the Sayan Mountains. He shot it and his wife wears the pelt as a jacket. I think we should be applying the same ruthlessness to *this* Snow Leopard.'

'We will have KGB marksmen at hand.'

'I've told you that he is very cautious. He's a professional, a nervous professional. To cover a building like that you would need ten or fifteen marksmen. They would create a presence which the Snow Leopard would pick up. It's possible, too, that he will give me very little notice. How are you going to position your men in an unknown building in, say, half an hour? No, General, no marksmen. There is only one way to be certain of catching this Snow Leopard. The person closest to him will have to shoot him. It's not something I want to do, or ever thought I would have to do, but I think it's the only way. I want you to supply me with a gun.'

Yakubovsky, the soldier now, looked into her to see if she had the mettle for this. He went back to his desk and took out a handgun from the top drawer. He checked that it was fully loaded, showed her how to operate it. He asked her if she'd ever fired a gun before.

'I was given small arms training during the war, General. Mr Gromov must have told you that I haven't always been a mathematician.'

She was taken back down to the car, her legs were weak, her stomach sick, the alcohol and coffee toxic in her blood. On the trip back to Invalidenstrasse she sat in the middle of the back seat, supporting herself with her hands on either side, exhausted by the performance.

The Snow Leopard stood over his sleeping wife at the end of the bed. She was lying on her back, her mouth slightly open, the air rushing in and out with her every breath. He tried to think of any memorable sexual moment they'd had together. He couldn't. A colleague had told him once that he'd known when he and his wife had conceived their first child. It had been special in some way. There'd been some extra surge that night. Schneider had been sceptical, had tried not to allow his imagination to tangle with the biology. Both his own conceptions had passed without any noticeable change in the electric current. And yet all he had to do was think of that room in Estrela, that bed, the sofa, the thick lash of her black hair, her brown coin-sized nipples, and he'd feel the blood uncoiling him. Yes, that had been memorable and they'd conceived too, although he still hadn't had any sense of that. Such is the persuasive power of self, he thought. We'll believe anything we want to.

He got into bed next to Elena. It was like an act of infidelity. He turned his back on her. She rolled and her hand rested on the fan of muscle below his shoulder and he found himself thinking of the job he had to do later that week, driving the two dissidents across the Gleinicke Bridge, and he thought about keeping on driving, and driving, and driving.

Chapter 38

Schneider arrived in the office early. He hadn't wanted to be around family that morning. He put a call through to an old friend in HVA Dept X and asked him where Rieff had gone to after he'd left Disinformation and Active Measures. He told him that he'd done three years on National Security running the Wall and the Curtain under the direct orders of Secretary Erich Honecker.

He went through his in-tray until he came to the report he'd been looking for. Her face looked up at him. A bad photograph but it still quickened his blood. He leafed through the surveillance report. Everything normal. They'd even lied about her taxi ride from Ernst Thälmann Park back to the hotel, saying she'd gone back directly.

At 9.00 a.m. he put a call through to Yakubovsky, who growled, but agreed to a corridor meeting outside HVA Dept XX. Schneider prepared himself for the meeting by running up the stairs so that he would arrive out of breath, panicked. He overdid it. Yakubovsky took one look at him from the end of the corridor and nearly bolted back into his office. Schneider calmed, drew alongside.

'I told you I couldn't help you,' said the Russian, annoyed.

'It's Rieff.'

'I also told you that Rieff was not our friend. It is up to you to deal with him in your own way.'

'But he's like a wild dog after me. He knows everything about Stiller, what he was doing in the West . . . he's even mentioned your name.'

'And what did you say?'

'I denied your involvement,' said Schneider. 'But that's not the problem. If it was just that sort of thing I could handle it . . . we could come to an arrangement. But this is not enough for him. He

424

wants my blood. He's accused me of being a double agent called the Snow Leopard. I've been through all the files at the AGA and I can't find any reference to a Snow Leopard. You have to help me on this. Corruption is one thing. Prison, or maybe a labour camp . . . But treason . . . treason's the guillotine.'

Yakubovsky stopped at the first mention of the Snow Leopard and let his eyebrows give Schneider their full attention.

'What did Rieff say about the Snow Leopard?'

'He's furious with the KGB, too.'

'But what did he say, Major?'

'He says the KGB never share their information. They conduct their operations without . . .'

'Major Schneider,' said Yakubovsky, gripping his shoulder, 'just tell me what Rieff said about the Snow Leopard.'

'He said . . . he asked me about the Snow Leopard and, when I said I'd never heard of him, he replied that he didn't think I would have, because . . . and these were his words: "I think *you* are the Snow Leopard."'

'Calm down, Major,' said Yakubovsky. 'You have nothing to be afraid of. You are not the Snow Leopard. The Snow Leopard is a KGB operation which will culminate in the next twenty-four hours. You are not to speak to anyone about this and especially not to Rieff. Afterwards, I will personally speak to Rieff.'

They parted, the Russian hitting him on the shoulder with his padded palm. Schneider went straight down to the toilets on the AGA floor, leaned his hot face against the cool cubicle wall and lit a cigarette, which did not calm him down.

Back in his office he put a call through to one of his patrol cars and ordered them to bring in a British national called Andrea Aspinall, a visiting maths postgraduate staying at the Hotel Neuwa and attending lectures with Günther Spiegel at Humboldt University. At lunchtime he was informed that the woman had been picked up and was waiting in Interrogation Room 4.

He shook himself down and felt for the passport and money in his pocket. He checked there was a full tape running for Interrogation Room 4 and went in. Andrea was sitting with her back to him, smoking.

'I am Major Schneider,' he said. 'Have you been offered coffee?'

'No,' she said, annoyed.

'I'm sorry. This isn't supposed to be anything threatening. It's just a routine matter, you understand. Our enemies have forced us to erect this anti-fascist protection barrier . . .'

'Is that what you call the Wall?'

'That's what it is, Miss Aspinall.'

'My God . . . when they sent your brain away, Major Schneider, it came back whiter than white.'

'I can, if I wish . . . if you want to be rude to me, make this go very badly for you.'

Silence.

'Sorry . . . you were saying . . . I think you were about to give me a lecture on enemies of state.'

'Yes . . . we have built this wall to protect our citizens, but our enemies continue to make frequent attempts to penetrate it. They send people to spy on us. People such as visiting mathematics postgraduates from Cambridge. It is my job at the Arbeitsgruppe Ausländer to weed out the false and leave the true. I have two conflicting reports here, which is why I've had to bring you here for questioning.'

'I'm not in East Berlin for very long, Major. This interruption cuts into my very short stay. I would be grateful if you could move it along.'

'Of course. You arrived yesterday, took lunch in your hotel, the Neuwa, went to see Dr Spiegel, had a coffee in the canteen, attended a lecture, went back to your hotel and then went out to dinner with Dr Spiegel in his apartment in Ernst Thälmann Park.'

'My God,' she said. 'I'd like to be able to say I find your surveillance comforting, Major, but I don't.'

'This is where we have the conflict. My report says you took a taxi back to the Neuwa Hotel.'

'Which I did.'

'The taxi picked you up at 21.55.'

'Probably.'

'The Neuwa Hotel reception reported that you came in at 23.10. That's an hour and a quarter to go from Ernst Thälmann Park to Invalidenstrasse, which would leave approximately one hour unaccounted for.'

Silence. Over a minute of it.

'I can't believe this country.'

426

'Believe it?'

'Is that all you do all day ... watch each other? Wait for each other to fall over so that you can report it? Ask the taxi driver. He took me on a tour of East Berlin. The Volkspark Friedrichshain, the statue of Lenin, the Volksbühne theatre, the ... the famous water tower where the Nazis murdered communists back in the thirties. It was all very instructive and time-consuming.'

'That still doesn't account for the hour, Miss Aspinall.'

'You said there was a conflict, Major. When did the surveillance people say I got back to the hotel?'

'At 22.15.'

'So who do you believe?'

'On this occasion the Hotel Neuwa reception,' said Schneider. 'And you're not going back to the university until that discrepancy's been explained to my satisfaction.'

'Before I left England they told me that the Stasi was no different to the Gestapo and, you know what ... they were wrong. You're worse.'

'I have all day, Miss Aspinall. The rest of the week. A month. We are blessed with time on this side of the Curtain.'

They sat in silence for ten minutes, smiling, looking at each other.

'This is ridiculous,' she said.

Schneider stood and walked around the room. He came back to her, brought his face down to her level and put the passport and money into her open handbag.

'Just tell me what happened in that hour, and as long as you weren't spying or taking photographs of sensitive buildings, making contact with people without authorization ... then you can go back to your hotel. If you don't, I will have you taken down to a holding cell and ...'

'I want to speak to General Oleg Yakubovsky,' she said, severe now.

Silence while Schneider blinked that information into his brain. Andrea slowly turned her head towards him. Their faces were only inches apart, their lips.

'Did you hear me, Major?'

'I did, yes,' he said. 'I'm just wondering why ... I mean, *how* you know General Yakubovsky.'

427

'I am operating under his authority . . . and that of Mr Gromov in London.'

Schneider stood, went back to his seat, his heart hammering away, even though he knew what was coming.

'What is this operation?'

'It is called Operation Snow Leopard and that is all I am saying, until General Yakubovsky is informed.'

Schneider stood, kicking his chair back as he did so. He offered his hand.

'Please accept my apologies,' he said. 'We were not informed of your presence here. I hope I haven't inconvenienced you unduly.'

'You have, Major,' she said. 'And I'm wondering why you don't call General Yakubovsky.'

'It's not necessary, Miss Aspinall. And . . . I would be very grateful if you could possibly not mention this to the general should you speak to him.'

She stood, picked up her handbag, refused his offered hand.

'I'll think about it.'

'Would you allow me to drive you back to the university or your hotel?'

'You're quite pathetic, Major, aren't you?' she said, and they left the room.

Schneider called up a car and, while they were waiting, retrieved the tape of the conversation. He drove her back to the university and returned to his office. He called General Rieff. The general was out and not due back until four o'clock.

General Rieff's secretary kept him waiting with his tape and file for thirty minutes before she put the call through. Rieff added on another fifteen minutes before asking him to be sent in. Schneider laid Andrea's file on the desk and asked permission to play the tape. He spooled it up and sat back to watch while General Rieff alternately rapped and slapped the arm of his chair, listening to the tape, half bored by what appeared to be the usual grind, until he heard her mention General Yakubovsky. Then he was still and listened intently through to the end.

'Why didn't you call General Yakubovsky?'

'I'd already spoken to him.'

'Why?'

'I'd asked him to help me. I told him that you'd accused me of being the Snow Leopard. I was desperate for him to intercede on my behalf. All he did was ask me how you knew about the Snow Leopard. And, of course, I didn't know. Then he put his hand on my shoulder and told me not to worry, that I wasn't the Snow Leopard, that the Snow Leopard was a KGB operation which would be concluded within the next twenty-four hours. He told me not to speak to anyone, and especially not to you.'

'Did he?'

'I've checked on Miss Aspinall and she's flying back to London tomorrow at 11.00 a.m.,' said Schneider. 'I also personally drove her back to the university in order to ingratiate myself, so that she would not report the incident to General Yakubovsky. She has agreed that it would be between us.'

'The Snow Leopard is *not* a KGB operation,' said Rieff. 'It is the codename of a double agent and we have as much right to him as the KGB. *More* right to him, because he is here, now, in this building giving away the names of our agents in the West, helping defectors . . .'

'I'll tap her phone and maintain surveillance on the Hotel Neuwa.'

'*You* and only you, Major, will listen to the phone tap, and all surveillance will report back to you if she moves. Nobody else in this building is to know about it,' he said, picking up the file. 'Is this hers? Have you done a background check on her?'

'I have, sir. There's nothing out of the ordinary. She has spent the last two years doing pure maths research in Cambridge and before that she was a maths postgraduate at Lisbon University. I also checked on Mr Gromov, who she mentions on the tape. He has diplomatic status in the Soviet embassy in London, but he also holds the rank of colonel in the KGB.'

At 7.30 p.m. Andrea got back to the Hotel Neuwa from Humboldt University. She sat on the bed with her head in her hands and looked at the telephone. Her gums itched and she had a fit of gaping yawns. She picked up the phone and dialled Yakubovsky's number.

'The Snow Leopard's made contact again,' she said.

'Where?'

429

'A note was given to me in the university canteen.'

'Has he asked for a meeting?'

'Of course, he has to, he needs my help.'

'Where is the meeting?'

'You remember what I said to you ... I don't want anybody there. We have to think of him as the kind of animal that he is.'

'Of course, but I will have to make my report.'

'The meeting will be above the arch on the third floor of the *dreiterhof* in the *Mietskasern* at number 11 Knaackestrasse in Prenzlauer Berg, at 22.00.'

At 7.38 p.m. Schneider relayed the phone tap to General Rieff.

'What do you think this means?' asked the general. 'When she says, "I don't want anybody there."'

'My understanding of that, sir, is that she is going to deal with the Snow Leopard herself.'

'No.'

'No?'

'I will not permit this to happen. The Snow Leopard must be interrogated. We have to find out the extent to which he has compromised our agents and who he is planning to help defect. If she kills him we will lose all this valuable information. We will lose the opportunity to become the Snow Leopard ourselves ... the possibilities for disinformation are enormous. I will not allow it.'

'Do you know this place where she's going to meet him?'

'Vaguely.'

'So you know why she's proposing to deal with the Snow Leopard herself?' said Schneider. 'It's the only way she can be certain.'

'You will leave me now and I shall think about this and decide on a course of action.'

'To control one of those *Mietskasernen* I would suggest you need a hundred men, and if you turn up with a hundred men I am sure you will not see the Snow Leopard.'

'Thank you for your advice, Major ... you have been indispensable.'

'May I add one other thing, General Rieff? That if you interfere I would suggest that it could lead to a lot of bad feeling between ourselves and the KGB.'

'Herr Major?'

'Yes, sir.'

'I shit on the KGB.'

At 9.00 p.m. Andrea checked the gun. It was still fully loaded, as it had been the last fifty times she'd looked at it. She left the hotel and walked straight into a waiting taxi and asked him to go to the Jewish cemetery near Kollwitzplatz. She stood in a dark corner and watched. Nobody was following. Yakubovsky appeared to have kept his word and Schneider had made sure that nobody was tailing her from the hotel. She went back up Husemannstrasse, turned left into Sredzkistrasse.

Her breath clouded the air and dispersed into the still, freezing night. Her heels on the silver cobbles were the only sound in the street. As she hit Knaackestrasse she bore left and walked straight into the entrance of the *Mietskasern*. She leaned against the wall and dragged the icy air up her nostrils, tried to clear her mind, prayed for it to be twenty-four hours later and everything done.

He'd told her not to think about it. He'd told her to keep acting, never stop, never pause for a fraction of a moment's thought. When she'd told him that she couldn't, he'd reminded her of the ruthlessness with which everybody else was acting.

'You just have to find your own values,' he'd said, 'the ones you're prepared to protect with the same ruthlessness.'

An image came to her from God knows where in her memory. One she'd never seen. Judy Laverne in the flaming cage of her car crashing down into the ravine. Lazard had been ruthless. Yes. Beecham Lazard. The sight of that bullet tearing out his throat, the crashing noise of the gun, the blood. That was the only time she'd ever seen anyone killed close up, as close as she was going to be to this man. This man, who she didn't know. The one who was going to save them. He'd told her how she would know the man, how she would know that he was there and the right man. He'd also told her the terrible thing she had to do, how to make it certain, how to make it look right. It was going to demand more of her than any other act in her life. Yes. Act, he'd said. Always act. It will not be you, he had said, but it was her.

She set off across the courtyard between the *ersterhof* and the *zweiterhof*, through the arch and into the next courtyard. She angled her walk towards the left-hand corner. She took out a torch she'd bought and walked up the stairs to the third floor, slowed down. She turned off the torch. Waited. She smelt the frozen air cut with the mustiness of degrading plaster, the mould of rotting timber. Her hand closed around the gun in her right-hand pocket. She walked steadily down the corridor until she arrived above the arch. She looked at her watch. A minute past ten. She shone her torch into the room, at the two piles of cement blocks on either side of the table. She sat on one of the piles, put her hand under the table and found the woollen ski mask, tucked it into the same pocket as the passport and money. She waited, desperate for a smoke but wanting to keep the air clear. Six minutes past ten. She turned off the torch and slipped out of her shoes.

She reached for the door, turned left down the corridor, one hand to the wall, the other holding the gun at waist height. She reached the first doorway, put her face into the blackness of the room, breathed in. She moved on to the next doorway. Nothing. Even before she reached the third doorway she could smell the unmistakable perfume of hair tonic. She stood in the doorway and clicked on her torch. Rieff was in the corner, gun hanging from his hand at his side, eyes wide in the torchlight. She fired quickly, three times. Three thuds into the heavy coat. His gun fell to the floor. She rushed at him as he began to fall forward and drove her shoulder into him so his knees buckled and he fell sideways against the wall. She tore the mask out of her pocket and stretched it over his head, not thinking, only acting, and to make it certain, to make it look right, fired a fourth shot through the ski mask into his face. His heavy head cracked back, destabilizing him, and he slid forward off the wall and ended face-down on the floor. She picked up his gun and stuffed it in his pocket. She took the passport and money out and put it into his other pocket. She ran out of the room, back down the corridor and into the room above the arch. She stepped into her shoes, sat on the cement blocks and put her head on the table and vomited between her feet.

Footsteps ran across the courtyard, sprinted up the stairs. Other, slower footsteps followed. Torch beams ricocheted down the corridor. Two armed men in combat gear appeared at the door. One stayed, the other moved on. The slower footsteps took forever to get up the stairs. They lumbered down the corridor. There was an exchange of Russian. Yakubovsky looked in on her and continued to where the other soldier was standing.

An order was given. The soldier reacted. There was a stunned silence. Another order was barked out. Yakubovsky moved back up the corridor, appeared in the doorway, passport in hand. He muttered something else and the soldiers staggered past with the body between them. He unhooked Andrea's fingers from the gun and put it in his pocket with the passport. He picked up the torch, offered Andrea his arm and they left the building.

'It's always distressing,' he said, 'to find that one of one's most valued colleagues is, in fact, a charlatan.'

In the morning, as a measure of respect due to a valued servant of the Soviet Union, General Yakubovsky ordered Major Kurt Schneider of the AGA to take Andrea to the airport. He picked her up at the hotel and they headed south out of the city, not talking for the first few minutes of the journey. Andrea sat in the back staring out at the greyscale of the framed cityscape.

'You're blaming yourself now, aren't you, for what I had to do?' she said to the back of his head.

'I keep thinking that there must have been another way.'

'I'm the strategist, remember, and there was no other way. The only uncertainty was that he would be there at all. When he was, I did as you said. It was ironic, that's all.'

'Ironic?'

'My piano teacher was killed by a direct hit on his house back in the Blitz in 1940. I was sixteen and I said to myself then that I would kill a German. When the time came for me to even the score . . . I couldn't find any of that old hate, only fear and certainty. I did it and there was no satisfaction.'

'Certainty?'

'From that ruthlessness you talked about.'

'You shouldn't have been put in that position in the first place.'

'Now you're going to blame Jim Wallis.'

'I am.'

'The way I see it is that I put myself in that position. I agreed to work for Gromov back in London. I took the step of going back to the Company. Jim Wallis just did his job,' she said. 'It surprised

433

me to find he had that kind of toughness in him. I thought he was soft . . . good-natured.'

He took a buff envelope out of his pocket, handed it to her between the seats.

'Your security,' he said.

'What is it?'

'Don't open it. Don't look at it. Just give it to Jim, and tell him the negative is in safe-keeping in East Berlin.'

'And what is it?'

'It's another one of those sad, seedy sideshows to our great intelligence industry,' said Schneider. 'It's a photograph of Jim Wallis being buggered in a public lavatory in Fulham.'

'Jim?' she said, astonished. 'Jim's on his second marriage.'

'Maybe that's why the first didn't work out,' he said. 'The glue that holds us together is, not infrequently, our shame.'

'Even with this I'm going to get a hard time for sacrificing the Varlamov defection.'

'Varlamov,' said Schneider to himself. 'Varlamov didn't smell right from the beginning.'

'Is this retrospective genius?'

'Probably. When I was told to set the defection up, they were very firm on one point . . . that I should never make contact with the subject until they gave the go-ahead. I'm still waiting. Varlamov was going to be leaving today.'

'Yakubovsky said they're going to take him back to Russia in chains.'

'I don't think Varlamov wanted to defect. Jim Wallis used him to keep the KGB distracted. They thought that he was the goal of the operation whereas . . . well . . . everything's worked. My cover is still intact, as is yours with the Russians, and Varlamov, a great servant of the State, has been discredited.'

They passed under the S-bahn between Schöneweide and Oberspree and the traffic eased up on the Adler-gestell. He put his hand back between the seats and she held it, stroked the knuckles with her thumb.

'Why did you tell me about that dissident exchange you're doing on Sunday night?' she asked.

He threaded his fingers through hers.

'I thought about going with them,' he said, and she squeezed his hand, suddenly anxious. 'I thought about driving them to the middle of the bridge for the exchange and then just keeping on driving. It . . . it would be possible . . . in my head.'

'So you're not going to do it.'

Their eyes connected in the rear view.

'Elena and the girls,' he said. 'They'd let them drop through the floor.'

She turned her head, let her eyes fall on the road markings flashing past the car, the dirty snow, the bare trees.

At Grünau he took his hand back and they peeled off the Adler-gestell, turned back underneath it and headed south-west on the autobahn to Schönefeld. They went through a document check at the police post to leave Greater Berlin and from there it was a few minutes to the airport.

'So this is it, for us?' she said. 'One day we might be on the same side.'

'Our ration for the next quarter of a century,' he said, putting his hand back to her again. 'And we *are* on the same side . . . *our* side . . . where nobody else matters.'

'Twenty-five years. That'll be 1996,' she said. 'I'll be seventy-two. They should have let me out of prison by then.'

'They won't send you to prison, and there's always *détente*,' he said. 'We have to have faith in *détente*. London thinks that Ulbricht's finished. Yakubovsky said that Rieff was well placed. Rieff used to work with Erich Honecker. I think Honecker will be Moscow's new man.'

'And what's he like?'

'A dry man but not arrogant like Ulbricht, not full of his own importance or hate for Willi Brandt . . . a better chance for *détente* . . . possibly.'

'Or a better chance for the Russians to retain control,' she said. 'Dry doesn't sound very flexible to me.'

'Maybe it's better . . . maybe he's breakable . . . crumbly.'

'In the end, Brezhnev dictates,' she said, and was suddenly depressed. 'You know why they use the word "*détente*"? I think it's because it doesn't sound as easy as "relaxation".'

He swung into the airport and parked up close to departures.

'We can add another two hours or so to our total,' he said. 'I worked it out once when I was in Krasnogorsk. We still haven't managed a whole day together . . . yet.'

He squeezed her hand. The moment suddenly on them.

'I know it hasn't been a day,' he said, 'but I know you. I said it once to myself out loud in the apartment in Lisbon. I am not alone. It sounded stupid, like all these things do, but it's what has mattered to me all this time, that at least there's been somebody.'

'When I flew back from Lisbon after putting Luís and Julião in the family mausoleum, I was panic-struck. I thought I'd become afraid of flying. But then I realized that it was the fear of suddenly finding myself alone. It was a sudden terror of crashing and dying in the company of strangers . . . unknown and unloved.'

'We're all strangers,' he said. 'Even more so in this business.'

'That's the point, Karl . . .'

'Or is it Kurt?' he said, his one operational eyebrow arched, and they both laughed.

She reached for the car door and he asked her for one last look at the photograph of Julião. He nodded it into his head.

He took her case, walked across the dry, frozen tarmac, cleared snow piled at the edges in solid ridges. He gave the case to a porter. They stood at the entrance, their breath joining in the icy air. He shook her hand and wished her a safe flight, stepped back and saluted her. He walked off without a backward glance, got into his car and drove away into his colourless world.

Wallis met her at the airport, took her by the arm as if he was going to march her straight into a waiting police car. They got into the back of a cab.

'Clapham,' he said, and sat back, pleased with himself.

'There's a police station at the top of the Latchmere Road,' she said.

'Come on, Andrea. No need for that. You did a great job.'

'By accident, rather than design.'

'Oh no, no, no, *I* think it was by design.'

'And now?'

'This isn't Russia, you know. We're not the KGB. No salt mines here, old girl. We take care of you. You go back to Admin, work hard, get your gong, take your pension.'

She checked him for sincerity. He returned her look. Karl had been right, he was still young behind that fat face, willing and eager to please. He made it all sound cosy.

'And, of course,' he said, 'in return, we hope you'll be amenable to maintaining a relationship with Mr Gromov.'

'And if I'm not?'

'Do not pass Go. Do not collect two hundred pounds. Go To Jail.'

'I told Gromov I'd only do one job for him.'

'Really? Why was that?'

'I wanted that pension you're talking about. I didn't want to live my life in a constant sweat. And, besides, the hate's gone. There's nothing left in me to keep me going.'

'Hate?' asked Wallis. 'Not sure what you're on about there, old girl.'

'How Louis Greig got me to work for Gromov in the first place.'

'But "hate"? Who do you hate? Louis Greig?'

'Louis turned pathetic,' she said, and after a laden pause: 'Perhaps I hate the same person you hate.'

'*I* don't hate anybody,' said Wallis, shifting to the corner of the taxi, turning to her. 'Hate ... you know, Andrea, it's not a very British thing that, is it? We don't have those sort of ... feelings.'

'I know, Jim, you don't even hate your traitors, do you? Or maybe you would if they were really close, right deep inside ... I mean, in the Hot Room ... that far inside.'

'We've cleaned our house, old girl. Bad show in the sixties, but we're spic-and-span now,' said Wallis, defensive, taking this as a strangely personal attack.

'Are you?' she asked, deflected for the moment. 'You know, when I told Gromov the contents of the Cleopatra file ... the names.'

'Yes, Cleopatra,' said Wallis, taking it away from her, relieved, back to being high on the hog, 'that was all a blind, just to test the ... er ... lines of communication between London, Moscow and Berlin. Moscow wanted to weaken Ulbricht, clear out his cronies, including Stiller. So Yakubovsky put Stiller on the list. You found out, told Gromov. Gromov presents the case to Moscow. Moscow ask Mielke what the hell is going on. Yakubovsky gets the order to execute. Andrea Aspinall passes her initiation test with Gromov.'

'I see ... so you planted the Cleopatra file on my desk and then *let* me get into the Hot Room?'

'You pilfered Speke's card.'

'How did you know I was working for Gromov?'

'Because we've been watching Louis Greig for the last five years.'

She nodded, remembering Rose's interest at the funeral party.

'You still haven't let me tell you what Gromov said.'

'After you gave him Stiller's name?'

'He said that the information would have to be checked. I was annoyed after the sweat I'd been through and asked him what he meant. He said: "Checked by somebody with Grade 10 Red status."'

'Pure mischief,' said Wallis.

'Is it? Why?'

Wallis tapped his lips with his forefinger, something not quite right. Day spoilt. Bloody shame.

'You're not going to turn me on Gromov,' said Andrea. 'There'd be no point until you've cleaned out your own house.'

'They'll stick you away, Andrea.'

'No, they won't,' she said. 'Because you'll give me your full support, Jim.'

'Only so far.'

'No . . . all the way,' she said and handed him the envelope. 'To the hilt.'

'What's this?'

'A gift from the Snow Leopard. He said that the negative was in East Berlin for safe-keeping. He also said you might not want to look in there. He told me not to and I didn't.'

'Not following you again, old girl,' he said. 'Bloody mysterious, aren't you? Always have been.'

'We're back to talking about that person, the one we hate, the one who's with us all the time, the one we can never get away from, the only one we can possibly know if we ever allow it.'

Jim Wallis shook his head. Cuckoo.

'Did they put something in your water over there, old girl? Flipped your marbles? Bleached your brain?'

He pushed his finger under the flap and drew it along. He eased out the photograph as if he was hoping it was a lucky card and even his thirty years of professional dissembling couldn't stop him from blanching.

On 3rd May 1971 Walter Ulbricht was delayed from attending the 16th Plenary Session of the Central Committee by two new bodyguards, appointed by the Stasi chief General Mielke. They took him for a long and exasperating walk along the River Spree. By the time he arrived at the session, Erich Honecker had been elected Secretary-General of the Central Committee and Chairman of the National Defense Council.

Book Three
The Walking Shadows

Chapter 39

September 1989, Andrea's cottage, Langfield, Oxfordshire.

'It was the only structural change I made, knocking down that wall,' said Andrea. 'I didn't want to spend my time endlessly walking from kitchen to dining room.'

'Talking of knocking walls down . . .' said Cardew.

'You promised not to mention him,' said Dorothy.

'Who?'

'You know damn well – Gorby.'

'My only conversational embargo is on property prices,' said Andrea.

'Hear, hear,' said Rose.

Only four of Andrea's guests for her first dinner party had not been honoured by the queen. Her next-door neighbours, Rubio and Venetia Raitio, were sculptors. He was Finnish. Sir Richard Rose had bought his Thai dancer boyfriend along, who was called Boo and occasionally called himself Lady Boo if Dickie became too pompous. Sir Meredith and Lady Dorothy Cardew and Jim Wallis MBE with his fourth wife, a Frenchwoman called Thérèse, made up the party.

'Where did you get this table?' asked Dorothy Cardew, determined to have her say. 'It's a Queen Anne refectory, isn't it?'

'A copy, Dorothy. A copy.'

'He says all the right things – *Gorby*,' said Cardew, scathing. 'All this *glasnost* and *perestroika* . . .'

Dorothy rolled her eyes.

'I always thought that was a horse-drawn sleigh,' said Venetia, trying to keep it light.

'That's a *troika*,' said Rose. '*Perestroika* is reconstruction.'

'How dull,' said Boo, who'd learned most of his vocabulary from Rose.

'I rather like the sound of sleigh bells,' said Dorothy, trying to pinch the conversation back.

'And *glasnost* is openness,' added Rose, explaining to the morons.

'I don't think you're right,' said Venetia, deciding to puncture Rose. 'I'm sure it's a Moscow directive that everybody should get out their open-top sleighs, put on their best fur mufflers and jingle about in the snow.'

Rose threw up his hands. Boo slapped him on the leg.

'Amounts to the same thing,' said Wallis. 'If you ask me, Gorby's a tricky customer. Whatever anybody says, he's still a red. We only like him because he's got a cracking wife.'

'It's *impossible* to hate someone with such a *tache de vin* on 'is 'ead,' said Thérèse. '*Il est très, très sympa.*'

'What's she on about?' asked Cardew.

'She likes Gorby's birthmark, dear,' said Dorothy. 'That archipelago on his head . . . it is rather endearing.'

'He'll come down with the iron fist eventually,' said Cardew. 'You'll see. The *politburo* will rough him over and he'll be breaking heads by Christmas.'

'I think he'll do it,' said Andrea.

'What?' said Cardew, spoiling for a fight.

'You said it yourself – "talking of knocking down walls". I think he'll open it all up. Get shot of all the satellite states. He can't afford them any more. He'll tell them to get on with it on their own.'

'Not in my lifetime, he won't,' said Cardew. 'Mind you, that might not be so long.'

'But you're so *young*,' insisted Thérèse, flashing her jewelled fingers. 'And so 'andsome.'

'He's depressed about being eighty in November,' said Dorothy.

'No need to go telling everybody,' said her husband.

Andrea bought a television and a dog at the beginning of October. They were both things she'd thought she'd never buy, but she liked the feeling of someone else in the house. The dog, a long-haired dachshund, seemed superior enough to be called Ashley.

A week later the television rewarded her. Gorbachev went to

Berlin and told that dry old stick Honecker, 'When we delay, life punishes us.' Andrea punched the air. Ashley was more circumspect.

She sat on the floor of the still empty living room and read the newspapers, watched and listened to every minute of news on the TV and radio. She felt that excitement again, the tug of the silver thread.

The beginning of November was even better, the boldness of the East Germans was building. She started living in her own world now, just as she'd seen other oldies, who'd committed themselves to a golf tournament, a tennis championship, or worst of all World Snooker. She didn't dare go out in case she missed something. She lived on coffee and cigarettes. Ashley went next door and was fed by Venetia.

On 9th November she'd just poured her first gin and tonic of the evening when she heard the bizarre announcement that free travel would be permitted for East Germans with immediate effect. Andrea didn't know what this meant. It was too banal. It sounded as if they'd just given up their strongest card – the Wall. Was this how such a régime ended . . . with a blunder?

Five hours later she was kneeling in the middle of the living room, a full ashtray and a bottle of champagne on her right and the phone on her left. The scenes on the television were beyond belief. People were standing on the Wall, Wessies were dancing with Ossies in the street, they were all drenched in beer and *sekt*, a lot of them were in their nightgowns and slippers, some were holding babies aloft and a drift of super-strength Kleenex was building up behind Andrea. Ashley lay with his chin on the ground, swivelling his eyes, wanting it all to be over so that they could go back to regular meals and walks.

Jim Wallis had been the first to call.

'Have you seen it?' he roared.

'Have I seen it? I've been living it, Jim. This is better than twenty-fifth April '74.'

'Twenty-fifth April?'

'The Portuguese Revolution. The end of European fascism, Jim.'

'Completely forgot about that, old girl. End of fascism, of course.'

'But this is the end, the real end of all that ... all that stuff.'

'Thought you were going to say the "H" word for a minute.'

She woke up at 4.00 a.m. lying on the floor, the television screen blank, the champagne bottle on its side, the ashtray overflowing and her mouth like the inside of an animal-feed sack. Was this any way for a pensioner to behave? She dragged herself up to bed. She slept and woke up feeling dead and empty, as if the whole point of her existence had been removed at a stroke. She drifted from room to room, most of them still empty of furniture because she'd sold every stick from the Clapham house. She decided that this was the day to give up smoking. When depressed, deepen the depression by doing something that's good for you.

She wanted the phone to ring. She wanted *him* to call, but how would he know where she was? Jim Wallis had dropped operational contact with him years ago. They'd lost track because it was too dangerous to keep track. She thought about flying to Berlin and trying to root him out. Then she started worrying because he was Stasi and there were bound to be reprisals, lynch parties. He'd have to keep his head down and it would do no good to have her poking about in the cadaver of the system, trying to find him.

She put it from her mind. She went to work on the house. She refurbished the attic for no other reason than it seemed right to start at the top, to reorder the head first. She redecorated the bedrooms, put beds in them even though she rarely had visitors who stayed. She made a study downstairs, bought a new computer which sat on her desk and had the same power as the one she'd used at Cambridge years ago which had occupied a whole room. She decided to involve herself more in village life and began to frequent the village shop, buying little and staying long because she liked the divorcée, Kathleen Thomas, who was running it with the proviso that she was always going to shut the next day because of the competition from Waitrose in Witney.

Only five people used the village shop until that Christmas, when a sixth joined this very expensive club. Morgan Trent was forty-five, he was a major who'd just left the army and was renting whilst trying to find somewhere to buy. He wanted to set up a garden centre. Andrea didn't like him. He fitted her mother's description of Longmartin, which seemed as good a reason as any

446

for some natural animosity. Also, Kathleen Thomas fancied him, which meant Andrea had to listen to their endless badinage while Morgan bought things that he didn't need three or four times a day.

Maybe it was because of Trent's business plans that she decided to start work on the garden in the spring. She didn't want to have to buy anything from him when his garden centre opened, although those plans didn't seem to be maturing with the speed that he implied. That summer she hired a skinny little kid from the council houses at the end of the village to come and mow her lawns. He was sixteen and called Gary Brock. She thought he was all right but Kathleen told her he was a glue sniffer and a threat to society. Morgan Trent agreed with her, but he was bedding her by now so he was bound to.

In the late summer Andrea came back from a treacherous shopping trip to Waitrose and found the lawn mower had gone. She mentioned it to Kathleen, who said that she'd seen Gary Brock walking it out of the village earlier that afternoon. Andrea announced she was going down to the council houses to speak to him.

'Watch those dogs,' said Kathleen.

'What dogs?'

'His father breeds pit bull terriers.'

'Sells them to drug dealers in Brixton,' shouted Morgan, from the living room.

'Shut up, Morgan,' said Kathleen.

'He bloody does.'

'Anyway, you've got the idea,' said Kathleen. 'Mr Brock senior isn't what you'd call genteel.'

'Not the type you fought the war for, Andrea,' shouted Morgan.

'How do you know I did anything in the war, Morgan?'

'Everybody did in your generation.'

On Marvin Brock's gate was a hand-painted plywood sign that said 'BE WEAR THE DOGS'. She rang the door bell, which set off savage barking from all over the house. She took two steps back as if that would give her a half-chance of escape. Through the frosted glass she could make out a large person struggling down the corridor.

'Come on now, matey,' said the voice.

Marvin Brock opened the door. Daytime TV blared from a room behind him. His head was shaved and he wore jeans and a Swindon Town football shirt; wrapped around his wrist was a thick leather lead, which was attached to a dog of such alarming power and potential ferocity that it didn't have a collar but a full leather harness. Andrea flinched at its name written in metal studs on the thick strap across its chest. Can you call a dog that nowadays? Isn't there a law? The dog was straining against the lead, pushing a twitching black nose in her direction.

'Come on, Clint,' said Marvin, 'back down, back down, there's a good lad.'

'Oh, Clint,' said Andrea, relieved.

'Yairs, after the actor. Greatest living actor. Clint Eastwood.'

'You're Gary's father, aren't you?'

'Yairs,' he said slowly, used to this opening question.

'I'm Andrea Aspinall. Your son Gary mows my lawn. He appears to have walked off with my mower.'

'Walked off?' said Marvin. 'Well, he's prob'ly gone to mow someone else's lawn.'

'I didn't give him permission.'

'I see.'

'Can you get him to bring it back please, Mr Brock.'

'No probs, Andy. No probs. Sorry about the mix-up.'

A week later there was still no mower and Andrea reported its theft to the police. Gary had stolen the mower and sold it, but it was just one in a long line of minor offences ending with a drugs charge. Andrea was called as a witness. She spent a full three minutes in front of the magistrates. Gary Brock was sent down for eighteen months.

In late May of 1991 she was mowing her own lawn and wondering why she'd ever bothered to pay Gary Brock to do it. It was so satisfying, even mathematical, especially that last square in the middle of all the other concentric squares.

As she put the lawn mower away she was aware of a presence leaning against her car in the garage.

'You remember me, Mrs A, don't you?' said a voice, with threat and lots of Oxfordshire threaded into it.

He was thickset, wearing tight jeans and mahogany Doc Martens. His T-shirt was stretched over slabs and ridges of muscle and clasped his biceps, which had a thick worm of a vein over them.

'Gary Brock, Mrs A.'

'You've been let out early, Gary.'

'Been on my best behaviour, 'aven' I, Mrs A?'

'You've been weight training too, haven't you, Gary?'

'Yair, I 'ave. You know why, Mrs A?'

'I expect being locked up's a bit boring, isn't it?'

'Not to start with, it isn't, no.'

'Why's that?'

'Because everyone wants to fuck a new arse, Mrs A.'

Silence.

'What are you doing here, Gary?'

'Just telling you what it's like inside, Mrs A.'

'You didn't got to jail because you stole my lawn mower, Gary.'

'You were quick to get up in that box against me though, weren' ya?'

She made for the door. Gary blocked her way. She was scared now. Rubio and Venetia were away and Gary would know that. The garage was hidden from the road at the back of the house. This was what happened, she thought, you survive the worst possible scenarios without a scratch only to be assaulted by a teenage lout in your garage at home on a summer's afternoon.

'What do you want, Gary?' she asked, angry now.

Gary's head suddenly twitched. Footsteps on the gravel drive. He stepped back to look. A tall male figure stood in the garage door, silhouetted against the bright light outside.

'Well . . . what *do* you want?' the man asked Gary in accented English.

She knew that voice. Gary lumbered over. Andrea moved into the light, made a negative sign with her hand.

'What *are* you doing here?' Voss asked, in a voice that had known men a lot worse than Gary. Voss put the terrible side of his face up to him. Gary pulled back from the power of such damage. A man, even in his seventies, who looked like that, who could walk around like that, had his own strength.

'I came to say hello to Mrs A, that's all,' he said, edging around Voss. 'Been away, I 'ave.'

Gary moved off, trying to look light and unselfconscious. Voss put an arm around her shoulders, gripped her tight.

'You have a talent, Karl Voss . . .' she said.

'I have my uses.'

Chapter 40

May 1989, Andrea's cottage, Langfield, Oxfordshire.

As soon as she sat him down in the kitchen and made him coffee she knew that he was different. They didn't just walk into each other's lives and take up residence as they had done before. Her instinctive understanding of him had disappeared. He'd made himself unreachable.

He told her he hadn't contacted her before because Elena had been ill. She'd died only last month. He'd just left his youngest daughter in Moscow after she'd got married to a research chemist two weeks ago. His eldest was in Kiev, married to a naval officer and pregnant with her second child. That was all he had to say about his two little girls. He mentioned, too, that he'd been ill himself and that he'd been working on a book but wouldn't be drawn on the subject. He was thin, and the good side of his face appeared haggard. He smoked constantly, roll-ups which he made with the economy of a prisoner. He didn't eat much of her celebration supper of loin of pork roasted with truffles and he drank heavily but with no change in his mood. He asked if he could stay – he needed a safe place to work. She felt ashamed at having to think about it for a fraction of a second. She showed him up to the attic room. That night she lay in her bed listening to him moving around, pacing, while she thought that he should have been with her, but she didn't want him in her bed. The stranger.

He'd arrived with very little clothing but two large suitcases filled with documents and files. A week later a trunk arrived with more paper. She felt invaded but still bought him a computer. He worked all the time. She heard him clacking on the keyboard at four in the morning. At meals he was distracted and withdrawn. In the afternoons she sat in her own study, looking up in his vague direction and feeling the terrible pressure coming down from the

451

top of the house. The unbearable weight of silent hate. It was overrunning her house, moving between the floors and walls like vermin, infecting the stairs and landings with its sharp stench.

She had to get out. She spent time at Kathleen's shop, confided in her, told her about Voss and how he'd seen off Gary Brock but now she couldn't bear to have him in the house. Kathleen told her to put him out, like a dog at night but never to return.

After a few weeks Voss started to take his meals at different times. He thought that by being absent it would relieve her of his oppressive presence, but it was equally intolerable because then he was *being* absent. He was still there even when he wasn't. This was not how it was meant to be.

She took refuge in the past, leafing through old papers, photographs, trying to recapture a sense of how she used to feel about him because, of course, there was no record, he was anonymous in her life. There were no old letters, no photographs, no mementoes even. Then she came across the letter from João Ribeiro's lawyer informing her of his death, which had happened two years after the revolution, in 1976. She had missed the funeral because, by law, burials have to take place within twenty-four hours in Portugal. João Ribeiro, who'd never taken up the offer of reinstatement to the central committee, had been carried out of the Bairro Alto in his coffin followed by hundreds of people. The lawyer's letter also said that he was holding something for her which had been left in João Ribeiro's possession.

She called the lawyer and booked two flights to Lisbon for 26th June. Voss had become so expert at avoiding her that she had to lie in wait like a hunter in a hide.

'I've bought you a present,' she said.

'What for?'

'Your birthday.'

'My birthday's not for three more days.'

'I know,' she said. 'The present is in Lisbon. We're flying tomorrow.'

'*Unmöglich,*' he said. Impossible. 'My work. I have to do my work.'

'Not *unmöglich,*' she said. 'We're going somewhere very important.'

'Nothing is more important that my work. Once that is finished

'. . . only then am I free,' he said, and his voice faltered over that last word as if he didn't believe it himself.

'Are you refusing to accept my gift?'

He looked tortured.

They flew into Lisbon on the afternoon of 26th June. The flight was pure torment for Voss, who had to endure two and a half hours without tobacco. He passed his time rolling cigarettes so that he had a hundred ready-made. They took a cab into the city through Saldanha, the Praça Marquês de Pombal, Largo do Rato and down Avenida Álvares Cabral to the Jardim da Estrela.

She was sitting on the ruined side of his face but she could see his eye, staring out from its gnarled and webbed nest, taking it all in, remembering. His head ducked down as they passed the Basílica da Estrela to catch sight of the façade of his old apartment building on Rua de João de Deus still intact – in fact, untouched, just a little more cracked and crumbled. Only then did she realize the brilliance of her gift. These parts of Lisbon hadn't changed at all in fifty years and some not since the 1755 earthquake.

They turned off into Avenida Infante Santo and into Lapa. The cab threaded through the streets to Rua das Janelas Verdes and the York House. They walked up the same stone steps as the monks had done in the seventeenth century, when it had been the Convento dos Marianos. Voss stood in the old courtyard, beneath the huge spread of the palm tree and remembered all those characters in all those other *pensões* in Lisbon reading their newspapers, waiting for the day's real information which was never in print in front of them.

They rested and in the evening walked back up to the Jardim da Estrela. They touched the tiles of the old apartment building's façade. Voss ran his hands up the iron swans' necks supporting the roof of the now disused kiosk, where he used to buy his cigarettes and newspapers. They sat and had a beer in the café in the gardens. They stood on the spot where he'd given himself up and he raised his eyes to the window of the old apartment, now open to the cool of the evening.

They walked the walk that they believed had been their undoing – down the Calçada da Estrela to São Bento and the National Assembly, into the edge of the Bairro Alto, around the church,

453

along Rua Academia Ciências, up the Rua do Seculo and right into the grid of the Bairro Alto. Andrea ate a meal of *rojões*, cubed pork with cumin, in a Minhote restaurant. Voss watched and drank the best part of a bottle of *Vinho Verde* red from Ponte da Lima. In the lamp-lit darkness they strolled past bars, restaurants and dodgy-looking characters offering a night of *fado*, as if it was a porno movie. They reached the Rua de São Pedro de Alcântara and walked up between the silver rails of the tramlines as they crossed the street to the *miradouro*. They stood at the railings, looking out across the city to the Castelo São Jorge, just as they had stood forty-seven years before, but not touching.

Voss still hadn't spoken much since they'd arrived, but it wasn't the hard, grim, obsessive silence of the month in Langfield. He seemed to be filling up, like a dry clay jug, darkening with moisture as it takes in water from a spring. She leaned with her back to the railings and pulled him to her by his lapels, looked into the good half of his face.

'Is this completely normal?' she asked.

He struggled. His eyes shifted over her face.

'I don't . . . I don't remember the words,' he said.

'You remember them,' she said. 'You told me them.'

'They've slipped my mind.'

'Is this completely normal?' she repeated, shaking him by the lapels.

'I don't . . . I don't know,' he said. 'I've only been in love once.'

'Who with?'

'You . . . crazy.'

He'd said it but it didn't carry the same conviction as forty-seven years ago.

'In that case,' she said, relenting, 'you're allowed into my hotel room.'

He joined her in bed that night and she slept with her back to him, their heads on the same pillow, hands joined over her stomach.

In the morning she went off on her own and found the lawyer's office in the Chiado. He gave her the wooden box, which she signed for. She bought some paper and wrapped it and went on to the bus station and booked two tickets to Estremoz for the next day.

They took the train from Lisbon out to Estoril along the glinting, panel-beaten Tagus, the silver carriages of the train visible ahead as they turned on the bright and shining rails. The surf broke against the Búgio lighthouse in the middle of the estuary and the hump of the sandbank lurked behind like a surfacing whale.

They were horrified by how tacky the casino had become – all naked girls and ostrich feathers. The passage up to the garden of the Quinta da Águia no longer existed. Houses had been built across it and up the hill behind. They had lunch on the promenade. He poked at his sardines. She showed him where she'd lived when she'd been married to Luís and they took the train back into the city in the late afternoon.

When they arrived in Estremoz the next day it was already brutally hot. They took a cab up to the *pousada* within the castle walls and flaked out for an hour. They went back down into the town for lunch and found a dark, cool *tasca* whose walls were lined with terracotta wine jars, each tall as a man. The place was packed with Portuguese, workers and tourists, all sitting on wooden benches and eating vast portions of food.

'Do you see these people?' asked Andrea.

'Yes, I see them,' said Voss, wary.

'What do you think about them?'

'That they might become very fat,' he said, the thin smug man.

'I think they don't give a damn about anything, except the food on their plates, the good wine in their glasses and the people around them. It's not such a bad way to be.'

He nodded and ate a quarter of his grilled fish and a leaf of lettuce.

They took a cab out to the small chapel and graveyard amongst the marble quarries on the outskirts of town. They walked the lanes of the graves and tombs until they reached the Almeida family mausoleum. Voss lagged behind, looking at the photographs of the dead, which were very formal, no better than mug shots, some of them. He fingered the flowers, some of which were plastic and others made out of material. He came alongside her, not knowing what they were doing in this place. She tapped Julião's photograph, faded in the years of draining sunshine. Voss took a closer look, peering at the outline of the face.

'You haven't asked me anything about him,' she said. 'So I

thought I'd start at the end. In his end is your beginning . . . something like that.'

Voss clung on to the wrought-iron bars of the gate to the mausoleum and took in the coffins, more coffins now, and the two urns of Julião and Luís on the same shelf. Andrea took out the old photograph and put in a new one. She handed the old one to Voss. They left the graveyard, Voss's head bowed over the bleached picture, and found a cab to take them back up to the *pousada*.

Outside the hotel she took his arm and walked him past the church and the statue of Rainha Santa Isabel and sat on the ramparts. She gave him the present, which he opened. He admired the African box and thanked her with an awkward kiss.

'Look inside,' she said. 'The present's inside.'

On top was the Voss family photograph. His hand shook as he took it out. His emaciated body shuddered as he looked from face to face, each one with its own sense of triumph at being someone in the family group, in front of a photographer. He took out his father's letters, leafed through them to the one asking him to get Julius out of Stalingrad. He read it, and then his own to Julius and finally the letter from one of Julius's men. He wiped his eyes with the back of his wrist.

'I took them from your room before I escaped on to the roof back in '44. I thought it might be the only thing I'd ever have of you so I kept them. They're yours,' she said. 'You probably don't have anything left yourself.'

He shook his head, chin resting on his chest.

'I lost you, Karl,' she said, standing up, looking down on his bowed head. 'This last time, you've turned up in my life but you're not here. You've been consumed by something else and I want you back. I hope this reminds you of the man you were, because you're still the only one who has meant anything and everything to me.'

They went up to the hotel room. Karl, exhausted, slept on his back with the box on his chest, its contents seeping into him like a new drug. In the evening they returned to the same *tasca* where they'd had lunch. This time he ordered beer and wine. He ate the cheese and olives. He ordered roasted pig's cheeks and ate it all, right down to the crackling skin. He had a pudding – cake with sugar plums – and coffee and he drank a *bagaço*, because he wanted to remember that harsh liquor, his demand for it when he'd been in Lisbon during the war. He still didn't say very much but he looked at her throughout, taking her in as if he'd noticed her for the first time. His eyes were still sunk in his head but they'd lost the haunted look, the tortured, pleading look.

Slightly drunk, they held on to each other and found a small café near some gardens by the barracks and ordered *aguardente velho*, less harsh, more refined, more suitable for pensioners. He toasted her:

'For what you've returned to me,' he said. 'And for reminding me what's important.'

'And?' she asked, severe, but eyes smiling with the booze.

He paused, smacked his lips.

'For being the most beautiful creature on earth that I've never stopped loving.'

'More,' she said, 'I think I deserve more of that stuff. Tell me how much you love me. Go on, Karl Voss, physicist from Heidelberg University. How much? Quantify it. I need measures.'

'I love you . . .' he said, and thought about it for thirty seconds.

'I'm glad this is taking so long to compute.'

'I love you more than there are water molecules in the oceans of the world.'

'Not bad,' she said. 'That *is* quite a lot. You may kiss me now.'

'This work,' he said, as they recklessly asked the waiter to leave the bottle of *aguardente velho* on the table, 'this book I've been working on, that I thought, until this afternoon, was so important, is called . . . I've named it *The Gospel of Lies*. It was to be a personal account of what it has been like to spend my whole life as a spy, always working against the states which have employed me. I thought that this would be the way to make sense of it all. But it wasn't just going to be that. I was also going to make an astounding revelation . . . that for the entire post-war period, until it became unimportant, the Russians had somebody installed at the very highest level of British Intelligence.

'In 1977 I was retired, but I asked to continue working in the Stasi archives. I had already stolen lots of documents, which I kept buried in the garden of a villa Elena and I had the use of on the outskirts of Berlin. From 1977 to 1982 I worked exclusively on stealing documents which would give me irrefutable proof that

457

there was a traitor permanently in the top five executives of the British SIS. In 1986, when Elena fell ill, I took her back to Moscow and there I managed to fit in the last piece of the puzzle. The final and verbal confirmation of all my documentary proof. I spoke to Kim Philby on three occasions before he died in 1988.

'It was difficult to work on the book in Moscow and later, as Elena got sicker, I became ill myself. I have cancer, which at my age is a slow-moving affair, but I've been told that it can suddenly get worse. So I've believed myself to be on this important mission, to tell the world everything I know, but without knowing how long I had to do it.

'I felt compelled to do this work because the man, this traitor, has been honoured by his country for his services and I didn't think it right that such a person should be so highly regarded for sending his own countrymen to their deaths.'

'And now?'

'And now, in the last forty-eight hours I've come to realize something. That what I thought was the most important thing, the work that would have left my stamp on this world, is as valuable as all the intelligence ever gathered and presented to those leaders who demanded it in order to make their brilliant decisions. It is worthless. It is dust. And now that I know that, or rather had you to help me remember it, and with all that you've shown me, with all that you've given me ... I am, at last, happy.'

Andrea sipped her *aguardente*, kissed him on the mouth so that he felt the sting of the alcohol on his lips.

'But who is it?' she asked. 'You've still got to tell who he is.'

They laughed.

'It is so worthless, such dust,' he said, 'that I don't think there's any point in telling.'

'You'll be sleeping on your own if you don't.'

'I wanted to tell you when we were on that walk yesterday. Our walk through the Bairro Alto. The one where we were seen by the *bufo* who reported it to General Wolters. That, for me, was the most amazing thing that Philby revealed. It was during my last meeting with him. I hadn't told him I'd been in Lisbon during the war. To begin with I thought that would be too risky, but Philby was completely finished by then. A very sad case. I think even the Russians were wary of him by the end. So I told him who I was. I even remembered my codename, because it was such an odd one. I told him I was "Childe Harold". He started laughing, laughing so hard I was worried about him. He grabbed my hand and breathed into my face, "And now we're on the same side." So I started laughing with him, willing him to tell me but not wanting to ask, because asking someone like that is different to them telling. He told me he had given the order that my name should be handed over to Wolters as a double agent and traitor . . . but that it must be done with subtlety. Nothing traceable.'

'Why did Philby want to get rid of you?'

'Because I was stuffing his British agents full of information which could possibly have given us, the Germans, a chance at a separate peace with the Americans and the British. He didn't want there to be any possibility that the Russians would be excluded. So, he ordered one of *his* men to give me up. It was this man who told the *bufo* to report it to Wolters and led to my arrest.'

'I knew it,' said Andrea. 'I knew it would be him.'

'Who?'

'Richard Rose.'

'This is very sad, Andrea, because I know how much this man means to you but . . .'

'Richard Rose means nothing to me . . . even less than nothing now. I invited him to my dinners because he's one of the gang. He's entertaining. But I've spent most of my life not liking him at all.'

'It wasn't Richard Rose. I always thought it would be, because he was so hard in the negotiations I had with him and Sutherland in the Monserrate Gardens.'

'No?'

'I couldn't believe it either . . . that he was already in position at such an early stage.'

'Philby was a liar, too.'

'I've got the documentary proof of his later work, Andrea. All those files I dug out of the Stasi archives. They're all at home.'

'If it's him, I want to hear it from his lips.'

'I'm not sure how wise that is, Andrea,' said Voss. 'Philby and Blake were both ruthless men. They sent hundreds of agents to their deaths, but I can assure you that Meredith Cardew was worse than the two of them put together.'

*   *   *

They slept heavily that night because of the drink. They woke late in the morning and made love for the first time, with the maids singing in the corridors outside.

By afternoon Voss was not feeling well and was in pain. They took a cab all the way to the airport and flew back to London. By eleven in the evening he was in the John Radcliffe Hospital in Oxford. By a quarter past he'd been transferred, in agony, to the Pain Relief Unit in the specialist cancer hospital, the Churchill, where they brought his condition under control. By morning he was stable.

The consultant told Andrea that it could be a matter of days, at the most a fortnight. Voss insisted on staying with her at home. Andrea paid for a private nurse who would come in twice a day. Voss was installed in her bed with a morphine drip, whose doses he could control by a hand-held self-administering device that computed the amount taken so that he couldn't overdose himself.

Andrea didn't go up into the attic. She didn't turn on Voss's computer. She never knew that all his data had been corrupted by a virus and that someone had taken a sample of the documents from the trunk. She stayed in the bedroom with Voss and read to him, because it was comforting to both of them.

At night she made a light supper and before she went up to bed at eleven o'clock, she let Ashley out into the garden. She stood at the back door under the light, the dog lost in the darkness. It was a balmy night but she wore a cardigan and held it tight around her chest though she realized the cold was coming from the inside out. She had tried not to think it, but she knew she was going to have to do it again. She was going to have to go through that whole painful process once more – coming to terms with the word 'never'. Not in a million years. From here to eternity. An infinity of absence.

She remembered coming out of the Basílica da Estrela back in 1944 having cried herself empty and the feeling of that breeze blowing straight through her. Had that been bad? Not entirely. There'd been a freeing up, a loosening of the moorings, her ship still linked to the landmass of her grief but the instinct already there to move on. That was her generation. Don't make a fuss. Get on with it. And now? After a life led with love hanging by a thread. And old age, and the only possible end of old age.

In the afternoon she'd walked through the graveyard of the

church looking at the headstones of married couples, wondering if this was a grim thing to be doing. She noticed that if the woman died first, the man always followed within a year. If the man died, the woman did not go gently into her husband's night. The women hung on in their decrepit bodies, hearts thumping through the years.

She was going to finish life how she'd started it. Alone. Except that this time there were connections and an image came to her of roped climbers up a sheer wall and the looks of encouragement between them.

She shouted for Ashley.

No response.

'Bloody dog,' she said, and set off down the path.

She found him by stumbling over his supine body. The dog was warm but completely inert and she could tell by the light coming up the garden from the back door that if there was any life in his visible eye it was the tiniest crack. She picked him up. Quite a weight for a dachshund. She went back to the light, inspected him briefly under it and took him inside and laid him on the refectory table at one end. She looked at him intently for some sign of what it was that had struck him down. The warm night air blew against her back. She prised open his jaws and saw vestiges of red meat in his teeth and, in the instant that it came to her that he'd been poisoned, a white silk scarf floated down in front of her eyes and snapped tight round her neck.

She grabbed at the reins of the scarf behind her neck and found that a pair of strong, male, gossamered hands held the loop of silk. She tried to move but the taut body behind her jammed her against the table. She kicked back at the shins, saw a pair of mahogany Doc Martens. He pushed her forward again with his hips, bending her down over the table so that she felt her last chance was to get her legs up on to the table, try to scrabble across it. The powerful hands reined her back, bore down on her. She rolled back towards him, clawing at his shoulders, trying to weaken him in any way she could but the fight was going out of her. Her face was swelling, her vision darkening at the rims. Blood blackened in her head and through the narrowing tunnel she saw his face. She mouthed his name with her thick, purple lips. Her last word, a soundless question:

'Morgan?'

Voss woke up. The only light in the room from the red digits of the clock which read 00.28. The pain had woken him. He clicked on the morphine dispenser but this time he didn't feel the trickle of Lethe, as they'd begun to call it. He looked at the pillow next to him. Empty. He moved his arm, which swung freely, and saw in the weak red light that the morphine-drip tube had been cut. The pain in his side was crushing, as if there was a steel hand in there relentlessly closing on an organ. He threw back the bedcovers, turned on the reading lamp, saw that the overhead drip-feed bag was empty when he knew it should have been at the halfway mark.

He launched himself out of bed, sent the drip clattering to the floor. He called out, 'Andrea!'

It was a weak cry. The steel hand was crushing the breath out of him as well. He reached the door frame, the cut tube, still with the intravenous needle taped to his arm, whipping around his face. He staggered down the stairs and turned into the kitchen and saw the bodies on the table. The dog at her feet.

What is she doing?

A spear of pain shot through his chest, so sharp and fast that neon flashed in his brain. He staggered to the edge of the table, gripped it with his fleshless hands and looked down into the face that was hers but not.

He coughed against a pain that was far greater than anything the steel hand could produce. He coughed against a whole agony in his chest, the departure of possibility, the flight of future. Drops darkened on the wool of her fuchsia cardigan as he put his face down to hers, touched her cheek with his good cheek, felt the residual warmth. He lay next to her on the table, clasped her hand in his and for one bright moment felt happy, saw her falling through the bubbles of water as he rushed down to meet her, to bring her up, to bring her back to the light. And then the pain in his chest tightened but this time didn't let go and, although he didn't want to resist it, his body arched against it, the last pain. And through it he saw her across the river from him, on the opposite bank, waving.

*   *   *

462

Morgan Trent, who'd been sitting at the dark edge of the room waiting for his bit of sadistic amusement, came forward. He inspected the bodies, drumming his chin with his fingers. He saw the hands clasped. How sweet, he thought, how very sweet. He looked over the faces, found himself mildly curious at the quizzical smile on the good side of Voss's face. As if he'd seen something. Received a welcome.

He checked for a neck pulse. None. He went up to the attic and brought down the trunk, which he passed over the wall into the garden of his rented cottage. He returned for the two suitcases of documents. He went back a third time, planted his foot firmly in the flower bed outside the dining-room window and broke a pane of glass. He climbed in through the window and walked out of the front door, closing it behind him.

He put the suitcases and the trunk in the back of his car. He removed the Doc Martens and put on a pair of crêpe-soled shoes. He trotted down to the Brocks' house and put the Doc Martens where he'd found them, in the garage. He drove to Swindon and made a call from a public phone box. They exchanged passwords and he said: 'It's done, I'm dumping the paper now.'

The nurse found the bodies in the morning. She had her own key. She called the police and an hour later three officers were standing around the bodies on the refectory table.

'You know what this looks like to me?' said the DC.

'Apart from murder, you mean?' said the DI.

'The way the bodies are positioned, with the dog at their feet, and the fact that he's holding her hand . . .'

'Odd that.'

'. . . it looks like a tomb,' he said. 'One of those old tombs, carved in stone. You know, the knight in armour and his lady wife.'

'You're right,' said the DI, 'and they've always got those little dogs at their feet.'

'There's a poem written about that,' said the third officer, who was young, new in the job.

'A poem,' said the DI. 'I didn't know they read poetry at Police College these days.'

'They don't, sir. I got a BA in General Arts from Keele University. We read a few poems.'

'All right,' said the DC, thinking – acceptable.
'I only remember the last line.'
'That's all right, we don't need the whole damn thing.'
'*"What will survive of us is love . . ."*, sir. That was the line.'
'Well, that's a load of crap, isn't it?'

Oxford Times 3rd December 1991
At 11.30 a.m. in the Oxford Crown Court Gary Brock was sentenced to life imprisonment for the murder of Karl Voss and Andrea Aspinall.

Oxford Times 3rd February 1992
Morgan Trent and Kathleen Thomas would like to announce their forthcoming marriage to take place at Langfield Church, Oxfordshire on 28th June 1992.

The Times 30th June 1993
On 28th June 1993 Sir Meredith Cardew died peacefully at home. He was 84 years old. There will be a memorial service at St Mary's in the Strand on 15th September 1993.

PRAISE FOR *KINTU*

'*Kintu* is an important book. It is also a very good one...
inventive in scope, masterful in execution, [Jennifer
Nansubuga Makumbi] does for Ugandan literature what
Chinua Achebe did for Nigerian writing.'

Guardian

'A multi-character epic that emphatically lives up to its
ambition.'

Sunday Times

'A highly ambitious, dense and tightly written narrative...
Makumbi succeeds in making us feel the emotional importance of uncovering family history.'

Times Literary Supplement

'A soaring and sublime epic. One of those great stories that
was just waiting to be told.'

Marlon James, Man Booker Prize-winning
author of *A Brief History of Seven Killings*

'*Kintu* is a triumph of east African literature.'

'Magisterial...epic... The great Africanstein novel.'

'Immediately engaging...as gruelling vignettes of gender injustice jostle with hallucinatory dream sequences.'

'Epic both in intention and execution, *Kintu* contains a vast number of characters, avenging ghosts and portentous visions...the final coming together of the entire Kintu clan, arrived at with precision and intricacy, makes for a satisfying and thoughtful denouement.'

'The most important book to come out of Uganda for half a century.'

'*Kintu* is an entertaining, engrossing, and, crucially, intimate read...an extraordinary novel that is unafraid and beautifully unashamed to examine Uganda's rich culture. It is a novel that is proudly Ugandan; it is a novel that deserves to be widely read.'

'*Kintu* is a masterpiece, an absolute gem, the great Ugandan novel you didn't know you were waiting for.'

'A masterpiece of cultural memory, *Kintu* is elegantly poised on the crossroads of tradition and modernity.'

Publishers Weekly (starred review)

'A work of bold imagination and clear talent.'

Ellah Wakatama Allfrey, editor of *Africa39*

'With crisp details and precise prose, Makumbi draws us into the dynamic and vast world of Uganda – its rich history, its people's intricate beliefs, and the collective weight of their steadfast customs.'

World Literature Today

'I recommend Jennifer Nansubuga Makumbi's *Kintu*, a sprawling, striking epic.'

Gabe Habash, author of *Stephen Florida*

'In this captivating multigenerational family saga, Makumbi has gifted us with an exquisite and powerful debut. Written in delightful prose, bold and ambitious, *Kintu* is easily one of the best novels I have read this year.'

Chika Unigwe, author of *On Black Sisters' Street*

'Impressive... Reminiscent of Chinua Achebe's *Things Fall Apart*, this work will appeal to lovers of African literature.'

Library Journal (starred review)

'A bold, sweeping epic, ambitious and very well crafted. The kind of book you hope everyone will read.'

Tendai Huchu, author of *The Hairdresser of Harare*

MANCHESTER

HAPPENED

JENNIFER
NANSUBUGA
MAKUMBI

ONEWORLD

Damian,
thank you has become inadequate.

To the fearless Ugandans in the diaspora,
olugambo tebalunkubira!

CONTENTS

AUTHOR'S NOTE

You know when your family is the poorest in the clan but you have these wheezing-rich cousins whose father sometimes helps out with your education, medical care and upkeep but sometimes threatens to withdraw his help if you don't do as he says? You think to yourself, hmm, if I lived with them, my prospects would improve, I'd be successful, help pull my family out of the hole and the world would be boundless. You approach Uncle. *Can I come and live with you?* He hesitates: he has heard your story before. He's impatient with your 'lazy', 'incompetent', 'backward' father who shouldn't have had so many children. But you're lucky; Uncle takes you in, and when you arrive at his home you join other relatives living with him and make a world. But Uncle's children, fed up with sharing their home with cousins from all over the clan, cry out, *We're squashed, Dad.* You shrink and try not to take up too much space, but it hurts when they presume things about your family. For you, the situation is more complex than an incompetent father.

Often, when things are not going right, cousins' resentment flares up and tantrums are thrown: *Get them out of here.* You shrink again, but privately you question their belief that your father should have had fewer children. After all, the cost of bringing up one of them, the pressure their needs put on the earth, could have brought up six, maybe even ten, of your siblings. Their childhood is long and indulgent; so is their old age. Still, when Uncle complains about the number of your siblings, you twist your lips and swallow the stories your father told you about Uncle's wealth. You keep your head down and try to make the most of your situation. You keep closer to the other relations Uncle is looking after – some of whom sneaked in after he said no, some of whom escaped abusive relatives, some seeking respite from strife, some who came to study but refused to go home. When we call this phenomenon 'extended family', you people at home insist that family is family, no one is extended. I thought, maybe I should let you see for yourselves? So, here are a few unfiltered snapshots of our world.

PROLOGUE

Christmas Is Coming

Luzinda sits curled in his favourite spot on the windowsill in his bedroom. The window overlooks Trafford Road, a park with green railings and the village beyond. This morning, the road, the gardens and the village are wet. But it is cosy where Luzinda sits. His room is warm, and he loves being in pyjamas. Yet he is agonising. Lip-biting, teeth-grinding agonising. Yesterday he turned thirteen.

He looks down three storeys below into the road. Strange cars have started appearing. Has the Premier League already started? It's not yet ten in the morning but all the parking spaces on his street have been taken. That means Man U will be playing at home today. The noise if they win. If he knew the number for the traffic wardens, those fans would come back to clamped cars.

Further down the road, an old couple, the idiots, are feeding the pigeons. They tear up slices of bread and throw, tear up and throw. The pigeons are frenzied. For the past six months, pigeons have made a nest on the balcony of the flat below. They fight and flap and stink when they come to roost. Their droppings are all over the balcony.

A memory intrudes and Luzinda's heart jumps. His birthday is in August, which means Christmas is coming. The demon in his house breaks loose on Christmas Day. At parties too.

His eyes wander back to the road. A cat sashays past the pigeons as if it's a vegetarian. It crosses the road and despite its chunky size slips through the narrow railings into the park. It stops. The tail, just the tail, makes slow wave-like motions above the ground but the rest of its body is dead still. Then it launches – puff-puff, snarling, yowling – into the bush and a fox yelps and scrums out. Luzinda scrambles up and stands on his toes to see the chase through the upper pane of the sash window but is too short. Cat and fox run out of view. He holds his mouth in disbelief. A whole fox? Chased yelping and scurrying by a cat? So wrong. Like a husband walloped by his wife. A moment later, the cat saunters back into view. Its coat and tail are still puffed. It stops for a moment and its body spasms. It looks back as if saying *Let me see you come back to my park again*, and struts past the pigeons and out of view.

'Ktdo.' Luzinda clicks his tongue because that's how upside down this country is. A cat walks past pigeons and chases a fox five times its size.

His door bursts open.

'Did you call?' Bakka, his seven-year-old brother, is breathless. Before he answers, Bakka steps in. 'You know you shouldn't sit on that windowsill; it totally creeps—'

Luzinda throws a styrofoam cup but Bakka jumps back just in time. The cup hits the door and falls to the floor. Bakka steps in again, happy to have elicited a reaction from his brother.

'That's why you're not growing tall,' he says. 'Curled up on that windowsill all the time.'

Luzinda ignores him.

'That's how stalkers start' – Bakka pretends to shudder – 'by spying on people.'

Luzinda rises from the windowsill in a *now you've gone too far* way.

'Don't let Mum catch you sitting there, not after yesterday.'

Both Luzinda's legs are on the floor now, his eyes narrowed.

Bakka bangs the door and runs downstairs giggling. He has banged the door so hard the picture of Christ on Luzinda's wall is askew. Luzinda sucks his teeth and starts to make his way to the understairs cupboard. He stumbles on something and looks down. It is the pile of his birthday presents from yesterday. He kicks them out of the way.

Outside his room, the house is silent. He runs down the stairs, fetches the stepladder and brings it to his bedroom. He stands on the top step and adjusts the picture so that Christ's hands are stretched towards his bed.

As he takes the stepladder back downstairs, yesterday returns so forcefully he can no longer block it from his mind. It awakens a snake of guilt, then fear. The first thing he realised was how close Christmas was. The other was that life hurts hardest at thirteen. He is more aware now; even thoughts hurt.

Best to go home. In Uganda God was hands-on. He watched and recorded every wicked deed, word and thought in his black book. Then he sent his angels to stockpile fire-wood in hell to burn you when you died. That's why grown-ups back home behaved – no messing about. But here in Manchester, where God gave up a long time ago, grown-ups are out of control. Children have no power to keep them in line. But how do you tell your parents, who keep telling you that they only came to give you a bright future, that the family needs to return home?

A month ago, Luzinda had told his mother that he did not want a birthday party this year. She had dismissed him with 'Nonsense; what child does not want a birthday party?' He had appealed to his dad, but he was useless. *Talk to your mother* is all he ever says.

Luzinda had always suspected that his birthday parties were as much for his parents as they were for him. And yester-day, when his mother ignored his wishes, confirmed this. How do you explain the amount of beer and wine she bought? And you know how on the way back from a party, your parents start digging into their so-called friends – *So-and-so is getting deported...so-and-so has bought a Mercedes yet lives like a rat... they are on benefits...so-and-so married for the visa...so-and-so's children have turned into British brats...that daughter of theirs must be a lezibian; did you see her haircut...so-and-so are same clan, same totem but cohabiting, spit, spit.* Luzinda had been certain that after his party, on their way home, guests would sink their talons into his parents. So, yesterday when the guests started to arrive, he locked himself in the bathroom. Asking where

4

the birthday boy was, uncle after uncle, then aunty after aunty stood outside the bathroom door, cajoling him to come out and open his presents, but Luzinda remained mute. Then that Nnalongo sighed, 'Children brought up in Bungeleza: they're impossible.'. And Aunty Poonah was quick to justify herself: 'That's why I left mine back home, hm-hm, I couldn't manage.' As if children brought up in Africa were perfect, as if grown-ups who grew up in Uganda weren't liars and—

'Still,' Nnalongo had whispered, 'something is wrong somewhere in this house.'

That made Luzinda sit up; he should have locked himself in the store. Too late; the guests were going to tear into his parents' backs anyway.

After a while his mum came to the door and he heard Aunt Nnambassa, Mulungi's mum, say to her, 'But this son of yours, Sikola! Something psychological is going on.'

'Yes, he's too quiet, too watchful for his age.'

'Talk to a psychiatrist and see,' Aunty Nnam suggested.

Mum did not respond. Instead she knocked on the door with renewed vigour. 'Luzinda, Luzinda? Come out, sweetie. Come tell Mummy what's wrong.'

At the sound of his mother's voice Luzinda had squeezed into the tiny space between the toilet bowl and the bathtub, put his chin on his knees, covered his ears and squeezed his eyes shut until she stopped. But Dad did not try to lure him out of the bathroom; not once. In the end, the grown-ups sucked their teeth at the door and gave up.

They left early. Normally, when Ugandans come around, they talk and drink, talk and drink way past midnight. But by eight o'clock they were all gone. They had drunk too much but there was no spare toilet. After the last guest had gone, Bakka came to the bathroom door and whispered, 'Luz, Luz, they've gone. Dad's gone to see them off!'

Luzinda opened the door a bit and listened. Silence. He opened it further and sniffed the air. Nothing. He stepped outside but did not let go of the door. He listened again. Finally, he walked a few steps into the sitting room and peered and sniffed. Then he turned to his brother. At the question in his eyes, Bakka shrugged: *I don't know why it didn't happen.* Luzinda had put his arm around his brother's shoulder, pulled him in and kissed his ear. Then he walked to his bedroom and got into bed.

At around nine, Dad came to his bedroom to check that he was properly tucked in. He said, 'Look, Luzinda, I've brought your presents.'

Luzinda pretended to be asleep. He heard Dad put the packages down on the floor. After he put the books away and turned the computer off, Dad turned out the lights and began to leave. But then he paused at the door as if thinking. He came back and Luzinda felt him sit on his bed. He felt Dad's breath on his cheeks before the feather of a kiss, then a warm hand on his shoulder, but Luzinda remained silent. He fell asleep before his father left the room.

The door opens again. Luzinda prepares to chase Bakka, but it's Mum. He looks away. Then steals a glance. Is she getting thinner? Her face is puffed as though liquids have collected beneath the skin. She has seen the unopened presents on the floor. Though her eyes are red and swollen, Luzinda has seen the hurt in them.

'Come and get something to eat, Luzinda.' Her voice is hoarse. She does not rebuke him for sitting on the window-sill; she does not mention yesterday; she does not comment on the unopened presents. Luzinda gets up and stomps past her. She sighs and closes the door.

At the end of September, Luzinda shoves his still-unopened birthday presents under the bed.

Christmas is two months away now, but Luzinda has done nothing about it except worry. But what is worrying going to achieve: grab Christmas's legs and tie them together so it won't come? Sundays are the hardest, especially when he doesn't have a book to read. He sits on the windowsill and conjures all kinds of Yuletide horrors. Now, determined that his family will return to Uganda before the dreaded day, he gets off the windowsill and kneels below the picture of Christ. He asks him to send the family back home. If he does, Luzinda will go to church every Sunday and get Saved. He will abandon his archaeologist dream and become a pastor when he grows up.

He gets off his knees and walks to his parents' bedroom. He knocks. No reply. Knocks again. He's sure his mother is in; she does not work on weekends and he heard her come home last night. Talking to Dad would be a waste of time. He would only say *Ask your mother*. He knocks insistently. A faint voice comes.

'Come in.'

He pushes the door and a warm wet stench wipes his face. He holds his breath. The room is so dark he can't see his mother.

'Morning, Mum.' He gulps the stench. 'Should I open the curtains?'

'No, darling, I've got a headache: what do you want so early in the morning?'

Luzinda resists the urge to say that it's past ten o'clock. He stands close to the chest of drawers to keep the door open.

'Mum, can we go home for Christmas?'

His eyes begin to adjust. Mum's head is up. She pats the pillow as if to fluff it before collapsing onto it. She lifts her head again.

'Darling, do you know the cost of flying four people to Uganda during the Christmas season?'

Luzinda keeps quiet. He would like to open the window and let in some fresh air. Mum attempts to sit up – she pants and grunts as if shifting a boulder – and fails.

'How about me and Bakka only?'

'I can't send you back on your own. We should eat Christmas together, as a family.'

Luzinda pauses. He pauses too long. As if there is something else to say, but then he steps back and out of the room. He closes the door and goes back to the windowsill. He curls up so tightly he can smell the fabric conditioner on his shirt. He does not see the fat cat cross the road and slip between the park railings. It would have cheered him up; he has respect for that cat now. He decides it's time to seek outside intervention.

A few days later, when he's alone with Bakka in the house – Dad's working the night shift and Mum's not yet back home – Luzinda picks up the phone and dials 999. A woman asks, 'Which service do you require?' Luzinda hesitates. 'Do you need the police, fire brigade or an ambulance?'

Stupid that those are the only options: what about Immigrations? What about Social Services? 'Police,' he says. It's the closest to Immigrations. But when he explains that his family are illegal immigrants, the woman tells him to put the phone down.

'This is for emergencies only.'

How dumb! Apparently he could be arrested for wasting their time. He rang to tell the police that he and his brother were home alone. He had heard Ugandans say that in Britain fourteen years old is the youngest that children can be left alone in the house. He changed his mind at the last minute: his parents would guess that one of them had rung the police.

Finally, towards the end of November, Children's Services arrive. Mum is out but unfortunately Dad is in. Luzinda had forgotten that he had rung the council a month earlier. At the time, he had given them all the family details, but they had not sounded convinced enough to come. In primary school, a teacher had told his class that it was child abuse for parents to smack their children and had made them write down the number for the NSPCC helpline. Luzinda had looked it up on the computer and found the number for the Manchester office.

Children's Services explain to Dad that they have come to check on the children, that they will talk to each child separately and without him. One woman talks to Bakka first. She takes him to the sitting room. One stays with Luzinda in his bedroom and another with Dad. But Luzinda can hear Dad pacing in the corridor. His voice is a whisper because he is close to tears. 'How can anyone say that I abuse my children? I live for my children, they're my world.'

Then it is Luzinda's turn. When the woman asks him whether his parents have ever beaten him or his brother, he thinks *Which Africans don't smack their children? Arrest them and deport us*, but the agony in his father's voice in the other room makes him shake his head. Did his father hit his mother? Luzinda barely masks his disdain. They don't ask whether his mum hit his dad. Had his father ever touched him sexually? *What?! These people!* You mention the word 'abuse' and the first thing they say is 'kiddy-diddler'. And see how they are so quick to suspect the dad! Why not the mum? The pain of Dad's footsteps pacing up and down in the corridor, the guilt of hearing him say to the woman, 'But what did they say we do to our children?' Good thing the social workers are all black. If they were white, Dad would ask *So black people don't know how to bring up their own children?*

When the interview ends, one of the women smiles at Dad. 'Sorry to put you through this, Mr Kisitu, but we have a call on our records' – she steals a glance at Luzinda – 'that stated children at this address were being neglected—'

'How?' Dad, now vindicated, interrupts. And when Dad is angry his Ugandan accent returns: 'Hawoo, hawoo, tell me ekizakitly haw my children are nejilekited.'

'We take such calls seriously. You agree that when it happens we should investigate.'

Dad nodded, tears wetting his eyes.

'You have beautiful children, Mr Kisitu' – the woman had touched Luzinda's arm sympathetically – 'and you're doing a good job of bringing them up.'

After they left, Dad clapped and shook his head Ugandanly. 'This is too much! Ugandans want Social Services to take away my children? Kdto!'

Bakka keeps glancing at Luzinda but says nothing.

If Luzinda thought that being thirteen was painful, this new guilt is in its own league. He gives up on outside intervention.

December is two weeks old. Luzinda has run out of options and Jesus does not care. Meanwhile, the days keep coming and falling away, coming and falling away. Christmas Day is heading straight for his house. On TV, the Coca-Cola advert enthuses that the holidays are coming, that holidays are coming, everywhere there are images of happy children and their wish lists, and the Coca-Cola advert, like a soundtrack, sings that the holidays are coming, Manchester city council has put up its decorations, the weatherman speculates that it will be a white Christmas, yet outside Luzinda's window the world is soulless. The wet street, the hunched lamp posts, cars parked half on the pavement half on the road, the drizzle only visible beneath the street light and the park now a shadow. What happened to the pigeons?

A car breaks the darkness. Its headlights flash past. Luzinda looks at his watch. It's nine o'clock; he thought it was seven. The car stops outside his block. It is a taxi. The driver – same as usual – gets out, comes around and opens the rear door. Mum tumbles out. The driver goes to the boot, grabs Mum's shopping bags and takes them to the doorstep. When he reappears, he closes the car boot, waves to Mum, gets into the car and drives away. Mum disappears under the canopy. Luzinda starts to count: 'One, two, three, four, five, si—'

The door bursts open and Bakka pushes Dad into the room. 'Get off that windowsill, Luz.' He throws orders like he pays the mortgage. He pushes Dad further into the room and kicks the door shut. Dad wears this smile as though he's only indulging in Bakka's game. Luzinda starts to get off the windowsill.

'Hurry up, Luz,' Bakka hisses. 'Get your homework book.'

Luzinda picks up his maths homework book and sits at his study desk.

'Dad, help Luz with his homework.'

Once Dad has sat down with Luzinda, Bakka steps back, looks around the room to make certain that everything is in order. Then he steps out of the room and closes the door.

Dad shakes his head in a *let's humour Bakka* way but says nothing. Luzinda opens his homework book and places it on the desk between him and his dad. He has done the homework. As his dad checks the answers, Luzinda wonders whether sometimes his father regrets not having a *no TV before you do your homework* kind of son. Being rebellious would bring excitement to the house. The door opens.

Mum stands at the door. She's so tired she holds the door frame to lean in.

Luzinda smiles and says, 'Hi Mum,' a little too cheerfully.

Before she replies Dad says, 'Welcome back, Sikola,' and they both go back to homework. Mum tries to reply, but her voice is strangled. She stands there not moving, she stands, stands.

Bakka appears. He holds a book as if he has been reading for hours. 'Hi Mum.' His smile is cherubic as he walks towards Luzinda's study desk. 'Dad, could you *please* help me with my homework when you've finished with Luz's?'

Dad caresses his hand. 'I'll be with you in a minute.'

Bakka turns with the smile of a homework enthusiast and as he walks past he says, 'Hi Mum,' again and Luzinda wants to scream *You greeted her already, idiot*.

Mum stares at Bakka as he walks past, until he closes his bedroom door. Then she turns and stares at Luzinda and her husband. There is amused suspicion on her face today, as if she suspects the three of them are up to no good but she's not sure why.

Under her scrutiny Dad focuses on one answer and frowns: 'Luzinda, how did you come to this figure?'

Luzinda looks at his calculation, reaches for the calculator and starts to punch figures in. His mother sighs, turns and shuffles towards their bedroom. She does not close the door. Luzinda carries on until he comes to the same answer. He shows the screen to his dad.

Dad speaks loudly enough for Mum to hear: 'You know that showing how you arrived at this figure step by step—'

'Is as important as the answer itself?'

Dad stands up. 'Get into your pyjamas.'

Luzinda slips his homework book back into his rucksack and gets dressed.

Dad tucks him in and says goodnight. At the door he asks, 'Light on or off?'

'Off.'

Luzinda hears his father walk towards Bakka's bedroom.

The Christmas tree arrived yesterday morning. Dad and Bakka dragged out old decorations for the tree, a large red candle that has never been lit, old Christmas cards with stale messages and tired Christmas CDs with Jurassic-era music by Philly Lutaaya, Boney M and Jim Reeves. They decorated the house. Luzinda did not join in. Last night when he went to the fridge for drinking water, the Christmas tree sat in a corner of the sitting room blinking in the dark like a witch.

Everyone is downstairs when Mum announces that they've been invited to a Christmas dinner. No surprise there. The whole Ugandan community will be there. Luzinda states that he'll not be going.

'Of course you will,' his mother says. 'Who eats Christmas on their own in this cold?' She talks about Christmas as if it's served on a plate.

Luzinda glares at her. Is she really that oblivious? Maybe her tiredness is starting to affect her mind as well. Recently, because she's on leave, Luzinda has taken to watching her face. He's worried about the swelling.

'And you need to stop following me around, Luzinda.'

He hadn't realised. He leans towards the cupboard where the microwave and the kitchen radio sit. She goes to the fridge and retrieves a bottle of Evian water. She drinks half of it in one go and sighs. Would the liquid burst out from underneath her skin like a blister if he pricked it? She walks past him. She takes the stairs, he takes them.

Bakka grabs his hand and pulls him back, hissing, 'She said don't follow her!'

Luzinda shakes him off. 'My bedroom's upstairs, idiot!'

'Then wait for her to go first!'

'Why?'

Bakka has no answer. Luzinda walks up the stairs defiantly. Bakka remains at the landing looking up, anxious, until Luzinda opens the door to his bedroom and bangs it shut.

Luzinda considers setting the house on fire – houses in Britain burn like paper. But British detectives will catch you no matter how clever you are. A few years ago, this dumb couple with a lot of children set their house on fire to frame someone else but six of their children died. Then they cried and cried on TV but the police sussed them out.

It's Christmas Eve and the sun, the sly one that appears in winter to taunt Africans, has come out. You've just arrived from home and discovered that Britain is inside a fridge. The novelty of snow wears off and you beg the sun to come out.

Who told you to leave Africa? it sneers. And then one morning it appears. You bolt outside to get some sunshine and *whack*, the winter cold wallops you. Luzinda is not interested in baking with Mum downstairs even though she has not been tired for three days. He stays on his windowsill looking out. Dad has locked himself in their bedroom wrapping presents as if he's a proper father. These days he looks at Luzinda worriedly. The other day, as they drove home from the West Indian Saturday School, he asked, 'You're righ'?' and laughed at his own Mancunian accent. When Luzinda did not respond Dad became more concerned. 'Is everything alright at school?'

Fancy him blaming school when the problem sleeps in his bedroom.

'Cos as I said before, if any bully picks on you, give him a proper thumping. You'll get in trouble, the teachers will call me in – *This is unacceptable, Mr Kisitu. In this country, we don't encourage violence, blah, blah, blah* – and I'll be suitably angry with you, but between you and the bully there'll be a new understanding.'

Luzinda shook his head. Somehow God picked the two most messed-up people in the world and made them his parents.

'How many people would I beat up, Dad? Yesterday a Caribbean boy beat a white boy for calling him African. Then there was this boy from Year Seven who apologised to me for calling me African. I said, "Dude, I am African."' Luzinda looked at his father with a *what do you do with that?* expression. When his dad did not respond he added, 'And by the way, when we first arrived, Lisa said right to my face, "I may not be white but at least I'm not African."'

'But Lisa is your best friend!'

'Exactly; now tell me who I should bea—'

'Dad.' Bakka has a talent for interrupting. 'I've promised to thump anyone who does clicks at me. You call me Spear Thrower, I thump you, no messing about.'

Luzinda did not know whether to slap or hug his brother, because he had been about to say *Sorry, Dad, you can't blame Britain for this one.*

Christmas Day arrives nice and early. It's a crisp morning: frosty on the ground, sunny in the sky. Smells of bacon, eggs and sausage waft into Luzinda's bedroom and, despite his apprehension, set him off stretching and yawning. In spite of his hunger, Luzinda stays on the windowsill. This must be how you feel on your execution morning.

At nine Dad opens the door looking all cheery, Father Christmas's red cap on his head, arms stretched out: 'Merry Christmas, my big man Luz.' He hugs and pulls Luzinda down from the windowsill and out of his bedroom to downstairs. He leads him to the Christmas tree and hands him his presents. He stands over him to make sure he opens them. Mum has bought him a pair of pyjamas, winter socks and underwear. Luzinda performs excitement. Dad has got him a PSP – the Vita console! He hurls himself at his father.

From that point on, Luzinda is lost in checking the features on his console. He does not see what he eats for breakfast. He does not see midday arrive. All the way in the car – dinner is in Moston – he's on the PSP.

But when they arrive, Mum confiscates it. 'It's rude to play games on your own when we've come all this way to be with other people. Give it to me.'

Luzinda hesitates.

His mother anticipates his reaction and warns, 'And don't you try that British brat behaviour, kicking things because you can't have your way – we don't behave like that.'

Luzinda drops the console on top of the handbrake and looks at his feet. He's sitting right behind his mother, who is in the passenger seat. Her words echo in his head. *We don't behave like that*, the superiority of it. *We don't behave like that*, the hypocrisy. He lifts his feet and puts them on the back of his mother's seat. His knees are so bent they almost touch his chin. As he contemplates kicking the seat into the dashboard, Bakka holds his breath. Luzinda looks at his brother. *You didn't really think I was gonna do it!* he smiles. He puts his feet down. They've arrived.

Dad steps out of the car and goes round to the boot. Someone has come out of the house. Grown-ups start making Ugandan noises at each other. Dad lifts the food out of the boot and carries it to the house. Luzinda storms out of the car and bangs the door. Without his PSP, apprehension has returned, especially as he realises that this is Tushabe's home. Tushabe goes to the same Saturday school.

Loud Ugandan music greets them. Chameleone is wale-waleing, imploring each of the African leaders – Kaguta, Kikwete, Kenyatta, Kabila, Kagame – as if they dance to his music. The house is packed. Smells of Ugandan food. As people see them, the greetings continue:

- *Bwana Kisitu, my Ffumbe brother; we're lost to each other.*
- *It's work, work, work; this British pound's going to kill us.*
- *The boys have grown, Sikola.*
- *Especially the younger one: he's already as tall as his older brother.*
- *Do these children of yours speak any Luganda?*
- *Do you know what we do in my house? As soon as we close the door we lock English outside.*
- *Very true, you take your children back home and they can't even talk to your parents.*
- *Leave them behind; wait until they are grounded in who they are first.*
- *Customs tried to confiscate my grasshoppers at the airport. I said, 'Border Control my foot; you won't control me.' I sat down and started eating—*
- *You ate grasshoppers in Customs?*
- *You should have seen the disgust on the officers' faces but I said, 'you eat prawns and mussels'.*

Mum and Dad join the older men in the lounge, more greeting, then catching up on what is happening back home:

- *This man will steal the votes again.*
- *Not this time; it will be too shameful after Nigeria, Kenya and Tanzania have had peaceful transitions.*

'Cameron is onto immigration again.' Dad, who believes that there are government spies in the Ugandan community, steers the conversation away from Ugandan to British politics.

'Every time he gets in trouble with his policies, he ups his ante on immigration.'

- *Police caught me walking on the motorway. The M60. How was I supposed to know you don't walk on the motorway? They put me in their car and I thought, I am finished. Instead, they drove me all the way to my house. They asked, where are you from originally, I said, not originally from; I am Ugandan. Does that mean you're going back? I said, of course. They were so polite; I couldn't believe it!*
- *Motorists in Britain are very polite, eh!*
- *Limes Nursing Home pays double time on Christmas Eve, Christmas Day, Boxing Day and New Year's.*
- *They call me Poonah Overtime at the airport, I always volunteer to work on these days, but this time I said, ah ah! Even the rich die.*
- *I've just come back from home but customer services in Uganda – yii? Especially in banks!*

As a small child, Luzinda had loved to sit and listen to their conversation. Not any more. Grown-ups imagine themselves intelligent and children essentially dumb. But by eleven he had started to see holes in things they said. By twelve he had decided that most grown-ups were dumb, especially his parents. It led to premature pubescent ire – temper flare-ups, followed by prolonged silences. Then came this obsessive need to look after his parents.

Now he gives his parents a once-over and decides that it's safe to leave them for the time being. He takes the stairs to

Tushabe's bedroom, where all the teenagers are congregating. When he comes back downstairs to check on them – you can't leave parents too long to their own devices – Dad is in the kitchen helping the women with the food the family brought while Mum sits in the lounge. Everything is alright: he goes back upstairs.

Next time he checks on them, his parents have started drinking. Dad holds a can of Stella, Mum a Carling. Sweat breaks out all over his head. But he has worried too soon: in half an hour dinner is served and the grown-ups stop drinking. He even enjoys dinner. Tushabe is making fun of her dad's accent. Recently, her dad threatened to send her back to Uganda because she hangs out with the wrong crowd, talks back, has started smoking and her skirts are the width of a belt.

'I'll *pac* you on a *plen* and fly you back to Uganda and then you shall see.'

The teenagers laugh.

'They don't *jok* over there! They'll *bit* all that madness out of your *hed* and then we shall see.'

Luzinda laughs too; Ugandan parents are the same everywhere.

With the eating over, the women clean up and join the men in the lounge to talk. Like the men, Mum never helps. Younger men and women, university students and all the unmarried remain standing in the dining area and kitchen. This time they are marvelling how they survived all that beating in high school. Teenagers bring down their plates, drop them on the table and return to Tush's bedroom without a care, without a care! How can a child with parents be without a care? Now even Mum has got hold of Stella.

An hour later, when he comes down to check on them, the signs have begun to manifest. First, her eyes become lazy. Then her lower lip droops. Luzinda runs back upstairs agitated. When he comes down again, there's a suspicious film of perspiration on Mum's face. There is nothing he can do but keep an eye on her. When he comes down for a drink, she's animated and laughing extravagantly.

By six o'clock, Luzinda cannot stay long upstairs. Mum's body has started to lose harmony. Her head drops fast and heavy. She's gone quiet. Luzinda's heart knots up. He glances at Dad: surely he has seen the signs. He wills his father to go to his wife and say *That's it, Sikola, you've had enough*, or *It's time to go home*, but Dad is talking to an uncle.

Luzinda turns away. The teenagers crowding Tush's bedroom are oblivious to his distress. Some are listening to music, trying out the latest dance moves in music videos. African music is all the rage now. Some are sharing songs on their phones; others are on Facebook and Instagram. Luzinda stares at them, at the way they laugh at mundane things, unaware that he's choking on fear. Where is Jesus?

He runs downstairs and out of the house, but winter is waiting. It clobbers him, *whack*, and he runs back into the house and upstairs. *Don't go back downstairs: stop watching her.* He even attempts to join the carefree teenagers, enthuses at Nigerian music. *Stay up here. Calm down.* He walks over to Mulungi, an intense girl, who rarely comes with her mother. Luzinda has heard his parents describe Mulungi's father as a rich, spoilt, Afghan brat with hair to below his backside. Apparently he could spend five hundred pounds on a book, or he could travel to France and check into a luxury hotel just to borrow a rare book from a nearby library. Mulungi is 'messed up'. Her mother tried to impose a Ugandan identity on her, but she rejected it. When she's fallen out with her mother she is Tajik and her name is Mulls. She's British when she hates her father. Today she is wearing a headscarf. Luzinda asks what her mother has done. She starts to explain that somewhere in Europe someone banned the niqab. After a while, Luzinda half-listens: his heart has run to the lounge. Soon he excuses himself.

Mum's face is so swollen her nose leans somewhat to one side. It would be hard for an outsider to notice but when she's really drunk her face swells more and her nose leans. And when it leans, you brace yourself: the monster is about to break loose. Luzinda's skin starts to itch like he's wearing low-grade cashmere. He claws at his arms and at his back.

He runs upstairs but stops on the landing, out of breath. There is a small window here but the glass is frosted. Three large vanilla candles stand on the windowsill. *Any minute now.* The staircase becomes claustrophobic. He is hot. He opens the window. He breathes in out, in out, until he cools down. Then the draught gets too cold and he closes the window. He plops onto the steps and holds his head. *Don't go back downstairs. Stay right here.*

Raised voices.

First, Luzinda runs to check on Bakka. Bumps into Tush going down the stairs. 'What's with you, Luz?' He stops, smiles. 'Nothing. I'm sorry,' but Tush does not wait long enough to listen. Thankfully, his brother has not heard: he's playing. This time Luzinda walks carefully downstairs. He's in time to hear his mother insult Aunty Katula; something about a sham marriage:

'Bring that husband you claim to have; let's see him.'

'That woman again; she's started!'

'I'm tired of her spoiling our parties.'

'She does it on purpose.'

'I know we're in Britain and we have our women's rights, but some women take it too far.'

'Equality or not, there's something ugly about a drunken woman.'

Luzinda hovers, prays.

Dad sits with his right hand propping his chin, defeated. It makes him look like a helpless wife.

'Leave her, don't argue with her,' Nnalongo says. 'She'll only get worse.'

'Why do you invite me? Stop inviting me, then.'

'Sikola, that's rude,' Dad pleads.

'Oh, you shut up.'

Mum looks up and sees Luzinda hovering. 'Heeeeeey.' She holds out her hands. 'There he is – my beautiful, beautiful boy.' Her hands invite him into a hug. Luzinda does not budge. 'This boy's so clever, have you seen the size of the books he reads? Come to Mummy, come, Luzinda, come to Mummy.' After a while, her hands fall at the rejection. She whispers to the guests, 'He doesn't approve of Mummy drinking – even a little like this.' She indicates a pinch. 'He's just finished *Long Walk to Freedom*. He's a real man now.'

'Go back upstairs, Luzinda,' Dad says, but Luzinda does not budge.

'All the *Harry Potters*' – Mum licks a finger – 'soup to him.' 'Leave him alone.'

Mum glares at Dad. Now she's really miffed. 'Leave him alone, leave him?' She grabs a cushion and whacks Dad with it. 'Isn't he my son?'

Dad takes the cushion off her as if she's being playful. Now Luzinda doesn't care for any other humiliation: he'll soon be the son of a battered husband. While Mum has lost her sense of judgement, she's still strong. If she's forced to go home, her frustration could turn Dad into a drum. And Dad never stops her. Unless, before she starts, Bakka acts fast and pushes Dad into Luzinda's bedroom, where the boys would protect him. Otherwise she would pace up and down the house, shouting, hitting him, while the boys cowered in their bedrooms. Now it's best to stay here and let her drink until she drowns. Luzinda hopes his dad's using his head.

Dad leaves the sitting room to pack the dishes and pans they brought. The party is dead. Most of the younger men and women have left. The few remaining are talking quietly; something about a celebrity sex tape back home. Uncle Mikka is calling his children, his face disdainful, his tolerance unwilling to extend to exposing his children to *such drunkenness*. Guiltily, Luzinda watches them leave. In the sitting room, only Mum yells. She tells the guests that she's not a labourer like them. Her husband was a paediatrician back home.

Luzinda realises too late that everyone is staring at him instead of her. He unclenches his fist and attempts to smile. The grown-ups look away but not the children – the children stare hard. He did not see them come downstairs; he did not see them break into little groups. Bakka is pushing the younger ones back upstairs. Somehow, he's got hold of Luzinda's console and he's offering it to anyone willing to go upstairs and play. But the children are not having it; they prefer to stay and stare.

Now Dad makes his way to her. He whispers that it's time to go home. Mum taunts him – 'Good for nothing,' she feeds him: 'Calls himself a man?' But Dad insists. Finally, she stands up. Is there a telltale wetness on her jeans?

'Why don't you man up and feed your family?'

She lunges at Dad. Dad does something he's never done before: he steps out of the way. Mum falls like a log. She remains motionless on the floor.

As Mum is being picked up, Bakka springs into action. He runs to the middle of the lounge, pulls down his trousers and whips out his willy as if to pee right there on the carpet, in front of everyone.

Uproar.

'Stop that boy!'

'Oh my goat, someone hold him.'

'What is this?'

'We're dead!'

Some hold their mouths, some clap, some go 'This is a calamity!'

When he sees Mum being led away, Bakka tucks his willy

back into his trousers, a triumphant grin on his face. Luzinda grabs him and pretends to slap his butt – 'What's wrong with you?' – but hits the jacket.

'I didn't do it.' Bakka laughs. 'Just joking.'

Mum must have fallen on her drink because when she was picked up off the floor, her jeans were wet.

The children whisper. They steal glances at Luzinda and Bakka and whisper. They don't laugh but whisper. Luzinda is mad that they are whispering. Why don't they laugh, the cowards? He turns and follows his mother being carried – feet dragging – through the dining room. One of her shoes slips off. Luzinda picks it up. Then the other: he picks it up, too. Mum has the softest, palest feet. See the folds? This house has the longest hallway in the whole world.

Outside, winter has stopped to stare. Bakka runs ahead and opens the rear door. Mum is thrown into the seat but Luzinda does not get in. He stands at the door. His mother is sprawled all over the back seat and Bakka has taken the passenger seat. Disgust twitches his nose. Dad, seeing him standing outside, comes around the car. He moves his wife into a sitting position. A huge bump has formed on her forehead where she fell.

When he has made space, Dad says, 'There, get in.'

The car stinks. Why does alcohol smell so foul on the breath? Wait until she goes to the toilet; then you'll know what stinking is. And if you go to their bedroom, that wet, warm stench of stale alcohol breath will wrap itself around you. God knows how Dad sleeps through it.

As Dad reverses the car, Mum tips and her head slips onto Luzinda's right shoulder. The disgustingness of it! As if a huge bluebottle fly has landed on his shoulders. He tries to shake her head off – he can't bear to touch her – but the head keeps coming. He shifts his shoulder, fidgets, but her head gets heavier. He tries to move away but she falls towards him. He looks up.

Dad is watching in the rear-view mirror. 'Luzinda, please! Your mother's tired.' That's Dad's favourite phrase: *your mother's tired, Mum's tired.* Luzinda is tired of pretending. 'Hold her head, Luzinda. Her neck will hurt if her head hangs like that.' But Luzinda will not touch her. She's drunk, not tired! Several times, he lifts his shoulder to shove his mother's head back onto her neck, but it keeps collapsing back on him. When they stop at a red light, Dad turns. 'Mum loves you, Luzinda. You cannot forget that.'

'Then let's go back to Uganda. Mum didn't drink in Uganda.'

The traffic lights turn amber. He does not tell his father that the lights have turned green.

'Alcoholism is a disease. It can come anywhere.'

'A disease? You walk into a pub and pay for a disease? She even hits you, Dad!'

The cars behind have started honking. Bakka is silent.

'She doesn't mean to. We'll get help.' Dad turns to drive.

As he pulls away, an impatient driver tries to overtake them. Dad drives faster. He races the man until he is level with him. He turns to the man and shouts, 'You want to kill my children, eh? You want to kill my family on Christmas Day?' Then he races forward.

Mum snores.

PART 1

DEPARTING

OUR ALLIES THE COLONIES

First he felt a rush of dizziness like life was leaving his body, then the world wobbled. Abbey stopped and held onto a bollard outside the Palace Theatre. He had not eaten all day. He considered nipping down to Maama Rose's for fried dumplings and kidney beans, but the thought of eating brought nausea to his throat. He steered his mind away from food. He gave himself some time then let go of the bollard to test his steadiness. His head felt right, and his vision was back. He started to walk tentatively at first then steadily, down Oxford Road, past the Palace Hotel, under the train bridge, upwards, towards the Grosvenor Picture Palace.

Abbey was set to return to Uganda. He had already paid for the first leg of the journey – the passage from Southampton to Mombasa – and was due to travel within six months. For the second and third legs of the journey – Mombasa to Nairobi, then Nairobi to Kampala – he would pay at the ticket offices on arrival. He had saved enough to start a business either dealing in kitenge textiles from the Belgian Congo or importing manufactured goods from Mombasa. Compete with the Indians even. As a starter, he had bought rolls of fabric prints from Summer Mist Textiles for women's dresses and for men's suits, to take with him. All that commercial development in Uganda he had read about – increased use of commercial vehicles; the anticipated opening of the Owen Falls Dam, which would provide electricity for everyone; he had even heard that Entebbe had opened an airport back in 1951 – was beckoning.

But his plan was in jeopardy. It was his one-month-old baby, Moses. Abbey had just returned from Macclesfield Children's Home, where the baby's mother, Heather Newton, had given him up for adoption, but he had not seen his son. In fact, he did not know what the baby looked like: he never saw him in hospital when he was born. Abbey suspected that Heather feared that one day she might bump into him and Moses. But Heather was fearful for nothing. Abbey was taking Moses home, never to return.

Suppose the children's home gave you the child, what then, hmm? the other side of his mind asked. What do you know about babies? The journey from Southampton to Mombasa is at least two weeks long on a cheap vessel. The bus ride from Mombasa to Nairobi would last up to two days. Then the following night you would catch the mail train from Nairobi to Kampala: who knows if it is still running? All those journeys with luggage and a six-month-old ankle-biter on your own. Yet Abbey knew that if he left Britain without his boy, that would be it. Moses would be adopted, given a new name and there would be no way of finding him. Then his son would be like those rootless Baitale children you heard of in Toro, whose Italian fathers left them behind.

He was now outside Manchester Museum, by the university. He was on his way to his second job, at the Princess Road bus depot, where he cleaned Manchester Corporation buses. His shift began at 9 p.m. It was almost 8 p.m., but the day was bright. He could not wait to get home and tell people how in Britain the sun had moods. It barely retired in summer yet in winter it could not be bothered to rise. He could not wait to tell them things about Britain. It was a shame he had stayed this long. But having a job and saving money made him feel like he was not wasting his youth away in a foreign land. His day job paid the bills while the evening job put savings away in his Post Office account. His mind turned on him again: Maybe Heather had a point – you don't have a wife to look after Moses while you work. You still have five months before you set off; if the home gives him to you, how will you look after him? But then shame rose and reason was banished. Blood is blood, a child is better off with his father no matter what.

He reached Whitworth Park. It was packed with people sunning themselves, young men throwing and catching Frisbees, families picnicking. At the upper end, close to Whitworth Art Gallery, he caught sight of a group of Teddy boys who, despite the warm evening, wore suits, crêpe-soled shoes and sunglasses, their greased hair slicked back. They looked like malnourished dandies. Even though Teddy Boys tended to hunt blacks in the night, Abbey decided against crossing the park. Instead, he walked its width to Moss Lane

East. The way the sun had defrosted British smiles. 'Enjoy it while it lasts,' strangers will tell you now.

Abbey arrived in Manchester aboard the *Montola*, a Dutch merchant ship, on 2 February 1950. That morning, the *Montola* limped into the Manchester Ship Canal on one engine and docked in Salford for repairs. It had been on its way to Scotland when it ran into difficulty. The crew had anticipated a delay of one or two weeks and would then carry on with the voyage. Abbey was hiding in the engine room when Ruwa, a Chagga colleague from Tanganyika, came down from the deck excited. 'Come up, Abu. Yengland is here.'

Since entering cold climes at sea, Abu had stayed in the engine room. Everywhere else on the ship was freezing. Ruwa, who was a 'specialist' on Europe, kept laughing: 'What will you do when we get to Scotland, the second coldest place on earth?' (According to Ruwa, Amsterdam held the trophy for coldness.) The unnatural heat in the engine room had so swollen Abu's hands and feet that his shoes were too tight. At the time, Abbey's name was Abu Bakri. He had named himself when he first arrived in Mombasa, even though he was not circumcised. Mombasa, especially the port, was run by Arabs and Zanzibaris who had a deep mistrust for non-Muslims and contempt for Africans. Luckily, his skin tone was light enough to pass for a Waswahili. Once he learnt the language, it was easy to pass himself off as Muslim. Soon, he was cursing and swearing like an Arab. When he arrived in Britain he changed Abu to Abbey like Westminster Abbey and

Bakri into Baker like Sir Samuel Baker. But his grandfather had named him Ssuuna Jjunju.

Wrapped in a blanket coat Ruwa lent him, Abu stepped out of the engine room and onto the short deck to see Yengland. The wind, like an icy blade, sliced through his lips, ears and nose. His puffed body deflated.

On approach, the Manchester Ship Canal seemed vast, wide. But then the *Montola* had to wait outside the canal as the *Manchester Regiment*, a monstrosity – imagine a whole village elevated to treetop level – trundled out, making the *Montola* seem like a dugout canoe. Then they started again, slowly, towards docked ships where everything seemed to be in a rush. Now the canal looked compact, tightly packed. Everywhere, ships, ships, ships. The horizon was masts and funnels and smoke. The mist was dark. Men climbing up and down hulls by means of ropes, men cleaning, men standing on suspended planks painting hulls, cranes loading, cranes offloading, ships departing, ships arriving. The way everyone rushed, the gods must have been stingy with time in England.

'Look, cotton bales have arrived too' – Abu pointed at a ship – 'they're from home!'

'They come from all over the world. Everything ends up here. See that building there? Cotton on that ship will go into that mill today, come out as fabrics tomorrow, get loaded on the same ship and head back to the colonies for us to buy.' Ruwa made a money-counting motion with his fingers. 'That's how they make money.'

'Ah ya, ya, ya! They're too rich.'

'Tsk, this is nothing.'

'Nothing?'

Ruwa did not respond because Abu was gawking and being backward and not hiding it.

'What's that smoke doing coming out of buildings; won't they catch fire?'

'In this country, you have to light fires to keep warm.'

'You mean people are in there roasting themselves right now?'

'Kdt.'

They docked.

A clock across on a building claimed 8.30 in the morning but the sun was nowhere. The world's ceiling was low and grey, the air was smoke-mist, the soil was black. After a silence of disbelief, Abu whispered, 'Where is the sun?'

Ruwa laughed.

'No wonder these people are just too eager to leave this place: the sun does not come out?'

'Sometimes it does. Mostly it rains.'

'All this wealth but no sun?'

'That's why they love it at ours too much. Always taking off their clothes and roasting themselves.'

Abu wanted to stay on the ship until it was repaired but Ruwa, who had been to Manchester several times, held his hand and led him into Salford. Abu, twenty-one years old, gripped Ruwa's hand like a toddler. They set off for a sea-men's club, the Merchant Navy Club in Moss Side, where they would know where his friend, Kwei, a Fante from the Gold Coast, lived. Even though he told Abu, 'Don't fear; Manchester is alright even to African seamen. It even has African places – Lagos Close, Freetown Close – where Africans stay, I'll show you', they walked all the way from Salford to Manchester city centre to Moss Side because Abu would not get on a tram.

'I know how to behave around whites,' he said. 'I've been to South Africa.'

'The British are different, no segregation here.'

'Who lied you, Ruwa? Their mother is the same.'

For Abu, being surrounded by a sea of Europeans in their own land brought on such anxiety that for the first time he regretted running away from home. To think that it all began with a picture on a stupid war recruitment poster – OUR ALLIES THE COLONIES. At the time, all he wanted was to join the King's African Rifles and wear that uniform. To his childish eyes the native in the picture looked fearless and regal in a fez with tassels falling down the side of his face and a coat of bright red with a Chinese collar of royal blue edged with gold. That palm tree trinket on the fez with the letters T.K.A.R. – Abbey coveted it. He wanted to hold a gun and hear it bark, then travel beyond the seas and be a part of the warring worlds. He had heard his father talk about the European war with breathless awe. He had wanted it so desperately he could not wait four years until he was eighteen to enlist. In any case, the war might be over by then. Besides, at fourteen, he was taller than most people. And the British were notoriously blind. Often, they could not tell girls from boys. Also, they were desperate for recruits because recently some Kapere had started to ask men who turned up to enlist 'Sex?', which the translator turned into

'Are you a man or a woman?' The men just walked away: who had time for that?

Unfortunately, a friend of his father saw him and pulled him out of the queue. When his father found out, he warmed his backside raw. That was when he swore to enlist in Kenya. After the war, he would come home elegant in his red uniform and fez and he would be made head of the royal army. Then his father would eat his words.

With a few friends, Ssuuna had jumped on a train wagon and hidden among sacks of cotton. What he remembered most about that journey was not the incessant jarring and grinding or screeching of rail metal, but the itching of sisal sacks. No one had warned them that Nairobi was frosty in June, especially in the morning. The boys had never known such cold. They thought they would die. And then the British turned them away. Ssuuna was told to come back in two years – the British were blind by two years – and his friends were told to go home to their mamas!

That was when his troubles began. Returning home was out of the question. Where would he say he had been? His father wanted him to stay in school, but studying was not for him. He wanted to be a soldier, shoot a gun, throw bombs and blow things up, and win a war.

While they waited to grow up, Ssuuna and his friends travelled to Mombasa. Everyone said that there was more life in Mombasa, the gateway to the world. He renamed himself and got a job as a deckhand on ships sailing at first to Zanzibar and Pemba Island, then to southern Africa's ports and later to West Africa.

But within a year he had lost interest in the European war. It was not just the cynical Arabs, it was seeing Indian coolies, Kenyans, Ugandans and Tanganyikans return on ships from Burma maimed. Lost limbs, lost sight, lost minds, lost comrades whose bodies were abandoned on foreign battlefields like they had no mothers. Apparently, one moment you were whispering to your friend, the next he was shredded meat. A man told of a soldier he saw gathering little pieces of his friend and then starting to put them back together as if bombs were not raining around him. When Abu found out that some of the soldiers never fired a gun but got blown up anyway, he was disgusted. Many of them were mere porters carrying European soldiers' luggage. Most heartbreaking was the fact that none of the soldiers returning wore the red jackets Abu had seen on the recruitment poster. The King's Rifles wore khaki and shorts. Apparently the red jacket was for Europeans only; can you imagine? The British were the very Kaffirs! Full of lies. And the way Arabs sneered at Africans who went to die in a war that did not touch them – 'Europeans are killing themselves, and you Africans want to die for them – why?' the nahodha of his boat had once laughed. Abu had cast his warrior dreams into the Indian Ocean.

It was approaching ten o'clock when Abu and Ruwa arrived in Manchester. The city centre was at once beautiful and scary. Here was his wish to travel beyond the seas coming true, without him even fighting in a war, but he was petrified just to walk through Manchester. The infrastructure alone – of brick and stone – was forbidding. The skyline – dotted by conical, sharp church steeples and tall chimneys – made him feel trapped. There was a church at every turn. Arches and arches, above doors and windows and on walls on every building. In Mombasa and Zanzibar the Arab culture along the East African coast had conjured a Muslim heaven of domes and large empty rooms with carpets and muezzins. Manchester brought to mind a Christian heaven of arches and arches, spires, steeples, pews and church bells. But why would the British sculpt snarling devils on their walls when they lived in such dark misty environs? Statues, some larger than humans, some tiny, some on horses, some gleaming black, frowned and grimaced. Everywhere he was surrounded by such tall buildings he was dizzy from turning and looking up. Neither gods nor spirits would ever make him go up there.

His neck started to ache.

At ground level, shops had bright striped canopies as if to cheer up the atmosphere. They sold glittering jewellery and sparkly watches and shimmering things for what Abu did not know. White women dressed in long blanket coats and wide-brimmed hats walked with their arms linked with their men's arms. Abu still hung onto Ruwa. Ruwa kept yanking him off the road, which was dangerous, especially those motorcycles with sidecars whizzing past, not to mention cars and buses everywhere. Then, once in a while, the horses and carts, especially that freaky horseshoe noise coming from behind you. But the pavements were not safe either; you could slip in horse dung or walk into the water and food troughs that had been put out for the horses.

Once they got away from the overpowering spectacle of the city centre, Abu exhaled. Now, bomb sites – former churches and houses – started to appear. Some were being cleared, some being rebuilt, some untouched.

'Did you see how the men hold the women's hands?'

'Because it's cold: that's how they keep warm.'

He laughed. 'But this coldness rules them too much!'

'Hmm.'

'Ha, but if Manchester, a younger city, looks like this, what is London like?'

Ruwa clicked his tongue in a *Like you even ask?* way. 'This Manchester is rags compared. London is where King George lives. At night, London blinks like a woman, even on the walls, mya, mya.' He made signs of flashing lights.

Abu pondered this, realised he could not picture a city that blinks like a woman and changed the subject. 'But why does everyone build similar houses? Does the king not allow different fashions? You could get lost here.'

'They don't build their own houses: the king does it for them.'

'What, he spoils them like that?'

'Stop asking stupid questions. They pay him, and look, all houses have numbers; you can't get lost.'

'Numbers? Like they are too stupid to find their own houses?'

Ruwa shook off Abu's hands. 'Walk by yourself; you're annoy-annoying me now.'

Later, after Abu had become Abbey and settled into Manchester and the city became less forbidding, he would go to Albert Square on a Sunday, when all shops were closed, and sit on a bench. He would marvel at the beauty of the Town Hall. Such intricate masonry. Sometimes he visited Piccadilly Gardens and sat on the slopes, a riot of colours – precise and controlled – below him. The backdrop of brick and stone made the flower gardens seem fragile. Who knew that living in a concrete city would make him yearn for nature? Who knew that one day he would roast himself in the sun? Now he could tell the British apart just from their clothing. If you saw a man wearing a white collar and a suit and a hat, those were the masters, the ones sitting in offices writing and giving orders. They spoke English the same way as the British in East Africa, smooth. The rest were workers. Their English was hard to understand when you had just arrived.

Occasionally, a man, a woman caught his eye and smiled discreetly. British humanity, when it flashed, took you by surprise. A stranger chatting to you about where you came from: *Let me buy you a cup of tea...What are you doing in England?... How do you chaps really feel about us being in your country?* and you said *We're very lucky, sir; you've brought for us civilisation and salvation,* and he shot you a look, clearly not buying your gratitude. It was a colleague asking about your leg, after a metal detergent bottle you nicked from work – to use as a bed-warmer – burnt you during an exhaustion-induced stupor. It was going to hospital sick with pneumonia and the doctor and nurses treating you delicately and the ambulance dropping you back at your house after you recovered without asking for any money. It was the ticket master at the booking agent for your travel back home who told you about cheaper tickets on a different ship with more comfortable berths, who knew you'd be overwhelmed by the procedures and did everything for you and said, 'My name is Mitch; when you're ready to travel, come and confirm your ticket, ask for me and make sure you don't wait too late because this ticket will expire in six months' time.' Then you asked yourself, But who are these other British people?

Abbey crossed Lloyd Street. On his left, on the site of a bombed-out church, children held sticks like guns, shooting Germans out of the sky and off the rubble and out of the burnt-out car nearby. When he reached the Royal Brewery, he turned left onto Princess Road. Down the road was the smaller of the two shopping centres at the heart of the black community in Moss Side. He crossed the road.

Halfway down the road, he caught sight of the Merchant Navy Club. From his side of the road, the club looked like a lazy woman waking up late. A touch of resentment crept up on him as if the club had conspired with Heather Newton to take his child away. The club had been at the centre of his life in Britain. The Africans who ran it had lived in Manchester for a long time: some had come as early as the 1910s; some had fought in the first war, some in the second; all were married to Irish women. They looked out for each other, especially the newcomers. They tipped each other off on available jobs and housing. When a ship arrived from

Africa, the club got wind of it first. When seamen Abbey knew arrived from Mombasa, it felt like home had come to visit. Now, as he walked past the club, Kwei's drunken warning when he and Ruwa had first arrived taunted him. On hearing that the *Montola* was to be scrapped, Kwei had had laughed, 'Don't stay here in Moss Side if you want to return to Africa; go somewhere like Stockport or Salford.' At first, Abbey thought it was Kwei's clumsy attempt to get rid of them because he and Ruwa were crowding his tiny room, but Kwei explained, 'Moss Side is a cruel mistress, pa! You know you have a home to go back to, but she treats you so right you keep saying *tomorrow*.'

Abbey had laughed. The idea of staying in cold Britain, where even ugly women crossed the road when they saw you coming, was absurd. Ruwa, who saw himself as a son of the sea, shook his head. 'Me, I can't stay here; the ground is too wobbly.'

'And the sea is steady?'

'That rocking, the swaying you feel on a ship, is steadiness to me.'

'You see,' Kwei had carried on drunkenly, 'in Moss Side people smile so wide, and talk so loud, pa!'

But later Ruwa had whispered to Abu, 'Me, I'm not working in a place where I am paid half the pay like a woman, however white' and moved to Southampton. But Abbey knew that Ruwa had money on him and was returning home.

Kwei took Abbey to the labour office on Oldham Street, where he registered as Abbey Baker, got a labour exchange card and National Insurance number. Abbey gave himself two years to work and save for his passage and return home. That was four years ago.

Abbey arrived at the shopping centre. Outside Nelson's Electrical Repairs, a group of West Indian men formed a circle, talking in Jamaican Patois. Abbey hurried around them. Black men standing in a group like that was the quickest way to get arrested for vagrancy, but West Indian men were defiant. Maybe it was okay for them to be defiant; after all, they had been invited to come and work after the war. Kwei had told him that back when the war ended, the British themselves went to the West Indies and asked people to come and help in the recovery of the mother country. But on arrival, doctors were turned away from hospitals, teachers were not allowed to teach in schools and engineers could only drive trains. Only nurses, cleaners, posties and drivers were wanted. In school, their children were told they could aspire either to singing, dancing or sports – nothing else. Abbey shook his head at the moniker 'mother country' because England was one wicked mother. But deep down he blamed the West Indians; why would you trust a mother who had brutalised you from the moment she laid eyes on you just because she had said *Come, I need your help*? Now many were stuck in poverty with no hope of going back home. He walked past the BP petrol station and crossed Great Western Street.

When he saw the tip of the tower on the bus depot, he slowed down. Most shops were closed. Empty buses whizzed past, drivers impatient to go home. Most bus services stopped at eight. The latest services, those going to hospitals and Ringway Airport, stopped at 10 p.m. Then they all drove back to the depot to be checked, cleaned and fuelled. As he crossed Claremont Road, the clock on the tower read 8.34 p.m. He stopped; now what? He had twenty-five minutes to burn before his shift started. He was contemplating running home to drop off his bag when he heard, 'Abbey, my friend!'

Berry walked towards him, his arm extended.

'Is your name still Abbey, as in Westminster Abbey?'

Berry was one of those *we're one people, one black nation, revolt against Babylon oppression* kind of people. He was well-meaning but a troublemaker nonetheless. He had wild, wild ideas of being equal to whites in their own country. He was a continual tenant at Greenheys Police Station, something which he wore as a badge of honour. Every time he came out of police custody he bragged about preaching to the policemen about their Babylon and how it was falling.

Berry made Abbey nervous. Not only because being with him could earn Abbey a stint in a Greenheys police cell, but because where Berry was a preacher man, Abbey was a chameleon, a *no need to aggravate your circumstances* kind of person. He was about to say that all he could remember from history at school was Sir Samuel Baker and Westminster Abbey, where Dr David Livingstone was buried, when Berry added, 'Africans take naming seriously; could your father have named you after Westminster Abbey, the seat of oppression, and Samuel Baker, the oppressor?'

Abbey looked away, his mouth twitching.

'Okay, I'll not hold you, my friend, but be true.' Berry shook his hand again.

That's the problem with Berry, Abbey thought as he walked away. Berry had a way of making him feel horrible about his name, but what would he say? That it was better to be West Indian than African? People like Berry did not realise that being black and African was too much. West Indians were 'at least' because there was a bit of Europe in them. To be called 'bongo bongo' was okay, but to hear *Do those chaps still eat each other* or *Even fellow blacks can't stand them* was crushing.

Another glance at the tower clock said that he still had fifteen minutes. Abbey stopped outside Henry George's Garments to kill time. He caught the eyes of Henry's 'almost-white' wife through the window and looked away. That woman, Henry's wife, hated blacks more than white people. Her Henry fought with the RAF, but he runs that shop now. People suspected her and Henry of being spies for the police. One tiny thing happened and the police swooped – how? But they denied it, claiming that Moss Side folk picked on them because they happen to be pale. The previous year at the queen's coronation, she carried on all euphoric and fluffy, decorating their shop and flag-waving like she was entirely white. Even now, in the window of their shop, she displayed a large portrait of the queen when she had still been Princess Elizabeth, with her children, four-year-old Charles and two-year-old Anne. Abbey stared at the picture. Princess Anne had been born just over six months after he arrived in England. That evening, Emmet their landlord had invited him and Kwei into his lounge to see the occasion on television. Gun salutes in Hyde Park and at the Tower of London, large crowds out to see the royal family, and Emmet cursing, 'Another one born to piss on our heads!' Abbey was so shocked to hear a white man curse the royal family he couldn't believe it. He had seen the notices NO BLACKS, NO IRISH, NO DOGS or HELP WANTED: IRISH NEED NOT APPLY, but he could not tell Irish from Scottish from Welsh from English. Who knew that Britain had tribes, who knew they suffered from tribalism? Still, every time they watched the Remembrance Day commemorations on television, Abbey looked at Emmet as former soldiers marched past being thanked. The fact that Emmet did not know about the coolies and Africans, the fact that those poor souls died for neither Africa nor their mothers but for an oppressor who thought they were less human anyway, churned his stomach.

Now, looking at how grown-up Princess Anne was in that picture, Abbey told himself, Ssuuna, if you're not careful, that boy Charles will become king before you leave this country.

He looked at the depot's clock: five minutes.

He bolted across Bowes Street and down the road until he came to the depot's main entrance. Neville, the supervisor, was talking to some drivers. Rather than walk past them, he decided to use the side door. Often drivers saw him, and even though he was only going up to Neville to ask for his allocation that day, he saw resentment rise in their eyes. Besides, he did not feel like hearing *Hey, Sambo, which jungle do you come from?* today. He tried the side door: it was locked. He walked to the end of the building and turned back to the Princess Road entrance. Luckily, the men were gone.

The vastness of the depot never ceased to overwhelm him. Rows and rows of buses stretched as far as he could see. Yet more buses were still arriving to park in rows 17 to 22 at the back. He wished he had a picture of it to take home with him. He turned to the right and walked down row 2, where the number 42 buses were parked. He took the ramp to the sluice to pick up his tools. He hoped Neville would give him row 8 with the number 53 buses as usual. They were the dirtiest because they went to Belle Vue Amusement Park, but Abbey liked that – the dirtier the bus, the more chances of coming across lost property. The rule was that all lost property be taken to the window marked LOST AND FOUND. Abbey always handed over toys, mittens, booties and other items of clothing. But not money. Often, he found halfpenny coins here and sixpences there. Once he found a cloth purse with sequins and pearls all over it and slid it into his underwear. Throughout the shift, it pressed heavily against his crotch. He only took it out when he got home. There were forty-two shillings in total. Abbey had patted the purse on his forehead feverishly, thanking family winds.

By the time he finished his three-hour shift at the depot, Moss Side was asleep, the streets dead. He got to the house without realising. Then stopped. Something was wrong. The lights in Emmet's quarters were still on. If Emmet was still up past midnight, then Emmet was unhappy. He tiptoed past his window to the back door. He opened it and the pungent smell of cow foot hit him. Kwei, Abbey's room-mate, was the kind to splash out on such delicacies. He justified it with *I don't know when my day is due: who am I leaving my money for? Let me eat well.* Abbey tiptoed up the stairs to the first floor, where his and Kwei's room was. Emmet was waiting on the landing. Emmet did not mind African tenants, but even he had limits.

'What's that horrible smell, Abbey?'

'I don't know, Mr Emmet, I've just returned.'

'Well, don't you smell it?'

Abbey sniffed the air and shook his head.

'How can you not! The whole house stinks.'

'I do not hear it, Mr Emmet.'

'Hear it? You mean you don't smell it?'

Abbey kept quiet.

'Tell your friend, Quway, that I'll not have you cook tripe or any of the horrible stuff you people eat.'

'I'll tell him, sir.'

Abbey walked past Emmet and down the corridor to their bedroom. He listened out before he opened the door. Emmet was going down the stairs muttering, 'They lie like little children.'

Abbey opened the door.

Kwei sat on the bed, pulling his shoes on. There was only one bed in the room but two mattresses. On the rare night when they were both at home, Abbey put his mattress on the floor. Except in winter, when it was too cold to squander each other's warmth. Abbey was surprised. Normally, by the time he came home, Kwei was gone for his night shift at the Dunlop tyre factory in Trafford Park.

Abbey hung up his fedora. 'Emmet is complaining again.'

'Let him complain. He knocked on the door and I ignored him.'

Abbey laughed.

'All he knows is how to boil rice, then wash it with cold water, add corned beef and call it dinner!'

'They eat cow tongue.'

'Disgusting people: I'll remind him next time.'

'Thanks for cooking.'

'How is Moses?'

Abbey's smile fell. He opened his hands in helplessness.

'You didn't see him, did you?'

'He was asleep.'

'Again? Twice you go all the way to Macclesfield for nothing?'

'What could I say, wake him up?'

'Yes. Wake him up for his father.'

'But they don't recognise me as important!'

'Force them – you're his father, you decide. The father always decides even among these people. Abbey, you're too soft.'

Abbey sat down on the bed and sighed. 'I don't know, Kwei. Heather said she didn't want the child to go to Africa into malaria and snakes and lions and diseases.'

'Didn't we grow up there? Stupid woman! Next time you go to see Moses, we go together. You're too timid. Now see how you've made me late because I am talking to you! By the way' – Kwei seemed to remember something – 'do you have any Blue Hearts?'

Abbey gave Kwei two of his awake pills. He had no use for them any more. He used to take them when he and Heather went out, then he would dance non-stop like a marine propeller. Kwei tossed both pills into his mouth without water. Unfortunately, Kwei had been taking Blue Hearts for too long; he no longer functioned well without them. He said goodbye, closed the door and his footsteps rang down the corridor, then the stairs. Abbey fell back on the bed. Heather Newton.

He met her at his day job at the Whit Knitwear factory on Wilmslow Road. She was working as a machinist while she waited for her nursing course to start in Scotland. At first, Abbey did not notice her. She was one of the girls in the tailoring pool, and there were over fifty girls and women in the main hall. The only girls he looked out for were the nasty ones. Besides, Abbey was so weighed down by being black and African he would never assume with white girls.

One day as she walked past Heather smiled *hello*. Abbey smiled back. It was brave of her to acknowledge him. She seemed like a good girl: not loud, did not swear and he had never seen her smoking behind the block.

Months later, Heather stopped to talk to him again. She asked what he did after work. Abbey explained that he had a second job at the Princess Road bus depot and that he was trying to save money to return home.

'Where is home?'

'Uganda.'

'Is that in the West Indies?'

'No, East Africa.'

'Really? You don't look African at all.'

Abbey beamed at the compliment.

'You don't have those big downturned lips, your eyes are not too close together and' – she felt his hair – 'your hair isn't wiry.' Then she went, breathless, 'Did you kill a lion to become a man?'

'No, we don't do that in Uganda.'

For a moment, as Heather walked away, Abbey wondered whether he should have lied, but he had never even seen a lion. Two weeks later, he bumped into her again. The other girls had walked on ahead and Abbey expected her to run and catch up with them, but she stopped and smiled.

'So where does Abbey from Uganda go on a night out?'

'At the Merchant Na—'

'The Merchant Navy? I've heard about it. Apparently, you blacks get up to all sorts there.' She prodded his chest playfully.

Rather than protest that nothing untoward happened at the Merchant Navy, Abbey just smiled. He held in each hand a bin full of cloth cuttings, thread and other couture rubbish. He had been on his way to the outside bin.

'I'd like to see the Merchant Navy. Would you show me?'

'Of course.'

Though they had agreed to meet that Friday night, Heather ignored him for the rest of the week. Abbey understood. Other girls would shun her if they found out she had fraternised with a black. Even then he began to doubt she had really meant it. He was therefore surprised to find Heather waiting outside the depot when he arrived for his shift that Friday. When she saw him, she motioned him to follow her. They went into a side corridor next to the depot. There, she told him that they would meet at the Merchant Navy entrance at 11.30 p.m., and disappeared.

He arrived at the Merchant Navy twenty minutes early and fretted. Suddenly the club seemed grubby, the people, especially their speech, coarse; look at that litter! Was that a whiff from the toilets at the entrance? He was sure that Heather would walk into the club, wrinkle her nose and walk out.

Heather was already excited when she arrived. She did not seem to notice anything amiss. Abbey was most attentive, buying her drinks he would never dream of wasting his savings on. The music was so loud, the hall so crowded, smoke everywhere, and Abbey was tense. It was not until Heather shouted above the music, 'This is fun,' that Abbey relaxed. They danced until Nelson turned off the music and forced the crowds out after 2 a.m. Abbey was wondering *what now?* – he had not expected Heather to stay this long – when she suggested that they go to the social centre on Wilbraham Road. Someone she knew was having a bash there. It was not a long walk. Then they arrived in a different world. White women with black men, mostly black Americans (who could not get over the fact that there was no segregation in Britain) and African students. Though there was a hall, the party was outdoors in the gardens. There was a lot of American alcohol as well. 'It's from the American air base,' Heather whispered.

Then she introduced him to her friends. One of them remarked, 'So, this is Heather's African.'

'Are you a prince?' another woman asked. Before Abbey answered, the woman turned to Heather and said, 'Most of these fellows claim to be princes.'

Abbey denied being a prince even though his grandfather was Ssekabaka Mwanga. He denied it because once he had heard a shine girl call her African father, who claimed to be a prince, a liar. Abbey had to stop himself from spitting in her face because how would she know that, on the one hand, princes in Africa tended to end up fugitives in Europe fleeing from assassination, and on the other, they were privileged to travel abroad? He had developed an unhealthy hate for shine people who seemed to hate the black in them, who presumed to be superior because of the whiteness in them.

He noticed that there were neither black nor shine girls at the party. The white men present were waiters, but Abbey did not ask why. A door to an exclusive world of white women going with black men had opened to him and he was going to enjoy it, however ephemeral. At the Merchant Navy, when people saw him with Heather, they had looked at him with concerned surprise, others with hurt astonishment as if it was an act of betrayal. Here, no one cared. They danced until six in the morning, when Heather caught the early bus back home.

The following weekend she suggested they go to the Mayfair. Abbey asked how she knew about black people's clubs.

'Girls say the most exciting things about black people's clubs. You must take me to the Cotton Club and Frascati.' They even went to Crown Kathy on Oldham Street, the only pub which admitted blacks.

When Kwei found out about Heather, he warned Abbey that for a seaman saving to return home, going out with a woman was an expensive venture. And for timid Abbey a white woman would devour him like mashed potatoes.

'It's a story to tell though, when I return home.'

'If you return.'

Abbey and Heather went out another three weekends. When he was with her, everyone noticed him. They glanced at her and then at him. When white men glared at him Abbey felt alive. When Heather said, 'You're painfully tall', he walked at his full height. Once an old white man spat in Heather's face and Abbey didn't know what to do. He pretended not to see when white people gave Heather dirty looks. Some black men glanced at him with a *so you're like that* look. But it was black women, even shine girls, who gave him the withering looks reserved for war deserters.

One time, Berry came to them on the dance floor. He was polite to Heather but turned to Abbey and said, 'I hope you don't have an Othello complex!'

'What's Othello?'

Heather went red and Berry smiled. 'Never mind, Abbey: be true.'

Abbey felt that black folk were being unfair. Black women were few; they were either circled or good churchgoing daughters. Shine girls would never look at an African man.

African girls who came to study had contempt for African men who lived in England. If you asked them out they said, 'I am sorry but I don't wish to be domiciled', meaning they would never go with a man paid as much as a white woman. 'I'll be *returning home* soon after my course', meaning to men who are not eunuched. But when you touched a white woman then it was betrayal.

One Friday, after close-down at the Merchant Navy, rather than go partying elsewhere as they normally did, Heather said she was tired and wanted to lie down. As she could not go home – it was past two in the morning – she asked Abbey to take her to his flat. Abbey could not believe his ears. Firstly, people said Africans stink: hadn't Heather heard? Secondly, what if Kwei had splashed out again and their room stunk of cow foot?

It was too late, because they were walking past Greenheys Police Station, towards his home. Mercifully, the room was clean and tidy. He had been ready to spend his savings on a hotel room if he saw Heather wrinkling her nose. She seemed too tired to notice that the room was bare save for the bed. He offered her their bed while he slept on the mattress on the floor. But after a while, Heather asked him to get in bed with her and hold her.

When he told Kwei about it the following day, Kwei prophesied, 'You're on the hook, Abbey: forget home.'

Abbey started looking forward to Fridays. At work, it started to hurt when Heather ignored him.

They had been seeing each other for five months when Heather stopped coming to work. Unfortunately, Abbey could not ask anyone why. Two months later, when he had decided that she had started her course in Scotland, she turned up at his house. It was a different Heather. She was fearful and angry. Abbey was confused. Heather needed a room to stay but would pay her own rent. She did not want him to look after her but she needed him to go to the shops for her. Yes, he was responsible for her condition but she was giving up the child for adoption. She cried a lot and blamed him for the loss of her job and course. Abbey insisted that as long as she carried his child he would come to see her. Sometimes he knocked on her door but she did not open up. Abbey was proud he was going to be a father, moreover to a shine child! Often, he laughed when she shouted at him. Until she handed his son up for adoption.

It was by chance that he found out when Heather went to have the baby. Her landlady told him that she had been taken to St Mary's Hospital the day before. When Abbey got to hospital, Heather was about to be discharged. The baby had been taken.

He made a scene. Who gives their child away to strangers? She did not even breastfeed him? What kind of woman does that? To get rid of him, the hospital gave him the name of the home the baby had been placed in. They told him and Heather to go and sort it out there. Before they left hospital, Abbey demanded to have his name put on the child's birth certificate. Heather disappeared.

*

The following week, when Abbey and Kwei arrived at the children's home in Macclesfield the matron pretended not to see them. This made Abbey more nervous but Kwei went up to her and said, 'We've come to see our son.'

'Who is *your* son?'

'Heather Newton's son; we call him Moses.'

'You're not his father.'

'In our culture, my brother's son is my son.'

'That child's process is complete. A nice couple have finalised the adoption process. They'll give him the life he deserves.'

'Ah?' Abbey, who had left Kwei to do the talking, gasped. 'But you say he's sleeping every time I come. Why lie?'

'His mother wanted him adopted. She never identified you as the father. We have her name on the records but we don't have yours.'

'Which mother, the woman who would not put him on her breast?'

'Show her a copy of the birth documents they gave you at the hospital, show her.'

The woman looked at them and shook her head. 'We never saw that one. We were never told about a father. Why didn't you come with the mother to confirm you're who you say?'

'She's hiding. Besides, why would I want a child that's not mine?'

'We're doing what is best for the child.'

'Ooh, you see them, Kwei? You see how they take people's children just like that?'

'I am only following instructions. In this country, it's brave and selfless to give up a child to people who will love him and meet his needs.'

'Brave? In my country, a parent will die first before they give up a child to strangers.'

'Bring his records. We need to see his records first.' Kwei banged the desk. 'Bring them here now.'

'You need to calm down, the both of you! I can't listen to—'

'Calm down, calm down, would you calm down when you're losing your child?'

'I'll bring the records,' the woman said, 'but you need to calm down.'

When she left the room Kwei whispered, 'They don't know how to deal with us when we're angry. We frighten them. But if you stand there speaking softly like they tell you how, then they've got you.'

The woman returned with a blue folder. ADOPTED was stamped across the cover. Abbey and Kwei stared in disbelief.

'He's been taken?'

'How would you look after him: are you married?'

'Why didn't you tell me, hmm? Why didn't you tell me every time I came?'

'He was only taken this morn—'

'Thieves, oh, but these people are thieves! They don't just steal kingdoms, they steal children too.'

'We want our child back.'

'There's nothing I can do, Mr Baker.'

Now Abbey broke down. 'How can I go home, Kwei, how can I leave my child here?'

Even the woman softened. 'Look, I am really sorry, but in this country—'

'Don't tell me about this country, you're not good people. You don't care who you hurt, you're selfish. You're—'

'We were thinking about the child, which obviously you have not!'

'Abbey,' Kwei started quietly. 'Write, write down everything. Our blood is strong, Moses will come looking.' He turned to the woman. 'You've made Moses an anonymous child, you'll take that to your grave.'

Abbey picked up a pen and opened the file. First, he wrote the child's name, *Moses Bamutwala Jjuuko*. Under FATHER, he wrote, *Ssuuna Jjunju*. In brackets, he wrote, *son of Mutikka Jjuuko of Kawempe, Kyadondo, Uganda*. He paused for a second and then he signed with the flourish of a man creating his self-worth on a piece of paper. He put the pen down and walked out. He heard Kwei say, 'I'll write down Uncle Kwei's contacts as well', but Abbey did not stop.

MANCHESTER HAPPENED

I watch my parents walk up to the scanners, their wheel-on luggage trailing. They stop and scan their boarding passes then stare into the red light of the retina readers. I am thinking I should have gone with them and helped, when the barriers open simultaneously and they spill into the security section. Dad – we call him Mzei – walks down the gangway as if the police might stop him and say *Where do you think you are going, Mzei?* He's in such a hurry to go home, he's refused to wait for an appointment to see the GP for a second opinion. Behind him, Mum – we call her Kizei – hobbles side-to-side the way big mamas who have been sniffy about exercising do. When her husband said no to waiting, she said, 'Leave your father alone, we have doctors in Uganda.' I step out of the way for other passengers streaming to the scanners and stand by the entrance to watch my parents go through Security. Neither is checked. They pick up their luggage and turn. Kizei waves like *I told you I would get my man back.* But

Mzei's wave is impatient: *Are you still standing there? Go home and get some sleep.* They turn and walk out of view.

Instead of sleeping, my mind flies back past this morning at the airport, past yesterday. I let it wander; it might find sleep along the way. It hurtles past Mzei pushing Nnalongo and the hospital/police palaver; past the birth of my daughter, Mulungi; past Aryan, my ex; past meeting Nnalongo. When it goes past my arrival in London in November 1988, to Ssalongo Bemba's death in Uganda, I hold my breath. Nothing good comes from delving so far back into the past. I turn on my side and curl up. I close my eyes like I've heard sleep coming, but my mind won't rest. It returns to the recent events during Mzei's visit to reconcile me with my sister Katassi.

Mzei wasted his time coming to Britain. I don't know how many times he has tried to make us sisters again. First, he talked to us separately, spouting that traditional nonsense of *Siblings are gourds: no matter how hard they knock each other they never break.* Then he rang to say, 'Katassi is going to call you to apologise – be nice.' That happened three times, but no call came. Then he invited us to go home. I travelled, Katassi didn't. The second time he begged, 'Come, Nnambassa: you're the eldest, show you're willing to reconcile, Katassi has assured me she's coming for Christmas.' No Katassi came. This final time he said, 'I am not going to die until you girls settle your differences', as if his cancer cared. 'If Katassi will not come home, I'll come to Britain.' It was a veiled threat, but neither Katassi nor I offered to travel to Uganda. Then he rang: 'I've bought the ticket.' He was sure that as soon as we saw his sick old self we would forget our feud and hug so he could die happily. I am susceptible to that kind of manipulation because I grew up with rebukes like *And you, Nnambassa, the eldest? You should know better, should show an example to the younger ones.* Katassi grew up watching me take the blame. That shit does not work on her.

Until Mzei pushed Nnalongo, I didn't know who Nnalongo really was. I mean, I knew her, I once lived with her, but I didn't know her roots in Uganda, or who she was before she came to Britain. Nnalongo is one of those people who bring Uganda with them to Britain. We call her house half-Luwero because it's littered with Ugandan paraphernalia – straw mats, masks with elongated faces, every ethnic basket from home, batiks, gourds and carvings. She eats Ugandan only. No speaking English in her house. But mostly it is that squeaky, monotonous kadongo kamu country music she plays. Her kadongo kamu, from the 1980s and 1990s, conjures home, but it is the woman-bashing Uganda. It decries the prostitutes of Kampala – who actually were city women – who couldn't cook, were near-naked, ate men's money but yielded nothing. It rebuked ugly women, old women, skinny women, dry-skinned women and even the dusty women of the slums. To me, that kadongo kamu was the cutting whip of Ganda patriarchy: why would Nnalongo lash herself with it in Britain?

Nnalongo, in her sixties, is one of the oldest members of the community. You can't go asking elderly people who they are. They might say things like *Where does my background touch you?* If they choose to tell you things about themselves, they tell you. If they don't, they don't. Nnalongo did not share her background with me, despite our mother–daughter relationship. Yet she's your traditional mother hen. If she sees young girls who have just arrived from home going astray, she says, *Mwana wange, don't do that, do this.* Or, *Watch the people you keep company with. Make sure they'll help you develop.* And if Manchester becomes too prohibitive and she feels you're worth her while, Nnalongo offers, *Move into my house, I have a spare bedroom. Save money and when you're steady on your feet, try again.* Afterwards, Nnalongo shrugs, *Don't bother thanking me, this country is not ours, we all help each other.*

But I've never heard Nnalongo say *I am going home to visit,* never heard her sigh about her twins or being wistful about being away from her family. The only sign of homesickness is her half-Luwero house. Yet she regularly visits the US. Another thing – you'll not take Nnalongo's photo. You whip out your phone or camera, she ducks. Apparently, Islam does not encourage taking photos. Yet at night beer is her duvet. She says her sleep needs a shove to come. I accepted these inconsistencies as human contradictions; we're all full of them.

In the early 1980s, Mzei did a two-year MA course at the London School of Economics through those British Council scholarships. Typically, he scrimped his upkeep money, joined a friend called Ssalongo Bemba in Peckham and worked while he studied. While there, he saw Ugandan teenagers arrive in Britain to work and study. These sixteen-, seventeen-, eighteen-year-olds were put on a plane with nothing more than *Aunt so-and-so will pick you up at the airport. Life will be tough at first, but since when has life been easy for us?* They arrived, set themselves up to work, studied and thrived. Apparently they became hardy, responsible and grew in character. With British degrees, the world belonged to them.

Mzei returned home excited and we all bought into it. When Mzei confirmed his plans for me to leave soon after my O levels, I could not wait. Those were the heady 1980s. Our parents, after the horrors of the 1970s, were looking overseas for the future of their children. Born in the 1940s and 1950s, they came from austere backgrounds. Then the 1970s had so lashed the middle classes that parents were wary of bringing up children entirely middle class. Pampered, spoilt and soft, we would be helpless in tough times. In any case, because of the incessant warring, wealth in Uganda was ephemeral – today you're cruising in a Mercedes, tomorrow you're hawking roast groundnuts. This made the middle class wobbly. Besides, what could be worse than Uganda fresh out of Idi Amin, the subsequent coups and now the new disease? And so, to see real life, to learn lessons, to grow hardy, to escape the dungeon that was Uganda, but most of all to get the coveted British degrees and grab that bright future, we were sent to Britain. It was at once a sacrifice and a privilege.

It was the wrong decade to send sixteen-year-olds unaccompanied to Britain. On the one hand, you had a Britain imploding under Thatcher – women's lib, gay rights, racial relations and the working class were rioting. On the other, you had a growing Ugandan community in London swelled by former regime politicians, embezzlers and wealthy widows and widowers of the new disease coming to Britain, where drugs trials needed guinea pigs. It was destination London because Britain was supposedly familiar – former colonial masters had set up the systems in Uganda to mirror systems in Britain. In school, we not only studied British history and geography but its literature. What could be difficult?

But 1988 London to sixteen-year-old me, newly arrived from Kampala, was Mabira Forest in the night. Like most middle-class children, I had been to boarding schools most of my life. When I came home, there was a maid, a gardener and I was chauffeured everywhere. My biggest concerns were my looks and public opinion. Now I was in a dense metropolis asking *What is NI?...Who is a GP? Why register with one?... Should I throw myself away, invent a new self and hand it in as an asylum seeker?*

The first thing I was told when I arrived was *You don't go gushing at someone just because you've heard them speak Luganda.* Ugandans would look at you in a *Mpozi, which car boot brought you here* way. There was distrust and intrigue within the community. You had to be careful who you sought to network with on jobs, housing and visa issues. You had to be careful how much of yourself you put out there. A lot of people hid from fellow Ugandans. A lot of people in public were hidden. Rumours were like rumours.

As for physical London, someone kind handed you the *London A–Z* booklet and said *Go.* In those first few months,

I would get lost and burst into tears. Then I would soothe myself: *Nnambassa mukwano, stop crying. Now try again.* I had no option but to love myself.

Don't start me on the Tube.

Take District Line, not southbound, northbound – which had nothing to do with the Northern Line – *Kwata Jubilee Line, leave Victoria Line, Vva ku Hammersmith – don't you hear English?* The first time I was like *Line? What line? I don't see any queues here.* Heh heh, let me laugh now because I could not laugh then. In moments of great distress English can sound Greek.

As for getting jobs, with a name like Nnambassa the first interview was on the phone to weed out nightmarish accents. If the interviewer started saying *I didn't catch what you said... can you spell that word for me please,* you knew you'd failed. So you swallowed your pride and applied to a nursing home. Meanwhile, budget the little money you have – bills, rent, transport. Don't worry about food, bread is cheap. Visa has expired? Stay well clear of the police – even if you're attacked. Exams are coming – ask for leave to prepare for them. In case you have forgotten, I was a sixteen-year-old from Kampala.

Ugandans who had arrived earlier – those who knew the system and how to make it work for them – preyed on the alone and frightened. Teenage girls moved in with men they would never look at twice at home. Boys serviced women older than their mothers. HIV acquired legs. Some teenagers struggled and got hooked on drugs. Some ended up among the homeless, some were sectioned in mental health facilities, some died with no one to cry for them. Girls turned tricks because some aunts never came to the airport to pick them up. Some aunts picked you up grudgingly and then proceeded to make your life so miserable you moved out of their homes as soon as you could. Even aunts who were happy to see you got fed up within six months. Then there was the ruthless aunt who picked you up, found you a job, registered you in her name, her National Insurance number and bank account. You worked your fingers to the bone but at the end of the month your salary was paid into her account. When you asked for your money she'd say, *Don't you eat, or do you imagine the bills pay themselves?* Sometimes the aunt introduced you to a man and said *You're lucky he's interested in you. Why don't you go and live with him? He has the right documents, maybe he'll marry you.* But why would he marry you when the following year some reckless parents would send another bunch of hapless daughters and he needed to sample them?

And yet we kept quiet when we returned home to visit – draped in high fashion, flashing cash and British accents. Nothing scared us like going back home looking like a failure. Being laughed at – *Did you see her? London scotched her!* Besides, the brave ones who tried to talk about it were accused of scaremongering: *If Britain is as harsh as you say, why don't you come back home?*

What do you say to that? That starting all over again in Uganda is scary? That you're saving to return but it may never happen? After all, there are those that made it, legitimately or otherwise. So we killed ourselves working, ensnared ourselves in debt so we could masquerade when we came home and perform success and perpetuate the dream. But inside? Inside we were dying.

Of course, there were savvy parents who knew the reality. The ultra-rich who came with their children, set them up in accommodation or paid the aunts. Parents who could afford to come regularly to see their children, who sent tickets for Christmas holidays because their children were on student visas. My parents were not among them. My aunt in London was no relation at all. She felt infringed upon. When I complained about the hardships, Mzei said, 'Look, Nnambassa, who is not suffering?'

That first year in London I survived on adrenaline. I retain some of that jumpiness. Every time I hear a siren – police or ambulance, it does not matter – I sweat. Then I say to my irritable bowels *Don't be silly!* Sometimes I look at Mulungi, my daughter, how she takes everything for granted, her entitlement to Britain, how my Ugandanness embarrasses her, her indifference to Uganda, and wonder whether to tell her the brutal truth.

I was lucky.

I don't know why Nnalongo came to London that day. I met her on a bus in Tottenham. She was looking for Uganda Waragi gin. At first, she spoke to me in faltering English. Her accent gave her away and I replied in Luganda. She almost died with relief. Then she went all native on me, *yii my child*, hugging, gesturing, laughing kiganda like we were in a kamunye taxi back home. She had met other Ugandans who had no patience with her old mama stance. I took her to Seven Sisters, where a shop stocked Uganda Waragi.

Along the way we got talking. She said, 'I don't know what is wrong with London. The first thing people do when they arrive in London is strip themselves of their humanity. But Manchester is not like this; people are human.' Then she offered, 'If London ever gets too much, come to Manchester. I'll help you settle in.' I was so grateful, I took her back to Victoria Coach Station to see her off back to Manchester.

When I came to Manchester, Nnalongo lived in Salford. Her main job was with Sodexo Cleaning Services, but she was bank staff for Apex Cleaners and had a few under-the-table jobs cleaning people's homes. The British still looked down on certain jobs – factory work, farm work, cleaning, nursing homes, working with people with learning disabilities. As long as you had a National Insurance number, no one asked to see your visa. Nnalongo enrolled me with Sodexo and we cleaned hospitals, schools, colleges and universities. We worked in unison like termites. I threw away all that Uganda had taught me socially and culturally and allowed Britain to realign me.

Things were going so well I moved out of Nnalongo's into a flat of my own and I started to buy new clothes from Peacocks instead of second-hand ones from charity shops. Guess what Mzei did when he heard? He sent my sister Katassi to live with me.

Katassi was fourteen years old; she could not get a job and contribute to the bills. That was 1993. I had been in Britain just over four years and to Mzei I had had enough time to

Jennifer Nansubuga Makumbi

establish myself. I tried to explain that it was unfair but Mzei thought I was being selfish: 'Give your sister the chance we gave you.' Apparently Katassi had been dreaming of joining me for the last two years. 'Besides,' he added, 'it's not good for you to be on your own in a foreign country.'

Katassi arrived full of the *I am going to Britain where you sweep money off streets* kind of bullshit. She had this unrealistic image of white people as generous, infinitely obliging, friendly and altruistic. She had grown up with the white figure conflated with images of a blond, blue-eyed Christ – sending money, arriving in Uganda to do charity work in hospitals and schools, starting projects, aid, adopting children, eyes melting at poverty – and took it at face value. She was unprepared for that disgusted gaze that questioned your humanity, for white people sleeping rough in London, for white beggars on the streets (how can they give us aid when their own people are begging?), for the rough area we lived in in Salford, for burglars (why would white people steal from us?), for the fact that she was going to be poorer in Britain than she had been at home. Her African heart must have told her that if white people can suffer in their own country, she was in trouble.

Within two weeks of starting school, Katassi froze. I mean zombie-like. Then, and I don't know when it happened, she started to smoulder. Do you know how the male turkey – I mean ssekkokko – puffs itself up and you hear small, sudden bursts of air like it has puffed itself too much? For three months Katassi walked around like that. Then she exploded and became this vicious, twisted creature who snarled. One moment she was saying racist things about white people, the

72

next she was saying vile things about black people. I became that nigger of a sister, the bitch. She wrestled with her own Africanness. I could see her pain and confusion but there was nothing I could do. It is a phase every new arrival from home goes through out here. The more hopes you have in Britain, the more arrogant and inadvisable you are, the bitterer the pain. It's like withdrawal symptoms from drugs. You suffer alone. In this phase, many teenagers denied ever having been on the African continent. They faked British accents, changed names and became British-born. I knew a Jjuuko who turned Jukkson and spoke like a Jamaican. On the other hand, you had grown-ups, especially intellectual types, who reacted by becoming pan-African fundamentalists. I mean aggressively African, in-your-face African. They dropped their Christian names like sin, turned away from things European the way newly saved Christians turn from heathenry. They wore the continent on their body as if not to be mistaken for anything else. I tell you, this transitional shit can be so bad it kills families. I had friends, a sister and a brother, whose parents had left them home in Uganda for twelve years. In the meantime, the parents gave birth to three other children while in Britain. When the family reunited in London, the older kids were strangers. The parents did not speak Luganda any more. The problem was not just that my friends lived with a strange family, but that the parents treated the British-born siblings as special. They got away with things the older kids would never have dreamt of in Uganda at the same age. They not only babysat their British siblings, but the siblings treated them as badly as their parents. My friends felt so unwanted they ran away and Social Services were involved. The last I heard they were asking to divorce their family entirely.

There is a belief out here that if your relationship with the person who received you in Britain survives this phase then it is for forever. It does not matter whether you're siblings, lovers, spouses, parents, children or friends, this phase kills relationships. Often you hear people say *he or she received me when I first came. I don't know where I would be without them.* You forever love that person unless you are an arsehole.

Katassi was a contradiction, like multiple personalities. The more I tried to help the more she lashed out. In her quest to fit in quickly, she dressed as if shock value epitomised Britishness. She acted out the way she saw teenagers do on soap operas. Do you know what a forced Mancunian accent with Ugandan inflections sounds like? I think the harder she tried to sound and act like them, the more the kids at school rejected her. It happened to me. She then brought all the pain from school home to me. She would not lift a finger to do chores. She wanted designer gear. I bought winter woollies from charity shops for her and she was like, *E mivumba? I am not wearing second-hand clothes in Britain.* And by the way, she needed to go to France with her friends in summer. I was the obstacle to her happiness – strict, stingy, mean and patronising. Apparently, I was terrible to her because we did not share a mother.

Looking back now, it was the moment she said it out loud that our kinship died.

Katassi's mother, Kizei, *is* Mum. Mine died in childbirth. We don't talk about it. Kizei brought me up without drama. I've never felt that stepmother vibe. And yet here was Katassi, who I was looking after, reminding me? That day, I rang Kizei and cried down the phone about Katassi reminding me of my aloneness.

Nnalongo stepped in. She said, 'Bring Katassi to me, you're too young to look after her.'

Katassi packed all her bullshit and took it to Nnalongo's half-Luwero house. She came and went in Nnalongo's house without a word. When Nnalongo told her off, Katassi said, 'You invited me to your house: deal with it.' A few months later, Nnalongo dealt with it when Katassi reminded her, 'This is Britain: children have rights. I don't have to do what you say.' Nnalongo said, 'But you'll pack your bags and leave my house.'

When I arrived at Nnalongo's, I asked, 'Katassi, what happened to you? Why are you like this?' She said, 'Manchester, babe, Manchester happened. You're no longer you, why should I be me?' And then I saw her, asaliita nyini, towards my car with her bags. I said, 'Where do you think you're going? Not to mine.' I was not going to watch myself fall mad because of her. I drove her to the nearest bed and breakfast and showed her how to get in touch with Social Services.

Boy, did Katassi celebrate when Social Services found her a place at a hostel in Moss Side. When we dropped her bags off, she went berserk: 'Good riddance to the hag and the nigger...Yo jaak shit...Yo twats...Yo nathin...wankaz!' White residents turned puce at the racial slurs, black residents bristled. When social workers started talking of sectioning her, I switched to Luganda, I said, 'Katassi, you better pack it in right now because these people have no religion! They're planning to take you to the Butabika of Britain.'

She fell silent. Every Ugandan knows Butabika Mental Hospital will sober the worst mental illness. That day I rang Mzei and said, 'Come and take Katassi back home, Social Services are no place for her,' do you know what he said? 'As long as they feed her and tell her to go to school, she'll be alright.' He would keep ringing the hostel to make sure everything was okay. In the subsequent calls, Mzei said that everyone at the hostel sang Katassi's praises. She had settled down, become a model resident, model student. I guess without me to come home to and scapegoat, Britain whipped her into shape. Or her transition was complete. Sadly, I missed telling her *Now you know what people mean when they say I did not know I was African until I came to the West.*

Half a year later, when Nnalongo said that Katassi had rung wanting to talk, I said, 'You keep mothering her, I don't want to know.' Luckily, I had moved to a new house. Never heard from Katassi again.

Eight years later – was it 2001 or 2002? – someone asked me, 'Yii, but Nnambassa, where were you?' I said, 'What do you mean?' She said, 'We didn't see you at your sister's graduation, why can't you forgive? It looked bad you not being there.' Apparently Katassi did nursing. My parents never mentioned it. Perhaps they had been expecting engineering – you know what Ugandan middle-class parents are like. I looked to the gods and said *Dunda, you've shepherded her.* Katassi had arrived safely.

★

The scam story is as old as the émigré story, but the impatience of people back home with diasporic victims, defrauded by family at home, is alarming. If it happens to you, just keep quiet. People at home will laugh in your face and call you stupid. Some say it's because at home they imagine we have it easy out here. Others claim it's resentment; we left instead of staying to build the nation.

That was the attitude that met Ssalongo Bemba, the guy Mzei lived with in Peckham as he did his MA. Bemba returned home in 1987, a year before I came to Britain. He spent three weeks at our house, but I didn't know why until Kampala got wind of the story and splashed it in the papers. Nnalongo Bemba, his wife, had not only failed to pick him up at the airport, but she had locked him out of the family home. Public opinion took Nnalongo's side:

- *Ten years is too long for a wife to sit there, looking at herself. And what did he imagine kept her blood flowing?*
- *How would she know he was coming back?*
- *Even if he did, how many men come back, find their wives threadbare old, dump them and marry a young wife who rhymes with the new wealth?*
- *Is he the first to be scammed? Get over it.*
- *Let him go back and live his dream life.*

Do you know what Bemba did? He climbed onto the roof of the house his Nnalongo built with his migrant money and plunged. Kampala stopped laughing. And you know how the media at home does not hold back on graphic images.

SSALONGO KILLS HIMSELF AFTER BETRAYAL. Another claimed NNALONGO TURNS TWIN DAUGHTERS AGAINST FATHER. Stories from Britain started to trickle into the papers. Apparently, in all his ten years in Britain, they never saw Bemba with another woman. He worked three jobs. Without legal documents, he could not visit Uganda and return to Britain.

Because there were no ambulances at the time, it was Mzei who paid the police to get off their backsides to pick up Bemba's body and take it to Mulago Hospital. But by then either Nnalongo Bemba and her lawyer boyfriend had fled the country or they had paid the police more money to be useless. It was Mzei who paid for Bemba's burial. Two days after his burial, the Bemba house was razed to the ground. It was the work of a bulldozer, but the villagers said they heard nothing all night. They speculated that someone did not want a cursed house standing in their village.

Bemba's story lingered as the papers looked for this and that angle, like sucking marrow from a bone. It came to light that Bemba had married his wife against his family's wishes, that she had married him for his money, that he had constantly been under pressure to sustain her love. When Uganda became too restricting moneywise, he went to Britain and promised to send for her. It did not happen because Bemba's status in Britain failed to become legal. Instead, he sent money. Along the way her love died. Some said she had always been a slut. Poor Bemba did not realise that he had lost his wife even though his family, his mother and siblings, warned him that Rebecca – that was his wife's name – was no longer missing him. She had been seen too happy, too often, in a certain lawyer's company. But why would Bemba believe them when they had been against the marriage right from the start? The more they told him, the more he resented them. Eventually he stopped talking to them entirely. So, when he returned and was locked out by his wife, his family crossed their arms and said *What do you want from us? We're the bad ones; go to your Nnalongo.*

It was against this background that Mzei met Nnalongo in Manchester, three weeks ago.

That day I cooked matooke, lumonde, off-layer chicken and fresh kanyebwa beans because Dad had brought a lot of food from home. I invited Nnalongo: Mzei wanted to thank her for looking after us. I had sent Mulungi over to Aryan because I needed her bedroom for Mzei. Mzei rang Katassi to come to talk. She said she was coming. Even I believed her this time. After all, Mzei had come all the way from home to reconcile us and he was dying. It was going to be intimate – me, Mzei, Katassi and Nnalongo.

I did not see it happen. Nnalongo arrived; I opened the door and took her raincoat. As I hung it up, she walked into the lounge. I heard a shriek and something shattered. I rushed in, Nnalongo lay on the floor, the glass coffee table shattered. Mzei, wild-eyed with fear, said, 'I only pushed her away, she tried to hug me, I only pushed her away!'

Amidst my calling the ambulance, telling them, 'She's dead, she's dead', and Mzei trying to explain to me, 'She killed him, mukazi mutemu, I didn't mean to push her too hard', I realised who Nnalongo the killer was. But with the police's arrival and questioning of us and the paramedics and Mzei's delirium, there was no time to be shocked.

I asked Mzei for Katassi's number and called her. Her phone rang for a while, but there was no answer. Meanwhile, I wondered who to follow in my car – Nnalongo in the ambulance, who was not dead after all and being taken to hospital, or Mzei being taken to the police station? I rang Katassi again; it went straight to voicemail. I decided to go with Mzei. I'd be of more use to him than to Nnalongo.

When we stepped outside my house, I counted at least five police cars, emergency lights flashing, interviewing our neighbours. I imagined them thinking, *Black people and violence.*

Sometimes events in Britain fail to translate into Luganda. Kizei kept asking, 'Did you say hospital or jail? You mean cancer has gone to his head?' I told her to talk to my siblings, they would make sense of things, but she asked how they would make sense when they were in Uganda. In the end she said, 'If your father is in police custody instead of hospital, then I am coming.' I said that the money she would blow on the visa application and ticket could be used for legal fees. She asked me if it was my money she was wasting. Meanwhile, Katassi had no idea that her Muzei was blinking behind bars and Kizei was coming. Our siblings at home said her phone was still switched off.

The only time you wish the British High Commission to deny someone a visa, they go and give it to her. Kizei arrived in Manchester with this sense of *Now that I am here everything is going to be alright.* But because Mzei had confessed to pushing Nnalongo, he was held in custody. The first time I visited him in jail, we looked at each other – me failing to deflate the sense of mortification in the air, him searching for redemption in my eyes. Then I realised that I could hug him and make small talk and show I was not ashamed of him. Afterwards, we sat down, his clasped hands digging between his legs, my arms crossed. Silence was tenacious. I said, 'It's cool and silent in here', like I envied him.

But he asked, 'Has Nnalongo returned to consciousness?' I shook my head and silence rolled in again. When he asked about people at home, I said his wife was coming. He perked up.

'She is?' As if Mum was the only thing he had got right in his life.

'I could not convince her otherwise.'

He grabbed me in a constricting hug and cried the tears of an old man. He cried the way you should never hear your old man cry. I remember thinking, where is cancer pain when you need it? Mzei needed another kind of pain, one he was not responsible for, to forget this one. When he let me go, I said, 'British weather is mean; the last three days have been hot and sunny.'

He wiped his tears. 'There is enough sunshine back home.' He did not ask about Katassi.

★

Nnalongo regained consciousness as if she had only fallen asleep. That day, we spoke at length without talking at all. She would not meet my eyes.

I told her the Ugandan community did not know what had happened yet. 'Do you want me to inform them?'

'No need,' she said. 'People have things they keep to themselves.'

'Anyone you need me to get in touch with back home or in the US?'

'Don't worry about that. Take my house keys' – she reached for her handbag, rummaged and removed a bunch – 'and check that everything is fine. Turn on the lights when it gets dark and turn them off at bedtime.'

But the facts – that Mzei had almost killed her, that she was Nnalongo Bemba, that Ssalongo Bemba had committed suicide in desperation, that she was not Muslim – sat right there on her hospital bed swinging their legs.

Just before Nnalongo was discharged from hospital, Kizei arrived. From the airport, we took her bags back to my house. Then, as if her legs were not as swollen as her bags, she said, 'Take me to see my one.' Mzei received her like the Second Coming – on his knees, holding out his hands. I stepped away because I am not used to them displaying their aged love. On our way back, Kizei asked to see Nnalongo. I said I had to ask Nnalongo first.

'What are you waiting for? Go and ask her.'

I told her the visiting hours were over. They were not. But I had to stop her. I took her home; she had a shower and put her feet up. Then she picked up the phone, called Katassi and told her a few horrors which would befall her if her father died with this anguish on his heart. The following day, when I asked Nnalongo whether she was happy to see my mother, she looked at me as if I was dumb.

'You mean she made this horrible journey too?'

I nodded.

'Of course, bring her; how can you ask?'

Kizei had a few tricks up her sleeve. As we came to Nnalongo's bed, she turned on the waterworks – like Nnalongo was dying and we were in Mulago Hospital. Nnalongo opened her arms and turned to soothing my mother: 'No need to cry, Maama Nnambassa! I am alright, aren't I? These things happen, we all make mistakes.' I drew the screen around them. But then Nnalongo too was overcome and they cried. Me, I was just dying of what we call 'African parents' in Britain. When they stopped, Nnalongo said, 'Can you imagine, this child asked me whether I would mind seeing you?' Kizei shook her head in despair: 'That's what happens when they live too long in these countries.'

Now Kizei looked at Nnalongo and asked, 'Tell me the truth: down inside yourself, how do you feel?'

Nnalongo flashed a smile. 'When you look at me, how do you see me?'

'Like every day England makes you younger!'

'How? When you're the one that looks like Nnambassa's sister. Tell me about the children.'

I asked if either wanted a hot drink. They looked at me in a *you mean you interrupted us for that nonsense?* way.

I told them I was going to the restaurant and walked out of there.

To the police Nnalongo denied everything. *Who said he pushed me...Don't listen to Mzei. He has cancer; it has got to his head...That Nnambassa was in the corridor when it happened. She didn't see anything...I am telling you it was an accident. Coerced? What do you call me? A child? Tsk, coerced indeed.* That's how Nnalongo talked to the police.

I did not witness the awkwardness of Kizei and Mzei visiting Nnalongo. Katassi was scheduled to see them and Nnalongo in hospital anyway. I could not go along in case Katassi turned her shame into anger against me again. I dropped Muzei and Kizei off at Manchester Royal Infirmary – Kizei knew her way to Nnalongo's ward now – and drove to Nnalongo's house to turn on the lights.

Because it was still daylight, I went into her bedroom to open the window and let natural light in. It was silent, like I was trespassing. I walked across the room, drew back the curtains and opened the window. Then I saw the pictures. For some reason, Nnalongo had recently filled the walls with her wedding and family pictures. I walked to a large wedding portrait. Nnalongo sat on the chair, staring into the camera. She was ridiculously skinny. A great beauty. No sign that she would 'kill' the handsome man standing behind her, both his hands on her shoulders. He was happy hereafter. It was an Afro Studio collection of the seventies, staged with fake backgrounds. I turned to one with the bride's and groom's families flanking them. Bemba's family didn't look like they would abandon him. Then there was a funny one. Nnalongo had put on some weight. She was dressed in one of those old-fashioned maxi dresses with frills everywhere. She and Bemba sat on chairs, fake bookshelves behind them, a tiered flower stand, with plastic flowers, on the side. They held the twins on their laps. The children looked nine, ten months old. One of those poses where children refuse to play along. One twin's head was thrown back in a mighty howl. The other rubbed her eyes searching for tears. Ssalongo and Nnalongo were laughing when the picture was taken. A chill swept over my arms. You don't forget a moment like that. I stopped looking at the pictures and walked back to close the window and get out of there. On the floor was a kakayi, one of the scarves Nnalongo used to cover her head with as a Muslim. I picked it up, folded it and put it on the bed. I closed the window, drew the curtains and tiptoed out of the room.

THE NOD

When I arrived at the party the guests were so natural around me I forgot myself because I didn't see myself in their eyes. I was just another person. It's true we see ourselves in the eyes that look at us. I didn't realise this until I came to Britain. When they look at you, people's eyes are mirrors. The problem is you're always looking at yourself.

Out here, especially when you've just come from your home country, whenever you arrive in an unfamiliar place, your eyes can't help scanning the guests, the crowd, the seminar group for someone like you. It's a reflex. I guess we do it because there's warmth in numbers. Your way of being, your behaviour on that occasion, won't carry the burden of representing your kind.

Once you've identified someone, you wait to catch their eye. In most cases, when you do, you smile or nod. Sometimes, however, you catch an eye that panics *Oh no, not one of you*, or one that flashes *Fuck off*. Some will avoid catching your eye intentionally and stay well clear of you. In most cases there is a flicker, an acknowledgement of *I'm glad you're here too*. Someone gave this acknowledgement a name; it's called the nod.

But when I arrived at the party I was made so comfortable I didn't look around for others. And that's when things went wrong. You see, I didn't see her; I didn't give her the nod.

Looking back now, I suspect that even if I had I might not have identified her. I think she saw me arrive, tried to catch my eye but I glanced past her. She must have thought I was one of those *Fuck off* types. And in terms of slights within the nation, that's one of the worst. They'll call you Oreo. Unfortunately for me, she was not the kind of sista you blanked and got away with it.

The party was in one of those rich areas, somewhere in Maple, where children stop playing and stare as you walk past. And if you catch them at it, they smile *hello*. Nothing rude, just that they don't see people like you often. Even though I'd just arrived in the country and everywhere in England looked the same to me, from houses, to the roads, to the shops: were the builders lazy or just lacking in imagination? I could tell that this was an exclusive area, like Kololo, from the distances the houses shrunk from the road. They had such large compounds you would build a second house. Hedges grew untamed. (Out here, in the areas where we live, you let your hedge grow high, your neighbours complain to the council that it blocks the sun.) Along the way, I came to parts where the woods were so dense it felt like walking in Mabira Forest. That's how wealthy this area was.

When I arrived, Annabelle's family were waiting. You would think I was a long-lost cousin. Everyone knew my name; everyone had been waiting. 'Let me take your coat, Lucky...Did you have a good journey on the train?...Cup of tea, Lucky?...Autumn's getting nippy...Ah, British weather: it must be awful for you...You must miss the weather at home...Red or white wine?...Try this cake, Lucky...I love your dress...You didn't get lost, did you?...We were worried...'

But our traditional upbringing, I tell you: it can be treacherous in Britain. You know how, as a visitor, it's rude to say no to food, especially when someone brings it to you. I accepted everything the women brought me. 'Try this, Lucky...You're gonna love this meringue cake...piece of lasagne...That is quiche...This is elderflower; you must try it...' In the end, there were plates and plates and glasses around me. Don't misunderstand me, it was new food and I was eager to try it all, but I was worried that the numerous plates made me look gluttonous. This is why Ugandans in Britain will tell you *The British didn't give your culture a visa: leave it at home.*

Annabelle came to my rescue, 'Oh my God, Lucky: they're gonna feed you to death. Here' – she picked up the plates – 'come with me.' She walked me to the kitchen. 'Put all that food away and get yourself what you want.' She dumped the food on work surfaces and walked back to the garden, where her engagement party was being held. But I was still too Ugandan. As soon as she left the kitchen, I tossed the food away and tied the bin liner. Yes, wasting food is abominable, but I was not going to leave my rudeness displayed like that! What if the people who served it to me saw that I had rejected their food?

I was reaching for the chocolate cake when a voice from behind me said: 'You have such lovely skin.'

I glanced at her, smiled, *thank you*, and turned back to the chocolate cake.

'It must be all that sun in Africa: the weather in this country is not right for *our* skin.'

'Yes,' I agreed without looking at her. My eyes were so focused on the delicate job of balancing a slice of cake on a spatula towards my plate that I didn't register the words *our skin*. In fact, when the slice was safe on the plate, I added, 'My grandmother says that sweat is the best moisturiser', to reinforce the notion that the sun in Africa was indeed good for our skin.

Truth be told, it was a lie. It was not my grandmother, it was my mother. My mother is what they call New Age out here. But the word 'grandmother' gave it a *je ne sais quoi*; let's call it the weight of African wisdom. It's something I turn on sometimes in Britain especially when among the nation, to play up on the difference, you know, African age-old wisdom (often common sense) vs Western research (the silly one). My grandmother is a city girl. She swears by Yardley products – soaps, talcum powder, deodorant and perfume. When she strays from Yardley she goes Avon. She would be seriously offended if she found out that I had attributed what she calls my mother's madness to her.

Then I realised the woman had said *our skin* and stopped. I looked at her properly. My mind was frantic: is she a

Zimbabwean, South African or Namibian white? But white Africans would never say *our skin*. They'll say *our weather, our economies, our politics,* never *our skin*. What I did not realise was that she was watching. She saw every wave of my frantic thoughts in my eyes as I tried to place her. Then I began to see markers of the sub-Sahara in her. Her hair, though long and straight, was suspiciously thick, perhaps straightened. Her eyes were too dark. And there were signs of 'the pride of Africa' around her posterior. It had been there all along; I'd have realised, if I had looked past the colour of her skin. But it was a delicate situation: out here you can't essentialise. Besides, there are blacks who don't want you to focus on the sub-Saharan in them, some who are wrathful at the suggestion.

Then I saw her anger. The *How dare you search my body for my blackness,* the *So I am not black enough!* In that moment, we spoke with just our eyes – hers fiery with outrage, mine withering with mortification. Finally, when she relented and the glare in her eyes flickered to a shade of *okay, I'll let you off this time,* she smiled. 'Really,' she said in response to my 'grandmother's wisdom'.

I flashed a sista smile (I was wont to overdo the comradery now). 'Well, sweat is nature's moisturiser, people don't realise. It has a perfect pH and it moisturises the skin from within, softening both layers. These creams we buy only work on the surface: they don't even penetrate the top layer. Our skin needs to sweat regularly.'

By now, I had turned on that conspiratorial tone we use in the nation when we discuss aspects like our food (we don't eat anything out of a tin, you don't need to be told that you need fruit and vegetables, we cook from scratch), our health (watch out, we put on a lot of weight in winter; take vitamin D supplements for the bones; go home to the islands or the continent at least once a year to get proper sunshine and to eat proper food to rejuvenate the body. For some reason, British weight drops off when we go home no matter how much we eat), and products specific to our bodies, (skin, hair, jeans that fit our thighs but don't betray our butts when we sit down).

'I go to the sauna four days a week' – I was talking too much but could not stop myself – 'and drink a lot of water just to sweat. It keeps my skin well moisturised. Besides, I've not yet found the right moisturiser. I use Vaseline.'

That was true at the time. For some reason, the air in Britain made my skin so dry that moisturisers marked *For very dry skin* lasted only a few minutes and my skin was dry again. Parts of me were desiccated: feet, ankles, knees, elbows and hands. I resorted to applying cream, waiting a few minutes, applying again and then using Vaseline Petroleum Jelly to lock it in. It took me a while to discover the ethnic beauty shops in Hulme which had appropriate creams. I thus expected her to step in and recommend a few moisturisers. She did not.

She reached for the chocolate cake, cut a piece, turned around and leant against the work surface. I waited as she bit into the cake because I could see she was about to say something.

'I've always wondered which one of my parents was black.'

I put my cake down. She had me by the scruff of my neck. The thing about the nation's sensibilities is that there is a danger of taking blackness too seriously. Then your skin becomes too heavy to carry. Black guilt, like the genocide in Rwanda, the Kill the Gays Bill, Tiger Woods' sex life, black on black crime, the ghettoism of blackness in the white world where the darker the skin the more ghetto and the 'failure' of Africa.

Out here, your skin carries such guilts intimately. In that moment, I was at once all the African, Caribbean and African-American men who had travelled to Britain, had had children but, for whatever reasons, had not brought them up. Don't ask why men. Black guilt was screaming 'absent fathers'. What could I say to her? I concentrated on looking guilty.

'I am now sure my father was African, a student,' she said. 'He was from either Liberia or Sierra Leone, though he could have been a South African coloured because, obviously, I am too pale.' The emphasis on 'obviously' said that she had not forgiven me.

Something, I don't know what, made me say, 'Some Africans, especially in Nigeria, Zimbabwe and other Southern African countries can be really pale.'

Her eyes flashed a *Don't correct me*, but she carried on.

'He finished his studies and returned to Africa. At the time, Africans that came to Britain were students and couldn't wait to go back to their countries after their courses. My mother was Irish, young and adventurous. He didn't realise she was pregnant when he left. And she didn't know his address in Africa.'

I looked at her for a while and then nodded. I imagined her as a child, lying in bed constructing herself. She began with the father and made him black. Then her mother, whom she made white. She constructed the circumstances of her birth and how she ended up wherever she was at the time. But as she grew older and more knowledgeable, she was forced to change things, make specific adjustments to her parents to fit what she looked like and the time of her birth. I was confident that at one time her father had been Caribbean complete with an island, he had also been African-American with a state and an accent. However, she had now settled on Africa and she was not going to be moved.

'Teta is a Liberian name, isn't it?'

'Oh!' I was put straight. Africa was guilty. I smiled. 'What a lovely name!' It was the first thing that came to mind. Then I regretted it. Why was everything that came out of my mouth either woefully inadequate or patronising? I should have said *Nice to meet you, Teta; my name is Lucky* and shaken her hand.

'It was the fifties,' she went on. 'In those days, more Irish women had relationships with black men. But she was young and could not bring up a child on her own. She selflessly gave me up for adoption.'

The fifties were like a rope thrown to me. I grabbed and clung onto them. 'You don't look like you were born in the fifties,' I said. And it was true. She did not look a year older than forty. 'Honestly, I thought you were in your thirties.'

'Oh, you're so kind.'

But Teta was not interested in looking young. I had blanked her and then dared to search her body for her blackness – I was going to pay for her abandonment as well.

'If you look at my wedding pictures, there are no black people. My husband is Italian and comes from a large family. There were so many people at the wedding, people imagined it was both our families. But of course, deep down they were thinking, Where are her black folks?'

'Ah, there you are.' I didn't see Brenda, Annabelle's mother, come in. 'It's your moment, Teta!' She grabbed Teta's hand and steered her towards the door. 'Wait till you hear Teta sing.' Brenda winked at me.

There was something about the way Brenda led Teta away: as if I was not the first person she had rescued from her. Yet the fact that she was going to sing at this party made me uncomfortable. I tell you, being in Britain can make you hypersensitive. Or maybe it's the nation's sensibilities. It's easy to give offence out here and even easier to take it. In that moment, Teta singing seemed a cliché.

As they got to the door, Teta looked back and asked, 'You're Lucky, aren't you?'

She saw that I understood and threw her head back with a large smile. 'Lovely name,' she said, and stepped out.

I closed my eyes. 'Sneaky bitch.'

Left alone in Annabelle's house, there was such silence that I felt the house's outrage. The corridor stared, mouth open. The door shook its head. A window tsked. Everything in the kitchen acted like they were the nation. I pushed the cake away and hurried out.

I sat at the back of the gathering and watched Teta sing. There were no traces of the earlier confrontation on her face whatsoever, only her happiness when the audience joined in and danced in a circle around her. She never looked at me again. I wondered whether she was one of those floating souls who, occasionally, made a landing. That day she had anchored on me, rattled me and taken flight again. Annabelle saw me sitting alone and came over. 'What are you doing hiding at the back, Lucky? Come sit with us.'

SOMETHING INSIDE SO STRONG

(Airport Diaries, 2006)

Poonah manoeuvred her Vauxhall Corsa into a parking bay in Area 20 reserved for airport staff. She turned off the engine and stepped out. It was 5.30 a.m. but there was no cold breeze, no wind and the sun was already comfortable in the sky. The weather was so perfectly warm you would think Britain loved tropical migrants. Perhaps the rain was taking a break.

She opened the rear door and picked up her rucksack. Armed with her customary *I came to work – Britain is not my home* attitude, she headed for Terminal 4 of the airport. She anticipated the usual inconveniences of a twelve-hour shift: aching feet, fatigue, clueless passengers, rude ones, ditzy ones, entitled celebrities and – courtesy of insufficient sunshine on African skin – the niggling pain in her knee. In her bag were painkillers, two cans of Red Bull and, if the worst came to the worst, Pro Plus, her turbo boost.

As she walked, a smidge of self-satisfaction fleeted across her face. Poonah was a success story. She had mastered that perfect combination of sheer hard work and stinting frugality that an immigrant with a deadline needed. Even when she visited home, Poonah dressed like she was visiting from Masaka. She did not carry gifts for relations except her children and her mother. She did not flash money helping this one, that one with their problems, reinforcing the idea that in Britain money grows on trees. She had bought two houses back home – one rented out, the other occupied by her mother and her children. She had accumulated savings in an ISA account in the region of £30,000. She had concluded that Ugandans who failed in Britain were the ones who came as an alternative. The idiots who had jobs back home but thought, Let me try Britain and see. They came expecting to get similar jobs but ended up as cleaners. Those rarely recovered. But if you had hit rock bottom and cried out to Uganda *Help* but it sucked its teeth, saying, *You can die if you want*, no matter what Britain threw at you, you thrived.

Mpona Watson was the name in her passport but she introduced herself as Poonah. Her mother had named her Mpony'obugumba. Her father, Ssenkubuge, added Nnampiima, one of the most beautiful girls' names in Buganda. That made her name Mpony'obugumba Nnampiima. Add Ssenkubuge when the West demands a 'family name' and she would be Mpony'obugumba Nnampiima Ssenkubuge. Poonah clipped it. Who cared about her mother's sentiments on barrenness or what the Ganda consider a beautiful name?

She had not come to Britain to showcase Uganda's naming creativity. And if you challenged her on altering her name or questioned her loyalty to African culture she would ask *What has Africa done for me?*

Poonah was not one of those middle- or upper-class Ugandans who, having grown up in the posh suburbs of Kampala and been fed on middle- or upper-class British images paraded on TV, in cinema and magazines, arrived in London's Peckham or Manchester's Rusholme and – because they had imagined that all of Britain was Buckingham Palace, Westminster Abbey, the Savoy and skyscrapers – whined in dismay *You mean this is England?* Or who on hearing the Mancunian dialect, ask *But these people; what happened to grammar?* Those privileged types did not realise that, despite their cushioned upbringing back home, they arrived in the roughest parts of Britain, to which Ugandans, rich or poor, tended to gravitate.

When Poonah arrived in Britain, she was in awe. Carl lived in Urmston, an upmarket area in Manchester where you asked for pumpkin and were told, 'Pumpkin comes out once a year, mate – Halloween.'

She was suitably intimidated by the absence of people in the streets, the orderly life, the silence of the world, the obsessive timekeeping, the hyper-politeness and the fact that though she spoke English well enough, she did not understand one word that was said.

Poonah would tell you that Carl had fished her out of Nakivubo Canal dripping with need. To her, Carl was a brave Briton who came to Uganda looking for his ancestry but afterwards did charity work. Some British people start charity organisations in Uganda, some adopt children; Carl Mpiima Watson defied British immigration laws, omitted Mpiima from his name in church (he had had no idea that no church in Buganda would marry a boy called Mpiima to a girl called Nnampiima) and brought her to Britain as his wife. When she met him, Poonah still used her proper name, Mpony'obugumba Nnampiima. In fact, it was the Nnampiima that got Carl interested.

'You mean we're brother and sister?'

'Same clan: we can't fall in love.'

Unfortunately, Carl could not say Mpony'obugumba. When she said *M-po, M-po Mponye*, he said *Pony*. She said *nye, nye*; he said *niye. Try Mpona.* He said *Poonah*. She became Poonah.

Carl brought her to Britain with the enthusiasm of a British subject giving the British establishment the middle finger. For three and a half years he looked after her like an older brother but held her like a wife in public. Three of those years, Poonah worked and saved. When she was ready to hunt for herself, Carl let her out in the British wild. By marrying her and guiding her through the maze of British systems, Carl raised Poonah, her three children and mother back at home out of necessity. That was far more than what the G20 achieved in a year.

Poonah left her children back home because British Ugandans warned that to take children to Britain was to tether yourself to the doorknob. What is the use of going to Europe if you can't leave the house to work? And if you do, childcare wolfs down your earnings. Besides, children used to African strictness get to Britain and, because they can't handle the kind of freedom Britain gives them, run wild. You chastise them, they call the police – parents' hands are tied: you either dance to your children's ntoli or Social Services takes them away.

Poonah did not need to be told twice. She told her children, 'You know what, stay here with your grandmother. I am going with Uncle Carl to find work so we can have a good life. Be good, be grateful and study hard because this world is tough. I'll come back as soon as I can.'

But there were people who brought kilemya, the kind of negativity designed to dishearten. *We hear you're going to Bungeleza, but do you know what they think of us over there?*

Poonah asked them one question: 'Are their thoughts bullets? As long as their thoughts don't take food off my plate or the roof off my house, as long as when I work I get paid, I don't care what they think.'

That attitude saw Poonah rise through the ranks. In the beginning, she sorted apples in a factory-like building – Gala from Pink Lady, russets from golden, Braeburns from Granny Smiths – on a conveyor. Soon she started to work out the British system (manager, team, team leader, minimum pay, overtime, National Insurance). Then she worked out the English language, how and where it discriminated against its own native speakers. Poonah decided to acquire the Mancunian twang. You don't do menial jobs and speak posh English – colleagues isolate you, claiming you have airs. Poonah climbed out of the factories into care work. For two years, she looked after old people in two nursing homes. In one, she worked nights Monday to Wednesday. In another she worked daytime Friday to Sunday.

From there she joined a company providing support to people with mental health problems. She worked seventy-two hours a week until she sprouted premature grey hairs. She cut back to forty hours and offered to do bank work occasionally. By then she had so mastered the rhythms of the Mancunian dialect you would have thought she had grown up in Moss Side.

After four years of support work and a few NVQ certificates, she applied for this job at the airport and became an ASO, an Aviation Security Officer. She registered for overtime and built a reputation of reliability. She planned, between 2008 and 2010, to join university to do a BA in social work. Afterwards, she would do social work in Britain for five years to boost her CV and then return home.

It was on account of her upward mobility and job training, besides the free medical care – letters from the NHS reminding her to go to breast screening – that Poonah couldn't stand Ugandans bad-mouthing Britain. You criticised Britain in her presence, she asked you *Why don't you go back home?*

She arrived at the concourse in Terminal 4 and the buzz of passengers queuing to check in was deafening. As she reached the lifts below the escalator, a woman lamented, 'I swear, passengers check in their brains when they check in their luggage!'

Poonah turned. A member of Monarch Airlines ground staff pointed at a family – a horrified woman and a guilt-ridden man – dashing across the concourse. Behind them, two teenagers ran after them grudgingly.

'What happened?'

'*He* left the urn with *her* mother's ashes in the toilets.'

Poonah said what a Briton would say: 'Says it all, doesn't it?'

Father and son disappeared into the gents while mother and daughter waited outside. Poonah was about to walk away when the woman asked about her shift.

'The big one,' Poonah said. 'Six to six.'

'Ouch, it's gonna hurt, I can tell you that, what with foreign students going home, sun-chasers on the move, stag and hen parties in bloody Benidorm, football fans travelling to Germany for the World Cup and' – she winked – 'that on top of the two notorious air carriers.' The two notorious airlines were PIA (Pakistan International Airlines) and Air Jamaica. They carried some of the most airport-nervous passengers.

'Oh, yeah,' Poonah remembered, 'they both fly on Wednesdays.'

'I finish at ten and I'm out of here before hell breaks loose.'

Poonah walked downstairs to the restrooms. She was not really worried about the busy shift ahead. At her job, busy made time fly. You didn't want to stand there counting the minutes. She arrived at the restrooms and swiped at the door. After clocking in, she decided to eat breakfast. If it was going to be as busy as the woman had suggested, she would not get a break for four hours. She sat down to open her bag and her belly sat on her lap. The lower buttons on her blouse gasped. She sucked in her stomach but it hardly shifted. She sucked her teeth and blamed eating and sleeping at irregular hours because of shift work. It messed with her metabolism.

Just as she finished her breakfast, she heard the Nights coming down the stairs from the search area to clock out from their shift. As their voices drew near, Poonah picked up a *Metro* nearby and pretended to read. There was a rift between Days and Nights. One of those feuds you walk into on a new job and take sides on without realising or knowing why. All she had heard was that Nights were a nasty bunch.

They lined up outside the swipe machine and waited for 5.45 a.m. to clock out. At 5.50 Poonah grabbed her bag and started towards the search area. Members of her group, five other ASOs, walked ahead. She was not buddy-buddy with them because today they smile at you, tomorrow they pretend not to know you. You meet a colleague in a supermarket and he looks away like he's ashamed to know you. Then there are those who are nice and expect you to suck up to them. The worst are friendly when no one is about but find them in the company of other ASOs and they look away. Soon, Poonah stopped playing along and glared everyone away Ugandan style. They declared her a nasty piece of work.

She arrived at the search area. From the sheer numbers of ASOs there, even Administration anticipated a mad day. All five X-ray machines and walk-in metal detectors were open. Each X-ray was manned by at least seven people – one on loading, helping passengers put their bags into trays before feeding them into the X-ray, one sitting down screening the bags and five stood at the back of the X-ray doing bag searches. There was a queue of passengers at each point of entry already.

The walk-in metal detectors were manned by four ASOs – two male and two female – 'frisking', as body searches were called. As Poonah looked for a space to insert herself, Hannah, the team leader, came up.

'Can you do bag search on the third machine, Poonah?'

She walked across the search area and stood at the back of the third X-ray machine. Trays, loaded with passengers' bags, slid out of the X-ray and the ASOs at the top pushed them down the rollers towards the bottom, where Poonah stood. She picked them up and arranged them on the search tables ready to be collected by passengers.

Soon, she was at the top of the queue receiving bags out of the X-ray machine and pushing them to the bottom where passengers picked them up. She searched a few random bags and it went on until she was at the top of the line for the fourth time. The ASO screening the bags stopped the X-ray to scrutinise an image.

'Can you find out what this is, Poonah?' He indicated an image on the screen. It was coiled, with both organic and inorganic material. He let the tray with the bag out.

Poonah picked up the tray and turned to the passengers waiting across the machine. 'Whose items are these?'

A priest, very tall, fortyish, put his hand up.

'Could you step over to the search tables, please?'

Poonah started with the routine questions: 'Did you pack this bag yourself?'

The priest nodded.

'Did anyone give you anything to carry for him or her?... Did you leave the bag unattended at any time?'

The priest shook his head at both questions.

'This is a specific bag search; there is an object in your bag we could not identify: do you mind if I look?'

'If you must.'

This prompted Poonah to whisper, 'Do you by any chance have a whip in here?', hoping to spare the priest embarrassment.

'I beg your pardon: I am a man of the cloth!'

Poonah emptied the bag – mobile phone, wallet, shaver, car and house keys, a pair of socks rolled into a ball, a camera, a pair of sunglasses. She put each item into the tray until she got to the bottom of the bag. There, coiled like a snake, was a whip – black, leather.

Poonah retrieved it and showed it to the priest. 'Is this yours?'

The priest's face went scarlet. Passengers who had been sneaking peeks looked away. Poonah picked up the bag with the tray and showed the whip to the ASO screening bags.

'Naughty, naughty.' He twirled his chair, saw the priest and turned back, sniggering, 'Oi oi, vicar!'

Poonah put the bag and tray with all the other items back into the machine for extra X-raying. When they came through, the screening ASO nodded his satisfaction.

Poonah walked back to the priest. 'I'm afraid you can't take the whip, Reverend. It's not allowed in the cabin.'

She threw it on the heap of confiscated items. After repacking the bag, she smiled. 'Have a nice flight, Reverend.'

As she put back the tray, one of the female ASOs on the frisk asked Poonah for a swap. She accepted reluctantly. ASOs hated the frisk. It was at the frisk that passengers staged their most devious resistance. She walked to one side of the metal detector and said hi to Alison, the other female ASO.

All went well for the first twenty minutes – women stepped through the metal detector and she and Alison rubbed down passengers who set it off to make sure they were not carrying items of threat airside and onto aircraft.

Just then Poonah pulled a woman: 'Could you step over to me, madam?' Because the passenger had not set off the machine, Poonah explained, 'This is a random search, madam,' even though her randoms tended to be every tenth female passenger. 'Do you mind being searched here, or would you rather go somewhere private?'

'You've pulled me because I am black. You think I am carrying drugs because I am Jamaican.'

Poonah wanted to say *I thought you were African*, but instead smiled. 'Really?'

'It's not the first time. We blacks are the worst to each other.'

Poonah ignored it. Every passenger had a reason for being pulled. Irish, Asians, blacks, Muslims, goths, people with tattoos or piercings, men with ponytails, all were persecuted by airport security.

She had done the passenger's neck, arms, under the breasts, back and stomach. She was reaching into the back of the waistband, bringing the passenger very close to herself, when the woman exclaimed, 'Eh, are you a lesbian?'

Poonah ignored her.

'I can tell a lesbian when I see one.'

'You mean you're so irresistible all lesbians want to touch you?'

'No, but I mean...'

Poonah started on the legs, but no matter how wide the woman stepped Poonah could not search between her thighs. She reached for the handheld metal detector and passed it around the passenger's front and back. She had squatted to rub the ankles when the woman let loose a fart on top of Poonah's head. Poonah stood up and stepped away.

'Oops,' she giggled. 'I am so sorry: it just escaped.'

'I am going to treat that as an attempt to obstruct me from searching you. Come' – Poonah pulled out a chair – 'take a seat. Take off your shoes, belt, bracelets, ring and danglers from your ears, please.' By now ASOs stole amused glances. They loved it when black people gave Poonah grief.

The woman pulled them off and dropped them into a tray. Poonah took them back for extra X-raying. Then she told the woman to get up and walk through the metal detector again without them. There was no need, but Poonah felt like it. As she gave back her belongings she smiled. 'Have a nice journey.'

Before she could get back to her post and whisper her outrage to Alison, a woman stepped through the detector and set it off. Poonah motioned to her. 'Step over to me, madam.'

'Did I set it off again?' The passenger looked up at the machine where it flashed red. 'I always do: too much iron in my blood.'

Alison rolled her eyes.

Luckily, the passenger knew the drill. She stood legs apart, arms stretched out to the sides without prompting. Then she sighed. 'I'm glad I changed my knickers.'

Poonah had long decided that body searches were so intrusive that some passengers said to themselves *If you're going to touch me everywhere you might as well hear my life's story.*

As soon as Poonah started rubbing her arms, the passenger went frolicsome: 'Uhhhh, I haven't been touched in years.'

Poonah kept a straight face.

She found a mobile phone in the passenger's trousers and told her, 'This is what set the machine off.' She put the phone in the machine to be X-rayed. After the search, she handed the phone back to the passenger and wished her a good flight. The woman leant in and whispered, 'I've heard that you blacks are good at this sort of thing, but I had no idea!'

By the time Poonah recovered, the passenger had gone.

Alison was seething. She whispered, 'I bet she left that phone in her pockets on purpose, I bet she wanted to be frisked, perv! You get all sorts in this place. We call them lesbos in this country. They disgust me. You Africans are right; don't let them destroy your culture.'

To Poonah, the passenger was not necessarily gay. Desperate, maybe. On the frisk, passengers said all sorts just to rattle you. One time after being frisked, this woman smiled at an ASO and said, 'I hope you enjoyed that more than I did!' The ASO was having none of it. She whispered back, 'Trust me: you're not all that!' Another time, a camp Somali lad walked through and set off the metal detector. Being Somali and camp was one thing; being terribly ticklish was another. He was so unprepared for being frisked that, as he was rubbed down, he yelped, hopping from one leg to the other as if walking barefoot on hot embers. Afterwards, as he picked up his tray, tears running down his face, an ASO turned to another and whispered, 'You mean they can be gay too?'

Poonah paused to catch her breath, and froze. Across from her at the back of the main machine stood Nnamuli. Poonah lost her rhythm and stood for too long. In the background, she felt a current of excitement run through the search area. She glanced towards where the commotion came from, but only to make sure that Nnamuli standing in the search area was not a dream. Wrestlers had arrived, but Poonah looked back to Nnamuli. Nnamuli still stood in the search area, not as a passenger but as a new ASO. Poonah called the next female passenger through.

As far as Poonah's shifts in Security at the airport went, this one had been so far unremarkable – until Nnamuli arrived. Nnamuli was not just another Ugandan; her family had once employed Poonah when she first arrived in Kampala, an A-level dropout from Buwama looking for a bright future. At the time, Nnamuli's dad had been an MP, not yet a cabinet minister. They had had a supermarket along Jinja Road. They had employed Poonah as one of the three shop attendants.

Because the shop closed late, Poonah, the youngest of the shop attendants, slept in a room above. Sometimes, after closing, Nnamuli's father would come to the shop to balance the books. After letting him in, Poonah would go to her room. He would call as he left and Poonah would lock the door.

One day, Nnamuli, who was the same age as Poonah, had come to get something from the shop and was shocked to find her father there balancing the books. Soon after she had gone home, Nnamuli's mother had arrived angrier than a cobra at midday.

'Pack your bags and get out.'

Poonah asked why.

'I said, get your stuff and get out.'

Poonah remembered that her husband was downstairs and understood. This was a world where women suspected that men were so blind with desire they would cheat with anything. Denying it was a waste of time. It was a wife saying to her husband *Watch me throw the object of your desire out of this place.* And the husband's silent contemptuous silence of *Go on: see if I care.*

When Poonah stepped outside, Nnamuli's mother waited for her husband to finish and locked up. She took the keys. Husband and wife got into separate cars and drove off, leaving Poonah spluttering into her hands outside the door. They hadn't even paid her.

That was the Nnamuli standing in the search area.

Luckily that night, Mutaayi, a special hire driver, had still been on the taxi rank next to the Diamond Trust bank. He was the only person Poonah knew in the city. The other person was her aunt who lived in Matugga, twenty miles away. Too late to find taxis going there at 11 p.m. Mutaayi had once taken Poonah out for a meal but all he had talked about was *my goats, my pigs, my chickens, my land back upcountry.* Poonah had left the rural specifically to escape goats, pigs, chickens and digging. Then he had taken her to the Pride Theatre, where he had kept up a running commentary on the performance. At the end of the evening, he had looked at Poonah like *I've spent all this money on you, what do I get in return?* When he had realised she was not sleeping with him, Mutaayi had sulked. Poonah had avoided him since.

Now she walked to him the picture of a rural damsel in distress – a makyala dress, plastic shoes, luggage in plastic bags and a teary story. He did not pretend to believe her. To him she was one of those girls who only dated a man if he spent money on them, who at the point when the relationship should transition to the next level, fled after 'eating' your money. He told Poonah to go back and wait for him outside the shop while he finished working.

Mutaayi knew how to break a girl. He finished work two hours later. By then Poonah was so desperate she was ready to pay for the meal, Pride Theatre and for much more if Mutaayi got her off the dark street.

The following morning, he asked: 'You're going to your aunt for what? How is a woman twenty miles away going to help you find a job in the city? Stay here, where I can help you.'

At first, he took her for job interviews and waited to drop her home afterwards. He gave her money for everything she needed while she job-hunted and Poonah got comfortable.

But before she got a job, she got pregnant and Mutaayi told her to forget working.

Pregnancy broke the remnants of her spirit and she became dependent on him. She received his money gratefully and accepted his rules. She had three children, cooked and maintained a stress-free home environment for him. Their ten-year relationship ended when Mutaayi found her stash of birth control pills and punished her so severely she could not go to the police to say it was not him. It was back in 1992, when those feminist lawyers, FIDA, were scary to a certain kind of man. By the time she came out of hospital, they were all over the case, brandishing words like *battered woman, domestic violence, internalisation*. Poonah told them, 'You put him away, my children will suffer,' but they were not moved. That was how she ended up peddling tea and chapati along Channel Street, where Carl Mpiima Watson found her.

Now, Poonah rolled her eyes skywards. Tears are a jerk. Sometimes they don't warn you before they spoil your cheery facade. She sucked her teeth and blamed Britain for making her soft. She looked across at Nnamuli and wondered, What are the odds? Here was Nnamuli – expensive education, sheltered life, daughter of a cabinet minister – doing the same job. Hadn't she become a lawyer or doctor or an engineer like her kind were supposed to? Then it dawned on her that perhaps Nnamuli was at university doing a second or third degree. She had that aura of *this situation is temporary* that you saw on middle-class Ugandan students doing menial jobs in Britain.

Poonah looked down. Let Nnamuli see her in her own time.

The wrestlers were mountains. They were in character – bouncing, flexing, rasping and huffing – to the kids' delight. They signed autographs. Passengers jumped out of queues to take pictures, which they were forced to erase, and the kids cried at the meanness of it.

When Poonah turned to call in another passenger, Nnamuli was staring: *This can't be true.* Poonah smiled: *Yes, it's me, Mpony'obugumba Nnampiima, the real one!* Nnamuli's face was so sickened with shock, she looked ready to throw up right there in the search area. Poonah's eyes said *Isn't Britain quite the leveller?*

Poonah went back to frisking.

Most PIA passengers travelled in large family groups, with lots of bags, excited kids and grown-ups wearing the beleaguered look of a people under suspicion. The men and women so looked you in the eyes to see your prejudice that you had to smile to reassure them that you were more intelligent than that. Unfortunately, most women passengers were pulled because bangles set off the detectors. It was impossible to convince them that they were not targeted. When metal detectors went off, they pointed to the bangles: 'Mine're pure gold. They don't go off.' And when you insisted, they became suspicious: 'You've set the machine off remotely to search us.'

Poonah, aware that Nnamuli was watching, explained patiently that gold was still a metal: it sets the machine off, that there was no way of setting the machine off remotely. But they were not having it. No gold-wearing passenger ever wanted to hear that gold was not above metal detection.

When she looked up again, Nnamuli had pulled a bag. It belonged to a family of three generations – grandkids, parents and grandparents. Unfortunately, all the women had set off the machine. The grandfather and his sons stood away from the body search area, watching livid but helpless, as Poonah and Alison frisked the women all over. The women, especially the grandmother, were scandalised. She gave Poonah the sour *Even you, joining them in humiliating us!* look that minorities gave each other.

Poonah had had enough of the frisk. As the family walked towards Nnamuli on bag search, she swapped and went to load bags into the X-ray. She kept an eye on Nnamuli to see how she handled the irate family.

The grandfather asked his family to pick up the rest of the bags and step back while he dealt with the bag search. After the preliminary questions, Nnamuli pulled a two-litre bottle of semi-skimmed milk from the bag.

'It's for drinking on the flight,' the old man said.

'You can't take liquids into the cabin.'

'Why not?'

'It could be a liquid bomb disguised as milk.'

Poonah smiled. You don't say *bomb* to a Muslim passenger in an airport. You stick to *It's not allowed.*

The man opened the lid, drank some milk. 'Would I drink it if it was dangerous?'

'I'm afraid that's the rule.'

The man opened the lid again, but this time lifted the bottle up and slowly poured the milk over his head. It flowed down his face, his white tunic and onto the floor. His family stared. Passengers stared. Airport staff glanced at each other and carried on unfazed. Nnamuli shrank. Poonah did not hide her satisfaction.

As soon as he put the empty bottle down, the cleaners kicked into full gear. Yellow WET FLOOR signs were put in place. Mops danced: *We're on top of this.*

Someone whispered, 'Imagine sitting next to him all the way to Karachi.'

When the family left, Hannah, the team leader, came to Nnamuli and commended her: 'I was watching; you did everything by the rules.'

Poonah looked away.

It was ten in the morning when Poonah went to the restroom as part of her hour's break. When she returned, she was sent to patrol duty-free shops, boarding gates, air bridges and the ramp. She did not come back to the search area until one o'clock. By then, the Air Jamaica passengers had been cleared and tucked away at their boarding gate. The area was quiet. Only a third of the ASOs remained. Nnamuli was chatting to other new ASOs. Her body language said *I'm going to be just fine.*

As Poonah settled on bag search, Liam from her group popped up behind her and asked, 'Do you know the new girl?'

Poonah looked at Nnamuli and shook her head.

'Apparently she's Ugandan: her name's Dr Mrs Jingle.'

Poonah doubled over. Delicious. It was so typically Ugandan middle-class to roll out all the pre-nominal letters to establish rank.

Poonah said, 'Yes, Jjingo is a Ugandan name.'

Gossip was rife in the search area about Dr Mrs Jingle. Of course, no one believed Nnamuli was a doctor. She had not realised that in Britain marriage was not an honour but a lifestyle choice. Poonah was tempted to mention that Nnamuli's father was a cabinet minister, then the ASOs would treat her to the full combo of contempt, disdain and disgust: *Her father is one of those greedy politicians who engorge themselves on public funds while their own people suffer.* But Poonah held back; it would not ring true with Nnamuli doing this kind of job.

By 3.30, passenger flow had dwindled to a trickle. Three of the five X-ray machines were shut down. The remaining ASOs spread out on the two machines around the main entrance. Nnamuli and Poonah ended up on the same machine. Poonah bristled.

At half past four, a woman, twenty-something, hair dyed green, large floral cloth bag, slender, smiley, airport-savvy, walked in. After being frisked, she thanked the ASO. As she got into her shoes, Nnamuli asked for a random bag search. The passenger smiled: 'Knock yourself out.'

As she emptied the bag, Nnamuli pulled out a gadget. From where Poonah stood, it looked like hair tongs in a sheath. But as Nnamuli put it down, she flicked a switch and the gadget bobbed.

Someone elbowed Poonah. 'Go help your friend.'

Poonah ignored the presumptuous *your friend* and looked again. She realised what the gadget was and giggled but did nothing. Luckily, the passenger deftly switched the gadget off without revealing it. Nnamuli was blissfully oblivious.

When she was done with the other contents, Nnamuli lifted the gadget (all gadgets had to be swabbed for traces of drugs and explosives) and asked the passenger: 'What is this?'

At first the woman looked at her like *Are you taking the piss?* But then she shrugged. 'You're the one searching my bag: open it and see.'

Nnamuli unzipped the sheath as if peeling a banana, then she shrieked and threw the vibrator into the tray. A female ASO stepped in and took the tray to the farthest search table. She beckoned the passenger and went through the bag again, toy covered from public view. The ASO swabbed the bag and tested it for narcotics and explosives. Satisfied, she passed it to the passenger with effusive apologies.

When she was gone, the stunned air turned to anger. First, Nnamuli's indiscretion – she shouldn't have exposed the toy. Part of their training dealt with how to handle sex toys discreetly. Secondly, Nnamuli's reaction – unprofessional. Hannah arrived and pulled Nnamuli out of the search area and into the manager's office.

The air took a turn for the worse.

A sense that Nnamuli had exposed the whole British culture to ridicule crept over the search area. Now the other ASOs avoided looking at Poonah, like she had conspired with Nnamuli to embarrass everyone. Normally, they would say

You'd think she'd have the common sense to check in her toys, but this time it was: 'People are entitled to carry whatever they want.'

Poonah had to make a decision. Either she condemned Nnamuli and joined the outraged brigade and muted the African/British binary, or she kept quiet and appeared complicit. She could not fake outrage, and kept quiet.

When Nnamuli returned, she walked across the search area and joined the machine opposite. The ASOs standing closest to her walked off and joined Poonah's machine. The others turned their backs to her. ASOs arriving for evening shifts were told about the incident and they stared at Nnamuli. There were whispers of 'Apparently, her name is Dr Mrs Jingle...don't like the look of her.'

It was like watching a plant being sprayed with weedkiller. Poonah started to get agitated. You know when you've fought with your sibling and a friend takes your side but hurts your sibling more than necessary? Poonah wanted to say, *Back off!*

Finally, Poonah caught Nnamuli's eye and flicked a sympathetic hand. Perhaps it was the unexpectedness of it, maybe Nnamuli realised that she had dragged Poonah's arse into it, but her head dropped and she cracked.

Poonah rushed over and grabbed her – 'You can't cry in the search area' – and steered her towards the toilets.

Hannah saw them and hurried over. She took Nnamuli and said, 'Leave her to me, Poonah. Go back to your post.'

'She genuinely didn't know what it was.'

'I know.'

Hannah led Nnamuli to the manager's office.

The air in the search area turned again. Now the ASOs were uncertain. Would their reaction be seen as racist? They asked Poonah, 'She'll be alright, won't she…It's a tough job, this one…We come from different cultures…to be fair, who wants to touch her bits, I mean!'

Nnamuli did not come back to the search area. Rumour had it that she was given the rest of the day off.

Hannah let Poonah and her group off the search area at 5.00 p.m. for their third and final break. Since their shift ended an hour after that, she told them not to come back. Nnamuli was in the restroom when Poonah arrived. 'Are you into cigs?' she asked. 'This is the smokers' room.'

Nnamuli began crying afresh. Poonah sat down beside her and dropped the Mancunian twang.

'Don't worry: it's just herd mentality. ASOs can be childish.'

'I'm not coming back.'

'Why? Because you made a mistake and they overreacted?'

Nnamuli sobbed.

'Are you a part-timer or a full-timer?'

'Part-time – twenty hours a week.'

'Tsk' – Poonah dropped English altogether – 'that's nothing. Stop acting spoilt. Do you need the money or not?'

Nnamuli sighed.

'Then quit playing. Let me tell you about this place. You come, you do your job, you keep your head down. Carry a lot of thank yous, I am sorrys and excuse mes. The way they make mistakes is not the way we make the same mistakes. Be careful: you fall out with one of them, they all turn against you – it's called closing ranks. Graduates don't do these kinds of jobs; don't tell people about your degrees. Play dumb; dumb protects you. They're gossipy; don't tell them things about yourself. They turn just like that – they turn on each other too. Don't tell them how rich you are back home: they won't believe you. When they ask *Do you like this country?* say *It's fantastic.* When they ask *Do you plan to stay?*, say *Of course not!* They ask *Would you like to become British?* say *I am proud to be Ugandan.* Finally, they have this thing of being nasty very politely: learn the skill.'

Nnamuli sighed. 'Is it as mad every day in the search area?'

'Mad? Apart from the milk incident and your reaction to the…whatever, that's every day. You'll get used. It's busy up to the end of September. Then it gets quiet until two weeks before Christmas, when things get manic. It gets a little busy in January with skiers and winter sports, but dies down again. Listen, you need to keep busy in this place: busy keeps your mind off things, busy is overtime.'

'Are you working tomorrow?'

'Four to ten in the morning.'

Nnamuli checked her roster. 'Same.'

'That's good. If you want, I can talk to Hannah so you're moved into my group. Then we'll be on at the same time.'

'Can you do that?'

'Sure. Hannah is nice.'

Nnamuli sniffed. 'After this kind of pain, earning just £6.10 an hour, someone back home rings and says *Can you send me £100?*'

Poonah laughed. She wanted to say *Your family is wealthy; who would send such a message?* but there were more important things to tell Nnamuli. She asked, 'Do you drive?...I can drop you...Are you at Manchester Met or Manchester Uni? I can't make up my mind where to do my BA.'

At 5.50 p.m., they swiped out from their shift and made their way to the car park. As they got to her car, Poonah clicked the doors open. 'It's a mess,' she apologised as she threw her rucksack into the back seat. When she turned the key in the ignition, 'Something Inside So Strong' by Labi Siffre burst out.

'Ooops,' Poonah said casually as she turned the volume down, 'I didn't realise how loud I had it,' but inside she was remembering how Nnamuli's parents had got in their cars that night.

'This version sounds African,' Nnamuli mused.

'It was written by a Nigerian.' Poonah reversed out of the space and drove to the barrier. She removed her pass from the lanyard and swiped it. 'Son of an immigrant.' The barrier opened.

'It doesn't mean the same when Kenny Rogers sings it.'

Poonah kept quiet for the rest of the journey and the air became bloated.

When Poonah dropped her outside her door, Nnamuli thanked and thanked her.

'I'll pick you up at three in the morning,' Poonah said. 'I prefer to get to the airport at least half an hour before my shift starts.'

'Isn't that too early?'

'Eyajj'okola teyebakka,' she snapped. 'Being in Britain is the proverbial prostituting: you know you came to work, so why get in bed with knickers on?'

'Absolutely,' Nnamuli agreed, too quickly.

When Nnamuli stepped inside her house, Poonah waved and drove away. She had decided to wait until Nnamuli trusted her entirely and then to ask *Do you know what happened to me that night?*

MALIK'S DOOR

This time the decision to leave came like a cramp, sudden and excruciating. Katula was standing in the corridor staring at Malik's bedroom door when she felt her heart curl into itself: *I'm leaving!* But then, just as quickly, the conviction faded. The same heart now palpitated, *After all he's done for you?* But the mind insisted – *You're leaving* – and she mouthed the words as if Malik's door had laughed at her.

She turned away and walked past her bedroom towards the end of the corridor, where their warm clothing hung. She sat down on the chair and started to pull on her winter boots. For the past two years, since she got British citizenship, she had swung with indecision like a bell around a cow's neck: *nkdi – I'm leaving, nkdo – how can I leave? Nkdi – this time I am going, Nkdo – going where?*

The problem was that Malik had outfoxed her. But it was not the cut-throat outsmarting of certain marriages Katula knew back home. In this was kindness blended with concealment, generosity mixed with arrogance. The biggest obstacle was her empathy. In Malik's position, perhaps she would have done the same. These things haunted her every time she tried to be strong. Strength in these circumstances was ruthless.

As she pulled on her gloves, the words of her mother, a cynic whose children each had a different father, came back to her. 'All things we humans do are selfish,' she once said.

'Even love?' Katula had asked.

'Kdt, especially love! It hides its selfishness behind selfless-ness: I got tired of pretending.'

Katula clicked at herself because in the beginning her love for Malik had been selfish. What she needed now was to convince herself that Malik's selfishness was worse than hers had been. Then she would use that to leave him.

As she put on the head warmer, her glance fell on his door again. All the doors in the house were shut but there was something final in the way his bedroom door was closed. Katula's eyes lingered as she adjusted the hat. She stood up, wrapped a scarf around her neck and called out: 'I'm going out to post the postal ballot forms.'

'Yeah' came from behind the door.

Yeah? Perhaps he hadn't heard what she said. Sometimes, because of her accent, Malik didn't catch the words and said 'yeah' to save her from repeating herself. She was about to rephrase the statement when the door opened a crack and Malik's head slipped through.

'Kat,' he said, 'I might be gone by the time you return. I'm going to spend the weekend with my mother.' Malik's eyes, like the marbles Katula used to roll on the ground as a child, looked at her, blinked and looked at her again.

'Okay,' she said, instead of *You're lying*. 'Say hello to her for me,' instead of *You think I am dumb?*

Malik pulled his head back and the door closed. Then it opened again and his head popped out again, just up to the neck. 'I'll leave the money for the plumber on the table.' He smiled. The smile spread from the lips, folding back his cheeks. It flowed into his eyes, lifting his eyebrows and creasing his forehead. Along the way, it massaged the resolve to leave out of Katula's jaws and she smiled.

'Thanks.'

There was a moment's hesitation, then Malik beamed. 'You know what, I'll leave an extra hundred pounds in case you want to go out with the girls...to the movies or for a meal.'

Katula's gaze dropped to the floor, her resolve returning. But when she lifted her eyes she smiled. 'You don't have to: I have my own money.'

'I am your husband: I take care of you.'

Malik's head withdrew and the door closed.

Katula picked up the house keys and walked towards the front door. She opened the door and was met by the brilliant whiteness of winter. The air was still the way only winter stills the world. The snow in her garden was fresh, crystalline and untrodden. The snow on top of Malik's Citroën Picasso was a pillow thick. She heard footsteps crunching and looked up. A woman and child in fur-lined padded coats walked past. Across the road, a double-decker bus pulled up at the bus stop, hissing and sneezing. Steam burst from its backside like a fart. Katula stepped out of the house and closed the door. As she walked down the driveway, the bus pulled away and the air became still again.

You're leaving him this time.

They met back in summer 2003 when Katula was still being hunted by Immigrations. Being hunted by Immigrations was somewhat like duka-duka during the Bush War. While there were no bullets to dodge or jungle to set on fire to flush you out in Britain, it was war nonetheless. When UK Border Force captured you, they had the same satisfied look of soldiers, and some people said you got kicked by enthusiastic officials in the vans. As in war, it did not matter whether you were in pyjamas or a vest – when they got you they took you as you were. And as in war, for a fee Ugandans would sell each other to Immigrations the way neighbours sold whoever supported the wrong politician back in the early 1980s. There came a time when Katula envied the oblivion of British tramps lying drunk and dirty on the streets (a waste of a British passport) the way she had envied the oblivion of trees during war. What made it painful was that in war everyone was on the run from the soldiers, while in Britain you're alone amidst the cries of *Get them out of here.*

Katula was a student nurse when her visa expired. At the time, Immigrations stipulated that to renew a student visa you needed to show a minimum of £600 in your account. Katula earned £1,200 a month from her job. She had thought that a steady income would suffice. As a precaution, she sent her renewal forms to Immigrations by post because a Ugandan friend had warned, 'These days Immigrations keeps a van ready and running: any failed applicants, *toop*, into the van, and *shoooop*, to the airport.'

After a month, UK Border Force wrote back to say that at one time in the past six months, Katula's account had dipped to below £600. That demonstrated that she didn't have sufficient funds for her maintenance in Britain: she should leave the country immediately. Katula moved to a new house and changed her job. Friends advised her to hook a British husband as soon as possible. To buy time while she hunted for a husband, she sent her passport back to UK Border Force for appeal, using a friend's address.

Malik fell like manna from heaven. She was standing at a bus stop outside the University of Manchester Students' Union when she saw him across the road standing near Kro Bar. She was waiting for the 53 bus. He was exceedingly tall; he held his head as though the clouds belonged to him. Katula looked again and thought, God must have been in an extravagant mood. She was less than pretty; exceedingly good-looking men made her uncomfortable. He was not a potential husband, anyway. Katula targeted white pensioners whom, she had heard, had a penchant for young African women. She was scanning the horizon for the 53 when she saw him standing at the same bus stop smiling at her.

'I think I know you: are you Ghanaian?'

'No, Ugandan.'

'You remind me of someone from Ghana.'

'A lot of people mistake me for a Ghanaian.'

Now that she had looked at him properly, he was odd. His jeans were not cropped as she had thought: he had shortened them rather shabbily above his ankles. On top was a long shapeless shirt. Was he trying to play down his good looks? It was the thick beard and clean-shaven head that made Katula realise that he could be Muslim. She asked: 'Are you Tabliq?'

'What is that?'

'A sect of devout Muslims.'

'I am Muslim, my name is Malik; how did you know?'

Katula explained that in Uganda, Muslims who wore their trousers above the ankles and had a beard were Tabliq. Tabliqs were devout and no-nonsense.

Malik's interest was piqued: was Uganda a Muslim country?

'Muslims are a minority.'

'African names have a meaning; what does Katula mean?'

The way he said Katula, as if it rhymed with spatula. She tried to laugh but it came out as a cough. How do you tell a man you dream to ensnare that your name is a warning? She decided to go with the absurdity of the truth.

'The katula is a tiny green berry which on the outside looks innocuous, but bite into it and it will unleash the most savage bitterness.'

Malik threw back his head and laughed. 'Who would call their child that?'

'To be fair,' Katula defended her parents, 'the katula is very good for cholesterol and heart problems. But my name is a warning against underestimating people because of their size.' Now she too laughed. 'You know us Africans, we don't dress things up.'

'Did you know that man Idi Amin?'

Every time Katula mentioned that she was Ugandan, Idi Amin was thrown at her as if he was Uganda's chief cultural export, but she smiled and said that she was born just after Amin was deposed. She started to hope. You could hook this man. On top of the British passport, he could give you two gorgeous daughters, one Sumin, one Sumaia, and a son, Sulait. But first you need to hint that you don't eat pork or drink alcohol and that there are Muslims in your family.

'When I saw you across the road,' Malik was saying, 'I knew you were African.'

Bus number 53 drove past.

'You are so dark-dark. I wish I was as dark as you.' He looked at her as if being dark-dark could actually be beautiful in Britain. Before Katula responded, he added, 'Only you Africans have that real dark, almost navy-blue skin. Look at me' – he showed Katula his inner arms – 'look at this skin, see how pale I am.'

Katula did not know what to say to that. No one had ever envied the darkness of her skin. Not even at home. In Britain, people with skin as dark as hers were not allowed to be black – not together with mixed-race people, Asians or other non-whites – they were called *blick*. Another 53 came along but she could not tear herself away. When she stopped the third 53, Malik asked to come along. She could not believe herself as he got on the bus with her. Perhaps he really was attracted to her. By the time they got to North Manchester General Hospital, she had learnt that Malik was not seven feet tall as she had thought but a mere six foot five. His mother was mixed race – her father came from Ghana but her mother was white. 'My maternal grandfather is my only claim to Africa, I'm afraid,' he said. Then he corrected himself: 'But then again, we are all African.' Malik's mother still lived in Sheffield, while his father had returned to Tobago. 'My big brother is dark because our dad is "dark-dark", but I turned out pale. The only time I get dark is when I go to the Caribbean.'

Malik walked Katula to the entrance of the hospital and they exchanged telephone numbers. That night as she worked, Malik's name, his soft voice, his perfect face and Britishness kept coming back and her heart would spread out in her chest.

Now holding the postal ballot forms, Katula walked until she came to the end of the last block of the Victorian semi-detached houses similar to hers and crossed the road. She came to the local pub, the Vulcan, with its Tudor facade. A monkey, the pub's insignia, swung on the sign. Men and women stood outside the door smoking despite the cold. The recent ban on smoking in public places was biting. Katula could see the red postbox where it stood next to a corner shop. Across the road from the postbox was the local primary school. Just as Katula prepared to cross Manchester Road, a gritting truck flew past. It dropped a few grains of sand, perhaps salt, on the road. The grains disappeared in the slush without effect. She made a mental note to pick up salt from the corner shop on her way back. There had been no salt in Tesco the previous weekend because of panic buying – they had used it on the snow on their driveways.

Dating was difficult. Malik could not be alone with a woman without a third person in the room. They met in halal restaurants in Rusholme. Even then, Malik sat away from her. As their relationship progressed, he told her that he had not been born Muslim. His name was Malachi until sometime in his twenties when he had gone astray.

'I got into some bad-bad, real crazy stuff,' Malik said, without going into details. To keep away from the bad stuff, he turned to God. However, he had found the Christian God rather lazy and laid-back. 'I went to all sorts of churches but nothing worked for me. I needed a God with a strong grip to put me straight.' Then he found Islam and changed his name from Malachi to Malik. Apparently, Islam's God had a tight grip: the five prayers a day kept a tight rein on him.

They had talked about the future: could Katula commit to wearing the hijab – *sure*. Could she take a Muslim name – *of course; Hadija*. Could she embrace Islam – she took a deep breath, but then she saw the redness of the British passport – *yes, of course!* And to demonstrate her commitment, Katula's dresses started to grow longer and wider even though Malik had not pressed her to dress differently. Eventually, he found a third person to be with them and invited her to his house.

That day Katula even wore bitenge wrappers on her head because Malik liked it when she dressed African. Malik's house was a two-bedroom semi-detached in Oldham. It had a very high ceiling and the rooms were spacious, but Malik had covered the floorboards with cardboard. In the windows, he had hung bed sheets. The kitchen was rotting. The house was dark and cold.

'Here is a job for a proper wife.' Katula surveyed the squalor with satisfaction. 'Three months in this place and all of this will be transformed.' She planned to make such an impact that Malik would not miss his bachelor days.

The living room doubled as Malik's bedroom even though the house had two empty bedrooms. As she walked in, she saw an African boy, no older than twenty-one, sitting on a settee close to the door. He was so astoundingly good-looking that Katula hesitated – when African men choose to be beautiful they overdo it. The lad wore a white Arab gown with a white patterned *taqiyah* on his head. The whiteness of his gown stood out in the grubby surroundings of Malik's house. He looked up at her as she entered the room and quickly looked away. Then he remembered to say hello and flung it over his shoulder. Katula dismissed him. From his accent, he was one of those *my parents are originally from Africa but I was born in Britain* types who tended to keep away from home-grown Africans as if the native African in them, which they had worked so hard to get rid of, might resurface. It's that shunning and bullying they suffer in schools that makes them run away from themselves. Katula wrinkled her nose.

She walked past him and sat on another settee; Malik sat on his bed facing the boy, whom he introduced as Chedi. Apart from the few times Malik asked Katula whether she wanted a drink, the two men were engrossed in their conversation. They talked about a certain sheikh's views on food, especially meats from supermarkets. Apparently not even tomatoes were safe to eat for a proper Muslim because they were genetically tampered with. He promised to lend Malik the sheikh's CD. Katula was uneasy about the way the two men did not invite her into their conversation. But she had grown up at a time when men, in the company of fellow men, ignored their wives because women could not be invited into masculine conversation. Probably they ignored her because she was non-Muslim, probably Islam did not allow women to join in men's conversation. Katula decided to play dumb.

The next time Malik invited her over to his house he was on his own, but she did not ask why. She sat on the sofa. He sat next to her and even held her hand as they talked. He sat so close she was tempted to kiss him. When she stood up to leave, he hugged her; Katula held him. This was her chance to feel how he felt her. Malik's body was rigid. She relaxed her body to encourage him a little, but his body did not notice: he could have been hugging his mother. When Katula reached up to kiss him on the neck he tore away, 'In Islam,' he said breathlessly, 'a man must guard his neck at all times.'

Katula crept out of Malik's house shrinking. On the way home, she chastised herself for pushing too hard – Malik falling in love and having children with you are toppings; focus on the main thing. She had never dated a British man; maybe that was the way they were. And you know what they say about Africans – hypersexual. The British are no doubt restrained. She cupped her hands around her mouth and blew into them. She smelt for bad breath: nothing. Her stomach chewed itself all the way home.

The following day Malik was waiting outside the hospital gate when she finished her shift. When she saw him, a feeling of pleasant surprise broke through her mortification. He invited her to come to his house the following weekend. For a moment, Katula looked away, but she overcame her embarrassment and smiled.

This time when she arrived Malik was wearing a towel. She stared. If she thought he was good-looking before, undressed he was magnificent. This time he had even tried to clean the house. He had the air of an expectant lover about him. He told her to make herself a cup of tea while he took a bath. As she had tea, he came out of the bathroom grinning.

'You know, the other day a man followed me all the way from Asda,' he said as he dried his hair with a towel. 'The man said I have the cutest legs, no?' He turned his legs to her.

Apart from the hairs, Katula wished Malik's legs were on herself. 'As far as I'm concerned, you're close to perfect.'

Malik's eyes shone as if no one had ever told him that he was gorgeous. He walked towards her and held her. Then he kissed her on the lips. She felt like a new flavour of ice cream. She was not sure he liked it.

'Do you like my body?' He smiled into her eyes.

'You're stunning.'

'Then I'm all yours, if you'll marry me.'

The earnestness in his eyes prompted Katula to tell him that she could not marry him because of her visa troubles. Instead of getting suspicious, Malik got angry. 'They make my blood boil.' To help her save on rent, Malik asked her to move in with him. She moved in the following day. However, he said that they could not share a bedroom until they were married. To make herself useful, Katula started to clean the house. The nagging fear that things were moving too quickly, that Malik would change his mind, that it was all too good to be true, was dispelled when he said that he wanted to fix the wedding date as soon as possible.

First, he gave her money to return home, where she sorted out her student visa. She returned to Britain a month later and, because she was a non-EU citizen, applied and paid for permission to marry a Briton. Ugandans called it a dowry. When it was granted, Malik asked for her shift roster.

Katula was due to work the night shift the day they got married. Malik informed her that they were getting married that morning because, as he explained, a couple had cancelled at the last minute and the imam had slotted them in.

'But I'm working tonight – should I call in sick?'

'No, you don't have to: we're getting married at midday.'

There was no time to dwell on the fact that Malik wanted her to work on their wedding night. Unknown to Katula, Malik had already bought the clothes she would wear for the nikah. 'I got them yesterday,' he said as he handed her an Indian gown similar to the ones she had seen in Asian boutiques in Rusholme. Turquoise, it had glittering sequins and beads. It had a scarf which she wore on her head.

At the wedding, Katula did not know any of the guests, not even her witness. Chedi, Malik's friend, did not turn up. His mother was not at the wedding either – she could not make it at such short notice. Afterwards, they went to a Lebanese restaurant for lunch. When they returned home, Malik offered to drop her at work. As she stepped out of the car at the hospital, he leant over and kissed her on the lips. 'See you tomorrow, wifie.'

Katula sensed that something was wrong when he did not pick her up in the morning. When she arrived at home he was in his bedroom, but the door was locked. His greeting, from behind the door, was curt. When he stepped out of his room, his face said *Don't come near me*. He rushed down the corridor and into the kitchen as if Katula would pounce on him. He didn't look at her. He ate in his bedroom. He left money for the house on the kitchen table.

That first week after the wedding, silence spread all over the house like ivy and held it tight. Then it grew thorns. There was no rejection like this rejection. Katula cried because this had nothing to do with the famous British reserve, nothing to do with Islam. And to think that he could be attracted to her darkness! Then she stopped the tears: Don't be stupid, focus.

She spent the early months of their marriage in her bedroom. She did not watch TV. She did not go to any rooms other than the kitchen and bathroom. She did a lot of overtime. Ahead of her were the two years before she could change her visa, then another year to get her citizenship; she would do it. In the meantime, she continued to refurbish and cook. After cooking, she would call out, 'Food is ready' to Malik's door. Then she would leave the kitchen so that he could come and get his food.

Six months after their wedding, Malik relaxed.

One day, Katula came home from work and found him waiting in the corridor. He told her that they were eating out because it was their six-month anniversary. She went along with the charade the way you do with a parent you suspect has lost their mind. When they came back home from the restaurant, Malik told her about mahr, a dowry, normally of gold, given to a bride in Islam. Then he gave her a satchel. Inside were a three-colour gold herringbone necklace with gold earrings, an engagement ring, a wedding ring and a gold watch with a matching bracelet. He had also bought himself a similar wedding band and a watch like hers, only his were larger.

'They're twenty-one carat: I bought them at a his and hers promotion at H. Samuel.'

Katula blinked and blinked. Then she sighed. Malik held his breath. When she accepted the dowry, he held her tight, really tight. Then he buried his head in her shoulder and his body started to shake.

'I'm not a bad person, Kat, I'm not.'

'I know.'

'I'll look after you, Kat. You trust me, don't you?'

'Of course I do.'

'Thank you.' He let go of her suddenly and walked to his bedroom and locked the door. Katula went to her bedroom and cried. Malik was at war with himself yet there was no room to say *I know*, or *I understand*. Or *Let's talk about it*. To think that she considered herself trapped. At least the door to her cell was open. Malik's was bolted from both inside and out.

*

One day, out of the blue, Malik told Katula that they should start sending money to her mother regularly because he knew how hard life was in the Third World. Tobago was in the Third World, but he never sent money to his father. In fact, his face clamped shut whenever Katula asked about his dad. 'Dad is a brute,' he once said.

When Katula rang home and told her mother about Malik's generosity, her mother said, 'God has remembered us.' The last time Katula rang, her mother begged, 'If doctors over there have failed, come home and see someone traditional. Sometimes, it's something small that hinders conception, Katula. You can't risk losing him: he's such a good man.'

'Malik is British, Mother: they don't leave their wives just because they're barren.'

'Listen, child, a man is a man: sooner or later he'll want a child.'

To get rid of her mother's nagging, Katula said that she would discuss it with Malik and let her know.

On payday, Malik transferred half his salary into Katula's account for the household. At first, Katula wanted to con-tribute, but he said: 'In Islam, a man must meet all his wife's needs. Your earnings are your own.'

Sometimes, however, Katula was overcome by irrational fury, especially when Malik gave her money unnecessarily, saying, 'Why don't you go and buy yourself some shoes or handbags? All women love shopping.'

In such moments, she wanted to scream *Stop apologising!*

Sometimes, Malik's strict adherence to the five prayers a day seemed slavish to her, as if he was begging God to change

him. She would clench her fists to stop herself from screaming *How can God create you the way you are and then say, 'hmm,
if you pray hard and I fancy it, I can change you?'* But instead she
would glower, avoiding him, banging her bedroom door. At
such times, silence returned to the house for days, but Malik
was patient. He would coax her out of her dark moods with
generosity. Katula knew that with a husband like that, a lot
of women back home would consider her extremely lucky.

She arrived at the postbox.

As she reached to slip the envelopes into the letter box,
she looked up. Near the school gate, a lollipop lady walked to
the middle of the road. She stopped and planted the lollipop
onto the road, blew her whistle and held her hand out to the
left. Cars stopped. Parents with little ones crossed the road.
Katula looked beyond them, down at the park covered in
barren snow. She let the envelopes fall through the postbox's
mouth and turned to walk back to the house she shared with
a husband who played at marriage the way children play at
having tea.

This time when he returns, she told herself, it is over: I
am done.

MEMOIRS OF A NAMAASO

My British name is Stow. I am sixteen human years old and I was born a pariah dog in Uganda; call me feral if you are contemptuous. I only became a pet when I arrived in Britain fifteen years ago. I have three or four weeks to live.

Some Ugandan dogs are basenji, some are African village dogs (don't ask); I am a Namaaso – we have beautiful eyes and when our tails are in the air we are a sight to behold, apparently. I am the first Namaaso to see the British Isles, and the story of how I ended up here, what I've seen, would blow the fur off your coat. Lately, because the days to my passing on are long and the nights are slow, memories have been coming. I thought I may as well write them down. Besides, that name Stow is full of lies – I should tell my side of the story. Bear with me if I don't remember everything in the right order.

★

The thing you need to know is that flying is like the dizziness you feel before you faint. I can't imagine why humans inflict it on themselves except for the possibility that they hate themselves as much as we real animals hate them. The hissing and rumbling and groaning in the pitch darkness of the hold. The tugging sensation just before a shooting speed as the plane launches itself, delirious. Then the weightlessness as luggage, below and above and everywhere, groans and we tilt back, rising. The way the smell of earth thins as gravity loses us. I must have passed out because next we were stable, but the earth was still lost. Though we were outside gravity, now and again the plane dropped and my body dropped slower and my organs slowest. Have you ever felt light-headed in your stomach? It was so cold in the sky I wondered what happened to the sun. Did you know oceans smell large and heady? These sensations went on and on until I sensed three cats and two dogs in the hold. I howled. They ignored me, but I was reassured by their lack of fear. Then Orora's scent came and I raised my head. The sweet, sweet scent of her concern when she responded. A cat snapped, *Shut up, you're on a plane, you're not going to die.* Another asked Orora, *Is your friend a Musenji?* The humiliation. Cats – scoundrels who eat cockroaches and rats – were talking down to me!

I don't know her breed, Orora replied, but I was beyond shock by then. Then I heard her whisper, *I think she's a stray,* and my humiliation was complete.

When I asked Orora whether she smelt the sea, the pets said all they could smell was my evacuation.

One moment I was ferreting around roadsides, nosing, roasting under the keen Ugandan sun, the heat off the ground stewing my brisket, the next I was on a plane and a pain so sharp was perforating my inner ears because gravity was back and earth reclaiming us. I died.

The night before the ordeal up in the air, I went to the lufula as usual, the one on Old Port Bell Road. Normally, I set off before midnight, when traffic trickles. When you've had so many roadkills in your family, you respect the five seconds it takes to cross a road in Kampala.

Work in the lufula started at midnight. Evilest hour if you are a meat-maker. By the time I arrived there, the butchering had started. I feasted on goat and cow entrails that were small enough to run through the gutters. It was two o'clock when I stopped eating and set off for home. A few paws and I realised I'd eaten too much – the problem of being a pariah: your stomach loses its brakes from constant hunger. I decided to lie down while the tightness in my stomach loosened. But then I thought, Kaweewo, why not stay the night? Find a space, sleep away from marked turfs and spend tomorrow exploring the territories in these parts. Tomorrow night you'll start eating as soon as the butchering starts and then set off for home. I walked to an open space that no one had laid claim to and lay down.

I woke with the sunrise and set off nosing the roadsides, ferreting out scurries to chase and sniffing out stupid pets on leashes or kennelled. I also needed to work off a lingering fullness from the previous night's feed. But by mid-morning I was bored. I decided to go home and yawn the day away in my familiar. I had a few bones marinating in the earth around the airstrip in case I did not feel like trotting back to the lufula in the night.

I reached Wampewo Avenue by noon and trudged up Kololo Hill towards my home at the airstrip. I branched off at Lower Kololo Terrace Road to take a break from the gradient and walk in the shade of the trees because the sun was just showing off that day. It was when I turned into Dundas Road that I caught a whiff of her. Naturally, I tracked her. I only trotted because there was no threat in her scent. However, she was a stranger and she felt too close to our turf. Then I saw her. I pranced, my manner half-playful, half-threatening because she had to be dumb beyond idiocy to be trespassing our streets unaccompanied. Closer up, she looked like a fat pup. By the time she realised, I was upon her. She yelped and backed into the hedge, shouting, *You big wolf.*

I laughed. I could not maintain my menace: not with that compliment.

It's not funny, you big bully.

Thank you very much, I said. *But what are you?*

What do you mean, what am I?

You're not from our parts and you seem grown, but you're so little rats would challenge you.

I am grown! Four years old already, thank you very much.

Full four years? And this is all you are? I am not yet a year old.

143

I puffed myself up but she didn't seem impressed. *You have too much fur*, I observed. *Is that how you puff yourself up, or are you conservation territory for fleas and ticks?*

Her fur stood on end and she shuddered and scratched. *Stop saying that.*

Never mind fleas and ticks; the heat under that coat will kill you first.

I was nosing the air up and down the road in case other pariahs came and saw me fraternising with not just a pet but a dog so small a musu rat would chase it. To be safe, I broke out into a prance, jumping at her and back, at her and back, in half-threats half-laughter.

Please stop that.

Got to do it. Pets could be watching behind these hedges. And you know how you pets gossip. I can't risk being outcasted for stooping so low. I pranced back and forth, back and forth. *Even I can't believe I'm talking to you right now. Normally, I have pride and haughtiness, but I must admit, you're a curiosity. I mean, I would be terribly embarrassed if I were four and so little.*

For a moment she seemed to have run out of breath to speak. She contemplated me, tilted her head this way, that way, as if to make me out. But just then I smelt cousin Njovu coming and barked: *Run, run, run! I need to chase and show you wrath because Njovu is coming.*

She was hesitating, asking, *Who is Njovu?* when I unleashed my scariest growl and she scurried back through the hedge into her human's field. I gave her a moment and then went after her. Luckily, it took me time to crawl through the narrow hole she had made in the hedge. When I reached the field on the other side, I dragged her further away from the road into the hedge at the back of the house. I lay down and told her to climb on top of me to disguise my scent. We lay quiet. Njovu got to the hedge and raised her nose to gauge how far off I was. Then she called. We kept quiet. She called again. She must have sensed I was okay because she walked away.

Once Njovu was out of scent, I threw the pet off my back and we came out of hiding. The pet said to me, *Welcome.*

*Welcome? What welcome, how dare...*but then I realised I was on her turf and turned to leave. Pet, despite her minuscule size, was getting bold. I said, *By the way, this whole road is my family's; so is the golf course. We don't tolerate trespassers. Either stay within your compound or in your hedge.*

She said, *Could we be friends? My name is Orora and I'm a Pomeranian, and my human and I visit Uganda often.* She was yapping so fast there was no time to be shocked by the outrage after outrage she was uttering. *When we're here, my human leaves me on my own for long periods; sometimes he doesn't come back for the entire day. I've always wanted to make Ugandan friends.*

I stared. This dog was so outside reality even the pet community in Uganda would be shocked. Even pets loved it when humans went to sleep and the world belonged to us. But here was a dog who complained about being left alone. I started to walk away – I was beyond words.

She followed me, so I said, *Look, whatever your name, truth is: you are a pet, I am a pariah. You enjoy captivity, I would die if anyone tampered with my freedom. You gave up ownership of yourself for food, we feed ourselves. You miss your human; to us, humans are the vermin destroying the earth. Tell me, what will I gain from being friends with you?* I knew pets were dumb, but I'd never come across this version of dumbness.

This territory, she offered, *including the hedge, the garden around the house and even inside the house, could be yours if you became my friend.*

Tempting, I said, but I kept walking. *Look, I've given you my time and I've held back on terrorising you; that's too much already. This tiny territory, enclosed territory, mind you, is not worth my dignity, my reputation and my place in my family.* I was by the hedge now.

Don't you want to see my house?

You mean your prison?

No, my human's house.

I stopped. At the time, I was fascinated by pet dogs' obsession with 'the house'.

In Uganda, dogs were not allowed indoors. Apparently, if a dog started snouting inside the house, the humans shouted *Out, out, get out,* but they allowed cats in. To tell the truth, I'd never seen the inside of a house before then. Curiosity won out and I turned back.

And just like that, the course of my life changed. All these years, I've looked back on that moment – I could have stayed in the lufula, I shouldn't have branched off at Lower Kololo Terrace Road, I should have chased Orora off the road, but all that doesn't matter; it was curiosity that brought me here.

The house was exactly what I had imagined, enclosed concrete. To make matters worse, we didn't make it out of the second room because Orora had asked me to taste her pebbles. I said fine. After all, we were inside a house and there were no strays or pets to see me. The pebbles were crunchy and tasty, but my pride was still high.

They're soggy like insects, I spluttered. *You know the roasted grasshoppers humans eat? Your food is like that.*

You're not all that big, you know, the pet said.

I menaced towards her. *What did you say, scurry? What did you say?*

She walked backwards but ended up on the wall. Standing on her hinds, her back against the wall, she said, *I mean, there are dogs bigger than you in Manchester, where I come from. As big as a lion.*

I contemplated her strangeness and laughed, *Yeah, right! I bet some canines are elephants where you come from.*

You don't have to make fun of me. I'm just saying that size doesn't matter to us because neither territory nor hunting matters.

Oh my tail, I sighed. *Because you're pets, small head, get it? You Are Pets.*

I walked to a huge trunk in the corner, which was a riot of meat essences. The smells were tight as if compressed and dry. They escaped in intense spurts. Thinking, Here is some food I recognise, I was beginning to isolate the smells one by one, when Orora shrieked, *My human is back*. I looked up; he was at the front door-opening. I nudged the lid of the trunk open, slipped in and the lid closed. I heard Orora jump on top of the trunk and sit down.

But her human wasn't alone; he came with two others. For some time, they moved about the house; their steps were heavy, like trudging, going out of the house, but quick and light coming back. Orora remained quiet on top of the trunk.

Then all three humans' footsteps came and stood around the trunk. Orora was lifted off. I heard her wriggle and yelp. I prepared to spring out and run as soon as they opened the trunk.

Instead, the lid was fastened then the trunk was lifted. I became weightless. One human remarked, *It's a bit heavy this time*, but the others just grunted. By now I could hear Orora below me jumping, yapping, *Don't worry, I'm coming along. Stay quiet. I'll see you soon. You'll be fine.* Her human shouted, *Stop that racket, Orora! She's normally placid*, he said to the others, but Orora didn't stop. *I won't bring you again*, her human threatened: then she was quiet. For me, all sorts of terrors had set in. The trunk was wrestled into a vehicle, doors banged, the ignition started and movements began, taking me along. I'll not lie, I soiled myself. Little did I know then that I was leaving my familiar for good.

All this time I've lived in Britain, I've not seen roadkill. Squirrels, yes, but not one dog or cat. In Uganda, roadkill for us was 'died of natural causes', like malaria to humans. Too many cars for dogs to grow old. Orora had dementia in her last days. It was hard watching her work out food from water, getting lost in the backyard, the trembles and the shakes. The heartbreak when she did not recognise me. That's when I started to resent longevity. To see a proud dog who used to hold their dung and urine until evening walks have accidents all over the carpet! Yet she was lucid enough to be horrified at herself. That is the darkest kennel in which to be held. It makes you long for Ugandan roads.

It's a month since my human, the second one, decided to put me down, but she's procrastinating. The moment she made the decision she gave off a stench of self-loathing and guilt. She wept to herself, stroking me, apologising until I licked her: *I'm ready, stop being selfish.* They're dead to our senses. I try to keep away from her pain for me but she won't let me alone. Her grief is killing my relief. It's the same scent she and her sister emitted just before they put Orora down. We were happy they had come to their senses, but their misery was unbearable. Unfortunately, they didn't take me along to the vet for Orora's passing. I would have liked to feel her go. Then perhaps the human stench of bereavement would have been bearable. The previous night we said good-bye, me and Orora. We squeezed onto my couch. She kept telling me to stop missing her because my scent was keeping her awake, that I should wait till she was gone. She hoped then that our humans would put me down soon afterwards. That was two years ago. Selfish, that's what it is.

The day Orora came to visit at the vet's clinic! I felt her the minute she leapt out of the car. Orora was a breed, no fault of her own, but she had a heart bigger than my mother's, the bravery of a wolf, the determination of a dingo, the per-sistence of a jackal and the cunning of a true fox. No truer canine. When she felt me alive, she bounded into the clinic, upsetting humans and their pets, jumped all over me, yapping as if someone had taken her pups and returned them. You have no idea what a familiar scent of a dog does to you when you come back to life in an animal clinic with pets odd and weird staring at you, in a strange country where you've been subjected to bizarre things like shampoo baths. We licked each other until our mouths went dry. I tried to get up but wooziness brought me down.

Orora yapped, *They didn't put you down, they didn't put you down.*

I said, *But they did; look, I'm right down on the floor.*

She said, *You're in England.* I said, *England is outside reality; look at the creatures you call dogs. Why is everyone so meek?*

Shhh, she laughed, *they'll hear you!*

After that day, we were inseparable. Even during walks, when pets laughed *Look what Orora dragged in,* she stood by me. And I confess it wasn't easy, because I didn't know how to hide my contempt for pets.

I don't know what happened at Manchester airport when we landed. I was comatose. Later, Orora told me that our human had special arrangements with friends in Customs. Whenever his trunks from Africa were deplaned, they were identified by the friends and diverted to a warehouse without going through the proper channels. In fact, Orora told me, she had never been through Customs because they quarantine pets returning from abroad.

When the human discovered me in the trunk, he almost died of shock. However, Orora fussed so much her human drove me straight to the vet. For me, I was yesterday's dead. I was resurrected in a clinic by a vet caressing my hocks. Two other vets came around and smiled and made noises as if I were a pup again. Resurrecting to the vicious smells in the clinic, I thought humans are lucky they're smell-dead. There were artificial concoctions grating my nostrils. Metallic flavours stinging my rhinarium. Then the smells of pain, of fear and of the animals passed on. I was still working out how I felt about being resurrected when I started shaking so violently my vision went. When I woke up again, I was in a cot, like a human pup, only on the floor.

Our human carried me from the vet's clinic and laid me on the back seat. Orora jumped in with me. She licked me. *It's fine, car rides are fine, just relax, you'll get used to it and start to enjoy them.* She couldn't stop bouncing on the seat, yelping, *My world isn't torture, just different*, there were things she couldn't wait to show me, she couldn't wait for me to meet other pets. Me, I was busy sensing out the pariahs in Manchester, plotting how soon I would escape and find a pariah family. I needed to locate where, what and who was who so I could map myself on the territory, but I was getting nothing. The air felt so dry my nose was parched. At first, I thought it was the medicines the vets had injected into me. I feared they had killed my senses. Finally, I confessed: *Orora, I think I've lost my sensing, I don't feel this place.*

She laughed so hard she fell off her seat. *You've not lost your perception. Compared to Kampala, which – with all due respect – is an assault on everything sensory, Manchester is tame.*

So how do you find your way home in case you run too far in the night?

Why would I run too far in the night?

When you've been out exploring because humans are sleeping or you run into hostiles who chase you far from your familiar.

Orora looked at me funny then laughed. *It won't happen.* She must have seen the worry on my face, for she added, *Maybe the car's moving too fast for you to register things? You'll soon get used to the sights and sounds around our area, don't worry.*

We arrived at the house. Car door unlocked, Orora bounded out. I stepped out unsteadily. Orora was already impatient at the entrance door. Our human opened and Orora bounded up the stairs. Me, I lingered below, looking up. Orora, up on the landing, said, *Come on.* I claimed wooziness but I was lying. I wasn't woozy. I was entering pet-hood. Our human lifted me and we went up two flights. Once again, Orora was impatient at the door.

But once inside, my pariah instincts kicked in and I nosed every inch of the house. It was carpet, carpet, coats hung. Only one human scent. Door, carpet, carpet, chairs, table, wall, sofa, gadgets, wall, carpet, carpet, linoleum, bathroom – humans drop dung in a bowl indoors! Strong sleep scents in the bedroom. My nose led me to the last room. Another trunk, empty but distant smells of snake, rhino horn, lion, cheetah, elephant lingered. Before I could say *I would love to sleep in this room*, Orora pulled me out by the ears: *Never, ever go sniffing in that room again.*

Apparently, one time our human saw her sniffing and gave off the foulest fear. Then he sniffed everywhere comically. Then he sprayed the house with that nauseating stuff. *You won't believe what humans call air-refresher*, she said. *Most revolting.*

I returned to the living room and Orora showed me my couch. I laughed because I couldn't believe her. I abhorred becoming a pet, but I looked forward to sleeping on that couch. Then I went to the kitchen, which I'd been putting off all this time. I walked nonchalantly as if I weren't fighting my nose, which wanted to raid the bin there and then. I already knew that the bin, hidden in the corner and a paradise of meats, was forbidden. Pets in Uganda used to say *If you want to see a human go dingo on you, tip the bin over.* I stopped. For the first time in my life, I won the battle against my nose.

Afterwards, our human sat down on his sofa with a can of beer. He burst the top, took a swig and then snapped his fingers at me. I stood up, took reluctant paws towards him.

'Sit.'

Orora sat. I flicked my tongue: *I'll sit when I'm ready.* But Orora whispered, *Sit on your hinds, please.* I sat.

'Right,' the human said, pointing at me, 'you need a name.'

My tail swept the carpet. In Uganda, pets have such original names, like Police, Simba, Askari. I thought, Maybe this human was more creative. I could see him thinking. A name arrived in his head and his eyes lit up. He snapped his fingers and pointed.

'Stow, for Stowaway.'

I looked at Orora: *Really?* She said, *Aww, I like Stow. Others don't have to know what it means.* I just walked away, curled up on my couch and put my head down.

*

One day I lost it.

Dogs in Britain had never heard of a Namaaso. The blank faces when I explained what a pariah is. They understood one thing only: stray. I laboured the fact that there was no pet blood in my family but the dogs thought I was just ignorant. As I explained myself, this pug laughed, *Stow, you're so anonymous you don't even have a breed!*

See, this was the pug who bragged about his pedigree. I asked him, *And what has being a thoroughbred done for you? That lazy nose?* I turned to the basset hound who had joined in the laughing and asked him, *Were you a seal in your former life?* Even that couple of spooky ghost dogs – they call themselves Irish wolfhounds – had been sniggering. I said, *And you, why don't you find a broom, fly in the moonlight and find yourselves a witch human?* The bull terrier started going all goody-goody on me: *Stow, you can't say things like that, we're all beautiful.*

I said, *Not you, sweetheart. You should sue the humans for what they did to your nature.*

She said, *I've never been subjected to such prejudice in my entire life.*

I said, *Somehow I don't believe that. Unless cats in Britain have lost their tongues.*

A Persian shouted, *Leave felines out of it.*

Poor Orora. She apologised, saying that I didn't mean what I said, that I didn't understand the nature of breeds, that it was those differences that made all dogs unique and beautiful and wonderful. She didn't talk to me for days. Maybe I was a bit of a dingo then.

*

The day I arrived, we stayed indoors all day, all night.

I had never known a night so dead. No insects, no lizards, a few birds and squirrels. I thought the silence would kill me. I was restless. Night was calling.

The following day I asked, *Orora, when do we skip outside to explore?*

She said, *In this country, we stay indoors. It can get very cold outside.*

I could not believe it: the house was a cage. Only you were not let out at night. I climbed up onto the sofa below the window and gazed outside. It was not cold when we arrived. Orora sensed my turmoil and said, *It was a good day yesterday, but you can't just go outside without a human. You can't run around unsupervised in this country. You need to be put on a lead.*

The L-word. Orora saw my fur standing on end and added, *Only during walks.*

I desperately needed to run around the village and sniff out the canine world – who is the alpha, who is his favourite, who is in season, what kind of males has she pulled, who has become roadkill, who did not return last night, who was attacked, who has been outcasted?

On our first walk, I couldn't believe this world. Dogs as fat as meat-makers. Even cats. I'd thought *cat* and *lean* were synonymous. Arrogant pigeons. No fear at all. They wouldn't even fly out of your way. You growled, they *orhoo*ed right back. Squirrels so contemptuous they laughed if you threatened. When I dropped dung, our human picked it up.

Embarrassment showered under my fur. Was I not supposed to drop a dump?

But there was no anger in our human. I thought, This is messed up in more ways than a hyena. Then I saw Orora being picked up after and I relaxed a bit. In Uganda, cats called us foulers because we don't dig a hole to do our business and bury it. It's the one thing that makes us insecure. Now I imagined the contemptuous things British cats said behind our backs and the following day I tried to bury, but Orora said, *Don't bother, you only make it harder for our human.* I saw other humans picking up after their dogs and left it. I had travelled to so far outside reality my nose would not find my way back even if I tried.

As for food, what can I say? At first, I was given those pebbles in a bowl. Then a bowl of water. When I tasted them in Uganda, they were good as a snack, but I'm sorry, pebbles and water simply do not constitute a meal. For pet food, I could tolerate mashed sweet potatoes in peanut butter sauce mixed with mukene fish or posho soaked in the juices of a lamb joint, preferably salted and raw. But pebbles are a joke. Dog biscuits are fake food. Luckily, the bin in the house was always bulging. Our first human loved chicken drumsticks and thighs. Often, they went out of date and he threw them away. Sausage, salami, bacon, gammon, burgers, hot dogs, cheese oh heavenly cheese, venison, elk, turkey and milk. I felt like a pariah again foraging in the bin. At first Orora was disgusted as I crunched chicken bones – *Stop it, Stow! You'll be sick.* I'd point at my stomach: *I have a crusher in there.* By the time she died, sausage and salami were Orora's favourites.

When the first human found out I ate out of the bin, he started sharing his food. I must confess, steak, rare, salted, dripping with blood, is the ultimate. I needed to drink a lot of water after a gammon or a pork shank. Hooked me on salt. The best times are at Christmas open markets when farmers bring meats straight from slaughter on their farms onto the fire. All forms of human cooking, BBQ, charcoal muchomo, grilled, baked, breaded and fried, cured; it's a madness of flavours. The human, the first one, would buy a lot of meat and we would eat together. Even Orora started to look forward to it. Even when we were taken to the dog sanctuary, the first human told them: 'Stow, the big one, eats meat cooked with salt. Orora, the Pomeranian, eats dog food.'

I'd never seen so many different natures of dogs in one place as I did in Manchester. I asked Orora, *Are you all native to Britain?* She said, *We're native to the world.* I looked at her because now she could say whatever she wanted to me. *However, humans call us breeds.* Then she told me how humans create breeds by selection. I was revolted. But she said, *Oh, it's not like Dolly the sheep.* I'd never heard of Dolly the sheep.

The first time I saw a Chihuahua, I thought it was a battery-powered toy. Eyes too big for the face, ears of a large dog, took tens of steps to keep up, squeaked like a two-month-old pup. I thought, This can't be right. I whispered to Orora, *Did humans do that to her?* She bit my ear and I kept quiet. But because British humans love travelling with their pets, I warned the Chihuahua, *Don't ever let your*

human take you to Uganda: a kite could swoop down and carry
you off for dinner.

The Chihuahua burst into tears, claimed it was traumatised.

The day humans took our first human away, we sensed nothing at all until it was too late. He didn't travel to Uganda any
more. But empty trunks kept coming and going. However,
on this night, I don't know what possessed him. A trunk with
animal bits arrived. I suspect that the smell of hides and skins
threw my now blunt nose off balance because I didn't smell
anything until it was too late.

We were asleep when I felt the agitation of strange foxhounds. Two of them downstairs, too close to our block.
Then strange humans, non-residents. I sat up and listened.
Their anticipation was mixed with worry and uncertainty
as if they were going on a hunt. I nudged Orora. She said, *It*
must be the neighbours downstairs; they do drugs, and went back
to sleep. But I hadn't lost my pariah instincts entirely. I told
her, *They're coming for us*, and went to the human's door. I
scratched and whimpered until he woke up. When he opened
the door, I ran up and down the house. Orora was irritated.
The human turned on the lights and the agitation outside
surged. I raised my voice, but he shushed me and ordered
me back to the couch. I slid under his worktable, tucked my
tail in and skulked. He understood. He turned off the light
and listened. Then he peered behind the curtain. It was like
a trigger; humans outside crept up the stairs. Instead of out
of the house the human ran to his bedroom.

The house was blitzed, humans shrieking orders, blinding torches, boots stomping like soldiers at the airstrip on Uganda Independence Day. The savages forced our human onto the floor and handcuffed him. Orora tried to disappear into me. The contemptuous foxhounds nosed the house like pariahs taking over a new territory. They laughed as they told us the human was a wildlife smuggler.

Lick him goodbye, you'll never see him again.

Yep, prepare for the impound.

As the humans dragged our human away, he told them that there were two dogs in the house; that if we were separated neither one would eat.

The trunk was carried out.

Humans were everywhere turning everything upside down, knocking on walls and listening. The house was under their guard for the rest of the night.

Later in the morning when the impound humans came for us, I saw Orora terrified. She was leaving her home forever. I had no such attachments, as long as Orora and I were together. At the sanctuary we were put in the same room. We huddled together day and night.

Orora became a star to prospective humans. She performed. I could not perform adorability if I tried. Dogs said I was grumpy and morose; I was ungrateful because they would give anything for a human like the one we had. I was holding Orora back; I should just be put down. I said, *Bring it on; better than being a pet.* Orora went, *Don't be like that, Stow. He pretends not to miss him, but he warned our human – didn't you, Stow?* I flicked my tongue, *Me? Miss a human, ppu!*

But then humans became interested in our refusal to be separated. One day, two men came and took pictures and watched us through their cameras for a week. After that, we were overwhelmed by attention. Even my grouchiness seemed to charm the humans. Eventually, we were matched to a couple of elderly sisters. We've been together nine human years now. And when Orora died, they never bought another dog. But then one of the sisters died too and it's just the two of us now. Luckily, I am passing on soon. My human will live another two years maybe and she too will go. Her liver is dying but she has no idea.

I'd not been in season when I arrived in Manchester. And I must confess there were some magnificent breeds; I thought I would be spoilt for choice when my season came. Orora didn't even know what being in season was. I told her it's the happiest time in a female's life. Twice a year you are bathed in this fragrance that sends males so crazy they must fight their way into your presence. Strong males within scenting radius hang around you hoping to be the lucky one. As many as fifteen males around you all day, all night making sure no one touches you. The love and worship showered on you for just a sniff and a lick! You stand up, they all stand up, you trot, they trot, you stop, they stop, you lie down, they sprawl around you.

In preparation for my first season, I drew a list of natures I could mate with. First, no dogs smaller than me. Corgis, terriers, spaniels, not even collies – too shaggy, they remind me of sheep. Don't mention Chihuahuas. Poodles? No thank you – too vain. Call me a bigot if you want, but flamboyance turns on she-birds, peacock tails and all – not me. Even greyhounds were off the menu – too skinny. No dachshunds either. I think in the beginning of time dachshunds aspired to be crocodiles but ended up half-reptile, half-canine. I couldn't bear the melancholy of the bloodhound. No Australian cattle dogs either, those dogs are glorified foxes.

Here are the breeds that made the final list:

- German shepherds. Grrrr. My number one – sheer wolf!
- Great Danes. Hatari! Canine royalty right there!
- Dobermann pinschers. Mwoto-mwoto! No-nonsense. Old-school.
- Akita. Must be a Ugandan name. The Akita are so beautiful you just want to have their pups.
- Siberian huskies. Wow! Wild kabisa. Killer eyes! Have you seen them dogs in motion? Agile, swift. I swear sometimes I think I prefer them to Alsatians.
- Dalmatians. Tamu-tamu. I call them white jaguars – so regal.
- Alaskan malamutes. Dishy but rather haughty. So into themselves, don't you think? Still, they would get an invite.
- Labradors. Lick, lick, lick. A bit tame but I suspect that a whiff of a female in season would let loose the wolf in them.

- St Bernards. They look kind of boring but would get an invite. You never know.

As you can imagine, I wanted big, I wanted fearless, I wanted speed and strength – males that promised sturdy pups – but I drew the line at the Newfoundland. Those monsters would break your back.

But at the time, I seemed to rub everyone the wrong way. They called me all sorts – sizeist, bigot, breedist. When we went for walks, not one male glanced at my butt let alone sniffed it. I thought, Wait till I'm in season, you'll come crawling on your bellies. I should've known something was wrong. The first day in season I woke up, climbed on the sofa and snouted between the curtains. I looked through the window expecting a crowd of males, restless downstairs. The car park was empty.

I wanted out of the house. If loving wouldn't come to me, I would go and get me some for myself, but the door was locked. When eventually time for the walk came, I was not just put on the leash, I was muzzled.

Picture this. You're a debutante, coming out on your first day in season – in a muzzle, on a leash! I couldn't walk beautiful if I tried.

In the park, there was not a flicker of interest from the males, neither sniffs nor licks, nada. Just snide remarks that the muzzle became me. Then the mongrel whispered to me: *Eunuchs!*

First I choked, then shivered, then I was filled with contempt. I wouldn't wish that on a hyena. For the rest of the day, I was frustrated, confused, angry, restless and disgusted. I needed male loving. But when I turned on poor Orora – I attacked her in the night, apparently – we visited the vet again. Never been in season since.

I had never seen dogs with issues – I mean deep-seated issues – like I saw at the dog shelter. In Uganda we had ticks, fleas, kawawa flies that ate flesh off your ears, worms, fungi and, more seriously, you could get rabies. There were also antisocial pariahs, but some of the things I saw at the sanctuary? No.

If you want to find out which breed has fallen out of human favour, go to dog shelters. I love ice cream, but how can a dog be addicted to chocolate? And when sanctuary staff stop giving it to her she suffers withdrawal symptoms? I saw a dog who freaked out every time she smelt cigarettes. Another arrived at the sanctuary shaved naked. One involuntarily evacuated at the sound of human footsteps. But if a human came talking or whistling then she was fine. I saw a dog who fell to the ground scratching in agony, I saw pugs who could not breathe, dogs with cigarette burns all over their coats. Yet all of them believed that the next human would be the one. This canine love for humans in Britain baffled me.

It is happening. I am going to Jirikiti. Even the sun is out. My tail is not what it used to be; I would have danced. My human is in her bedroom getting dressed. They found out about her liver. Unlike other humans, she's not going to fight it. She's a tough one, my human. Did I tell you we're the same age, me and my human? Eighty-four. In Uganda, they call my kind Mbwa ya Namaaso…

PART 2

RETURNING

SHE IS OUR STUPID

My sister Biira is not: she's my cousin. Ehuu!

Ever heard of King Midas's barber, who saw the king's donkey ears and carried the secret until it became too much to bear? I could not hold it in any longer. I stumbled across it five years ago at Biira's wedding and I have been carrying it since. But unlike Midas's barber – stupid sod dug a hole in the earth, whispered the secret in there and buried it – my family does not read fiction. A bush grew over the barber's words and every time the wind blew, the bush whispered, *King Midas has donkey ears*. I have also changed the names. Of course, the barber was put to death. But for me, if this story gets back to my family, death will be too kind.

Back in 1961, Aunty Flower went to Britain on a sikaala to become a teacher – sikaala was scholarship or sikaalasip. Her name was Nnakimuli then. At the time, Ugandan scholars to Britain could not wait to come home, but not Aunty Flower;

she did not write either. Instead, she translated *Nnakimuli* into *Flower* and was not heard from until 1972.

It was evening when a special hire from the airport parked in my grandfather's courtyard. Who jumped out of the car? Nnakimuli. As if she had left that morning for the city. They did not recognise her because she was so skinny a rod is fat. And she moved like a rod too. Then the hair. It was so big you thought she carried a mugugu on her head. And the make-up? Loud. But you know parents, a child can do things to herself but a parent will not be deceived. It was Grandfather who said, 'Isn't this Nnakimuli?'

Family did not know whether to unlock their happiness because when her father reached to hug her, Nnakimuli planted kisses – on his right cheek and on his left – and her father did not know what to do. The rest of the family held onto their happiness and waited for her to guide them on how to be happy to see her. When she spoke English to them, they apologised: *Had we known you were coming we would have bought a kilo of meat...haa, dry tea? Someone run to the shop and get a quarter of sugar...Remember to get milk from the mulaalo in the morning...Maybe you should sit up on a chair with Father; the ground is hard...The bedroom is in the dark...Will you manage our outside bathroom and toilet?...Let's warm your bathwater – you won't manage our cold water.* And when Nnakimuli said her name was Flower, the disconnect was complete. Their rural tongues called her *Fulawa*. When she helped them, *Fl, Fl, Flo-w-e-r*, they said *Fluew-eh*. Nonetheless, she had brought a little something for everyone. People whispered *There's a little of Nnakimuli left in this Fulawa.*

Not Fulawa, maalo, it's Fl, Fl, Flueweh, and they collapsed in giggles.

The following morning, Flower woke up at five, chose a hoe and waited to go digging. She scoffed when family woke up at 6 a.m. Now she spoke Luganda like she never left. Still, family fussed over her bare feet, chewing their tongues speaking English: 'You'll knock your toes, you're not used.' But she said, 'Forget Flower; I am Nnakimuli.'

She followed them to the garden where they were going to dig. When they divided up the part that needed weeding, they put her at the end in case she failed to complete her portion. She finished first and started harvesting the day's food, collected firewood, tied her bunch and carried it on her head back home. She then fetched water from the well until the barrel in the kitchen was full. She even joined in peeling matooke. When the chores were done, she bathed and changed clothes. She asked Yeeko, her youngest sister, to walk her through the village greeting residents, asking about the departed, who got married – *How many children do you have?* – and the residents marvelled at how Nnakimuli had not changed. However, they whispered to her family *Feed her; put some flesh on those bones before she goes back*. Nnakimuli combed the village, remembering, eating wild fruit, catching up on gossip. For seven days, she carried on as if she were back for good and family relaxed. Then on the eighth day, after the chores, she got dressed, gave away her clothes and money to her father. She knelt down and said goodbye to him.

'Which goodbye?' The old man was alarmed. 'We're getting used to you: where are you going?'

'To the airport.'

'Yii-yii? Why didn't you tell us? We'd have escorted you.'

Entebbe airport had a waving bay then. After your loved one checked in, you went to the top and waited. When they walked out on the tarmac, you called their name and waved. Then they climbed the steps to the plane, turned at the door and waved to you one last time and you jumped and screamed until the door closed. Then the engine whirred so loud it would burst your ears and it was both joyous and painful as the plane taxied out of sight and then it came back at a nvumulo's speed and jumped in the air and the wheels tucked in and you waved until it disappeared. Then a sense of loss descended on you as you turned away.

'Don't worry, Dad' – she spoke English now – 'I'll catch a bus to Kampala and then a taxi to the airport.'

Realising that Fulawa was back, her father summoned all the English the missionaries taught him and said, 'Mankyesta, see it for us.'

'Yes, all of it,' her siblings chimed as if Manchester were Wobulenzi Township, which you could take in in a glance.

'Take a little stone,' Yeeko sobbed, 'and throw it into Mankyesta. Then it'll treat you well.'

That was the last time the family saw her sane. She did not write, not even after the wars – the Idi Amin one or the Museveni one – to see who had died and who had survived. Now family believes that when she visited, madness was setting in.

Don't ask how I know all of this. I hear things, I watch, I put things together to get to the truth. Like when I heard my five grandmothers, sisters to my real grandmother who died giving birth to Aunty Yeeko, whisper that Aunty Zawedde should have had Biira. Me being young, I thought it was because Biira is a bit too beautiful. Aunty Zawedde is childless.

In 1981, a Ugandan from Britain arrives looking for the family. He says that Flower is in a mental asylum. Family asks, 'How?' Apparently she started falling mad, on and off, in the 1970s. 'How is she mad?' The messenger didn't know. 'Who's looking after her?' You don't need family to look after you in a mental asylum. 'You mean our child is all alone like that?' She's with other sick people and medical people. 'Who put her there?' Her husband. 'Husband, which husband?' She was married. 'Don't tell me she had children as well.' No. 'Ehuu! But what kind of husband dumps our child in an asylum without telling us? How did he marry her without telling us?' Also, ask yourselves, the messenger said, how Flower married him without telling you. The silence was awkward. However, love is stubborn. Family insisted, 'Us, we still love our person'; Nnakimuli might have been stupid to cut herself off from the family, but she was their stupid. 'Is her husband one of us or of those places?' Of those places. 'Kdto!' They had suspected as much. The messenger gave them the address and left. Family began to look for people who knew people in Britain. Calls were made; letters were written: *We have our person in this place; can you check on her and give us advice?* In the end, family decided to bring Aunty Flower back home: 'Let her be mad here with us.' The British were wonderful; they gave Aunty Flower a nurse to escort her on the flight.

Aunt Flower had got big. A bigness that extended over there. She smoked worse than wet firewood. Had a stash of Marlboros. 'Yii, but this Britain,' family lamented, 'she even learnt to smoke?' With the medicine from Britain, Aunt Flower was neither mad nor sane. She was slow and silent.

Then the medicine ran out and real madness started. People fall mad in different ways. Aunty Flower was agitated, would not sit still, as if caged. 'I am Flower Down, Down with an e.' 'Who?' family asked. 'Mrs Down with an e.' Family accepted. 'I want to go.' 'Go where?' 'Let me go.' 'But where?' 'I could be Negro, I could be West Indian – how do you know?' They let her go. Obviously, England was still in her head. But someone kept an eye on her. All she did was roam and remind people that she was Down with an e. But by 6 p.m., she was home. After a month, the family stopped worrying. Soon the bigness disappeared, but not the smoking. Through the years, Flower Downe roamed the villages laughing, arguing, smoking. She is always smart, takes interest in what she wears. However, if you want to see Aunty Flower's madness properly, touch her cigarettes.

Then in 1989 someone remarked, 'Isn't that pregnancy I see on Flower?' The shock. 'Yii, but men have no mercy – a madwoman?' An urgent meeting of her siblings, their uncles and aunts was called: 'What do we do, what do we do?' There were threats: 'If we ever catch him!' They tried to coax her: 'Flower, who touched you there?' But when she smiled dreamily, they changed tactics: 'Tell us about your friend, Mrs Downe.' She skipped out of the room. A man was hired again to tail her. Nothing.

A few months later, Aunt Flower disappeared. When I came home for the holidays, she was not pregnant. I imagined they had removed it. Meanwhile, Mum had had Biira but I don't remember seeing her pregnant. I was young and stupid and did not think twice about it.

There is nothing to tell about Biira. I mean, what do I know? I am the eldest – she is the youngest. She came late, a welcome mistake, we presumed. Like late children, she was indulged. She is the loving, protective, fiercely loyal but spoilt sister with a wild sense of fashion. We grew up without spectacle, close-knit. However, we do not have a strong family resemblance – everyone looks like themselves. So there is nothing about Biira to single her out apart from being beautiful. But all families have that selfish sibling who takes all the family looks – what can you do? However, if you want to see Biira's anger, say she resembles Aunty Flower.

Then Biira found a man. We did the usual rites families do when a girl gets engaged. Then on the wedding day, Aunty Flower came to church. No one informed her, no one gave her transport, no one told her what to wear, yet she turned up at church decked out in a magnificent busuuti like the mother of the bride. Okay, her jewellery and make-up were over the top, but she sat quiet – no smoking, no agitating, just smiling – as Biira took her vows. And why were Dad and his sibling restless throughout the service? Later they said, 'Flower came because Biira resembles her.' I thought, Lie to yourselves. Aunty Flower never came to any of my cousins' weddings.

The day of Biira's wedding, I looked at Aunt Flower properly and I am telling you the way Biira resembles her is not innocent – I mean gestures, gait, fingers, and even facial expressions. How? I have been watching Aunt Flower since. There is no doubt that her mind is absent – deaths, births, marriages in the family do not register. However, mention Biira and you will see moments of lucidity in Aunt Flower's eyes.

MY BROTHER, BWEMAGE

Up to the moment Nnaava made the announcement that she and Mulumba were getting engaged traditionally, returning to Uganda had not crossed my mind. Uganda had become extended family, cousins you played with as a child but had drifted away from. Occasionally, you remember them when something happens – a death, a marriage or a birth – and ask your mum, *Mpozi, who was that?* But when I realised that we had to go home for Nnaava's rituals, memories started to pop up – City Parents', my former school; church; kamunye taxis; the dust; power cuts; and the pesky boda boda. But these were general recollections. Then the date for the rituals was set and we bought the tickets. That was when details returned.

First were my grandparents. I dreaded that first contact, especially with Dad's parents, when they would look at me like *Even you? To abandon us like that?*

Then there was Dad. Let's put Dad aside.

Then our home. For some reason, it was the outdoors that I remembered best. The compound, especially in the morning under a languid sun before the shadows folded, the ripened guavas, the jackfruit tree laden with browned nduli and long oval pawpaws hanging down the neck of the tree. In the garden by the hedge, Mum had two matooke shrubs and a few stalks of maize and vegetables. The mango tree near the gate was young then. Avocados so big the fruit cracked when they fell. Their skin turned purple when they softened. I could even hear our neighbour, Maama Night, sweeping her yard. But for some reason the inside was hazy. I remembered my bed when I got up and ran to the window to look outside, I remembered the darkness when I woke up thirsty in the night and went to the fridge, I remembered running through the corridor to Mum and Dad's bedroom and throwing myself on their bed. We walked barefoot indoors; we left our shoes and slippers by the door.

To tell the truth, I didn't want to go back. Not after the way we left. I would have gladly stayed in Britain and pretended that Uganda did not exist. But Nnaava, ever the dutiful elder daughter to whom rebellion was sheer selfishness, was going to introduce her fiancé. Dad and the wider family had to be present with all the trappings of kwanjula rites. I had to be there.

As for Mum, God help us. Our mother was very Ugandan when it came to marriage. For her, getting hitched to a man was a coup, far greater than graduating. She would revel in people saying *Well done on getting your eldest married!* then turn to me: 'You're next, Nnabakka; don't let us down.' What bothered me most was the way Nnaava's marriage seemed to have erased the scandal. It was as if we had never fled.

In June 2013, we flew back.

Immigrations at Entebbe did not disappoint. It's a tiny airport, one terminal handling a few flights a day, but the chaos was unbelievable. There was only one queue for all passengers even though there were four desks – two marked UGANDAN PASSPORTS, one marked EAST AFRICAN PASSPORTS and one for INTERNATIONAL PASSPORTS. People jumped out of the queue and walked past you like you were dumb to line up. There were no instructions on the tannoy to guide passengers, no gangway, no staff at the gate to give you directions, no signposts for different queues. We were home. I was beginning to embrace it when we came to the Immigrations desk and had to pay for our visas. We were not Ugandan in Uganda the way we were in Britain. The lady, though she had recognised our names, reminded us not to outstay our visitor visas. That was it. I said, tapping every word on her desk, 'Excuse me, madam; Nze Nnabakka. Ndi Muganda. My totem is Ffumbe, A kabiro Kikere. My sister's name is Nnaava. That means our mother is a royal.' All the Luganda came rushing back. 'Tuli baana ba ngoma, ba kungozi' – I had no idea what that meant – 'ba nvuma. Baganda wawu!' I walked away.

After collecting our bags, I did not realise that I was walking ahead of Mum and Nnaava until I stepped outside Arrivals and a man leapt out of the waiting crowd yelping, 'Nnabakka?' I looked back for Mum; she was not there. I looked at the man again. 'Dad?'

He had wilted: shorter, skinny, dry. His eyes were old. He held me quietly as if savouring the moment. Then he shrieked, 'Nnaava', let go of me and ran to my sister. Then he was back. 'God, Nnabakka: where are you going with this tallness?' Then back to Nnaava: 'Yii, yii, you're getting married!' Back to me: 'At least I still have you...' Then Mum arrived and Dad deflated.

There was no pretending things away any more. Luckily, Mum smiled and Dad rushed to her. They hugged as if he had knocked into her and was steadying her. Then he grabbed her trolley and channelled the rest of his emotions into pushing it. A man stepped out of the waiting crowd and took my trolley. I frowned at Dad. He explained, 'That's Kajja, the driver.'

We followed Dad and Kajja through a tunnel-like walkway until we came to the car park.

Someone clicked a car lock and the lights of two large vans came on. As I started towards the vans, a group of Chinese men and women rushed past, got into the vans and, without lingering, drove off. Kajja, the driver, saw me staring and laughed, 'Ah, the Chinese: Ugandans abandon this country like it's a desert, but to them it's an oasis.'

I felt the sting in 'abandon' and gave Nnaava a *what has it got to do with him?* look. Kajja wheeled our luggage towards a car while Dad steered Mum's to another. Nnaava frowned at me then glanced in Mum and Dad's direction. I looked. Nnaava squeezed my hand. As Kajja put our luggage in the boot, we got in the back of the car and Nnaava whispered, 'I'm glad we're not travelling with them; can you imagine?'

Before I replied, Kajja got into the car and our awareness of what was going on in Mum and Dad's car intensified. It was like hearing moans from your parents' bedroom. And Kajja, like an older sibling distracting the younger ones from their parents' moment, launched into telling us about the development that had taken place in the country since we left. But as we drove from the airport, I couldn't help glancing back at Mum and Dad's car. It followed ours like a bad reputation.

Kajja enjoyed our surprise at the good roads.

'The tender for road maintenance was given to a Chinese company. They repair road surfaces every other year. China has injected life into our economy.'

We wowed. There were new buildings everywhere along Entebbe Road.

'You know that *your* European countries no longer allow *our* corrupt officials to put their money in *your* banks?'

We exchanged looks.

'Eh eh! These days they pack the money in suitcases and buy land and build flats and shopping malls and things like that.'

I contemplated the possibility that development had come to Uganda partly because 'our' European countries had finally banned 'his' corrupt Ugandan officials from banking with them and partly because China had injected life into the economy. Kajja did not realise that it takes more than holding a British passport to make you British. Clearly, he knew what had happened and had taken Dad's side.

'The owner of that building committed suicide,' he was saying. 'Tsk, he was stupid! Anti-corruption caught him and was forcing him to regurgitate the money he ate. He hanged himself, poor guy.'

Mum and Dad's car made to overtake ours. Dad drew level. He hooted to indicate that Kajja was driving too cautiously. I smiled. I had forgotten what a speed junkie Dad was. Kajja stepped on the pedal, but the distance between ours and their car was great.

'That building is empty. No one can afford to rent it. It was built for the CHOGM when your queen came for the Commonwealth.'

A huge neon sign, Xhing Xhing, glowing red atop a high building, welcomed us into Greater Kampala. But in Katwe, shanty structures still stood defiant as if testimony to a hidden truth. We applauded Katwe's heroism but knew it was desperation.

'Katwe is still Katwe.' Kajja was apologetic. It will be the grandchildren of our great-grandchildren who will eradicate it.

The cityscape had changed so much we kept reminding ourselves of what had been. 'That used to be...There was a market there...' turning to the right, to the left, looking for familiar features. Had I been on my own, I would have missed the turning to our house. Huang Fei luxury flats stood where the road used to be.

'What happened to the old woman who lived here?'

'Yeah, her guavas were pink inside and sweet rather than salty.'

'Development swept her away.'

'But she looked after her family graveyard; it used to be—'

'Yes, it used to be around here. She kept it neat with flowers; was it removed?'

'I'm telling you, her children were negotiating with buyers even as she gasped her last breath.'

Mum and Dad were getting out of their car when we arrived. There were huge security lights on every side of the house, but the compound was asleep. Still, I could see that the mango and guava trees were so tall they came to window level on the first floor. Even the hedge was higher. The trees had eaten up so much space the compound looked smaller. The pawpaw tree was gone.

It was close to two in the morning but instead of heading for the door, I retraced my steps along the veranda like I used to, swinging and skipping, to the back of the house. Everything – the outdoor toilet and bathroom, the outdoor kitchen, the kennel, the clothes lines – was still the same. I walked back to the front. It was then, as I got to the front door, that I realised that something was wrong. Dad was unlocking the door rather than someone opening it from inside.

'Dad lives alone?'

Don't ask me, Nnaava shrugged.

There is a knowledge that returns to you the minute you arrive home. It is not just unusual, it is downright suspicious for a man Dad's age and stature to live alone in a big house. It makes people uncomfortable. They whisper, 'What does he get up to in that house on his own?' They even ask you, smiling, 'But why are you hermiting yourself like that? Living alone is not good for your mind.'

I stopped at the doorstep, leant forward and peered inside.

The house was bare.

Only one sofa of the old set stood in a corner of the sitting room. No carpet, no coffee table, no TV, no bookshelves, no curtains. The wedding pictures, our photographs, batiks, even the banner, CHRIST IS THE CENTRE OF OUR HOME, were all gone. I turned to Dad. He tried to conceal his pleasure at my confusion. I looked at Mum: her face was stone. Nnaava anticipated my reaction and looked away before I turned to her. Why was I the only one shocked?

I stepped in. I felt like a ghost returning home after decades of being dead. It was our house, but not the home I had left behind. The emptiness made the rooms large. It made our crumpled flat in Stockport seem like a matchbox. I wanted to laugh at the lone chair at the small dining table. What happened to the glass dining table we had?

No fridge? The security lights outside illuminated the rooms eerily.

I opened the door to the kitchen and turned on the light. An earthen sigiri without any ash squatted on the floor.

Stains of the grime the cooker had made on the floor where it once stood were indelible. A pan, a plate, a cup, a spoon, a fork. They had not been used in a long time. The cupboards were empty. Someone had cleaned hastily.

As I walked back to the sitting room, Nnaava came down the stairs saying, 'All the bedrooms are empty except theirs.'

'This is how you left the house.' Dad came towards us, his voice apologetic. I turned to Mum but Dad, perhaps to spare her, added, 'What you left behind for me was enough. Tonight, and for the three weeks you're going to be around, we can bring mattresses. On the other hand, we can furnish the house, even tomorrow if you want, provided that you're coming back to use it.'

Silence fell and then stretched.

The question of coming back had arisen too soon. We needed to sit down, catch our breath and recover from the ten years. Then consider thinking about it.

'Can we get mattresses for tonight?'

It was right that Mum should say that. After all, she stole us away while Dad was on a pastors' retreat in the US. Nostalgia is a bitch. I had missed home after all. I was not just confused, I was hurt that my home had been gutted so ruthlessly, that Dad looked as abandoned as the house.

'*The girls* will be in a better position to take that decision after they have rested.' Mum distanced herself from any decision of coming back.

Dad stepped out of the house and told Kajja, who sat in the car, to bring the mattresses.

Within no time, Kajja arrived with two new foam mattresses. He dropped them on the floor in the sitting room. We looked at him like *there are three of us, where is the third?*

'That's it,' he said.

Silence came again.

'Take one of them to a spare bedroom for me,' Mum said. 'The girls will share.'

Awkwardness hissed. There is nothing more excruciating than watching your father make a fool of himself trying to get your stony mother into his bed. We had just arrived after a decade of separation and so far he had made two clumsy passes at her. I wished I were a toddler.

Kajja heaved one of the mattresses above his head and walked towards the stairs. Dad, humiliated in front of his man, closed his face. But it did not last.

'Okay.' He clapped, then rubbed his hands. Looking at me and Nnaava he asked, 'Do you wish to eat first or take baths?'

We looked at each other.

'Will the food be brought here?' I asked. 'There are no plates or cutlery.'

'As I said before, you swept the house clean when you left.' He smiled at me even though he was talking to Mum. 'We could go to Fang Fang: you like Chinese?'

'I'm too tired to go out again.' Mum was irritable. 'Besides, I didn't come home to eat Chinese.'

I threw myself on the remaining mattress and Nnaava joined me. Mum and Dad remained standing. Tension tightened around the lone chair: Mum's injured anger and Dad's desperate guilt. Mum had declined the chair. Nnaava and I maintained our neutrality as if unaware. To break the silence, Nnaava said that we would bathe while Dad went to look for food. As soon as Dad and Kajja left, Nnaava and I wheeled our suitcases to the bedrooms.

God knows where Dad found Ugandan food at that time of the night. He and Kajja came back with two women. They had everything – plates, cutlery and all the Ugandan food I had forgotten. I was starving. Dad must have booked them in advance.

Later, as I slipped onto the mattress next to Nnaava, I asked how we had 'swept the house clean'. Nnaava was fifteen when Mum stole us away, I was eight. Nnaava was bound to know.

'Mum, partly out of anger and partly to raise the money for our flight, pawned everything in the house, save for a single item for him…Who knew he would leave everything the way we left it for ten years?'

I remembered the day we left. Mum woke us up very early in the morning – she was with her militant sister, Aunt Ndagire – and told us to get dressed: 'We're leaving.' We ate breakfast hastily. I did not read much into 'leaving' even though we spent three days at Aunt Ndagire's before flying out. At the time, I thought we were going abroad for a visit. Mum and Dad travelled a lot. Abroad was a place you visited and did a lot of shopping for family. I didn't see Mum strip the house. I didn't find out that we had left Dad for good until two months later in Manchester, when, after I had been badgering her about Dad and when we would go home, Mum said, 'We're not going back to your father: we're on our own now.'

I didn't ask why. It was the way she said *your father* as if she were no longer related to him. I first got suspicious when we were enrolled in school and joined a surgery. But I dismissed my suspicions because you trust your mother. Looking back, I should have realised when we left Uganda during term time. But that's being young for you.

Then Mum stopped speaking in muted tones on the phone to Aunt Ndagire and I heard that Pastor – Mum called

Dad Pastor – had almost collapsed when he returned from the retreat to an empty house. Apparently, he went around Mum's relatives and friends asking for information about us. None of them knew where we were except Aunt Ndagire, who would not talk to him. He begged, prayed and fasted for a telephone number, but God was mute. I heard Mum say, 'Let that woman cook also.'

It tore flesh to hear it. It hurt that Mum had told Aunt Ndagire about it. It should have been a family secret. Parents ought to know that children are awfully protective of their family. That while they've fallen out with each other, we haven't. Why humiliate each other within our hearing? It hurts in unspeakable ways to hear them say horrible things about each other. It doesn't matter what the other parent has done, children are slow, even reluctant, to apportion blame.

And so, through Mum's conversation on the phone, I found out that we had fled Uganda amidst a scandal. My father, a whole pastor, had fathered a child on the side. Mum, unable to take the scandal (a pastor's wife patched with another woman, as if she were not enough), had fled to Britain. I refused to think about it. I did not think about the child either. But it hurt daily that we were in a strange country, that Mum was struggling to make ends meet. For a long time, I hated Mum for bringing us to Britain.

Now I asked Nnaava why we weren't staying at Aunt Ndagire's: 'Why come back to a house we stripped and fled?'

'Dad paid for our tickets.'

'Do you think she'll forgive him?'

'Who knows? Ten years ago she couldn't bear to hear his voice; today she's sleeping in the same house as him. Maybe she's tired of the poverty in Britain.'

'Maybe it's for your engagement rites: we have to put on a show of togetherness. Besides, she has to prepare the house to receive Mulumba's family.'

'You know what a reconciliation between Mum and Dad means? You come back with Mum!'

I put my head down. That question again. I lifted my head and said, 'I'm about to start university: there's no way I'm coming back before I finish.'

'Kdt,' Nnaava clicked. Mum's decision would not affect her. She had a job and would be moving in with Mulumba after the wedding.

'You can't undo ten years of living in Britain just like that!'

'Maybe they won't reconcile.' Nnaava did not seem to care either way.

I wanted them to get back together. I liked the sound of 'Mum and Dad', I liked the idea of coming home to them, them growing old together, of bringing grandchildren to them in the same house.

The fact that Mum had not asked for a divorce in the last ten years was hope.

'Look' – I sat up – 'Mum's resistance is weakening. I mean, why is she sleeping in a separate bedroom? It's an invitation to Dad to sneak in with her while we sleep. If she really wanted to send him a clear message, she would have slept here with us.'

Nnaava giggled, 'Ten years without Dad: she's as horny as a nun!'

Dad walked in and I jumped. I heard myself say, 'Dad, can you bring back my chair and bed and plate and cup?'

He stopped, smiled and shook his head in disbelief. 'Come here.' He hugged me.

Then he looked at Nnaava expectantly and she was obliged to say, 'Mine too.' Then she added matter-of-factly, 'We need to furnish the house before Mulumba's clan arrives.'

I had spoken too soon. Perhaps it was because I resented Mum for using me and Nnaava as a whip to flog Dad. I should have been allowed to gather my own anger against him. I should have been asked if I wanted to leave him, especially as it was such a drastic departure.

Surprisingly, Nnaava was the one that sneaked, after three years in Britain, and rang Dad. She had started university and was broke. For a long time, I thought she had got a boyfriend until one day the phone rang while she was in the bathroom and I saw the Ugandan area code. I answered it. I too agreed not to tell Mum that we were in touch with him. Dad was forthright about his infidelity. He had accepted the punishment God had imposed on him – that of losing his family. He would never marry as long as Mum was single, but he would look after the child he had fathered. He rang twice a week and sent me and Nnaava money regularly. Though I felt that I deserved my father and Mum had neither the right to deprive me of him nor to inflict a life of poverty in Britain on me, I still felt guilty going behind her back.

★

That first Sunday at Dad's church.

We were guided to the front row to our former seats set aside for the pastor's family. The three chairs were empty. Nnaava and I sat down on the sides leaving the middle seat for Mum like we used to. I looked back, wondering where she had gone. Mum sat on the row behind us. Her chair, empty between Nnaava and me, formed a gap that told the whole church things that I would rather have kept private. I was tempted to sit on it and gag it, but it was too loud.

Nnaava leant across and whispered, 'Looks like Mum's legs are still crossed.'

I did not laugh.

But Dad was unruffled. Our presence had energised him. He did not look so desiccated any more. He wore one of the suits Nnaava and I had bought for him. When he stood up to go to the pulpit, he walked tall. He opened his sermon, entitled 'Hope in a Hopeless World', with: 'Is God good?'

'All the time.'

'All the time?'

'God is good.'

I had forgotten how it felt to be part of Dad's congregation. Because I was born into it, it had been a routine, unquestioned, expected; it was life. Now I stood outside, a spectator. The thing is, it's easy to lose your faith in Britain, where everything is under scrutiny. You can't live life without questioning it. And when it comes to Christianity and faith, British scrutiny is vicious. I still went to church in Manchester, but for Mum's sake. Church had become theatre. I enjoyed dressing up, meeting up with friends, the performance and the music. Mum felt it was the safe place to meet future husbands and I could see her conniving with other mothers to make introductions between sons and daughters.

But I had become increasingly aware of the entrepreneurial nature of evangelical churches like Dad's. Looking around at people way poorer than us parting with their money as offerings, hoping for blessings, money which I suspected ended up at our table, was distressing. I stopped mentioning that Dad was a church minister when I read that article about Ugandan pastors cruising around in Hummers, showing off their lavish lifestyles, ostensibly to demonstrate that they were true prophets because God had blessed them with wealth. Dad had numerous businesses, but it was not clear whether they were his businesses or church properties. Often I wondered whether to stop taking his money, but I was too weak.

Still, even though I stood outside faith, the emotions in the air that first Sunday were tangible. Dad whipped them up. They rose and ebbed: now outrage, then sadness, now anger, then love, now fear, then triumph.

'For ten years,' he was saying, 'three seats on this row' – he pointed to where we sat – 'have been empty, to remind me of what I did, amen?'

'Amen!'

'But today, two of them have been filled. Is God good?'

'All the time!'

'I said, is my God good?'

The response almost broke my ears.

He paused. Silence fell.

'I am not saying that everything is back to normal – how? After what I did? When you break your skin, it will heal, but the scar is indelible. The skin is saying, *This is what happens when you are careless with your body*, amen?'

'Amen.'

'But today, though I stand here covered in scars, I look down there and I see my beautiful girls. Nnaava there reminds me of her mother when I first met her. Nnabakka is so tall she wants to touch the roof of this church. Then I ask myself, is God good or is God good?'

'Aaaaall the tiiiime!'

'They'll be going back to Britain because Nnabakka is starting university in September, but today, right now, my family, all of it, is heeeeere in this rooooom and I—'

The congregation did not wait for him to finish. We all stood up clapping, nodding at the goodness of God, Dad wiping away his tears, Nnaava sniffing, and even I allowed Dad's pain to flow down my face. I could not glance at Mum. But I felt the static in the air around her. As if everyone was trying not to glance at her. I prayed that she had stood up, that she had at least sniffed. The congregation was loving Dad, it forgave him a long time ago, and Mum had better be receiving him too. Otherwise she would seem like a bitter woman.

At the end of the sermon, we stepped outside and the brethren came to greet us. We had taken care to hide the fact that we were broke in Britain. We dared not look less than First World. People would laugh at Mum: *She stole the children away from their father but they look worse than us*

Third Worlders! I wore a lace bodycon dress; Nnaava, being a bride-to-be, wore sheer silk. But once we stepped outside church, Birabwa, Aunt Ndagire's eldest daughter, joined us. She pointed at my dress.

'We have that fashion here already: you can get that dress for fifty thousand shillings in town.'

'Oh really?' That was about £15. I bought that dress for £80 in Debenhams.

'Yeah, these days we don't have to wait for hand-me-downs from the West four years after they're out of fashion. As soon as your summer ranges are out, the Chinese duplicate them for us, and by Christmas we're wearing them.'

Birabwa must have seen the disbelief on my face because she added, 'Obviously, it's a cheaper imitation, but who cares?'

'China my ass,' Nnaava mumbled.

When Mum finally exploded, it was at Red Dragon Supermarket, near Kobil in Kawempe. It was not at Dad but at a Chinese woman working on the till. As soon as she saw her, Mum's eyes darkened. By the time she finished paying, her mouth was so elongated it could have touched her nose. She grabbed her bags and, ignoring the woman's 'thank you', stomped out. We had hardly stepped outside when she burst out: 'You mean she wrote *cashier in a supermarket* on her visa application? Have we no cashiers here that we have to import them from China?'

Mum was like that. She conveniently forgot that she was an immigrant in Britain. I was about to remind her but Nnaava beat me to it. As we got back into the car – the heat raging in the air, a coating of sweat and dust caking my skin, and a man who reminded me of a hornbill screeching, 'Jesus is coming' at us – Nnaava said: 'But Mum, when you applied for your British visa, did you write *cleaner*?'

Mum waited until she had sat down in the car and closed the door. Then she turned to us in the back seat, eyes blazing *how dare*.

'There is a difference between me, an African from one of the poorest economies in the world going to Britain and becoming a cleaner, and a Chinese woman who has come to invest in my country ending up working on the till. These people are blinding us, building a stadium here and a road there. Soon they'll have our economy in their hands!'

'I don't mind them running our economy,' Kajja said as he started the car. 'I'm fed up with the thieves. Uganda is not a cake that you cut a slice from and eat. A hundred years ago the British came and created a European-like economy to extract as much wealth as they could for themselves. Let the Chinese come too. Let's see what model they have to offer. If we don't like it, we'll start a war and they'll pack their bags. They know it; we know it.'

'Listen to that!' Mum waved her hands in despair. 'So, you drive the lizards out and let the geckos in?'

'Mum!'

'What? Do you know what's happening to Ghana? Hordes and hordes of illegal Chinese immigra—'

Kajja stepped on the brakes and hurled us forward. He had been reversing into the road when he almost backed into a boda boda with two Chinese men squeezed on the back.

'Look at that.' Mum's voice was savage. 'Did you see that? Two of them squeezed on the back of a motorcycle. They're going to die here.' She waved an angry hand at the disappearing boda boda.

'Don't worry about Chinese people,' Kajja said, 'They are like us. Some are even poorer. They live among us. They don't even have servants. You never see them parading wealth like whites. Besides, they have no intention of staying here. They've been here how long now – fifteen, twenty years – but I've not seen a mixed-race child.'

Mum's mouth clamped tight.

'Look at what happened after the Italians were evacuated from Abyssinia to Toro – was it in 1945?' Kajja saw me look at Nnaava and explained, 'Those Italians did not stay long but they left behind a legion of children called a Baitale, fatherless all their lives – but not the Chinese.'

Still Mum did not join in. Her mouth remained fastened. Nnaava noticed and touched my hand like *shut up.*

To me, immigration was something that Europe and the USA suffered. In Britain, the way they go on about it you feel as though the whole of Africa is in transit on boats, planes and foot, gunning for the UK. But then you returned home and Kampala was no longer the city you left behind. Areas that were just Sudanese. Little Mogadishu in Kisenyi. Nigerians were no longer a curiosity. Neither were Afrikaners. Yet Ugandans did not seem bothered. It was Mum who, ironically, was British.

Later in the evening Nnaava told me about Mum's brother Ssimbwa. He was finishing at Peking University. China had invited him to go. Then the Nanjing anti-African riots took place. Grandfather asked him to come home but he said the riots were far from where he was. Next, the Ugandan embassy rang to say that Ssimbwa had committed suicide, jumped out of a window. The body was repatriated with specific instructions not to open the coffin – the embalming chemicals were lethal if inhaled. They underestimated the Gandas' relationship to their dead. Grandfather and his sons took axes to the coffin. *You could bury all sorts among our dead.* It was Uncle Ssimbwa alright. Sealed in a see-through plastic bag like a fish. No broken bones. Just torture marks, eyes gouged out. When he reported it to the embassy, Grandfather was told, 'Go home and bury your son; you're lucky you got him back.'

The weekend of Nnaava's rituals arrived. Mum's and Dad's families came on Saturday evening to help with chores. Aunt Muwunde, Dad's eldest sister, was chosen to be Nnaava's official aunt for the rites and to oversee her marriage afterwards. Nnaava chose her because Muwunde had lived in the US back in the 1980s. She would understand the complexities of a diasporic marriage.

I liked Aunt Muwunde but I had reservations. Firstly, while Nnaava and Mulumba were Saved, Aunt Muwunde was not. Secondly, Aunt Muwunde did not shy away from confrontation. On the eve of the rites, as we had supper, in the presence of all other relatives, she called Dad over.

'Muwanga?'

Dad had discarded that name. To him, Muwanga, a Ganda God, was heathen. Dad's surname was Ssajjalyayesu. But Aunt Muwunde had rejected it because it had neither clan nor totem. But being older than Dad she could talk to him in any way she wished.

'Where is our other child?' she asked. 'Eh, you did it, it's done. Stop hiding him and let's love our child.'

Mum can be smooth when she's ready. If her husband was to be flogged publicly, *she* would be the one to do it. She took the words out of Aunt Muwunde's mouth and said rather softly: 'Yes, Pastor, bring him to his sister's rites. Let him wear his kanzu. He's the muko.'

Mum, uttering those words – *He's the muko* – cut off the head of the serpent that had been stalking us since we arrived. She was not only acknowledging him, she was inviting him. But for me, the child, who for the last ten years had been nameless and faceless, took on a new significance. Brothers give away their sisters.

He arrived quite late the following day, at 1.30 p.m., an hour before Mulumba's clan arrived. When I saw mother and son, I groped for Nnaava, but she was not there to die with me. Here was Dad's act personified. The physicality blew common sense out of me. Mum's outrage became mine. This was no longer an accident but intentional. Where was Nnaava?

I texted her: *They're here. Hurry, I am dying.*

And the boy's mother? I couldn't take my eyes off her. *Where are you, Nnavs? You need to see for yourself.*

The mother wore an orange and blue Shanghai gown. It was clearly a ceremonial dress but in my anger I thought that she should have worn a busuuti if she wanted to blend in. And then from afar she looked ridiculously young: not much older than Nnaava.

Mum must have seen me scowl, for she leant forward and whispered, 'She's a teacher: teaches Mandarin.'

'Mandarin, who needs Mandarin?'

'People doing business in China. Now she has a Ugandan passport.'

'What use is it to her?'

'Free movement within East Africa and other African countries.'

I looked at the woman again. She had brought a Ugandan friend, a woman. They were talking. The way she rubbed her back and cast her eyes on the ground, she knew we were watching. Mum crossed her legs aggressively. The left leg, on top, swung as if it would kick the woman out of the marquee.

I turned my eyes to the boy. He was greeting everyone in the marquee, coming towards us. My pulse accelerated. Nnaava had not arrived.

In some ways, he was a typical ten-year-old – big front teeth, legs too long for the rest of his body, perfect skin. But in other ways there was something about his Chinese-African look with a Huey Freeman afro that made you stare beyond politeness. His forehead was shaved and manicured Ganda-style. His hue was darker than mixed race. He was smiling, confident even. Very comfortable. Everyone stared, and

Ugandans stare hard, but he was not bothered. I suspected he was enjoying it.

Nnaava arrived, but there was no time to die of shock because the boy was upon us.

I pointed with my mouth towards him: 'That's him!'

Nnaava gasped. Her grip on my hand was all I needed.

Aunt Muwunde must have been aunting that boy all along; the way she was familiar with him! She introduced us.

'These are your sisters. Look at them properly.' Then she asked, 'Have you seen them, Bwema?'

'Bwema?' I blurted the name before I could stop myself.

'Bwemage.'

That shut me up. Mum's mouth wriggled from side to side as if rinsing the warning in the name out of her mouth. I suspected Aunt Muwunde. She was the kind to name such a child Innocent.

'Happy to see you, Nnaava,' the boy mumbled, extending his hand, but Nnaava hugged him so I hugged him too. He moved on to greet other relatives.

Before we could whisper anything to each other, a woman behind us made throaty clicks and whispered, 'Our blood tends to pull children towards us, no matter the race they are born into, but he refused. All we got is hair and colour.'

'Yes, the mother pulled him towards herself,' another agreed.

I closed my eyes and dropped my head because Ugandan tongues know no bounds! Nnaava slapped my back: *Hold yourself together.*

But Mum replied – there was no doubt that she was responding to the woman even though she spoke to Dad:

'You've done well to teach him his language, Pastor. Another person would have left him to float in the middle, speaking English only.'

It was like a cue for everyone else to compliment Dad on 'our' child speaking proper Luganda. But the women behind us were not going to let Mum and Dad play happy families.

'Aha,' one of them sighed. 'China too has arrived.'

'Bwoleka, in a special way, it came into this house: straight for the hearth.'

I stood up, turned to the women. 'Is that why you came?'

'Yeah' – Nnaava joined me – 'to eat, to count the children in the family and to give them positions?'

'That's not what we meant.' The women looked around as people shifted restlessly, sucking their teeth, clicking.

'The girls are putting words in our mouths; it's not what we meant.'

Mum raised her voice. 'Pastor, give Bwema his kanzu. He must get ready for his role. Has he been coached on what to say?'

We were in the middle of the rites. Nnaava and I sat on a mat facing Mulumba and his clan. Nnaava had changed into a different busuuti for this phase of the rites. Aunt Muwunde had done her part. As Nnaava's mouthpiece, she had told Dad's spokesman that she was old enough to leave home and start a home of her own, that she had found someone to do it with.

Dad's spokesman was reluctant to let her go, citing the bad ways of such random men as you meet on the road, besides, she was still too young, but Aunt Muwunde insisted that she was going with her man. Dad's spokesman, heartbroken, agreed to let her go. He asked her to show the family the specific person she intended to make a home with.

Now Aunt Muwunde put a garland around Mulumba's neck and there was applause.

'Wait a minute.' Dad's spokesman brushed the clapping aside.

Mulumba's spokesman looked up, feigning worry.

So far, the negotiations had been about language and wit. Mulumba's spokesman had hitherto spoken beautifully, backing out of any corners Dad's spokesman tried to put him in, without offence. But he was yet to convince our spokesman to let Mulumba be born into our house. Dad's spokesman was focused on making it impossible for him to ask by humiliating him, stalling and pouring scorn on his words. And so, although the garland was draped around Mulumba's neck, his request, to become part of our family, was yet to be accepted.

'You can wear the garland,' Dad's spokesman said, 'It's nothing special: that's how we treat our visitors. However, if you are serious about being born in our house, you must have talked to our son, who would be your muko.'

The confusion on Mulumba's face was priceless. His spokesman tried to hide his surprise behind a smile.

Our side of the family stirred: *Ahaa, we've got you!*

I looked at Nnaava like *Didn't you tell Mulumba about the boy?* She closed her eyes: *Oh my God.* Bwemage was our family's secret weapon.

Mulumba's spokesman asked for a moment to confer with the groom. It was embarrassing to ask for a timeout, in fact, humiliating to confer – a sign that Mulumba's family had not done their homework – but under the circumstances, there was no way around it. For them to say that they did not know about a son would be deeply offensive: they could be thrown out of the marquee and told to go back and get their facts right. But to lie that they knew him was to walk into a trap.

After conferring, Mulumba's spokesman came back and claimed, 'Of course we know our muko: how could we not?' Perhaps he thought Dad's spokesman was bluffing.

There was silence at the blatant lie. I wondered how Mulumba's spokesman would extricate himself, especially when he realised that there was an actual son. Dad's spokesman stood up. He turned to our family and said, 'He says he knows his muko even though he had to confer first', and there were derisive noises from our relations. He turned to Mulumba's spokesman and said, 'If you know him very well, what's his name?'

I stole a look at Mulumba and mouthed, 'Bwemage.'

Dad's spokesman saw me and shouted, 'Nnabakka: keep your eyes on the ground.' To Mulumba's spokesman he warned, 'Be careful, we don't give birth to liars in this house!'

Nnaava's hand was shaking. I put mine on top of it.

For a moment, Mulumba's spokesman was tongue-tied.

Dad's spokesman went in for the kill: 'Do you still want our girl, or have you changed your mind? Look, we have crops to bring in from the fields and animals to collect from grazing ku ttale – we don't have time to sit here and look at a suitor who doesn't even know the name of the muko who will give him the woman he has come for. You can leave when you are ready. Children,' Dad's spokesman called like he was going back to running his house, 'have you finished doing your homework? We need to—'

'Of course we know his name.' Mulumba's spokesman was fraught. 'But sir, you know we don't articulate important people's names, faa, like that!'

Dad's spokesman paused: he had not anticipated this recovery.

'What name do you call him when you meet?'

'I refer to him by his office – muko. I say, Muko-muko! And he asks, "But you Mulumba, when are you bringing my cockerel? If you're not careful, I'll give my sister away." So today I said to myself, "Mulumba, why don't you take muko's cockerel before he gives your lovely away?"'

Nnaava stole a relieved glance at me.

'What if I bring him out here and he says that he doesn't know you?'

'Go ahead, sir: bring him. As soon as he sees me, we'll be hugging: you'll see.'

Mulumba's spokesman was doing well: you'd rather have a muko in the marquee saying that he doesn't know you than one hiding away in the house where you can't appeal to him.

'Bring my son,' Dad's spokesman called to the people in the house. He turned to Mulumba's spokesman and said, 'If he doesn't know you, you see the gate over there? Take a walk!'

Bwemage stepped out of the house. He wore a kanzu and a coat on top like all the men. Mulumba's spokesman looked the boy over, took in the fact that he was not only very young but mixed race and decided that there was nothing to be afraid of. In fact, there was a stir of relief in Mulumba's clan, a sense that the negotiations were done.

Bwemage went and stood next to Dad's spokesman. The man put a loving hand around his shoulders.

'Son, these people say they're your friends.'

'Which ones? Them?' Bwemage pointed at Mulumba's clan, his face saying *How can I be friends with them?* 'Never seen them before.' He did not even bother to look at them again.

Mulumba's clan froze not just at Bwema's crisp Luganda but at his confident voice and the belligerent attitude. Realising that the boy was trouble, Mulumba sneaked a fat envelope to his spokesman. Dad's spokesman was saying, 'That's all I needed, son. Go back and play.'

'Wait' – Mulumba's spokesman grabbed Bwemage's hand deferentially – 'Muko, yii, vvawo nawe, Muko! You, my very own, to forget me like this in my moment of need?'

'Who are you?'

'It's me, your very best friend.' Mulumba's spokesman draped a loving hand around Bwema's shoulders and pulled him towards himself while he slipped the envelope into Bwemage's hand. 'How could you forget me so soon?'

Bribery is traditionally Ganda, I swear! Bwemage grabbed the envelope and hid it behind his back and flashed a toothy smile at Mulumba's spokesman. 'Oh, it's you, tsk. For a moment there I didn't recognise you. Finally, you've come. You're lucky you're in time. I was about to give my sister away.' He turned to Dad's spokesman. 'I know him. He's a good person.'

Mulumba's clan broke out ululating.

Dad's spokesman was suspicious. 'Where is he from?'

'Yii yii, Mulumba was born in Kabowa but his father and grandfather and grandfather twice over come from Kiboga. I know them very well. They're of the Musu clan.'

Mulumba's clan ululated again. His spokesman did a dance and twirled.

Everyone stared at a boy of ten addressing a gathering of no fewer than a hundred people with such audacity.

'So, are you going to give them your sister?'

'Of course.'

Mulumba's clan applauded again. Our side deflated. Bwemage had sold out too easily.

'Just like that?'

'On one condition.'

Dad's spokesman perked up. 'What condition, son?'

'You know, Father, that Nnaava is my favourite sister.' Dad's spokesman nodded as if he had known all along. 'She understands me. The thought of losing her makes me sad.' Bwemage, hand on heart, closed his eyes. 'But of course, Mulumba promised that if I gave her up he would replace her with something equally precious.'

'Do you know what this precious thing is?'

'No, I am waiting to see what he thinks can replace my sister, because as you know I have everything I need.'

'Go back to your games, son! You have spoken so well I've got nothing to add.'

The little monkey was beginning to walk away when he added: 'Oh, Father, I've remembered.'

'What is it?'

'For the last three weeks, I've not leaked on an ounce of sleep.'

'Why, son?'

'All sorts of men bothering me – waiting in the house, calling on my phone and waylaying me on the road.'

'What do they want?'

'What else? To marry my sister. Can you imagine, one offered me a car? I said, "I am just a boy: I can't drive a car." He said, "I'll give you a driver to take you wherever you want", but I said no. Then another one gave me a whole house. But when I told him that I have a home, he said that I would need it when I grow up. I told him that I don't take bribes.' The imp looked at the fat envelope in his hands and smirked. 'Even just now, as I was coming out of the house, this man grabbed my hand and I think he had been to see a wizard who broke into my dreams.'

'He did not!'

'He must have! This man was holding one of my dreams in his hands.'

'No! Which one?'

Everyone leant forward to hear what this boy's dream could possibly be. He whispered in the microphone.

'A ticket to Disney World – Orlando!'

Everyone was laughing and clapping as Bwemage walked back to the house. Our side of the family cheered because Mulumba's spokesman had run out of words. Even his clan was clapping.

Soon after, Nnaava and I were asked to leave the marquee as Dad's spokesman considered taking pity on Mulumba and accepting his request to be born in our house. When we got back to the house, Nnaava ran up to Bwema and lifted him, shrieking, 'You, you, you, I could eat you.' She put him down. 'You went beyond! Just beyond. At first, I was worried that I didn't tell Mulumba about you but now I am glad I didn't. You've made the whole negotiations seem so real and entertaining!'

The women coming into the house to get the food ready hugged Bwema, pinched his cheeks and told him how he had done us proud, and he was very happy. I smiled at him from a distance. Through the window, I saw his mother and her friend come to the backyard. They held large dishes with Chinese patterns. I wanted to nudge Nnaava to tell her that Bwema's mother had brought food, that she had come to help the women with lunch, but just then Dad's spokesman came and said that the final rite – when Bwema would receive Nnaava's fiancé into the house, give him a tour and then serve him his first meal as part of the family – was about to begin. Nnaava and I, because we were daughters, were asked to step outside.

As I walked out of our house I glanced back. Bwema stood alone in the sitting room, filling it with his presence. There was not a shred of unease about him. As if he had grown in that sitting room all his life. I marched to where Mum sat and whispered, 'Mum, you're not coming back to Britain with us.'

'Excuse me?'

'You're staying behind to—'

'You can't tell me what—'

'You're not hearing me, Mum.' I was shaking. 'Sort things out. Find out for real if, when all the anger is done, you still don't want to be with Dad. I deserve to know that if something happened to Dad, this house is still my home.'

I walked away before people heard us.

THE AFTERTASTE OF SUCCESS

When I step outside, after a week of hibernating, I feel like a traditional bride coming out of the honeymoon bedroom to start a new life. Every sense is attuned to the difference. A loud cockerel, goats bleating, someone chopping wood; I smell ripe jackfruit and my eyes search for the tree. A boda boda whizzes down the hill, raising a cloud of dust. The morning is cool but Ddembe, my older sister, and Mugabi, who has come to open the gate, are shivering. Manchester has hardened me. But then my lips twist. A long day lies ahead. Fifteen years away is not long enough to forget things, but it is long enough to yearn for a certain Britishness, like hyper-politeness, political correctness, queuing up and those tiny rights I'd learnt to demand – *This is unacceptable; can I speak to the manager.* You pull those tricks here, you suffer. They accuse you of bringing your luzunguzungu. And yet the lack of hurry in the air, the ntangawuzi chai and yellow bread with Blue Band spread I had for breakfast, then the morning bath in a plastic basin, say *You'll be alright, you'll get back in the rhythm*. Ddembe drives out first and I follow her in her second car.

Kampala city centre feels like a toddler learning to walk. There is exuberance despite the many falls. Manchester was middle-aged, around 220 years old. The thought of Kampala growing is at once optimistic and depressing. You want those kids off the streets, but the idea of that concrete used to build megacities sunk into these virginal hills of Kampala is almost sacrilegious. Sometimes, Manchester city centre felt like a steamed-up bus. As if someone were breathing too close to your nostrils. Kampala is dust. It makes the buildings look weather-beaten. It's a waste of time getting irritated by boda bodas. They own the country now. Young people are skinny. So are most men. As if middle-aged women eat all the food. The build of the women's bodies, their gaits, the hairstyles, the mannerisms, the colourful clothes. I never realised how good-looking Ugandans are until I left the country.

All but one of the messages I carried for Ugandans in Manchester have been collected by their loved ones. Two days after I arrived, I rang them and they collected their envelopes. Today, I'll deliver Mikka's, the last one. It's for his parents: they are elderly and it's a lot of money. Mikka and I were quite close, which is rare. Friendship among Ugandans in Britain is transient. People are too busy, too guarded, too jittery. You can't expect someone who goes to bed not sure where she will be when the sun rises, or someone who had been betrayed back home, or people who walk on tiptoes because they fall in love the other way, to offer you firm friendships. But Mikka was always there, generous and quiet. We had to be careful, though: that nonsense that men and women can't be best friends.

I am going to start by announcing myself to family. People take it personally if you don't tell them that you're back. You never know when you'll need their help. Then they'll click, *Ktdo, she came back, didn't even tell us, now she wants our help?* I'll start with Mother, then Nnakazaana, my grandmother, then lunch with my sisters, and finally I'll go to Mikka's parents'.

On second thoughts, I'll start with Grandmother. Nnakazaana is mother, father, aunt, grandmother all in one. My parents are supplements. But Nnakazaana is not your typical melting grandmother; wait till you meet her. She is a tough girl. Even age is struggling to chew her. I so love my grandmother, there is not enough water in the Nalubaale, but if I find her arguing with someone, my heart will go out to the other person. In the late 1950s, she was a trailblazer. The first woman to do business in Kenya, or so she says. When other traders flocked to Kenya, she turned to Zaire. In the 1980s, she changed to Dubai, and when other people flooded Dubai she went to Japan to import reconditioned cars, then Denmark for bitenge. She has always held a British passport. Her reasons? She was born in the British Empire and her father fought in World War II. She says that in those days saying *I am British* opened doors around the world. She had an address in London long before she set foot in Britain. Renewals of her passport were sent there. Because of the merchandise shop she set up in the sixties, then the famous Bunjo Boutique in Uganda House and finally, in the

eighties, the Mobil petrol station that doubled as a reconditioned Nagoya car dealership, tongues that whipped women
into domesticity lashed. You can feel the welts in her hoarse
voice, the spikes in her temperament and in her confrontational attitude. Tongues said she made her money by selling
herself – first in Mombasa, then Dubai, London and finally
Amsterdam. But in Zaire she smuggled gold, they said. The
rumours about Dubai were most hurtful. Apparently, Arabs
made such African women fuck their dogs. Kids in primary
school would shout at me *Ki Kitone, is your grandmother still a*
malaya? Consequently, Nnakazaana grew thorns on her skin.
But sometimes her thorns tear into loved ones. It's best to
get her out of the way first thing in the morning.

I get to Kawempe and stop to buy meat, matooke, cooking
stuff, sugar, washing soap – the kind of things you take to old
ones you've not visited in a long time. The butcher has sussed
me out; he speaks English: 'Ah, my Muzungu, come to me.'

I am still too black British to find the 'compliment' *muzungu*
palatable. I take a breath: *Calm down, Kitone, that's what people*
call you before they overcharge you. I smile. 'Have people in
Kawempe abandoned Luganda entirely?'

'Tsk' – he switches to Luganda – 'you kivebulayas pretend
to have forgotten our language, speaking mangled Luganda.
I was only helping you.'

I buy goat meat, two pieces – one for Mother, one for
Nnakazaana. Then I cross the road to the fresh market and
buy matooke, fresh beans, peas, greens and then carry on.

Along the way, places that used to be bush, swamps, shambas or gardens are built-up. The crowds are out along the road, even though it is still early in the morning. Matugga is now suburbia. I see my grandmother's house long before I turn off Bombo Road.

Nnakazaana hurries out of the house. She's in trousers. I smile and shake my head. At her age she's expected to wear either a busuuti or long bitenge robes, not jeans. Back in the nineties, traders on Luwum Street used to call her Mukadde takadiwa because she was a grandmother but not acting it.

'Kitone,' she claps.

'Jjajja.'

My grandmother is magical, beautiful, intelligent, regal, loving, but no one else sees it. She looks the same as she did two years ago but has abandoned her trademark wigs. There is a softness to her when she wears her own hair. She had never put on that midriff weight that middle-aged women do. There was a time when she was prickly about her slender frame, but times have changed. Now she claims *I watch my figure*, rather than commend a bad-tempered metabolism. Had she put on weight, she would have claimed credit: *Age does not look good skinny; it was time to put on some.* Recently, she owned up to being seventy-eight rather than sixty-five. When I rang on her birthday, she spoke in the plural: 'Yes, we're seventy-eight: what are we hiding any more? We've devoured the years.'

As I reverse to park, she follows the car back and forth as if I might drive away. Most old people move out of large houses into smaller ones; Nnakazaana recently moved into this house. Dad built it in 1986, soon after I was born. A wing for his mother and one for himself when he visited. Apparently, he had hoped his mother would stop hustling in Kampala and move to the quiet of what was rural Matugga then. But Nnakazaana was not ready. She loved the city and thrived on hustling: 'Who says a woman has to give up her life to bring up a child?' She did not say this to Dad. She let him finish the house, said *Thank you very much* and waited for him to fly back to Britain. Then she built another house, smaller, on the compound and rented the properties to a non-government organisation. Her rent was quoted in dollars. Then she informed her son that she had a new idea for the property. Recently, after her birthday, she said, 'I am going to enjoy my son's labours before I die' and moved into the property. When I told her I was returning, she said, 'Otyo! The half-mansion is vacant; it's waiting for you.'

By the time I finish parking, she has made so much noise the neighbours have come to see. They greet me and withdraw. But not before Nnakazaana tells them that, unlike the brainless lot who go to Britain and get stuck there, meaning Dad, I've returned.

First, she walks me around the bigger house to show me what she's done with it. It has been decorated tastefully, professional work; but it's overwhelmingly big. I suspect that she only moved in because she could not find worthy tenants. The whole left wing is unoccupied. After greetings, she asks, 'So, you people really Brexited!'

I shrug. For someone who went into a semi-depression after the referendum, I am surprised by my indifference.

'Jjajja, these nations are growing old and it has taken them by surprise. For the first time, they are worried by the youth, energy, optimism of younger nations. They're afraid they'll be devoured like they did us in the eighteenth and nineteenth centuries.'

'But things were improving. The Europe of the seventies and eighties was a dark place, but now when I come, everyone is nice and polite. You even have African MPs.'

'But then the economy shrank. On the one hand Britain had embroiled itself in two wars it couldn't afford, while on the other machines took the jobs. What did they do? They blamed us. Liberalism was a luxury they indulged in when things were good.'

'Oh well,' she sighs, 'who knew that Britain would one day claim an Independence Day? We saw it on TV and asked ourselves: did Europe colonise Britain?'

'All this time I've been in Britain I saw a genuine attempt to eradicate prejudice.'

'I hope our children also Brexit and come home.'

'Oh, they will. Anyone who has a home to come back to is laying down plans. When we woke up that morning after the referendum, the clouds spelt *Go home!*'

'Good, come home, all of you. Otherwise, how was everyone else?'

By 'everyone else' Nnakazaana means Bunjo, my father. There is no shielding her from the reality: Dad did not send a word. She and he don't talk. Nnakazaana takes credit for the breakdown of Dad's marriage. Just because she lived here while Bunjo's wife, Melanie, was in Britain did not mean that Nnakazaana could not be the mother-in-law from hell. She had warned Bunjo against marrying European women who *marry your son and swallow him, who are so possessive it's unhealthy.* The relationship between Nnakazaana and Melanie became so bad that Bunjo's visits to Uganda stopped altogether. Nnakazaana blamed Melanie and would fly to Manchester to terrorise her. I've heard her say, 'I asked Melanie, "Do you think our sons fall from trees that you pick one up and do as you please?" He left relations in Africa.'

I take a breath before I tell my grandmother that Dad is fine but did not send her a message.

'Heh heeh.' She does that contemptuous laugh old women do. 'You know, Kitone' – she points at me as if I am my father – 'when I first ran away from Bunjo's father, people talked: *Eh, she has run away from her husband. Look, she's burrowed with a child in a tiny hole like a rodent. Eh, she'll have to slut herself. Eh, that boy will amount to nothing.* But if that did not move me, why would Bunjo, a child I brought into the world just the other day?'

I shrug.

'So next time you talk to your father, tell him that I've known more pain than he can inflict.'

I keep quiet. Nnakazaana's contemptuous laugh was not contemptuous: it was a sob. Luckily her tough face is in place. If it slips, she will collapse into tears. I get up and hug her again. It's not an *I'm sorry* hug – Nnakazaana does not do sympathy – it's *I'm so happy to see you again*. Strong people are exoskeletal. One crack in the shell and they're dead. Experience has taught me to reinforce Nnakazaana's facade of strength before cracks appear.

'But I think Dad pretends to hate you.'

'You think so?'

'He calls you *my mother*, very possessive. And he talks about you, your achievements, with pride. When you were sick, he paid the hospital bills. He was always on the phone with the doctors.'

Nnakazaana beams. 'I know, the doctors asked me, "Who was that on the phone, is he a doctor?" Apparently, he asked medical questions. I said he's my son. But he didn't speak to me.'

'He says you hate white people.'

'How?'

'I don't know: maybe because of Melanie.'

'That woman again.' She pulls away to look in my eyes. 'All I said to Bunjo was, "Don't marry Europeans." White women come with too much power into a marriage with us. The relationship is lopsided against your son. Do you see?'

I nod because her hands are gesturing the imbalance.

'Your son becomes the woman. They know how to emasculate African men. And for those they give visas to, ho.' She claps horror. 'The stories you hear. Your son does something trivial and she threatens him with deportation. But if I hate white people, why did I tell Bunjo to apply for the RAF scholarship? Ask him who told him, after his studies, to apply to international airlines? Why would I encourage him if I don't like Europeans? Didn't I tell you that I don't mind you marrying a white man?'

'You did. But, Jjajja, not all European women are like that.'

'What are you talking about, child? It's their culture. I've heard a woman, with my very own ears, compliment another about her husband: "You trained him well." I said, "Twaffa dda, is he a dog?" In Britain, children belong to their mothers. You divorce your wife, she takes the children. The court gives you visitation rights! The woman uses those rights to strangle you. Only a few women realise that it's child abuse to deny their children their fathers.'

Hmm is the only safe response when my grandmother starts on this topic.

'Melanie told my son that she did not want children. And Bunjo, like the sheep he is, said, *Okay, madam, no problem*. I tell you, Kitone, your father followed Melanie like a trailer of an articulated lorry – blindly. But I said, "No way, I am going to be a grandmother, come what may!"'

'But, Jjajja, Dad and Melanie have been divorced twenty years now; Dad has not had any more children.'

'How can he? He does long-haul flights which means he's away for at least five days a week. Besides, once Melanie sowed that seed in his mind, that was it.'

This is not strictly true. In one of our candid conversations, Dad told me that if it had not been for his mother, he'd not have had a child. But I can't say that to my grandmother's face; I can't keep contradicting her.

'If it's true that Bunjo does not want children, how come he worships you? Tell me he doesn't love you.'

I smile and she knows she has won.

'Kitone, people don't sit down and ask themselves *Do I want children?* When the time is right to have children, children come. The only question is how many. Love for children is like breast milk; a child arrives, ba pa, you're overwhelmed.'

'Hmm.'

'If I hadn't fought to have you, I would be destitute right now.'

What Nnakazaana doesn't know is that Bunjo can't get enough of white women. The more she's against them the more he wants them. Of all Dad's girlfriends I've met, only Juana, a Mexican artist, and Lorena, a Brazilian student, were non-white. And to describe them as non-white is to stretch the fact: they were white. Once, when Dad was going on about his mother being prejudiced, I said, 'But Dad, you don't date black women either.'

Ho ho! It was as if I had opened his door by the hinges. He didn't talk to me for days. It didn't help that soon after he had a flight to Sydney and didn't come back for a week. When he spoke to me again, he made it clear that he would not tolerate that kind of talk in his house. Then he relented and explained that black women, especially Africans, bring too much baggage into a relationship.

'They come looking for stability,' he said, 'with plans to marry you, have children, and while you are at it, you must act married – *Sports cars are for young men*; you have to act your age – *tight jeans?…nothing says bad boy like a leather jacket*; and by the way, *Why don't you go to church? Oh, Mother rang, she's asking about you, when will you visit them?* I'll never inflict my mother on another woman again but, equally, I don't want a family inflicted on me. Everyone must carry their stability in themselves. Don't look to me to give it to you.'

Like mother like son, I had thought, but I kept quiet about his essentialising African women in case he sulked at me again.

After a cup of tea, I give Nnakazaana the stuff I brought for her from Britain. A pack of Chloé perfume and body lotion, shoes, Marks and Spencer bras and underwear – she insisted on them – a handbag, a watch and other toiletries. Then I give her the foodstuff I bought in Kawempe. We walk to the half-mansion – that's what we call the smaller house Nnakazaana built on the premises – and look around the house I'll be moving into once my containers arrive. The walls need a lick of paint. Nothing I can do about the small windows. I don't like the red cement floor. I think I'll carpet it all. That will give me something to do while I wait to start my job.

'You know, Jjajja,' I say, 'because it needs a little bit of work, I'll move in with you in a few days and start working on it.'

That puts a smile on her face. As we walk back to the main house she puts her hand on my shoulders. 'You're enough for me, Kitone,' she whispers. 'You're me.'

'Maybe I love you more, Jjajja.'

'Maybe.' Her smile is sceptical.

When the time comes to leave, it's a struggle to extricate myself. She thought I would spend the entire day with her. But when I explain that I am going to see Mother, she smiles because I visited her before my mother, especially as Mother lives in the city where I came from. To say that Nnakazaana and Nnazziwa, my mother, don't get along is to say that Mr Lion and Little Miss Antelope don't see eye to eye.

Mother lives in Wankulukuku, just after the stadium as you go towards Bunnamwaya. My mother doesn't wrestle with life. What comes her way she accepts; what does not, is not hers. From rumours and whispers I've heard, I imagined Nnakazaana marching up to my mother soon after I was born and saying *Where is my grandchild?*, plucking me out of her arms and handing her a cheque for her troubles – *Thank you very much* – then giving Mother terms of visitation. Mother could not fight back; she doesn't know how to. Tradition was on Nnakazaana's side, being Dad's mother. Besides, Nnakazaana had a lot of resources at her disposal, but that does not mean that Mother did not hurt. Like today, when she finds out that I visited Nnakazaana first, she looks down to hide her pain. I had not planned to tell her, but she asked, 'So how is Nnakazaana?' and I was tempted to say *Why ask me? Who's just arrived from Britain*, but I said, 'Same old Nnakazaana.'

If my mother were a car, my father clicked the central locking button and walked away. She's still parked where he left her. I suspect I'm the result of a one-night stand. Probably a drunken night, because Mother's not the kind of woman Dad would go for sober. Besides, there is no record of their relationship – no pictures, no stories, not even anecdotes. Some parents hear a song and sigh *Oh, that song reminds me of your father*, or point to a place and say *That's where me and your father once lived*, or *Kdto, we ate life in that club, me and your mother.* The only record of their relationship is me. It makes me nervous, Mother not knowing Dad. When I started a relationship with Dad, I visited him once a year. Every time I came back from Britain, I brought pictures of him and Mother pored over them like an opportunity lost.

Mother has a tiny house. Smaller than the half-mansion. Word has it that she built it with the money Nnakazaana paid her for me. Mother is mumsy in a Ganda way. The kind of woman a Ganda husband would not lose whatever he did. The kind of wife who says *I came to cook; I am not leaving, whatever he does.* Their ability to endure marital abuse is the epitome of Ganda feminine strength. Mother is appropriately plump. She only wears kitenge gowns or busuuti. She still bleaches. Her hair is very long and worn in a straight perm. When I arrived, I saw her worried glance at my hair – short, natural and uncombed.

I only agree to have tea with her because it would be rude if I left her house without eating something. Thank God I am going to meet my sisters for lunch, thank God they've told her about it, otherwise I would have had lunch to compensate for seeing Nnakazaana first. I give Mother the bag containing all the stuff I brought for her from Britain. I always bring her more than I do for Nnakazaana. If Nnakazaana needs stuff from Britain, she gives money to her friends who are travelling.

I pass on the pictures I printed off. In all of them, I am with Dad: I know it's him she wants to see. For a moment, she is silent as she riffles through them. Then she sighs, 'Yes, that's him: those are the eyes.' Then she looks up. 'When did his head start cutting bald?'

I smile without replying.

Mother has always treated me like an indulgence. With her, I feel like an ornament. As a child, whenever she visited she brought presents – you don't need presents from your mother every time you see her. When she picked me up for holidays, funerals, weddings or baptisms in her family, I was stared at. She never told me off. I imagine that relationships with parents come from moments of intense emotion. When they scream at you or spank you, when they praise you, or save you from danger and you see their fear, horror, or when they embarrass you, when you hate them, when you fear for them or miss them – it's all those emotions, and more, that coalesce and congeal with the sensations of feeling their heart beat when they carry you, that form a bond. There is none of that in my relationship with Mother – only stares and smiles.

At her house, she treated me as if she dared not return me to Nnakazaana's chipped or cracked. My sisters seemed unsure of what to do with me. They liked and resented me equally. Ddembe, the eldest, would pinch me for no reason and run. If I did not make a noise, she'd run back and dig a deeper pinch and twist until I winced. She preferred to take me by surprise because I would jump. Now I know why I never complained. If our mother was going to pamper me, Ddembe was going to hurt me. Then we were equal.

One day she got a pair of scissors and shredded all my clothes. Mother bought me new ones before I went back home.

I don't know when my sisters and I normalised. The change crept up on us like puberty. Later my sisters told me that whenever I was around Mother fed us sumptuously. They also said that once they started to come around to Nnakazaana's house they understood Mother's behaviour. But Mother never normalised. My conversation with her skims on the surface. Thus, Mother asking when Dad started going bald is skimming the surface. After all, ever since I first visited Dad – I was thirteen then – he's been going bald. All the pictures I brought back since then have showed Dad at some stage of balding.

Dad does not feel paternal either. He loves me, but sometimes I suspect he would rather be my best friend. The first time I visited him back in 1999, he picked me up in a convertible sports car. Talked to me like a friend. He was too sleek, too well-groomed, too into his gym body, expensive clothes and his pleasure-seeking life to feel like a dad. His home was a bachelor pad. Two bedrooms and two bathrooms. The rest were spaces filled with gadgets, vinyl records, DVDs, PlayStation games, books. Every room had speakers inset into the ceiling. Coloured lights. When he introduced his girlfriend, it was clear from their body language that it was all about having a good time. What shocked me most was him telling me I didn't have to call him Dad. After all, he said he had not been a dad so far. I snapped, 'I'll call you Dad.'

'Look,' he said, 'I don't know what my mother has told you; I mean, about the circumstances of your birth.'

'What's there to tell? You're here in Britain, I'm there in Uganda.'

'Oh.' He had stared at me for a while. Then he asked the weirdest thing: 'Do you have a relationship with your birth mother?'

'My birth mother? What does that even mean? Why wouldn't I have a relationship with my mother?'

'I just want to know.'

'Of course,' I said. 'I don't live with her, but I see her all the time.'

At the time, Dad cleaned and washed up and did the laundry. At first, I thought he just didn't want me to touch his gadgets. Then one time he had a long-haul flight and I asked him to show me how to use the washing machine and the dryer. He said, 'I don't want you to think that I'm making you my servant.'

I was like *What?* I mean, how Zungucised is that? I said, 'Am I your daughter or not?'

He was startled.

I said, 'Let me put it this way: are you still a Muganda?'

'Why?'

'Because this Britishness is killing me, Dad. Back home, children do chores; it's not child abuse.'

He laughed. 'You take after my mother. She must be proud.'

I didn't know whether it was a reprimand or amusement. I didn't care. From that day, our relationship improved. One thing about Dad: he's dutiful. Back then, I didn't have to carry clothes when I travelled. I always found my wardrobe full of clothes. He bought them on his travels. I started wearing labels before I knew what they were. He took care of all my needs, from tampons, knickers, deodorant and perfume to going with me to Marks and Spencer to get my bust measured for bras. Even now, Dad books my visits to the dentist and GP for check-ups.

'Is Bunjo still single?' Mother asks.

'No, he has a girlfriend.'

She laughs. 'Only you young people have girlfriends. We have a man or a woman.' She pauses. 'White again?'

'No, Kenyan.'

'Hmm,' she laughs. 'He learnt his lesson!'

There it was again. Evil Melanie. Then again, why did I say Kenyan? To protect Mother from the suspicion that Dad rejected her because he prefers white women, which in her mind elevates white women above her? To protect my father from Mother's suspicion that he's an insecure African man on a trophy trip? I would like to believe that I don't challenge my mother because I'm exhausted, but something far worse has happened to me. After America voted Trump I started to rationalise Uganda's right-wing views. After all, liberalism is a by-product of prosperity.

I barely make it to lunch with my sisters, Nnannozi and Nnalule.

★

I am in a taxi to Ntinda after walking out on my sisters. My head is boiling.

People talk a bit too straight. And by the time I met my sisters my nerves were already frayed. Apparently, my failure to look right, like a kivebulaya, disconcerts them. I am too skinny and my hair looks like I've just walked into civilisation. 'You're even wearing lesbian shoes!' Nnalule had moaned.

In the past when I visited, I played to the kivebulaya expectations – the latest fashion in Britain, outrageous accessories, going out every night. It was easy then because I visited for two weeks and returned to Britain. But I am back for good; I am older and no longer interested in wearing the First World on my body.

'Look,' I tried to explain, 'Dad's not buying me clothes any more and I'm not interested in labels.'

'But still, Kitone, you try. People will think you were deported.'

'I don't mind.'

'Come on, like you've just returned but already are scraping the bottom? Have mercy on us.'

So it was not about me per se; it was about them. They've spent years constructing themselves through dress, associates, cars, jobs, boyfriends, houses and even the areas they live. In my absence, I was co-opted into the masquerade. Now they needed me to perform kivebulaya.

'You people! This keeping up of appearances is tragic. We're in the developing world, for heaven's sake.'

'That's exactly why,' Nnalule said. 'We poor people are embarrassed by poverty. We hide it. There's no need to look at a person saying *I've tried Britain and failed.* Where is the hope for a dreamer?'

'Looking poor while rich is a virtue in the West. Here you just look crude!'

'Yeah, the West is so rich it performs poverty. Aspects of poverty have become fashionable. They started with faded jeans, then they frayed their jeans, now it's gaping holes like they miss wearing rags.'

'Look, Kitone, we know you've never been poor. We get it. You may even look down on us pretending to be rich. But this idea of *I'm in the Third World and it's vulgar to display wealth* is just depressing.'

I ate quietly. Did not respond to what they said. Finally, they too fell silent. After eating I stood up, went to the counter and paid the bill even though it was their treat. I waved good-bye and walked out. I drove Ddembe's car back to Mutungo and caught a taxi to Ntinda. Only one day in Kampala and already I've disappointed my mother and fallen out with two of my three sisters. I can already hear them saying *Kitone came back, but she's too white for life.*

Mikka's home is a grand old house, like the ones in Mmengo built back in history when architecture was still indulgent. Obviously, Mikka's family owned the land in the village then. His parents must have sold to the new money clans in Kampala. The compound is too large for Naalya, an upscale village. It is well kept with high hedges. An old royal palm fell and lies in the compound as if still being mourned. The falawo trees are so tall and old you hear them sigh up above in the breeze. The house is square. Sprawling roof. Bland front. Two large windows on either side of the door. A huge veranda, wider than an extravagant corridor. The outdoor kitchen of perforated red bricks is annexed to the main house by a tunnel walkway. Mikka's parents must have inherited this house.

I peer in before knocking. The front door opens into the sitting room, but there is no one around. On the walls, with wood panelling halfway up, are fading black-and-white pictures of former kings: Mwanga, Ccwa and Muteesa II in informal moments. I recognise Sir Apollo Kaggwa and Ham Mukasa. The decor is frozen in the 1970s. The floor is overlaid with a thin red carpet. On top of the carpet are mats spread in the spaces between the furniture.

'Koodi abeeno?'

'Karibu.' A woman's voice comes from further inside the house. 'We're home: come in.'

I don't step in. Not until I see who is inviting me.

The door to the inner house squeaks as it is pulled back. Mikka's mother steps out. He does not look like her, but there is that labelling that parents do to their children, like mannerisms. She is early seventies or late sixties. Her hair is dyed and relaxed in leisure curls. Her eyebrows are pencilled, lips glossed.

'Is this Mr Mutaayi's home?' It's unnecessary but I've got to start somewhere.

'This is it, come in.'

'Mikka sent me.' I am still standing at the door.

'Oh.' The woman twirls and claps. 'Bambi! You're Mikka's friend? What a good person to be our friend. Yii yii, come in, get out of the doorway, come in.' She ushers me towards the chairs but common sense tells me to grab a mat. I sit with my legs neatly tucked under my bottom like I was brought up properly.

The greeting is lengthy – *how are your people, is the sun as mean over there, what is the city saying? What lies is the world telling?*

I say what everyone usually says: 'Life is like that, hard.'

'Hardship is not illness,' she says. 'As long as there is peace, there is life. We too here are contemplating time. And Manchester, have you been there long?'

When I say that I am not going back, she leans in and shakes my hands. 'Well done; your parents are lucky.'

'You've got such lovely photographs here.' I motion to the walls to change the subject.

'Those?' She looks up. 'They're old – ancient people the world has forgotten.' But then she stands up and pulls down a family picture. There are other pictures on the wall behind me I had not seen from outside. They are in colour and of young families. The one she has pulled down is black-and-white and of a whole family. She points out Mikka as a boy. I peer at it. Mikka sucked his thumb. He was a lot younger than his siblings. As if his parents had already been finished. She points out each of Mikka's siblings: 'That one is in Germany, that one in California, this one was in Sweden but she passed away. That one is in Canada; he has no family yet.'

'All Mikka's siblings are abroad?'

'All gone and lost,' she sighs as she hangs back the picture before sitting down again. 'We have no children, no grand-children, not even in-laws to find fault with.' She claps. 'They went to study but never returned. Now all we get are phone calls telling us to expect money as if they're paying us off.'

'You could visit them.'

'You get tired of begging for visas. And then it's awkward when you get there. The houses are so tiny, there is no space to stretch your legs. And then you lock yourselves indoors all day like a prison. Ah, ah.' She throws her arm out in refusal. 'They should visit us, not the other way around. Why should we go guba-guba all the way to Bulaya where they're scattered?'

'Even Mikka does not visit?'

'Especially Mikka. And when he comes, he doesn't bring the children.'

'Yii, yii? But in Manchester whenever I see him, he's with his children.'

'The wife confiscated the children's passports.'

'What? Tell him to apply for Ugandan passports.'

'They would need visas to go back.'

I shake my head. I have no other suggestion. I ponder Mikka. The thing with quiet people…Mikka never talks about himself. I call him, complaining about this and that, but he never does the same. I look at his mother's pain and decide to deliver the message and get the hell out of there. But then the grandfather clock, which has tick-tocked quietly up to that point, sets off the bell. She stands up. 'Time to wake up my one otherwise he'll not sleep tonight. You'd have gone without seeing him.'

The door protests as she opens it and disappears. A long pause. The door creaks again. She steps out first and holds it. Mikka so took after his father now that I know what he'll look like when he is old. His father's legs are not good but he has that well-preserved look of the upper-class. After greeting him, I pass Mikka's envelope on to his mother. She passes it over to her husband without opening it. 'You count it.'

'But it was given to you.'

'But I've given it to you.'

Wife and husband go back and forth like a lovable old couple until she wins with, 'You know I have no eyes any more.' The smile on her face says she's used to getting her own way.

Mikka's father counts the notes, licking his forefinger now and again, until he's finished. He slips the notes back into the envelope. I notice that the wife has been staring at me rather than listening to the counting. The husband asks, 'One thousand five hundred pounds?'

I nod.

'Thanks for carrying it, child,' Mikka's mother says without interest. Then she leans forward. 'But how was my boy really?'

I smile as I realise that Mikka is her boy. 'He was well.'

'What does well look like?'

'Healthy, not struggling financially.'

'How old are the children now?'

I remember taking photos with Mikka and his children just before leaving. And because Mikka always brought his children to the Ugandan community gatherings, I have a few others. His wife, however, is a different case. Like Dad, she's never been to the Ugandan community gatherings. No one knows what she looks like. Mikka never talks about her. Mikka has never invited me to his house even though he walks into Dad's house and mine easily, most times with his children. There are issues in his marriage, it is written all over him, but I've never asked. I suspect he is hanging on for the children's sake. I get my phone and retrieve the pictures. 'I have pictures of him and the children.' I get up and kneel beside his mother. 'Here, that's Nnassali, the big girl, then Nnakabugo, the middle one, and that's Kiggundu, the youngest. They were learning how to drum.'

'You mean our drums?'

'They even learnt to play nsaasi.'

She claps in happy wonderment.

'Here they're learning kiganda dance.' I scroll. 'Here they're singing the Buganda anthem. Mikka always talks to his children in Luganda.'

'Really?'

'He's very keen. Everyone in the Ugandan community knows you don't talk to Mikka's children in English. Here, hold the phone and scroll down yourself.'

As soon as she's got the phone, the anger melts and she gasps and giggles and exclaims. Her legs stretch out on the mat, her eyes shining as she pores over each frame. At one picture, she catches her breath, then looks at her husband. 'Yii yii.' She stands up and goes over to him. 'Look at what you did, look how you gave this poor girl your wide feet!'

'Oh, kitalo' – he holds his mouth in delighted mortification – 'my ugly feet.'

'That nose is ours too: see how it is sat like luggage,' she says, and they fall over each other giggling.

For a long time Mikka's parents are in their own world, looking for themselves in Mikka's children. When their excitement wanes, she returns the phone. I promise to print off the pictures and bring them.

'Are you married, child?' Mikka's mother takes me by surprise.

'No.'

'Yii yii, you're alone, bwa namunigina like this.' She wags a lone finger. 'Surely there must be someone you have hopes in?'

'No, not at the moment.'

'At least you have a child?'

I shake my head.

'Would you like to have children?'

'In the future, yes.'

She flashes a happy smile at her husband. Then she leans in and says, 'You see all of this?' She indicates the property. 'It belongs to no one. Me and my one' – she points at her husband – 'we're useless. We can't develop it. Mikka's children belong to England. They can't come into our dust and flies.' She strokes her lower lip in thought. 'Ssali, Mikka's older brother, has not married. We can't even have the grandchildren in Sweden. When our daughter died, our son-in-law refused to bring her home for burial. We trudged all the way to Stockholm. Never seen a more desolate funeral; only a handful of mourners. Oh! The last we heard was that her Swede husband remarried and put the children in welfare because they don't get on with his wife. Apparently they are uncontrollable.'

'But they could have sent them to you!'

'They are Swedish, you see.'

'That's the thing! They won't let them come out here because all Africa is starving.'

'It's our fault. As parents, we lost our way. We – me and my one there – were the clever parents, quite trendy in our time. You educated your children, then sent them abroad to get international qualifications, widen their horizons. That was the trend in the 1980s.'

'Hmm!'

I notice that Mikka's quietness is the same as his father's.

'Now we're the childless, grandchildless couple! People our age are grandparenting, but our hands are empty.' She draws a huge breath and sighs, 'Aha, the bitter aftertaste of success.'

'Hmm.'

'Sometimes we look at people coming to us pleading, *You have a child in this country, can you help mine to go as well?* Don't we, wamma?' She turns to her husband, who nods. 'But if you tell them that to send your children abroad is to bury them they won't believe you.' Now she looks at me. 'Tell me what's wrong with our country? Look at us. Don't we look well? Don't we eat, don't we sleep?'

'You do.'

'But what are children looking for abroad any more?'

'Hmm.'

'If there is nothing good about Uganda, why is everyone coming here? West Africans, South Africans, the Chinese, all of them; haven't you seen them?'

'We're blind to what we have,' the husband sighs.

'Now, what our children do is send money. Money-money, money-money, money-money' – she swings her arm to the rhythm – 'as if money is life. If you go to our bank, all their money is sitting idle like this.' She makes a sign of a heap. 'But who said we don't have our own money? Me and my one, we keep it in a foreign account. We don't touch it. One day they'll come to visit, when one of us is dying or dead, and we shall show them their heaps of money. But I digress.' She leans forward, speaking in earnest. 'What I meant to ask, child, is which clan are you?'

'Mmamba. My clan name is Nnabunjo. Kitone Nnabunjo.'

'Mmamba clan?' She turns to her husband in an excited *you see?* Then back to me: 'We're of Monkey clan.' She recites some Monkey Clan names – 'We're Kabugo and Nnakabugo, Ssali and Nnassali.'

I keep my face neutral.

'What I am saying is, but really, I am just suggesting, because that is all it is, a suggestion, because if you don't ask you die in ignorance; what if you and Mikka get together and have a child or two? Don't answer immediately, child.' She flips her hand. 'You see, a squirrel that failed to adapt to urbanisation died crossing the highway. If our children are lost in the world, we must come up with ways of making alternative grandchildren. I tell you, if we die now, every-one – our children, grandchildren, great-grandchildren – will scatter because they have no anchor. Mikka and his siblings will come, sell off all of this and melt into the world. But this here is their centre. This is what will hold them together.

Everyone who is curious, even fifty years from now, should be able to come here and say *This is where I come from.'*

'Child' – the husband leans forward – 'new laws say that if you are non-Ugandan, you can't own property here. All our children and their children have NATO passports.'

'Do you see our problem now?'

'Aah—'

'As I said, don't answer right away. Go home and think yourself through. You said you want to have children; didn't you?'

'Yes, but—'

'Do you have a job yet?'

'Yes, but I don't start until next month.'

'Good, but with our proposal you don't need a job. As soon as you get pregnant, ba ppa.' She cracks a knuckle. 'We prepare a house, we look after you. The child is born, we take him or her for a blood test, because you know girls these days can be clever...'

'Kdto, they don't joke,' the husband laughs.

'We don't care whether it is a girl or a boy; we just want someone our own to take over after us. As soon as the child is confirmed ours, we write the will.'

'Maama,' Mikka's father calls, but I don't register that he could be addressing me like that. 'Anzaala mukadde?' I turn. He leans in with that respect old men bestow on daughters-in-law. 'Will you think about it?'

I have no choice but to nod.

'We're not bad people and not the ugliest either,' his wife says. 'We promise love, thick, cordial love for the child.

Meanwhile I'll talk to Mikka. He's going to call to see whether the money has arrived. And then I'll say *But isn't Nnabunjo beautiful, have you noticed?*'

A week later, I visit Mother. She rang to ask how I was settling in at Nnakazaana's, but I knew it was to gauge my attitude towards my sisters. I agreed to go for lunch. So far, neither she nor I have mentioned the bust-up with my sisters. I had expected them to join us, but they are not here. We are sitting outside on the veranda. Mother has been talking about an Indian soap on TV, some girl called Radhika and her exploits. I am struggling to stay awake when she remembers Mikka's parents and asks whether I found them. I describe the house to her.

'Oh, those Mutaayis. They're old money.'

'You won't believe what they asked me.' I explain everything.

'Of all people, why ask you?'

I shrug.

'What did you say?'

'What could I say? They're old people, why break their hearts? They told me to think about it.'

'Tell me you're not thinking about it.'

Instead of saying *Of course not*, I hear myself saying: 'Well, these days, you don't have to wait for a man to come along, weigh you up, decide you're right for him, do the courtship dance, marry and then have children. These days you can find a man you share mutual like and respect with and say *By the way, can you give me one or two children? No strings attached, no financial support. All I need are names, a clan and perhaps extended family for the children.* That way a woman can have children on her own terms.' Seeing the horror on her face I add, 'Mother, for the first time a woman can own her children.'

Mother smiles. She even looks relieved. 'You're trying to scare me.'

'Three of my friends here in Kampala have done it.'

Her face changes again. She does not respond, though.

I smile. 'Don't worry, Mother, I might meet someone tomorrow and fall in love.'

She remains silent for a moment, then clicks in self-pity, 'What you eat beautiful today will come back ugly tomorrow. That's the truth.'

I don't pay attention to her proverb because two of her sisters arrive and we have lunch. By the time I leave, the whole thing is forgotten. I visit another friend who I met in Manchester years ago and we go out. It's past ten when I get home. Nnakazaana is up waiting even though I rang to say I was eating out. Before I even drop my bag, she starts:

'Your mother was here, hysterical.'

I frown.

'Apparently you're planning to have a child like yourself.'

'A child like myself? What does she mean, like myself?'

'No relationship between the parents.'

I laugh. 'That's most people I know. I was joking. Besides, if I ever do it, it would be artificially.' But now I am really peeved. 'What's wrong with Mother? I told her it was a joke!'

'She's frightened because that's what happened with you.'

'What?' I look at my grandmother.

She leans against the door frame, arms folded. Her stare does not negate my suspicion.

'You mean Mother did not, I mean, never went with Dad?'

'Nope.' She walks to the sofa, pats the cushions. 'It was artificial.'

'What?'

'I paid her for everything, including breastfeeding.'

'You mean you sat down and negotiated the terms of my birth? I thought you paid her for giving me up.'

'Don't get angry with her, it was me, I approached her. Part of me hoped that when Bunjo met her he would fancy her. Nnazziwa was beautiful, well-mannered, the kind of girl you wished your son would marry. Unfortunately, she had had three children; no one married such women then. I sent Bunjo her pictures – he had separated from Melanie then – we discussed it over the phone. He came, I introduced them, I told Nnazziwa, "It's now up to you to hook him." They went out once, twice, thrice, but in the end Bunjo said, "We're doing it in a fertility clinic." Poor Nnazziwa, she had fallen in love.' She shrugs. 'What we didn't know was that at one point, Bunjo reconciled with Melanie. Apparently to get me off his back, Melanie agreed to go on with it. So Bunjo was not touching Nnazziwa whatsoever.'

'Wow.'

'I flew with her to Britain. But Bunjo didn't come once to see us, forget inviting us to his house. She was with me all the time. I suspect Melanie supervised everything on his part. I was going to pay for the procedure, but your father would not let me. All I paid for was surrogacy. I looked after Nnazziwa for almost two years. To be fair, Bunjo visited when you were born and kept coming regularly until you were four or five.'

'Hmm.' I fail to look at her.

'You're angry with me.' She comes towards me. 'I've hurt you?'

When she holds me, I feel like I am a child again. When I have held my emotions in check, I pull away.

'No, but it's hurled me quite afar.' There is silence. 'In Britain, you go to a fertility clinic and pick a picture of a man you like, read up on him – his education and medical evaluation – and say, That one.' I shrug. 'But I have a father and a mother and all their relatives; it doesn't matter how I happened. What has shocked me is that you and Mother and Father did this kind of thing back in the eighties.'

She holds me again. I hold her too. Relieved, she says, 'If you want to have children the same way, go on. I won't lie, I would love to see you walk down the aisle with someone, but I am not stupid. Besides, the Mutaayis are a decent family. Children don't only inherit wealth but a family's attitude to life too.'

I smile. 'Let's wait and see what life says.'

I've stayed so long in the bath the water has gone cold. It's hard to come to terms with the fact that I was commissioned like a piece of art. No one ever thinks about their conception, but now that I'm forced to contemplate it, I would have liked to imagine myself the product of a bout of passion. That my parents' love for me started with a strong attraction to each other. The image of your dad jerking off into a sterilised beaker. Why name me Kitone? Certainly I am not an unexpected gift. On the other hand, I couldn't have been a mistake.

I didn't need to know.

I miss Mikka. These are the kinds of things I would ring breathless to talk about. Crazy Dad. Crazier grandmother. *Mother sold her egg. AI is for artificial insemination.* But then I would laugh. *Your parents have gone rogue, Mikka. You won't believe their indecent proposal.* His quiet laughter. His disbelief. I am a sucker for quiet men. Dad was suspicious: 'Are you shagging a married man, Kitone?' But at the time I was going out with Caryl, a Liberian guy. I like Mikka's family. I like the look of his children. Marriage is a business transaction. Love is not blind; that's why we don't fall in love with vagabonds. Mikka has never attempted to cheat on his wife. Dad would love a grandchild.

I get out of the bath, unplug the water and scrub the bathtub. I wrap a towel around myself but instead of the bedroom, I tiptoe to the cabinet in the sitting room where I had seen Nnakazaana's wines. I pick up a quarter-full Uganda Waragi and a liquor glass and slip into my bedroom. I toss back a swallow before I pick up the phone from where it was charging. I go to the box where I keep my passports, British bank cards, NI card and foreign currency. I retrieve the British phone and take both phones to the bed. I switch it on and while it plays its start-up images and tunes, I toss back more Uganda Waragi. I go into Contacts, scroll down until I come to Mikka. I write down his number, switch off the British phone and take it back to the box. It's 10 p.m. in Britain. WhatsApp's ringing is muted when you call. I start to rehearse what I am going to say but before the words form, there is crackling and Mikka's quiet voice: 'Hello, Kitone?' I hold my breath. I've been poisoned. We're no longer Mikka and Kitone, close friends. He's Mikka with potential.

LET'S TELL THIS
STORY PROPERLY

If you go inside Nnam's house right now the smell of paint will choke you but she enjoys it. She enjoys it the way her mother loved the smell of the outside toilet, a pit latrine, when she was pregnant. Her mother would sit a little distance away from the toilet, whiff-wards, doing her chores, eating and disgusting everyone until the baby was born. But Nnam is not pregnant. She enjoys the smell of paint because her husband Kayita died a year ago but his scent lingered, his image stayed on objects and his voice was absorbed into the bedroom walls: every time Nnam lay down to sleep, the walls played back his voice like a recording. This past week, the paint has drowned Kayita's odour and the bedroom walls have been quiet. Today, Nnam plans to wipe his image off the objects.

A week ago, Nnam took a month off work and sent her sons, Lumumba and Sankara, to her parents in Uganda for

Kayita's last funeral rites. That is why she is naked. Being naked, alone with silence in the house, is therapy. Now Nnam understands why when people lose their minds the first impulse is to strip naked. Clothes are constricting but you don't realise until you have walked naked in your house all day, every day for a week.

Kayita died in the bathroom with his pants down. He was forty-five years old and should have pulled up his pants before he collapsed. The more shame because it was Easter. Who dies naked at Easter?

That morning, he got up and swung his legs out of bed. He stood up but then sat down as if he had been pulled back. Then he put his hand on his chest and listened.

Nnam, lying next to the wall, propped her head on her elbow and said, 'What?'

'I guess I've not woken up yet,' he yawned.

'Then come back to bed.'

But Kayita stood up and wrapped a towel around his waist. At the door, he turned to Nnam and said, 'Go back to sleep; I'll give the children their breakfast.'

Lumumba woke her up. He needed the bathroom, but 'Dad won't come out'. Nnam got out of bed, cursing the builders who put the bathroom and the toilet in the same room. She knocked and opened the bathroom door, saying, 'It's only me.'

Kayita lay on the floor with his head near the heater, his stomach on the bathroom mat, one end of the towel inside the toilet bowl, the other on the floor, him totally naked save for the briefs around his ankles.

Nnam did not scream. Perhaps she feared that Lumumba would come in and see his father naked. Perhaps it was because Kayita's eyes were closed like he had only fainted. She closed the door and, calling his name, pulled his underwear up. She took the towel out of the toilet bowl and threw it in the bathtub. Then she shouted, 'Get me the phone, Lum.'

She held the door closed as Lumumba gave it to her.

'Get me your father's gown too,' she said, dialling.

She closed the door and covered Kayita with his grey gown.

On the phone, the nurse told her what to do while she waited for the ambulance to arrive: 'Put him in the recovery position…keep him warm…you need to talk to him…make sure he can hear you…'

When the paramedics arrived, Nnam explained that the only thing she had noticed was Kayita falling back in bed that morning. Tears gathered a bit when she explained to the boys, 'Daddy's unwell, but he'll be fine.' She got dressed and rang a friend to come and pick up the boys. When the paramedics emerged from the bathroom, they had put an oxygen mask on Kayita, which reassured her. Because the friend had not arrived to take the boys, Nnam did not go with the ambulance. The paramedics would ring to let her know which hospital had admitted Kayita.

When she arrived in Casualty, a receptionist told her to sit and wait. Then a young nurse came and asked, 'Did you come with someone?'

Nnam shook her head and the nurse disappeared.

After a few moments, the same nurse returned and asked, 'Are you driving?'

She was, and the nurse went away again.

'Mrs Kayita?'

Nnam looked up.

'Come with me.' It was an African nurse. 'The doctor working on your husband is ready.'

She led Nnam to a consultation room and told her to sit down.

'The doctor will be with you shortly,' the nurse said, and closed the door behind her.

Presently, a youngish doctor wearing blue scrubs came in and introduced himself.

'Mrs Kayita, I am sorry, we could not save your husband: he was dead on arrival.' His voice was velvety. 'There was nothing we could do. I am sorry for your loss.' His hands crossed each other and settled on his chest. Then one hand pinched his lips. 'Is there anything we can do?'

In Britain grief is private – you know how women throw themselves about, howling this, screaming that back home? None of that. You can't force your grief on other people. When Nnam was overcome, she ran to the toilet and held on to the sink. As she washed her face before walking out, she realised that she did not have her handbag. She went back to the consultation room. The African nurse was holding it.

Her name was Lesego. Was there something she could do? Nnam shook her head. 'Is there someone you need me to call? You cannot drive in this state.' Before Nnam said no, Lesego said, 'Give me your phone.'

Nnam passed it to her.

She scrolled down the contacts calling out the names. When Nnam nodded at a name, Lesego rang the number and said, 'I'm calling from Manchester Royal Infirmary...I'm sorry to inform you that...Mrs Kayita is still here...yes, yes... yes of course...I'll stay with her until you arrive.'

Looking back now, Nnam cannot remember how many people Lesego rang. She only stopped when Ugandans started to arrive at the hospital. Leaving the hospital was the hardest. You know when you get those two namasasana bananas joined together by the skin: you rip them apart and eat one? That is how Nnam felt.

Nnam starts cleaning in the bathroom. The floor has been replaced by blue mini mosaic vinyl. Rather than the laundry basket, she puts the toilet mats in the bin. She goes to the cupboard to get clean ones. She picks up all the toilet mats there are and stuffs them in the bin too: Kayita's stomach died on one of them. Then she bleaches the bathtub, the sink and the toilet bowl. She unhooks the shower curtain and stuffs it into the bin too. When she opens the cabinet, she finds Kayita's razor-bumps powder, a shaver and cologne. They go into the bin. Mould has collected on the shelves inside the cabinet. She unhooks the cabinet from the wall and takes it to the front door. She will throw it outside later. When she returns, the bathroom is more spacious and breezy. She ties the bin liner and takes it to the front door as well.

Kayita had had two children before he met Nnam. He had left them back home with their mother but his relationship with their mother had ended long before he met Nnam. On several occasions Nnam asked him to bring the children to Britain but he said, 'Kdt, you don't know their mother; the children are her cash cows.'

Still, Nnam was uneasy about his children being deprived of their father. She insisted that he rang them every weekend: she even bought the phone cards. When he visited, she sent them clothes.

Kayita had adapted well to the changing environment of a Western marriage, unlike other Ugandan men, married to women who immigrated before they did. Many such marriages became strained when a groom, fresh from home, was 'culture shocked' and began to feel emasculated by a Britain-savvy wife. Kayita had no qualms about assuming a domestic role when he was not working. They could only afford a small wedding, they could only afford two children. At the end of the month, they pooled their salaries: Kayita worked for G4S, so his amount was considerably smaller, but he tried to offset this by doing a lot of overtime. After paying the bills and other household expenses, they deducted monies to send home to his children and sometimes for issues in either family – someone had died, someone was sick, someone was getting married.

Nnam had bought a nine-acre tract of land in rural Kalule before she met Kayita. After decades in Manchester, she dreamt of retiring to rural Uganda. But when Kayita came along, he suggested that they buy land in Kampala and build a city house first.

'Why build a house we're not going to live in for the next two decades in rural Kalule, where no one will rent it? The rent from the city house will be saved to build the house in Kalule.'

It made sense.

They bought a piece of land at Nsangi. But Nnam's father, who purchased it for them, knew that most of the money came from his daughter. He put the title deeds in her name. When Kayita protested that he was being sidelined, Nnam told her father to put everything in Kayita's name.

Because they could not afford the fare for the whole family to visit, Kayita was the one who flew home regularly to check on the house. However, it was largely built by Nnam's father, the only person she could trust with their money and who was an engineer. When the house was finished, Kayita found the tenants that would rent it. That was in 1990, six years before his death. They had had the same tenants all that time. Nnam had been to see the house and had met the tenants.

Nnam is cleaning the bedroom now. The windowsill is stained. Kayita used to put his wallet, car keys, spectacles and G4S pass on the windowsill at night. Once he put a form near the window while it was open. It rained and the paper got soaked. The ink dissolved and the colour spread on the windowsill, discolouring it. Nnam sprays Mr Muscle cleaner on the stains but the ink will not budge. She goes for some bleach.

After the window, she clears out the old handbags and shoes from the wardrobe's floor. She had sent Kayita's clothes to a charity shop soon after the burial but she finds a belt and a pair of his underwear behind the bags. Perhaps they are the reason his scent has persisted. After cleaning, she drops a scented tablet on the wardrobe floor.

Ugandans rallied around her during that first week of Kayita's death. The men took over the mortuary issues, the women took care of the home; Nnam floated between weeping and sleeping. They arranged the funeral service in Manchester and masterminded the fundraising drive, saying, 'We are not burying one of us in snow.'

Throughout that week, women worked shifts sleeping at Nnam's house, looking after the children then going to work. People brought food and money in the evening and prayed and sang. Two of her friends took leave and bought tickets to fly back home with her.

It was when she was buying the tickets that she wondered where the funeral would be held back home, as their house had tenants. She rang and asked her father. He said that Kayita's family was not forthcoming about the funeral arrangements.

'Not forthcoming?'

'Evasive.'

'But why?'

'They are peasants, Nnameya: you knew that when you married him.'

Nnam kept quiet. Her father was like that. He never liked Kayita. Kayita had neither the degrees nor the right background.

'Bring Kayita home; we'll see when you get here,' he said finally.

As soon as she saw Kayita's family at Entebbe airport, Nnam knew that something was wrong. They were not the brothers she had met before, and they were unfriendly. When she asked her family where Kayita's real family was, they said, 'That's the *real* family.'

Nnam scratched her chin for a long time. There were echoes in her ears.

When the coffin was released from Customs, Kayita's family took it, loaded it on a van they had brought and drove off.

Nnam was mouth-open shocked.

'Do they think I killed him? I have the post-mortem documents.'

'Post-mortem, who cares?'

'Perhaps he was ashamed of his family,' Nnam was beginning to blame her father's snobbery. 'Perhaps they think we're snobs.'

She got into one of her family's cars to drive after Kayita's brothers.

'No, not snobbery,' Meya, Nnam's eldest brother said quietly. Then he turned to Nnam, who sat in the back seat, and said, 'I think you need to be strong, Nnameya.'

Instead of asking *What do you mean?*, Nnam twisted her mouth and clenched her teeth as if anticipating a blow.

'Kayita is...*was* married. He has the two older children he told you about, but in the few times he returned, he had two other children with his wife.'

Nnam did not react. Something stringy was stuck between her lower front teeth. Her tongue, irritated, kept poking at it. Now she picked at it with her thumbnail.

'We only found out when he died, but Father said we should wait to tell you until you were home with family.'

In the car were three of her brothers, all older than her. Her sisters were in another car behind. Her father and the boys were in another; uncles and aunts were in yet another. Nnam was silent.

Another brother pointed at the van with the coffin. 'We need to stop them and ask how far we are going in case we need to fill the tank.'

Still Nnam remained silent. She was a kiwuduwudu, a dismembered torso – no feelings.

They came to Ndeeba roundabout and the van containing the coffin veered into Masaka Road. In Ndeeba town, near the timber shacks, they overtook the van and flagged it down. Nnam's brothers jumped out of the car and went to Kayita's family. Nnam still picked at the irritating something in her teeth. Ndeeba was wrapped in the mouldy smell of half-dry timber and sawdust. Heavy planks fell on each other and rumbled. Planks being cut sounded like a lawnmower. She looked across the road at the petrol station with its car wash and smiled, *You need to be strong, Nnameya,* as if she had an alternative.

'How far are we going?' Meya asked Kayita's brothers. 'We might need to fill the tank.'

'Only to Nsangi,' one of them replied.

'Don't try to lose us: we shall call the police.'

The van drove off rudely. The three brothers went back to the car.

'They are taking him to Nsangi, Nnam; I thought your house in Nsangi was rented out?'

Like a dog pricking up its ears, Nnam sat up. Her eyes moved from one brother to another to another, as if the answer were written on their faces.

'Get me Father on the phone,' she said.

Meya put the phone on speaker. When their father's voice came, Nnam asked, 'Father, do you have the title deeds for the house in Nsangi?'

'They are in the safe deposit.'

'Are they in his name?'

'Am I stupid?'

Nnam closed her eyes. 'Thanks Father thanks Father thanks thank you.'

He did not reply.

'When was the rent last paid?'

'Three weeks ago. Where are you?'

'Don't touch it, Father,' she said. 'We're in Ndeeba. We're not spending any more money on this funeral. His family will bury him; I don't care whether they stuff him into a hole. They're taking him to Nsangi.'

'Nsangi? That doesn't make sense.'

'Not to us either.'

When Nnam switched off the phone she said to her brothers, 'The house is safe', as if they had not heard. 'Now they can hold the vigil in a cave if they please.'

The brothers did not respond.

'When we get there' – there was life in Nnam's voice now – 'you will find out what's going on; I'll be in the car. Then you will take me back to town: I need to go to a good salon and pamper myself. Then I'll get a good busuuti and dress up. I am not the widow any more.'

'There is no need—' Meya began.

'I said I am going to a salon to do my hair, my nails and my face. But first I'll have a bath and a good meal. We'll see about the vigil later.'

Then she laughed as if she were demented.

'I've just remembered' – she coughed and hit her chest to ease it – 'when we were young' – she swallowed hard – 'remember how people used to say that we Ganda women are property-minded? Apparently, when a husband dies unexpectedly, the first thing you do is to look for the titles of ownership, contracts, car logbook and keys and all such things. You wrap them tight in a cloth and wear them as a sanitary towel. When they are safe between your legs, you let off a rending cry, Bazze wange!'

Her brothers laughed nervously.

'As soon as I realised that my house was threatened – *pshooo!*'

She made a gesture of wind whizzing over her head. 'Grief, pain, shock – gone.'

As the red-brick double-storeyed house in Nsangi came into view, Nnam noted with trepidation that the hedge and compound had been taken good care of. When the van containing the coffin drove in, Kayita's people, excitable, surrounded it. The women cried their part with clout. Kayita's wife's wail stood out: a lament for a husband who had died alone in the cold. The crying was like a soundtrack to Kayita's coffin being offloaded and carried into the house. But then the noise receded: Nnam had just confirmed that Kayita's wife had been the tenant all along. She had met her. Kayita had been paying his wife's rent with Nnam's money. Nnam held her mouth in disbelief.

'Kayita was not a thief: he was a murderer.' She twisted her mouth again.

Even then, the heart is a coward – Nnam's confidence crumbled as her brothers stepped out of the car. Travelling was over. The reality of her situation stared her straight in the face. Her sisters arrived too. They came and sat in the car with her. Her father, the boys, her uncles and aunts parked outside the compound. They were advised not to get out of their cars. The situation stared in Nnam's face without blinking.

People walked in and out of her house while she was frightened of stepping out of the car. She did not even see an old man come to the car. He had bent low and was peering inside when she noticed him. He introduced himself as Kayita's father. He addressed Nnam: 'I understand you are the woman who has been living with my son in London.'

'Manchester,' one of Nnam's sisters corrected rudely.

'Manchester, London, New York, they are like flies to me: I can't tell male from female.' The old man turned back to Nnam. 'You realise Kayita had a wife.' Before Nnam answered, he carried on, 'Can you to allow her to have this last moment with her husband with dignity? We do not expect you to advertise your presence. The boys, however, we accept. We will need to show them to the clan when you are ready.'

The sisters were speechless. Nnam watched the man walk back to her house.

The two friends from Manchester arrived and came to the car where Nnam sat. At that point, Nnam decided to confront her humiliation. She looked in the eyes of her friends and explained the details of Kayita's deception the way a doctor explains the extent of infection to a patient. There was dignity in her explaining it to them herself.

There is nothing much to clean in the kitchen, but she pulls out all the movable appliances to clean out the accumulated grime and rubbish. Under the sink, hidden behind the shopping bags, is Kayita's mug. Nnam bought it on their fifth wedding anniversary – WORLD'S BEST HUSBAND. She takes it to the front door and puts it into a bin. On top of the upper cabinets are empty tins of Quality Street that Kayita treated himself to at Christmas. Kayita had a sweet tooth: he loved muffins, ice cream, ginger nuts and eclairs. He hoarded the tins, saying that one day they would need them. Nnam smiles as she takes the tins to the front door – Kayita's tendency to hoard things now makes sense.

Nnam, her friends and family returned to the funeral around 11 p.m. From where she sat, she could observe Kayita's wife. The woman looked old enough to be her mother. That observation, rather than giving her satisfaction, stung. Neither the pampering, the expensive busuuti and jewellery, nor the British airs that she wore could keep away the pain that Kayita had remained loyal to such a woman. It dented her well-choreographed air of indifference. Every time she looked at his wife, it was not jealousy that wrung her heart: it was the whisper *You were not good enough.*

Just then, Nnam's aunt, the one who had prepared her for marriage, came to whisper tradition. She leant close and said, 'When a husband dies, you must wear a sanitary towel immediately. As he is wrapped for burial, it is placed on his genitals so that he does not return for—'

'Fuck that shit!'

'I was only—'

'Fuck it,' Nnam did not bother with Luganda.

The aunt melted away.

*

As more of Nnam's relations arrived, so did a gang of middle-aged women. Nnam did not know who had invited them. One thing was clear, though: they were angry. Apparently Nnam's story was common. They had heard about her plight and had come to her aid. The women looked like former nkuba kyeyo – the broom-swinging economic immigrants to the West. They were dressed expensively. They mixed Luganda and English as if the languages were sisters. They wore weaves or wigs. Their make-up was defiant as if someone had dared to tell them off. Some were bleached. They unloaded crates of beer and cartons of Uganda Waragi. They brought them to the tent where Nnam sat with her family and started sharing them out. One of them came to her and asked, 'You are the Nnameya from Manchester?' She had a raspy voice like she loved her Waragi.

Nnam nodded and the woman leant closer.

'If you want to do the crying widow thing, go ahead, but leave the rest to us.'

'Do I look like I am crying?'

The woman laughed triumphantly. It was as if she had been given permission to do whatever she wanted to do. Nnam decided that the gang were businesswomen, perhaps single mothers, wealthy and bored.

Just then a cousin of Nnam's arrived. It was clear she carried burning news. She sat next to Nnam and whispered, 'Yours are the only sons.' She rubbed her hands gleefully, as if Nnam had just won the lottery. She turned her head and pointed with her mouth towards Kayita's widow. 'Hers are daughters only.'

Nnam smiled. She turned and whispered to her family, 'Lumumba is the heir: our friend has no sons,' and a current of joy rippled through the tent as her family passed on the news.

At first the gang of women mourned quietly, drinking their beer and enquiring about Britain as if they had come to the vigil out of goodness towards Kayita. At around two o'clock, when the choir got tired, one of the women stood up.

'Fellow mourners,' she started in a gentle voice as if she were bringing the good tidings of resurrection.

A reverent hush fell over the mourners.

'Let's tell this story properly.' She paused. 'There is another woman in this story.'

Stunned silence.

'There are also two innocent children in the story.'

'Amiina mwattu.' The amens from the gang could have been coming from evangelists.

'But I'll start with the woman's story.'

According to her, the story started when Nnam's parents sent her to Britain to study and better herself. She had worked hard and studied and saved but along came a liar and a thief.

'She was lied to,' the woman with a raspy voice interrupted impatiently. She stood up as if the storyteller were ineffectual. 'He married her – we have the pictures, we have the video, he even lied to her parents – look at that shame!'

'Come on,' the interrupted woman protested gently. 'I was unwrapping the story properly: you are tearing into it.'

'Sit down: we don't have all night,' the raspy woman said.

The gentle woman sat down. The other mourners were still dumbfounded by the women's audacity.

'A clever person asks,' the raspy woman carried on, 'where did Kayita get the money to build such a house when he was just broom-swinging in Britain? Then you realise that, ooooh, he's married a rich woman, *a proper lawyer in Manchester*.'

'How does she know all that?' Nnam whispered to her family.

'Hmmm, words have legs.'

'He told her that he was not married but this wife here knew what was going on,' the woman was saying. 'Does anyone here know the shock this woman is going through? No, why? Because she is one of those women who emigrated? For those who do not know, this is her house built with her money. I am finished.'

There was clapping as she sat down and grabbed her beer. The mourning ambience of the funeral had now turned to the excitement of a political rally.

'Death came like a thief.' A woman with a squeaky voice stood up. 'It did not knock to alert Kayita. The curtain blew away, and what filth!'

'If this woman had not fought hard to bring Kayita home, the British would have burnt him. They don't joke. They have no space to waste on unclaimed bodies. But has anyone had the grace to thank her? No. Instead, Kayita's father tells her to shut up. What a peasant!'

The gang had started throwing words about haphazardly. It could turn into throwing insults. An elder came to calm them down.

'You have made your point, mothers of the nation, and I add it is a valid point because, let's face it, he lied to her and, as you say, there are two innocent children involved—'

'But first let us see the British wife,' a woman interrupted him. 'Her name is Nnameya. Let the world see the woman this peasant family has used like arse wipes.'

Nnam did not want to stand up, but she did not want to seem ungrateful for the women's effort. She stood up, head held high.

'Come.' A drunk woman grabbed her hand and led her through the mourners into the sitting room. 'Look at her,' she said to Kayita's family.

The mourners, even those who had been at the back of the house, had come to stare at Nnam. She looked away from the coffin because tears were letting down her *hold your head high* stance.

'Stealing from me I can live with, but what about my children?'

At that moment, the gang's confrontational attitude fell away and they shook their heads and wiped their eyes and sucked their teeth.

'The children indeed…Abaana maama…yii yii but men also…this lack of choice to whom you're born…who said men are human?…'

The vigil had turned in favour of Nnam.

It was then that Nnam's eyes betrayed her. She glanced at the open coffin. There is no sight more revolting than a corpse caught telling lies.

Nnam is in the lounge. She has finished cleaning. She takes all the photographs that had been on the walls – wedding, birthdays, school portraits, Christmases – and sorts them out. All the pictures taken before Kayita's death, whether he is in the picture or not, are separated from the others. She throws them in the bin bag and ties it. She takes the others to the bedroom. She gets her nightgown and covers her nakedness. Then she takes the bin with the pictures to the front door. She opens the door and the freshness of the air outside hits her. She ferries all the bin bags outside, one by one, and places them below the chute's mouth. She throws down the smaller bags first. They drop as if in a new long-drop latrine – the echo is delayed. She breaks the cabinet and throws the bits down it. Finally, she stuffs the largest bag, the one with the pictures, down the chute's throat. The chute chokes. Nnam goes back to the house and brings back a mop.

In her mind, her father's recent words are still ringing: 'We can't throw them out of the house just like that. There are four innocent children in that house and Lumumba, being Kayita's eldest son, has inherited all of them. Let's not heap that guilt on his shoulders.'

She uses the handle to dig at the bag. After a while of the photo frames and glass breaking, the bin bag falls through. When she comes back to the house, the smell of paint is overwhelming. She takes the mop to the kitchen and washes her hands. Then she opens all the windows and the wind blows the curtains wildly. She takes off the gown and the cool wind blows on her bare skin. She closes her eyes and raises her arms. The sensation of wind on her skin, of being naked, of the silence in a clean house is so overwhelming she does not cry.

LOVE MADE IN MANCHESTER

(Airport Diaries, 2016–18)

Poonah was at the Civic Centre in Oldham when Kayla rang. Not to ask her to babysit little Napule as usual, but to meet up. Poonah said she could do three o'clock. Kayla suggested they meet at the Town Hall, in the Sculpture Hall Cafe on the ground floor. Before she put down the phone, Poonah asked, 'Are you sure you're okay?' Kayla said, 'We'll talk.' That had made Poonah's heart race. The Ugandan woman in her imagined the worst – Wakhooli was playing up. She would kill him if he wrecked their marriage.

When Poonah arrived at the cafe, Kayla had already ordered. They hugged.

'How's social work?'

Poonah shrugged: *same old, same old,* and instead commented on the Town Hall. 'Wow, this is one handsome building.' She looked up. 'That's some serious craft on the ceiling. Very olde England.'

'Not that old, 1800s. You should see the first floor, dead stunning.'

'Really?'

'Me, me mum and dad and me sisters, Freya and Athol, used to come here when we was little. It's open to visitors on certain days of the week if you're interested.'

'I'll definitely visit.' Poonah was fascinated by European architecture, from prehistoric to contemporary. Whenever she got a chance to go to London, she spent a day on those hop-on hop-off tour buses just to ogle the buildings in central London. 'Before I return home, I'll travel across Europe just to see buildings – can't wait to see those great Russian palaces.'

She ordered a tuna sandwich and tea, then asked Kayla what the matter was.

'It's Masaaba.'

Poonah sat back. If it was the son playing up, that she could handle. But Masaaba was not playing up like normal British teenagers – he wanted to be circumcised traditionally.

Poonah threw back her head and laughed. A helpless rib-hurting laugh. When she took a breath, she saw Kayla's eyes and stopped. 'You're kidding me, Kayla.'

Kayla shook her head.

'But how did he even know about imbalu?'

'YouTube?'

'Does he know what actually happens – I mean, what really happens?'

'Wakhooli's told him. But he had already told his frickin' friends at school and there's this dare and one of them's gone and put it online.'

Poonah pictured Masaaba – basketball, manga comics, huge afro, KFC, metrosexual. He would collapse at the sight of the knife. 'Tell him it's done in public, the entire world watching. Tell him, you're covered in a paste of millet flour, standing still, no blinking, no shaking. Tell him they don't just cut the foreskin, there's a second layer: they don't like it either.'

'He's like, *If Ugandan boys can do it, so can I*. Now the dare's spread online.'

'Pull it, say it was a hoax.'

'He won't.'

'Tsk.' Poonah was dismissive. 'Don't worry; he'll change his mind.'

'What if he doesn't? What would you do?'

'Me? Girdle myself like a woman.' Poonah started to laugh but stopped. 'Sorry, Kayla, I'm laughing because I can't see it happening. But in case he's serious and I were you, I would say, *Baby, if this is what you want, you have my support*.'

'You're joking me.'

'I wouldn't be the one to discourage him. Let Wakhooli do it; it's his culture.' Poonah bit into the sandwich and sat back. Then sipped at tea. As an afterthought she added, 'Talk to the family back home; what do they think? Masaaba is what, fifteen? Next imbalu season will be in two years, he'll have changed his mind.'

That was then.

★

For the first time, as they drove from the airport, Poonah was mortified that Entebbe Road had no street lights. Even in Britain, she had become sensitive to things that embarrass 'us' – the loud man holding up the bus, arguing with the driver in an African accent, the woman angry on the phone in her language as if she is alone on the train, the secondary school girls fighting their invisibility by being disruptive in libraries and on buses. Right now, Kayla's silence was putting her on edge. Was she frightened of the dark? Was it the imbalu? But when did Uganda start to embarrass her? Is this how Kayla had felt when she had protected her at the airport?

It must have been 2008. An African came through Security. Kayla stood with Poonah because her group had come over to Terminal 4 to help with a high volume of passengers. On the X-ray, the African's bag showed five round objects of organic material. The bag was pulled. It was food. He worked in Amsterdam but flew back every weekend. His wife cooked and froze five meals for him. The containers were packed in plastic bags. The ASO removed one container, opened the cover and brought it to his nose. Poonah clicked: few Africans tolerate the sniffing of their food. The ASO explained that he was going to open them all. The passenger asked him to wear gloves before he touched his food. The ASO did, but he went to town opening each container, smelling it, and Poonah was disgusted. The ASO must have seen her disgust because when he let the passenger go, he came to where she and Kayla stood and said: 'I had to check; he said it was his food, but you never know – could've been human heads.'

Poonah held her breath.

Kayla turned to her, mouth open, hands on cheeks, eyes wild. 'He didn't! Tell me he didn't just say what I think he said.'

'Kdto!'

Kayla had turned to the ASO. 'Did you just say that that passenger, because he's African, could be a cannibal?' She turned to Poonah again. 'Holy shit, I can't believe he's just said that. Who says things like that any more? Wow.' She held her head like it was exploding. Then she turned back to him, pointing her finger in his face. 'Those are the disgusting lies white people put about to dehumanise black people in the past, so they could ensla— Oh my days—' She burst into tears. 'My children are black. I can't bear the thought of what people like him put them through.'

Poonah was laughing inside – *Yerere, that's the shit I put up with* – but on the outside she said, 'I'm just numb, me', because when someone helps you to cry for your dead, you cry louder.

By the time Kayla was through with him, the ASO had lost his job, the managers were sufficiently horrified, training on 'racial intolerance in the workplace' was rolled out across all terminals and counselling put in place. From then, Poonah became aware that when they worked together, Kayla was on the alert for any whiff of racism. Did Kayla feel this kind of anxiety too? She looked through the window: they were in Kajjansi. She wondered how Kayla and the boys saw those shops, the inadequate lighting, the people. But the boys were busy identifying stars in the sky.

★

Wakhooli had arrived in Uganda two weeks earlier to prepare for his family and to liaise with local authorities about the programme in Mbale, where imbalu would take place. The family planned to stay in Uganda for six weeks. Two weeks in Kampala while Masaaba learnt imbalu dance and songs and did the interviews Jerry the agent had arranged with the local media. Then two weeks in Mbale – the first five days would be for the rites, the rest would be for Masaaba's post-op seclusion. The last two weeks, while Masaaba healed, the family would do touristy stuff. Such was the plan, but you know our Uganda. You can plan all you want but, in the end, it will impose its will. Like the ngeye, the headdress and back gear for Masaaba's regalia which should have arrived in Uganda a week earlier, but had not.

For decades the Ministry of Culture had banned the wearing of even imitation colobus monkey skin for fear it would become endangered. Then came Masaaba, a mixed-race boy from Britain, whose agent had a slick tongue and international media attention. The Ministry of Culture caved in but insisted that Masaaba's crown should be visibly fake. Preferably a change of colours. Luckily, sample pictures sent from a fur company in China were more ornate and more beautiful than the real thing. The ministry made approvals and the family chose the colours. That had been three months earlier.

At first, the dare spread only among Masaaba's school friends, their friends and friends' friends. That was in 2016, when a Facebook account and a website introducing 'Masaaba, the British Mumasaaba' were set up. Anyone who wished to join paid a minimum of £5 into the dare. But then the following year Africans joined the conversation and scoffed at the Muzungu who thought circumcision was a joke. The dare stagnated at £20,175. In June 2017, panic that it was a scam spread online. Poonah prayed that Masaaba would come to his senses and pull it. He did not. Said he was not doing it for the dare. Poonah wondered whether someone had questioned the boy's masculinity. He loved the gym too much lately. Maybe it was a publicity stunt. Masaaba wanted to pursue a career on stage and kids these days were sharp.

Then in December 2017 Jerry the agent came along.

Jerry was a Chuka Umunna lookalike, right down to the shaven head to hide nature's merciless razor. Spoke as smooth, too. He wore three-piece suits beneath long winter coats. Carried a large umbrella like a walking stick, like he was lord of the manor. But unlike Chuka, Jerry was so muscle-bound beneath the suits Poonah suspected a neurotic relationship with the gym. He said his name was Jerry Stanton, but on his business card he was Jeremiah Were Stanton. When Masaaba read it as a sentence, Jerry corrected him: '*Weh-reh*, not *were*. My father was Ugandan, Jopadhola.' He smiled. 'Dad died when I was young.' As if it explained why he had opted for his British mother's name and middle-named his Ugandan father's. By now the irony that Poonah's name was Mpony'obugumba Nnampiima Ssenkubuge, whose ex-husband was Carl Mpiima Watson, had lost its sharp edges. She had become wary of people who hid their African roots.

Wakhooli's family fell under Jerry's spell, especially as they did not need to worry about paying him. He would charge 15% commission on deals he arranged in Britain and 20% on foreign ones. 'If anyone from the media gets in touch,' he told the parents, 'send them to me. My job is to free up your time so you focus on what is important, your son.'

Little did the family know that Jerry's intention was to whip up media attention and harvest his commission. He started small. BBC4 did a documentary on adult circumcision in Eastern and Southern Africa. That was his springboard. He arranged for a feature, 'Meet Masaaba, the British Mumasaaba', in *Metro*. He briefed the family on what aspects to talk about. One paper did a piece on how Masaaba and his brothers found out about imbalu; another on Masaaba and Zoe, his girlfriend; another on how Kayla and Wakhooli met; another on Kayla ('On Being the Mother of an Initiate'). The dare skyrocketed to £100,000.

In February 2018, Jerry asked for dates. The circumcision window in Uganda was small compared to the number of initiates – from August to the end of the year. At the end of February, the announcement went up on the website – Masaaba would be circumcised on 18 August 2018 – and a countdown began. Unbeknownst to the family, Jerry was already in talks with TV channels for documentary rights to the rituals. In March, BBC4 started shooting the documentary, inexplicably called *Love Made in Manchester*.

*

For all her apprehension, Poonah was too Ganda to pass up an opportunity to travel home all expenses paid. And you know about taking Western spouses back home – the special arrangements you have to make for them, the cleaning up and painting, the need to make sure everything and everyone is civilised. You have to be careful what you say. Your partner hears you and your siblings laugh at how your mother used to whip you raw when you were up to no good, stops talking to your mother entirely, but you so love your mother the earth is not enough. Then you have to be with them all the time, explaining things, holding hands, kiss-kissing, honey-honey-ing all over the place. And you know our Uganda: it sees that stuff, it sucks its teeth: *Spare us*. Wakhooli asked Poonah to come along and keep Kayla and their sons company while he ran around organising things.

Kayla must have sensed their anxiety, for she said, 'Look, Poonah, I married Wakhooli knowing our cultures are different. The last thing I need is to get to Uganda and be treated like I am fragile.'

'Of course not!'

But a nervous condition is a nervous condition. Wakhooli whispered to Poonah, 'Wamma, you'll take care of her for me: you understand?'

'Of course, leave her to me.'

By then Poonah and Wakhooli had become siblings in their Ugandanness even though she was Ganda and he was Masaaba, even though she was closer to Kayla than to him.

*

271

They pulled up to a gate in Nagulu. Wakhooli hooted. As they drove in, the security lights flooded the car and Poonah caught Kayla giving Wakhooli that stern look women give their men. She got out first and motioned to Wakhooli. In the back, the boys were peering: *Is this it?*

The BBC crew van pulled in. Two cameramen jumped out – BBC4 had been joined by the World Service in Uganda – and started filming. Poonah opened the door and as she stepped out, she heard Kayla say, 'We agreed not to spend money on posh accommodation.'

'This is Wetaya's house.'

'You mean this is your brother's house?'

Poonah ducked, at once proud and indignant. *What did you expect, huts?*

As Kayla and Wakhooli came back to the car, Poonah lifted sleeping Napule off the seat and held him over her shoulders. She heard the boys ask, 'Dad, is this Uncle Wetaya's house?'

'It is – grab your bags.'

Poonah walked to Wakhooli. 'Show me where to rest, Napule; he's gone.'

Wakhooli took him off her and told her to get her luggage. 'Come on, boys.'

By the time she came back with her bags, a camera operator was at the door filming as they walked in. Poonah hung back until he finished.

In the sitting room, Julie the producer arranged the family for a quick interview for the arrival shots. Masaaba had become dexterous at answering Julie's sappy questions, like:

'Help us understand how it feels to travel to a world so different from your own…to do something out of this world like adult public circumcision. It's mind-boggling.'

Masaaba talked about being tired but was not one bit scared. 'My father did it; boys younger than me routinely do it.'

The crew told them that a clip of their departure at Manchester airport had made the six o'clock news. Mwambu, the second son and the family nerd, rummaged through his bag for his tablet to see whether Jerry had uploaded it to the website. He had. But as he opened the link, his battery died. Poonah sat out of shot watching. When the interviews were done, the BBC crew told them what time they would arrive the following day and drove away. Poonah's bedroom was on the ground floor, while the family went upstairs.

As she showered, Poonah remembered Kayla's surprise at Wetaya's house and thought of ways to get Kayla and the boys over to her house. It was not as grand as this one, but compared to their council house in Hyde, it was luxury. She imagined Kayla going back to the airport with pictures on her phone, showing ASOs in the search area: *Remember Poonah who worked on Terminal 4? This is her house in Uganda, I kid you not. She's got two. Dead posh, innit? But then again, she is a social worker for Oldham Council now.*

Who would have known, the way they met, that one day Poonah would escort Kayla to Uganda? It was 2005. Poonah's group had been sent to Terminal 5 to process a flight from

Lahore bound for New York. At the time, the airport had a contract with JFK for flights from Pakistan to be rechecked in Europe before arriving in New York. Poonah was doing bag search when she saw Kayla come towards her smiling as if they knew each other. Poonah looked behind to see whom she was smiling at. She did not return the smile, but this did not faze Kayla. She came to her and asked: 'Are you Poonah from Uganda?'

'Yeah.'

'I am Kayla Wakhooli. My Wakhooli is Ugandan.'

Kayla brushed Poonah's handshake aside: 'Let's hug properly.' When she let go, she added, 'When British people first hear my name, they imagine I'm African, which I am in a way…by marriage.' She tried and failed to tuck a stray lock behind her ear. 'Whereabouts in Uganda do you come from?'

'Central.'

'Kampala?'

'Close, Buwama.'

'Muganda?'

'Yes.'

'My Wakhooli is from the east.'

'I know, Mugishu.'

'Not Mugishu!' Kayla went red in the face as if Poonah had said something racially insensitive. 'Mumasaaba. It's not even Mugishu, it's Mugisu.'

'Oh!'

'Gisu is just another name for Mwambu, the ancestor of the Badadili.'

'Who?'

'I forgive you.' Kayla smiled. 'You're Muganda.'

Poonah wanted to ask *How long have you been Ugandan, Nambozo?*, but said, 'Badadili, you even know the Budadili region?'

'Of course! The Badadili are northern Bamasaaba.'

'Wow, this is awful! Here I am in Manchester being schooled by an English person about *my* culture.'

'Scottish.'

'Corrected; have you been?'

'Not yet, but it's not my fault; it's Wakhooli's. He seems to think he needs to save a lot of money before we go. I said, "I'm family, don't fuss", you know what I mean?'

Poonah nodded, thinking, how can you even begin to know?

'But his parents, Mayi and Baba, have been to visit.'

'Have they?'

'Three times now.' Kayla waggled three fingers. 'First, for our wedding, then for Wakhooli's graduation. Lovely, wonderful people. Couldn't have married into a nicer family.' She whispered, 'Like Wakhooli, they're softly spoken. My parents said, "Do his parents realise how gobby our Kayla is?"'

They laughed so hard Kayla wiped away a tear.

'Wakhooli's parents lived in Kampala for a long time. Baba was a surveyor, Mayi a high-school teacher, but they've retired now and gone back to Mbale.'

'Okay.'

'I would like to see Mount Masaaba and the caves and the cursed rivers.'

'Mount Masaaba? Oh, Elgon.'

'I know we – I mean we…British' – she flushed red again – 'named it Mount Elgon, I apologise.'

'You know your Masaaba region well.'

At that point, Kayla, perhaps realising she had stayed away from her post too long, tapped Poonah on the hand. 'What shift are you on?'

'Finishing at two.'

'Good, I'm finishing at midday. I'll see you before I go.' She made to leave. 'You must meet my boys: we have three.' She flashed three fingers. Little Napule was not yet born then. 'Our oldest is called Masaaba…'

'Wow,' said Poonah, thinking, But this Wakhooli is intense on his Masaaba culture.

'Mwambu is our second, then Wabuyi. So happy to meet you.'

Poonah watched Kayla hurry away and clicked. She suspected Kayla was one of those people you meet in the West who knows too much about your culture and tries to show you up. Yet she had seemed genuinely happy to meet her, like she had married her Wakhooli, his culture, country and continent. Had they met back home, Poonah would have been awed, but Britain had made her suspicious.

At 11.45, when Kayla came to say goodbye, she asked, 'Do you know where I can buy Ugandan food? My Wakhooli is suffering white people's food.'

Poonah suppressed a smirk. That disarming moment when a person you gossip about owns the things you say behind her back. She smiled. 'That's not true, Kayla. I'm sure he loves it, but I know a few Asian shops that sell matooke—'

'Yes, matooki! Now you know what I am talking about. Every time Wakhooli goes to Uganda he brings matooki.' She whispered, 'Between me and you, I find it's absolutely tasteless; don't you?'

Poonah frowned. 'Are you taking the mick out of ethnic food?'

Kayla burst out laughing. 'No, just doing what Wakhooli told me: be straight with Ugandans.'

'Ah, tell you what, why don't we get together and I'll show you where to get Ugandan food.'

'Yay,' Kayla clapped. 'I knew we would be friends.' And they hugged. 'Oh my God, you're so kind, wait till I tell my Wakhooli!' They exchanged numbers and Kayla ran off.

At around 4 p.m. the BBC arrived to shoot the British family meeting the Ugandan one for the first time. Wakhooli had two sisters and three brothers. They all had children. They started to arrive at five. As blood relationships were established, Poonah's position started to wobble. When Kayla said, 'This is Poonah. She's auntie to the boys', Wakhooli's siblings smiled. When she added, 'Poonah so kindly agreed to come and help us with the culture and language', Nabwiile, Wakhooli's eldest sister, shot Poonah a look like *Which culture?* Others weighed her up and down like *Only a Muganda would be that deceitful.*

Poonah reverted to being Kayla's best friend rather than Wakhooli's sister. But even that was undermined by her Ugandanness. Like you're only her best friend because you're

Ugandan. She retreated into herself. Kayla kept pulling her into the conversation, but she didn't want to intrude. Besides, it was intriguing to watch the families interact. The cousins, especially the teenagers, were most interesting. They had none of the finesse of the grown-ups. Perhaps it was the Britishness and biracialness of the Wakhooli brothers; some cousins were uneasy, some were downright awkward, some showed off, some hogged the attention. They asked questions about the royal family, Man United, Lewis Hamilton and serial killers. Poonah had never seen Wakhooli's sons so patient and polite. Like Kayla, their Mancunian twang had been dropped.

Napule had no such problems. There was only one cousin for him, Khalayi, a bossy little girl. When Poonah noticed them, Khalayi was issuing orders and Napule, malleable as a cat's tail, was taking them. He called her Car Lye. Khalayi spoke Ugandan English like a six-year-old does, Napule spoke Mancunian English, but they understood each other perfectly. The only time there was trouble was when Khalayi had to leave and they both sulked and refused to say goodbye to each until Wakhooli promised to drop Napule off to his other sister's, Nambozo's, the following day. Still, when Khalayi wailed as they drove away, Napule lost his bravery and hid his face in his mother's skirts. The camera rolled.

Poonah was shocked when Masaaba's initiator arrived. Initiators are a secret cult. Absolutely no contact between the initiator and the initiate until the final moment of the knife blade. But then this was no ordinary imbalu. The initiate was British, half-white and spoke English. The fact that the rite would be conducted in English was already disrupting the ways of imbalu. The initiator did not wait to be introduced; he went straight to Masaaba: 'You must be my man Masaaba, I recognised you immediately, been following you on social media. I am your number one fan.' They hugged. 'Ah, but your father named you well. You're a true Mumasaaba!' The camera rolled.

Wakhooli introduced him as Dr Wafula, the man who would perform the cut. Now Poonah realised: he had been chosen because he was a medical doctor.

'I'm your man.' He shook Masaaba's hand. 'Me and you alone in that moment, no one else.' He took a breath. 'We thought it would help if the umusinde, that's you, and the initiator, that's me, get to know each other so you learn to trust me. I understand on Thursday you start to learn the kadodi?'

Masaaba nodded.

'Kadodi is the fun part; you'll love it.'

As Dr Wafula left, Julie the producer ran to him and introduced herself. She asked, 'Is there a way you can give us an interview and perhaps walk our viewers through imbalu?'

'Ah.' Wafula looked her over like *Do you realise imbalu is manly business?* He said, 'Maybe certain things, but the cut itself is out of bounds.'

'So you won't be able to demonstrate how the cut is done? I mean...er...using a prosthetic or something.'

Wafula realised what was being asked of him and turned away. Had it been a Ugandan woman she would have been put in her place there and then, but Julie was not just white, she was BBC. 'Er…no, absolutely not. You've got to realise that though imbalu is done in public, it's a secret ritual. By the way, you won't see a thing.'

'That's exactly the kind of thing our viewers would like to know. The contradictions, this public but secret rite, perhaps the history, the changes it has undergone and its significance to your people. Your view, the view of the initiator who performs the cut, will be critical.'

'Perhaps you can prepare your questions in advance and I'll let you know what I can and can't answer.'

'That will be fantastic, sir, thank you, we appreciate it. And if you don't mind' – Poonah closed her eyes like *Journalists don't know when to stop* – 'could we have one interview before Masaaba's imbalu and another afterwards to talk us through your feelings in that moment and how you prepared yourself?'

'We'll see.' Wafula started to walk away.

Julie thanked him and hurried back to her crew.

At around seven, the family drove to Hotel Africana – Masaaba wanted to find a gym. As the boys swam, Poonah asked Kayla about her first impressions of Uganda.

'It's not what I expected at all, but I suppose I haven't seen much. So far, I'm loving it and Wakhooli's family is super.'

'What did you think of his sisters?'

'They're way too kind; I mean, I'm not surprised. Everyone is so polite.' Then she frowned. 'I hope this is the way they treat all in-laws, not just the Mzungu.'

Poonah laughed. 'It's the way sisters-in-law are welcomed into families, but they might fuss a little because you're not Ugandan.'

'Oh no, I...I don't want to be treated—'

'Relax, Kayla, they would do the same if you were black British or Nigerian.'

'Oh, okay.' She smiled. 'This is exactly why I need you here.'

'And the initiator?'

She gasped. 'What a lovely, lovely man. I'm so relieved. He's a real doctor, not that I care, but when he said he'll walk Masaaba through everything I saw the worry fall off my boy's face like *ah*.' She made a gesture of a falling face.

Masaaba's schedule in Kampala began the following day. First Kayla and Wakhooli dropped Napule off at Khalayi's and then they went to the Ministry of Culture to collect the permit allowing Masaaba to wear the fake colobus monkey skin. Poonah suspected Wakhooli took Kayla along to put the bureaucrats on their best behaviour, especially as the BBC World Service was filming everything.

Poonah travelled with the older boys to Ndere Troupe's studios in Kisaasi for Masaaba's kadodi practice. The BBC4 crew came with them. First, Masaaba picked out his regalia. He tried on the bead sashes. Two wide ones, multicoloured beads sewn on a cloth that dropped down to the hips. Wakhooli had them made especially for him. Now Poonah understood why Masaaba had been keen to find a gym. For all his rituals he would be shirtless save for those sashes crisscrossing his chest. Then he picked out a flywhisk and mock-danced with it. The thigh rattles were not a problem; they were adjustable.

Next, he was introduced to the young dancers who had been hired to dance kadodi with him on the streets like sisters and cousins. His cousins were typical middle-class Kampala kids. Everything traditional embarrassed them. Wakhooli did not expect them to join in. The previous day, faced with their biracial British cousins who treated imbalu as something sacrosanct, Poonah had seen their predicament. While the British wanted to hear their cousins' imbalu experiences or plans, the Ugandans were uncomfortable, preferring to chat about computer games or something British. Yet, this morning the teenagers, who were off school, were at the studio eager to show off their kadodi dancing while Masaaba was filmed learning to dance. When the dancing started, the dance floor was crowded. Everyone wanted to see themselves dance in the large mirror on the wall. Because the camera was focused on Masaaba, they stood as close to him as possible. Until Wanyentse, the choreographer, stopped the music and said, 'If you're not going to take part in Masaaba's kadodi in Mbale, step out please.'

Silence. Masaaba looked at the floor. No one moved. Poonah sucked her teeth in: *Get rid of them; they're wasting time.* Wanyentse spread them out across the floor and they resumed.

Masaaba was a peacock. With girls and boys dancing for him, him learning the steps while watching himself in the mirror, kadodi music filling the room, he was loving himself too much. He couldn't believe that once he learnt the steps he would have a live band, that he would lead his dancers, that the dancers would do his will, that the band would watch his steps and play accordingly, that sometimes he would be carried shoulder high so as not to tire himself out. This being Masaaba, a Mumasaaba was fate. That he should come to Mbale to do imbalu was inevitable.

Mwambu, the second brother, had to be asked to put the iPad away and get on the floor. All the years Poonah had known the family, Mwambu, now fifteen, had never looked her in the eye. Was it coyness, was it haughtiness; she was not sure. He was polite, said hi, but by the time you looked up he had looked away. All this time, he had hidden behind the iPad, taking pictures for uploading, pretending not to see the drama on the dance floor. Now he put the tablet away and joined Masaaba at the front. He was a quick learner but painfully self-conscious. In all his interviews, he had made it clear that under no circumstances would he even contemplate doing imbalu. He would be circumcised now that he was aware, but in hospital under general anaesthesia like most of his cousins. *Why? Because it's my roots, obviously. While I am British, I am also Mumasaaba, and this is what we do...I am going to learn the dance and the songs, but I've not decided whether I'll join in the kadodi yet...I love my brother and I am here to support him but we're different, I mean...We'll see.* Since their arrival, Mwambu had been moaning about the sluggish internet even though Wakhooli had bought him a high-powered modem. You'd find him eating breakfast mid-morning because he stayed up late when internet speed improved.

Wabuyi, the third brother, would follow Masaaba to the moon. Right now, he was dancing, proper tribal, blowing a whistle, flicking a flywhisk, wowing the dancers who thought he was too cute for life. Out of the four boys, he looked more like Wakhooli but had his mother's open disposition. Too trusting. Self-consciousness had not occurred to him. He was still at that beautiful age when his parents were superheroes and his brothers were cool. Right now, he was dressed like Masaaba because there were extra pieces of regalia. They were oversized on him, but he did not care. He wanted facial paint, leaves around his head, waving branches, the whole shebang. In his interviews he said he was waiting to see what the physical circumcision was really like before he committed to doing imbalu when he came of age.

By the end of the second week, Masaaba was saying things in his interviews like: *I've even been to Dad's former school… Now Mum is talking about buying a house here…England is green, but this place is out of this world. The soil is red; never seen anything like it…I grew up with images of a barren Africa, like sheer poverty, you know, in those humiliating charity organisation ads of skeletal children drinking dirty water cows are pooing in and people are washing in at the same time, or fat mothers holding starving children, that made you think, what is wrong with these people? Until you realise the nature of editing. I mean, there is poverty, obviously, but I've seen poverty in New York…I know what I signed up for…*

By the time the family set off for Mbale, Masaaba's ngeye crown and the monkey skin to drape over his back had arrived and he had learnt to dance with them on. A picture of him in full regalia had been put up on the website. And then the Ministry of Culture had casually informed the family that dignitaries from other countries might be coming to what they had dubbed the 'Imbalu Special': *Don't worry, we'll take care of everything.*

It had been such a busy fortnight that Masaaba only started to catch up on social media on the way to Mbale. Mbale was 120 miles from Kampala but the boys were so busy on chats with friends back in Britain, they did not see the journey. Occasionally, they broke out in laughter as they shared a comment on social media. An academic had some-how connected Masaaba's imbalu to Trump. Mwambu read out the title: 'Masaaba's Imbalu and the Rise of Traditional Masculinities in the Trump Era.' He passed his tablet to his mother, who could not believe it and afterwards passed it to Poonah. The article was illustrated with an image of Trump, chin up after shoving the Montenegrin president out of the way.

Critical material had accumulated on the internet. The most worrying came from animal lovers. Someone had taken Masaaba's image in full regalia and written: 'Another colobus monkey dies in vain!' Another wrote: 'This nobbit did not cringe at wearing an imitation of the barbaric killing of beau-tiful defenceless animals.' In another place, CENSORED had been stamped across Masaaba's picture. Mwambu uploaded everything; Jerry had told him not to discriminate among material. But Wabuyi was angry. He found the article and typed a response: 'Shaka Zulu's leopard prints are in vogue, mate.' He attached Theresa May's shoes and tapped Enter. Then he went to another item, typed, 'The rug in our living room is a zebra skin', and attached an image from some website.

Previously non-existent consultants – university professors and researchers – on adult circumcision in Africa had popped up online, offering insights, promoting their blogs and vlogs. Then there were the anti-circumcision groups – especially the one with the imagery of blood-soaked crotches – preaching doom and gloom. They accused Masaaba of gentrifying genital mutilation. They brandished statistics of deaths from adult circumcision each year. They called it MGM, an acronym quickly acquiring the notoriety of FGM. They talked about how boys in Africa were coerced, how women were used to spy on uncircumcised men who were captured and forcibly circumcised. Then this headline: CONSERVATIVES FAIL TO CONFIRM THEY WOULD BAN IMBALU IF IT HAPPENED IN BRITAIN. Mwambu uploaded everything.

Napule had become a stranger. Occasionally his Aunt Nambozo brought him to visit the family, but he lived across town in Bunga with Khalayi. Kayla had surprised Poonah. She did not bat an eyelid at being separated from him, even when Napule chose to stay in Kampala with Khalayi while they travelled to Mbale.

The earlier plans to hold the rites at Masaaba's grandparents' home had been thrown out. Anticipating international attention, the mayor of Mbale, the Ministry of Tourism, Wildlife and Antiquities, and regional MPs had remapped the route for Masaaba's kadodi, taking in the major features of the city. Wakhooli's Ugandan family was all for it; the bigger the better.

Meanwhile tension was building between Poonah and Nabwiile, Wakhooli's eldest sister. To her, Poonah was a hanger-on. Her attitude sneered *We can ease Kayla into our family, thank you very much*. She had started by arranging visits to all Wakhooli's siblings' homes. Then she hijacked a visit to Nakivubo. Poonah had arranged to take Kayla shopping for bitenge gowns when Nabwiile said she knew someone who had the best and cheapest on Kampala Road. Apparently, her someone brought lovely shirts from Ghana too; Wakhooli and the boys would love them. Poonah kept quiet; she had planned to give Kayla a local market experience, besides, she knew how expensive shops on Kampala Road were and Kayla and Wakhooli were not exactly rich. Kayla sensed the tension and asked what was going on.

'It's me arriving into *their* world to ease *their* sister-in-law into *their* family and *their* culture like they can't do it.'

Kayla gasped. 'I didn't realise.'

'Neither did I! Add to that, I am Ganda: don't even speak Lumasaaba.'

She held her mouth. 'Do you want to leave?'

'Wakhooli paid my fare for a reason. You carry on being you and I'll be discreet.'

They arrived at Hotel Elgonia around six and checked in.

Poonah did not join the family until midday the following day. By then the boys had gone to meet Masaaba's kadodi band and check out the dance route. Local MPs, the mayor and people from the government had been to welcome the family to Mbale and talk about the programme on the eighteenth. In the afternoon the family went to Wakhooli's parents' house. They had supper there.

Kayla's sisters, Athol and Freya, arrived in Kampala that night. So did Masaaba's British friends. Wakhooli had arranged for them to be picked up at the airport at the same time and be taken to the Kabira Hotel in Kampala, then to Mbale the following day. But he had put his foot down against Zoe, Masaaba's girlfriend, coming to Uganda for imbalu. 'It's common sense,' he said. Jerry the agent was staying in Tororo with his grandmother and would commute to Mbale. He was to handle post-op interviews, and he had handled the insurance in case Masaaba needed emergency repatriation to England. Masaaba, his dancers and the cousins who had arrived spent the following day rehearsing with the band.

Time in Mbale ran too fast. After lunch on the first day of the kadodi, a group of elders came to whisper with Masaaba. It was excitement, happiness and pride. By 1.30, members of the press had started to lurk. At 2 p.m., Masaaba came down dressed. You heard the rattles first as he walked and turned. That ngeye crown would transform a toad into a prince; Masaaba was killing it. And those bands enhancing his biceps! A woman went *Airiririri* over him and there were answers of *Ayii*. He posed for pictures, answered some questions for BBC4 and got into the transport to meet with the band and the dancers. At the gate, locals had collected; kids chased the car as it disappeared. Poonah felt constrained by her maternal aunt status. She would have liked to go along and watch the kadodi, perhaps dance a bit.

Meanwhile, Wakhooli's family was expanding. Earlier, before the kadodi started, there was confusion. Rumour had it that you had to be vetted before you joined Masaaba's kadodi carnival. People arrived, introduced themselves, reminding Wakhooli or his siblings how they were related, demanding that their children be included in Masaaba's procession: 'We understand that you hired English-speaking dancers, that you have to speak English to be a part. Since when?' And Wakhooli denied that he would ever think of doing such a thing. He had presumed they would not want to be part of it. 'Really, how? Because we even heard you hired men to carry our son when he danced on the shoulders.' Wakhooli explained and apologised.

The new relations were impressed by Kayla. They shook her hand – *Thank you for holding our tradition dear* – then they would turn to Wakhooli: *You chose well.* No doubt Masaaba's love for his culture was down to good parenting...*You see, some of our own people here are not encouraging it any more. But a Musungu, coming all the way from England, ah.* Kayla would go red in the face and Poonah would nudge her to smile.

Later, Kayla would be like, *I hate it when people say terrible things about Ugandans and make me out like I'm some sort of angel. I want to say, I'm not, I'm just like you.* Poonah would twist her lips. How would she say *But you're not like everyone else, that the British had no idea that the white exceptionalism they worked so hard to inculcate in the colonies would one day become a burden*, but she said, 'They'd say the same if you were Jamaican.'

That evening, the boys came back at around seven, exhausted and excited. Mwambu was laughing: 'Mum, Masaaba's gonna start a farm in Manchester.'

Kayla was shocked. 'They've given him live animals?'

'Not yet. But so far they've promised him four goats, I don't know how many chickens and a baby cow, and that's just the first day! We saw them. They asked Masaaba to touch them. If he's – I mean, *when* he's brave, they're his.'

'Oh my God, Poonah, what do we do?'

Auntie Nabwiile stepped in. 'We'll give them to your grandparents to rear for you, Masaaba. But the chickens and goats will be used for the party when you come out of seclusion.'

Silence as 'used' sank in.

It was Wabuyi who asked, 'You mean we're gonna eat them cute goats?'

'Yes, Wabuyi,' Auntie Nabwiile smiled. 'Cute animals are where meat burgers come from.'

Poonah expected him to run to his mother demanding they rescue the animals but Mwambu had given him a warning eye. Wabuyi smiled. 'Of course, Auntie.'

As Mwambu uploaded pictures of Masaaba touching the animals, Masaaba explained, 'Mum, in the past, Dad should've built me a hut already; the animals would be a kind of wealth to start adulthood with.'

'Yeah,' Mwambu sniggered, 'like getting a council flat and an uncle gives you a sofa, an aunt gives you pans and pots, another gives you a telly, a bed, whatever.'

'Well then,' Kayla laughed, 'time to kick you out of our house.'

It happened on the second day when the boys were out for the kadodi carnival. Kayla's two sisters, Athol and Freya, monopolised her now even Nabwiile had eased off. They had this kind of protective aura as if Kayla were going through the mother of all trauma. When they arrived, interviews of them with Kayla picked up. Twice now, Kayla had come out upset. Poonah, who had noticed in Britain that when there was a mixed-race couple on TV – parents of a sports, musical or dance hero, or of a child protégé – cameras focused more on the white half of the parents, became suspicious. The second time, Poonah went up to Kayla and asked what was wrong.

'Nothing,' she said, and stormed off to her room.

Poonah went after her, but Athol stopped her: 'Can't you see she wants to be left alone?'

But she opened the door anyway and went in. Freya joined them.

Don't beg to help, pack your bags and go back to Kampala. If she needs you she will call. Then she relented. *Kayla is British; brushing you off does not mean she's being rude.* Poonah walked back to her room. But it hurt. All the years she had known Kayla, she had never known the sisters to show interest in their nephews. At the boys' birthdays they tended to nip in and nip out, but now that there was a camera they were displaying concern. She sent Wakhooli a text: *We need to talk. Urgently. Give me a call.*

When they got together, Poonah told him, 'Something's been going on with Kayla since her sisters arrived. I don't know why, but twice…you know that BBC woman?'

'Julie?'

'Twice she's interviewed them, and both times Kayla's come out upset.'

'Why were you not with her?'

'Her sisters are here.'

'I know what they're doing. Ever since they started this documentary business, Julie's been trying to tear-jerk her and Masaaba. Like, *Oh, it must be terrifying for you as a mother, knowing your baby is going…?* They need her to cry. That's what they do. With Masaaba I had to step in and say, "Do not introduce fear into my boy's mind." Now they're trying to milk Kayla through the sisters.'

'Problem is showing Kayla crying on TV. They'll edit it to seem like she's regretting…You know what they're like. They edit their programmes to show this fragile white woman who married an African now traumatised by his barbaric culture. Can you imagine the backlash online when Africans see it?'

Wakhooli sighed exhaustion. 'I'll talk to Julie.'

'Also tell them you want to see the final edit. Tell them you don't want your wife to be shown crying.'

On Saturday the eighteenth it rained in the morning. A loud, gusty rain that brought everything to a standstill. By the time Poonah got downstairs for breakfast, the hotel lobby was packed. People stood everywhere, some fretting because preparations were held up, some waiting to escort Masaaba to face the knife. For the first time Wakhooli was not running around. He and his brothers sat with Masaaba plus some other elders. A bunch of men, suspicious and menacing, stood around them, watching. Dr Wafula had warned them back in Kampala that on the last day, things would turn dark. Masaaba would not be left on his own in case he bolted. Mwambu and Wabuyi sat away from everyone. They stole worried glances at their brother, then at the menacing gang.

Poonah's eyes fell on Jerry. He had gone to whisper with Masaaba, but the menacing gang pushed him away like he would help Masaaba escape. Thankfully, he had left his lord-of-the-manor look in England. As he walked away, two white men approached him, shook his hand and he led them to a table. Poonah wondered what they wanted. The day before, Jerry had arrived at the hotel with three items in his hands. First, there had been film offers. 'But I said to them, it's early days. Let's wait and see how Masaaba's circumcision pans out and then decide who will do my man here' – he shook Masaaba by the shoulders – 'justice.' The second item was a project with CNN, something to do with the spectacular landscape in Eastern Uganda, bringing it to the attention of the world. 'It's in the future; if Masaaba is interested, let me know.' However, the major issue was the dare money. 'It's become toxic. Public opinion has changed. It was about £625,000 last time I checked—'

'£642,545,' Mwambu corrected.

'There you go. It's too much money. Ugandan kids get circumcised all the time without money or fanfare. The presumption is that because you're British you're rich and privileged and shouldn't make money out of an African ritual.'

'Let me speak for once.' Poonah stood up, gesturing Ugandanly. 'This has nothing to do with Ugandans. Masaaba, Ugandans don't begrudge you your money. They don't care because it's not their money. It's the rich, white, middle-class people in the West who, disgusted with their own wealth, are trying to guilt-trip everyone—'

Mwambu joined in: 'Bloody leftists; they do my head in.'

'We call them *We Are the World*,' Wakhooli laughed. 'They consider themselves the conscience of the world regardless of the circumstances. And they impose their conscience ruthlessly.'

'We're not touching that money,' Kayla interrupted. 'End of discussion.' But her outburst said *You're not the white ones; all that shit will be aimed at my face.* She turned to Jerry. 'What do you suggest?'

'I was thinking of perhaps a clinic for imbalu initiates here in Mbale. Somewhere they can go for seclusion with good medical facilities, good meals, peace and quiet. The circumcision season is very small and happens every two years. The rest of the time, the hospice would serve the community. Any profit would fund the initiates' wing. I think Dr Wafula might be useful. We must be seen to be doing something.'

Silence fell as the performance of *We must be seen to be doing something* sunk in. Images of Western celebrities, *The X Factor* and shows which had been 'seen to do something in Africa' flashed in Poonah's mind and she clicked.

'We'll discuss it when we return home,' Wakhooli said softly. 'There's no hurry.'

Now, Poonah's eyes travelled to where Kayla sat playing Scrabble with her sisters. Kayla could win an Oscar so far.

Rain stopped like God had plugged it. Bang at midday. People rushed outdoors. Men carrying tools, others loading plastic chairs onto a lorry, mops drying the entrance. Thirty minutes later, reporters were setting up in the garden, some speaking into mics, staring into cameras and pointing at the hotel. Next time she looked outside, a crowd had built up outside the gate. Poonah's heart fell into her stomach. Then she chided herself: You'll jinx the boy if you don't stop worrying. She walked to her room and picked up a Bible from next to a table lamp. The Old Testament. Psalms. She thumbed to 23 and read. 'The Lord is my shepherd; I shall not want...' She put it down, closed her eyes and recited in Luganda, 'Mukama ye musumba wange, seetagenga...' It was still as calming as it had been when she lived with Mutaayi. When she finished she sighed, 'Masaaba, you're in God's hands now.' She reached for the TV remote control. Rice screens. CNN. A religious channel. Football. She settled on a Nollywood film.

A band struck up and she woke.

Masaaba's kadodi band had come to the hotel? She jumped out of bed. The music filled the place. She had heard that Masaaba's band was a combination of two bands – one that Wakhooli had paid for before the politicians got involved and the biggest band in Mbale, which the politicians had hired. Poonah ran through the corridors. Kadodi music is like that: you hear it, you can't stay away. She ran across the foyer to the main entrance. The band filled the garden. People beyond the gate were dancing. Kayla and her sisters were taking pictures. Poonah ran to them.

'Is this what the boys have been dancing to?'

'Isn't it just great?'

'We've missed the fun part,' Freya moaned.

'That's being a mother for you.'

'I'm glad the boys have had fun,' Athol added. 'I wish it lasted a week instead of three days.'

Kayla wiped her tears away.

Poonah looked back in the foyer for Masaaba. He was being led away from his lunch table, but the food was untouched. She followed them with her eyes. An uncle found a space in a corner and motioned to the rest to join him. Poonah hurried and grabbed a chair close by and draped her sweater over it. She went to the water fountain, filled a glass and came back to the seat. By then, Masaaba was surrounded by his relations. The menacing gang formed the outer ring.

Someone was saying: 'I can't say the merrymaking is over because you still have your band, your crown and people are going to dance for you, but it's serious business now. As you can see, only men surround you and not all of them have good intentions. Some are here to provoke your fear, to make you stumble, to frighten you so they can say you are not ready to become a man. We won't stop them because we know our son is strong. In fact, we'll be laughing because your bravery will be even sweeter when you shame them…'

'Bring it on…'

'Did you hear that, haters?'

The gang did not bother with English as they jeered, making derisive noises.

'Okay, Wakhooli, take Masaaba and get him ready.'

As they led him away, the gang broke out in celebration, brandishing sticks, clubs and branches: *He'll shake and tremble…yeah, he'll cry for Mummy…he's been showing off on the internet and whatnot! Let's see what he is made of.* Even folks watching the kadodi turned as the haters made a show of the savagery they would mete out to Masaaba if he dared tremble. They followed him to the lift.

The Masaaba who stepped out of the lift was subdued. In the foyer, apart from the camera clicks, silence fell. Forget the abs and biceps and all the handsomeness his parents gave him – it was all covered under a layer of white millet flour paste. No amount of clowning could break through. Just then the gang – they must have given them the slip – were heard coming down the stairs shouting, 'Where is he? Where is he?' When they saw him covered in millet flour, looking like a squirrel, they laughed, clapped, celebrating like finally the stage was theirs to show off bad blood. Masaaba's British friends joined the haters in laughter. But all the laughing and clowning in the world could not lift the heaviness in the air. Outside, the band played, people danced. As they led him out, Masaaba waved to his mother. 'When you see me again, Mum, I'll be a man.'

'You'll always be my baby.'

He waved to his aunties but Poonah called, 'You have made us proud and—'

'Not yet, Auntie, not yet. See you on the other side.'

Wakhooli stepped out and got on one knee, Masaaba mounted on his shoulders, and he rose, hoisting his son. The crown on Masaaba's head almost touched the ceiling; the skin on his back came down to Wakhooli's shoulders. Wild *Airiririri* rang out and Kayla answered with *Ayii*. Even her sisters joined in this time. They took a few more pictures as a family. Then Wakhooli stepped out of the front entrance. A roar rose and the band's drumming became critical. When Wakhooli twirled and did a jig, the crowd went wild. After a while, Masaaba raised his hand. The band, the dancers, onlookers, everyone stopped.

Then, punching the air, he called, 'Bamusheete?'

'Eh!' everyone answered.

'Bamusheete?'

'Sheet' omwana afanane babawe!'

The band joined in and Wakhooli danced down the stairs, Mwambu and Wabuyi dancing beside him like *Behold, we bring the hero*. Masaaba flywhisked the cobwebs out of the sky and then low, each swat swishing *Out of my way*, then eyes closed he nodded, casual as you like, and the crown did its magic.

As Wakhooli danced down the driveway, the hired dancers and cousins joined him, then the band fell in step, the crowd joined at the back pulsing, singing, blowing whistles.

By then, all you saw was the back of Masaaba's crown, the fur bouncing. Poonah, Kayla, her sisters and other guests followed them down to the gate. They stayed there until the last of the dancers disappeared.

For some time, Poonah, Kayla, her sisters and Julie, who, because she was a woman, could not follow Masaaba to certain points, rode on the euphoria of the crowd and the band that had escorted Masaaba. Without it, the effort not to think about five o'clock would have failed them. They played Scrabble. When 4.30 came, none of them was keen to get into the van. Eventually, as 5 p.m. approached, they were driven to the venue. You realised the gravity of the occasion when you saw Mbale's streets quieter than Sunday mornings.

Cars, bicycles, boda boda, pedestrians; all roads led to Manafwa High School. The school's games pitch was covered with three large tents and a small one at the head. In the quadrangle at the centre was a dais, where the cut would take place. Now it was occupied by traditional performers. The tents were full. Tourists occupied one tent, dignitaries another. Then the miscellaneous. The van drove past all that to a white tent further away at the edge of the pitch.

The tent was carpeted, a sofa set and a low table in the middle. A waitress asked if anyone wanted a drink. Kayla and her sisters asked for wine. Poonah opted for Bell lager. They resumed their game of Scrabble, but Julie had disappeared. Poonah had started to appreciate Freya and Athol's presence. It was a relief to have them occupy Kayla after all.

It was a quarter to six when the waitress ran into the tent breathless; she had seen Masaaba sprint to the dais. They listened. Outside was total silence. Someone clutched Poonah's hands. Poonah did not breathe. Then a cry cut the air, *Airiririri*. Everyone looked at everyone else.

Kayla turned to Poonah. 'What does that mean?'

Before she could say *I don't know*, Kayla emitted a scream like it had escaped. She stopped like she had transgressed. Outside, more *Airiririri* rang out. Someone said, 'It's done.' But no one attempted to run out and look.

Kayla set off an *Airiri*. Then, as if she had not screamed, she asked, 'Does it mean he was brave?'

Now they ran out of the tent but stopped outside. They could see people jumping up and down but still they dared not celebrate. Then Jerry came running, waving.

'He's legend, Kayla,' he waved, 'Your son is legend.'

Kayla exploded like a well-shaken bottle of Coke, releasing all the emotion she had bottled up. She screamed, leaping in the air shaking her head like a British schoolgirl at a One Direction show.

Jerry went to her and they held each other, jumping up and down. 'I swear to God…I mean…I didn't doubt him… but heck, Masaaba's got balls the size of Tororo Rock.'

Athol and Freya were crying.

Poonah ran towards the tent area. A white man in shorts lay flat out on the ground being fanned. Further down, Julie stood alone wiping tears away. In a gap between two tents three white men were bent over throwing up. Kids were laughing at them. Then she saw Masaaba sat in the wheelchair. His crown was still on his head.

She ran back to the tent. 'He's wearing his crown, it's the first thing they pull off if you tremble.'

But Mwambu had reached his mother and she was holding him and everywhere was crowded with women and it was hard to get to Kayla. Next Mwambu was pushing his way out. He sat down beside the tent and held the bridge of his nose to hide the tears. His face was so red the freckles had disappeared.

Poonah asked, 'Did you see it?'

'I did,' he sniffed. 'I mean, I didn't. He was surrounded by so many men you couldn't see. I saw him run to the podium, saw him steady himself with the pole. Then that dude, the surgeon. Next the knife flashed with blood, then again and men screamed, and I sat down 'cause I couldn't stand. Next, they had wrapped a sheet around him and he was helped into a wheelchair. It happened too fast. I wanted to go and hold him, but I couldn't get up.' Now he looked at Poonah. 'I was afraid I might hurt him and spoil everything.'

Wakhooli came running. 'Kayla, Kayla, where's Kayla?'

'Dad's bonkers.' Mwambu attempted to laugh.

Wakhooli grabbed Kayla and kissed her bang on the lips like it was an imbalu ritual. They were mobbed. Before she realised, women had lifted Kayla, carrying her towards the tents. The sheer anxiety in her glance screamed *Put me down: can't you see I am a white woman, put me down.* Poonah pointed at Wakhooli. 'Relax, they're carrying him too.' Kayla tried to smile but history was stalking her. Poonah turned back to Mwambu. She pulled him off the ground and held him. For a while he was still. Then she felt his stomach crunch and hold, then blew out as he sucked air; it crunched again, then distended. After a while, he pulled away and wiped his face. Then he smiled like his bravado had returned.

'Didn't even take any pictures. Been recording the most mundane stuff but not the one most important moment.'

'Someone did – Jerry, the World Service, BBC4, other journalists.'

'He didn't flinch, Auntie Poonah. Bastard stood still like it was nothing.'

'Of course he didn't!' After a while she asked, 'You're okay now?'

He nodded. 'Cheers, Auntie.'

'Let's go see him before the ambulance takes him to seclusion.'

When they got to the tent area, people had broken into groups. The mayor, MPs and dignitaries were saying goodbye to Masaaba and his parents. Photographers peered at camera screens, scrolling through pictures: *Did you get it?* Haters were dancing like they had forgotten themselves. People dropped money like leaves at Masaaba's feet. Mwambu broke away and ran to his brother.

Masaaba's wheelchair sat between his parents. Kayla held Wabuyi, but her face was white. She seemed suspended between this world and another. Women still airiried around them. Masaaba sat manspreading. He was covered from waist to above the ankles with a kanga. Too many people congratulating him for Poonah to get close. She looked on the ground between his feet. A little patch of the soil was soaked. Then a drop. Another. Another. She was thinking of the symbolism when she began to feel light-headed. She was thinking of sitting down when she heard, 'Hold that woman.' When she came to, the concerned faces of Freya, Kayla, Athol and Julie were bent over her.

When he emerged from seclusion, Masaaba had lost so much weight he looked fifteen again. He wore a kilt. He must have noticed everyone's shock and, ever the clown, he twirled and the kilt blew out. The twirl went wrong and came to an excruciating end. Bending to limit the damage, he bit back a scream. His brothers ran to him, but he held up his hand. Ugandans were in stitches. He inserted a finger in a hole on the front of the kilt and held it away from his wounds. He waddled to his seat, sat at the edge, spread his legs out and arranged the kilt. Kayla smiled as if to say *Oh, he'll be fine*. Wakhooli, still laughing, said, 'Now you understand why Zoe couldn't come.'

ACKNOWLEDGEMENTS

- Great thanks to the Ludigo sisters, Martha Ludigo-Nyenje, Janet Ludigo-Mawuba and Irene Ludigo-Katamba, who received me in Manchester in September 2001. But especially you, Martha, for insisting that I join you, and your patience with me those first six months. I hope, when you read these stories, you will remember Rusholme, Heald Avenue. I think you're a hero.
- Martin De Mello, where would my writing be without your brutal reading, generous counsel, cynical eye and everything else?
- Vimbai Shire for the sheer scrutiny of the collection; I cannot thank you enough.
- Cultureword's short story group (2014), which pushed me to write a short story every month; this collection is the result.
- Uncle Tim (Professor Timothy Wangusa) for the generous critique, gentle encouragement and cultural insight for the final story.

- Sui Annuka for the sincere, candid and lavish critique. I'm lucky to be writing buddies with you.
- Nicole Thiara for making me feel like I am doing great.
- To my literary godfather, Michael Schmidt, for keeping an eye on me, my writing, my career and reassuring me when I hit a wall that there is a door close by.
- Enock Kiyaga for all things traditional – Luganda and kiganda.
- Marie Nandago Senyomo for everything in Uganda, the US and London. For loving me through these years.
- To Ken and Cath Kakiiza-Okwir and the little ones – for opening your door to me when I come home. Love you, Cath.
- My agent, James Macdonald Lockhart, for your quiet counsel.
- The Windham-Campbell Prize, for the relief and opportunities opened up.
- Juliet Mabey, Margot Weale and the rest of the team at Oneworld for getting behind my books.
- Sarah Terry for the thorough cleaning-up of my prose.
- Manchester Metropolitan University's Writing School for the space and the time off.
- Jess Edwards, my line manager and head of department, for the open door, for listening.